汉英经典文库

汉英对照

LIBRARY OF CHINESE AND ENGLISH CLASSICS
Chinese-English

三国演义
Three Kingdoms
IV

罗贯中　著

罗慕士　译

Attributed to Luo Guanzhong

Translated by Moss Roberts

外 文 出 版 社

Foreign Languages Press

目　录

CONTENTS

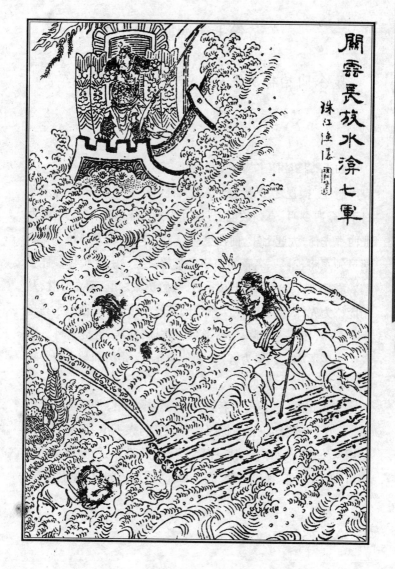

關雲長放水淹七軍

珠江漁隱

第七十四回

庞令明抬榇决死战　关云长放水淹七军

　　却说曹操欲使于禁赴樊城救援,问众将谁敢作先锋。一人应声愿往。操视之,乃庞德也。操大喜曰:"关某威震华夏,未逢对手;今遇令明,真劲敌也。"遂加于禁为征南将军,加庞德为征西都先锋,大起七军,前往樊城。这七军,皆北方强壮之士。两员领军将校:一名董衡,一名董超;当日引各头目参拜于禁。董衡曰:"今将军提七枝重兵,去解樊城之厄,期在必胜;乃用庞德为先锋,岂不误事?"禁惊问其故。衡曰:"庞德原系马超手下副将,不得已而降魏;今其故主在蜀,职居'五虎上将';况其亲兄庞柔亦在西川为官:今使他为先锋,是泼油救火也。将军何不启知魏王,别换一人去?"

　　禁闻此语,遂连夜入府启知曹操。操省悟,即唤庞德至阶下,令纳下先锋印。德大惊曰:"某正欲与大王出力,何故不肯见用?"操曰:"孤本无猜疑;但今马超现在西川,汝兄庞柔亦在西川,俱佐刘备:孤纵不疑,奈众口何?"庞德闻之,免冠顿首,

Chapter 74

Pang De Carries His Coffin to His Final Battle
Lord Guan Floods the Enemy's Seven Armies

Pang De was the man who promptly answered Cao Cao's call for a volunteer to take the vanguard of Yu Jin's rescue force. Elated, Cao Cao said, "That fellow Guan has terrified the entire north; he has yet to meet his match. But Pang De will be a formidable opponent." He promoted Yu Jin to General Who Conquers the South, and Pang De to Vanguard Leader Who Conquers the West. They brought seven armies into the field and headed for Fan.

The seven armies were formed of the northerners' toughest fighters. That day the two subcommanders, Dong Heng and Dong Chao, brought the various captains before Yu Jin to offer their respects. Dong Heng said, "General, today you have called up seven strong units to break the siege at Fan. This is a battle we must win. Yet you have placed in the van a man sure to ruin our campaign." Yu Jin was startled and asked Dong Heng to explain himself. "Pang De once served Ma Chao as deputy commander," Dong Heng replied. "He surrendered to Lord Cao by force of circumstance. Now his former lord is in the Riverlands, holding the position of 'Five Tiger General.' In addition, his brother Pang Rou is an official in the Riverlands. To make him vanguard leader is like pouring oil on a fire. General, why don't you and the king of Wei find another leader?"

Yu Jin went to speak to Cao Cao that same night. Cao Cao understood the problem; he summoned Pang De and ordered him to hand over his seal of vanguard leader. Astonished, Pang De said, "This is the day before I will show Your Highness what I can do. Why are you unwilling to use me now?" "I myself have no reservations," Cao Cao replied, "but Ma Chao is in the Riverlands, as is your brother Rou. And both serve Liu Bei. Even if you have my confidence, what about the troops?" At these words Pang De removed his cap and knocked his head on the

流血满面而告曰:"某自汉中投降大王,每感厚恩,虽肝脑涂地,不能补报;大王何疑于德也?德昔在故乡时,与兄同居,嫂甚不贤,德乘醉杀之;兄恨德入骨髓,誓不相见,恩已断矣。故主马超,有勇无谋,兵败地亡,孤身入川,今与德各事其主,旧义已绝。德感大王恩遇,安敢萌异志?惟大王察之。"操乃扶起庞德,抚慰曰:"孤素知卿忠义,前言特以安众人之心耳。卿可努力建功。卿不负孤,孤亦必不负卿也。"

德拜谢回家,令匠人造一木榇。次日,请诸友赴席,列榇于堂。众亲友见之,皆惊问曰:"将军出师,何用此不祥之物?"德举杯谓亲友曰:"吾受魏王厚恩,誓以死报。今去樊城与关某决战,我若不能杀彼,必为彼所杀;即不为彼所杀,我亦当自杀:故先备此榇,以示无空回之理。"众皆嗟叹。德唤其妻李氏与其子庞会出,谓其妻曰:"吾今为先锋,义当效死疆场。我若死,汝好生看养吾儿;吾儿有异相,长大必当与吾报仇也。"妻子痛哭送别,德令扶榇而行。临行,谓部将曰:"吾今去与关某死战,我若被关某所杀,汝等即取吾尸置此榇中;我若杀了关某,吾亦即取其首,置此榇内,回献魏王。"部将五百人皆曰:"将军如此忠勇,某等敢不竭力相助!"于是引军前进。有人将此言报知曹

ground until blood covered his face. "I surrendered to Your Highness in Hanzhong; and I have never forgotten your generous favor, which my very life's blood could not repay. Why does Your Highness doubt me? Long ago in my home village when I was living with my elder brother, his wife did not behave as a virtuous sister-in-law; while I was drunk I killed her. My brother has hated me ever since, swearing never to see me again. We have severed all relations. My former lord, Ma Chao, was brave but foolish. His army defeated, his territory lost, he went alone to the side of the Riverlands. Now he and I serve different masters, and our bonds too are broken. After all your kind treatment, how could a disloyal thought sprout in me? If only Your Highness would consider this." Cao Cao helped Pang De to his feet and consoled him, saying, "I have always believed in your loyalty and honor. What I said was simply to quiet the minds of the others. Strive and accomplish! If you are true to me, so will I be to you."

Pang De prostrated himself in gratitude; then he returned home, had a coffin made, and invited a few friends to view it at a banquet the following day. They reacted with astonishment. "General," they said, "what use has something so inauspicious before the campaign?" Raising his cup, Pang De replied, "Honored by the generous favor of the king of Wei, to whom my very life is sworn, I go today to Fan to fight Lord Guan to the finish. If he does not die at my hands, then I will die at his. This coffin demonstrates my determination not to return without achieving my objective." The company was aghast. Pang De called his wife, Lady Li, and his son Pang Hui. "This time I go in the vanguard," he said to her. "For honor's sake I face death on the field of battle. If I die, take good care in bringing up our boy. He has unusual signs and will grow up to avenge me." Lady Li and the child wept sorely, seeing him off. Pang De had the coffin carried along as he prepared to set out.

Before departing, Pang De said to his commanders, "I will fight Guan to the finish. If he kills me, put my body in this coffin. If I kill him, I will use it to carry his head back to the king." His five hundred commanders answered in unison, "General, we will spare no effort in supporting one so loyal and brave." After that, Pang De led the advance.

Someone reported the incident to Cao Cao, who said, "Pang De is

操。操喜曰："庞德忠勇如此，孤何忧焉！"贾诩曰："庞德恃血气之勇，欲与关某决死战，臣窃虑之。"操然其言，急令人传旨戒庞德曰："关某智勇双全，切不可轻敌。可取则取，不可取则宜谨守。"庞德闻命，谓众将曰："大王何重视关某也？吾料此去，当挫关某三十年之声价。"禁曰："魏王之言，不可不从。"德奋然趱军前至樊城，耀武扬威，鸣锣击鼓。

　　却说关公正坐帐中，忽探马飞报："曹操差于禁为将，领七枝精壮兵到来。前部先锋庞德，军前抬一木橔，口出不逊之言，誓欲与将军决一死战。兵离城止三十里矣。"关公闻言，勃然变色，美髯飘动，大怒曰："天下英雄，闻吾之名，无不畏服；庞德竖子，何敢藐视吾耶！关平一面攻打樊城，吾自去斩此匹夫，以雪吾恨！"平曰："父亲不可以泰山之重，与顽石争高下。辱子愿代父去战庞德。"关公曰："汝试一往，吾随后便来接应。"关平出帐，提刀上马，领兵来迎庞德。两阵对圆，魏营一面皂旗上大书"南安庞德"四个白字。庞德青袍银铠，钢刀白马，立于阵前；背后五百军兵紧随，步卒数人肩抬木橔而出。关平大骂庞德："背主之贼！"庞德问部卒曰："此何人也？"或答曰："此关公义子关平也。"德叫曰："吾奉魏王旨，来取汝父之首！汝乃疥癞小儿，吾不杀汝！快唤汝父来！"平大怒，纵马舞刀，来取庞德。德横刀来迎。战三十合，不分胜负，两家各歇。

loyal and brave; we have nothing to fear." But the adviser Jia Xu said, "Pang De is counting on raw physical courage for his battle. But I have my doubts." Cao Cao agreed and had a warning communicated to Pang De: "Lord Guan has a full measure of wit and courage. Do not underestimate him. If you can take him, take him; if not, defend with caution." Pang De acknowledged the command and said to his commanders, "Why does His Highness place such emphasis on Guan? I predict that this time I will put an end to his reputation of thirty years." To this boast Yu Jin responded, "What the king of Wei wishes we must obey." Pang De urged his army on to Fan; and there to the sound of gongs and the beat of drums he flaunted his martial powers.

Meanwhile, Lord Guan had received a surveillance report in his command tent: "Cao Cao has sent Yu Jin in command of seven detachments of picked troops. Pang De, the vanguard, has brought a coffin with him and defiantly vows to fight you to the finish, General. They're some thirty *li* from here." At these words Lord Guan's face darkened and his fine curly beard quivered. Wrathfully he cried, "Heroes of the realm cower at the sound of my name. How dare this punk scorn me! Guan Ping, you attack Fan. I myself will dispatch this skunk to vent my outrage." But Guan Ping replied, "Father, does mighty Mount Tai challenge a common stone? Let me engage Pang De." "Try one turn," Lord Guan replied. "I will follow and relieve you." Guan Ping left the tent, armed himself, and rode off with his men to meet Pang De.

The oppposing lines formed. Above the northern camp flew a black flag inscribed "Pang De of Nan'an." Pang De had a black battle gown and silvery armor, a steel sword, and a white horse. Thus he stood before his line, five hundred warriors close behind. Several foot soldiers appeared bearing the coffin. Guan Ping denounced Pang De: "Traitor! Villain!" Pang De turned to his men and asked, "Who is that?" "Guan's adopted son," was the reply. Pang De called over to him: "I hold the mandate of the king of Wei to take your father's head. Scabby urchin, you're not worth the killing. Call out your father." Guan Ping dashed forth swinging his blade. Pang De leveled his own and they closed. The combat raged for thirty clashes; then the fighters broke and rested. Neither had prevailed.

早有人报知关公。公大怒，令廖化去攻樊城，自己亲来迎敌庞德。关平接着，言与庞德交战，不分胜负。关公随即横刀出马，大叫曰："关云长在此，庞德何不早来受死！"鼓声响处，庞德出马曰："吾奉魏王旨，特来取汝首！恐汝不信，备榇在此。汝若怕死，早下马受降！"关公大骂曰："量汝一匹夫，亦何能为！可惜我青龙刀斩汝鼠贼！"纵马舞刀，来取庞德。德轮刀来迎。二将战有百余合，精神倍长。两军各看得痴呆了。魏军恐庞德有失，急令鸣金收军。关平恐父年老，亦急鸣金。二将各退。庞德归寨，对众曰："人言关公英雄，今日方信也。"正言间，于禁至。相见毕，禁曰："闻将军战关公，百合之上，未得便宜，何不且退军避之？"德奋然曰："魏王命将军为大将，何太弱也？吾来日与关某共决一死，誓不退避！"禁不敢阻而回。

却说关公回寨，谓关平曰："庞德刀法惯熟，真吾敌手。"平曰："俗云：'初生之犊不惧虎。'父亲纵然斩了此人，只是西羌一小卒耳；倘有疏虞，非所以重伯父之托也。"关公曰："吾不杀此人，何以雪恨？吾意已决，再勿多言！"次日，上马引兵前进。庞德亦引兵来迎。两阵对圆，二将齐出，更不打话，出马交锋。

Lord Guan was furious at the news from the field. He sent Liao Hua to attack Fan and went himself to deal with Pang De. Guan Ping met his father and described his battle with Pang De. Lord Guan rushed out, sword leveled, and hurled his challenge at De. "Yunchang is here!" he cried. "Come quickly — and die!" To the beat of drums Pang De emerged. "I hold the king of Wei's command to take your head. If you doubt it, the coffin stands ready. If you fear death, dismount and surrender." Lord Guan hurled back his curses: "What can a low-down nobody do to me? What a shame to waste my dragon blade on a rodent like you." Racing forward, blade dancing, Lord Guan made for Pang De. De met him, making circles with his sword. The two warriors clashed more than one hundred times, but their energies seemed only to redouble. On both sides the armies watched, transfixed. Finally, the northern army of Wei, fearing for Pang De, sounded the recall gongs. And Guan Ping, concerned for his father who was no longer young, also rang the gong; the two generals returned to their lines.

Back at camp, Pang De said to his followers, "Lord Guan is reputed to be a great hero. Today I am convinced." At that moment Yu Jin entered and said to him, "I heard that you had fought over a hundred bouts with Lord Guan but could not get the better of him. Why not pull the army back for a while and avoid the enemy?" Pang De replied hotly, "You are the king of Wei's chief general. Don't be chicken-hearted! Tomorrow I will fight Guan to the finish. As for pulling back — never!" Yu Jin could not object further, and returned to his camp.

Back at his camp, Lord Guan said to his son, "Pang De is a past master of swordsmanship. Truly my equal." Guan Ping replied, "You know the saying, 'The newborn calf has no fear of tigers.' Even if you kill him, Father, he's no more than a run-of-the-mill Qiang warrior. And what if something goes wrong? What a way to show respect for our weighty charge from Uncle Xuande!" Lord Guan replied, "There is no other way to settle the score. My mind is made up. The matter is closed."

The following day Lord Guan rode forth, and Pang De met him. The armies deployed into lines as the opposing generals came out. No time was wasted on words. They joined battle at once. After some fifty clashes Pang De drew his horse around and fled, letting his sword drag behind

斗至五十余合，庞德拨回马，拖刀而走。关公随后追赶。关平恐有疏失，亦随后赶去。关公口中大骂："庞贼！欲使拖刀计，吾岂惧汝？"原来庞德虚作拖刀势，却把刀就鞍鞒挂住，偷拽雕弓，搭上箭，射将来。关平眼快，见庞德拽弓，大叫："贼将休放冷箭！"关公急睁眼看时，弓弦响处，箭早到来；躲闪不及，正中左臂。关平马到，救父回营。庞德勒回马轮刀赶来，忽听得本营锣声大震。德恐后军有失，急勒马回。原来于禁见庞德射中关公，恐他成了大功，灭禁威风，故鸣金收军。庞德回马，问："何故鸣金？"于禁曰："魏王有戒：关公智勇双全。他虽中箭，只恐有诈，故鸣金收军。"德曰："若不收军，吾已斩了此人也。"禁曰："'紧行无好步'，当缓图之。"庞德不知于禁之意，只懊悔不已。

却说关公回营，拔了箭头。幸得箭射不深，用金疮药敷之。关公痛恨庞德，谓众将曰："吾誓报此一箭之仇！"众将对曰："将军且暂安息几日，然后与战未迟。"次日，人报庞德引军搦战。关公就要出战。众将劝住。庞德令小军毁骂。关平把住隘口，分付众将休报知关公。庞德搦战十余日，无人出迎，乃与于禁商议曰："眼见关公箭疮举发，不能动止；不若乘此机会，统七军一拥杀入寨中，可救樊城之围。"于禁恐庞德成功，只把

him. Lord Guan pursued closely, followed by Guan Ping, who feared some mishap. "Scoundrel!" cried Lord Guan, cursing. "You think that old trick will scare me!" In fact, Pang De's "trailing-sword trick" was only a pretense. He had actually hooked the weapon onto his saddle and stealthily drawn his bow; then fitting an arrow, he made his shot. The acute Guan Ping had spotted Pang De's maneuver and shouted, "Villain! No sneak shot!" But even as Lord Guan watched, the bow hummed and the shaft struck his left arm. Riding alongside, Guan Ping saw his father safely back to camp. Pang De, stabbing the air with his weapon, started to give chase when the gongs in his own camp sounded furiously. Fearing trouble in his rear ranks, Pang De rode back.

What had happened was this: Yu Jin had seen Pang De's arrow hit Lord Guan and rang the gongs of retreat to prevent Pang De from achieving merit that would eclipse his own reputation. Riding back, Pang De demanded, "Why were the gongs sounded?" Yu Jin replied, "The king of Wei warned us, Lord Guan is a master of strategy and combat. Although he was hit, I was afraid of deception." "If you had not recalled us, I would have killed the man by now," retorted Pang De. "You know, 'A swift course, an easy fall.' Let's plan this more carefully," was the explanation, and Pang De, never realizing Yu Jin's true motive, had to resign himself to his frustration.[1]

Lord Guan returned to camp and had the arrow removed from his arm. It had not penetrated far, luckily for him, and the wound was treated with medicine for injuries from weapons. With intense hatred Lord Guan said to his commanders, "I will avenge this wound." The commanders answered, "Rest a few days first, General, before fighting again." But the next day when Pang De came and delivered his challenge, Lord Guan wanted to go forth. The commanders pleaded with him not to go. Pang De had his men hurl abuse at Lord Guan. Guan Ping kept the points of access closed, however, and ordered all commanders to report nothing to his father.

Pang De issued challenges for more than ten days; but when no one responded, he said to Yu Jin, "It seems that the wound is having its effect. He cannot act. This is our chance to storm their positions with our seven armies and relieve the siege at Fan." But again, fearing Pang De's

魏王戒旨相推，不肯动兵。庞德累欲动兵，于禁只不允，乃移七军转过山口，离樊城北十里，依山下寨，禁自领兵截断大路，令庞德屯兵于谷后：使德不能进兵成功。

却说关平见关公箭疮已合，甚是喜悦。忽听得于禁移七军于樊城之北下寨，未知其谋，即报知关公。公遂上马，引数骑上高阜处望之，见樊城城上旗号不整，军士慌乱；城北十里山谷之内，屯着军马；又见襄江水势甚急。看了半晌，唤向导官问曰："樊城北十里山谷，是何地名？"对曰："罾口川也。"关公喜曰："于禁必为我擒矣。"将士问曰："将军何以知之？"关公曰："'鱼'入'罾口'，岂能久乎？"诸将未信。公回本寨。时值八月秋天，骤雨数日。公令人预备船筏，收拾水具。关平问曰："陆地相持，何用水具？"公曰："非汝所知也。——于禁七军不屯于广易之地，而聚于罾口川险隘之处；方今秋雨连绵，襄江之水必然泛涨；吾已差人堰住各处水口，待水发时，乘高就船，放水一淹，樊城、罾口川之兵皆为鱼鳖矣。"关平拜服。

却说魏军屯于罾口川，连日大雨不止，督将成何来见于禁

success, Yu Jin reiterated the king of Wei's insistence on caution and would not accede to Pang De's pleas for military action. Instead, Yu Jin shifted the armies over to the approaches to the hills and established new positions some ten *li* north of Fan. Yu Jin took his army to cut off the main road and had Pang De station his forces at the rear of the gorge, thus preventing him from winning any victories.

*　*　*

Guan Ping was overjoyed to see that his father's wound had closed. Suddenly he learned that Yu Jin had shifted his seven armies north of Fan. Unable to decide what they were planning, he went to inform his father. Lord Guan rode with a few companions to a high knoll to observe the city. He saw that the flags on the walls were disorderly and the soldiers slovenly. He noted that troops were deployed in a ravine ten *li* north of the city and that the waters of the River Xiang were unusually swift. After looking over the terrain for some time, he summoned a local guide and asked, "What do they call that ravine north of Fan?" "Zengkou, 'Open Net Stream,'" was the reply. Lord Guan said with satisfaction, "Then Yu Jin is mine!" "How do you know that?" his officers asked. "Once a fish enters the mouth of the net," Lord Guan answered, "how long can it live?"[2] The commanders looked skeptical. Lord Guan returned to his camp.

It was autumn, the eighth month (A.D. 219). Heavy rainstorms struck and lasted for several days. Lord Guan ordered his men to prepare rafts, poles for punting, and the like. Guan Ping asked him, "We will confront them on land; why do we need these things?" "You wouldn't understand," Lord Guan replied. "Yu Jin has not positioned his forces on broad and open ground but has concentrated them by the narrow point called Open Net Stream. Now the seasonal rains have been coming down for days; the Xiang is bound to overflow. I have already had several points dammed. When the flood crests, we'll take to our boats. Then we'll release the waters and turn the troops around Fan and Open Net into fishes and turtles." Guan Ping expressed admiration for his father's strategy.

The forces of Wei kept to their positions at Open Net as the rains continued unabated. Army Inspector Cheng He came to Yu Jin and said,

曰:"大军屯于川口,地势甚低;虽有土山,离营稍远。即今秋雨连绵,军士艰辛。近有人报说荆州兵移于高阜处,又于汉水口预备战筏;倘江水泛涨,我军危矣;宜早为计。"于禁叱曰:"匹夫惑吾军心耶!再有多言者斩之!"成何羞惭而退,却来见庞德,说此事。德曰:"汝所见甚当。于将军不肯移兵,吾明日自移军屯于他处。"

计议方定,是夜风雨大作。庞德坐于帐中,只听得万马争奔,征鼙震地。德大惊,急出帐上马看时,四面八方,大水骤至;七军乱窜,随波逐浪者,不计其数。平地水深丈余,于禁、庞德与诸将各登小山避水。比及平明,关公及众将皆摇旗鼓噪,乘大船而来。于禁见四下无路,左右止有五六十人,料不能逃,口称"愿降"。关公令尽去衣甲,拘收入船,然后来擒庞德。时庞德并二董及成何,与步卒五百人,皆无衣甲,立在堤上。见关公来,庞德全无惧怯,奋然前来接战。关公将船四面围定,军士一齐放箭,射死魏兵大半。董衡、董超见势已危,乃告庞德曰:"军士折伤大半,四下无路,不如投降。"庞德大怒曰:"吾受魏王厚恩,岂肯屈节于人!"遂亲斩董衡、董超于前,厉声曰:"再说降者,以此二人为例!"于是众皆奋力御敌。自平明战至日中,勇力倍增。关公催四面急攻,矢石如雨。德令军士用短兵接战。

"It's low ground here at the mouth of the stream where the army is stationed. The elevations are too far from our main camps. The rains have made the troops miserable. The latest news is that the men of Jingzhou have moved to higher ground and are preparing rafts for combat at the mouth of the River Han. Now — before the waters rise and endanger our army — now is the time to plan for them." Yu Jin rebuked the speaker sharply, saying, "A nobody like you wants to disturb the army? The next man to complain dies." Humiliated, Cheng He withdrew and went to Pang De, who said, "I agree with you. If General Yu won't move the men tomorrow, I will." They worked out a plan.

During that night of fierce wind and heavy rain Pang De, sitting in his tent, heard the restless movements of ten thousand horses and the ground-shaking roll of war drums. Alarmed, he went outside and rode off to look. From all sides, floodwaters were rushing in; the seven armies, thrown into panic flight, had already lost untold numbers in the tide. On level ground the water reached a depth of more than ten spans. Yu Jin, Pang De, and the commanders climbed to safe heights. By dawn Lord Guan and his commanders, waving flags and beating drums, were bearing down in large ships. Yu Jin saw no way out and, with barely fifty or sixty men around him, declared his willingness to surrender. Lord Guan ordered Yu Jin and his men to strip off their armor and took them on board under guard. He then went for Pang De.

At this time Pang De, Dong Heng, Dong Chao, and Cheng He were standing on an embankment with five hundred foot soldiers; none had armor. At Lord Guan's approach, Pang De went boldly to meet him. Lord Guan had his boats ring the group; then his archers went to work, killing the greater part of the northern troops. Dong Heng and Dong Chao pleaded with Pang De: "More than half our men are gone. We are trapped here. Surrender is our only hope." But Pang De, enraged, replied, "As a beneficiary of the king's favor, I will never bow to another," and cut down the two men with his own blade. He cried sternly, "Whoever else urges surrender will follow them!" This stand roused his troops, and they battled the enemy from dawn to midday with redoubled vigor.

Lord Guan urged his own forces to strike harder; they poured stones and arrows down on the enemy. Pang De ordered his men into close

德回顾成何曰："吾闻'勇将不怯死以苟免，壮士不毁节而求生'。今日乃我死日也。汝可努力死战。"成何依令向前，被关公一箭射落水中。众军皆降，止有庞德一人力战。正遇荆州数十人，驾小船近堤来，德提刀飞身一跃，早上小船，立杀十余人，余皆弃船赴水逃命。庞德一手提刀，一手使短棹，欲向樊城而走。只见上流头，一将撑大筏而至，将小船撞翻，庞德落于水中。船上那将跳下水去，生擒庞德上船。众视之，擒庞德者，乃周仓也。仓素知水性，又在荆州住了数年，愈加惯熟；更兼力大，因此擒了庞德。于禁所领七军，皆死于水中。其会水者料无去路，亦皆投降。后人有诗曰：

夜半征鼙响震天，襄樊平地作深渊。

关公神算谁能及，华夏威名万古传。

关公回到高阜去处，升帐而坐。群刀手押过于禁来。禁拜伏于地，乞哀请命。关公曰："汝怎敢抗吾？"禁曰："上命差遣，身不由己。望君侯怜悯，誓以死报。"公绰髯笑曰："吾杀汝，犹杀狗彘耳，空污刀斧！"令人缚送荆州大牢内监候："待吾回，别作区处。"发落去讫。关公又令押过庞德。德睁眉怒目，立而不跪，关公曰："汝兄现在汉中；汝故主马超，亦在蜀中为大将：汝如何不早降？"德大怒曰："吾宁死于刀下，岂降汝耶！"骂不绝

combat with short swords. Turning to Cheng He, he said, "You know the saying, 'Not even death can make the brave general look for an easy out or try to survive at the cost of his integrity.' This is the day I will die. And I want all of you to fight to the death."

Cheng He advanced as ordered. A single arrow from Lord Guan dropped him into the river. The rest of the soldiers surrendered. Pang De alone fought on. He came upon a few dozen Jingzhou soldiers guiding a small craft near his embankment. Pang De shouted and sprang to the deck. At once his whirling sword claimed ten men. The rest jumped into the water. Pang De, his sword in one hand, the boat's rudder in the other, tried to escape to Fan. But a large raft hit his boat, overturning it and dumping him into the river. The commander of the raft — Zhou Cang — leaped into the water and captured Pang De. Zhou Cang was used to the water, and his many years in Jingzhou had made him all the more adept. In addition, he had great physical strength; thus, he captured Pang De. The seven armies under Yu Jin's command perished; the others, who saw no way out, surrendered. A poet of later times has left these lines:

> Battle drums beat hard throughout the night
> As Lord Guan sent a flood across their flats.
> Inspired tactics forced the foe's defeat:
> Immortal now, the name the heartland feared.

1831

Lord Guan returned to his high vantage point, entered his tent, and seated himself. A throng of armed guards hustled Yu Jin into his presence. Jin threw himself to the ground, begging piteously for his life. "How dared you resist me?" Lord Guan said. "I acted on orders," Yu Jin answered. "It was not my own doing. Have mercy, Your Lordship, and I will repay you with lifelong devotion." Fondling his beard, Lord Guan laughed. "Killing you would be like killing a dog or a pig," he said at last. "Why dirty a good axe?" He ordered Yu Jin sent back to jail in Jingzhou, adding, "I'll deal with you when I return." And thus he disposed of Yu Jin.

Lord Guan then ordered Pang De brought before him. Pang De stared Lord Guan full in the face, rage in his glare, and refused to kneel. "Your elder brother is now in Hanzhong," Lord Guan said. "And your former lord, Ma Chao, is a chief general in the Riverlands. Why not surrender to

口。公大怒，喝令刀斧手推出斩之。德引颈受刑。关公怜而葬之。于是乘水势未退，复上战船，引大小将校来攻樊城。

却说樊城周围，白浪滔天，水势益甚，城垣渐渐浸塌，男女担土搬砖，填塞不住。曹军众将，无不丧胆，慌忙来告曹仁曰："今日之危，非力可救；可趁敌军未至，乘舟夜走：虽然失城，尚可全身。"仁从其言。方欲备船出走，满宠谏曰："不可。山水骤至，岂能长存？不旬日即当自退。关公虽未攻城，已遣别将在郏下。其所以不敢轻进者，虑吾军袭其后也。今若弃城而去，黄河以南，非国家之有矣。愿将军固守此城，以为保障。"仁拱手称谢曰："非伯宁之教，几误大事。"乃骑白马上城，聚众将发誓曰："吾受魏王命，保守此城；但有言弃城而去者斩！"诸将皆曰："某等愿以死据守！"仁大喜，就城上设弓弩数百，军士昼夜防护，不敢懈怠。老幼居民，担土石填塞城垣。旬日之内，水势渐退。

关公自擒魏将于禁等，威震天下，无不惊骇。忽次子关兴来寨内省亲。公就令兴赍诸官立功文书去成都见汉中王，各求

me?" "I'll die under the knife first," was Pang De's angry retort, and curses poured from his lips. In a fury Lord Guan barked the order for execution to the axemen, and Pang De stretched forth his neck, eager for the blow. Afterward Lord Guan, touched by Pang De's spirit, had him buried properly. Then, while the flood waters were still high, Lord Guan and his men took to their war-boats and began the attack on Fan.[3]

* * *

Around the besieged city white breakers surged against the horizon, and the increasing pressure of the water undermined the city walls. The entire population worked relentlessly with earth and brick but could not shore them up. Fear-stricken, the northern military leaders rushed to Cao Ren. "The crisis is past relieving," they said. "Let us flee tonight by boat before the enemy arrives. We can save ourselves even if we lose the city." Cao Ren agreed and was about to order the withdrawal, when Man Chong objected. "It is a mistake," he said, "Among these mountains the floods come on in a flash, but never remain for long. They are sure to recede within ten days. Before attacking, Lord Guan sent auxiliary commanders on to Jiaxia, which shows that he cannot advance at will for fear we will ambush him from behind. If we abandon the city of Fan today, nothing south of the Yellow River will remain in the possession of the dynasty. I urge you, General, to maintain the defense of this point, the outer shield of our security."

Clasping his hands before his chest, Cao Ren expressed appreciation. "If not for your advice, Man Chong," he said, "everything might have been ruined."[4] Ren rode his white horse up to the wall and swore before his commanders: "The king of Wei has mandated me to defend this city, and I will execute anyone who speaks of deserting it." The commanders responded by vowing to hold the city to the death. Well pleased, Cao Ren placed several hundred archers and crossbowmen on the wall. Day and night the soldiers mounted strict guard, never slackening for a moment, while the old and young worked at carrying earth to fortify the walls. Within ten days the waters had begun to recede.

Lord Guan's capture of General Yu Jin made him a power feared throughout the realm. Unexpectedly Guan's second son, Xing, came to see his father at the camp. Lord Guan ordered him to go to Chengdu and

1833

升迁。兴拜辞父亲,径投成都去讫。

却说关公分兵一半,直抵郏下。公自领兵四面攻打樊城。当日关公自到北门,立马扬鞭,指而问曰:"汝等鼠辈,不早来降,更待何时?"正言间,曹仁在敌楼上,见关公身上止披掩心甲,斜袒着绿袍,乃急招五百弓弩手,一齐放箭。公急勒马回时,右臂上中一弩箭,翻身落马。

正是:

　　水里七军方丧胆,城中一箭忽伤身。

未知关公性命如何,且看下文分解。

present the king of Hanzhong with a list of the accomplishments of his officers and requests for promotion. Guan Xing bade his father good-bye and headed for the capital of the Riverlands.

Next, Lord Guan sent half his army against Jiaxia while he led the other half in a four-sided assault on Fan. That day Lord Guan went himself to the north gate of the city. Astride his horse, he flourished a whip and issued a challenge: "The time to surrender has long passed, you rats!" At that very moment, from his watchtower Cao Ren noticed that Lord Guan was wearing only his breastplate and that from the side his green battle gown was exposed. Ren hurriedly summoned five hundred bowmen to let fly at him together. Lord Guan swung his horse swiftly around, but a bolt caught his right arm, and he dropped from his horse. Indeed:

> Amid the flood, the seven armies quailed;
> From the wall, a single shot — a leader felled.

Would Lord Guan survive?[5]

Read on.

第七十五回

关云长刮骨疗毒　吕子明白衣渡江

　　却说曹仁见关公落马，即引兵冲出城来；被关平一阵杀回，救关公归寨，拔出臂箭。原来箭头有药，毒已入骨，右臂青肿，不能运动。关平慌与众将商议曰："父亲若损此臂，安能出敌？不如暂回荆州调理。"于是与众将入帐见关公。公问曰："汝等来有何事？"众对曰："某等因见君侯右臂损伤，恐临敌致怒，冲突不便。众议可暂班师回荆州调理。"公怒曰："吾取樊城，只在目前；取了樊城，即当长驱大进，径到许都，剿灭操贼，以安汉室。岂可因小疮而误大事？汝等敢慢吾军心耶！"平等默然而退。

　　众将见公不肯退兵，疮又不痊，只得四方访问名医。忽一日，有人从江东驾小舟而来，直至寨前。小校引见关平。平视其人：方巾阔服，臂挽青囊；自言姓名："乃沛国谯郡人，姓华，名佗，字元化。因闻关将军乃天下英雄，今中毒箭，特来医治。"平曰："莫非昔日医东吴周泰者乎？"佗曰："然。"平大喜，即与众

Chapter 75

Hua Tuo Scrapes the Poison from
Lord Guan's Bone
Lü Meng Sends Mariners Across
the River in Disguise

The moment he saw Lord Guan fall, Cao Ren and his men came charging out of the city for the kill. But Guan Ping fought the northerners off and brought his father safely back to camp. There the arrow was removed from his right arm. The arrowhead, however, had been poisoned; ulceration had reached the bone, and the arm, greenish and swollen, would not move. Guan Ping hastily convened the commanders and said, "If my father loses his arm, he will never fight again. It will be best to go back to Jiangling and take care of it." He then went with the commanders to see their leader. "What have you come for?" Lord Guan asked. "In view of Your Lordship's wound," they replied, "We are afraid the shock of battle could be bad for you. Our consensus is for all to return to Jiangling with you for treatment."

Lord Guan responded angrily, "Fan is within our grasp, and once we have it, we can reach Cao's capital at Xuchang by forced march. Then we can flush out the traitor, destroy him, and secure the house of Han. I cannot ruin this enterprise for the sake of a minor wound. Don't sap the morale of the troops." Guan Ping and the rest retired silently.

Lord Guan would not retreat, and the wound would not heal. His commanders were searching high and low for a good doctor when one arrived unexpectedly by boat from the Southland. A petty officer led him to Guan Ping, who studied the man. He had a square cap and loose-fitting clothes. A black satchel hung from his arm. Volunteering his name, he said, "I am Hua Tuo (styled Yuanhua) from the Qiao district in the fief of Pei. Hearing that General Guan, the world-renowned hero, has been wounded by a poisoned arrow, I have come especially to cure him." "I believe you are the man who once treated Zhou Tai of the Southland," Guan Ping said. "That is true," Tuo replied. Guan Ping was delighted,

1837

汉英经典文库

将同引华佗入帐见关公。时关公本是臂疼，恐慢军心，无可消遣，正与马良弈棋；闻有医者至，即召入。礼毕，赐坐。茶罢，佗请臂视之。公袒下衣袍，伸臂令佗看视。佗曰："此乃弩箭所伤，其中有乌头之药，直透入骨；若不早治，此臂无用矣。"公曰："用何物治之？"佗曰："某自有治法。——但恐君侯惧耳。"公笑曰："吾视死如归，有何惧哉？"佗曰："当于静处立一标柱，上钉大环，请君侯将臂穿于环中，以绳系之，然后以被蒙其首。吾用尖刀割开皮肉，直至于骨，刮去骨上箭毒，用药敷之，以线缝其口，方可无事。——但恐君侯惧耳。"公笑曰："如此，容易！何用柱环？"令设酒席相待。

公饮数杯酒毕，一面仍与马良弈棋，伸臂令佗割之。佗取尖刀在手，令一小校捧一大盆于臂下接血。佗曰："某便下手。君侯勿惊。"公曰："任汝医治。吾岂比世间俗子，惧痛者耶！"佗乃下刀，割开皮肉，直至于骨，骨上已青；佗用刀刮骨，悉悉有声。帐上帐下见者，皆掩面失色。公饮酒食肉，谈笑弈棋，全无痛苦之色。

须臾，血流盈盆。佗刮尽其毒，敷上药，以线缝之。公大笑而起，谓众将曰："此臂伸舒如故，并无痛矣。先生真神医也！"佗曰："某为医一生，未尝见此。君侯真天神也！"后人

and in company with the commanders he took Hua Tuo in to Lord Guan.

Lord Guan was in terrible pain and worried about morale in the army. He was playing chess with Ma Liang to divert himself when they arrived. He invited the doctor in and, after the formalities, offered him a seat. Tea was served and drunk. Hua Tuo then asked to examine the wound. Lord Guan bared his arm and stretched it out. "This is from a crossbow," Hua Tuo said. "There is aconite infiltrating the bone. The arm will be useless if not treated soon." "What would you use?" Lord Guan asked. "I can save it," Hua Tuo answered, "but I am afraid Your Lordship would shrink from the treatment." With a smile Lord Guan responded, "To me, death is my homecoming. I will not shrink."

Hua Tuo continued, "In a quiet room we will have to set up a post with a loop nailed to the top. I will ask you to put your arm through the loop and let us tie it. We will cover your head with a blanket. I will cut through to the bone with a razor and scrape the poison off the bone; then after applying some medicine, I will sew up the wound. Nothing will happen to you; I am only afraid you will shrink from the surgery." "Is that all? It won't bother me a bit," Lord Guan replied. "And you can dispense with post and loop." With that he ordered a feast set forth.

After a few cups, Lord Guan resumed his game of chess with Ma Liang as he extended his arm and instructed the doctor to start the operation. An attendant held a basin under the arm to catch the blood. Hua Tuo took up his knife and said, "I am ready. Have no fear, Your Lordship." "Do what is required," said Lord Guan. "Don't think I shrink from pain like any common fellow." Hua Tuo parted the flesh, exposing the bone: it was already coated green. The knife made a thin, grating scund as it scraped the surface, until everyone present blanched and covered his face. But Lord Guan continued eating and drinking, laughing and talking as he played, showing no sign of pain.

In a short time the basin filled with blood. Hua Tuo finished the scraping, applied medicine, and sewed the wound shut. Lord Guan got up, smiled, and said to his commanders, "The arm is as flexible as ever. There is no pain at all. Master, you are a marvelous physician." Hua Tuo replied, "In a lifetime of practice I have never seen anything like this! It is Your Lordship who is more than human!" A poet of later times left

有诗曰：

治病须分内外科，世间妙艺苦无多。

神威罕及惟关将；圣手能医说华佗。

关公箭疮既愈，设席款谢华佗。佗曰："君侯箭疮虽治，然须爱护。切勿怒气伤触。过百日后，平复如旧矣。"关公以金百两酬之，佗曰："某闻君侯高义，特来医治，岂望报乎！"坚辞不受，留药一帖，以敷疮口，辞别而去。

却说关公擒了于禁，斩了庞德，威名大震，华夏皆惊。探马报到许都，曹操大惊，聚文武商议曰："某素知云长智勇盖世，今据荆襄，如虎生翼。于禁被擒，庞德被斩，魏兵挫锐；倘彼率兵直至许都，如之奈何？孤欲迁都以避之。"司马懿谏曰："不可。于禁等被水所淹，非战之故；于国家大计，本无所损。今孙、刘失好，云长得志，孙权必不喜；大王可遣使去东吴陈说利害，令孙权暗暗起兵蹑云长之后，许事平之日，割江南之地以封孙权：则樊城之危自解矣。"主簿蒋济曰："仲达之言是也。今可即发使往东吴，不必迁都动众。"操依允，遂不迁都；因叹谓诸将

these lines:

> Physic and surgery — two branches of one art —
> The rare and subtle science of the mortal world.
> For superhuman might, Lord Guan may take the crown;
> For sacred skill in healing, Hua Tuo wins renown.

When his wound was better, Lord Guan held a banquet to thank Hua Tuo. "Your Lordship's wound is cured," the doctor said, "but it must still be protected from any shock of anger. It will take a hundred days before everything is normal." Lord Guan offered Hua Tuo one hundred taels of gold, but the physician said, "I seek no reward. Your reputation for a high-minded sense of honor brought me here." Firmly refusing payment, Hua Tuo left a prescription for medicine to put on the wound; then he took his leave and departed.[1]

After Lord Guan's stunning victories — the capture of Yu Jin and the execution of Pang De — his name resounded across the northern heartland, impressing one and all. When spies reported Lord Guan's triumph in the capital, Cao Cao summoned his advisers and said in alarm, "I have always known that Lord Guan surpassed all others in wisdom and valor. Now he holds Xiangyang: the tiger has grown wings! Yu Jin has been captured, Pang De killed, and our own keen mettle blunted. What if they come straight to the capital? I think we should take the precaution of transferring the government."

Sima Yi objected to this proposal: "Yu Jin's men drowned in the flood, not in battle. Jin's defeat does not affect the government's position. Moreover, current discord between the Liu and Sun houses means that if Lord Guan gets what he wants, Sun Quan will be very unhappy. This is the time, Your Highness, to send someone down there who, by judicious argument — and by offering the entire Southland to Sun Quan as his fief once peace is restored — will be able to convince Sun Quan to muster a force and quietly pounce on Lord Guan from behind. That is how to relieve the siege at Fan."[2]

First Secretary Jiang Ji added, "Sima Yi is right. Send a man to the Southland. There's no need to move the capital and disturb the people. Cao Cao assented, and the idea of moving the capital was dropped. In a tone of dismay Cao said to his commanders, "Yu Jin followed me for

1841

曰:"于禁从孤三十年,何期临危反不如庞德也!今一面遣使致书东吴,一面必得一大将以当云长之锐——"言未毕,阶下一将应声而出曰:"某愿往。"操视之,乃徐晃也。操大喜,遂拨精兵五万,令徐晃为将,吕建副之,克日起兵,前到阳陵坡驻扎;看东南有应,然后征进。

　　却说孙权接得曹操书信,览毕,欣然应允,即修书发付使者先回,乃聚文武商议。张昭曰:"近闻云长擒于禁,斩庞德,威震华夏,操欲迁都以避其锋。今樊城危急,遣使求救,事定之后,恐有反覆。"权未及发言,忽报:"吕蒙乘小舟自陆口来,有事面禀。"权召入问之,蒙曰:"今云长提兵围樊城,可乘其远出,袭取荆州。"权曰:"孤欲北取徐州,如何?"蒙曰:"今操远在河北,未暇东顾,徐州守兵无多,往自可克;然其地势利于陆战,不利水战,纵然得之,亦难保守。不如先取荆州,全据长江,别作良图。"权曰:"孤本欲取荆州,前言特以试卿耳。卿可速为孤图之。孤当随后便起兵也。"

　　吕蒙辞了孙权,回至陆口,早有哨马报说:"沿江上下,或二十里,或三十里,高阜处各有烽火台。"又闻荆州军马整肃,

thirty years. It surprised me that at the moment of truth he didn't measure up even to Pang De. Now I want a man to take the letter to the Southland, and I also want a ranking commander to check Lord Guan's advance." Even as he spoke, a commander standing below volunteered. Cao Cao turned to him. It was Xu Huang. Well pleased, Cao Cao put fifty thousand picked men in Xu Huang's command, with Lü Jian as his deputy. On the appointed day the army advanced to Yangling Slope and camped there, waiting for an answer from the Southland before marching on.

* * *

On receiving Cao Cao's letter, Sun Quan readily accepted the proposed plan and swiftly dispatched his answer. He then assembled his counselors. Zhang Zhao made the first argument: "The recent news is that the north is so shaken by Lord Guan's victories over Yu Jin and Pang De that Cao Cao wants to move the capital and thus avoid the brunt of Guan's attack. Now that Fan may fall, he sends to us for help. But after the situation is stabilized, he will only go back on his word." Before Sun Quan had time to speak, a report came in: "Commander Lü Meng has arrived by boat from Lukou with important business to present in person." Sun Quan summoned the commander, who said, "Lord Guan has deployed around Fan. Now is the time to attack Jingzhou, when he is on a far-off campaign." "I was thinking rather of going north and taking Xuzhou," Sun Quan replied. "Cao Cao, too, is far from his base on the north side of the Yellow River," Lü Meng said, "and has no time to look east to Xuzhou, it's true. Moreover, the province is lightly defended and should fall easily. However, the terrain favors the army rather than the navy. Even if we capture it, holding it will be another matter. I would take Jingzhou first; and then with the whole of the Great River secured, we can consider our next move." "Exactly my thought," Sun Quan responded. "I only wanted to sound you out. Quickly devise a plan. I will follow you with my army."[3]

Lü Meng bade Sun Quan good-bye and returned to Lukou. There, mounted scouts informed him: "Up and down the river there are warning-fire beacons, some twenty, some thirty *li* apart." Lü Meng also learned that the Jingzhou forces were magnificently marshaled and fully

预有准备,蒙大惊曰:"若如此,急难图也。我一时在吴侯面前劝取荆州,今却如何处置?"寻思无计,乃托病不出,使人回报孙权。权闻吕蒙患病,心甚怏怏。陆逊进言曰:"吕子明之病,乃诈耳,非真病也。"权曰:"伯言既知其诈,可往视之。"陆逊领命,星夜至陆口寨中,来见吕蒙,果然面无病色。逊曰:"某奉吴侯命,敬探子明贵恙。"蒙曰:"贱躯偶病,何劳探问。"逊曰:"吴侯以重任付公,公不乘时而动,空怀郁结,何也?"蒙目视陆逊,良久不语。逊又曰:"愚有小方,能治将军之疾,未审可用否?"蒙乃屏退左右而问曰:"伯言良方,乞早赐教。"逊笑曰:"子明之疾,不过因荆州兵马整肃,沿江有烽火台之备耳。予有一计,令沿江守吏,不能举火;荆州之兵,束手归降,可乎?"蒙惊谢曰:"伯言之语,如见我肺腑。愿闻良策。"陆逊曰:"云长倚恃英雄,自料无敌,所虑者惟将军耳。将军乘此机会,托疾辞职,以陆口之任让之他人,使他人卑辞赞美关公,以骄其心,彼必尽撤荆州之兵,以向樊城。若荆州无备,用一旅之师,别出奇计以袭之,则荆州在掌握之中矣。"蒙大喜曰:

prepared for attack. Startled, he said, "If that is how things stand, our plans are in trouble. A day ago I was trying to convince Lord Sun to capture Jingzhou. And now — how am I going to put my words into deeds?" Unable to come with a solution, Lü Meng hid from his lord under cover of illness.

Sun Quan was deeply saddened by the news of Lü Meng's illness. Another commander, Lu Xun, came forward and said, "Lü Meng's illness is not real; it is put on." "If you are sure of that," Sun Quan said, "look into it." As ordered, Lu Xun went to Lukou and saw Lü Meng, whose face, as he had expected, showed no sign of illness. Lu Xun said to him, "I have been instructed by Lord Sun to inquire most respectfully into what has given discomfort to your esteemed self." Lü Meng replied, "Some unforeseen disorder afflicts my humble person — hardly worth troubling yourself to inquire after." "Lord Sun has entrusted a heavy responsibility to you," Lu Xun went on. "But instead of seizing the time to act, you vainly nurse this melancholia. Why?" Lü Meng studied his visitor a long while but said nothing. Lu Xun continued, "I would be so foolish as to proffer a little prescription that should remedy your disorder, General. However, I am not certain it applies." Lü Meng dismissed his attendants and said, "Vouchsafe the precious remedy, and soon." With a smile Lu Xun said, "Your disorder is due to the magnificent marshaling of the Jingzhou army and its flare warning system along the river. But I have a plan to keep the guardians of the flare stations from raising the signal, a plan that will bring the armies of Jingzhou to surrender tamely. Would that suit you?" Lü Meng blurted out startled thanks, saying, "You speak as if you could see into my vitals. I would learn your worthy plan."

"Lord Guan counts too much on his heroic valor," Lu Xun explained, "and assumes he has no equal. You alone cause him concern. General, take this opportunity to resign your office, pleading ill health. Yield your command here at Lukou to someone else, someone whom we will instruct to acclaim and exalt Lord Guan with self-deprecatory phrases in order to feed his arrogance. Then he will be sure to pull back from Jingzhou and concentrate on Fan. If he leaves Jingzhou unprepared, a surprise attack by one of our contingents will yield control of it with a minimum of

"真良策也！"

由是吕蒙托病不起，上书辞职。陆逊回见孙权，具言前计。孙权乃召吕蒙还建业养病。蒙至，入见权，权问曰："陆口之任，昔周公谨荐鲁子敬以自代，后子敬又荐卿自代：今卿亦须荐一才望兼隆者，代卿为妙。"蒙曰："若用望重之人，云长必然提备。陆逊意思深长，而未有远名，非云长所忌；若即用以代臣之任，必有所济。"权大喜，即日拜陆逊为偏将军、右都督，代蒙守陆口。逊谢曰："某年幼无学，恐不堪重任。"权曰："子明保卿，必不差错。卿毋得推辞。"逊乃拜受印绶，连夜往陆口；交割马步水三军已毕，即修书一封，具名马、异锦、酒礼等物，遣使赍赴樊城见关公。

时公正将息箭疮，按兵不动。忽报："江东陆口守将吕蒙病危，孙权取回调理，近拜陆逊为将，代吕蒙守陆口。今逊差人赍书具礼，特来拜见。"关公召入，指来使而言曰："仲谋见识短浅，用此孺子为将！"来使伏地告曰："陆将军呈书备礼：一来与君侯作贺，二来求两家和好。幸乞笑留。"公拆书视之，书词极其卑谨。关公览毕，仰面大笑，令左右收了礼物，发付使者回去。使者回见陆逊曰："关公欣喜，无复有忧江东

effort." Lü Meng was delighted with the ruse. He persisted in claiming he was too sick to appear, and finally submitted a written resignation.

Lu Xun returned and explained the strategy to Sun Quan, who accordingly summoned Lü Meng back to Jianye to convalesce. Coming before Lord Sun, Lü Meng was told, "Originally, Zhou Yu recommended Lu Su as his replacement for the post you hold; Lu Su recommended you. Now you, too, should recommend someone able and well regarded to replace you." "If we appoint an important person," Lü Meng said, "Lord Guan will be on his guard. Lu Xun is a profound strategist and, having no more than a local reputation, is unlikely to cause Lord Guan anxiety. If you appoint him in my place, our plan should carry." Delighted, Sun Quan made Lu Xun subordinate commander and inspector on the Right, replacing Lü Meng as defender of Lukou.[4]

Lu Xun declined the honor, saying, "I am too young and inexperienced to assume so heavy a task." But Sun Quan said, "Lü Meng's recommendation could not be wrong. I will not take no for an answer." And so Lu Xun accepted the seal of office and departed at once for Lukou. After assuming command of all infantry, cavalry, and naval forces, Lu Xun drew up a letter to Lord Guan and sent it by messenger together with champion horses, rare silk damasks, wine, and other gifts.

While Lord Guan was recuperating from his wound and refraining from military action, the announcement came: "The Southland's chief commander at Lukou, Lü Meng, is dangerously ill. Sun Quan has recalled him for treatment and assigned Lu Xun to replace him. Lu Xun has sent a man with a letter and gifts as a gesture of respect." Lord Guan summoned the messenger and, pointing at him, said, "It seems rather shortsighted of Sun Quan to appoint a mere boy as general." The messenger bowed down to the ground and said, "General Lu presents this letter and these ceremonial gifts not only to honor Your Lordship, but with an earnest desire for accord and amity between the houses of Liu and Sun. I pray your indulgence in accepting them."

Lord Guan unsealed the letter and studied it. The language was the ultimate in self-deprecation and reverence. After perusing it, Lord Guan looked up and laughed, ordered his aides to receive the gifts, and sent the messenger back. The messenger told Lu Xun: "Lord Guan was appre-

之意。”

逊大喜，密遣人探得关公果然撤荆州大半兵赴樊城听调，只待箭疮痊可，便欲进兵。逊察知备细，即差人星夜报知孙权。孙权召吕蒙商议曰：“今云长果撤荆州之兵，攻取樊城，便可设计袭取荆州。卿与吾弟孙皎同引大军前去，何如？”孙皎字叔明，乃孙权叔父孙静之次子也。蒙曰：“主公若以蒙可用则独用蒙；若以叔明可用则独用叔明。岂不闻昔日周瑜、程普为左右都督，事虽决于瑜，然普自以旧臣而居瑜下，颇不相睦；后因见瑜之才，方始敬服？今蒙之才不及瑜，而叔明之亲胜于普，恐未必能相济也。”

权大悟，遂拜吕蒙为大都督，总制江东诸路军马；令孙皎在后接应粮草。蒙拜谢，点兵三万，快船八十余只，选会水者扮作商人，皆穿白衣，在船上摇橹，却将精兵伏于𦩷𦪇船中。次调韩当、蒋钦、朱然、潘璋、周泰、徐盛、丁奉等七员大将，相继而进。其余皆随吴侯为合后救应。一面遣使致书曹操，令进兵以袭云长之后；一面先传报陆逊，然后发白衣人，驾快船往浔阳江去。昼夜趱行，直抵北岸。江边烽火台上守台军盘问时，吴人

ciative and delighted. The Southland should not concern him any further."

Lu Xun could not have been more pleased. He sent spies into Jingzhou who reported that Lord Guan had indeed shifted most of his men to the siege at Fan and was waiting only for his wound to heal before launching the attack. After verifying the details, he dispatched the news to Sun Quan overnight. Sun Quan summoned Lü Meng and told him, "As expected, Lord Guan has pulled troops out of Gong'an and Jiangling in order to attack Fan. We can prepare the tactics to surprise the province. You and my younger cousin, Sun Jiao, shall lead the offensive. What do you say?" Sun Jiao (Shuming) was the second son of Quan's uncle Sun Jing.

Lü Meng responded, "If Your Lordship has confidence in me, use me alone. If you have confidence in Sun Jiao, use him alone. You must remember how much conflict there was when Zhou Yu and Cheng Pu were left and right field marshals; that was because Cheng Pu felt his senior status compromised by Zhou Yu's authority to make decisions. Cheng Pu had to see Zhou Yu's talents at work before he paid him the respect he deserved. My own talents fall far short of Zhou Yu's, and Sun Jiao is closer to you than Cheng Pu was; I'm afraid things wouldn't balance out."

1849

Sun Quan saw the wisdom of Lü Meng's point and made him chief commander with authority over all armed forces. He ordered Sun Jiao to oversee supply and support operations from the rear. Lü Meng prostrated himself in gratitude; then he called up thirty thousand men and eighty swift craft. He selected a group of able sailors, disguised them in the plain clothes that merchants usually wear, and placed them at the oars. Concealed in the hulls were crack troops. Next, he assigned seven ranking commanders — Han Dang, Jiang Qin, Zhu Ran, Pan Zhang, Zhou Tai, Xu Sheng, and Ding Feng — to advance in series. The rest of the commanders were to remain with Sun Quan to provide support and reinforcement. The preparations complete, Lü Meng sent a letter to Cao Cao telling him to attack Lord Guan from the rear; and Lu Xun in Lukou was informed of all steps taken. Finally, the sailors dressed as merchants began their mission. They steered their light craft to the Xunyang River,

答曰："我等皆是客商；因江中阻风，到此一避。"随将财物送与守台军士。军士信之，遂任其停泊江边。约至二更，𦩷𦪌中精兵齐出，将烽火台上官军缚倒，暗号一声，八十余船精兵俱起，将紧要去处墩台之军，尽行捉入船中，不曾走了一个。于是长驱大进，径取荆州，无人知觉。将至荆州，吕蒙将沿江墩台所获官军，用好言抚慰，各各重赏，令赚开城门，纵火为号。众军领命，吕蒙便教前导。比及半夜，到城下叫门。门吏认得是荆州之兵，开了城门。众军一声喊起，就城门里放起号火。吴兵齐入，袭了荆州。吕蒙便传令军中："如有妄杀一人，妄取民间一物者，定按军法。"原任官吏，并依旧职。将关公家属另养别宅，不许闲人搅扰。一面遣人申报孙权。

　　一日大雨，蒙上马引数骑点看四门。忽见一人取民间箬笠以盖铠甲，蒙喝左右执下问之，乃蒙之乡人也。蒙曰："汝虽系我同乡，但吾号令已出，汝故犯之，当按军法。"其人泣告曰："某恐雨湿官铠，故取遮盖，非为私用。乞将军念同乡之情！"蒙曰："吾固知汝为覆官铠，然终是不应取民间之物。"叱左右推

moving at full speed day and night until they hit the north shore.

When challenged by Lord Guan's soldiers at the signal-flare stations, the Southlanders replied, "We are all merchants from afar. The wind blocked our course on the river, so we have come to take refuge here." They offered gifts to the station guards, who took their word and permitted them to anchor along the shore. Toward the second watch, the troops hidden in the boats emerged as a body, seizing and binding the station guards. At a silent signal the troops in all eighty boats appeared, captured the soldiers at the key signal stations, and hustled them back to the boats. Not one escaped. The Southlanders then struck out for Jiangling in unimpaired secrecy.

As they approached Jiangling in Jingzhou, Lü Meng used fair words to placate the men he had captured by the river; by means of various generous gifts he got them to agree to deceive the gate guards and, once inside, to start signal fires.[5] The captives followed orders. Lü Meng had them lead the way. Late that night when they reached the walls, the gatekeepers recognized their own men and opened at their call. A united shout arose from the crowd of soldiers, and just inside the gate they set the signal fires. The Southlanders rushed in and took the city by surprise.

Lü Meng immediately issued a decree: "If any soldier kills one man or takes one article, he will be dealt with by strict military law." The city's administrators were told to continue in their current duties. Lord Guan's family was moved to different quarters and placed under protective custody. A report was sent to Sun Quan.

1851

During a day of heavy rains, Lü Meng and his attendants were riding around inspecting the four gates of the city. They spotted one of Meng's men wearing a common cape and straw hat over his armor. Meng ordered the man held and interrogated; he turned out to be a fellow villager of Lü Meng's. "Although you come from my home region," the commander said, "You have violated my publicly proclaimed order and military law must therefore be applied." Tearfully, the man appealed: "I only feared that the rains would damage the armor issued to me, so I took the cape and cap to protect it. It was not for my personal use. Please, General, consider our bond as fellow townsmen." "I fully appreciate your intention," Lü Meng replied, "but when all is said and

下斩之。枭首传示毕,然后收其尸首,泣而葬之。自是三军震肃。

不一日,孙权领众至。吕蒙出郭迎接入衙。权慰劳毕,仍命潘濬为治中,掌荆州事;监内放出于禁,遣归曹操;安民赏军,设宴庆贺。权谓吕蒙曰:"今荆州已得,但公安傅士仁、南郡糜芳,此二处如何收复?"言未毕,忽一人出曰:"不须张弓只箭,某凭三寸不烂之舌,说公安傅士仁来降,可乎?"众视之,乃虞翻也。权曰:"仲翔有何良策,可使傅士仁归降?"翻曰:"某自幼与士仁交厚;今若以利害说之,彼必归矣。"权大喜,遂令虞翻领五百军,径奔公安来。

却说傅士仁听知荆州有失,急令闭城坚守。虞翻至,见城门紧闭,遂写书拴于箭上,射入城中。军士拾得,献与傅士仁。士仁拆书视之,乃招降之意。览毕,想起"关公去日恨吾之意,不如早降。"即令大开城门,请虞翻入城。二人礼毕,各诉旧情。翻说吴侯宽洪大度,礼贤下士;士仁大喜,即同虞翻赍印绶来荆州投降。孙权大悦,仍令去守公安。吕蒙密谓权曰:"今云长未获,留士仁于公安,久必有变;不若使往南郡招糜芳归

done, it is forbidden to take any article belonging to the people." He ordered the man removed and executed, and then ordered his head displayed publicly. Afterward he had head and body gathered up and buried. At the interment Lü Meng wept. From then on, strict discipline prevailed throughout the armed forces.

Within a day Sun Quan and his forces arrived; Lü Meng received his lord outside of the city walls. After paying tribute to the achievement of the troops, Sun Quan ordered Pan Jun to resume control of civil administration of all Jiangling's affairs. He released Yu Jin from jail and sent him home to Cao Cao. Then he comforted the population, rewarded his men, and held a great banquet to celebrate the victory. On that occasion Sun Quan said to Lü Meng, "Jingzhou is now ours. But how can we recover Gong'an, which Fu Shiren holds, and Nanjun district, which Mi Fang governs?" As he spoke, someone stepped forward and said, "I think I can talk Fu Shiren into surrendering, and save us the effort of military action." The assembly turned to Yu Fan. Sun Quan said to him, "You must have some exceptional plan to induce Fu Shiren to surrender." "He and I have been close friends since childhood," Yu Fan responded. "If I can show him where his true interests lie, I am sure he will come over." Sun Quan was delighted and sent Yu Fan with five hundred soldiers straight to Gong'an.[6]

Fu Shiren, when he learned of the loss of Jingzhou, ordered a strict defense of his city. Yu Fan arrived to find the gates shut tight, so he wound a letter round an arrow and shot it over the wall. It was brought to Fu Shiren who studied carefully its call to surrender. Putting the letter aside, he thought, "When he departed, Lord Guan showed hatred for me.[7] I'm better off surrendering." So he opened the gates and bade Yu Fan enter. The two men exchanged courtesies and discussed their old friendship. Yu Fan spoke of Sun Quan's magnanimity and honorable treatment of able men. Shiren was delighted and went with Yu Fan to Jiangling to deliver the seal of his office.

Greatly pleased, Sun Quan asked him to resume control of Gong'an. But Lü Meng whispered to Sun Quan, "Don't put him back in Gong'an while Lord Guan is still free, or he will turn on us before too long. Why not send him on to Nanjun to urge Mi Fang to surrender?"

降。"权乃召傅士仁谓曰："糜芳与卿交厚，卿可招来归降，孤自当有重赏。"傅士仁慨然领诺，遂引十余骑，径投南郡招安糜芳。

正是：

　　　　今日公安无守志，从前王甫是良言。

未知此去如何，且看下文分解。

Accordingly, Sun Quan said to Shiren, "You and Mi Fang are old and good friends. If you can induce him to join our side, you will be richly rewarded." Fu Shiren agreed eagerly. Taking a dozen riders, he went to Nanjun. Indeed:

> Fu Shiren lacked the will to defend his post.
> If only Lord Guan had heeded Wang Fu's warning!

What was the outcome of Fu Shiren's mission?[8]
    Read on.

第七十六回

徐公明大战沔水　关云长败走麦城

　　却说糜芳闻荆州有失,正无计可施。忽报公安守将傅士仁至,芳忙接入城,问其事故。士仁曰:"吾非不忠。势危力困,不能支持,我今已降东吴。——将军亦不如早降。"芳曰:"吾等受汉中王厚恩,安忍背之?"士仁曰:"关公去日,痛恨吾二人;倘一日得胜而回,必无轻恕:公细察之。"芳曰:"吾兄弟久事汉中王,岂可一朝相背?"正犹豫间,忽报关公遣使至,接入厅上。使者曰:"关公军中缺粮,特来南郡、公安二处取白米十万石,令二将军星夜解去军前交割。如迟立斩。"芳大惊,顾谓傅士仁曰:"今荆州已被东吴所取,此粮怎得过去?"士仁厉声曰:"不必多疑!"遂拔剑斩来使于堂上。芳惊曰:"公如何斩之?"士仁曰:"关公此意,正要斩我二人。我等安可束手受死?公今不早降东吴,必被关公所杀。"正说间,忽报吕蒙引兵杀至城下。芳大惊,乃同傅士仁出城投降。蒙大喜,引见孙权。权重赏二人。

Chapter 76

Xu Huang Wages War on the River Mian
Lord Guan Flees to Mai in Defeat

The news of the loss of Jiangling left Mi Fang completely nonplussed. Suddenly the arrival of Fu Shiren was announced. Mi Fang received him excitedly and asked his purpose in coming. "It is not that I am disloyal," Fu Shiren began, "but circumstances overwhelmed me. I could not maintain my position, and have surrendered to the Southland. I think, General, that an early surrender would be in your best interests, too." "We here," Mi Fang responded, "have enjoyed the favor of the king of Hanzhong. I could not bear to betray him." Shiren said, "At the time of his departure Lord Guan had little love for either of us. And the day he returns victorious, there will be no easy clemency for us, you can be sure. Look clearly at the situation." "My brother and I have long served the king of Hanzhong," Mi Fang went on. "I cannot simply turn against him without warning."

1857

Torn between two choices, Mi Fang was informed of the arrival of a messenger from Lord Guan. Ushered into the reception room, the messenger said, "The army is short of grain. Lord Guan is looking particularly to Gong'an and Nanjun for one hundred thousand piculs of rice. He orders both of you generals to deliver it to the front immediately." [1] Astounded, Mi Fang said to Fu Shiren, "Jiangling has been taken by the south. How can I send this grain over to him?" Shiren retorted sharply, "Enough shilly-shallying!" He drew his sword and killed the messenger right in the main hall. "Why did you do that?" Mi Fang exclaimed. Shiren replied, "Guan's purpose was nothing less than to have us killed. Are we supposed to tie our hands and wait quietly for that? If you don't surrender to the south, Guan is sure to kill you." At that moment it was reported that Lü Meng was marching on the city, and so the frightened Mi Fang went with Fu Shiren outside the walls and surrendered. Lü Meng was

安民已毕，大犒三军。

时曹操在许都，正与众谋士议荆州之事，忽报东吴遣使奉书至。操召入，使者呈上书信。操拆视之，书中具言吴兵将袭荆州，求操夹攻云长；且嘱："勿泄漏，使云长有备也。"操与众谋士商议，主簿董昭曰："今樊城被困，引颈望救，不如令人将书射入樊城，以宽军心；且使关公知东吴将袭荆州。彼恐荆州有失，必速退兵，却令徐晃乘势掩杀，可获全功。"操从其谋，一面差人催徐晃急战；一面亲统大兵，径往洛阳之南阳陵坡驻扎，以救曹仁。

却说徐晃正坐帐中，忽报魏王使至。晃接入问之，使曰："今魏王引兵，已过洛阳；令将军急战关公，以解樊城之困。"正说间，探马报说："关平屯兵在偃城，廖化屯兵在四冢：前后一十二个寨栅，连络不绝。"晃即差副将徐商、吕建假着徐晃旗号，前赴偃城与关平交战。晃却自引精兵五百，循沔水去袭偃城之后。

且说关平闻徐晃自引兵至，遂提本部兵迎敌。两阵对圆，关平出马，与徐商交锋，只三合，商大败而走；吕建出战，五六合亦败走。平乘胜追杀二十余里，忽报城中火起。平知中计，急

delighted and brought Mi Fang before Sun Quan, who rewarded both defectors richly. After reassuring the population, Sun Quan held a grand feast for the entire army.

*　*　*

Cao Cao was in Xuchang meeting with his counselors on the Jingzhou situation when a messenger from the Southland arrived with Sun Quan's letter. The letter described the coming attack on Jingzhou and appealed to Cao Cao for joint operations against Lord Guan, closing with an admonition not to disclose the contents and thereby give Lord Guan the chance to prepare. In the ensuing discussion Cao Cao's first secretary, Dong Zhao, argued, "Lord Guan has Fan surrounded. The people there are desperate for relief. I think we should have this letter shot into the city of Fan to improve the morale of the troops and also to let Lord Guan know that the south is going to attack Jingzhou. Guan will withdraw rather than lose Jingzhou. We should then have Xu Huang fall upon Guan and his men and complete the victory." Cao Cao adopted Dong Zhao's proposal. He sent a man to urge Xu Huang to fight at once; and he took personal command of a large force and marched to Yangling Slope, south of Luoyang, to aid Cao Ren.

Xu Huang was in his tent when Cao Cao's messenger arrived. "Today the king of Wei and his troops have passed Luoyang," he announced. "He commands you, General, to do battle with Lord Guan and relieve the siege at Fan without delay." At this moment a spy reported: "Guan Ping has encamped at Yan and Liao Hua at Sizhong in a string of twelve well-constructed bases in good communication with each other." Xu Huang immediately sent his lieutenant commanders, Xu Shang and Lü Jian, to fight Guan Ping at Yan — but they were to fly Xu Huang's colors as a decoy. Xu Huang himself took five hundred picked troops and, skirting the River Mian, went to surprise Yan from the rear.

When Guan Ping heard that Xu Huang was marching toward him, he went to meet the enemy with his own unit. The two armies faced off and Guan Ping rode forth. After three clashes with Xu Shang, Guan Ping was victorious and Xu Shang fled. The second lieutenant commander, Lü Jian, took the field; but he too fled in defeat after five or six clashes. Guan Ping gave chase some twenty *li,* dealing bloody slaughter as he

勒兵回救偃城。正遇一彪军摆开，徐晃立马在门旗下，高叫曰："关平贤侄，好不知死！汝荆州已被东吴夺了，犹然在此狂为！"平大怒，纵马轮刀，直取徐晃；不三四合，三军喊叫，偃城中火光大起。平不敢恋战，杀条大路，径奔四冢寨来。廖化接着。化曰："人言荆州已被吕蒙袭了，军心惊慌，如之奈何？"平曰："此必讹言也。军士再言者斩之。"忽流星马到，报说正北第一屯被徐晃领兵攻打。平曰："若第一屯有失，诸营岂得安宁？此间皆靠沔水，贼兵不敢到此。吾与汝同去救第一屯。"廖化唤部将分付曰："汝等坚守营寨，如有贼到，即便举火。"部将曰："四冢寨鹿角十重，虽飞鸟亦不能入，何虑贼兵！"于是关平、廖化尽起四冢寨精兵，奔至第一屯住扎。关平看见魏兵屯于浅山之上，谓廖化曰："徐晃屯兵，不得地利，今夜可引兵劫寨。"化曰："将军可分兵一半前去，某当谨守本寨。"

是夜，关平引一枝兵杀入魏寨，不见一人。平知是计，火速退时，左边徐商，右边吕建，两下夹攻。平大败回营，魏兵乘势追杀前来，四面围住。关平、廖化支持不住，弃了第一屯，径投四冢寨来。早望见寨中火起。急到寨前，只见皆是魏兵旗号。

rode. A report of fire in his city brought him up short. Realizing he had
fallen into a trap, Guan Ping wheeled around and went back to save Yan.
But a force of well-deployed troops confronted him; at their head was Xu
Huang. Poised on his horse, banners flying above him, he called out, "Guan
Ping, worthy nephew. Have you no fear of death? The southerners hold
your Jingzhou now, yet you refuse to behave yourself here!"

In great anger Ping gave rein, wheeling his blade and making straight
for Xu Huang. But after they had locked weapons and broken three or
four times, his men began shouting: Yan was burning down. No longer
able to give himself to the fight, Guan Ping cut a great bloody swath as he
charged headlong toward the second camp at Sizhong. Liao Hua received
him, saying, "I hear that Lü Meng has taken Jingzhou. Our troops are
close to panic. What are we going to do?" "It's a lie!" retorted Ping.
"Execute anyone repeating it!" At that moment an express messenger
brought word that Xu Huang had attacked the first position north of Yan.
Guan Ping said to Liao Hua, "If that position is lost, our camps will not be
secure. Here, however, we are right on the River Mian. The bastards
won't dare approach. Let's go and relieve it."

Liao Hua instructed his own unit commanders: "You are to hold these
camps and outworks at all costs. Signal by fire if the bastards come."
The commanders replied, "The outworks at Sizhong are guarded by many
rings of tree branches and defensive stakes. Not even a bird could get
through. Never mind them!" So Guan Ping and Liao Hua mustered their
best troops and headed for the first camp. Observing northern soldiers
stationed on a low hill, Ping said to Liao Hua, "Xu Huang did not exploit
the geography of this place. We can raid that camp tonight." "General,"
Liao Hua said, "you take half the troops and make the raid. I will hold the
fort with the rest."

That night Guan Ping and a detachment of men fell upon the northern
camp. Finding it empty, Ping realized he had entered a trap and withdrew
swiftly, but Xu Shang and Lü Jian struck from both sides. Ping, badly
defeated, made it back to the first camp. Pressing their advantage, the
northerners surrounded it. Guan Ping and Liao Hua abandoned the camp
and struck out for Sizhong; but it was too late. Already flames were
visible in the distance, and they arrived to find the walls of Sizhong flying

关平等退兵，忙奔樊城大路而走。前面一军拦住，为首大将，乃是徐晃也。平、化二人奋力死战，夺路而走，回到大寨，来见关公曰："今徐晃夺了偃城等处；又兼曹操自引大军，分三路来救樊城；多有人言荆州已被吕蒙袭了。"关公喝曰："此敌人讹言，以乱我军心耳！东吴吕蒙病危，孺子陆逊代之，不足为虑！"

言未毕，忽报徐晃兵至。公令备马。平谏曰："父体未痊，不可与敌。"公曰："徐晃与吾有旧，深知其能；若彼不退，吾先斩之，以警魏将。"遂披挂提刀上马，奋然而出。魏军见之，无不惊惧。公勒马问曰："徐公明安在？"魏营门旗开处，徐晃出马，欠身而言曰："自别君侯，倏忽数载，不想君侯须发已苍白矣！忆昔壮年相从，多蒙教诲，感谢不忘。今君侯英风震于华夏，使故人闻之，不胜叹羡！兹幸得一见，深慰渴怀。"公曰："吾与公明交契深厚，非比他人；今何故数穷吾儿耶？"晃回顾众将，厉声大叫曰："若取得云长首级者，重赏千金！"公惊曰："公明何出此言？"晃曰："今日乃国家之事，某不敢以私废公。"言讫，挥大斧直取关公。公大怒，亦挥刀迎之。战八十余合，公虽武艺绝

northern flags. Guan Ping withdrew and fled down the main road to Fan.

Guan Ping and Liao Hua, blocked on the road by a detachment led by Xu Huang, managed to get away in desperate fighting. Back at camp they came before Lord Guan and said, "Xu Huang has taken Yan and the other bases. Cao Cao is bringing a major force in a three-pronged advance to the relief of Fan. And other reports say that Lü Meng has taken Jingzhou." "Lies!" Lord Guan shouted. "Lies spread by the enemy to weaken our morale. Lü Meng is seriously ill; some young fellow, Lu Xun, took his place. Nothing to worry about."

At this moment Xu Huang's army arrived. It was reported to Lord Guan, who called for his horse. Guan Ping said, "You cannot engage the enemy, Father, while your strength is still impaired." "I've known Xu Huang many years," Lord Guan replied, "and am fully aware of what he can and cannot do. If he doesn't pull back, I will take the initiative and kill him; that'll give the generals of the north a good scare!"

Lord Guan emerged, vigorous and fearless, appointed with sword and armor. As he rode, he struck fear into the northmen who saw him. He reined in and called out his challenge: "Xu Huang, where are you!" Where banners parted at the entrance to the northerners' camp, Xu Huang rode forth. He bowed deeply. "My lord," he began, "since we parted, many years have fled. Who would have thought your hair and beard would turn so grey! Yet well and fondly do I remember the lusty years of our companionship, when I gained much from your tutelage. Today the effect of your triumphs is felt throughout our land. It makes an old friend sigh in admiration. Here fortune grants us a meeting, and long-endured yearnings are appeased."

To this Lord Guan replied, "The friendship between us is deep indeed — deeper than any other. Why, then, have you time and again driven my son so utterly to the limit?" Xu Huang turned to the commanders behind him and cried out harshly, "A thousand pieces of gold to the man who takes his head!" Lord Guan was astonished. "My friend," he said, "how can you say this?" Xu Huang answered, "Today I serve the government. I am not one to set public duty aside for personal sentiment." With that, he took on Lord Guan in direct combat, his poleaxe whirling. In a fury Lord Guan met him with circling blade. After some eighty bouts Lord

伦,终是右臂少力。关平恐公有失,火急鸣金,公拨马回寨。忽闻四下里喊声大震。原来是樊城曹仁闻曹操救兵至,引军杀出城来,与徐晃会合,两下夹攻,荆州兵大乱。关公上马,引众将急奔襄江上流头。背后魏兵追至。关公急渡过襄江,望襄阳而奔。忽流星马到,报说:"荆州已被吕蒙所夺,家眷被陷。"关公大惊,不敢奔襄阳,提兵投公安来。探马又报:"公安傅士仁已降东吴了。"关公大怒。忽催粮人到,报说:"公安傅士仁往南郡,杀了使命,招糜芳都降东吴去了。"

关公闻言,怒气冲塞,疮口迸裂,昏绝于地。众将救醒,公顾谓司马王甫曰:"悔不听足下之言,今日果有此事!"因问:"沿江上下,何不举火?"探马答曰:"吕蒙使水手尽穿白衣,扮作客商渡江,将精兵伏于䑽舻之中,先擒了守台士卒,因此不得举火。"公跌足叹曰:"吾中奸贼之谋矣!有何面目见兄长耶!"管粮都督赵累曰:"今事急矣,可一面差人往成都求救,一面从旱路去取荆州。"关公依言,差马良、伊籍赍文三道,星夜赴成都求救;一面引兵来取荆州,自领前队先行,留廖化、关平断后。

却说樊城围解,曹仁引众将来见曹操,泣拜请罪。操曰:"此乃天数,非汝等之罪也。"操重赏三军,亲至四冢寨周围阅

Guan finally felt his right arm begin to weaken, though his fighting skill was at its peak. Fearful for his father, Guan Ping hastily sounded the gongs, and Lord Guan rode back to the base.

All of a sudden a deafening clamor surrounded the camp. What had happened was this: the moment Cao Ren had heard that Cao Cao was coming to relieve Fan, he had led his troops out of the city and joined forces with Xu Huang. Together they attacked and routed the Jingzhou troops. Lord Guan took flight, riding pell-mell with his men to the upper reaches of the Xiang River, the troops of Wei in hot pursuit. Lord Guan crossed quickly and headed south for Xiangyang. On the way, an express courier found him and informed him that Jiangling had fallen and that Lü Meng had his family in custody. Lord Guan began to panic. Xiangyang was no longer safe, so he led his men toward Gong'an. But scouts brought a new report: "Fu Shiren has surrendered Gong'an to the south." Lord Guan was furious. Then his quartermaster arrived and announced, "Fu Shiren has gone to Nanjun, killed your messenger, and induced Mi Fang to surrender."

At this latest news, Lord Guan exploded in anger. His wound split open, and he passed out on the ground. When his commanders revived him, he said to Major Wang Fu, "Things would never have turned out so badly had I only heeded your advice." Lord Guan then asked, "What happened to the beacon flares along the river?" The scout replied, "The guards never got to raise their flares. Lü Meng crossed the river with his mariners dressed like merchants. The boats held crack troops, who overwhelmed the station guards." Lord Guan staggered and groaned. "Trapped by the cunning enemy! How can I face my elder brother again?" Commissariat Chief Zhao Lei said, "The situation is critical. We must send to Chengdu for help. And we must take the land route to try and recapture Jiangling." Lord Guan agreed. He sent Ma Liang and Yi Ji racing west to Chengdu with letters seeking aid. Lord Guan himself set out for Jiangling; he took the van, Guan Ping and Liao Hua the rear.

*   *   *

The siege of Fan was lifted. Cao Ren led his commanders to see Cao Cao, before whom he prostrated himself and tearfully confessed his fault.[2] Cao Cao said, "What Heaven ordains is no fault of yours." Cao Cao

1865

视，顾谓众将曰："荆州兵围堑鹿角数重，徐公明深入其中，竟获全功。孤用兵三十余年，未敢长驱径入敌围。公明真胆识兼优者也！"众皆叹服。操班师还于摩陂驻扎。徐晃兵至，操亲出寨迎之，见晃军皆按队伍而行，并无差乱。操大喜曰："徐将军真有周亚夫之风矣！"遂封徐晃为平南将军，同夏侯尚守襄阳，以遏关公之师。操因荆州未定，就屯兵于摩陂，以候消息。

　　却说关公在荆州路上，进退无路，谓赵累曰："目今前有吴兵，后有魏兵，吾在其中，救兵不至，如之奈何？"累曰："昔吕蒙在陆口时，尝致书君侯，两家约好，共诛操贼，今却助操而袭我：是背盟也。君侯暂驻军于此，可差人遗书吕蒙责之，看彼如何对答。"关公从其言，遂修书遣使赴荆州来。

　　却说吕蒙在荆州，传下号令：凡荆州诸郡，有随关公出征将士之家，不许吴兵搅扰，按月给与粮米；有患病者，遣医治疗。将士之家，感其恩惠，安堵不动。忽报关公使至，吕蒙出郭迎接入城，以宾礼相待。使者呈书与蒙。蒙看毕，谓来使曰："蒙昔日与关将军结好，乃一己之私见；今日之事，乃上命差遣，不得自主。烦使者回报将军，善言致意。"遂设宴款待，送归馆驿安歇。于是随征将士之家，皆来问信；有附家书者，有口传音信

rewarded the army richly and then personally inspected the outworks at the recently conquered Sizhong. Turning to his commanders, he said, "For Xu Huang to have penetrated their moat and barricades of branches is a great achievement. In more than thirty years of soldiering I have never been able to break through enemy outworks straightaway. Xu Huang excels in tacitcs as well as courage." The commanders, too, expressed great admiration.

Cao Cao withdrew and repositioned at Mopo. When Xu Huang arrived, Cao Cao received him outside of the base, noting with satisfaction how Xu Huang's troops moved in orderly ranks with great precision. "General Xu upholds the great tradition of Zhou Yafu!"[3] Cao Cao exclaimed, and he honored Xu Huang with the title General Who Vanquishes the South. Xu Huang and Xiahou Shang then went to Xiangyang to check Lord Guan while Cao Cao posted his troops at Mopo, awaiting word of the pacification of Jingzhou.

* * *

Lord Guan had no base and nowhere to turn. He said to Zhao Lei, "The southern forces are ahead, the northern behind. I am caught in the middle, and no rescue has come.[4] What are we to do?" Zhao Lei answered, "Lü Meng once wrote to Your Lordship from Lukou committing himself to the common effort to punish the traitor Cao. Now, instead, he is helping Cao Cao by attacking us. I advise you to station the army here, Your Lordship, and write to Lü Meng reproving him for betraying the alliance. See what he says." Lord Cuan sent a messenger to Jiangling.

In Jiangling in Jingzhou, Lü Meng had issued orders that the families of the warriors accompanying Lord Guan, whatever district they might be in, were to be issued monthly rations, shielded from any harassment, and provided with medical care. The grateful families went on with their lives peacefully. When Lord Guan's representative arrived, Lü Meng met him outside the wall and welcomed him into the city as an honored guest. On delivery of Lord Guan's letter, Lü Meng told the messenger, "In concluding an accord with General Guan, I acted on my own. Today I am under orders. I am not my own master here, and I must trouble you, when you report back to the general, to convey my view as amicably as you can." Lü Meng ordered a banquet for the representative and es-

者,皆言家门无恙,衣食不缺。

使者辞别吕蒙,蒙亲送出城。使者回见关公,具道吕蒙之语,并说:"荆州城中,君侯宝眷并诸将家属,俱各无恙,供给不缺。"公大怒曰:"此奸贼之计也!我生不能杀此贼,死必杀之,以雪吾恨!"喝退使者。使者出寨,众将皆来探问家中之事;使者具言各家安好,吕蒙极其恩恤,并将书信传送各将。各将欣喜,皆无战心。

关公率兵取荆州,军行之次,将士多有逃回荆州者。关公愈加恨怒,遂催军前进。忽然喊声大震,一彪军拦住,为首大将,乃蒋钦也,勒马挺枪大叫曰:"云长何不早降!"关公骂曰:"吾乃汉将,岂降贼乎!"拍马舞刀,直取蒋钦。不三合,钦败走。关公提刀追杀二十余里,喊声忽起,左边山谷中韩当领军冲出,右边山谷中周泰引军冲出,蒋钦回马复战:三路夹攻。关公急撤军回走。行无数里,只见南山冈上人烟聚集,一面白旗招扬,上写"荆州土人"四字,众人都叫:"本处人速速投降!"关公大怒,欲上冈杀之。山崦内又有两军撞出:左边丁奉,右边徐盛;——并合蒋钦等三路军马,喊声震地,鼓角喧天,将关公困在垓心。手下将士,渐渐消疏。比及杀到黄昏,关公遥望四山之

corted him to the post station, where the families of Lord Guan's warriors surrounded him for news. Some pressed letters on him and some gave him spoken messages, all to the effect that the families were well and had enough food and clothing. Lü Meng escorted Lord Guan's courier outside the city.

When the messenger brought back Lü Meng's answer and the tidings of Lord Guan's and his commanders' families, Lord Guan was moved to rage. "Treacherous, treasonous tricks!" he cried. "But I will take revenge, for I will kill him while I live, or else after I am dead!" Lord Guan roughly sent the messenger out, and the man was quickly surrounded by commanders seeking news of their families. As they took in hand the letters from home and learned of the security and comfort their loved ones enjoyed and the pains Lü Meng had taken to be considerate, the commanders felt grateful and began to lose their will to fight.

Lord Guan led his army on toward Jiangling, but during breaks in the march many there deserted and fled. Hate and anger rose up in him, and he pressed the army to advance. Suddenly there was a thunderous clamor. A band of soldiers blocked his way, at the head a chief commander — Jiang Qin. Reining in, he raised his spear and shouted, "Guan! Surrender now!" Lord Guan swore back, "I am a Han general and will never surrender to a rebel!" Laying on the whip, his blade dancing, Guan went for Jiang Qin. The clash was brief. Qin fled in defeat. Lord Guan had pursued him some twenty *li,* when more shouting began. On the left Han Dang came charging out of a ravine; on the right Zhou Tai came out of another. Then Jiang Qin reversed direction and gave battle. Caught between three forces, Lord Guan pulled back and fled.

After proceeding several *li* Lord Guan saw groups of men on the ridges of some hills to the south. Near them, a white flag bearing the words "Natives of Jingzhou" caught the breeze. They shouted down a plea: "All native warriors surrender quickly!" Lord Guan wanted to rush the hills and kill them. But he was assaulted by two more units, which had sprung from the shady side of the hills: to the left, Ding Feng; to the right, Xu Sheng. Their men now joined those of Jiang Qin, Han Dang, and Zhou Tai. Amid earth-shaking yells and drums and horns that filled the sky with noise, they closed in. Lord Guan's immediate commanders were

1869

上,皆是荆州土兵,呼兄唤弟,觅子寻爷,喊声不住。军心尽变,皆应声而去。关公止喝不住,部从止有三百余人。杀至三更,正东上喊声连天,乃是关平、廖化分两路兵杀入重围,救出关公。关平告曰:"军心乱矣,必得城池暂屯,以待援兵。麦城虽小,足可屯扎。"关公从之,催促残军前至麦城,分兵紧守四门,聚将士商议。赵累曰:"此处相近上庸,现有刘封、孟达在彼把守,可速差人往求救兵。若得这枝军马接济,以待川兵大至,军心自安矣。"

正议间,忽报吴兵已至,将城四面围定。公问曰:"谁敢突围而出,往上庸求救?"廖化曰:"某愿往。"关平曰:"我护送汝出重围。"关公即修书付廖化藏于身畔,饱食上马,开门出城。正遇吴将丁奉截往。被关平奋力冲杀,奉败走,廖化乘势杀出重围,投上庸去了。关平入城,坚守不出。

且说刘封、孟达自取上庸,太守申耽率众归降,因此汉中王加刘封为副将军,与孟达同守上庸。当日探知关公兵败,二人正议间,忽报廖化至。封令请入问之。化曰:"关公兵败,现困于麦城,被围至急。蜀中援兵,不能旦夕即至。特命某突围而出,来此求救。望二将军速起上庸之兵,以救此危。倘稍迟延,

slowly being eliminated as the fighting wore on into the sunset. Lord Guan saw Jingzhou troops on the surrounding hills, brothers calling to brothers, sons searching for fathers and fathers for sons. It went on and on; the men were turning against him, quitting in response to the calls, ignoring Lord Guan's commands. Soon he was left with only three hundred followers.[5]

The fighting went on into the third watch. Due east a great cry went up. It was Guan Ping and Liao Hua. They had broken through the encirclement to rescue Lord Guan. Guan Ping said, "The troops are out of control. We have to get to a fortified place and hold it unitl help comes. The town of Mai, though small, should serve." Lord Guan approved and urged his remnant force toward the town. After entering, they sealed the four gates tight. Then they took counsel. Zhao Lei said, "We are close to Shangyong. Liu Feng and Meng Da are defending it. Send to them for help. Even a small contingent, just to relieve us until a larger force comes from the Riverlands, will restore morale."

At this moment it was reported that Southland troops had surrounded Mai. Lord Guan asked, "Who will break out and go to Shangyong for help?" Liao Hua volunteered, and Guan Ping agreed to escort him through the enemy lines. Lord Guan composed a letter, which Liao Hua concealed on his person. The two volunteers supped well, mounted, and went out the gate. Ding Feng of the Southland confronted them. Guan Ping attacked valiantly and drove him off. Seizing the moment, Liao Hua got through the siege and made for Shangyong. Guan Ping reentered the city and resolutely refused to appear.

1871

* * *

Liu Feng and Meng Da, since occupying Shangyong, had received the submission of Shen Dan, the district governor. As a result, the king of Hanzhong appointed Liu Feng deputy general to guard the city together with Meng Da. Liu Feng and Meng Da were conferring about Lord Guan's defeats when Liao Hua arrived and was conducted to their quarters. "Lord Guan's army is defeated," Liao Hua announced. "He is under siege at Mai. The danger is great, and the Riverlands relief force needs time to get there. He sent me through the enemy lines for help. We are counting on you two to rally your troops to aid us. The slightest delay

1872

公必陷矣。"封曰:"将军且歇,容某计议。"

化乃至馆驿安歇,尚候发兵。刘封谓孟达曰:"叔父被困,如之奈何?"达曰:"东吴兵精将勇;且荆州九郡,俱已属彼,止有麦城,乃弹丸之地;又闻曹操亲督大军四五十万,屯于摩陂:量我等山城之众,安能敌得两家之强兵?不可轻敌。"封曰:"吾亦知之。奈关公是吾叔父,安忍坐视而不救乎?"达笑曰:"将军以关公为叔,恐关公未必以将军为侄也。某闻汉中王初嗣将军之时,关公即不悦。后汉中王登位之后,欲立后嗣,问于孔明,孔明曰:'此家事也,问关、张可矣。'汉中王遂遣人至荆州问关公,关公以将军乃螟蛉之子,不可僭立,劝汉中王远置将军于上庸山城之地,以杜后患。此事人人知之,将军岂反不知耶?何今日犹沾沾以叔侄之义,而欲冒险轻动乎?"封曰:"君言虽是,但以何词却之?"达曰:"但言山城初附,民心未定,不敢造次兴兵,恐失所守。"封从其言。次日,请廖化至,言:"此山城初附之所,未能分兵相救。"化大惊,以头叩地曰:"若如此,则关公休矣!"达曰:"我今即往,一杯之水,安能救一车薪之火乎?将军速回,静候蜀兵至可也。"化大恸告求,刘封、孟达皆拂袖而

could mean the fall of my lord." Liu Feng suggested that Liao Hua rest himself while he considered the request. Liao Hua went to the guesthouse to await the muster of the troops.

Liu Feng said to Meng Da, "Uncle Guan is in deep trouble. What can we do?" "The Southland has superb troops and fearless commanders," Meng Da replied. "Moreover, all of Jingzhou now belongs to them. He has only Mai — a pitiful piece of ground. Further, we have heard that Cao Cao has marched to Mopo with four or five hundred thousand. I don't see how our little mountain-town army can do anything about two powerful enemies. We should not risk it." "That makes sense to me," Liu Feng replied. "But Lord Guan is my uncle. I can't sit back and watch without doing something." Meng Da smiled as he replied, "You say you hold him as your uncle, General. I am afraid he does not necessarily hold you as his nephew. I have heard that Lord Guan was awfully upset earlier when the king of Hanzhong adopted you. After the king of Hanzhong formally assumed the kingship, he asked Kongming about the selection of the heir apparent. Kongming said he was reluctant to interfere in family affairs and suggested the king ask Lord Guan and Zhang Fei, so the king sent a man to Jingzhou for Lord Guan's opinion. Lord Guan said that a foster son[6] could not rightfully be instated and advised the king to send you to this remote outpost to avoid trouble in the future. This matter is widely known. I am surprised that you know nothing of it. Why should you now run the risk of going to war out of sentimental attachment to 'the bond of uncle and nephew'?"

To this advice Liu Feng responded, "What you say is true, but what excuse can I make?" "Simply tell him," Meng Da answered, "that the town has just become part of our kingdom and we might lose it if we rush into war before the people have fully accepted us." Liu Feng agreed. The next day he summoned Liao Hua and told him: "We have just established ourselves here and cannot spare any troops for the rescue." Liao Hua was astounded. He knocked his head on the ground, crying, "Then my lord is done for!" "Even if we went," Meng Da said to him, "how could one cup of water put out a cartload of burning wood? Return, General, and await patiently the forces of the Riverlands." Liao Hua pressed his appeal passionately. But Liu Feng and Meng Da flicked their sleeves

1873

入。廖化知事不谐，寻思须告汉中王求救，遂上马大骂出城，望成都而去。

却说关公在麦城盼望上庸兵到，却不见动静；手下止有五六百人，多半带伤；城中无粮，甚是苦楚。忽报城下一人教休放箭，有话来见君侯。公令放入，问之，乃诸葛瑾也。礼毕茶罢，瑾曰："今奉吴侯命，特来劝谕将军。自古道：'识时务者为俊杰。'今将军所统汉上九郡，皆已属他人类；止有孤城一区，内无粮草，外无救兵，危在旦夕。将军何不从瑾之言：归顺吴侯，复镇荆襄，可以保全家眷。幸君侯熟思之。"关公正色而言曰："吾乃解良一武夫，蒙吾主以手足相待，安肯背义投敌国乎？城若破，有死而已。玉可碎而不可改其白，竹可焚而不可毁其节：身虽殒，名可垂于竹帛也。汝勿多言，速请出城，吾欲与孙权决一死战！"瑾曰："吴侯欲与君侯结秦、晋之好，同力破曹，共扶汉室，别无他意。君侯何执迷如是？"言未毕，关平拔剑而前，欲斩诸葛瑾。公止之曰："彼弟孔明在蜀，佐汝伯父，今若杀彼，伤其兄弟之情也。"遂令左右逐出诸葛瑾。瑾满面羞惭，上马出城，回

and withdrew. Liao Hua knew the situation was hopeless and decided to appeal to the king of Hanzhong. With a great shout of defiance, then, he left the city and headed for Chengdu.[7]

* * *

In Mai, Lord Guan waited expectantly for relief from Shangyong. But no sign came. Only five or six hundred men remained to him, and most of those had been wounded. A shortage of rations was causing severe suffering. Suddenly a man appeared at the town wall; he called out, "Hold your arrows!" and asked for an audience. Lord Guan ordered the gates opened, and Zhuge Jin entered. The formalities concluded, tea was served. Zhuge Jin began, "At the command of my lord, Sun Quan, I come to appeal to your reason. The ancient saying runs, 'Whoever recognizes the exigencies of the occasion is a paragon of men.' The nine districts of Jingzhou no longer belong to you. You are reduced to this single paltry town, bereft of resources within and assistance without. If you do not fall in the morning, you will in the evening. Therefore take this advice: give your allegiance to the lord of the Southland, and he will restore your position as guardian of Xiangyang and preserve your family. Favor this suggestion, my lord, with your fullest consideration."

His expression all rectitude, Lord Guan replied, "I am but a warrior from Jieliang. By my lord's favor he and I became brothers. I cannot betray my honor and throw in my lot with the enemy. If this town falls, what is left to me is death. Jade may break, but its whiteness will never change. Bamboo may burn, but its joints will always remain. The man may fall, but his name will come down through history. You may say no more. Be pleased to withdraw. I wish to decide all with Sun Quan in a fight to the finish." To this, Zhuge Jin replied, "Lord Sun wanted to form an alliance with you, based on marriage, so that we could unite against Cao Cao and uphold the house of Han. We harbor no other ambition. Why must you cling to these misconceptions, my lord?" Before Zhuge Jin could finish, Guan Ping had pulled his sword and was making for the visitor. Lord Guan stopped him. "His younger brother Kongming is in the Riverlands serving as your uncle's right-hand man. If you kill him, you will offend his brother." Lord Guan then ordered Zhuge Jin driven away. His face suffused with humiliation, Zhuge Jin left Mai and rode back to

见吴侯曰："关公心如铁石，不可说也。"孙权曰："真忠臣也！似此如之奈何？"吕范曰："某请卜其休咎。"权即令卜之。范揲蓍成象，乃"地水师卦"，更有玄武临应，主敌人远奔。权问吕蒙曰："卦主敌人远奔，卿以何策擒之？"蒙笑曰："卦象正合某之机也。关公虽有冲天之翼，飞不出吾罗网矣！"

正是：

龙游沟壑遭虾戏，凤入牢笼被鸟欺。

毕竟吕蒙之计若何，且看下文分解。

see Sun Quan. "Adamant," Jin reported to Sun Quan, "no one can persuade him." "A model of loyalty," said Sun Quan. "What is our next step?"

Lü Fan suggested, "Let me forecast with the Book of Changes." Sun Quan ordered the forecast. Lu Fan drew the milfoil and the stalks formed a pattern — the hexagram "Master" composed of earth above water.[8] In addition, Dark Tortoise, the northern quadrant of the sky, hovered overhead, meaning that an enemy would flee a great distance. "If the hexagram indicates distant flight," Sun Quan said to Lü Meng, "what would be the manner of apprehending the fugitive?" Lü Meng smiled as he said, "The hexagram's patterns fit perfectly with our plans. Lord Guan may have Heaven-mounting wings, but he cannot outfly our nets!" Indeed:

> When a dragon's in a ditch, the shrimp will tease it;
> When a phoenix enters the coop, the hens will mock it.

How did Lü Meng intend to capture Lord Guan?

Read on.

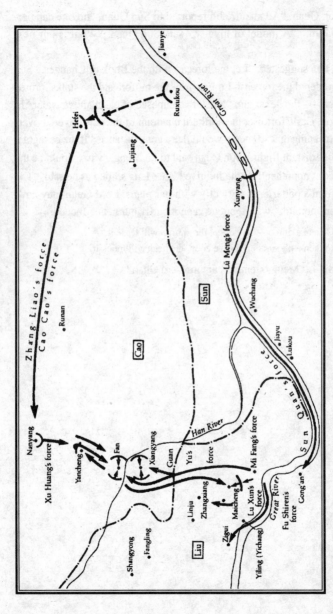

MAP 7. The Southland retakes Jingzhou: key places and persons. Source: Wuhan budui silingbu junshi ziliao yanjiuzu, ed., *Zhongguo gudai zhanzheng yibai li* (Wuhan: Hubei renmin chubanshe, 1979), p. 214.

1879

第七十七回

玉泉山关公显圣　洛阳城曹操感神

　　却说孙权求计于吕蒙。蒙曰："吾料关某兵少，必不从大路而逃，麦成正北有险峻小路，必从此路而去。可令朱然引精兵五千，伏于麦城之北二十里；彼军至，不可与敌，只可随后掩杀。彼军定无战心，必奔临沮。却令潘璋引精兵五百，伏于临沮山僻小路，关某可擒矣。今遣将士各门攻打，只空北门，待其出走。"权闻计，令吕范再卜之。卦成，范告曰："此卦主敌人投西北而走，今夜亥时必然就擒。"权大喜，遂令朱然、潘璋领两枝精兵，各依军令埋伏去讫。

　　且说关公在麦城，计点马步军兵，止剩三百余人；粮草又尽。是夜，城外吴兵招唤各军姓名，越城而去者甚多。救兵又不见到。心中无计，谓王甫曰："吾悔昔日不用公言！今日危急，将复何如？"甫哭告曰："今日之事，虽子牙复生，亦无计可施也。"赵累曰："上庸救兵不至，乃刘封、孟达按兵不动之故。何不弃此孤城，奔入西川，再整兵来，以图恢复？"公曰："吾亦欲如此。"遂上城观之。见北门外敌军不多，因问本城居民："此去往

Chapter 77

At Mount Yuquan Lord Guan Manifests
a Divine Presence
In Luoyang City Cao Cao Feels
the Force of His Soul

Lü Meng offered Sun Quan the following plan: "Guan has few troops
and is unlikely to flee by the main road. He'll take the steep path just
north of Mai. Have Zhu Ran place five thousand of our best men there in
ambush twenty *li* down the way and strike after the enemy passes. They'll
be in no mood to fight and will flee toward Linju. Then let Pan Zhang hide
another five thousand men in the hills by Linju — we will have Lord Guan!
For now, attack Mai on all sides except the north and wait for them to go
out through there." Sun Quan agreed and asked Lü Fan to judge the
prospects of this plan in the light of the *Book of Changes*. When the
hexagram had been formed, Lü Fan announced, "The hexagram signifies
an enemy fleeing northwest. Well before midnight[1] Guan is sure to be
caught." Satisfied, Sun Quan ordered Zhu Ran and Pan Zhang to carry
out Lü Meng's plan.

Inside Mai,[2] Lord Guan counted up his forces. Of infantry and cavalry there remained a mere three hundred all told. His grain and fodder
were exhausted. During the night southern soldiers called out the names
of their brethren within the walls, many of whom slipped over and fled,
for no sign of rescue was to be seen. At his wits' end, Lord Guan said to
Wang Fu, "How I regret ignoring your good advice. In the present crisis,
what more can be done?" Wang Fu wept as he answered, "Not even the
ancient strategist Jiang Ziya could find a way out!" And Zhao Lei said,
"We have had no relief from Shangyong because Liu Feng and Meng Da
won't act on our appeal. Why not abandon this isolated town and flee for
the Riverlands, reorganize an army and plan the reconquest of Jingzhou?"
"That's my own inclination," Lord Guan replied. Then he ascended the
wall and saw few enemy troops around the north gate.

Lord Guan asked a resident of Mai, "What is the terrain like going

北,地势若何?"答曰:"此去皆是山僻小路,可通西川。"公曰:"今夜可走此路。"王甫谏曰:"小路有埋伏,可走大路。"公曰:"虽有埋伏,吾何惧哉!"即下令:马步官军,严整装束,准备出城。甫哭曰:"君侯于路,小心保重!某与部卒百余人,死据此城;城虽破,身不降也!专望君侯速来救援!"

公亦与泣别。遂留周仓与王甫同守麦城,关公自与关平、赵累引残卒二百余人,突出北门。关公横刀前进,行至初更以后,约走二十余里,只见山凹处,金鼓齐鸣,喊声大震,一彪军到,为首大将朱然,骤马挺枪叫曰:"云长休走!趁早投降,免得一死!"公大怒,拍马轮刀来战。朱然便走,公乘势追杀。一棒鼓响,四下伏兵皆起。公不敢战,望临沮小路而走,朱然率兵掩杀。关公所随之兵,渐渐稀少。走不得四五里,前面喊声又震,火光大起,潘璋骤马舞刀杀来。公大怒,轮刀相迎;只三合,潘璋败走。公不敢恋战,急望山路而走。背后关平赶来,报说赵累已死于乱军中。关公不胜悲惶,遂令关平断后,公自在前开路,随行止剩得十余人。行至决石,两下是山,山边皆芦苇败草,树木丛杂。时已五更将尽。正走之间,一声喊起,两下伏兵尽出,长钩套索,一齐并举,先把关公坐下马绊倒。关公翻身落马,被潘璋部将马忠所获。关平知父被擒,火速来救;背后潘璋、朱然

north?" "North of here," the reply went, "are paths in the foothills that lead to the Riverlands." "That's the route I want to take," Lord Guan said. But Wang Fu objected: "Small roads are vulnerable to ambush. Take the main road." "Even so," Lord Guan answered, "I'm not afraid." With that, he issued an order for all his soldiers and officers to pack and dress for the evacuation. Again Wang Fu wept as he said, "My lord, take care on the roads. I will remain here with one hundred men and hold Mai to the death. If they take the town, we will not submit but wait for you to rescue us."

Lord Guan and Wang Fu parted tearfully. Then, leaving Mai in the hands of Wang Fu and Zhou Cang, Guan bolted out the north gate accompanied by Guan Ping, Zhao Lei, and two hundred followers. Lord Guan rode with his sword leveled for action. By the end of the first watch, when he had gone about twenty *li,* drums and gongs began sounding from the pockets and hollows in the hills. Voices rang in the air as a band of troops appeared, Zhu Ran at the head. He charged, spear raised, and shouted: "Go no further! Surrender or die!" Lord Guan advanced, whirling his blade. Zhu Ran fled at once; Lord Guan pursued hotly. At the sound of the drum, troops sprang up on all sides. Resistance was unthinkable; Lord Guan fled by a narrow road toward Linju. Zhu Ran harried the rear, reducing Lord Guan's retinue.

After another four or five *li* Lord Guan was confronted with earth-shaking cries and sky-reaching flames as Pan Zhang charged in for the kill. Maddened, Lord Guan met him. After three clashes Pan Zhang fled in defeat; but Lord Guan could not afford to continue fighting, and headed out toward the hills. Guan Ping overtook him and reported that Zhao Lei had fallen in the melee. Sorrow and despair overcame Lord Guan. He ordered Ping to cover the rear while he forged ahead. A dozen followers were all that remained to him.

Lord Guan came to a place called Breach in the Rocks where the hills squeezed the road. Reeds and shriveled grass grew against the hills, crowded by tangles of shrubs and trees. The fifth watch had nearly ended. Suddenly a voice cried out, springing another ambush. Spear-length hooks and loops reached out and yanked Lord Guan from his mount. As he tumbled to the ground, Pan Zhang's commander, Ma Zhong, took him prisoner. Guan Ping rushed to his father's aid. But Pan Zhang and Zhu

率兵齐至，把关平四下围住。平孤身独战，力尽亦被执。至天明，孙权闻关公父子已被擒获，大喜，聚众将于帐中。

少时，马忠簇拥关公至前。权曰："孤久慕将军盛德，欲结秦、晋之好，何相弃耶？公平昔自以为天下无敌，今日何由被吾所擒？将军今日还服孙权否？"关公厉声骂曰："碧眼小儿，紫髯鼠辈！吾与刘皇叔桃园结义，誓扶汉室，岂与汝叛汉之贼为伍耶！我今误中奸计，有死而已，何必多言！"权回顾众官曰："云长世之豪杰，孤深爱之。今欲以礼相待，劝使归降，何如？"主簿左咸曰："不可。昔曹操得此人时，封侯赐爵，三日一小宴，五日一大宴，上马一提金，下马一提银：如此恩礼，毕竟留之不住，听其斩关杀将而去，致使今日反为所逼，几欲迁都以避其锋。今主公既已擒之，若不即除，恐贻后患。"孙权沉吟半晌，曰："斯言是也。"遂命推出。于是关公父子皆遇害。时建安二十四年冬十二月也。关公亡年五十八岁。后人有诗叹曰：

汉末才无敌，云长独出群：

Ran had surrounded him. Ping fought on, alone, until he was spent; then they took him, too. As the day broke, Sun Quan was informed of the capture of Lord Guan and his son. Immensely pleased, he called his commanders together.

After a short while Ma Zhong hustled Lord Guan into Sun Quan's tent. Sun Quan said, "General, out of long-standing admiration for your splendid virtues, I sought to work out a liaison through marriage. Why did you spurn the offer? You have ever clung to the view that you are without peer in the empire. How has it come about that you are my prisoner today? Do you, General, acknowledge yourself beaten?" Lord Guan damned him harshly: "Green-eyed scamp! Red-whiskered rodent! I gave my allegiance to Imperial Uncle Liu in the peach garden when we swore to uphold the house of Han. What would I be doing in the ranks of traitors in revolt such as you? Now that I have blundered into your treacherous devices, death alone remains. There is no more to say."

Sun Quan turned to his assembled officers. "Lord Guan," he said, "is one of the valiant champions of our time, a man I cherish deeply. I propose that we treat him with the utmost courtesy to encourage him to come over to us. What do you say?" First Secretary Zuo Xian said, "It will not work. That time when Cao Cao had him, he enfeoffed him as a lord, granted him rank, and feasted him — every third day a minor banquet, every fifth day a major one. Whenever he got on his horse, Cao handed him gold. Whenever he got down from his horse, Cao handed him silver. With such kindnesses Cao failed to hold him, and saw Guan leave and kill his pass guards on the way. And today Cao Cao is on the verge of shifting his capital to avoid the thrust of Guan's offensive. My lord, Guan is our captive. If you do not do away with him immediately, I fear the consequences."

1885

Sun Quan pondered for some time until he admitted the truth of the secretary's words and ordered the prisoner removed. And so Lord Guan and his son, Ping, were beheaded in the twelfth month of the twenty-fourth year of Jian An (A.D. 220). Lord Guan was fifty-eight years of age. A poet of later times has left these lines expressing his sorrow and admiration:

Unrivaled in the latter years of Han,

汉英经典文库

1886

神威能奋武，儒雅更知文。

天日心如镜，《春秋》义薄云。

昭然垂万古，不止冠三分。

又有诗曰：

人杰惟追古解良，士民争拜汉云长。

桃园一日兄和弟，俎豆千秋帝与王。

气挟风雷无匹敌，志垂日月有光芒。

至今庙貌盈天下，古木寒鸦几夕阳。

关公既殁，坐下赤兔马被马忠所获，献与孙权。权即赐马忠骑坐。其马数日不食草料而死。

却说王甫在麦城中，骨颤肉惊，乃问周仓曰："昨夜梦见主公浑身血污，立于前；急问之，忽然惊觉。不知主何吉凶？"正说间，忽报吴兵在城下，将关公父子首级招安。王甫、周仓大惊，急登城视之，果关公父子首级也。王甫大叫一声，堕城而死。周仓自刎而亡。于是麦城亦属东吴。

却说关公一魂不散，荡荡悠悠，直至一处：乃荆门州当阳县一座山，名为玉泉山。山上有一老僧，法名普净，原是氾水关镇国寺中长老；后因云游天下，来到此处，见山明水秀，就此结

Lord Guan towered high above all men.
Bold in arms by dint of godlike might,
He knew his letters in a scholar's right.
Like glare of day, his heart reflected true,
His *Spring and Autumn* honor touched the clouds —
A shining spirit to live through history,
Not just the crowning glory of a world in three.

Another verse says:

For the paragon of men, look back to Jieliang;
There men vie to honor Lord Guan of the Han.
For the peach grove brother oath he sealed one day,
A thousand autumns' tribute of royal rites.
His manly soul had power like wind or thunder;
His glowing purpose shone like sun or moon.
And now the realm abounds in statued shrines
With winter-braving crows on olden boughs.

After the passing of Lord Guan, his glorious steed, Red Hare, cap-tured by Ma Zhong, was presented to Sun Quan, who made Ma Zhong a gift of the horse. But Red Hare refused to eat and died after several days.

Inside the town of Mai, meanwhile, Wang Fu, trembling and fearful, asked Zhou Cang, "Last night our lord came to me in a dream. Covered with gore, he stood before me. As I questioned him, I woke with a violent start. What does it signify?" Then came the report: the southerners were at the gate with the heads of Lord Guan and Guan Ping, calling for the surrender of the town. Wang Fu and Zhou Cang quickly climbed the wall and looked down at the heads. The report was all too true. Wang Fu let out a cry and fell to his death. Zhou Cang cut his throat. Thus, the town of Mai, too, came into the possession of the Southland.

The vapor from Lord Guan's soul remained undissolved, floating at-tenuated until it came to rest on Jade Springs Hill in Dangyang county, Jingmenzhou. On the hill lived an old monk whose Buddhist name was Pujing, or Universal Purity. He was the abbot of Zhenguo Temple at the Si River pass.[3] In his jaunts through the realm, he had come to the moun-tain and, attracted by its charming scenery, had built himself a thatched

草为庵，每日坐禅参道；身边只有一小行者，化饭度日。是夜月白风清，三更已后，普净正在庵中默坐，忽闻空中有人大呼曰："还我头来！"普净仰面谛视，只见空中一人，骑赤兔马，提青龙刀，左有一白面将军、右有一黑脸虬髯之人相随，一齐按落云头，至玉泉山顶。普净认得是关公，遂以手中麈尾击其户曰："云长安在？"关公英魂顿悟，即下马乘风落于庵前，叉手问曰："吾师何人？愿求法号。"普净曰："老僧普净，昔日汜水关前镇国寺中，曾与君侯相会，今日岂遂忘之耶？"公曰："向蒙相救，铭感不忘。今某已遇祸而死，愿求清诲，指点迷途。"普净曰："昔非今是，一切休论；后果前因，彼此不爽。今将军为吕蒙所害，大呼'还我头来'，然则颜良、文丑、五关六将等众人之头，又将向谁索耶？"于是关公恍然大悟，稽首皈依而去。后往往于玉泉山显圣护民，乡人感其德，就于山顶上建庙，四时致祭。后人题一联于其庙云：

　　赤面秉赤心、骑赤兔追风，驰驱时、无忘赤帝。

shelter there. In this hermitage he would seat himself for meditation each day, searching for the truth of life. Beside him was a single novice; they lived on the food they could beg.

The night Lord Guan died, the moon glowed pale and a breeze blew cool and fresh. Some time after the third watch, as the monk was sitting in meditation, a voice in the sky called out, "Return my head." Pujing scrutinized the air. A man was riding the steed Red Hare and brandishing the sword Green Dragon. Two men were in his train, a general of fair complexion and a swarthy man with curling whiskers. Together the three alighted from a cloud onto the summit of Jade Springs Hill. Pujing realized that it was Lord Guan and struck the door with a deer-tail whisk for protection against the spirit. He said, "Lord Guan, where are you now?" Lord Guan's glowing cloud-soul seemed to comprehend instantly as it dismounted and dropped on the wind before the monk's hut. Palms together, the wraith spoke: "Who are you, master? I would know your name-in-Buddha." "This old monk is known as Pujing," he replied. "We met once before at the Zhenguo Temple, my lord. Can you have forgotten?"

Replied Lord Guan: "My gratitude for the help you once gave me is engraved in my memory. A calamity has befallen me, and I appeal to you now for the redeeming counsel that will point me out of the darkness of my wandering." "Right and wrong, past and present are relevant no more; retribution follows human action with the certainty of fate," the monk answered. "Now you cry out for your head, having met your death at the hands of Lü Meng. From whom shall Yan Liang, Wen Chou, Cao Cao's six pass guards, and the countless others whom you killed seek their heads?" In a flash Lord Guan realized the truth and, bowing his head in submission to Buddha's law of Karma, he departed.[4] Thereafter he frequently manifested himself in divine form on Jade Springs Hill to afford protection to the common people. And the local dwellers showed their gratitude by building a temple on the summit, where they made offerings each season. Later someone inscribed the following couplet on the temple wall:

> Behind the ruddy face, a ruby heart —
> Lord Guan astride Red Hare outrode the wind.

青灯观青史、仗青龙偃月，隐微处、不愧青天。

却说孙权既害了关公，遂尽收荆襄之地，赏犒三军，设宴大会诸将庆功；置吕蒙于上位，顾谓众将曰："孤久不得荆州，今唾手而得，皆子明之功也。"蒙再三逊谢。权曰："昔周郎雄略过人，破曹操于赤壁，不幸早殁。鲁子敬代之：子敬初见孤时，便及帝王大略，此一快也；曹操东下，诸人皆劝孤降，子敬独劝孤召公瑾逆而击之，此二快也；惟劝吾借荆州与刘备，是其一短。今子明设计定谋，立取荆州，胜子敬、周郎多矣！"

于是亲酌酒赐吕蒙。吕蒙接酒欲饮，忽然掷杯于地，一手揪住孙权，厉声大骂曰："碧眼小儿！紫髯鼠辈！还识我否？"众将大惊，急救时，蒙推倒孙权，大步前进，坐于孙权位上，两眉倒竖，双眼圆睁，大喝曰："我自破黄巾以来，纵横天下三十余年，今被汝一旦以奸计图我，我生不能啖汝之肉，死当追吕贼之魂！——我乃汉寿亭侯关云长也。"权大惊，慌忙率大小将士，皆下拜。只见吕蒙倒于地上，七窍流血而死。众将见之，无不恐惧。权将吕蒙尸首，具棺安葬，赠南郡太守、孱陵侯；命其

But far as he rode, he served the Fire King.[5]
By oil lamp light he studied history;
In war he trusted to his dragon sword.
His inmost thought would welcome light of day.[6]

Now that Lord Guan was dead, Sun Quan consolidated his hold on all
the territories of Jingzhou. After rewarding all units of the army, he held a
grand banquet for the commanders in honor of Lü Meng. Turning to the
assembly, Sun Quan said, "After long frustration, our easy acquisition of
Jingzhou is owing to the meritorious service of Lü Meng." Lü Meng tried
repeatedly to decline the testimonial, but Sun Quan continued, "At an
earlier time, Zhou Yu, a man of exceptional talent and vision, defeated
Cao Cao at Red Cliffs. Alas, he died prematurely and was replaced by
Lu Su, who in his very first interview with me broached a grand imperial
strategy for the Southland — the first boon. When Cao Cao descended
upon us, I was universally counseled to surrender. Lu Su alone urged me
to call in Zhou Yu, to oppose and attack Cao Cao — the second boon. The
only fault I found in Lu Su is that he talked me into allowing Liu Bei to
borrow Jingzhou. But today it is you, Lü Meng — you worked out the
strategy for retaking Jingzhou, and thus you excel the other two by far."

Sun Quan personally poured out wine and presented it to Lü Meng.
Lü Meng received it and was about to drink, when he dashed the cup to
the ground instead and seized Sun Quan with one hand. "Green-eyed
scamp!" he screamed. "Red-whiskered rodent! Have you forgotten me?
Or not?" The assemblage looked aghast. Everyone moved to rescue Sun
Quan, but Meng knocked him to the ground, strode to his throne, and
seated himself upon it. Meng's eyebrows arched, his eyes grew round
and prominent as he bellowed, "I have crisscrossed the empire for thirty-
odd years since defeating the Yellow Scarves, only to have your treacherous trap sprung on me. But if I have failed to taste your flesh in life, Lü
Meng, I shall give your soul no peace in death — for I am Guan Yunchang,
lord of Hanshou precinct!"[7]

Fear-stricken, Sun Quan led the assemblage in offering obeisance.
But lo! Lü Meng collapsed on the ground, blood ran out of his orifices, and
he died. There was general terror. Sun Quan had Lü Meng's corpse

1891

子吕霸袭爵。孙权自此感关公之事，惊讶不已。

　　忽报张昭自建业而来。权召入问之。昭曰："今主公损了关公父子，江东祸不远矣！此人与刘备桃园结义之时，誓同生死。今刘备已有两川之兵；更兼诸葛亮之谋，张、黄、马、赵之勇。备若知云长父子遇害，必起倾国之兵，奋力报仇：恐东吴难与敌也。"权闻之大惊，跌足曰："孤失计较也！似此如之奈何？"昭曰："主公勿忧。某有一计，令西蜀之兵不犯东吴，荆州如磐石之安。"权问何计。昭曰："今曹操拥百万之众，虎视华夏，刘备急欲报仇，必与操约和：若二处连兵而来，东吴危矣。不如先遣人将关公首级，转送与曹操，明教刘备知是操之所使，必痛恨于操，西蜀之兵，不向吴而向魏矣。吾乃观其胜负，于中取事：此为上策。"

　　权从其言，随遣使者以木匣盛关公首级，星夜送与曹操。时操从摩陂班师回洛阳，闻东吴送关公首级至，喜曰："云长已死，吾夜眠贴席矣。"阶下一人出曰："此乃东吴移祸之计也。"操视之，乃主簿司马懿也。操问其故，懿曰："昔刘、关、张三人

confined and buried, and posthumously appointed Meng governor of Nanjun and lord of Chanling; Meng's son, Ba, inherited his rank. Thereafter Sun Quan was tormented with anxiety over the execution of Lord Guan.

Unexpectedly, Zhang Zhao arrived from the southern capital, Jianye; he was summoned by Sun Quan. "My lord," Zhang Zhao said, "when you put Lord Guan and his son to death, you brought the Southland to the verge of disaster, for the man had bound himself to Liu Bei. By the peach garden oath they swore to live and die as one. Today Liu Bei controls the forces of all the Riverlands. Add to that the cunning of Zhuge Liang and the valor of the remaining 'Tiger Generals,' Zhang Fei, Huang Zhong, Ma Chao, and Zhao Zilong — when Liu Bei learns how Lord Guan and Guan Ping died, he will mobilize the whole kingdom and do his utmost for revenge, a threat the Southland is going to find difficult to meet." Badly shaken by Zhang Zhao's words, Sun Quan stamped his feet as he said, "I have miscalculated. What can we do about it?"

"All is not lost, my lord," Zhang Zhao replied. "I have a plan to keep the westerners from attacking and thus keep Jingzhou as secure as a rock." "Tell us," said Sun Quan. Zhang Zhao went on, "Cao Cao has command of a million men. His glance scours the empire like a tiger's. But Liu Bei's urgent wish for revenge will require him to come to terms with Cao Cao. The Southland will hardly survive if those two combine forces and invade, so you would be well advised to make the first move. Have Lord Guan's head sent to Cao Cao in such a way as to make it appear to Liu Bei that it was all at Cao's direction. His animosity will be redirected toward Cao Cao and his armies will turn on the kingdom of Wei while we observe the fortunes of both and from a neutral vantage seize our opportunity."

1893

Sun Quan agreed, and the head was taken in a wooden box to Cao Cao. At the time Cao Cao had just returned to Luoyang from Mopo. Hearing that Sun Quan had sent Lord Guan's head, Cao Cao exclaimed delightedly, "With him dead, I shall spend my nights secure indeed." But a member of the court stepped forward and said, "This is actually a device for transferring disaster away from the Southland." Cao Cao studied the speaker, First Secretary Sima Yi. Cao Cao demanded an explana-

桃园结义之时，誓同生死。今东吴害了关公，惧其复仇，故将首级献与大王，使刘备迁怒大王，不攻吴而攻魏，他却于中乘便而图事耳。"操曰："仲达之言是也。孤以何策解之？"懿曰："此事极易。大王可将关公首级，刻一香木之躯以配之，葬以大臣之礼；刘备知之，必深恨孙权，尽力南征。我却观其胜负：蜀胜则击吴，吴胜则击蜀。——二处若得一处，那一处亦不久也。"操大喜，从其计，遂召吴使人。呈上木匣，操开匣视之，见关公面如平日。操笑曰："云长公别来无恙！"言未讫，只见关公口开目动，须发皆张，操惊倒。众官急救，良久方醒，顾谓众官曰："关将军真天神也！"吴使又将关公显圣附体、骂孙权追吕蒙之事告操。操愈加恐惧，遂设牲醴祭祀，刻沉香木为躯，以王侯之礼，葬于洛阳南门外，令大小官员送殡，操自拜祭，赠为荆王，差官守墓；即遣吴使回江东去讫。

却说汉中王自东川回成都，法正奏曰："王上先夫人去世；

tion, and Sima Yi replied, "At the time when Liu, Guan, and Zhang pledged their honor in the peach garden, they swore to die for one another. Now, having put Lord Guan to death, the Southland fears the brothers' reprisal. That is why Sun Quan presented the head to Your Majesty — to make Liu Bei shift his hatred and attack us instead of them, while they look for ways to exploit the situation."

"What you say is correct," Cao Cao responded to Sima Yi, "but how do we get out of it?" "It is not difficult at all," Sima Yi replied. "Let Your Highness have Lord Guan's head fitted with torso and limbs carved of fragrant wood so that he may be buried whole with the ceremony due a high minister. When Liu Bei learns of it, his hatred for Sun Quan will deepen, and he will concentrate on the southern expedition. Then we can sit back and await developments. If the Riverlands is winning, we attack the Southland; if the Southland is winning, we attack the Riverlands. Once one falls, the other cannot last."

Delighted with the scheme, Cao Cao called in the messenger from the Southland. The messenger presented the wooden box. Cao Cao opened it and saw Lord Guan's face, just as it had been in life. With a smile, Cao Cao said, "You have been well, I trust, General, since we parted?"[8] Before Cao Cao could finish, the mouth opened, the eyes moved, and the hair and beard stood up like quills. Cao fell in a faint, reviving only after a long spell. He said to the officers who had rushed to his aid, "General Guan is no mortal!" The messenger told Cao Cao how Lord Guan had taken possession of Lü Meng, reviled Sun Quan, and then hounded Meng himself. Cao Cao shivered at the report. Adopting Sima Yi's advice, he held a grand ceremony with sacrificial animals and libations honoring the great man as a prince before burying his head and the wooden corpse outside the southern gate of Luoyang. Cao Cao ordered officials of all ranks to attend the funeral, and he personally made offerings and advanced Lord Guan's rank to prince of Jingzhou. Guards were then dispatched to the tomb, and the Southland messenger was sent home to report.

1895

*　　*　　*

When the king of Hanzhong returned to Chengdu from the eastern Riverlands, Fa Zheng petitioned him: "Your Majesty's former wife has

孙夫人又南归，未必再来。人伦之道，不可废也，必纳王妃，以襄内政。"汉中王从之。法正复奏曰："吴懿有一妹，美而且贤。尝闻有相者，相此女后必大贵。先曾许刘焉之子刘瑁，瑁早殁。其女至今寡居，大王可纳之为妃。"汉中王曰："刘瑁与我同宗，于理不可。"法正曰："论其亲疏，何异晋文之与怀嬴乎？"汉中王乃依允，遂纳吴氏为王妃。——后生二子：长刘永，字公寿；次刘理，字奉孝。

且说东西两川，民安国富，田禾大成。忽有人自荆州来，言东吴求婚于关公，关公力拒之。孔明曰："荆州危矣！可使人替关公回。"正商议间，荆州捷报使命，络绎而至。不一日，关兴到，具言水淹七军之事。忽又报马到来，报说关公于江边多设墩台，提防甚密，万无一失。因此玄德放心。

忽一日，玄德自觉浑身肉颤，行坐不安；至夜，不能宁睡，起坐内室，秉烛看书，觉神思昏迷，伏几而卧；就室中起一阵冷风，灯灭复明，抬头见一人立于灯下。玄德问曰："汝何人，黄夜至吾内室？"其人不答。玄德疑怪，自起视之，乃是关公，于灯影下往来躲避。玄德曰："贤弟别来无恙！夜深至此，必有大故。吾与汝情同骨肉，因何回避？"关公泣告曰："愿兄起兵，以雪弟

1897

left the world, and Lady Sun has gone home to the south, unlikely to return. But this great principle of human relations cannot be ignored forever. You shall have to take another royal wife to aid in domestic matters." When the king consented, Fa Zheng continued, "Wu Yi has a younger sister who is attractive and virtuous. Once a reader of faces predicted that she would rise high. She had been promised to Liu Mao, son of the late Protector Liu Yan. But due to Mao's premature death, she has lived in widowed retirement. She would make a suitable consort for Your Highness." The king replied, "It is unthinkable. Liu Mao was my kinsman." "In terms of propinquity," Fa Zheng argued, "how is it different from the case of Duke Wen of Jin, Chong Er, and Huai Ying?"[9] And so the king of Hanzhong relented and accepted Lady Wu as his royal consort. Later, she bore him two sons, Liu Yong (Gongshou) and Liu Li (Fengxiao).

* * *

In both the eastern and the western sections of the Riverlands the population was contented, the kingdom was prosperous, and the harvests were large. Suddenly a report came from Jingzhou that the Southland had sought a state marriage with Lord Guan and that he had rejected it. "Jingzhou will fall," Kongming said. "Lord Guan must be recalled and someone sent to replace him." As they were speaking, more reports streamed in, followed by Guan Xing, who told them how Lord Guan had flooded seven armies at Fan. Soon another rider brought word that Lord Guan had set up an impenetrable net of signal stations along the river. This last report eased Xuande's worries.

One day, however, Xuande was seized with trembling. Walking or sitting, he could find no peace. That night, unable to sleep, he sat in his inner chamber reading by candlelight. Feeling his senses darken, he sank, unconscious, onto the table. A chilly gust sprang up inside the room; the candle blew out, then rekindled. Xuande raised his head and saw a man's form standing by the lamp. "Who comes to my room in dead of night?" he demanded, but there was no reply. Puzzled, Xuande arose to examine him: it was Lord Guan, moving back and forth evasively beside the lamp. "Worthy brother, have you been well since we parted?" Xuande asked. "You must have some serious reason for coming here in the dead of

恨！"言讫，冷风骤起，关公不见。玄德忽然惊觉，乃是一梦：时正三鼓。玄德大疑，急出前殿，使人请孔明来。孔明入见，玄德细言梦警。孔明曰："此乃王上心思关公，故有此梦。何必多疑？"玄德再三疑虑，孔明以善言解之。

孔明辞出，至中门外，迎见许靖。靖曰："某才赴军师府下报一机密，听知军师入宫，特来至此。"孔明曰："有何机密？"靖曰："某适闻外人传说，东吴吕蒙已袭荆州，关公已遇害！故特来密报军师。"孔明曰："吾夜观天象，见将星落于荆楚之地，已知云长必然被祸；但恐王上忧虑，故未敢言。"二人正说之间，忽然殿内转出一人，扯住孔明衣袖而言曰："如此凶信，公何瞒我！"孔明视之，乃玄德也。孔明、许靖奏曰："适来所言，皆传闻之事，未足深信。愿王上宽怀，勿生忧虑。"玄德曰："孤与云长，誓同生死；彼若有失，孤岂能独生耶！"

孔明、许靖正劝解之间，忽近侍奏曰："马良、伊籍至。"玄德急召入问之。二人具说荆州已失，关公兵败求救，呈上表章。未及拆观，侍臣又奏荆州廖化至。玄德急召入。化哭拜于地，细奏刘封、孟达不发救兵之事。玄德大惊曰："若如此，吾弟休矣！"孔明曰："刘封、孟达如此无礼，罪不容诛！王上宽心，亮亲提一旅之师，去救荆襄之急。"玄德泣曰："云长有失，孤断不

night. You and I are as kindred. Why do you avoid me?"

Lord Guan appealed through his sobs: "I beg my brother, raise an army; avenge me." So saying, he was no more as another chilly gust swept by. Waking from the dream to the beating of the third drum, Xuande rushed bewildered from his room calling for Kongming. Kongming came, and Xuande reported his alarming dream, "This is all because Lord Guan is much on Your Highness's mind. Do not vex yourself so." Xuande voiced his anxieties, and Kongming tried his best to soothe him.

After taking leave of his lord, Kongming came upon Xu Jing at the gate. Jing said, "I was just at your residence, Director General, to deliver a secret report. They said I'd find you here in the palace." "What is it?" saked Kongming. "The rumor is that Lü Meng of the Southland has surprised Jingzhou and that Lord Guan has been killed." "Last night I was observing the heavens," Kongming said. "A martial star fell over the Jingzhou area. It told me that Lord Guan must have met his doom. But I chose to keep silent because of His Highness's anxieties." As the two men were speaking, someone came out of the building and seized Kongming's sleeve. "How can you try to keep such evil news from me!" It was Xuande! Kongming and Xu Jing made obeisance and said, "These rumors cannot be taken seriously. Let Your Highness be calm and free of anxiety." "Yunchang and I swore to die as one," Xuande cried. "I would not be able to live on without him."

Kongming and Xu Jing tried to calm him. But at that moment an attendant announced the arrival of Ma Liang and Yi Ji. The two men were rushed before Xuande. They reported the fall of Jingzhou, Lord Guan's defeat, and his request for aid; they also submitted his letter of appeal. Before Xuande had time to read it, the arrival of Liao Hua from Jingzhou was announced. He too was brought swiftly before Xuande. Liao Hua threw himself to the ground, weeping as he told how Liu Feng and Meng Da had refused to send forces to rescue Lord Guan. Xuande was astounded. "In that case, my brother is done for," he exclaimed. Kongming added, "For spiting us so, death is too gentle for those two. Stay calm, Your Highness, and I will take an army to Jingzhou myself and save the province." But Xuande cried out, "I cannot endure life without my brother. I will go to his rescue tomorrow myself." Xuande sent someone to

独生！孤来日自提一军去救云长！"遂一面差人赴阆中报知翼德，一面差人会集人马。未及天明，一连数次，报说关公夜走临沮，为吴将所获，义不屈节，父子归神。玄德听罢，大叫一声，昏绝于地。

正是：

　　　　为念当年同誓死，忍教今日独捐生！

未知玄德性命如何，且看下文分解。

Langzhong to notify Zhang Fei while he himself set about mustering the army.

Before day had dawned, reports of the catastrophe in Jingzhou were streaming in, telling of Lord Guan's night flight to Linju, his capture by the southerners, his refusal to dishonor his pledge of loyalty to Xuande, and his final dispatch together with his son, Ping. After hearing the whole tale, Xuande uttered a dreadful cry and fell unconscious to the ground. Indeed:

> Thinking of their vow to die as one,
> Could he bear to let him die alone?

Would Xuande revive?[10]

Read on.

第七十八回

治风疾神医身死　传遗命奸雄数终

　　却说汉中王闻关公父子遇害，哭倒于地，众文武急救，半晌方醒，扶入内殿。孔明劝曰："王上少忧。自古道'死生有命'；关公平日刚而自矜，故今日有此祸。王上且宜保养尊体，徐图报仇。"玄德曰："孤与关、张二弟桃园结义时，誓同生死。今云长已亡，孤岂能独享富贵乎！"言未已，只见关兴号恸而来。玄德见了，大叫一声，又哭绝于地。众官救醒。一日哭绝三五次，三日水浆不进，只是痛哭；泪湿衣襟，斑斑成血。孔明与众官再三劝解。玄德曰："孤与东吴，誓不同日月也！"孔明曰："闻东吴将关公首级献与曹操，操以王侯礼祭葬之。"玄德曰："此何意也？"孔明曰："此是东吴欲移祸于曹操，操知其谋，故以厚礼葬关公，令王上归怨于吴也。"玄德曰："吾今即提兵问罪于吴，以雪吾恨！"孔明谏曰："不可。方今吴欲令我伐魏，魏亦欲令我伐吴：各怀谲计，伺隙而乘。王上只宜按兵不动，且与关公发丧。

Chapter 78

Treating an Affliction, a Famous Practitioner Dies
Delivering the Last Command, the Tyrant
Ends His Days[1]

The king of Hanzhong dropped to the ground, grieving for Lord Guan
and his son. Military officers and court officials rushed to offer him assistance. Finally the king revived, and they helped him to his rooms. "Try to
stay calm," Kongming urged him. "From the beginning of time, death has
been ordained. Lord Guan's willful arrogance caused this catastrophe.[2]
Your Highness must guard your precious health while we plan revenge
step by step." "I took an oath of brotherhood with Lord Guan and Zhang
Fei," Xuande answered. "We vowed to die as one. With Lord Guan
gone, what meaning do wealth and honor have for me?"

As Xuande was speaking, Guan Xing entered, wailing piteously. At
the sight of Lord Guan's son, Xuande cried out and fainted again. Officers rushed to his side. Five times Xuande fell from grief that day. For
three days, refusing all food and drink, he howled out his pain until his
cries brought flecks of blood to his tear-soaked robes. Kongming and the
officers pressed him to desist, but he said, "Neither this sun nor this moon
shall I share with the Southland: so I swear." "They say," Kongming
responded, "that the Southland has presented Lord Guan's head to Cao
Cao who has interred him with royal ceremony." "What does it mean?"
Xuande asked. "It means," Kongming replied, "that the Southland is trying to shift the blame for his death to Cao Cao — who, however, has seen
through the scheme and buried Lord Guan with full honors so that your
revenge may fall on the Southland." "Then," Xuande answered, "we
must bare our weapons now and visit that vengeance on the south."[3]

Kongming objected: "That we must not do, for the south would have
us embroiled in the north just as the north would have us in the south,
each evolving its own schemes and awaiting the opportunity to strike.
Your Highness needs to refrain from action for now and simply initiate

1903

待吴、魏不和,乘时而伐之,可也。"众官又再三劝谏,玄德方才进膳,传旨川中大小将士,尽皆挂孝。汉中王亲出南门招魂祭奠,号哭终日。

却说曹操在洛阳,自葬关公后,每夜合眼便见关公。操甚惊惧,问于众官。众官曰:"洛阳行宫旧殿多妖,可造新殿居之。"操曰:"吾欲起一殿,名建始殿。恨无良工。"贾诩曰:"洛阳良工有苏越者,最有巧思。"操召入,令画图像。苏越画成九间大殿,前后廊庑楼阁,呈与操。操视之曰:"汝画甚合孤意,但恐无栋梁之材。"苏越曰:"此去离城三十里,有一潭,名跃龙潭;前有一祠,名跃龙祠。祠傍有一株大梨树,高十余丈,堪作建始殿之梁。"

操大喜,即令人工到彼砍伐。次日,回报此树锯解不开,斧砍不入,不能斩伐。操不信,自领数百骑,直至跃龙祠前下马,仰观那树,亭亭如华盖,直侵云汉,并无曲节。操命砍之,乡老数人前来谏曰:"此树已数百年矣,常有神人居其上,恐未可伐。"操大怒曰:"吾平生游历,普天之下,四十余年,上至天子,下及庶人,无不惧孤;是何妖神,敢违孤意!"言讫,拔所佩剑亲自砍之:铮然有声,血溅满身。操愕然大惊,掷剑上马,回至宫

the funeral services for Lord Guan. When the accord between north and south breaks down, we can start our punitive expedition."[4] The assembly of officials joined in earnest appeal, and Xuande finally accepted food; then he ordered the armed forces from the generals down to the rank and file to go into mourning. In front of the southern gate of the capital the king personally led the rites for summoning the souls of the dead and performed the sacrifices. His lamentation continued the entire day.

* * *

Lord Guan had been interred at Luoyang, but he continued to appear in Cao Cao's mind's eye. Cao put the matter to his officials, who said, "Vengeful ghosts haunt the old buildings in the supplementary palace here. You must build a new residence." "I have been planning," Cao Cao responded, "to construct a residence to be called Foundation Hall, but I lack a skilled architect." "Su Yue is one of Luoyang's best," Jia Xu suggested. As Cao Cao's invitation, Su Yue designed a large-scale building of nine sections, surrounded by corridors, elevated galleries, and towers. The drawings were presented to Cao Cao. After examining them, he said, "Exactly what I had in mind. But we do not have the lumber for the main beams." Su Yue replied, "Thirty *li* from the city in front of the Vaulting Dragon Pool there is a temple of the same name. Beside the temple grows a giant pear tree over a hundred spans tall. That should provide the beams for Foundation Hall."

1905

Elated, Cao Cao sent workmen to cut the tree down. But they could not penetrate it with saws or open it with axes. In disbelief Cao Cao led several hundred men to the shrine to inspect the tree, which soared straight up and spread out a leafy canopy that seemed to reach to the Milky Way. Cao Cao ordered his men to cut the pear tree down, but some local elders came forward to object. "The tree is already several hundred years old," they said, "and a spirit has always occupied it. It should not be cut." Cao Cao made an angry reply: "In all my time, over forty years, I have gone far and wide across the realm. And I am held in fear and respect by all, from the Son of Heaven himself to the common man. What perverse spirit here dares challenge my wishes?" He struck at the tree with his sword. There was a metallic sound; then blood splashed over Cao, who threw his sword to the ground and rode home in hysteria.

内。是夜二更，操睡卧不安，坐于殿中，隐几而寐。忽见一人披发仗剑，身穿皂衣，直至面前，指操喝曰："吾乃梨树之神也。汝盖建始殿，意欲篡逆，却来伐吾神木！吾知汝数尽，特来杀汝！"操大惊，急呼："武士安在？"皂衣人仗剑砍操。操大叫一声，忽然惊觉，头脑疼痛不可忍。急传旨遍求良医治疗，不能痊可。众官皆忧。

华歆入奏曰："大王知有神医华佗否？"操曰："即江东医周泰者乎？"歆曰："是也。"操曰："虽闻其名，未知其术。"歆曰："华佗字元化，沛国谯郡人也。其医术之妙，世所罕有：但有患者，或用药，或用针，或用灸，随手而愈。若患五脏六腑之疾，药不能效者，以麻肺汤饮之，令病者如醉死，却用尖刀剖开其腹，以药汤洗其脏腑，病人略无疼痛。洗毕，然后以药线缝口，用药敷之；或一月，或二十日，即平复矣：其神妙如此！一日，佗行于道上，闻一人呻吟之声。佗曰：'此饮食不下之病。'问之果然。佗令取蒜齑汁三升饮之，吐蛇一条，长二三尺，饮食即下。广陵太守陈登，心中烦懑，面赤，不能饮食，求佗医治。佗以药饮之，吐虫三升，皆赤头，首尾动摇。登问其故，佗曰：'此因多食鱼腥，故有此毒。今日虽可，三年之后，必将复发，不可救也。'后

That night at the second watch, unable to sleep, Cao Cao was seated
in his chamber, resting against a low table. Suddenly he saw a man dressed
in black, hair disheveled, hand on sword, advancing straight at him and
shouting, "I am the spirit of the pear tree. Building Foundation Hall sig-
nals your intent to usurp the dynasty. That explains your striking at a
sacred tree.[5] I know your number is told, and I come to take your life!"
Cao Cao called in panic for his guards. The black-robed figure swung his
sword. Cao Cao screamed and awoke, his head throbbing unbearably.
Physicians were sought, but none could bring relief. The court officials
were depressed.

Hua Xin submitted a proposal: "Your Highness knows of the marvelous physician Hua Tuo?" "The man who cured Zhou Tai of the
Southland?" Cao asked. "The same," Hua Xin said. "I have heard the
name, but am unacquainted with his technique," Cao said. Hua Xin continued, "Hua Tuo (styled Yuanhua) is from the Qiao district in the fief of
Pei. He has worked miraculous cures unknown to any other doctor. For
the sufferer he prescribes salves or acupuncture or moxibustion, and pa-
tients seem to heal at his touch. In cases of disease of the internal organs,
where applied compounds will not work, he feeds the patient a narcotic
potion to induce a deep sleep; then he cuts open the stomach and irrigates
the affected areas with medicinal fluids. The patient feels not the slightest pain, and after the irrigation Hua Tuo sews up the wound with treated
sutures and spreads salve over it. Recovery takes a month, maybe twenty
days. That's the kind of skill he has!

"Traveling one day, he heard someone groaning. 'Inability to ingest,'
he said — which turned out to be the case. Hua Tuo had three pints of
garlic and leek juice given to the sufferer, who spit up a worm over two
feet long. After that the man could ingest once again. Governor of
Guangling Chen Deng suffered from severe indigestion and inflamed
complexion. Unable to eat, he summoned Hua Tuo. After taking medicine, the governor vomited up three pints of worms; their tails wriggled
and their heads were reddish. Chen Deng asked for the cause. The doctor told him his condition came from eating too much fish, and that the
symptoms could well recur in three years and become incurable even
though he was normal at the moment. Three years later the governor

1907

陈登果三年而死。又有一人眉间生一瘤，痒不可当，令佗视之。佗曰：'内有飞物。'人皆笑之。佗以刀割开，一黄雀飞去，病者即愈。有一人被犬咬足指，随长肉二块，一痛一痒，俱不可忍。佗曰：'痛者内有针十个，痒者内有黑白棋子二枚。'人皆不信。佗以刀割开，果应其言。此人真扁鹊、仓公之流也！现居金城，离此不远，大王何不召之？"

操即差人星夜请华佗入内，令诊脉视疾。佗曰："大王头脑疼痛，因患风而起。病根在脑袋中，风涎不能出，枉服汤药，不可治疗。某有一法：先饮麻肺汤，然后用利斧砍开脑袋，取出风涎，方可除根。"操大怒曰："汝要杀孤耶！"佗曰："大王曾闻关公中毒箭，伤其右臂，某刮骨疗毒，关公略无惧色；今大王小可之疾，何多疑焉？"操曰："臂痛可刮，脑袋安可砍开？汝必与关公情熟，乘此机会，欲报仇耳！"呼左右拿下狱中，拷问其情。贾诩谏曰："似此良医，世罕其匹，未可废也。"操叱曰："此人欲乘机害我，正与吉平无异！"急令追拷。

华佗在狱，有一狱卒，姓吴，人皆称为"吴押狱"。此人每日以酒食供奉华佗。佗感其恩，乃告曰："我今将死，恨有《青囊书》未传于世。感公厚意，无可为报；我修一书，公可遣人送与

died.

"Another time, a man had a tumor by his eyebrow. It itched intolerably, so the sufferer summoned Hua Tuo. After studying the growth, the doctor said that something winged was inside. Everyone laughed, but when he cut it open, a little sparrow flew out, and the man was healed.

"Another time, a dog bit a man's toes, and two lumps of flesh grew there. One hurt and one itched excruciatingly. Hua Tuo said, 'There are ten needles inside the one that hurts, and two chess pieces, one black, one white, inside the other.' No one thought this diagnosis credible; but when Hua Tuo cut them open, it was exactly as he said. He is of the same caliber as Bian Que of the Spring and Autumn period or Master Cang of the Former Han. At present Hua Tuo lives in Jincheng, not too far from here. Your Highness should call for him."

Hua Tuo was speedily summoned and ordered to examine the ailing king. "Your Highness's severe headaches are due to a humor that is active. The root cause is in the skull, where trapped air and fluids are building up. Medicine won't do any good. The method I would advise is this: after general anesthesia I will open your skull with a cleaver and remove the excess matter. Only then can the root cause be removed." "Are you trying to kill me?" Cao Cao protested angrily. "Your Highness must have heard how I treated Lord Guan's right arm after he was wounded by a poisoned arrow," Tuo replied. "I had to scrape the bone, yet he betrayed no sign of fear. Why is Your Highness so apprehensive over a minor affliction?" "An arm can be scraped. How can the skull be opened? You must be Lord Guan's close friend, hoping to use this occasion for revenge." So saying, Cao Cao ordered Hua Tuo imprisoned and interrogated. Jia Xu objected: "So excellent and rare a physician should not be wasted." But Cao Cao replied sharply, "The man was looking for a chance to murder me, as Ji Ping was," [6] and ordered the interrogation to proceed.

One of the jailers where Hua Tuo was confined was known as Wu the Bailiff. Every day the man provided wine and food for Hua Tuo. Gratefully, Tuo said to him, "My death is imminent. What I regret most is that my *Book of the Black Bag* will be lost to posterity. You have been

我家,取《青囊书》来赠公,公继吾术。"吴押狱大喜曰:"我若得此书,弃了此役,医治天下病人,以传先生之德。"佗即修书付吴押狱。吴押狱直至金城,问佗之妻取了《青囊书》;回至狱中,付与华佗检看毕,佗即将书赠与吴押狱。吴押狱持回家中藏之。旬日之后,华佗竟死于狱中。吴押狱买棺殡殓讫,脱了差役回家,欲取《青囊书》看习,只见其妻正将书在那里焚烧。吴押狱大惊,连忙抢夺,全卷已被烧毁,只剩得一两叶。吴押狱怒骂其妻。妻曰:"纵然学得与华佗一般神妙,只落得死于牢中,要他何用!"吴押狱嗟叹而止。因此《青囊书》不曾传于世,所传者止阉鸡猪等小法,乃烧剩一两叶中所载也。后人有诗叹曰:

华佗仙术比长桑,神识如窥垣一方。

惆怅人亡书亦绝,后人无复见《青囊》!

却说曹操自杀华佗之后,病势愈重,又忧吴、蜀之事。正虑间,近臣忽奏东吴遣使上书。操取书拆视之,略曰:

臣孙权久知天命已归王上,伏望早正大位,遣将剿灭刘备,扫平两川,臣即率群下纳土归降矣。

操观毕大笑,出示群臣曰:"是儿欲使吾居炉火上耶!"侍

so kind to me, but I have been unable to repay you. Now I will write to my family. Have someone take them the letter, and they will present the book to you so that my methods can be carried on." Delighted, the bailiff said, "With that book I can be done with this kind of work and cure the sick. That way, master, your benevolence will reach the generations to come." Hua Tuo composed the letter, and Wu the Bailiff took it to Jincheng. Tuo's wife gave him the book, and he brought it back to Hua Tuo, who read it through and then gave it as a gift to the jailer. Wu the Bailiff took it home and kept it there.

Ten days later Hua Tuo died. Wu the Bailiff purchased a coffin and had the body readied for burial. He then resigned his office and returned home, ready to begin his study of Hua Tuo's book. Once home, he could hardly believe his eyes: his wife was putting the book in the fire. Up in arms, Wu the Bailiff tried desperately to retrieve it, but it was already destroyed. Only a couple of pages remained. When the bailiff angrily cursed his wife, she said, "Even if you could become as great a physician as Hua Tuo, you would only end up dead in jail. What's the good of it?" Wu the Bailiff sighed his heart out before he desisted. This is why Hua Tuo's writings have never come down to us, except for the few lines about capons and gelded pigs on the unburned pages. A poet of later times left these lines in praise of the renowned physician:

> Hua Tuo's transcendent skill beyond compare
> Enabled him to see inside of men.
> Alas, his text was lost upon his death;
> The book of cures was never seen again.

Cao Cao's condition worsened after he had killed Hua Tuo, and he was depressed over his problems with the Southland and the Riverlands. As he pondered the situation, an attendant brought a letter from Sun Quan. Cao Cao opened it and studied the contents: "Your subject, Sun Quan, recognizing that the Mandate of Heaven has come to Your Highness, humbly anticipates your early ascension to the imperial throne. If you would dispatch your generals to destroy Liu Bei, I will forthwith lead my subordinates in tendering our lands in loyal submission." Cao Cao laughed aloud and showed the note to his courtiers. "The bastard wants to roast me on the fire!" he said.[7] But a group around Chen Qun peti-

1911

中陈群等奏曰："汉室久已衰微，殿下功德巍巍，生灵仰望。今孙权称臣归命，此天人之应，异气齐声。殿下宜应天顺人，早正大位。"操笑曰："吾事汉多年，虽有功德及民，然位至于王，名爵已极，何敢更有他望？苟天命在孤，孤为周文王矣。"司马懿曰："今孙权既称臣归附，王上可封官赐爵，令拒刘备。"操从之，表封孙权为骠骑将军、南昌侯，领荆州牧。即日遣使赍诰敕赴东吴去讫。

操病势转加。忽一夜梦三马同槽而食，及晓，问贾诩曰："孤向日曾梦三马同槽，疑是马腾父子为祸；今腾已死，昨宵复梦三马同槽。主何吉凶？"诩曰："禄马，吉兆也。禄马归于曹，王上何必疑乎？"操因此不疑。后人有诗曰：

　　三马同槽事可疑，不知已植晋根基。

　　曹瞒空有奸雄略，岂识朝中司马师？

是夜，操卧寝室，至三更，觉头目昏眩，乃起，伏几而卧。忽闻殿中声如裂帛，操惊视之，忽见伏皇后、董贵人、二皇子，并伏完、

tioned him: "The house of Han has long been declining,[8] while Your Majesty's merits and virtues mount ever higher. All living souls look up to you. Now Sun Quan declares his allegiance — a human reflection of the divine, different orders with corresponding signs. You should respond to Heaven and accord with men, Your Majesty, and quickly assume the dynastic throne."[9]

Cao Cao smiled and said, "Many years have I served the Han, and perhaps some merit or virtue of mine has benefited the people. When I was raised to the status of king of Wei, my name and position reached their peak. What further dare I dream of? But if somehow the Mandate of Heaven should come to rest with me, I would remain loyal to the dynasty nonetheless, like King Wen of the Zhou."[10] "Since Sun Quan declares his allegiance," Sima Yi added, "Your Highness could confer rank and office upon him with instructions that he resist Liu Bei." Cao Cao adopted the suggestion and submitted a memorial to the throne recommending that Sun Quan be made general of the Flying Cavalry and lord of Nanchang, as well as protector of Jingzhou. The documents were dispatched that day to the Southland.

Cao Cao's condition worsened. One night he dreamed that three horses (*ma*) were feeding from the same trough (*cao*). The next morning he described the dream to Jia Xu and said, "I've had this dream before. I thought then it meant trouble from Ma Teng and his sons.[11] Ma Teng is dead, but the dream has recurred; does it signify something dire or auspicious?" Jia Xu responded, "They are boon (*lu*) horses — a sign of good luck.[12] A boon horse comes home to Cao. There is no need for Your Majesty to be disturbed." Later, a poet left this verse:

> Three horses at one trough troubled Cao Cao's mind;
> Meanwhile, he overlooked the rooting tree of Jin.[13]
> How fruitless all his tyrant treachery.
> The men who broke his clan came from within.

Toward the third watch, as he lay in his chambers, Cao felt his head and eyes begin to swim. He got up and rested against a low table. Something sounded like cloth tearing. Frightened, Cao Cao looked up in amazement. Suddenly he saw the murdered queens, Empress Fu and Lady Dong, and the two royal sons, along with Fu Wan, Dong Cheng, and some twenty

1913

董承等二十余人，浑身血污，立于愁云之内，隐隐闻索命之声。操急拔剑望空砍去，忽然一声响亮，震塌殿宇西南一角。操惊倒于地，近侍救出，迁于别宫养病。次夜，又闻殿外男女哭声不绝。至晓，操召群臣入曰："孤在戎马之中，三十余年，未尝信怪异之事。今日为何如此？"群臣奏曰："大王当命道士设醮修禳。"操叹曰："圣人云：'获罪于天，无所祷也。'孤天命已尽，安可救乎？"遂不允设醮。

次日，觉气冲上焦，目不见物，急召夏侯惇商议。惇至殿门前，忽见伏皇后、董贵人、二皇子、伏完、董承等，立在阴云之中。惇大惊昏倒，左右扶出，自此得病。操召曹洪、陈群、贾诩、司马懿等，同至卧榻前，嘱以后事。曹洪等顿首曰："大王善保玉体，不日定当霍然。"操曰："孤纵横天下三十余年，群雄皆灭，止有江东孙权，西蜀刘备，未曾剿除。孤今病危，不能再与卿等相叙，特以家事相托。孤长子曹昂，刘氏所生，不幸早年殁于宛城；今卞氏生四子：丕、彰、植、熊。孤平生所爱第三子植，为人虚华少诚实，嗜酒放纵，因此不立。次子曹彰，勇而无谋；

other high courtiers. Smeared with blood, they stood in the gloom and called for his life in muted voices. Cao Cao jerked his sword free and sliced at the empty air. Then came a crash as the southwest corner of the building fell in. Cao collapsed and was rushed to another part of the palace.

The next night Cao Cao could hear the incessant wails of men and women outside. At dawn he assembled the officials and said, "Throughout the campaigns of thirty years I have never given credence to the monstrous or the abnormal. But what do these things mean?" They replied, "Your Highness should command a Taoist priest to perform rites to ward off evil." But Cao sighed, commenting, "As the sage Confucius said, when you give offense to Heaven, to whom can you pray? My mandate is exhausted; I am beyond rescue." He did not allow the services to be held.

By morning Cao Cao felt a pounding in his head, and he could not identify forms. He called Xiahou Dun to his side. But when Dun reached the entrance to Cao's residence, he too had a vision of the murdered Empress Fu and Lady Dong, the royal sons, Fu Wan, Dong Cheng, and the others standing in the gloom. Dun took fright and collapsed. His attendants helped him out, but he never regained his health. Cao Cao called for Cao Hong, Chen Qun, Jia Xu, and Sima Yi; when they were at his bedside, he instructed them on the matter of the succession. Cao Hong and the others touched their heads to the ground and said, "Let Your Highness care well for his precious self. This spell is sure to pass, and soon."

Cao Cao responded, "I have made conquests the length and breadth of the realm these thirty years, and all manner of heroes have I annihilated. There remain but Sun Quan of the Southland and Liu Bei of the Riverlands to be removed. But I will not be able to remain among you, and I shall have to entrust my house to you. My eldest, Ang, son of Lady Liu, died young at Wancheng. Of my other four sons by Lady Bian — Pi, Zhang, Zhi, and Xiong — my favorite has always been Zhi, the third. But I will not have him as heir because he is vain and insincere, as well as overindulgent in wine and unrestrained in conduct. The second, Zhang, is bold but tactless; the fourth, Xiong, is sickly and will not live long. Only

四子曹熊,多病难保。惟长子曹丕,笃厚恭谨,可继我业。卿等宜辅佐之。"

曹洪等涕泣领命而出。操令近侍取平日所藏名香,分赐诸侍妾,且嘱曰:"吾死之后,汝等须勤习女工,多造丝履,卖之可以得钱自给。"又命诸妾多居于铜雀台中,每日设祭,必令女伎奏乐上食。又遗命于彰德府讲武城外,设立疑冢七十二:"勿令后人知吾葬处,恐为人所发掘故也。"嘱毕,长叹一声,泪如雨下。须臾,气绝而死。寿六十六岁。时建安二十五年春正月也。后人有《邺中歌》一篇,叹曹操云:

> 邺则邺城水漳水,定有异人从此起:
> 雄谋韵事与文心,君臣兄弟而父子;
> 英雄未有俗胸中,出没岂随人眼底?
> 功首罪魁非两人,遗臭流芳本一身;
> 文章有神霸有气,岂能苟尔化为群?
> 横流筑台距太行,气与理势相低昂;
> 安有斯人不作逆,小不为霸大不王?
> 霸王降作儿女鸣,无可奈何中不平;
> 向帐明知非有益,分香未可谓无情。

the eldest, Pi, is reliable, generous, respectful to others, and scrupulous in word and deed — fit, therefore, to succeed to my estate. I hope you will give him all support and assistance."[14]

Cao Hong and the rest wept as they received their king's last command. After they left, Cao Cao had an attendant bring out the rare perfumes he had collected; he apportioned these valuable substances to his harem ladies and instructed them as follows: "After my death devote yourselves diligently to needlework. Make plenty of silk shoes, and you will be able to survive on the sales." Cao Cao also commanded many of the women to remain in the Bronze Bird Tower in order to offer sacrifices to nourish his spirit each day in ceremonies to be attended by female entertainers and accompanied by music.[15]

In addition, Cao Cao ordered seventy-two decoy tombs erected outside Jiangwu in Zhangde county lest anyone discover his burial place and excavate it. Shortly afterward, with a long sigh and copious tears Cao Cao passed away at the age of sixty-six. It was the first month of the twenty-fifth year of Jian An (A.D. 220).[16] Cao Cao is mourned in the following "Song of Ye" :

> From Ye, the Ye that stands upon the Zhang,
> Was sure to come a greatly gifted man:
> Grand schemes and poetry from his genius sprang —
> Genius shared by liege men, brothers, sons!
> The hero who transcends the common scope
> Can't tailor his career to please the world.
> High merit and great evil — from a single hand,
> Fair honors with foulest crime conjoined.
> In letters, divine powers; as hegemon, great force —
> Could he tamely blend among the mass?
> Athwart the tide by Taihang he built towers;
> The buildings' spirit fit their setting well.
> Here was a man to challenge all tradition!
> First he rose to hegemon, then to king.
> But in decline he whined as any child.
> He can fight no more; fate ordains his lot.
> Turning to his womenfolk, he has no hope of help.
> Doling out the rare perfumes — call him not unkind.

呜呼！

古人作事无巨细，寂寞豪华皆有意；

书生轻议冢中人，冢中笑尔书生气！

却说曹操身亡，文武百官尽皆举哀；一面遣人赴世子曹丕、鄢陵侯曹彰、临淄侯曹植、萧怀侯曹熊处报丧。众官用金棺银椁将操入殓，星夜举灵榇赴邺郡来。曹丕闻知父丧，放声痛哭，率大小官员出城十里，伏道迎榇入城，停于偏殿。官僚挂孝，聚哭于殿上。忽一人挺身而出曰："请世子息哀，且议大事。"众视之，乃中庶子司马孚也。孚曰："魏王既薨，天下震动；当早立嗣王，以安众心。何但哭泣耶？"群臣曰："世子宜嗣位；但未得天子诏命，岂可造次而行？"兵部尚书陈矫曰："王薨于外，爱子私立，彼此生变，则社稷危矣。"遂拔剑割下袍袖，厉声曰："即今日便请世子嗣位。众官有异议者，以此袍为例！"百官悚惧。忽报华歆自许昌飞马而至，众皆大惊。须臾华歆入，众问其来意，歆曰："今魏王薨逝，天下震动，何不早请世子嗣位？"众官曰："正因不及候诏命，方议欲以王后卞氏慈旨立世子为

Alas! Great men of old took care in every deed;
Deserted or in pomp, their purposes held firm.
The pedant lightly speaks about the dead;
From the grave they mock his pedant's airs.[17]

The entire court raised the cry of mourning. The funeral announcement was carried to Cao Cao's heir, Cao Pi; to Cao Zhang, lord of Yanling; to Cao Zhi, lord of Linzi; and to Cao Xiong, lord of Xiaohuai. The officials placed the king's body in a golden coffin with a silver outer casing. The bier was rushed from Luoyang to Ye. Cao Pi broke into unrestrained lamentation at the news. Leading a crowd of officials of all ranks, he prostrated himself in the road ten *li* outside the city to receive his father's coffin; then he had it carried to a side chamber of the palace. The entire court wore mourning vestments and wept together in the main hall of the palace.

Then someone stood and came forward. "Let the heir grieve no more," he said. "We must consider the succession." The assembly turned to the man. It was Sima Fu, attendant to the heir apparent. "The king of Wei is no more," Fu went on, "and the empire trembles. We must instate his successor as soon as possible to calm the minds of the people. Why are you simply wailing and weeping?" "The heir apparent should succeed," the courtiers cried, "but without a mandate from the Son of Heaven, we are not free to act." Chen Jiao, minister of war, said, "The king has died away from the capital. If his sons strive for the succession, causing dissension among themselves, the dynastic shrine itself could fall." So saying, he drew his sword and slashed the sleeve of his surcoat. He cried fiercely, "Today we beg the heir apparent to mount the throne. Any official opposing will suffer the fate of this coat." The assembly shook with fear.[18]

The arrival of Hua Xin, who had ridden at top speed from Xuchang, caused fresh consternation. He entered the court and explained his purpose in coming: "The king of Wei is no more. The empire trembles. Shouldn't we instate his successor as soon as possible?" The officials responded, "Because we could not wait for the imperial mandate, we were discussing getting Lady Bian's royal approval for installing the heir apparent." But Hua Xin answered, "I already have a mandate from the

王。"歆曰:"吾已于汉帝处索得诏命在此。"众皆踊跃称贺。歆于怀中取出诏命开读。原来华歆谄事魏,故草此诏,威逼献帝降之;帝只得听从,故下诏即封曹丕为魏王、丞相、冀州牧。丕即日登位,受大小官僚拜舞起居。

正宴会庆贺间,忽报鄢陵侯曹彰,自长安领十万大军来到。丕大惊,遂问群臣曰:"黄须小弟,平日性刚,深通武艺。今提兵远来,必与孤争王位也。如之奈何?"忽阶下一人应声出曰:"臣请往见鄢陵侯,以片言折之。"众皆曰:"非大夫莫能解此祸也。"

正是:

　　　　试看曹氏丕彰事,几作袁家谭尚争。

未知此人是谁,且看下文分解。

Emperor with me." The courtiers elatedly voiced their congratulations. Hua Xin produced the document and read it out. Hua Xin, a fawning follower of the house of Wei, had drafted and compelled the Emperor to issue the decree, which honored Cao Pi as king of Wei, prime minister, and protector of Jizhou.[19] That same day Cao Pi assumed his father's position and accepted the fervent felicitations of the court.

In the midst of the celebration feast it was reported that Cao Zhang, lord of Yanling, was bringing an army of one hundred thousand from Chang'an. In great alarm, Cao Pi turned to his advisers: "My yellow-bearded brother has always been willful. And he knows the martial arts well. For him to come so far with troops means he wants to contest the kingship of Wei. What is to be done?" Below the dais a man came forward and said, "Let me go to see the lord of Yanling. I can turn him around with a few words." The courtiers cried, "Only a great man like yourself could avert this crisis!" Indeed:

> Cao Cao's two sons were falling out
> As Yuan Shao's sons once did.

Who volunteered to dissuade Cao Zhang?

Read on.

1921

兄逼弟曹植

賦詩

紫文偉史

1923

第七十九回

兄逼弟曹植赋诗 侄陷叔刘封伏法

　　却说曹丕闻曹彰提兵而来，惊问众官；一人挺身而出，愿往折服之。众视其人，乃谏议大夫贾逵也。曹丕大喜，即命贾逵前往。逵领命出城，迎见曹彰。彰问曰："先王玺绶安在？"逵正色而言曰："家有长子，国有储君。先王玺绶，非君侯之所宜问也。"彰默然无语，乃与贾逵同入城。至宫门前，逵问曰："君侯此来，欲奔丧耶？欲争位耶？"彰曰："吾来奔丧，别无异心。"逵曰："既无异心，何故带兵入城？"彰即时叱退左右将士，只身入内，拜见曹丕。兄弟二人，相抱大哭。曹彰将本部军马尽交与曹丕。丕令彰回鄢陵自守，彰拜辞而去。

　　于是曹丕安居王位，改建安二十五年为延康元年；封贾诩为太尉，华歆为相国，王朗为御史大夫；大小官僚，尽皆升赏。谥曹操曰武王，葬于邺郡高陵，令于禁董治陵事。禁奉命到彼，只见陵屋中白粉壁上，图画关云长水淹七军擒获于禁之事：画云长俨然上坐，庞德愤怒不屈，于禁拜伏于地，哀求乞命之状。原来曹丕以于禁兵败被擒，不能死节，既降敌而复归，心鄙

Chapter 79

**Brother Oppresses Brother; Cao Zhi Composes a Poem
Nephew Entraps Uncle; Liu Feng Answers to the Law[1]**

The man who volunteered to stop Cao Zhang's onslaught was Imperial Officer First Grade Jia Kui.[2] Delighted, Cao Pi ordered him to go to meet his brother Zhang. The first question Cao Zhang put to the officer was, "Where is the late king's seal?" With a dignified expression Jia Kui replied, "Every family has its eldest; every state has its appointed heir. It is not appropriate for Your Lordship to inquire about the late king's seal." Cao Zhang kept silent and rode into the city with Jia Kui. When they reached the palace, Jia Kui asked him, "Has Your Lordship come to attend the funeral or to contest the succession?" "For the services only," Cao Zhang replied. "I have no hostile intentions." "In that case," responded Jia Kui, "why have you brought an army?" Cao Zhang dismissed his guard and entered the palace alone. He paid his respects to Cao Pi, and the brothers embraced and wept. Cao Zhang turned his armed force over to Cao Pi, who ordered his brother to return to Yanling and guard it. Cao Zhang took his leave and departed.[3]

Cao Pi was now secure on the throne. He changed the reign year from Jian An 25 to Yan Kang 1 (A.D. 220). He made Jia Xu his grand commandant, Hua Xin his prime minister, and Wang Lang his chief censor. The entire court was given promotions and rewards. Cao Cao, posthumously titled King Wu, was interred at Gaoling in Ye.[4] Yu Jin was given charge of all matters concerning the tombs.

When Yu Jin reached the site, however, he saw a painting on the chalky wall of the crypt depicting the battle between Lord Guan and himself. The drowning of Cao Cao's seven armies and the capture of Yu Jin were graphically shown, with Lord Guan seated grandly, Pang De defiant and indignant, and Yu Jin pressing himself to the ground, pleading piteously for his life. It so happened that Cao Pi had lost all respect for Yu

1925

其为人，故先令人图画陵屋粉壁，故意使之往见以愧之。当下于禁见此画像，又羞又恼，气愤成病，不久而死。后人有诗叹曰：

　　三十年来说旧交，可怜临难不忠曹。

　　知人未向心中识，画虎今从骨里描。

　　却说华歆奏曹丕曰："鄢陵侯已交割军马，赴本国去了；临淄侯植，萧怀侯熊，二人竟不来奔丧，理当问罪。"丕从之，即分遣二使往二处问罪。不一日，萧怀使者回报："萧怀侯曹熊惧罪，自缢身死。"丕令厚葬之，追赠萧怀王。又过了一日，临淄使者回报，说："临淄侯日与丁仪、丁廙兄弟二人酣饮，悖慢无礼：闻使命至，临淄侯端坐不动；丁仪骂曰：'昔者先王本欲立吾主为世子，被谗臣所阻；今王丧未远，便问罪于骨肉，何也？'丁廙又曰：'据吾主聪明冠世，自当承嗣大位，今反不得立。汝那庙堂之臣，何不识人才若此！'临淄侯因怒，叱武士将臣乱棒打出。"

　　丕闻之，大怒，即令许褚领虎卫军三千，火速至临淄擒曹植等一干人来。褚奉命，引军至临淄城。守将拦阻，褚立斩之，

汉英经典文库

Jin when, defeated and captured, he failed to die honorably and then returned north after surrendering. In order to humiliate Yu Jin, Cao Pi had ordered an artist to make the painting before sending him to the tomb. The moment Yu Jin looked at the wall, he felt shame and vexation, and the force of his anger made him so ill that he died soon after. A poet of later times has left these lines:

> Thirty years bespeaks a friendship rare;
> But facing death, Jin proved disloyal to Cao.
> Cao Cao never saw into his heart.
> To paint a tiger, the bones are where to start.

Hua Xin petitioned Cao Pi: "The lord of Yanling has turned his forces over to you and returned to his own fief. But Cao Zhi, lord of Linzi, and Cao Xiong, lord of Xiaohuai, have not attended the funeral and should be called to account." Cao Pi approved the suggestion and sent messengers to each to demand explanations.

Within a day there was an answer from Xiaohuai: "Cao Xiong, lord of Xiaohuai, has hanged himself for fear of giving offense." Cao Pi ordered his brother buried with honors and posthumously titled king of Xiaohuai. The following day there was an answer from the envoy to Linzi: "The lord of Linzi spends his days with the Ding brothers, Zhengli and Jingli, indulging in wine. Their manner is rude and arrogant; they violate all norms of civil conduct. When the edict arrived, the lord of Linzi remained seated, erect and motionless. His companion Ding Zhengli chided me, saying, "The late king wanted my master to be his heir, but slanderers stood in the way. Now they are making flesh and blood answer for offenses so soon after the king's death. Why?' Then his brother, Jingli, added, 'We are of the view that our brilliantly capable master, the foremost man of the age, should have succeeded to the throne as a matter of course. Instead, he has been unable to. But your kind of courtier can ignore a man as able as our lord!' Then the lord of Linzi himself grew angry and had his personal guard drive me from his presence with blows."

Cao Pi, angered by the report, ordered Xu Chu to take three thousand of his personal Tiger Guard to Linzi and bring Cao Zhi and his company before him. When Xu Chu arrived at the town of Linzi, he was stopped by the commander in charge. Xu Chu swiftly cut him down and entered

直入城中，无一人敢当锋锐，径到府堂。只见曹植与丁仪、丁廙等尽皆醉倒。褚皆缚之，载于车上，并将府下大小属官，尽行拿解邺郡，听候曹丕发落。丕下令，先将丁仪、丁廙等尽行诛戮。丁仪字正礼，丁廙字敬礼，沛郡人，乃一时文士；及其被杀，人多惜之。

却说曹丕之母卞氏，听得曹熊缢死，心甚悲伤；忽又闻曹植被擒，其党丁仪等已杀，大惊。急出殿，召曹丕相见。丕见母出殿，慌来拜谒。卞氏哭谓丕曰："汝弟植平生嗜酒疏狂，盖因自恃胸中之才，故尔放纵。汝可念同胞之情，存其性命。吾至九泉亦瞑目也。"丕曰："儿亦深爱其才，安肯害他？今正欲戒其性耳。母亲勿忧。"

卞氏洒泪而入。丕出偏殿，召曹植入见。华歆问曰："适来莫非太后劝殿下勿杀子建乎？"丕曰："然。"歆曰："子建怀才抱智，终非池中物；若不早除，必为后患。"丕曰："母命不可违。"歆曰："人皆言子建出口成章，臣未深信。主上可召入，以才试之。若不能，即杀之；若果能，则贬之，以绝天下文人之口。"丕从之。须臾，曹植入见，惶恐伏拜请罪。丕曰："吾与汝情虽兄弟，义属君臣，汝安敢恃才蔑礼？昔先君在日，汝常以文章夸示

the town. Unopposed, he went into the official headquarters, where he found Cao Zhi and the Ding brothers intoxicated. Xu Chu tied them up, put them on a wagon, and headed back to Ye; he also took into custody all subordinate officials. Cao Pi disposes of the offending Ding brothers by having them publicly executed. They were noted literary men from the Pei district, and many deplored their deaths.

When Lady Bian, mother of Cao Pi, learned of Cao Xiong's death, she was bitterly aggrieved. The news of Cao Zhi's capture on top of that, and the killing of his companions, caused her great alarm. She hurried out of her chambers and summoned Cao Pi before her. Seeing that his mother had left her chamber, Cao Pi rushed to greet her. Tearfully, Lady Bian said, "Your younger brother Zhi has indulged himself in wine and wild behavior all his life; because he counted only on his inborn talents, he let himself go. You are to be mindful of your fraternal ties and spare his life. Only then I will be able to rest in peace in the netherworld." "I, too," Cao Pi replied, "deeply cherish my brother's talent. How could I harm him? I only meant to curb his temper. Put your worries to rest, Mother."

Lady Bian returned to her quarters, crying freely. Cao Pi ordered that Cao Zhi be brought into his presence. Hua Xin asked Pi, "Is it not true that the queen mother just now urged you not to kill Cao Zhi?" "That is so," Pi answered. Hua Xin went on, "Given Cao Zhi's talents and knowledge, he will never be content with what he has and will cause no end of trouble unless you act now." "I cannot violate my mother's command," Cao Pi said. "Everyone says," Hua Xin continued, "that Cao Zhi is so gifted that the very words he speaks become poems, though I myself have never believed it. My lord, summon him and put his reputed abilities to the test. If he fails, kill him. If he really shows talent, then lower his status and put an end to the carping of the literary men." Cao Pi adopted the advice.

Soon after, Cao Zhi came before Cao Pi and anxiously prostrated himself, begging forgiveness for his offenses. "Although in private sentiment we are brothers," Pi said, "in public responsibilites we are lord and vassal. How dare you presume upon your talents to set at naught the formalities of this relaionship? When our late father was alive, you were

于人,吾深疑汝必用他人代笔。吾今限汝行七步吟诗一首。若果能,则免一死;若不能,则从重治罪,决不姑恕!"植曰:"愿乞题目。"时殿上悬一水墨画,画着两只牛,斗于土墙之下,一牛坠井而亡。丕指画曰:"即以此画为题。诗中不许犯着'二牛斗墙上,一牛坠井死'字样。"植行七步,其诗已成。诗曰:

> 两肉齐道行,头上带凹骨。

> 相遇块山下,欻起相搪突。

> 二敌不俱刚,一肉卧土窟。

> 非是力不如,盛气不泄毕。

曹丕及群臣皆惊。丕又曰:"七步成章,吾犹以为迟。汝能应声而作诗一首否?"植曰:"愿即命题。"丕曰:"吾与汝乃兄弟也。以此为题。亦不许犯着'兄弟'字样。"植略不思索,即口占一首曰:

> 煮豆燃豆萁,豆在釜中泣。

> 本是同根生,相煎何太急!

曹丕闻之,潸然泪下。其母卞氏,从殿后出曰:"兄何逼弟之甚耶?"丕慌忙离坐告曰:"国法不可废耳。"于是贬曹植为安乡侯。植拜辞上马而去。

曹丕自继位之后,法令一新,威逼汉帝,甚于其父。早有细

always boasting of your compositions, but I always suspected someone else was actually doing the writing. Here is my challenge: walk seven paces and make a poem before you finish. If you succeed, I will spare your life; if not, your offenses will be heavily punished without the slightest mitigation." "On what theme?" Cao Zhi asked. Cao Pi pointed to an ink drawing on the wall. It depicted two bulls by a wall, one of which — after a fight — had fallen dead into a well. "There is your theme," Cao Pi said. "But your poem must avoid the words 'Two bulls fought by a wall, one fell dead in a well.'" Cao Zhi took seven steps and in that time produced this poem:

> Upon a narrow road two meat hunks closed
> (A U-bone topped each head)
> And met by a mound of dirt:
> In a flash they butted and gored.
> Two foes, but one less tough —
> That meat prone in a pit.
> Not that his might was less,
> But his vital force had been clipped.

Cao Pi and his court were astonished at Cao Zhi's performance. "Still," Pi said, "seven paces takes some time. Can you create a poem on a moment's notice?" "I shall address whatever theme you suggest," Zhi replied. "Our relation as elder and younger brother, then. But you are not to use the word 'brother,'" Cao Pi said. Without pausing to reflect, Cao Zhi spoke these lines:

> Beans asimmer on a beanstalk flame
> From inside the pot expressed their ire:
> "Alive we sprouted on a single root —
> What's your rush to cook us on the fire?"

Cao Pi burst into tears. Lady Bian, advancing from the rear of the hall, said, "An elder brother should not push a younger brother so." Pi hastily left his seat and appealed to her: "It is simply that the law can not be ignored." Accordingly, he reduced Cao Zhi's position to lord of Anxiang. Cao Zhi then took his leave and departed on horseback.

Since his succession to his father's throne, Cao Pi had thoroughly remade the laws and regulations of the dynasty; and he harassed the Han

作报入成都。汉中王闻之,大惊,即与文武商议曰:"曹操已死,曹丕继位,威逼天子,更甚于操。东吴孙权,拱手称臣。孤欲先伐东吴,以报云长之仇;次讨中原,以除乱贼。"言未毕,廖化出班,哭拜于地曰:"关公父子遇害,实刘封、孟达之罪。乞诛此二贼。"玄德便欲遣人擒之。孔明谏曰:"不可。且宜缓图之,急则生变矣。可升此二人为郡守,分调开去,然后可擒。"

玄德从之,遂遣使升刘封去守绵竹。原来彭羕与孟达甚厚,听知此事,急回家作书,遣心腹人驰报孟达。使者方出南门外,被马超巡视军捉获,解见马超。超审知此事,即往见彭羕。羕接入,置酒相待。酒至数巡,超以言挑之曰:"昔汉中王待公甚厚,今何渐薄也?"羕因酒醉,恨骂曰:"老革荒悖,吾必有以报之!"超又探曰:"某亦怀怨心久矣。"羕曰:"公起本部军,结连孟达为外合,某领川兵为内应,大事可图也。"超曰:"先生之言甚当。来日再议。"超辞了彭羕,即将人与书解见汉中王,细言其事。玄德大怒,即令擒彭羕下狱,拷问其情。羕在狱中,悔之无及。玄德问孔明曰:"彭羕有谋反之意,当何以治之?"孔明

Emperor even more harshly than his father had. Spies quickly brought word of these changes to the king of Hanzhong in Chengdu.

Gravely concerned by the new situation, the king took counsel with his civil and military officials. "Cao Cao is dead," he said to them, "and Cao Pi, his successor, harasses the Emperor far worse than Cao Cao ever did, while Sun Quan of the Southland submissively declares allegiance to the new order. It is my desire first to scourge the south and avenge my brother's death, and then to smite the north and rid the land of sedition." Even as Xuande spoke, Liao Hua stepped forward from the ranks and, prostrating himself, said through his tears, "It is the fault of Liu Feng and Meng Da that Lord Guan and his son are dead. I beg Your Lordship to punish the traitors." Xuande would have seized the two at once, but Kongming opposed it. "You had better take your time," he said. "Move too quickly and they'll defect. Instead, make them governors and assign them to separate districts before you arrest them." Accordingly, Xuande appointed Liu Feng governor of Mianzhu.

It so happened that Peng Yang, a close friend of Meng Da, learned of this and rushed home to send a letter to Meng Da. His carrier was apprehended outside the city's south gate, however, and brought before the commander Ma Chao. In order to investigate the matter Ma Chao went to Peng Yang's home, where he was welcomed and offered wine. After several rounds Ma Chao said pointedly, "The king once treated you most handsomely. I wonder why he seems to have grown indifferent." Under the influence of the wine, Peng Yang said heatedly, "That perverse, ridiculous old war-horse. He'll get what he deserves!" Ma Chao probed further, saying, "I, too, have had to bear many grievances." "If you put your own units into action," Peng Yang replied, "and coordinate with Meng Da from without, I'll work with some Riverlands troops from within, and we can carry the day." "Your views are quite to the point," Ma Chao said. "Tomorrow we will discuss this further."

After taking leave of Peng Yang, Ma Chao brought the captured messenger and letter before the king and gave him a detailed account of his conversation with the author of the letter. Xuande was furious and had Peng Yang thrown into jail and interrogated; his regrets availed him not. Xuande asked Kongming, "How should we handle Peng Yang's con-

曰:"羕虽狂士,然留之久必生祸。"于是玄德赐彭羕死于狱。

羕既死,有人报知孟达。达大惊,举止失措。忽使命至,调刘封回守绵竹去讫。孟达慌请上庸、房陵都尉申耽、申仪弟兄二人商议曰:"我与法孝直同有功于汉中王;今孝直已死,而汉中王忘我前功,乃欲见害,为之奈何?"耽曰:"某有一计,使汉中王不能加害于公。"达大喜,急问何计。耽曰:"吾弟兄欲投魏久矣;公可作一表,辞了汉中王,投魏王曹丕,丕必重用。吾二人亦随后来降也。"达猛然省悟,即写表一通,付与来使;当晚引五十余骑投魏去了。使命持表回成都,奏汉中王,言孟达投魏之事。先主大怒。览其表曰:

> 臣达伏惟殿下:将建伊、吕之业,追桓、文之功,大事草创,假势吴、楚,是以有为之士,望风归顺。臣委质以来,愆戾山积;臣犹自知,况于君乎?今王朝英俊鳞集,臣内无辅佐之器,外无将领之才,列次功臣,诚足自愧!

> 臣闻范蠡识微,浮于五湖;舅犯谢罪,逡巡河上。夫际

汉英经典文库

spiracy?" "He may be only an idiosyncratic scholar," Kongming responded, "but he will make trouble later if you spare him." And so Peng Yang's fate was sealed, though in consideration of his status Xuande allowed him to die by his own hand.

Meng Da was deeply disturbed by the news of Peng Yang's death. Subsequently he received Kongming's order for his partner Liu Feng to return to Mianzhu to serve as governor. Meng Da quickly called the military commanders of Shangyong and Fangling, the brothers Shen Dan and Shen Yi, to a meeting. "I have done no less for the cause of the king of Hanzhong than Fa Zheng has," he said. "Now Fa Zheng is dead, and the king forgets my former service.[5] He would even see me harmed. What is to be done?" Commander Shen Dan replied, "I think I know how to prevent the king of Hanzhong from doing you injury." Delighted, Meng Da asked his plan. "My brother and I have long wanted to join the cause of the kingdom of Wei. You might prepare a formal document severing ties with the king of Hanzhong and offering allegiance to Cao Pi, king of Wei — who is sure to use you well. My brother and I will follow you in surrender." Instantly, Meng Da saw the wisdom of his proposal and wrote out a document for Kongming's messenger to take back. The same night, taking fifty riders, he went to serve the king of Wei.

The messenger returned to Chengdu bearing Meng Da's note and the news of his defection. The First Ruler[6] angrily read over the document, which said:

1935

> As your servant, I humbly lay myself at your feet. In the beginning, Your Majesty strove to guide the dynasty toward greatness in the manner of Yi Yin of the Shang and Taigong Wang of the Zhou, to recover something of the grandeur of the hegemon-patriarchs Huan and Wen. Then, the southern powers, Jingzhou and the Southland, lent their strength to your cause. As a result, ambitious and capable talents, attracted by your prestige, tendered their allegiance. Since committing my humble self to your enterprise, I have compiled a long record of errors and offenses. Even I know that; how much more clearly must you see it. Now at Your Highness's court, brilliant men of talent are beyond numbering. But I, lacking the talent to assist the government and the ability to lead an army, would be truly ashamed to take my place among your meritorious vassals.
>
> I am mindful of Fan Li, who knew when he was no longer of use and

会之间，请命乞身，何哉？欲洁去就之分也。况臣卑鄙，无元功臣勋，自系于时，窃慕前贤，早思远耻。昔申生至孝，见疑于亲；子胥至忠，见诛于君；蒙恬拓境而被大刑，乐毅破齐而遭谗佞。臣每读其书，未尝不感慨流涕；而亲当其事，益用伤悼！

迩者，荆州覆败，大臣失节，百无一还；惟臣寻事，自致房陵、上庸，而复乞身，自放于外。伏想殿下圣恩感悟，愍臣之心，悼臣之举。臣诚小人，不能始终。知而为之，敢谓非罪？臣每闻"交绝无恶声，去臣无怨辞"。臣过奉教于君子，愿君王勉之。臣不胜惶恐之至！"

玄德看毕，大怒曰："匹夫叛吾，安敢以文辞相戏耶！"即欲起兵擒之。孔明曰："可就遣刘封进兵，令二虎相并；刘封或有功，或败绩，必归成都，就而除之，可绝两害。"玄德从之，遂遣使到绵竹，传谕刘封。封受命，率兵来擒孟达。

却说曹丕正聚文武议事，忽近臣奏曰："蜀将孟达来降。"丕召入问曰："汝此来，莫非诈降乎？"达曰："臣为不救关公之

set himself adrift on the lakes and rivers; mindful too of Uncle Fan, who, acknowledging his offenses, bade his lord good-bye on the banks of the Yellow River.[7] At the opportune moment they begged to be released from their vassal's oath. Why? To resolve cleanly the dilemma of leaving or staying. For I, lowliest of those who serve you, can boast no high merit or striking achievement, having merely temporized. These examples of admired ancient worthies help me in my resolve to leave rather than endure the shame of remaining.

In olden days no son was more filial than Shen Sheng, yet his father doubted him; no minister more loyal than Zixu, but his king had him executed. General Meng Tian extended the northern borders for the state of Qin, but he suffered capital punishment. Yue Yi destroyed the enemy state of Qi but fell victim to slander. The stories of these men always move me to passionate tears. Now a like fate confronts me, and I despair.[8]

After the recent catastrophe in Jingzhou, the high officials surrendered. If others fled, I persevered in my duties. But after going to Fangling and Shangyong, I again ask your permission to seek my fortune elsewhere. I humbly hope that your sagely compassion and sympathetic understanding will enable you to indulge my wish and accept, if with sadness, my departing.

Truly unworthy of respect is the man who does not finish what he has begun. No man can excuse the offense committed with knowledge aforethought. It is often said that 'friendships should end without harsh words' and that 'in parting, let lord and vassal utter no complaint.' I have always taken to heart the teachings of the worthies, and I beg Your Highness to do likewise. I am overcome by trepidation.

1937

The letter put Xuande in a rage. "This underling in revolt! How dare he mock me with these fine words?" Xuande's impulse was to send the army, but Kongming checked him, saying, "Simply send Liu Feng and let the two tigers fight it out. Whether he wins or loses, Liu Feng will have to return here. Then we can easily get rid of him — killing two birds." On Kongming's suggestion, Xuande sent a man to Mianzhu with orders for Liu Feng to arrest Meng Da.

*   *   *

Cao Pi had convened his civil and military officials when one of his aides announced suddenly: "The Riverlands general Meng Da comes to surrender!" Cao Pi summoned the man and challenged him: "Is this not

危,汉中王欲杀臣,因此惧罪来降,别无他意。"曹丕尚未准信,忽报刘封引五万兵来取襄阳,单搦孟达厮杀。丕曰:"汝既是真心,便可去襄阳取刘封首级来,孤方准信。"达曰:"臣以利害说之,不必动兵,令刘封亦来降也。"丕大喜,遂加孟达为散骑常侍、建武将军、平阳亭侯,领新城太守,去守襄阳、樊城。原来夏侯尚、徐晃已先在襄阳,正将收取上庸诸部。孟达到了襄阳,与二将礼毕,探得刘封离城五十里下寨。达即修书一封,使人赍赴蜀寨招降刘封。刘封览书大怒曰:"此贼误吾叔侄之义,又间吾父子之亲,使吾为不忠不孝之人也!"遂扯碎来书,斩其使。次日,引军前来搦战。

孟达知刘封扯书斩使,勃然大怒,亦领兵出迎。两阵对圆,封立马于门旗下,以刀指骂曰:"背国反贼,安敢乱言!"孟达曰:"汝死已临头上,还自执迷不省!"封大怒,拍马轮刀,直奔孟达。战不三合,达败走,封乘虚追杀二十余里,一声喊起,伏兵尽出,左边夏侯尚杀来,右边徐晃杀来,孟达回身复战。三军夹攻,刘封大败而走,连夜奔回上庸,背后魏兵赶来。刘封到城

a false surrender?" "I refused to rescue Lord Guan," Meng Da replied, "so the king of Hanzhong has decided to kill me. I came to avoid punishment, for no other reason." But Cao Pi remained unconvinced. It was reported that Liu Feng was coming to Xiangyang with fifty thousand men for the sole purpose of doing battle with Meng Da. "If you are sincere, then," Cao Pi said to Meng Da, "go to Xiangyang and bring me Liu Feng's head — and I will believe your story." "Let me explain the situation to Liu Feng," Meng Da answered, "and without any action on your part, Liu Feng too will offer his surrender." Delighted, Cao Pi appointed Meng Da mounted royal guard[9] and General Who Establishes by Arms, as well as lord of Pingyang precinct and governor of Xincheng, to hold Xiangyang and Fan.

It happened that generals Xiahou Shang and Xu Huang had already established the king of Wei's power in Xiangyang[10] and were preparing to take over Shangyong. Meng Da reached Xiangyang and exchanged greetings with the two northern generals. Liu Feng was camped fifty *li* from the city. Meng Da sent him a letter inviting surrender.[11] But Liu Feng responded to Meng Da's suggestion angrily: "This villain would break the bond between nephew and uncle and sunder the love of father and son, making me disloyal and unfilial." So saying, he tore up the letter and executed the messenger. The next day he went forth to challenge the foe.[12]

Enraged by Liu Feng's defiance, Meng Da met him in the field. The opposing armies assumed their formations, and Liu Feng rode out beneath the banners marking the entrance to his position. "Traitor to the house of Han, speak no nonsense!" he cried, pointing his sword toward Meng Da. "Death is at your shoulder; still you dream on!" Meng Da shot back. Feng slapped his steed, flourished his blade, and went for Meng Da. They clashed briefly. Meng Da fled in defeat; Feng pursued his advantage, unopposed for twenty *li*. Then voices cried out, and an ambush was sprung. Xiahou Shang came from the left, Xu Huang from the right, and Meng Da turned and fought again. Squeezed between three armies, Liu Feng fled, badly defeated, and rode straight on to Shangyong, the troops of Wei in hot pursuit. Reaching the town, Liu Feng was met with a barrage of arrows.

1939

下叫门，城上乱箭射下。申耽在敌楼上叫曰："吾已降了魏也！"封大怒，欲要攻城，背后追军将至。封立脚不住，只得望房陵而奔，见城上已尽插魏旗。申仪在敌楼上将旗一扬，城后一彪军出，旗上大书"右将军徐晃"。封抵敌不住，急望西川而走。晃乘势追杀。刘封部下只剩得百余骑，到了成都，入见汉中王，哭拜于地，细奏前事。玄德怒曰："辱子有何面目复来见吾！"封曰："叔父之难，非儿不救，因孟达谏阻故耳。"玄德转怒曰："汝须食人食、穿人衣，非土木偶人！安可听谗贼所阻！"命左右推出斩之。汉中王既斩刘封，后闻孟达招之，毁书斩使之事，心中颇悔；又哀痛关公，以致染病。因此按兵不动。

且说魏王曹丕，自即王位，将文武官僚，尽皆升赏；遂统甲兵三十万，南巡沛国谯县，大飨先茔。乡中父老，扬尘遮道，奉觞进酒，效汉高祖还沛之事。人报大将军夏侯惇病危，丕即还邺郡。时惇已卒，不为挂孝，以厚礼殡葬。

是岁八月间，报称石邑县凤凰来仪，临淄城麒麟出现，黄

From the forward tower Commander Shen Dan shouted down: "I have surrendered to the Wei!" Enraged, Liu Feng made ready to assault the wall, but as his pursuers closed in, he fled to Fangling — only to find the flags of Wei flying on the city wall. From the tower Commander Shen Yi described an arc with his signal banner, and a company of men appeared from behind the wall; their standard read "General of the Right Xu Huang."

Liu Feng could offer no resistance and made a desperate dash westward; Xu Huang gave chase. Hardly a hundred riders remained in Feng's command. Finally he reached Chengdu and was received by the king of Hanzhong before whom he flung himself to the ground and wept as he recounted the events up to his arrival in the Riverlands. But Xuande said angrily, "Scapegrace! Have you the face to come before me again?" Liu Feng tried to defend himself, saying, "When my uncle was in trouble, Meng Da stopped me from going to him. It was not that I refused." But Xuande's anger only rose higher. "You eat as men do," he said to his adopted son, "wear what men wear. You're not made of clay or wood. How could a slandering traitor 'stop' you?" So saying, Xuande ordered Liu Feng executed. Only after the execution did the king learn how Liu Feng had spurned Meng Da's offer to surrender.[13] Overcome by remorse and pining for Lord Guan as well, Xuande was taken ill and made no military moves.[14]

* * *

Cao Pi, king of Wei since assuming his father's throne, promoted and rewarded all his civil and military officials. Next, he led three hundred thousand armored troops on a southern tour of Qiao county in the fief of Pei,[15] where he held a magnificent feast at the ancestral graves. The village elders swarmed out to greet their native son, bearing flagons of wine as gifts as their forefathers had once done on the Supreme Ancestor's triumphant return. During the festivities, however, Regent-Marshal Xiahou Dun was reported to be ill, and Cao Pi returned early to Ye. By the time he arrived, the famous general had already died. Cao Pi went into mourning and arranged a burial of the most elaborate ceremony for the late regent-marshal.

In the eighth month of the year (A.D. 220), strange manifestations

龙现于邺郡。于是中郎将李伏、太史丞许芝商议：种种瑞征，乃魏当代汉之兆，可安排受禅之礼，令汉帝将天下让于魏王。遂同华歆、王朗、辛毗、贾诩、刘廙、刘晔、陈矫、陈群、桓阶等一班文武官僚，四十余人，直入内殿，来奏汉献帝，请禅位于魏王曹丕。

正是：

魏家社稷今将建，汉代江山忽已移。

未知献帝如何回答，且看下文分解。

were reported: in Shiyi county a phoenix showed itself, in Linzi a unicorn appeared, and in Ye itself a yellow dragon was seen. Imperial Corps Commander Li Fu and Grand Astrologer's Assistant Xu Zhi agreed between themselves that these various signs and omens foretold the replacement of the Han dynasty by the Wei and called for a ceremony of abdication at which Emperor Xian would yield the empire to the king of Wei.

Following this, a delegation of more than forty civil and military officials — including Hua Xin, Wang Lang, Xin Pi, Jia Xu, Liu Yi, Liu Ye, Chen Jiao, Chen Qun, and Huan Jie — went directly into the imperial chamber to petition Emperor Xian to yield the throne to Cao Pi, king of Wei. Indeed:

> The shrines of Wei were about to be established;
> The land of Han was about to pass into another's hands.

What would the Emperor say? And the king of Hanzhong?

Read on.

1945

第八十回

曹丕废帝篡炎刘　汉王正位续大统

　　却说华歆等一班文武，入见献帝。歆奏曰："伏睹魏王，自登位以来，德布四方，仁及万物，越古超今，虽唐、虞无以过此。群臣会议，言汉祚已终，望陛下效尧、舜之道，以山川社稷，禅与魏王：上合天心，下合民意，则陛下安享清闲之福，祖宗幸甚！生灵幸甚！臣等议定，特来奏请。"帝闻奏大惊，半晌无言，觑百官而哭曰："朕想高祖提三尺剑，斩蛇起义，平秦灭楚，创造基业，世统相传，四百年矣。朕虽不才，初无过恶，安忍将祖宗大业，等闲弃了？汝百官再从公计议。"

　　华歆引李伏、许芝近前奏曰："陛下若不信，可问此二人。"李伏奏曰："自魏王即位以来，麒麟降生，凤凰来仪，黄龙出现，嘉禾蔚生，甘露下降：此是上天示瑞，魏当代汉之象也。"许芝

Chapter 80

Cao Pi Deposes the Emperor, Usurps
the Liu Throne
The King of Hanzhong Assumes the Throne,
Continues the Han Line

Accompanied by a delegation of civil and military officials, Hua Xin
entered the court and addressed Emperor Xian: "Reverently we observe
that since the new king of Wei has come to the throne, his virtue has
spread throughout the land to the benefit of all. Not even the sage founders
of our civilization, Tang and Yu, surpass the king. The assembly of the
court, after collective consultation, now deeming that the sacrifices of
Han have come to term, beseech Your Majesty to emulate the ancient
sage-king Yao by ceremonially relinquishing the mountains, rivers, and
dynastic shrines to the new king of Wei. This will fulfill the will of Heaven
and satisfy the minds of men and also will enable Your Majesty to secure
the blessings of untroubled leisure, a boon to your ancestral clan and the
living souls of the realm. Our conclusion having been reached, we come
to deliver this formal appeal."

The Emperor listened in fear and shock. After a long silence, he turned
his gaze to the court of officials and began to sob. "I think back to the
time," he said, "when the Supreme Ancestor, founder of the Han, slew
the white serpent with his three-span sword and led the rebellion that
quelled Qin and crushed Chu. He thus founded this house whose rule has
passed from generation to generation in the Liu clan for four hundred
years. Small though my talent be, what offense have I committed, what
fault have I that justifies abandoning my ancestral right? Let the court
reopen discussion!"

Hua Xin then brought forth two astrologers, Li Fu and Xu Zhi, and
continued, "If Your Majesty has doubts, let these two answer them." Li
Fu addressed the throne: "Since the accession of the king of Wei, the
unicorn has descended, the phoenix has manifested itself, the yellow dragon
has appeared, prize grains grow luxuriantly, and sweet dew has dropped

1947

又奏曰："臣等职掌司天，夜观乾象，见炎汉气数已终，陛下帝星隐匿不明；魏国乾象，极天际地，言之难尽。更兼上应图谶，其谶曰：'鬼在边，委相连；当代汉，无可言。言在东，午在西；两日并光上下移。'以此论之，陛下可早禅位。'鬼在边'，'委相连'，是'魏'字也；'言在东，午在西'，乃'许'字也；'两日并光上下移'，乃'昌'字也：此是魏在许昌应受汉禅也。愿陛下察之。"帝曰："祥瑞图谶，皆虚妄之事；奈何以虚妄之事，而遽欲朕舍祖宗之基业乎？"王朗奏曰："自古以来，有兴必有废，有盛必有衰，岂有不亡之国、不败之家乎？汉室相传四百余年，延至陛下，气数已尽，宜早退避，不可迟疑；迟则生变矣。"帝大哭，入后殿去了。百官哂笑而退。

　　次日，官僚又集于大殿，令宦官入请献帝。帝忧惧不敢出。曹后曰："百官请陛下设朝，陛下何故推阻？"帝泣曰："汝兄欲篡位，令百官相逼，朕故不出。"曹后大怒曰："吾兄奈何为此乱逆之事耶！"言未已，只见曹洪、曹休带剑而入，请帝出殿。曹后大骂曰："俱是汝等乱贼，希图富贵，共造逆谋！吾父功盖寰区，威震天下，然且不敢篡窃神器。今吾兄嗣位未几，辄思篡

from the skies. Thus does Heaven give sign and token that Wei shall replace Han." Xu Zhi added: "We who monitor the divine configurations can see that the allotted time of the fire-signed Han has expired. Your Majesty's imperial star has dimmed, while stellar configurations representing Wei, from the cope of Heaven to the margins of the horizon, outnumber all telling. Furthermore, the occult auguries show first the graphs *gui*, 'ghost,' and *wei*, 'consign,' in association. Thus the supplanting of Han is indisputable.[1] Next the auguries show *yan*, 'word,' and *wu*, 'meridian,' side by side; and finally they show two suns, *ri*, vertically aligned. The conclusion is clear: Your Majesty must abdicate, for the graphs properly joined together read 'Wei Xuchang' — that is, 'Wei to receive the abdication of Han in the capital at Xuchang.' I beg Your Majesty to take heed."[2]

To this Emperor Xian responded, "Your tokens, your graphic riddles — all hollow and preposterous! Would you have me set aside my patrimony on the strength of baseless delusions?"[3] Wang Lang came forward next and addressed the throne: "From time immemorial, what has flourished must decay; what has prospered must decline. Every dynasty ends; every house falls. The house of Han has reigned more than four hundred years; with Your Majesty its line expires. Retire now, do not delay — or who knows what may happen next." Aggrieved, the Emperor retired to his rear chambers. The officials left smirking.

The next day the courtiers reassembled in the great hall and sent a eunuch to request the presence of Emperor Xian. The sovereign, anxious and fearful, refused to appear. Empress Cao[4] said, "How can Your Majesty obstruct an official request to hold court?" The Emperor sobbed as he replied, "Your brother, who intends to usurp my throne, has instructed the officials to coerce me. That is why I will not go." Angrily the Empress said, "How dare my brother commit lese majesty?" As she was speaking, Cao Hong and Cao Xiu, armed, entered and requested the Emperor to appear before the officials in the great hall. The Empress denounced them. "This comes of your sedition and treachery!" she cried. "Angling for wealth and power has led you into treason and conspiracy. Never did my father, whom the world admired above all others for his high and glorious deeds, covet the hallowed instruments of supreme au-

1949

汉，皇天必不祚尔！"言罢，痛哭入宫。左右侍者皆歔欷流涕。

　　曹洪、曹休力请献帝出殿。帝被逼不过，只得更衣出前殿。华歆奏曰："陛下可依臣等昨日之议，免遭大祸。"帝痛哭曰："卿等皆食汉禄久矣；中间多有汉朝功臣子孙，何忍作此不臣之事？"歆曰："陛下若不从众议，恐旦夕萧墙祸起，非臣等不忠于陛下也。"帝曰："谁敢弑朕耶？"歆厉声曰："天下之人，皆知陛下无人君之福，以致四方大乱！若非魏王在朝，弑陛下者，何止一人？陛下尚不知恩报德，直欲令天下人共伐陛下耶？"帝大惊，拂袖而起。王朗以目视华歆。歆纵步向前，扯住龙袍，变色而言曰："许与不许，早发一言！"帝战栗不能答。曹洪、曹休拔剑大呼曰："符宝郎何在？"祖弼应声出曰："符宝郎在此！"曹洪索要玉玺。祖弼叱曰："玉玺乃天子之宝，安得擅索！"洪喝令武士推出斩之。祖弼大骂不绝口而死。后人有诗赞曰：

　　奸宄专权汉室亡，诈称禅位效虞唐。

　　满朝百辟皆尊魏，仅见忠臣符宝郎。

thority. And yet my brother, who has hardly succeeded to the kingship of Wei, boldly yearns to supplant the Han. August and luminous Heaven will never confer its blessing." So saying, the distraught Empress withdrew to her palace, leaving the attendants weeping emotionally.[5]

Cao Hong and Cao Xiu strenuously urged the Emperor to attend the court session. Unable to resist further, he donned his formal attire and proceeded to the front of the hall. Hua Xin addressed the throne: "Let Your Majesty be guided by our discussions of yesterday lest disaster strike." The Emperor cried bitterly, "All of you have long enjoyed rich recompense as servants of the Han. Can the many sons and grandsons of renowned vassals among you bear to commit this act of insubordination?" "If Your Majesty will not comply with the consensus," Hua Xin continued, "I fear disorder in the inner sanctum could erupt at any time. This is not a case of our disloyalty to Your Majesty." "Who would dare to murder me?" the Emperor demanded.

Stridently Hua Xin replied, "All the empire knows that Your Majesty, lacking the 'great blessing' by which Heaven mandates the ruler of men, must take responsibility for the chaotic state of the realm. If not for the king of Wei, Cao Cao, there would have been more than one who would have put Your Majesty to the sword. But still you refuse to acknowledge his past concern and repay his erstwhile kindness, and seem to want a general assault upon your imperial person." Appalled, the Emperor rose with a sweeping motion of his sleeves. Wang Lang eyed Hua Xin meaningfully. Hua Xin advanced boldly, laid hands on the sacred dragon robe and, his face contorted, said, "Agreed? Or not? Speak. Now."

The trembling Emperor could not respond. Cao Hong and Cao Xiu drew their swords and called for the keeper of the regalia. The keeper, Zu Bi, responded, "Present." Cao Hong demanded the jade seal. Zu Bi protested, "The jade seal is the treasure of the Son of Heaven. How dare you demand it?" Cao Hong called for his guards who removed the keeper and cut off his head. Zu Bi continued to protest until the moment of his death. A poet of later times left these lines of tribute to Zu Bi:

> Treachery reigned; the Han passed from the scene:
> "Thus Yao yielded to Shun," they falsely cried.[6]
> A courtful of courtiers paid homage to the Wei;

帝颤栗不已。只见阶下披甲持戈数百余人,皆是魏兵。帝泣谓群臣曰:"朕愿将天下禅于魏王,幸留残喘,以终天年。"贾诩曰:"魏王必不负陛下。陛下可急降诏,以安众心。"帝只得令陈群草禅国之诏,令华歆赍捧诏玺,引百官直至魏王宫献纳。曹丕大喜。开读诏曰:

朕在位三十二年,遭天下荡覆,幸赖祖宗之灵,危而复存。然今仰瞻天象,俯察民心,炎精之数既终,行运在乎曹氏。是以前王既树神武之迹,今王又光耀明德,以应其期。历数昭明,信可知矣。夫"大道之行,天下为公";唐尧不私于厥子,而名播于无穷:朕窃慕焉。今其追踵尧典,禅位于丞相魏王。王其毋辞!

曹丕听毕,便欲受诏。司马懿谏曰:"不可。虽然诏玺已至,殿下宜且上表谦辞,以绝天下之谤。"丕从之,令王朗作表,自称德薄,请别求大贤以嗣天位。帝览表,心甚惊疑,谓群臣曰:"魏王谦逊,如之奈何?"华歆曰:"昔魏武王受王爵之时,三辞而诏不许,然后受之。今陛下可再降诏,魏王自当

In defense of the seal a single vassal died.

The Emperor shook violently. At the base of the stairs leading to his throne all he could see were hundreds of armed men of Wei. Tearfully, the Emperor addressed the assemblage: "We intend here solemnly to abdicate our rule, transferring all under Heaven to the king of Wei. Kindly spare what breath still remains to me, that I may live out my natural years." Jia Xu said, "The king would never dismay Your Majesty. Quickly issue the edict and give peace to the hearts of all." The Emperor had no choice. He ordered Chen Qun to draft the edict; next, he ordered Hua Xin to receive the document and the imperial seal and then to bring the whole court to the king's palace to make the ritual presentation.

Cao Pi was delighted. He unsealed the edict and read it:

> My reign of thirty-two years has seen great trouble in the empire. Fortunately, the spirits of my forefathers have rescued me from peril. But today, searching the configurations of the heavens and examining the hearts of the people, I see that the cycle of the fire element has expired and that a new element corresponding to the Cao clan now prevails. Indeed, that change of period is attested by the late King Cao's martial success and the present King Cao's manifest and glorious virtue. The new succession thus fulfills the expectations of all.
>
> It is said, "When the way of the sages prevails, the empire belongs to all." For not favoring his own son, Yao earned an immortal name. I venture to emulate him. Today, abdicating to the prime minster and king of Wei, I follow in the footsteps recorded in the "Canon of Yao." Let Your Highness not decline.

1953

When the edict had been read, Cao Pi was anxious to accept the decree, but Sima Yi warned him, "That would be wrong. Even though the edict and seal were brought here, let Your Highness decline in due modesty so as to forestall criticism in the outside world." On this advice Cao Pi had Wang Lang prepare a memorial which declared his virtue too meagre to assume the throne and advised searching elsewhere for someone of true worth.[7] The Emperor, perplexed by the memorial, said to his vassals, "The king is modest and self-effacing. What shall I do?" Hua Xin replied, "Previously, when his father, Cao Cao, was offered the kingship of Wei, he declined three times but finally accepted as the edict

允从。"

帝不得已，又令桓阶草诏，遣高庙使张音，持节奉玺至魏王宫。曹丕开读诏曰：

　　咨尔魏王，上书谦让。朕窃为汉道陵迟，为日已久；幸赖武王操，德膺符运，奋扬神武，芟除凶暴，清定区夏。今王丕缵承前绪，至德光昭，声教被四海，仁风扇八区；天之历数，实在尔躬。昔虞舜有大功二十，而放勋禅以天下；大禹有疏导之绩，而重华禅以帝位。汉承尧运，有传圣之义，加顺灵祇，绍天明命，使行御史大夫张音，持节奉皇帝玺绶。王其受之！

曹丕接诏欣喜，谓贾诩曰："虽二次有诏，然终恐天下后世，不免篡窃之名也。"诩曰："此事极易：可再命张音赍回玺绶，却教华歆令汉帝筑一坛，名'受禅坛'；择吉日良辰，集大小公卿，尽到坛下，令天子亲奉玺绶，禅天下与王，便可以释群疑而绝众议矣。"

丕大喜，即令张音赍回玺绶，仍作表谦辞。音回奏献帝。帝问群臣曰："魏王又让，其意若何？"华歆奏曰："陛下可筑一坛，

required. Let Your Majesty send down another edict. The king should accept it."[8]

The Emperor had no recourse. He ordered Huan Jie to draft another edict, and sent Zhang Yin as envoy of the Ancestral Temple to deliver document and seal to the palace of the king of Wei. Cao Pi opened the memorial, which read:

> Let the king of Wei be advised with regard to his humble refusal of our throne: we have recognized the slow decline of the Han. How fortunate we were to have the help of King Wu, Cao Cao, whose virtue proved able to cope with all that destiny demanded, eliminating baneful violence, purging and securing our heartland.
>
> The present king, Cao Pi, continues in that great tradition. His splendid virtue shines brilliantly forth. His sagely teachings cover the realm. His humane influence spreads in every direction. In his person the divine succession rests.
>
> In ancient times after Shun had effected twelve accomplishments, Yao resigned the empire into his charge; and after Yu the Great distinguished himself in managing the floodwaters, Shun abdicated in his favor. The Han, in the tradition of Yao, is obliged to transfer its rule to a worthy sage, conforming to the spirits above and below, properly responding to Heaven's clear Mandate. Thus, we have empowered Imperial Censor Zhang Yin to proffer the imperial seal. Let His Majesty now receive it.

1955

Cao Pi accepted the edict with delight. Turning to Jia Xu, he said, "Despite this second edict, I still fear that the world as well as future generations will condemn the usurpation." "There is a simple solution," Jia Xu replied. "Command Zhang Yin to take the edict back once again with instructions for Hua Xin to have the Emperor build an Altar for Acceptance of the Abdication. Then, on a propitious day, convene the senior and junior officials at the foot of the altar and have the Emperor personally tender the seal as he abdicates. That should resolve all doubts and check all criticism."[9]

Delighted with this advice, Cao Pi had Zhang Yin return the regalia and prepare another memorial announcing his humble refusal of the imperial place. When Zhang Yin presented the new memorial, the Emperor asked his courtiers, "What is the king of Wei's purpose in declining a second time?" Hua Xin said to the Emperor, "Your Majesty, build an

名曰'受禅坛',集公卿庶民,明白禅位;则陛下子子孙孙,必蒙魏恩矣。"帝从之,乃遣太常院官,卜地于繁阳,筑起三层高坛,择于十月庚午日寅时禅让。

至期,献帝请魏王曹丕登坛受禅,坛下集大小官僚四百余员,御林虎贲禁军三十余万,帝亲捧玉玺奉曹丕。丕受之。坛下群臣跪听册曰:

汉英经典文库

> 咨尔魏王!昔者唐尧禅位于虞舜,舜亦以命禹:天命不于常,惟归有德。汉道陵迟,世失其序;降及朕躬,大乱滋昏:群凶恣逆,宇内颠覆。赖武王神武,拯兹难于四方,惟清区夏,以保绥我宗庙;岂予一人获乂,俾九服实受其赐。今王钦承前绪,光于乃德;恢文武之大业,昭尔考之弘烈。皇灵降瑞,人神告徵;诞惟亮采,师锡朕命。金曰:尔度克协于虞舜,用率我唐典,敬逊尔位。於戏!"天之历数在

Altar for Acceptance of the Abdication, then gather the high officials and commoners around it so that the abdication will be plain and public. That way, the future generations of your line will enjoy the grace of the Wei." The Emperor complied. He sent an officer of the Department of Imperial Sacrifices to divine for a favorable site in Fanyang. There an altar of three levels was set up. They designated the predawn hours of *gengwu*, the seventh cyclical day in the tenth month, for the abdication ceremony to take place.[10]

When the appointed time came, Emperor Xian invited Cao Pi, king of Wei, to ascend the altar. Around the base clustered a vast assemblage of four hundred officials, major and minor, as well as some thirty thousand warriors including the Royal Guard, the Imperial Guard, and the Palace Guard. The Emperor held the jade seal in both hands and transferred it respectfully to Cao Pi. Below, the assembly kneeled to hear the declaration of transmission:

> Be it known to you, O King of Wei, that anciently Yao solemnly relinquished the mandate to Shun, who in turn passed it to Yu. For the Mandate of Heaven does not abide but finds its home only where virtue is. The way of Han is failing; our generations have lost their proper sequence. When the succession reached my own person in the spreading gloom of great upheaval, a multitude of malefactors ran unchecked and havoc was all within our sphere.
>
> Thanks to the martial genius of King Wu, Cao Cao, who retrieved our empire from rebellions in all quarters, the integrity of our northern region was preserved, and our ancestral sanctum kept safe. Not I alone benefited; the capital and its nine subject domains stand in his debt. You, King, have honorably followed in his footsteps and added glory to his great virtue; you have magnified the great cause of the founders of the Zhou, kings Wen and Wu; and you have given new luster to the boundless fame of your late father.
>
> The spirits of former emperors send down auspicious signs; men and gods affirm the auguries: Cao Pi is the ideal successor to manage the dynasty's affairs. To all I confer my sovereign charge. All concur in enjoining you to model yourself after Shun, so that I may reverently abdicate to you in accordance with the "Canon of Yao." Oh, heed this! "The Heavenly calendar is invested in your person." May you conform to this

尔躬"，君其祗顺大礼，飨万国以肃承天命！

读册已毕，魏王曹丕即受八般大礼，登了帝位。贾诩引大小官僚朝于坛下。改延康元年为黄初元年。国号大魏。丕即传旨，大赦天下。谥父曹操为太祖武皇帝。华歆奏曰："'天无二日，民无二主'。汉帝既禅天下，理宜退就藩服。乞降明旨，安置刘氏于何地？"言讫，扶献帝跪于坛下听旨。丕降旨封帝为山阳公，即日便行。华歆按剑指帝，厉声而言曰："立一帝，废一帝，古之常道！今上仁慈，不忍加害，封汝为山阳公。今日便行，非宣召不许入朝！"献帝含泪拜谢，上马而去。坛下军民人等见之，伤感不已。丕谓群臣曰："舜、禹之事，朕知之矣！"群臣皆呼"万岁"。后人观此受禅坛，有诗叹曰：

　　　　两汉经营事颇难，一朝失却旧江山。

　　　　黄初欲学唐虞事，司马将来作样看。

　　百官请曹丕答谢天地。丕方下拜，忽然坛前卷起一阵怪风，飞砂走石，急如骤雨，对面不见；坛上火烛，尽皆吹灭。丕惊

great ritual with humility before the spirits and thus solemnly receive
Heaven's Mandate to preside over the regions and districts of the realm.

After the ceremonial reading, Cao Pi undertook the eight-round inauguration ceremony and ascended the imperial throne. Below the altar Jia
Xu led the body of officials in paying homage to the new sovereign. They
then changed the reign period from Yan Kang, "Prolonged Prosperity,"
year l, to Huang Chu, "Commencement of the Yellow,"[11] year l of a new
dynasty called Great Wei. Next, Cao Pi issued a general amnesty. He
gave his father Cao Cao the posthumous title Great Ancestor and August
Martial Emperor.

Hua Xin memorialized the new Emperor: "'Two suns do not shine in
heaven; two sovereigns cannot rule.' The Han Emperor should now retire to a remote feudatory kingdom. We petition for your sage instruction
on the enfeoffment of the leader of the Liu clan." With these words, he
helped Emperor Xian kneel below the altar to listen to the imperial word.
Cao Pi directed that the Han Emperor be honored as lord of Shanyang
and depart forthwith. Hua Xin placed his hand on his sword and, pointing
at Emperor Xian, said harshly, "Putting one emperor in power and re-
moving another was routine in the old days. The present sovereign is
humane and merciful and wishes you no harm; he honors you as lord of
Shanyang. You are to leave at once, never to enter the court again except
on official summons."

Holding back tears, Emperor Xian made the ritual gesture of appreciation, bowing low; then he mounted and set off under the grieving gaze
of the commoners and soldiers around the altar. Cao Pi said to the assembly, "Now I can appreciate the succession of Shun and Yu." The courtiers shouted, "Long life to the sovereign!" In later times a poet, viewing
the Altar for Acceptance of the Abdication, left these lines:

> The two Hans' governance made a heavy task;
> Then all at once they had no "hills and streams."
> The Wei in Yao and Shun had found their model;
> Too soon the Simas learned this lesson well.

The assembly invited Cao Pi to offer Heaven and earth his thanks.
But as the new emperor began descending to prostrate himself, a freak
storm sprang up, driving sand and stones before it like a sudden down-

倒于坛上，百官急救下坛，半晌方醒。侍臣扶入宫中，数日不能设朝。后病稍可，方出殿受群臣朝贺。封华歆为司徒，王朗为司空；大小官僚，一一升赏。丕疾未痊，疑许昌宫室多妖，乃自许昌幸洛阳，大建宫室。

早有人到成都，报说曹丕自立为大魏皇帝，于洛阳盖造宫殿；且传言汉帝已遇害。汉中王闻知，痛哭终日，下令百官挂孝，遥望设祭，上尊谥曰"孝愍皇帝"。玄德因此忧虑，致染成疾，不能理事，政务皆托与孔明。孔明与太傅许靖、光禄大夫谯周商议，言天下不可一日无君，欲尊汉中王为帝。谯周曰："近有祥风庆云之瑞；成都西北角有黄气数十丈，冲霄而起；帝星见于毕、胃、昴之分，煌煌如月：此正应汉中王当即帝位，以继汉统，更复何疑？"

于是孔明与许靖，引大小官僚上表，请汉中王即皇帝位。汉中王览表，大惊曰："卿等欲陷孤为不忠不义之人耶？"孔明奏曰："非也。曹丕篡汉自立，王上乃汉室苗裔，理合继统以延

pour. All went dark; the altar lanterns blew out. Cao Pi collapsed in fright and had to be carried down, regaining consciousness only after a long while. Attendants took him into the palace, where he remained for several days, unable to hold court. Then, feeling stronger, he appeared in the main hall to accept the courtiers' congratulations on assuming the sovereignty. He honored Hua Xin as minister of the interior and Wang Lang as minister of works. Other officials were promoted and rewarded.

Cao Pi did not completely recover, however, and he began to suspect that the capital buildings were haunted. He therefore moved from Xuchang to Luoyang and built a palace complex there.

* * *

Word soon reached Chengdu that Cao Pi had taken the throne as august emperor of the Great Wei and was constructing a new palace in Luoyang. And there were rumors that the Han Emperor had already been killed. The king of Hanzhong grieved the whole day at the news and ordered his court into mourning. He also arranged sacrifices for the distant Han Emperor, honoring him posthumously as August Emperor Min the Filial.

These events made Xuande too ill to administer government affairs, and he turned everything over to Kongming. Kongming consulted Imperial Guardian Xu Jing and Imperial Steward Qiao Zhou;[12] the three decided to establish the king of Hanzhong as emperor on the grounds that the empire may not be without a sovereign even for a single day. Qiao Zhou said, "Recently we have had the good omen of auspicious winds and clouds. In the northwest corner of Chengdu a yellow haze several hundred spans high rose into the evening sky.[13] The imperial star was seen in the area of Stomach, Mane, and Net,[14] shining with an august fire and bright as the moon. These correspondent signs indicate that the king of Hanzhong should assume the imperial throne and continue the great line of Han. Their meaning is unmistakable."

And so Kongming, together with Xu Jing, led a general assembly of officials to petition the king of Hanzhong to take the imperial throne. The king read over the memorial and said in astonishment, "Would you urge on me a course both disloyal and dishonorable?"[15] Kongming addressed the king: "Not at all! Cao Pi has usurped the Han and taken power. As a

1961

汉祀。"汉中王勃然变色曰:"孤岂效逆贼所为!"拂袖而起,入于后宫。众官皆散。三日后,孔明又引众官入朝,请汉中王出。众皆拜伏于前。许靖奏曰:"今汉天子已被曹丕所弑,王上不即帝位,兴师讨逆,不得为忠义也。今天下无不欲王上为君,为孝愍皇帝雪恨。若不从臣等所议,是失民望矣。"汉中王曰:"孤虽是景帝之孙,并未有德泽以布于民;今一旦自立为帝,与篡窃何异!"孔明苦劝数次,汉中王坚执不从。孔明乃设一计,谓众官曰:如此如此。于是孔明托病不出。

汉中王闻孔明病笃,亲到府中,直入卧榻边,问曰:"军师所感何疾?"孔明答曰:"忧心如焚,命不久矣!"汉中王曰:"军师所忧何事?"连问数次,孔明只推病重,瞑目不答。汉中王再三请问。孔明喟然叹曰:"臣自出茅庐,得遇大王,相随至今,言听计从;今幸大王有两川之地,不负臣夙昔之言。目今曹丕篡位,汉祀将斩,文武官僚,咸欲奉大王为帝,灭魏兴刘,共图功名;不想大王坚执不肯,众官皆有怨心,不久必尽散矣。若文武

kinsman of the Han, Your Majesty should by rights succeed in the line so as to maintain the ritual sacrifices." The king of Hanzhong, his countenance altered, said angrily, "Shall I emulate the conduct of renegade traitors?" Flicking his sleeves, he arose and retired to the rear of the palace; the assembly dispersed.

Three days later Kongming returned to court with the body of officials and requested that the king come forth. The courtiers prostrated themselves when he appeared. Xu Jing addressed the king: "Cao Pi has murdered the Emperor of Han. Unless Your Majesty assumes the royal seat and takes the field to suppress the renegades, you will fail in your obligations of loyalty and honor. The whole world desires Your Majesty to reign and redeem the humiliation suffered by the August Emperor Min the Filial, Emperor Xian. You will fail the hopes of the people if you decline." The king replied, "Though a descendant of Emperor Jing, I lack sufficient virtue to extend to all the people. Were I suddenly to establish myself, how would it differ from the crime of usurpation?" Kongming's strenuous appeals could not move the king, so he conceived a plan that he shared with the officials. Then, claiming to be ill, he went home and remained unavailable.[16]

When the king heard that Kongming's illness was serious, he went to Kongming's quarters, walked straight to his bedside, and asked, "What ails you, Director General?" "A burning anguish," Kongming replied, "so sharp, I fear I have little time to live." "The cause?" the king asked. He repeated the question a number of times, but Kongming, intending to look too sick to reply, lowered his lids. The king pressed him until finally, with a long sigh, Kongming said, "Since the day I left my thatched hut to serve Your Majesty down to the present, I have stayed beside you. You have had implicit faith in me and heeded my every counsel. Good fortune has placed the whole of the Riverlands in Your Majesty's hands, exactly as I predicted long ago. Now that Cao Pi has usurped the throne, and terminated the ritual sacrifices of the Han, all our officers and officials, both civil and military, earnestly desire to serve Your Majesty as emperor and to share in the glory of eliminating the Cao clan and reviving the Liu. Your refusal was unthinkable; but now the whole court may soon disperse in dismay, leaving the Riverlands vulnerable if Wei and Wu were to

皆散，吴、魏来攻，两川难保。臣安得不忧乎？"汉中王曰："吾非推阻，恐天下人议论耳。"孔明曰："圣人云：'名不正，则言不顺。'今大王名正言顺，有何可议？岂不闻'天与弗取，反受其咎'？"汉中王曰："待军师病可，行之未迟。"孔明听罢，从榻上跃然而起，将屏风一击，外面文武众官皆入，拜伏于地曰："王上既允，便请择日以行大礼。"汉中王视之，乃是太傅许靖、安汉将军糜竺、青衣侯向举、阳泉侯刘豹、别驾赵祚、治中杨洪、议曹杜琼、从事张爽、太常卿赖恭、光禄卿黄权、祭酒何宗、学士尹默、司业谯周、大司马殷纯、偏将军张裔、少府王谋、昭文博士伊籍、从事郎秦宓等众也。

汉中王惊曰："陷孤于不义，皆卿等也！"孔明曰："王上既允所请，便可筑坛择吉，恭行大礼。"即时送汉中王还宫，一面令博士许慈、谏议郎孟光掌礼，筑坛于成都武担之南。诸事齐备，多官整设銮驾，迎请汉中王登坛致祭。谯周在坛上，高声朗读祭文曰：

　　惟建安二十六年四月丙午朔，越十二日丁巳，皇帝备，敢昭告于皇天后土：汉有天下，历数无疆。曩者，王莽

attack. How could your devoted servant not despair?"

The king replied, "I do not decline on pretext. I fear the adverse judgment of the world." Kongming said, "Confucius said that incorrect names make for illogical positions. Now Your Majesty would be entirely justified in taking such an action. There is nothing to criticize. But can you have forgotten the saying, 'What Heaven grants is refused only at peril'?" The king said, "When your illness improves, there will be time enough to act." At these words Kongming sprang up from his couch and knocked the screen aside. A host of civil and military officials strode in and flung themselves to the ground. "With Your Majesty's agreement, we shall select a day for the ceremony." From the crowd before him the king recognized Imperial Guardian Xu Jing; Mi Zhu, General Who Secures the Han; Xiang Ju, lord of Qingyi; Liu Bao, lord of Yangquan; Zhao Zuo, lieutenant governor; Yang Hong, provincial secretary; Du Qiong, a counselor; Zhang Shuang, an aide; Lai Gong, minister of protocol; Huang Quan, the palace director; He Zong, the libationer; Yin Mo, the scholar-official; Qiao Zhou, the imperial steward; Chief Commander Yin Chun; Auxiliary Commander Zhang Yi; Treasurer Wang Mou; Academician Who Sheds Light on Texts, Yi Ji; Assistant Aide Qin Mi; and many others.

With trepidation the king said, "You are forcing me into a dishonorable position." "Since Your Majesty has already granted our request," Kongming said, "we may build the altar and select a propitious day for the reverent performance of the inauguration." He sent the king back to the palace and ordered Imperial Academician Xu Ci and Court Counselor Meng Guang to take charge of the ceremonies and have an altar built south of Mount Wudan.[17]

1965

When all arrangements had been made, the officials had the royal carriage escort the king to the altar, where he performed the sacrifice. Qiao Zhou was on the altar and read out the accompanying text in a loud, clear voice:

It being the day *dingsi*, fifty-fourth of the cycle, twelve days after the beginning of the fourth moon on *bingwu*,[18] the twenty-sixth year of Jian An,[19] I, Bei, the August Emperor, resolve to proclaim to the august shining Heaven and the fruitful earth that the Han hold the empire in unbroken succession. There was one instance of usurpation: Wang Mang seized

篡盗，光武皇帝震怒致诛，社稷复存。今曹操阻兵残忍，戮杀主后，罪恶滔天；操子丕，载肆凶逆，窃据神器。群下将士，以为汉祀堕废，备宜延之，嗣武二祖，躬行天罚。备惧无德忝帝位，询于庶民，外及遐荒君长，佥曰：天命不可以不答，祖业不可以久替，四海不可以无主。率土式望，在备一人。备畏天明命，又惧高、光之业，将坠于地，谨择吉日，登坛告祭，受皇帝玺绶，抚临四方。惟神飨祚汉家，永绥历服！

读罢祭文，孔明率众官恭上玉玺。汉中王受了，捧于坛上，再三推辞曰："备无才德，请择有才德者受之。"孔明奏曰："王上平定四海，功德昭于天下，况是大汉宗派，宜即正位。已祭告天神，复何让焉！"文武各官，皆呼"万岁"。拜舞礼毕，改元章武元年。立妃吴氏为皇后，长子刘禅为太子；封次子刘永为鲁王，三子刘理为梁王；封诸葛亮为丞相，许靖为司徒；大小官僚，一

the throne, but August Emperor Guang Wu made his fury felt, executed the traitor, and restored our sacred shrines.

Now Cao Cao has committed atrocities and cruelly murdered the reigning sovereign, a hideous crime that assails the very skies. His son Pi gives free rein to nefarious treason, unlawfully seizing the sacred instruments of rule. The whole of our civil and military hold that, with the services of the Han lapsed and void, it is proper for me, Bei, to resume them and, as heir to our founders, personally carry out Heaven's retribution.

Fearful lest my virtue prove unequal to the station, I have taken counsel among the common people and the chieftains around our borders. All agree that the Mandate of Heaven must be heeded, that the patrimony must not remain displaced, and that the realm must not be without its ruler. Throughout the land expectation rests on me, Bei.

Yet do I tremble before that clear mandate. Yet do I fear that the estate of the two founders, Han Gao Zu and Emperor Guang Wu, may come to ruin. With deep reverence have we selected an auspicious day to ascend the platform and offer sacrifice, that our acceptance of the royal seal may bring solace throughout the realm. May the gods relish the dynastic offerings and bestow lasting harmony on our domain.

When the reading was done, Kongming led the assembly in tendering the jade seal. The king took it in his hands and placed it reverently on the altar. Again and again he declined the honor, saying "I, Bei, have neither talent nor virtue; you should find someone else who has, and elevate him." But Kongming addressed the throne thus: "In bringing order to the realm, Your Majesty has illumined the empire with merit and virtue. And since you are a member of the royal house, it is fitting that you occupy the proper seat. The gods above have already received the sacrifice and the announcement. To defer is not possible any longer." A chorus of "Long live the Emperor!" went up from the assembly.

At the conclusion of the ceremonies, they changed the reign title to Zhang Wu, Manifest Might. The Emperor's consort, lady Wu, was made Empress.[20] His eldest son, Shan, was appointed heir apparent; his second son, Yong, was honored as king of Lu; and his third son, Li, was named king of Liang. Zhuge Liang became prime minister; Xu Jing minister of the interior; and all the other officials, high and low, were advanced. An

一升赏。大赦天下。两川军民,无不欣跃。

次日设朝,文武官僚拜毕,列为两班。先主降诏曰:"朕自桃园与关、张结义,誓同生死。不幸二弟云长,被东吴孙权所害;若不报仇,是负盟也。朕欲起倾国之兵,剪伐东吴,生擒逆贼,以雪此恨!"言未毕,班内一人,拜伏于阶下,谏曰:"不可。"先主视之,乃虎威将军赵云也。

正是:

　　君王未及行天讨,臣下曾闻进直言。

未知子龙所谏若何,且看下文分解。

amnesty was declared throughout the empire, and the people of the Riverlands, soldier and civilian alike, rejoiced.

The next day in full court, before the civil and military in their respective stations, the First Ruler[21] delivered his first edict: "With Lord Guan and Zhang Fei we bound ourselves in honor and allegiance in the peach garden, swearing to live or die as one. Alas! My second brother, Lord Guan, met his doom at the hands of Sun Quan of the Southland. Unless we take revenge on this enemy, the covenant is betrayed. Therefore we intend full mobilization for war against the south to take alive the renegade traitor and to redeem our shame." But before the First Ruler had finished, someone stepped out from the ranks and threw himself at the First Ruler's feet to object: "No!" he cried. It was one of the "Five Tiger Generals," Zhao Zilong. Indeed:

> Before the Emperor could execute the punishment ordained,
> His vassal Zhao Zilong brought forward a complaint.

How did the great warrior remonstrate?

Read on.

第八十一回

急兄仇张飞遇害　雪弟恨先主兴兵

却说先主欲起兵东征，赵云谏曰："国贼乃曹操，非孙权也。今曹丕篡汉，神人共怒。陛下可早图关中，屯兵渭河上流，以讨凶逆，则关东义士，必裹粮策马以迎王师；若舍魏以伐吴，兵势一交，岂能骤解。愿陛下察之。"先主曰："孙权害了朕弟；又兼傅士仁、糜芳、潘璋、马忠皆有切齿之仇：啖其肉而灭其族，方雪朕恨！卿何阻耶？"云曰："汉贼之仇，公也；兄弟之仇，私也。愿以天下为重。"先主答曰："朕不为弟报仇，虽有万里江山，何足为贵？"遂不听赵云之谏，下令起兵伐吴；且发使往五谿，借番兵五万，共相策应；一面差使往阆中，迁张飞为车骑将军，领司隶校尉，封西乡侯，兼阆中牧。使命赍诏而去。

却说张飞在阆中，闻知关公被东吴所害，旦夕号泣，血湿

汉英经典文库

Chapter 81

Eager for Revenge, Zhang Fei Is Assassinated
To Avenge His Brother, the Emperor Goes to War

Zhao Zilong spoke against the expedition: "Cao Cao is the traitor, not Sun Quan. Cao Pi has usurped the Han throne, to the common indignation of gods and men. Let Your Majesty first make the land within the passes your target. Station your men along the upper Wei River in order to bring these hateful renegades to justice; and the Han loyalists east of the passes will then bundle their grain and urge on their horses to welcome the royal host. But if, instead of the northern kingdom of Wei, you attack the southern kingdom of Wu, once your forces are engaged, they cannot be quickly recalled. May Your Majesty consider this carefully."[1]

1971

The Emperor replied, "Sun Quan murdered my brother, and others have earned their share of my hatred: Fu Shiren, Mi Fang, Pan Zhang, Ma Zhong. Until I've gnawed their flesh and exterminated their clans, my humiliation will not be effaced. Why would you stand in my way?" Zhao Zilong answered, "War against the traitors to Han is a public responsibility. War for the sake of a brother is a personal matter. I urge Your Majesty to give priority to the empire." To this the Emperor replied, "If I should fail to avenge my brother, the possession of these ten thousand *li* of mountains and rivers would make an unworthy prize." Ignoring Zhao Zilong's opposition, the Emperor ordered mobilization, sending envoys to Wuxi to borrow fifty thousand troops from the Qiang nation. At the same time he promoted Zhang Fei, who was in Langzhong, to general of Chariots and Cavalry and commander of the Capital Districts, and further honored him as lord of Xixiang and protector of Langzhong. An envoy took the edict to him.

* * *

Zhang Fei was in Langzhong when he learned that the revered Lord Guan had been murdered in the Southland. Day and night he howled and

衣襟。诸将以酒解劝,酒醉,怒气愈加。帐上帐下,但有犯者即鞭挞之;多有鞭死者。每日望南切齿睁目怒恨,放声痛哭不已。忽报使至,慌忙接入,开读诏旨。飞受爵望北拜毕,设酒款待来使。飞曰:"吾兄被害,仇深似海;庙堂之臣,何不早奏兴兵?"使者曰:"多有劝先灭魏而后伐吴者。"飞怒曰:"是何言也!昔我三人桃园结义,誓同生死;今不幸二兄半途而逝,吾安得独享富贵耶!吾当面见天子,愿为前部先锋,挂孝伐吴,生擒逆贼,祭告二兄,以践前盟!"言讫,就同使命望成都而来。

却说先主每日自下教场操演军马,克日兴师,御驾亲征。于是公卿都至丞相府中见孔明,曰:"今天子初临大位,亲统军伍,非所以重社稷也。丞相秉均衡之职,何不规谏?"孔明曰:"吾苦谏数次,只是不听。今日公等随我入教场谏去。"当下孔明引百官来奏先主曰:"陛下初登宝位,若欲北讨汉贼,以伸大义于天下,方可亲统六师;若只欲伐吴,命一上将统军伐之可也,何必亲劳圣驾?"先主见孔明苦谏,心中稍回。忽报张飞到

wept until his shirt was damp with blood. Wine, which his commanders urged on him to calm him, served only to inflame him; whoever crossed him — whether of high rank or low — he had flogged immediately, and many deaths resulted. Each day he would stare into the south, gnashing his teeth in the fury of humiliation, venting cries of anguish. At this time the messenger from the Emperor arrived. He was rushed into Zhang Fie's presence, where he read the edict. After accepting his new honors and offices, Zhang Fei faced north and prostrated himself to show his devotion to the Emperor. He then regaled the messenger.

"My will to avenge my brother's murder is deep as the sea," Zhang Fei said. "Why have the members of court made no appeals to the throne for a general mobilization?" The envoy replied, "The majority urge that Wei be annihilated before we take up arms against Wu." "What words!" Zhang Fei cried out angrily. "We three brothers took an oath to live and die as one. The second has passed from us before his time. What are wealth and station to me without him? I shall see the Son of Heaven myself and offer to serve in the vanguard. Under the banner of mourning I shall wage war upon the south, bring the traitor home to sacrifice to my second brother, and thus fulfill the covenant." Zhang Fei headed back to Chengdu, capital of the Riverlands, with the envoy.

The Emperor went regularly to the training field to direct army maneuvers. He set the day for the expedition, which he intended to lead personally. The high officers of the court went to the prime minister's quarters and complained to Kongming: "The Son of Heaven has held the throne for too brief a time to be taking personal command of the army. The sacred shrines will be neglected as a result. Your Excellency, you hold the most influential position. Could you not urge him toward a better course?" Kongming responded, "I have protested — many times — to no avail. Come with me today to the training grounds and I'll try again." [2]

Kongming, at the head of the assembly, addressed the Emperor: "Your Majesty has assumed the throne so recently; if it is your purpose to bring the northern traitors to justice so that the principle of allegiance to legitimate authority may prevail in the empire, then it is altogether right for you to take command of the entire army yourself. But if you simply mean to attack the Southland, ordering one of your superior commanders to lead

1973

来，先主急召入。飞至演武厅拜伏于地，抱先主足而哭。先主亦哭。飞曰："陛下今日为君，早忘了桃园之誓！二兄之仇，如何不报？"先主曰："多官谏阻，未敢轻举。"飞曰："他人岂知昔日之盟？若陛下不去，臣舍此躯与二兄报仇！若不能报时，臣宁死不见陛下也！"先主曰："朕与卿同往：卿提本部兵自阆州而出，朕统精兵会于江州，共伐东吴，以雪此恨！"飞临行，先主嘱曰："朕素知卿酒后暴怒，鞭挞健儿，而复令在左右：此取祸之道也。今后务宜宽容，不可如前。"飞拜辞而去。

　　次日，先主整兵要行。学士秦宓奏曰："陛下舍万乘之躯，而徇小义，古人所不取也。愿陛下思之。"先主曰："云长与朕，犹一体也。大义尚在，岂可忘耶？"宓伏地不起曰："陛下不从臣言，诚恐有失。"先主大怒曰："朕欲兴兵，尔何出此不利之言！"叱武士推出斩之。宓面不改色，回顾先主而笑曰："臣死无恨，但可惜新创之业，又将颠覆耳！"众官皆为秦宓告免。先主曰："暂且囚下，待朕报仇回时发落。"孔明闻知，即上表救秦宓。其略曰：

the campaign should suffice. Why should your own sagely self bear the burden?" In view of Kongming's strenuous objections, the Emperor was experiencing some uncertainty about the invasion when Zhang Fei's arrival was announced.[3] The Emperor summoned him at once. Zhang Fei bent to the ground before the reviewing stand, weeping as he hugged his lord's feet. The Emperor wept too.

"Today Your Majesty reigns," Zhang Fei said, "and already the peach garden oath is forgotten! Can you leave our brother unavenged?" "Many officials oppose taking revenge. I cannot act rashly." was the reply. "What do others know of our covenant? If you will not go, I will avenge him whatever the cost to myself. Should I fail, I shall be content to die and see you no more." "Then I shall go with you," the Emperor said. "You start out from Langzhou with your own troops. I shall meet you with an elite force at Jiangzhou. Our joint campaign against the Southland will redeem our shame." Zhang Fei was about to leave when the Emperor added a warning, "You have often turned violent after wine, beaten your stalwarts, and then reassigned them in your personal guard. That is a good way to destroy yourself. Hereafter change your ways; make an effort to be tolerant and understanding." Zhang Fei bowed low, took leave, and departed.

The next day the Emperor organized his forces for the march. Scholar Official Qin Mi addressed the throne: "For Your Majesty to jeopardize the imperial person in pursuit of a trifling point of honor is a course no sage of olden times would approve.[4] I beg you to reconsider." "Yunchang is I — in sacred union," the Emperor responded, "and I am Yunchang. Who could forget the great obligation this entails?" Qin Mi flung himself to the ground and would not get up. "Heed me," he cried, "lest your plan miscarry." "How dare you speak of failure on the eve of the mobilization?" the Emperor demanded angrily. He ordered the guards to remove Qin Mi and behead him. But Qin Mi, his expression unaltered, turned back and smiled at the Emperor. "I go to die without regret," he said, "but the collapse of your new enterprise makes me sad." All the officials pleaded for Qin Mi, and so the Emperor said, "Imprison him for the time being. We'll deal with him after completing our mission of revenge." Kongming learned of this incident and submitted a memorial in defense of

臣亮等切以吴贼逞奸诡之计，致荆州有覆亡之祸；陨将星于斗牛，折天柱于楚地：此情哀痛，诚不可忘。但念迁汉鼎者，罪由曹操；移刘祚者，过非孙权。窃谓魏贼若除，则吴自宾服。愿陛下纳秦宓金石之言，以养士卒之力，别作良图，则社稷幸甚！天下幸甚！

先主看毕，掷表于地曰："朕意已决，无得再谏！"遂命丞相诸葛亮保太子守两川；骠骑将军马超并弟马岱，助镇北将军魏延守汉中，以当魏兵；虎威将军赵云为后应，兼督粮草；黄权、程畿为参谋；马良、陈震掌理文书；黄忠为前部先锋；冯习、张南为副将；傅彤、张翼为中军护尉；赵融、廖淳为合后。川将数百员，并五谿番将等，共兵七十五万，择定章武元年七月丙寅日出师。

却说张飞回到阆中，下令军中：限三日内制办白旗白甲，三军挂孝伐吴。次日，帐下两员末将范疆、张达，入帐告曰："白旗白甲，一时无措，须宽限方可。"飞大怒曰："吾急欲报仇，恨

Qin Mi:

> It is my earnest belief that the treachery of the Southland led to the disaster in Jingzhou. We lost our leading star; our pillar of Heaven was broken. But however keen our grief, however unforgettable, we must also remember that the crime of displacing the sacred dynastic vessels of Han arose through Cao Cao. The removal of the holy offerings of the Liu was not Sun Quan's fault. And I would presume to say that if the traitors of the Wei are removed, then the Southland will submit to us of its own accord. I implore you to accept the precious advice of Qin Mi and husband the strength of our armies. There are other worthwhile strategies that will bring great good fortune to our shrines and to our realm.[5]

But the Emperor threw the petition to the ground and said, "We are resolved. Let there be no further opposition." So saying, he commanded Prime Minister Zhuge Liang to take the heir apparent, Ah Dou, into his charge and defend the Riverlands; Flying Cavalry General Ma Chao and his cousin Ma Dai to assist Queller of the North, General Wei Yan, in the defense of Hanzhong against the northern army; Tiger Might General Zhao Zilong to coordinate relief from the rear and to supervise supply operations; Huang Quan and Cheng Ji to serve as military advisers; Ma Liang and Chen Zhen to take charge of documents; Huang Zhong to serve as vanguard of the forward army; Feng Xi and Zhang Nan to serve as lieutenant commanders; Fu Tong and Zhang Yi to be posted as commander's aides in the central army; and Zhao Rong and Liao Chun to coordinate the rear. The expedition, which included several hundred Riverlands generals as well as a number of leaders of the Miao and Yao peoples from the Wuxi region — altogether seven hundred and fifty thousand strong — was to begin on the *bingyin* day, fifty-first of the cycle, in the seventh month of Zhang Wu 1.[6]

* * *

Zhang Fei returned to his camp in Langzhong, where he allotted but three days to prepare white banners and white armor so that his armies might set forth against the Southland under the color of mourning. The next day two minor commanders, Fan Jiang and Zhang Da, entered his tent and announced, "The allotted period will have to be extended if we are to arrange for white banners and white armor." Violently angered by these words, Zhang Fei shouted, "My vengeance will brook no delay.

LIBRARY OF CHINESE
AND ENGLISH CLASSICS

1977

不明日便到逆贼之境,汝安敢违我将令!"叱武士缚于树上,各鞭背五十。鞭毕,以手指之曰:"来日俱要完备!若违了限,即杀汝二人示众!"打得二人满口出血。回到营中商议,范疆曰:"今日受了刑责,着我等如何办得?其人性暴如火,倘来日不完,你我皆被杀矣!"张达曰:"比如他杀我,不如我杀他。"疆曰:"怎奈不得近前。"达曰:"我两个若不当死,则他醉于床上;若是当死,则他不醉。"二人商议停当。

却说张飞在帐中,神思昏乱,动止恍惚,乃问部将曰:"吾今心惊肉颤,坐卧不安,此何意也?"部将答曰:"此是君侯思念关公,以致如此。"飞令人将酒来,与部将同饮,不觉大醉,卧于帐中。范、张二贼,探知消息,初更时分,各藏短刀,密入帐中,诈言欲禀机密重事,直至床前。原来张飞每睡不合眼;当夜寝于帐中,二贼见他须竖目张,本不敢动手。因闻鼻息如雷,方敢近前,以短刀刺入飞腹。飞大叫一声而亡。时年五十五岁。后人有诗叹曰:

安喜曾闻鞭督邮,黄巾扫尽佐炎刘。
虎牢关上声先震,长坂桥边水逆流。
义释严颜安蜀境,智欺张郃定中州。
伐吴未克身先死,秋草长遗阆地愁。

却说二贼当夜割了张飞首级,便引数十人连夜投东吴去

The shame is that we can't reach the traitor's borders tomorrow! And yet you dare contravene my command!" He shrieked for them to be bound to a tree and lashed on the back fifty times. Then he pointed at them menacingly and cried, "Everything is to be ready tomorrow! If you fail, I will make a public example with your heads!" And he beat them until blood ran from their mouths.

The two returned to camp to think of a way to save themselves. Fan Jiang said, "After a beating like this, how are we going to carry out our orders? The man's as violent as fire. And unless everything's ready tomorrow, we both will die!" "Better him than us," Zhang Da answered. "But we couldn't get near him," Fan Jiang replied. "If we are fated to live, he will fall asleep drunk. If we are fated to die, he will stay sober," Zhang Da said. Thus, the two men prepared themselves to act.

That night in his tent, anxious and restless, Zhang Fei asked his commanders, "I no longer know peace; I cannot rest — what does it mean?" The officers responded, "It comes from thinking of the revered Lord Guan, Your Lordship." Zhang Fei ordered wine and drank with his officers. Before realizing it, he fell into a drunken stupor. Informed of Zhang Fei's condition, Fan Jiang and Zhang Da slipped into his tent at the first watch with concealed knives. Claiming to have an important secret petition to present, they approached his couch. Now, Zhang Fei always slept with open lids, and the two traitors, watching the sleeping man's bristling beard and staring eyes, stood paralyzed. Then, hearing the loud drone of breath in his nostrils, they stepped up and plunged their daggers into Zhang Fei's belly. Zhang Fei gave a single cry and died. He was fifty-five years of age. A poet of later times has left these lines:

1979

> At Anxi town he flogged the state inspector [7]
> And aided the Liu in clearing out the Scarves.
> At Tiger Trap his voice rang clear and loud;
> By Steepslope Bridge he turned back Cao Cao's horde.
> His release of Yan Yan secured the Riverlands;
> He tricked Zhang He and gave Liu Bei Hanzhong.
> But by dying before the Southland could be won,
> He left a lasting sadness in Langzhong.

The two traitors severed Zhang Fei's head and proceeded to the south

了。次日，军中闻知，起兵追之不及。时有张飞部将吴班，向自荆州来见先主，先主用为牙门将，使佐张飞守阆中。当下吴班先发表章，奏知天子；然后令长子张苞具棺椁盛贮，令弟张绍守阆中，苞自来报先主。时先主已择期出师。大小官僚，皆随孔明送十里方回。孔明回至成都，怏怏不乐，顾谓众官曰："法孝直若在，必能制主上东行也。"

却说先主是夜心惊肉颤，寝卧不安。出帐仰观天文，见西北一星，其大如斗，忽然坠地。先主大疑，连夜令人求问孔明。孔明回奏曰："合损一上将。三日之内，必有惊报。"先主因此按兵不动。忽侍臣奏曰："阆中张车骑部将吴班，差人赍表至。"先主顿足曰："噫！三弟休矣！"及至览表，果报张飞凶信。先主放声大哭，昏绝于地。众官救醒。次日，人报一队军马骤风而至。先主出营观之。良久，见一员小将，白袍银铠，滚鞍下马，伏地而哭，乃张苞也。苞曰："范疆、张达杀了臣父，将首级投吴去了！"先主哀痛至甚，饮食不进。群臣苦谏曰："陛下方欲为二弟报仇，何可先自摧残龙体？"先主方才进膳；遂谓张苞曰："卿与

with a few dozen followers. By the time the deed was known the next day, pursuit was impossible.

At the time of the murder Wu Ban, one of Zhang Fei's commanders, earlier from Jingzhou, had been assigned by the Emperor as garrison commander to help defend Langzhong. This Wu Ban prepared the memorial announcing Zhang Fei's death. After completing it, he had Zhang Fei's eldest son, Zhang Bao, prepare the coffins, inner and outer, and place the body inside; he had the younger son, Zhang Shao, guard Langzhong while Zhang Bao went ahead to inform the Emperor.

The Emperor had already gone forth with the army on the day selected. Kongming, followed by a grand assembly of officials, escorted the Emperor some ten *li*. Afterward, the prime minister, filled with foreboding, returned to Chengdu, where he told the court officials, "Fa Zheng, were he alive, could have prevented this expedition."[8]

* * *

The Emperor spent an anxious night. Unable to sleep, he stepped outside his tent and looked into the sky: in the northwest he saw a meteor large as a dipper plunge toward the horizon. The Emperor sent to Kongming for an explanation of the phenomenon. Kongming responded, "It represents the loss of a senior general. We'll have upsetting news within three days." Kongming's reply kept the Emperor from advancing. Suddenly, an attendant addressed the throne: "General Zhang Fei's commander Wu Ban has sent a man to deliver a memorial." The Emperor stamped his foot on the ground and cried, "Alas! Third brother must be gone!" Then he learned the awful truth from Wu Ban's memorial. The Emperor let out a terrible cry and fell faint. His officers rushed to revive him.

The next day it was reported that a company of troops was fast approaching. The Emperor left his tent to see for himself; after a long wait he saw a young commander in white battle gown and silver-gilt armor ride up, dismount briskly, and prostrate himself, crying. It was Zhang Fei's son, Zhang Bao. "Fan Jiang and Zhang Da," he cried, "have slain your vassal's father and taken his head to the Southland." The Emperor, grief-stricken, refused all food and drink. His officers pleaded, "If Your Majesty means to avenge the death of your two brothers, you must maintain your health." Finally the Emperor accepted food. He asked Zhang Bao,

1981

吴班，敢引本部军作先锋，为卿父报仇否？"苞曰："为国为父，万死不辞！"先主正欲遣苞起兵，又报一彪军风拥而至。先主令侍臣探之。须臾，侍臣引一小将军，白袍银铠，入营伏地而哭。先主视之，乃关兴也。先主见了关兴，想起关公，又放声大哭。众官苦劝。先主曰："朕想布衣时，与关、张结义，誓同生死；今朕为天子，正欲与两弟同享富贵，不幸俱死于非命！见此二侄，能不断肠！"言讫又哭。

众官曰："二小将军且退。容圣上将息龙体。"侍臣奏曰："陛下年过六旬，不宜过于哀痛。"先主曰："二弟俱亡，朕安忍独生！"言讫，以头顿地而哭。多官商议曰："今天子如此烦恼，将何解劝？"马良曰："主上亲统大兵伐吴，终日号泣，于军不利。"陈震曰："吾闻成都青城山之西，有一隐者，姓李，名意。世人传说此老已三百余岁，能知人之生死吉凶，乃当世之神仙也。何不奏知天子，召此老来，问他吉凶，胜如吾等之言。"遂入奏先主。先主从之，即遣陈震赍诏，往青城山宣召。震星夜到了青城，令乡人引入出谷深处，遥望仙庄，清云隐隐，瑞气非凡。

"Are you and Wu Ban willing to put your men in the vanguard to avenge your father?" Zhang Bao replied, "Yes. For my kingdom and for my father's sake, I will welcome death ten thousand times if need be."

The Emperor was about to dispatch Zhang Bao to ready his troops, when another body of soldiers arrived. The Emperor directed his attendant to find out who they were. Presently the attendant escorted in a young general dressed in a white surcoat and silvered armor; he prostrated himself and cried. It was Guan Xing. The sight of the lad reminded the Emperor of the revered Lord Guan, and he gave voice to his grief. The officials could not assuage him. "I remember when we were commoners in obscurity," the Emperor said. "We pledged our honor to live and die for each other. Now, as the Son of Heaven, I should be enjoying wealth and prestige with my brothers. Alas, both met violent ends. And the sight of these two nephews breaks my heart." So saying, he began to cry again.

The officials said to the young commanders, "Withdraw for now; our liege lord needs rest." The imperial attendants addressed the throne: "Such excess of emotion could be harmful, Your Majesty; you are more than sixty years of age." "Can I carry on alone, without my brothers?" the Emperor said. He knocked his head on the ground and wept. The body of officials asked each other, "How can we relieve the Son of Heaven's distress?" Ma Liang replied, "For our lord to grieve all day when he is personally commanding this great campaign bodes the army no good." Chen Zhen added, "I have heard that west of Azure City Mountain lives an old recluse named Li Yi, said to be over three hundred years old, who can divine a man's years and his fortune. He is one of the holy immortals of our age. Let us petition the Son of Heaven to summon this man and ask his reading of what lies in store. It will be worth more than any suggestions of ours."

Chen Zhen presented this proposal to the Emperor, who approved and sent Chen Zhen to deliver his edict and summon the divine. That night Chen Zhen reached Azure City Mountain and had a man from the area guide him to a recess in the valley from which he could observe the divine's cottage.[9] Clouds enshadowed it, and a magical aura marked it. Suddenly a lad greeted him and said, "You must be Chen Zhen." The

1983

忽见一小童来迎曰："来者莫非陈孝起乎？"震大惊曰："仙童如何知我姓字？"童子曰："吾师昨者有言：'今日必有皇帝诏命至；使者必是陈孝起。'"震曰："真神仙也！人言信不诬矣！"遂与小童同入仙庄，拜见李意，宣天子诏命。李意推老不行。震曰："天子急欲见仙翁一面，幸勿吝鹤驾。"再三敦请，李意方行。即至御营，入见先主。先主见李意鹤发童颜，碧眼方瞳，灼灼有光，身如古柏之状，知是异人，优礼相待。李意曰："老夫乃荒山村叟，无学无识。辱陛下宣召，不知有何见谕？"先主曰："朕与关、张二弟结生死之交，三十余年矣。今二弟被害，亲统大军报仇，未知休咎如何。久闻仙翁通晓玄机，望乞赐教。"李意曰："此乃天数，非老夫所知也。"先主再三求问，意乃索纸笔画兵马器械四十余张，画毕便一一扯碎。又画一大人仰卧于地上，傍边一人掘土埋之，上写一大"白"字，遂稽首而去。先主不悦，谓群臣曰："此狂叟也！不足为信。"即以火焚之，便催军前进。

张苞入奏曰："吴班军马已至。小臣乞为先锋。"先主壮其志，即取先锋印赐张苞。苞方欲挂印，又一少年将奋然出曰：

astonished visitor replied, "How do you know me, young immortal?" "Yesterday my master told me that today Chen Zhen would bring an imperial edict," was the reply. "A true seer!" he exclaimed. "What people say is no lie." He accompanied the lad to the cottage, paid his respects to the sage, and announced the imperial summons. But Li Yi declined the summons, pleading his great age. Chen Zhen pursued the matter: "The Son of Heaven urgently desires an interview with the divine elder. Please do not begrudge him this visit." After repeated pleas, Li Yi agreed to go.

Li Yi came to the royal camp. Receiving him, the Emperor observed the old man's crane-white hair and youthful face, his greenish eyes and broad pupils glistening with an inner light, and his body that seemed to have assumed the configuration of an ancient cypress. Recognizing in Li Yi a man of unique gifts, the Emperor treated him with the sincerest cordiality.

"This old man," Li Yi began, "from a remote mountain village lacks both art and wisdom. Your Majesty has graciously summoned me, but what your command may be, I do not know." The Emperor responded, "I formed a life-and-death bond with my brothers, Guan and Zhang, more than thirty years ago. The two have been murdered, and I have undertaken to lead this great army to exact revenge, but I wonder what outcome the future holds. I have long known, divine elder, that you understand the mysterious workings of fate, and I look forward to the benefit of your instruction." Li Yi answered, "What Heaven ordains is beyond my ken." The Emperor pleaded again and again. Finally Li Yi called for brush and paper and drew some forty illustrations of soldiers, horses, and weapons. He then tore each drawing into tiny pieces. Next, he drew a giant sleeping face up on the ground. Beside him someone was digging a grave to bury him. At the top of the paper Li Yi wrote the word "white." He knocked his head respectfully to the ground and departed. Displeased, the Emperor said to his company, "A mad old man! Not worth our trust!" He burned the paper and dispatched the order for his army to advance.[10]

Zhang Bao entered the command tent and addressed the Emperor: "Wu Ban's forces have come. I beg to be placed in the vanguard." Impressd by Zhang Bao's ardor, the Emperor presented the seal of the

"留下印与我!"视之,乃关兴也。苞曰:"我已奉诏矣。"兴曰:"汝有何能,敢当此任?"苞曰:"我自幼习学武艺,箭无虚发。"先主曰:"朕正要观贤侄武艺,以定优劣。"苞令军士于百步之外,立一面旗,旗上画一红心。苞拈弓取箭,连射三箭,皆中红心。众皆称善。关兴挽弓在手曰:"射中红心何足为奇?"正言间,忽值头上一行雁过。兴指曰:"吾射这飞雁第三只。"一箭射去,那只雁应弦而落。文武官僚,齐声喝采。苞大怒,飞身上马,手挺父所使丈八点钢矛,大叫曰:"你敢与我比试武艺否?"兴亦上马,绰家传大砍刀纵马而出曰:"偏你能使矛!吾岂不能使刀!"

二将方欲交锋,先主喝曰:"二子休得无礼!"兴、苞二人慌忙下马,各弃兵器,拜伏请罪。先主曰:"朕自涿郡与卿等之父结异姓之交,亲如骨肉;今汝二人亦是昆仲之分,正当同心协力,共报父仇;奈何自相争竞,失其大义!父丧未远而犹如此,况日后乎?"二人再拜伏罪。先主问曰:"卿二人谁年长?"苞曰:"臣长关兴一岁。"先主即命兴拜苞为兄。二人就帐前折箭为誓,永相救护。先主下诏使吴班为先锋,令张苞、关兴护驾。水陆并进,船骑双行,浩浩荡荡,杀奔吴国来。

1987

vanguard commander to him. Zhang Bao was about to take the seal, when another young commander rushed forward and said, "Leave the seal for me!" It was Guan Xing. "But I have the edict," Zhang Bao protested. "Are you fit for the task?" Guan Xing asked. "I have trained in the military arts since my youth," he replied. "My every arrow finds its mark." The Emperor said, "Let our worthy nephews show their skills, and we shall decide between them." Zhang Bao had some soldiers plant a banner with a red center one hundred paces away. Zhang Bao held his bow and drew three arrows. Each shot hit the center. The crowd shouted its acclamation.

Guan Xing snatched his own bow and cried, "Nothing remarkable about that!" Suddenly a line of geese flew overhead. Guan Xing pointed up and said, "I'll shoot down the third." He shot into the sky and the bird fell as the string hummed. The officials hailed Guan Xing in unison. Angered, Zhang Bao mounted swiftly and, gripping the eighteen-span spear his father had used, shouted, "A trial of arms with me?" Guan Xing mounted, raised a sword handed down from his father, and dashed out to meet the challenge. "Use your spear; I'll use my sword!"

The two commanders had started to close, when the Emperor cried, "No more wrangling, lads!" The two hastily dismounted, threw down their weapons, and prostrated themselves as they begged the royal pardon. The Emperor continued, "In the district of Zhuo your fathers and I bound ourselves in friendship. Though of different surnames, we were as kinsmen. Now you two must join as brothers and commit yourselves utterly to avenge your fathers. What's the point of pitting yourselves against each other, neglecting the greater duty? Your fathers have been lately slain. If you go on like this, what will it lead to?" The two nephews bowed low and acknowledged their fault.

The Emperor asked, "Which of you is older?" Zhang Bao replied, "I am, by one year." The Emperor commanded Guan Xing to honor Zhang Bao as elder brother, and the two sealed the pledge by breaking an arrow in front of the royal tent, vowing always to help one another. The Emperor placed Wu Ban in the vanguard and ordered Zhang Bao and Guan Xing to serve as his guards. By water and land the western force advanced: war-junks parallel to the cavalry, a vast tide bearing down on the

却说范疆、张达将张飞首级，投献吴侯，细告前事。孙权听罢，收了二人，乃谓百官曰："今刘玄德即了帝位，统精兵七十余万，御驾亲征，其势甚大，如之奈何？"百官尽皆失色，面面相觑。诸葛瑾出曰："某食君侯之禄久矣，无可报效，愿舍残生，去见蜀主，以利害说之，使两国相和，共讨曹丕之罪。"权大喜，即遣诸葛瑾为使，来说先主罢兵。

正是：

两国相争通使命，一言解难赖行人。

未知诸葛瑾此去如何，且看下文分解。

汉英经典文库

Southland.

*　*　*

Meanwhile, Fan Jiang and Zhang Da had transported Zhang Fei's head to Sun Quan. Hearing their account of the incident, the lord of the south accepted them and then addressed his officials: "Liu Bei has assumed the imperial throne, and now seven hundred thousand seasoned troops under his personal command are marching toward us. How shall we meet this mighty force?" The officials paled and stared at one another helplessly. Zhuge Jin came forward and said, "Long have I enjoyed Your Lordship's bounty without having rendered due service. I wish, whatever the risk, to go to meet the sovereign of the Riverlands and persuade him of the advantage of restoring friendship between our two states, that we may jointly scourge Cao Pi for his crimes." Well pleased, Sun Quan sent Zhuge Jin as his representative to persuade the Emperor to halt his armies. Indeed:

> A man was sent to the power bent on war;
> All hopes for peace rested with the message-bearer.[11]

What was the fate of Zhuge Jin's mission?

Read on.

第八十二回

孙权降魏受九锡　先主征吴赏六军

　　却说章武元年秋八月，先主起大军至夔关，驾屯白帝城。前队军马已出川口。近臣奏曰："吴使诸葛瑾至。"先主传旨教休放人。黄权奏曰："瑾弟在蜀为相，必有事而来。陛下何故绝之？当召人，看他言词。可从则从；如不可，则就借彼口说与孙权，令知问罪有名也。"先主从之，召瑾入城。瑾拜伏于地。先主问曰："子瑜远来，有何事故？"瑾曰："臣弟久事陛下，臣故不避斧钺，特来奏荆州之事：前者，关公在荆州时，吴侯数次求亲，关公不允。后关公取襄阳，曹操屡次致书吴侯，使袭荆州；吴侯本不肯许，因吕蒙与关公不睦，故擅自兴兵，误成大事。今吴侯悔之不及。此乃吕蒙之罪，非吴侯之过也。今吕蒙已死，冤仇已息。孙夫人一向思归。今吴侯令臣为使，愿送归夫人，缚还降将，并将荆州仍旧交还，永结盟好，共灭曹丕，以正篡逆之

Chapter 82

Sun Quan Submits to Wei, Receives the Nine Dignities
The First Ruler Marches on Wu, Rewards All Armies

In autumn, during the eighth month of the first year of Zhang Wu, the Emperor's army reached Kui Pass and pitched camp at the town of Baidi (which means "White Emperor"); ahead, vanguard squads had already passed beyond Riverlands territory. A close attendant informed the Emperor that Zhuge Jin had come. The Emperor declined to receive the Southland envoy, but Huang Quan said, "Jin is the older brother of Your Majesty's own prime minister. He has not come for naught, and he should be received. Let's hear him out. Perhaps we can satisfy his request. At the least, we can use him to inform Sun Quan that we intend to make him answer for his crime." On this advice the Emperor called Zhuge Jin into Baidi.

Zhuge Jin prostrated himself before the Emperor, who asked him, "What is the purpose of this visit?" Jin replied, "My younger brother has long served Your Majesty. I come today — even at the risk of execution — to put the question of Jingzhou before you once again. While Lord Guan held Jingzhou, Lord Sun of the Southland made several offers of alliance through marriage, which were always refused. After Lord Guan captured Xiangyang, Cao Cao sent several letters to Lord Sun urging him to attack Jingzhou.[1] Lord Sun refused but Lü Meng, whose relations with Lord Guan were never good, took action against him without Lord Sun's authorization. Lü Meng thus created an unfortunate incident, which Lord Sun deeply regrets; yet the fault was Lü Meng's, not my lord's. Now that Lü Meng is dead, the quarrel between us ends. Moreover, Lady Sun thinks only of returning to her husband.[2] Lord Sun has sent me here, therefore, to communicate our desire to deliver Lady Sun and to repatriate those commanders of Lord Guan's who surrendered to us. Finally, we desire to restore Jingzhou to you to seal our amity in perpetu-

罪。"先主怒曰："汝东吴害了朕弟，今日敢以巧言来说乎！"瑾曰："臣请以轻重大小之事，与陛下论之：陛下乃汉朝皇叔，今汉帝已被曹丕篡夺，不思剿除；却为异姓之亲，而屈万乘之尊：是舍大义而就小义也。中原乃海内之地，两都皆大汉创业之方，陛下不敢，而但争荆州：是弃重而取轻也。天下皆知陛下即位，必兴汉室，恢复山河；今陛下置魏不问，反欲伐吴：窃为陛下不取。"先主大怒曰："杀吾弟之仇，不共戴天！欲朕罢兵，除死方休！不看丞相之面，先斩汝首！今且放汝回去，说与孙权：洗颈就戮！"诸葛瑾见先主不听，只得自回江南。

却说张昭见孙权曰："诸葛子瑜知蜀兵势大，故假以请和为辞，欲背吴入蜀。此去必不回矣。"权曰："孤与子瑜，有生死不易之盟；孤不负子瑜，子瑜亦不负孤。昔子瑜在柴桑时，孔明来吴，孤欲使子瑜留之。子瑜曰：'弟已事玄德，义无二心；弟之不留，犹瑾之不往。'其言足贯神明。今日岂肯降蜀乎？孤与子瑜可谓神交，非外言所得间也。"正言间，忽报诸葛瑾回。权曰："孤言若何？"张昭满面羞惭而退。瑾见孙权，言先主不肯通和

ity that we may strive to eliminate the traitor and usurper Cao Pi."

The Emperor retorted hotly, "You southerners murdered our brother. Don't ply us with clever arguments!" But Zhuge Jin continued, "Allow me to weigh the merits of the case. Your Majesty is an imperial uncle of the Han; the Han Emperor has been unlawfully deprived of his throne by Cao Pi. Yet instead of dedicating yourself to eliminating the traitors, you compromise your imperial dignity for a kinsman by oath, not by blood, and thereby forsake a sacred obligation for a lesser one. The northern heartland is the core of the realm; Chang'an and Luoyang are the recognized capitals of Han. Your Majesty, forsaking the north to fight for Jingzhou means forsaking what is important to pursue what is petty. The whole empire knows that by assuming the throne you could revive the Han and bring the mountains and rivers of this land within its rule once again. I venture to advise Your Majesty not to ignore Wei in order to wage war against Wu."

In a fury the Emperor said, "That enemy who slew my brother will never share one sky with us. Nothing — save my death — will stop these troops. Were not the prime minister your brother, you would have already lost your head. However, you may return and tell Sun Quan to wash his neck: the executioner is coming." Thus, the Emperor stood firm, and Zhuge Jin betook himself home to the Southland.

* * *

Zhang Zhao said to Sun Quan, "Zhuge Jin knows the strength of the Riverlands army and intends to defect. His peace mission is a cover. He will not be back." Sun Quan replied, "Zhuge Jin and I are fast friends, friends to the death. He would never betray me, nor I him. The last time Kongming came to Chaisang, Jin was here. I tried to get him to win his brother over, but he said, 'My brother serves Xuande with single-minded loyalty. He could no more remain with us than I could go over to them.' Such words even the gods can hear. Zhuge Jin would never submit to the Riverlands. Our sacred friendship stands proof against outside intrusion." As he was speaking, Zhuge Jin returned. "You see?" Sun Quan said, and Zhang Zhao retreated shamefacedly.

Sun Quan received Zhuge Jin, who told him that the Emperor had rejected reconciliation. Alarmed, Sun Quan said, "In that case, the

之意。权大惊曰:"若如此,则江南危矣!"阶下一人进曰:"某有一计,可解此危。"视之,乃中大夫赵咨也。权曰:"德度有何良策?"咨曰:"主公可作一表,某愿为使,往见魏帝曹丕,陈说利害,使袭汉中,则蜀兵自危矣。"权曰:"此计最善。但卿此去,休失了东吴气象。"咨曰:"若有些小差失,即投江而死,安有面目见江南人物乎!"

权大喜,即写表称臣,令赵咨为使。星夜到了许都,先见太尉贾诩等,并大小官僚。次日早朝,贾诩出班奏曰:"东吴遣中大夫赵咨上表。"曹丕笑曰:"此欲退蜀兵故也。"即令召入。咨拜伏于丹墀。丕览表毕,遂问咨曰:"吴侯乃何如主也?"咨曰:"聪明、仁智、雄略之主也。"丕笑曰:"卿褒奖毋乃太甚?"咨曰:"臣非过誉也。吴侯纳鲁肃于凡品,是其聪也;拔吕蒙于行阵,是其明也;获于禁而不害,是其仁也;取荆州兵不血刃,是其智也;据三江虎视天下,是其雄也;屈身于陛下,是其略也:以此论之,岂不为聪明、仁智、雄略之主乎?"丕又问曰:"吴主颇知学乎?"咨曰:"吴主浮江万艘,带甲百万,任贤使能,志存经略;

Southland may fall." But below the platform a man stepped forth and said, I have a plan to avert the danger." It was Zhao Zi, a ranking adviser at court. "What plan?" Sun Quan asked. "Let Your Lordship declare submission to Cao Pi, Emperor of Wei. Delegate me to deliver the petition, and I will show him that his advantage lies in attacking Hanzhong. That will exert pressure on the Riverlands army." Sun Quan responded, "An excellent plan. But do not lose the Southland's honor on this trip." Zhao Zi replied, "I would throw myself into the river first, for I could never face my countrymen if I committed the least fault in this."

Sun Quan was delighted. He wrote the memorial declaring his allegiance to the Emperor, Cao Pi, and Zhao Zi bore it swiftly to Xuchang. There he was received by Grand Commandant Jia Xu and a number of major and minor officials. The next day at morning court Jia Xu stepped forth from the ranks and addressed the throne: "The Southland has sent Senior Adviser Zhao Zi to present a memorial." Cao Pi smiled and said, "That's because they want the army of Shu driven back." He summoned the envoy, who threw himself to the ground in the vermillion courtyard of the palace.

After reading the memorial, Cao Pi asked Zhao Zi, "What manner of master is the lord of the Southland?" A man of understanding and insight, humanity and wisdom, valor and military judgment," was the reply. Cao Pi smiled and said, "Perhaps you overpraise him?" Zhao Zi said, "I cannot too much honor my lord. He took Lu Su, a man of ordinary rank, into his confidence: that shows his understanding. He raised up Lü Meng from the ranks of the army: that shows his insight. He seized Yu Jin but spared him: that shows his humanity. He captured Jingzhou without staining his swords: that shows his wisdom. From the vantage of his river-girded realm he has held the empire in awe: that shows his valor. And now he submits to Your Majesty's authority: that shows his judgment. He thus proves no less than all I claim."

Next, Cao Pi asked him, "And is he also a man of learning?" "Lord Sun," Zhao Zi replied, "has a fleet of ten thousand ships and a million men under arms. The men serving him are honest and able. He concerns himself with administrative order, and with what leisure he has he reads

1995

少有余闲，博览书传，历观史籍，采其大旨，不效书生寻章摘句而已。"丕曰："朕欲伐吴，可乎？"咨曰："大国有征伐之兵，小国有御备之策。"丕曰："吴畏魏乎？"咨曰："带甲百万，江汉为池，何畏之有？"丕曰："东吴如大夫者几人？"咨曰："聪明特达者八九十人；如臣之辈，车载斗量，不可胜数。"丕叹曰："'使于四方，不辱君命'，卿可以当之矣。"

于是即降诏，命太常卿邢贞赍册封孙权为吴王，加九锡。赵咨谢恩出城。大夫刘晔谏曰："今孙权惧蜀兵之势，故来请降。以臣愚见：蜀、吴交兵，乃天亡之也；今若遣上将提数万之兵，渡江袭之，蜀攻其外，魏攻其内，吴国之亡，不出旬日。吴亡则蜀孤矣。陛下何不早图之？"丕曰："孙权既以礼服朕，朕若攻之，是沮天下欲降者之心；不若纳之为是。"刘晔又曰："孙权虽有雄才，乃残汉骠骑将军、南昌侯之职。官轻则势微，尚有畏中原之心；若加以王位，则去陛下一阶耳。今陛下信其诈降，崇其位号以封殖之，是与虎添翼也。"丕曰："不然。朕不助吴，亦不助蜀。待看吴、蜀交兵，若灭一国，止存一国，那时除之，有何难

the classics and commentaries and studies historical records, extracting their main ideas; he never follows the trifling example of pedantic scholars." Cao Pi responded, "I want to invade the south. Will I succeed?" Zhao Zi answered, "If your great kingdom has the forces for a campaign, our lesser kingdom has strategies for meeting the threat." "Does Wu fear Wei?" Cao Pi asked. "Why should we," Zhao Zi replied, "with a million men under arms and the Great River for our moat?" Cao Pi went on, "And how many like you are there in the Southland?" "We have eighty or ninety men of insight, vision, and accomplishment," he replied. "As for men like me, we come in cartloads, in bushels." "'Where'er you send him round the land, he never fails his king's command' — the saying fits you," Cao Pi concluded.

Cao Pi issued an edict ordering Master of Ceremonies Xing Zhen to deliver documents honoring Sun Quan as king of the Southland and investing him with the Nine Dignities. Zhao Zi gave thanks for this gracious generosity and left the capital. A high courtier, Liu Ye, protested, "Sun Quan fears the army of Shu, which is why he offered to submit. My humble opinion is that war between those two kingdoms is Heaven's way of destroying them. This is the time to send your best commanders with tens of thousands of troops across the river to surprise Wu. Hit by Shu, their declared enemy, and Wei, their supposed ally, the Southland kingdom should fall in ten days' time; Shu will then be isolated. May Your Majesty take the necessary steps without delay."

Cao Pi responded, "Sun Quan has officially submitted. To attack him will discourage others who might follow his example. The correct course is to accept his surrender." Liu Ye went on, "Brave and capable as Sun Quan is, under the fallen Han he was merely a Flying Cavalry general and lord of Nanchang. His offices were not high and so his influence was limited, yet still the northern lands stand in awe of him. Raise him now to king, and he will be but one step removed from Your Majesty. To put faith in Sun Quan's false surrender, augment his titles, and enrich him with fiefs is but to serve the enemy's ends, to 'lend the tiger wings,' as they say." "I disagree," Cao Pi replied. "I mean to help neither Wu nor Shu but to wait to destroy the one that survives their conflict. How easy it will be then! My mind is made up. Do not refer to this again." With that, Cao

1997

哉？朕意已决，卿勿复言。"遂命太常卿邢贞同赵咨捧执册锡，径至东吴。

却说孙权聚集百官，商议御蜀兵之策。忽报："魏帝封主公为王，礼当远接。"顾雍谏曰："主公宜自称上将军、九州伯之位，不当受魏帝封爵。"权曰："当日沛公受项羽之封，盖因时也；何故却之？"遂率百官出城迎接。邢贞自恃上国天使，入门不下车。张昭大怒，厉声曰："礼无不敬，法无不肃，而君敢自尊大，岂以江南无方寸之刃耶？"邢贞慌忙下车，与孙权相见，并车入城。忽车后一人放声哭曰："吾等不能奋身舍命，为主并魏吞蜀，乃令主公受人封爵，不亦辱乎！"众视之，乃徐盛也。邢贞闻之，叹曰："江东将相如此，终非久在人下者也！"

却说孙权受了封爵，众文武官僚拜贺已毕，命收拾美玉明珠等物，遣人赍进谢恩。早有细作报说："蜀主引本国大兵，及蛮王沙摩柯番兵数万，又有洞溪汉将杜路、刘宁二枝兵，水陆并进，声势震天。水路军已出巫口，旱路军已到秭归。"时孙权

Pi ordered Minister of Ceremonies Xing Zhen to accompany Zhao Zi back to the south to present the credentials and ceremonial articles to Sun Quan.

At this time Sun Quan had summoned his court to discuss the Riverlands invasion. Suddenly a courier reported: "The Emperor of Wei honors Lord Sun as king of the Southland. Ceremony requires welcoming his envoy on the road." But the adviser Gu Yong protested: "Your Lordship should declare himself commander in chief and lord of the Nine Provinces and should not accept any title from the Wei emperor." Sun Quan replied, "Did not Liu Bang accept the title king of Han from Xiang Yu? It was appropriate at the time. Why should I refuse this honor?" So saying, he led the court beyond the city wall to welcome the northern envoy.[3]

Xing Zhen felt so confident in his position as imperial emissary that he did not come down from his carriage after passing through the capital gates. Zhang Zhao, angered by this arrogance, shouted at him, "There can be no disrespect in ceremonies, nor levity in protocol. What are these high and mighty ways? Don't think the Southland is a kingdom without swords!" Xing Zhen hurriedly stepped down and was received by Sun Quan, who escorted him into the city. But someone behind the carriage wailed, "Oh, shame! To allow our lord to accept rank and title from others when we should rouse ourselves and lay down our lives to annex both kingdoms, Wei and Shu, for him!" The assembly turned to Xu Sheng. Hearing this, Xing Zhen reflected, "If the Southland has such generals and ministers, it will never remain under our rule."

In the end, Sun Quan accepted the kingship from Cao Pi. After receiving the congratulations of the entire court, Sun Quan gathered jade and pearls and other articles, which he sent to Xuchang to express his gratitude. But spies had already reported to him: "The lord of Shu is marching against us, leading a mighty army of his own together with tens of thousands of Miao and Yao tribesmen under Chief Shamoke. In addition, they have naval and land forces under Du Lu and Liu Ning, two Han generals from Dongxi. The very heavens are atremble from the scale of this army. The naval force has already come through Wu Gorge, and the land force is now at Zigui."

虽登王位,奈魏主不肯接应,乃问文武曰:"蜀兵势大,当复如何?"众皆默然。权叹曰:"周郎之后有鲁肃;鲁肃之后有吕蒙;今吕蒙已亡,无人与孤分忧也!"言未毕,忽班部中一少年将,奋然而出,伏地奏曰:"臣虽年幼,颇习兵书。愿乞数万之兵,以破蜀兵。"权视之,乃孙桓也。桓字叔武,其父名河,本姓俞氏,孙策爱之,赐姓孙,因此亦系吴王宗族;河生四子,桓居其长,弓马熟娴,常从吴王征讨,累立奇功,官授武卫都尉;时年二十五岁。权曰:"汝有何策胜之?"桓曰:"臣有大将二员:一名李异,一名谢旌,俱有万夫不当之勇。乞数万之众,往擒刘备。"权曰:"侄虽英勇,争奈年幼;必得一人相助,方可。"虎威将军朱然出曰:"臣愿与小将军同擒刘备。"权许之,遂点水陆军五万,封孙桓为左都督,朱然为右都督,即日起兵。哨马探得蜀兵已至宜都下寨,孙桓引二万五千军马,屯于宜都界口,前后分作三营,以拒蜀兵。

　　却说蜀将吴班领先锋之印,自出川以来,所到之处,望风而降,兵不血刃,直到宜都;探知孙桓在彼下寨,飞奏先主。时先主已到秭归,闻奏怒曰:"量此小儿,安敢与朕抗耶!"关兴奏曰:"既孙权令此子为将,不劳陛下遣大将,臣愿往擒之。"先主

Although now a vassal king, Sun Quan despaired of significant help from the Wei ruler. He asked his advisers, "How do we meet this formidable force of Shu?" No one had an answer. Sun Quan sighed aloud and said, "After Zhou Yu we had Lu Su; and after Lu Su, Lü Meng. But Lü Meng is dead, and there is no one now to share my trials." Even as he spoke, a young commander stepped forward boldly, touched his head to the ground, and said to the king, "Though I am young, I know something of the art of war. I would like to ask for troops — several tens of thousands — with which I will defeat the Riverlands armies." Sun Quan regarded the speaker. It was Sun Huan (Shuwu). His real father was Yu He. Sun Ce had kindly allowed Yu He to assume the surname Sun and affiliate with the clan. Sun Huan was the eldest of Sun He's four sons, expert in both marksmanship and horsemanship. He frequently followed the Southland king on his campaigns and had striking achievements to his credit, for which he had been appointed commander of the Military Guard. Sun Huan was twenty-five years old.

"What plan do you have?" Sun Quan asked Sun Huan. "I have two commanders under me," he replied, "Li Yi and Xie Jing — both men of unconquerable courage. I ask for thirty to fifty thousand troops to take Liu Bei alive." Sun Quan responded, "Despite your splendid courage, nephew, you are still too young. Find someone to assist you, and I will grant your request." Tiger General Zhu Ran came forward and said, "Let me accompany the young commander to seize Liu Bei." Sun Quan approved and detailed fifty thousand marine and ground troops. He appointed Sun Huan field marshal of the Left and Zhu Ran field marshal of the Right and began the mobilization. Scouts had already brought word that Riverlands troops were camped at Yidu. Sun Huan took twenty-five thousand men and stationed them at the access point to Yidu, where they drew up a line of three camps to repel the Riverlanders.

The commander of the Riverlands vanguard, Wu Ban, had overawed all opposition since entering Southland territory and had reached Yidu by this time without bloodying a single sword. Informed that Sun Huan had camped there, Wu Ban sent word to the Emperor, who was already in Zigui. Angered, the Emperor said, "How dare that brat Sun Huan oppose us!" Guan Xing then addressed the Emperor: "If Sun Quan saw fit to

曰:"朕正欲观汝壮气。"即命关兴前往。兴拜辞欲行,张苞出曰:"既关兴前去讨贼,臣愿同行。"先主曰:"二侄同行甚妙;但须谨慎,不可造次。"

二人拜辞先主,会合先锋,一同进兵,列成阵势。孙桓听知蜀兵大至,合寨多起。两阵对圆,桓领李异、谢旌立马于门旗之下,见蜀营中,拥出二员大将,皆银盔银铠,白马白旗:上首张苞挺丈八点钢矛,下首关兴横着大砍刀。苞大骂曰:"孙桓竖子!死在临时,尚敢抗拒天兵乎!"桓亦骂曰:"汝父已作无头之鬼;今汝又来讨死,好生不智!"张苞大怒,挺枪直取孙桓。桓背后谢旌,骤马来迎。两将战有三十余合,旌败走,苞乘胜赶来。李异见谢旌败了,慌忙拍马轮蘸金斧接战。张苞与战二十余合,不分胜负。吴军中裨将谭雄,见张苞英勇,李异不能胜,却放一冷箭,正射中张苞所骑之马。那马负痛奔回本阵,未到门旗边,扑地便倒,将张苞掀在地上。李异急向前轮起大斧,望张苞脑袋便砍。忽一道红光闪处,李异头早落地。——原来关兴见张苞马回,正待接应,忽见张苞马倒,李异赶来,兴大喝一声,劈李异于马下,救了张苞。乘势掩杀,孙桓大败。各自鸣金收军。

send this boy as his commander, Your Majesty need not bother sending a top general against him. Allow me to go and capture him." "I am eager for a display of your mettle!" the Emperor responded and ordered Guan Xing to proceed forthwith. As Guan Xing was taking leave, Zhang Bao stepped forth and said, "I wish to join him in punishing the traitors." The Emperor replied, "Although it is a fitting touch, my nephews, for both of you to go, caution is essential. Go, but do not act in haste."

The two young warriors bade the Emperor good-bye and, joining as a vanguard, set out together, their troops in fine formation. Sun Huan soon heard that the Riverlands forces had arrived en masse and established themselves in a string of encampments. The armies formed opposing lines, and Sun Huan led Li Yi and Xie Jing on their mounts to the entrance to his formation. He saw two leading commanders emerge from the Riverlands camp. Each wore a silver-gilt helmet and armor and had a white horse and white banner: Zhang Bao menacingly raised his eighteen-span spear, and Guan Xing held his great sword leveled for combat.

Zhang Bao denounced Sun Huan: "Little scamp! Prepare to die if you still dare to stand against Heaven's ordained army!" Sun Huan returned the taunt: "Your father is already a headless ghost. And now you come courting death — in all folly!" Zhang Bao raised his spear and made for Sun Huan. From behind Sun Huan, Xie Jing sprang forward and fought more than thirty bouts with Zhang Bao, then fled. Zhang Bao pursued, pressing his advantage. Li Yi, seeing Xie Jing defeated, flourished his gilt-metal axe and rushed against Zhang Bao. But neither prevailed in a battle lasting some twenty passes.

Tan Xiong, a lieutenant commander in the Southland army, saw that Li Yi could not best his brave opponent and so shot at him from a concealed position. But the arrow hit Zhang Bao's horse, and sent the wounded animal galloping back. It collapsed before it had reached the home line, throwing Zhang Bao to the ground. Li Yi again rushed forward wheeling his axe and aimed a blow at Zhang Bao's head. But a streak of red cut the air, and Li Yu's head fell first. Guan Xing had seen Zhang Bao racing back and was about to join the fight himself, when he saw the rider fall and Li Yi approach for the kill. Guan Xing shouted, then cut down Li Yi, saving Zhang Bao's life. Guan Xing pressed the attack, and Sun Huan

次日，孙桓又引军来。张苞、关兴齐出。关兴立马于阵前，单搦孙桓交锋。桓大怒，拍马轮刀，与关兴战三十余合，气力不加，大败回阵。二小将追杀入营，吴班引着张南、冯习驱兵掩杀。张苞奋勇当先，杀入吴军，正遇谢旌，被苞一矛刺死。吴军四散奔走。蜀将得胜收兵，只不见了关兴。张苞大惊曰："安国有失，吾不独生！"言讫，绰枪上马。寻不数里，只见关兴左手提刀，右手活挟一将。苞问曰："此是何人？"兴笑答曰："吾在乱军中，正遇仇人，故生擒来。"苞视之，乃昨日放冷箭的谭雄也。苞大喜，同回本营，斩首沥血，祭了死马。遂写表差人赴先主处报捷。

孙桓折了李异、谢旌、谭雄等许多将士，力穷势孤，不能抵敌，即差人回吴求救。蜀将张南、冯习谓吴班曰："目今吴兵势败，正好乘虚劫寨。"班曰："孙桓虽然折了许多将士，朱然水军现今结营江上，未曾损折。今日若去劫寨，倘水军上岸，断我归路，如之奈何？"南曰："此事至易：可教关、张二将军，各引五千军伏于山谷中；如朱然来救，左右两军齐出夹攻，必然取胜。"班曰："不如先使小卒诈作降兵，却将劫寨事告与朱然；然见火

2005

suffered a great defeat. Finally, each side recalled its men.

The next day Sun Huan again appeared in force; Zhang Bao and Guan Xing advanced toward him. Guan Xing rode into position before his line and, standing alone, challenged Sun Huan. Roused to fury, Sun Huan raced toward him, wheeling his sword. After more than thirty bouts with Guan Xing, Sun Huan retired in defeat, exhausted. The two young commanders, Zhang Bao and Guan Xing, pursued Sun Huan and fought their way into his base camp, while Wu Ban led Zhang Nan and Feng Xi in a swift assault on the southerners. Zhang Bao, swept forward by his boundless courage, had crossed into the southern army's line when Xie Jing confronted him. Zhang Bao speared him with one thrust. The Southland forces fled every which way; the Riverlands army recalled its victorious troops. But Guan Xing was not to be seen.

In alarm, Zhang Bao said, "I cannot live without Guan Xing," and remounted, holding his spear. After riding several *li* in search of Guan Xing, Zhang Bao came upon him holding a sword in one hand and an enemy commander fast in the other. "Who is that?" Zhang Bao asked him. Guan Xing smiled as he replied, "I found this foe in the thick of battle and took him alive." Zhang Bao recognized Tan Xiong, the archer who had shot at him from ambush the day before, and took pleasure in bringing the prisoner back to camp, where Bao beheaded him and offered the drained blood in sacrifice to his dead horse. A report of the victory was sent to the Emperor.

The loss of commanders Li Yi, Xie Jing, and Tan Xiong as well as a number of officers and men had left Sun Huan too weak to resist; he called for help from the Southland. Riverlands commanders Zhang Nan and Feng Xi said to Wu Ban, "The southern army is through. This is the moment to raid their camps." Wu Ban answered, "Sun Huan has taken great losses, but Zhu Ran's marine force remains intact on the river. If we raid their camps, the sailors could come ashore and cut off our retreat — what then?" "That's easy enough," Zhang Nan answered. "Have commanders Zhang Bao and Guan Xing place five thousand each in ambush in the valleys. If Zhu Ran comes, he'll be trapped between our two forces and the day will be ours." Wu Ban said, "Why not first send a few soldiers to Zhu Ran to feign surrender and inform him of our planned

起,必来救应,却令伏兵击之,则大事济矣。"冯习等大喜,遂依计而行。

却说朱然听知孙桓损兵折将,正欲来救,忽伏路军引几个小卒上船投降。然问之,小卒曰:"我等是冯习帐下士卒,因赏罚不明,待来投降,就报机密。"然曰:"所报何事?"小卒曰:"今晚冯习乘虚要劫孙将军营寨,约定举火为号。"朱然听毕,即使人报知孙桓。报事人行至半途,被关兴杀了。朱然一面商议,欲引兵去救应孙桓。部将崔禹曰:"小卒之言,未可深信。倘有疏虞,水陆二军尽皆休矣。将军只宜稳守水寨,某愿替将军一行。"然从之,遂令崔禹引一万军前去。是夜,冯习、张南、吴班分兵三路,直杀入孙桓寨中,四面火起,吴兵大乱,寻路奔走。

且说崔禹正行之间,忽见火起,急催兵前进。刚才转过山来,忽山谷中鼓声大震:左边关兴,右边张苞,两路夹攻。崔禹大惊,方欲奔走,正遇张苞;交马只一合,被苞生擒而回。朱然听知危急,将船往下水退五六十里去了。孙桓引败军逃走,问部将曰:"前去何处城坚粮广?"部将曰:"此去正北彝陵城,可以屯兵。"桓引败军急望彝陵而走。方进得城,吴班等追至,将城四面围定。关兴、张苞等解崔禹到秭归来。先主大喜,传旨将

raid? When Zhu Ran sees the camps afire, he will go to relieve them and we can spring our ambush then. Our triumph will be complete." Feng Xi and the other leaders were satisfied with the plan and proceeded at once to carry it out.

Zhu Ran was preparing to relieve Sun Huan when his sentries led the false defectors onto his boat. When the soldiers expressed their desire to surrender, Zhu Ran asked for an explanation. "We are Feng Xi's men," one of them said. "Because of his unfair rewards and punishments, we have come to submit — and to report an important secret as well." "What secret?" Zhu Ran asked. One of the soldiers continued, "Tonight Feng Xi wants to raid General Sun Huan's base camp. Fire will be the signal." Zhu Ran immediately forwarded this information to Sun Huan; his messenger was intercepted by Guan Xing and killed. Zhu Ran met with his commanders to plan the rescue of Sun Huan. Lieutenant Commander Cui Yu said to Zhu Ran, "Their story is doubtful. If this is a trick, our marine and land forces will both be done for. General, I suggest you defend our naval camp and let me go in your place." Zhu Ran approved this plan and gave Cui Yu a command of ten thousand. That night Feng Xi, Zhang Nan, and Wu Ban divided their Riverlands men into three armies and fell upon Sun Huan's camp. Fires rose on all sides as the southern troops panicked and fled.

In the meantime, Cui Yu had been advancing. Seeing the fires, he pressed forward and rounded a hill. Suddenly the beating of drums animated the valley as Zhang Bao and Guan Xing sprang their two-sided ambush. Cui Yu struggled to escape but found himself face to face with Zhang Bao, who took him prisoner after a single exchange of arms. Zhu Ran soon learned of this unfavorable turn of events and withdrew his fleet fifty or sixty *li* downstream. Sun Huan, escaping with his defeated men, asked a lieutenant, "Is there a stout-walled town with ample provisions anywhere ahead of us?" The lieutenant replied, "Due north is Yiling. We can station there." Sun Huan hurried in that direction; he had hardly entered the town, when Wu Ban's pursuit arrived and encircled the walls.

Guan Xing and Zhang Bao took Cui Yu to Zigui. The Emperor was delighted and ordered the prisoner beheaded. Afterward he rewarded his

2007

崔禹斩却,大赏三军。自此威风震动,江南诸将无不胆寒。

却说孙桓令人求救于吴王,吴王大惊,即召文武商议曰:"今孙桓受困于彝陵,朱然大败于江中:蜀兵势大,如之奈何?"张昭奏曰:"今诸将虽多物故,然尚有十余人,何虑于刘备?可命韩当为正将,周泰为副将,潘璋为先锋,凌统为合后,甘宁为救应,起兵十万拒之。"权依所奏,即命诸将速行。此时甘宁已患痢疾,带病从征。

却说先主从巫峡建平起,直接彝陵界分,七百余里,连结四十余寨;见关兴、张苞屡立大功,叹曰:"昔日从朕诸将,皆老迈无用矣;复有二侄如此英雄,朕何虑孙权乎!"正言间,忽报韩当、周泰领兵来到。先主方欲遣将迎敌,近臣奏曰:"老将黄忠,引五六人投东吴去了。"先主笑曰:"黄汉升非反叛之人也;因朕失口误言老者无用,彼必不服老,故奋力去相持矣。"即召关兴、张苞曰:"黄汉升此去必然有失。贤侄休辞劳苦,可去相助。略有微功,便可令回,勿使有失。"二小将拜辞先主,引本部军来助黄忠。

army. As a result of this victory, the Emperor was feared throughout the Southland.

*   *   *

The men Sun Huan had sent to ask for help reached the Southland. Astounded at the news they brought, the king of Wu summoned his counselors. "Sun Huan is trapped in Yiling," he told them, "and Zhu Ran was badly defeated on the river. The Riverlands army is indeed formidable. What are we to do?" Zhang Zhao addressed the king: "Although many generals have been lost, more than ten remain. Need we fear Liu Bei? Make Han Dang principal general, Zhou Tai his lieutenant, Pan Zhang vanguard leader, and Ling Tong rear commander; hold Gan Ning in readiness to assist where he's needed, and with one hundred thousand men we can resist them." Sun Quan ordered his commanders to carry out Zhang Zhao's proposal. Though suffering from dysentery, Gan Ning went with the army.

*   *   *

Meanwhile, the First Ruler had created a string of forty camps that stretched from Jianping at Wu Gorge some seventy *li* along the Great River to the vicinity of Yiling. Inspired by the great victories of Guan Xing and Zhang Bao, he exclaimed, "The commanders who have followed me from the early days are getting old; they're not good for much. But now that I have such splendid heroes in these nephews of mine, Sun Quan does not bother me!" At this moment the approach of southern troops under Han Dang and Zhou Tai was reported. The Emperor wanted to send a general to meet them, but an attendant told him, "Our general from the old days, Huang Zhong, has defected to the Southland with five or six men." "He's no turncoat," the Emperor said smiling. "It was a slip of the tongue when I said the old generals were not much use, and Huang Zhong, who will never give in to his years, has hustled off to the front."

The Emperor summoned Zhang Bao and Guan Xing and said to them, "Something is bound to happen to Huang Zhong this time. My worthy nephews, do not shirk hardship. Go after him and help him. After he accomplishes a little something, order him to return. See that nothing happens to him." The two commanders bade the Emperor good-bye and

2009

正是：

　　老臣素矢忠君志，年少能成报国功。

未知黄忠此去如何，且看下文分解。

set out with their men. Indeed:

> The old vassals were steeped in loyalty to their lord;
> The fresh commanders could do great deeds for their land.

What was to be Huang Zhong's fate?[4]

Read on.

2011

第八十三回

战猇亭先主得仇人 守江口书生拜大将

却说章武二年春正月，武威后将军黄忠随先主伐吴；忽闻先主言老将无用，即提刀上马，引亲随五六人，径到彝陵营中。吴班与张南、冯习接入，问曰："老将军此来，有何事故？"忠曰："吾自长沙跟天子到今，多负勤劳。今虽七旬有余，尚食肉十斤，臂开二石之弓，能乘千里之马，未足为老。昨日主上言吾等老迈无用，故来此与东吴交锋，看吾斩将，老也不老！"

正言间，忽报吴兵前部已到，哨马临营。忠奋然而起，出帐上马。冯习等劝曰："老将军且休轻进。"忠不听，纵马而去。吴班令冯习引兵助战。忠在吴军阵前，勒马横刀，单搦先锋潘璋交战。璋引部将史迹出马。迹欺忠年老，挺枪出战；斗不三合，被忠一刀斩于马下。潘璋大怒，挥关公使的青龙刀，来战黄忠。交马数合，不分胜负。忠奋力恶战，璋料敌不过，拨马便

Chapter 83

**Fighting at Xiaoting, the Emperor Takes a Foe
Defending the River, a Scholar Takes Command**

In spring, the first month of the second year of Zhang Wu (A.D. 222), Martial Might, General of the Rear Huang Zhong was marching with the First Ruler against the Southland, when someone told him that the ruler had disparaged the older generals. Zhong took up his sword, leaped to horse, and headed straight for the vanguard camp at Yiling with half a dozen followers. Commanders Wu Ban, Zhang Nan, and Feng Xi welcomed him. "Why have you come, elder general?" they asked. Huang Zhong replied, "I have followed the Son of Heaven through every hardship since we met at Changsha. Today, over seventy, I can still eat ten catties of meat a day, draw a bow two hundred pounds strong, and ride the best of horses. I am not so old. But after our lord cast a slur on us old soldiers the other day, I have come to do battle — to let you see whose heads I will take and whether I should be counted old or not!"

The arrival of the Southland van was reported even while he spoke. As enemy scouts approached the camp, Huang Zhong left the tent with energetic zeal and mounted for battle. Feng Xi and others tried to dissuade him, saying, "Don't plunge into this lightly, elder general." Huang Zhong ignored Feng Xi and rode off. Wu Ban had Feng Xi follow with some troops to support him.

Huang Zhong reined in before the southern line, leveled his sword, and challenged the enemy leader Pan Zhang to single combat. Pan Zhang sent out a lieutenant Shi Ji to answer. Shi Ji scorned Huang Zhong for his years and rode forth, working his spear. But Huang Zhong unhorsed him and killed him in a brief clash. Angered, Pan Zhang spun the dragon blade Lord Guan had once wielded and confronted Huang Zhong. In several exchanges neither prevailed. Huang Zhong fought with vicious fury until Pan Zhong weakened, wheeled, and fled the field. Huang Zhong

走。忠乘势追杀，全胜而回。路逢关兴、张苞。兴曰："我等奉圣旨来助老将军；既已立了功，速请回营。"忠不听。

　　次日，潘璋又来搦战。黄忠奋然上马。兴、苞二人要助战，忠不从；吴班要助战，忠亦不从；只自引五千军出迎。战不数合，璋拖刀便走。忠纵马追之，厉声大叫曰："贼将休走！吾今为关公报仇！"追至三十余里，四面喊声大震，伏兵齐出：右边周泰，左边韩当，前有潘璋，后有凌统，把黄忠困在垓心。忽然狂风大起，忠急退时，山坡上马忠引一军出，一箭射中黄忠肩窝，险些儿落马。吴兵见忠中箭，一齐来攻。忽后面喊声大起，两路军杀来，吴兵溃散，救出黄忠——乃关兴、张苞也。二小将保送黄忠径到御前营中。忠年老血衰，箭疮痛裂，病甚沉重。先主御驾自来看视，抚其背曰："令老将军中伤，朕之过也！"忠曰："臣乃一武夫耳，幸遇陛下。臣今年七十有五，寿亦足矣。望陛下善保龙体，以图中原！"言讫，不省人事。是夜殒于御营。后人有诗叹曰：

　　　　老将说黄忠，收川立大功。

　　　　重披金锁甲，双挽铁胎弓。

　　　　胆气惊河北，威名镇蜀中。

followed up with a murderous assault, then headed back to camp in triumph. On the way, he met Zhang Bao and Guan Xing. Guan Xing said, "Elder general, we bear the sacred imperial command to assist you. Now that you have distinguished yourself, return to camp quickly; we implore you." Huang Zhong would not listen to them.

The next day Pan Zhang again issued his challenge. Zhang Bao and Guan Xing tried to assist, but Huang Zhong refused; nor would he accept Wu Ban's offer of help. Instead, he went out himself with five thousand to meet the enemy. After several bouts Pan Zhang fled, trailing his sword. Huang Zhong galloped after him, crying hotly, "Stand your ground, traitor! Today I will avenge Lord Guan." Huang Zhong had run for thirty *li,* when shouts erupted on all sides and he was caught in an ambush: to his right, Zhou Tai; to his left, Han Dang; in front, Pan Zhang; and behind, Ling Tong. Suddenly a fierce storm began blowing. Huang Zhong moved swiftly to retreat as Ma Zhong guided his mount down one of the hillsides and shot Huang Zhong in the armpit, nearly unhorsing him. At the sight of the wounded enemy leader, the southern troops poured into the field. But war cries rang out behind them; two companies attacked the southerners and broke their mass: Guan Xing and Zhang Bao had saved Huang Zhong.

The two young generals escorted Huang Zhong directly to the royal camp. Lacking the vigor of a younger warrior, Huang Zhong suffered keenly from the open wound and was in mortal danger. The Emperor came to see him and, stroking his back, said, "I am to blame for getting you wounded, elder general." Huang Zhong replied, "I am only a warrior whose great good fortune was to serve Your Majesty. Now at seventy-five, I have lived long enough. I pray Your Majesty will keep his sacred person safe for the coming struggle for the northern heartland." So saying, he lost consciousness and passed away later that night in the royal camp. A poet of later times left these lines in his praise:

> Huang Zhong, veteran general par excellence,
> Won vast renown in the Riverlands campaigns.
> He bore again his ringed and gilded mail;
> His sturdy hands could strain a bow of steel.
> Virile in war, he kept the north in fear;
> His prodigies subdued the western sphere.

2015

临亡头似雪，犹自显英雄。

先主见黄忠气绝，哀伤不已，敕具棺椁，葬于成都。先主叹曰："五虎大将，已亡三人。朕尚不能复仇，深可痛哉！"乃引御林军直至猇亭，大会诸将，分军八路，水陆俱进。水路令黄权领兵，先主自率大军于旱路进发：时章武二年二月中旬也。

韩当、周泰听知先主御驾来征，引兵出迎。两阵对圆，韩当、周泰出马，只见蜀营门旗开处，先主自出，黄罗销金伞盖，左右白旄黄钺，金银旌节，前后围绕。当大叫曰："陛下今为蜀主，何自轻出？倘有疏虞，悔之何及！"先主遥指骂曰："汝等吴狗，伤朕手足，誓不与立于天地之间！"当回顾众将曰："谁敢冲突蜀兵？"部将夏恂，挺枪出马。先主背后张苞挺丈八矛，纵马而出，大喝一声，直取夏恂，恂见苞声若巨雷，心中惊惧；恰待要走，周泰弟周平见恂抵敌不住，挥刀纵马而来。关兴见了，跃马提刀来迎。张苞大喝一声，一矛刺中夏恂，倒撞下马。周平大惊，措手不及，被关兴一刀斩了。二小将便取韩当、周泰。韩、周二人，慌退入阵。先主视之，叹曰："虎父无犬子也！"用御鞭一

Though at the end his head was white as hoar,
He showed himself a hero all the more.

The Emperor grieved inconsolably for Huang Zhong. He had a coffin prepared for interment in Chengdu. With a sigh the Emperor said, "Of the 'Five Tiger Generals,' three are gone. In sorrow I reflect that they remain unavenged." So saying, he led the Imperial Guard directly to Xiaoting for a general meeting with his generals and commanders. Afterward he divided his forces into eight field armies, which advanced by land and by water. Huang Quan commanded the naval forces; the Emperor himself led the march of the land armies. It was the middle of the second month, Zhang Wu 2 (A.D. 222).

When Han Dang and Zhou Tai learned of the Emperor's approach, they advanced to oppose him. The two armies drew up in formation, and Han Dang and Zhou Tai rode forth. They watched the Emperor emerge from the bannered entrance to his camp: above him a yellow silk gold-woven canopy; to his left, a white yak-tail banner; to his right, a golden battle-axe; before him and behind, golden and silver insignia. Han Dang called out, "Your Majesty is now the sovereign of Shu; why risk your person so lightly? What if something unforeseen happens? What use will regrets be then?" The Emperor shook his finger at the southern generals as he shouted, "Dogs of Wu! I'll never share this earth with my brother's murderers!" Han Dang turned to his commanders and said, "Who dares set upon them?" Lieutenant Xia Xun cocked his spear and rode out. Behind the Emperor, Zhang Bao held out his eighteen-span spear and, shouting lustily, charged into the field, making straight for Xia Xun. Xia Xun, quaking from the thunderous cry, started to flee; but Zhou Ping, the younger brother of Zhou Tai, raced out, his sword whirling, to support the wavering Xia Xun. Guan Xing, who had been watching the action unfold, now raised his sword and galloped into the fray. At this moment Zhang Bao vented a fierce cry and speared Xia Xun, unhorsing him. Zhou Ping panicked and lost his balance; Guan Xing laid him low with a stroke of his sword.

Next, the two young commanders made for Han Dang and Zhou Tai and sent them scrambling back to their line. Observing the combat, the Emperor exclaimed, "Tigers beget tigers!" Then, answering the motion

指，蜀兵一齐掩杀过去，吴兵大败。那八路兵，势如泉涌，杀的那吴军尸横遍野，血流成河。

却说甘宁正在船中养病，听知蜀兵大至，火急上马，正遇一彪蛮兵，人皆披发跣足，皆使弓弩长枪，搪牌刀斧；为首乃是番王沙摩柯，生得面如噀血，碧眼突出，使一个铁蒺藜骨朵，腰带两张弓，威风抖擞。甘宁见其势大，不敢交锋，拨马而走；被沙摩柯一箭射中头颅。宁带箭而走，到于富池口，坐于大树之下而死。树上群鸦数百，围绕其尸。吴王闻之，哀痛不已，具礼厚葬，立庙祭祀。后人有诗叹曰：

　　吴郡甘兴霸，长江锦幔舟。

　　酬君重知已，报友化仇雠。

　　劫寨将轻骑，驱兵饮巨瓯。

　　神鸦能显圣，香火永千秋。

却说先主乘势追杀，遂得猇亭。吴兵四散逃走。先主收兵，只不见关兴。先主慌令张苞等四面跟寻。原来关兴杀入吴阵，正遇仇人潘璋，骤马追之。璋大惊，奔入山谷内，不知所往。兴

of his whip, the soldiers of Shu poured onto the field and slaughtered the men of Wu. The eight western armies advanced like a mighty flood, strewing the ground with enemy corpses. The blood ran in rivers.

*　*　*

Recuperating from his wounds aboard ship, Gan Ning heard of the westerners' advance. He mounted at once and rode for the front. On the way, he encountered the western contingent of warriors from the Man nation. All wore their hair loose and went barefoot. Their weapons consisted of bows, crossbows, long spears, shields, swords, and battle-axes. The leader of these soldiers was the Qiang king, Shamoke. Shamoke had a deep bloodshot complexion and bulging greenish eyes. He wielded a steel-spiked mace and carried two bows at his waist; he flaunted his martial bearing. Unwilling to engage so formidable an opponent, Gan Ning swung his horse around and took flight; but Shamoke shot an arrow into his skull. With the arrow lodged in his head, Gan Ning rode to Fuchikou, sat down beneath a tree, and died. Strangely, hundreds of crows flew out of the branches and circled his corpse. King Sun Quan of Wu, grief-stricken, had him sumptuously buried. Afterward he built a temple in Gan Ning's honor so that sacrifices and services could be performed. A poet of later times wrote these lines in Gan Ning's praise:

> First among Southland heroes, Gan Xingba —
> Feared along the Yangzi for his silken sails —
> Pledged fealty to the lord who knew his worth,
> And befriended the son of the man he slew.
> Before his famous raid on Cao Cao's camp,[1]
> He let his fighting men carouse their fill.
> Gan Ning's ghost ensouled those sacred crows;
> His temple flame shall burn forevermore.

The Emperor, riding on the momentum of his victory, captured Xiaoting. Their ranks broken, the southern troops ran for their lives. But when the Emperor called a halt, he could not find Guan Xing; anxiously he sent Zhang Bao and others to make a search.

This is what had happened to Guan Xing. After penetrating the southern battle line, he met up with his archenemy Pan Zhang and raced after him. Pan Zhang panicked and darted into a ravine, where he soon lost

寻思只在山里，往来寻觅不见。看看天晚，迷踪失路。幸得星月有光，追至山僻之间，时已二更，到一庄上，下马叩门。一老者出问何人。兴曰："吾是战将，迷路到此，求一饭充饥。"老人引入，兴见堂内点着明烛，中堂绘画关公神像。兴大哭而拜。老人问曰："将军何故哭拜？"兴曰："此吾父也。"老人闻言，即便下拜。兴曰："何故供养吾父？"老人答曰："此间皆是尊神地方。在生之日，家家侍奉，何况今日为神乎？老夫只望蜀兵早早报仇。今将军到此，百姓有福矣。"遂置酒食待之，卸鞍喂马。

三更已后，忽门外又一人击户。老人出而问之，乃吴将潘璋亦来投宿。恰入草堂，关兴见了，按剑大喝曰："歹贼休走！"璋回身便出。忽门外一人，面如重枣，丹凤眼，卧蚕眉，飘三缕美髯，绿袍金铠，按剑而入。璋见是关公显圣，大叫一声，神魂惊散；欲待转身，早被关兴手起剑落，斩于地上，取心沥血，就关公神像前祭祀。兴得了父亲的青龙偃月刀，却将潘璋首级，摽于马项之下，辞了老人，就骑了潘璋的马，望本营而来。老人自将潘璋之尸拖出烧化。

且说关兴行无数里，忽听得人言马嘶，一彪军来到；为首

2021

himself. Guan Xing assumed he was in the hills and searched about, but without success. The day was ending, and Guan Xing could not find his way. Luckily, the moon and stars were bright. As Guan Xing pursued his enemy in the hills, he came upon a farm during the second watch. Dismounting, he knocked at the door. An old man appeared and asked who he was. "A warrior," Guan Xing replied, "lost, who comes by chance to beg a bowl of food." The old man conducted him into a chamber lit with candles burning before a portrait of Lord Guan. With a cry Guan Xing flung himself to the ground. "What does this mean?" the old man asked. "That is my father," Guan Xing answered. The old man prostrated himself, too. Guan Xing asked, "Why these offerings to my father?" The old man replied, "His spirit is most revered in these parts. Every family revered him when he lived, and all the more so now that he is gone. I have prayed for the western army to avenge his death swiftly. Your coming, General, is a blessing to the people." The old man put food and drink before him; then he unsaddled Guan Xing's horse and fed it.

After the third watch another man knocked on the farmhouse gate. The old man went out to the door; it was the southern commander Pan Zhang seeking a night's refuge. The moment Guan Xing saw the commander come into the thatched cottage, he gripped his sword and cried, "Filthy traitor! Halt!" Pan Zhang had turned to leave, when another man came to the door. He had a face ruddy as dates, eyes like the crimson-faced phoenix's, brows like nestling silkworms; his beautiful beard in three strands moved delicately. He entered, hand to sword, wearing a green battle gown and metal armor. Pan Zhang recognized the divine presence of Lord Guan. A cry burst from him, and panic seized his faculties. He tried to turn, but Guan Xing cut him down, plucked out his heart, drained off the blood, and offered it in sacrifice before his father's portrait. Guan Xing recovered from Pan Zhang his father's crescent-moon blade, Green Dragon, and hung Pan Zhang's head from the neck of his mount. Bidding the old man good-bye, he climbed onto Pan Zhang's horse and rode back to camp. The old man dragged off the corpse and cremated it.

Guan Xing had not gone far when he caught the sound of human voices and horses neighing. Suddenly, a body of soldiers flashed into view;

一将，乃潘璋部将马忠也。忠见兴杀了主将潘璋，将首级摽于马项之下，青龙刀又被兴得了，勃然大怒，纵马来取关兴。兴见马忠是害父仇人，气冲牛斗，举青龙刀望忠便砍。忠部下三百军并力上前，一声喊起，将关兴围在垓心。兴力孤势危。忽见西北上一彪军杀来，乃是张苞。马忠见救兵到来，慌忙引军自退。关兴、张苞一处赶来。赶不数里，前面糜芳、傅士仁引兵来寻马忠。两军相合，混战一处。苞、兴二人兵少，慌忙撤退，回至猇亭，来见先主，献上首级，具言此事。先主惊异，赏犒三军。

却说马忠回见韩当、周泰，收聚败军，各分头守把。军士中伤者不计其数。马忠引傅士仁、糜芳于江渚屯扎。当夜三更，军士皆哭声不止。糜芳暗听之，有一伙军言曰："我等皆是荆州之兵，被吕蒙诡计送了主公性命，今刘皇叔御驾亲征，东吴早晚休矣。所恨者，糜芳、傅士仁也。我等何不杀此二贼，去蜀营投降？功劳不小。"又一伙军言曰："不要性急，等个空儿，便就下手。"

糜芳听毕，大惊，遂与傅士仁商议曰："军心变动，我二人性命难保。今蜀主所恨者马忠耳；何不杀了他，将首级去献蜀主，告称：'我等不得已而降吴，今知御驾前来，特地诣营请罪。'"仁曰："不可。去必有祸。"芳曰："蜀主宽仁厚德；目今阿斗太子是我外甥，彼但念我国戚之情，必不肯加害。"二人计较

their leader, Ma Zhong, a subordinate commander under Pan Zhang. Ma Zhong spied his master's head swinging from Guan Xing's horse and the dragon blade that Guan Xing had seized. Overcome by anger, he raced for Guan Xing. Guan Xing recognized his father's murderer, and his fury mounted to the stars. He raised the Green Dragon in preparation to strike, when Ma Zhong's three hundred yelling soldiers surrounded him. In mortal danger, the outnumbered Guan Xing spotted a troop of riders to the north-west fighting their way toward him: Zhang Bao had come to his rescue. Rather than fight on, Ma Zhong led a retreat. Guan Xing and Zhang Bao both started out after him; after a few li's chase they came upon Mi Fang and Fu Shiren looking for Ma Zhong. The two companies skirmished; then Guan Xing and Zhang Bao, having too small a force, hastily returned to Xiaoting. They offered the Emperor the captured head and delivered their tale, which he followed with amazement. The Emperor ended by rewarding the whole armed forces.

Ma Zhong reported back to Han Dang and Zhou Tai, regathered his defeated fighters, and posted them to various positions. An appalling number had been wounded. Ma Zhong then led Fu Shiren and Mi Fang to occupy a spit of land in the river. That night at the third watch the soldiers vented their grief and despair as Mi Fang listened silently. One group said, "We are all Jingzhou men, fooled by Lü Meng into sending Lord Guan to his doom. Now the imperial uncle has started a war the Southland is sure to lose. But if we killed those he hates most — the two traitors Mi Fang and Fu Shiren — and surrendered ourselves in the western camp, it would be well appreciated." Another group of soldiers said, "Not so fast. Wait for the right moment to act."

Astounded by all he had heard, Mi Fang said to Fu Shiren, "The soldiers have turned against us. Our lives are at risk. The one man the ruler of Shu, Liu Bei, hates is Ma Zhong. What if we took his head to him and said, 'We joined the South against our will. The moment we heard of Your Majesty's approach, we came to answer for our crime'?" Fu Shiren said, "No! That would be our ruin." "The ruler of Shu," Mi Fang persisted, "is tolerant and humane, a man of ample virtue. The present crown prince, Ah Dou, is my late sister's son. His father is bound to keep us from harm, if only for the sake of family feeling." Thus, the two

已定，先备了马。三更时分，入帐刺杀马忠，将首级割了，二人带数十骑，径投猇亭而来。伏路军人先引见张南、冯习，具说其事。次日，到御营中来见先主，献上马忠首级，哭告于前曰："臣等实无反心；被吕蒙诡计，称言关公已亡，赚开城门，臣等不得已而降。今闻圣驾前来，特杀此贼，以雪陛下之恨。伏乞陛下恕臣等之罪。"先主大怒曰："朕自离成都许多时，你两个如何不来请罪？今日势危，故来巧言，欲全性命！朕若饶你，至九泉之下，有何面目见关公乎！"言讫，令关兴在御营中，设关公灵位。先主亲捧马忠首级，诣前祭祀。又令关兴将糜芳、傅士仁剥去衣服，跪于灵前，亲自用刀剐之，以祭关公。忽张苞上帐哭拜于前曰："二伯父仇人皆已诛戮；臣父冤仇，何日可报？"先主曰："贤侄勿忧。朕当削平江南，杀尽吴狗，务擒二贼，与汝亲自醢之，以祭汝父。"苞泣谢而退。

此时先主威声大震，江南之人尽皆胆裂，日夜号哭。韩当、周泰大惊，急奏吴王，具言糜芳、傅士仁杀了马忠，去归蜀帝，亦被蜀帝杀了。孙权心怯，遂聚文武商议。步骘奏曰："蜀主所

men concluded their little dispute and readied their horses. During the third watch they entered Ma Zhong's tent and severed his head, then headed for Xiaoting with a few dozen followers.

Sentinels brought them first before Zhang Nan and Feng Xi, to whom the defectors told their story. The next day they offered Ma Zhong's head to the Emperor, explaining bitterly as they stood before him, "We never meant to rebel . Lü Meng tricked us. He said Lord Guan was dead, and induced us to open the gate and surrender the city against our will. But once we heard Your Lordship was marching east, we killed the traitor to satisfy Your Majesty's desire for revenge. We humbly beg forgiveness."

In great anger the Emperor said, "You never came to confess before, in all the time since I left Chengdu! Only now do you come forth with cunning fables to save your skins in a moment of peril. If I spared you, I could not face Lord Guan in the world below." So saying, the Emperor ordered Guan Xing to set up a tablet to Lord Guan in the royal camp; he then personally carried Ma Zhong's severed head in both hands and offered it in sacrifice before the altar. Finally, he commanded Guan Xing to remove Mi Fang's and Fu Shiren's clothing and to have them kneel before the altar while he personally sliced them up as an offering to Lord Guan.[2]

Zhang Bao suddenly came into the Emperor's tent and flung himself to the ground before the Emperor. "My uncle's enemies," he cried, "have all been executed. When will my own father's death be avenged?" "Do not be anxious, good nephew," the Emperor replied. 'When I have conquered the Southland and slain every southern dog, we will catch the two traitors who murdered him and you can make mincemeat out of them as an offering to your father's spirit." Zhang Bao retired with tearful thanks.

By this time the Emperor's awesome reputation had so intimidated the southerners that they wept aloud day and night. In alarm Han Dang and Zhou Tai urgently informed King Sun Quan of Wu that Mi Fang and Fu Shiren had killed Ma Zhong and offered their allegiance to the western king only to be executed themselves. Feeling his own courage failing, Sun Quan gathered his advisers for a conference.

恨者，乃吕蒙、潘璋、马忠、糜芳、傅士仁也。今此数人皆亡，独有范疆、张达二人，现在东吴。何不擒此二人，并张飞首级，遣使送还，交与荆州，送归夫人，上表求和，再会前情，共图灭魏，则蜀兵自退矣。"权从其言，遂具沉香木匣，盛贮飞首，绑缚范疆、张达，囚于槛车之内，令程秉为使，赍国书，望猇亭而来。

　　却说先主欲发兵前进。忽近臣奏曰："东吴遣使送张车骑之首，并囚范疆、张达二贼至。"先主两手加额曰："此天之所赐，亦由三弟之灵也！"即令张苞设飞灵位。先主见张飞首级在匣中面不改色，放声大哭。张苞自仗利刀，将范疆、张达万剐凌迟，祭父之灵。

　　祭毕，先主怒气不息，定要灭吴。马良奏曰："仇人尽戮，其恨可雪矣。吴大夫程秉到此，欲还荆州，送回夫人，永结盟好，共图灭魏，伏候圣旨。"先主怒曰："朕切齿仇人，乃孙权也。今若与之连和，是负二弟当日之盟矣。今先灭吴，次灭魏。"便欲斩来使，以绝吴情。多官苦告方免。程秉抱头鼠窜，回奏吴主曰："蜀不从讲和，誓欲先灭东吴，然后伐魏。众臣苦谏不听，如

Bu Zhi addressed the king: "The ruler of Shu hated Lü Meng, Pan Zhang, Ma Zhong, Mi Fang, and Fu Shiren. Now they are all dead, although Fan Jiang and Zhong Da are still alive in our homeland. Why not send them, along with Zhang Fei's head, back to the ruler of Shu, hand Jingzhou over to him, return his wife Lady Sun, and submit a memorial suing for peace so that you two kings can meet again in the former spirit of friendship and concert your efforts for the elimination of the kingdom of Wei? That should make the western soldiers withdraw." Sun Quan approved the suggestion. He had Zhang Fei's head put in a fragrant aloeswood case, and the two defectors bound and put in cage-carts. Sun Quan entrusted the mission to Cheng Bing, provided him with his personal letter, and sent him to Xiaoting.

* * *

As the Emperor was preparing his invasion, a personal vassal addressed him thus: "The Southland has sent an envoy with General Zhang Fei's head, together with the two murderers Fan Jiang and Zhang Da under guard." The Emperor touched both hands to his forehead in a gesture of rejoicing and said, "This comes from Heaven! And the spirit of third brother has helped!" He immediately ordered Zhang Bao to set up an altar to his father. When the Emperor looked at Zhang Fei's head, its features unchanged, a sharp cry broke from his lips. Zhang Bao took a sharp knife and slowly sliced the murderers to death as an offering to his father's spirit.

2027

When the ritual was over, the Emperor, still unassuaged, reaffirmed his intention to destroy the Southland. But Ma Liang said, "The culprits are dead; your grievance is answered. Cheng Bing, a high official, has come to return Jingzhou, send back Lady Sun, and seal an everlasting amity with a view to the destruction of Wei. He humbly awaits your royal decree." But the Emperor said angrily, "Sun Quan I hate. To ally with him now would be to betray my fraternal covenant. We will destroy Wu first, and then Wei!"[3] The Emperor would have executed the southern envoy, but was dissuaded by his officers. Cheng Bing fled in humiliation and reported to the lord of Wu: "The kingdom of Shu will not talk peace. They have sworn to destroy the south first and then attack Wei; they are deaf to the protests of their officials. What are we to do?"

之奈何？"

权大惊，举止失措。阚泽出班奏曰："现有擎天之柱，如何不用耶？"权急问何人。泽曰："昔日东吴大事，全任周郎；后鲁子敬代之；子敬亡后，决于吕子明；今子明虽丧，现在陆伯言在荆州。此人名虽儒生，实有雄才大略，以臣论之，不在周郎之下；前破关公，其谋皆出于伯言。主上若能用之，破蜀必矣。如或有失，臣愿与同罪。"权曰："非德润之言，孤几误大事。"张昭曰："陆逊乃一书生耳，非刘备敌手；恐不可用。"顾雍亦曰："陆逊年幼望轻，恐诸公不服；若不服则生祸乱，必误大事。"来骘亦曰："逊才堪治郡耳；若托以大事，非其宜也。"阚泽大呼曰："若不用陆伯言，则东吴休矣！臣愿以全家保之！"权曰："孤亦素知陆伯言乃奇才也！孤意已决，卿等勿言。"

于是命召陆逊。逊本名陆议，后改名逊，字伯言，乃吴郡吴人也；汉城门校尉陆纡之孙，九江都尉陆骏之子；身长八尺，面如美玉；官领镇西将军。当下奉召而至，参拜毕，权曰："今蜀兵临境，孤特命卿总督军马，以破刘备。"逊曰："江东文武，皆大王故旧之臣；臣年幼无才，安能制之？"权曰："阚德润以全家保

Sun Quan was in a quandary. Kan Ze stepped forward to address him: "We have among us a pillar of strength. Why not use him?" Sun Quan eagerly asked whom he meant, and Kan Ze continued, "In times past all great affairs of the south were entrusted to Zhou Yu. After Zhou Yu's death, Lu Su assumed the responsibility, and after he died, Lü Meng. Now Lü Meng, too, is dead. But in Jingzhou we have Lu Xun (styled Boyan). Though known only as a scholar, Lu Xun's ability compares, I judge, to Zhou Yu's. Lord Guan's defeat was entirely his doing. If Your Lordship can use his talents, we will surely defeat the kingdom of Shu. If he fails, I beg to share whatever punishment Lu Xun is condemned to suffer." Sun Quan replied, "Kan Ze, your words have saved the day."

But Zhang Zhao said, "Lu Xun is a mere pedant, no match for Liu Bei. I doubt that he can be of service to us." Gu Yong seconded this opinion. "Lu Xun," he said, "is too young and too little known for our leaders to accept his authority. His appointment will cause disorder and ruin our cause." Bu Zhi added his view: "Lu Xun may have the talent to administer a district but not to undertake such a major responsibility." To these negative views Kan Ze shouted back, "Without Lu Xun's services, the Southland is done for! I will guarantee him with the lives of my family." "I have long known of Lu Xun's rare ability and have decided to employ him. You gentlemen need say no more," Sun Quan said, and he summoned Lu Xun.

Lu Yi was the man's original name; later he changed it to Lu Xun and adopted the style Boyan. He was a southerner from the district of Wu. His grandfather was Lu Yu, commandant of the City Gates; his father Lu Jun, military commander of Jiujiang. Lu Xun stood eight spans tall; his face was like exquisite jade. The office he held was General Who Quells the West. On receiving Sun Quan's summons, Lu Xun came at once.

Lu Xun's obeisance completed, Sun Quan said to him, "The western army is bearing down on our border. I am giving you overall command of our forces to destroy Liu Bei." Lu Xun replied, "Among the Southland's civil and military officers, Your Majesty has vassals long in service. How can someone as young and lacking in talent as I keep control of them?" To this Sun Quan responded, "Kan Ze has pledged his family in recom-

卿,孤亦素知卿才。今拜卿为大都督,卿勿推辞。"逊曰:"倘文武不服,何如?"权取所佩剑与之曰:"如有不听号令者,先斩后奏。"逊曰:"荷蒙重托,敢不拜命;但乞大王于来日会聚众官,然后赐臣。"阚泽曰:"古之命将,必筑坛会众,赐白旄黄钺、印绶兵符,然后威行令肃。今大王宜遵此礼,择日筑坛,拜伯言为大都督,假节钺,则众人自无不服矣。"权从之,命人连夜筑坛完备,大会百官,请陆逊登坛,拜为大都督、右护军镇西将军,进封娄候,赐以宝剑印绶,令掌六郡八十一州兼荆楚诸路军马。吴王嘱之曰:"阃以内,孤主之;阃以外,将军制之。"

逊领命下坛,令徐盛、丁奉为护卫,即日出师;一面调诸路军马,水陆并进。文书到猇亭,韩当、周泰大惊曰:"主上如何以一书生总兵耶?"比及逊至,众皆不服。逊升帐议事,众人勉强参贺。逊曰:"主上命吾为大将,督军破蜀。军有常法,公等各宜

2031

mending you; I too have long known of your talents. Please do not decline my offer to make you chief commander." "What if the officers and officials refuse to accept my authority?" he asked. Sun Quan handed Lu Xun his sword, saying, "Whoever disobeys, execute; and report to me afterward." "I am obliged by your heavy charge and can only honor your command, but I beg Your Majesty not to bestow the sword and formally empower me until you assemble the officials."

Kan Ze said, "In ancient times they always built an altar and assembled the court when empowering a general. The white command banner and golden battle-axe, the seal, the seal-cord, and the military tally were publicly transferred in order to make the general's authority effective and his orders strictly executed. Your Majesty should observe this ceremony. Select a day for building the altar, honor Lu Xun as chief commander, bestow the battle-axe of authority, and no one will deny his allegiance." Following this suggestion, Sun Quan had the altar built without delay, assembled his court, and invited Lu Xun to ascend. Before the officials he installed Lu Xun as chief commander, honored him as guardian of the Right and General Who Quells the West, and raised his status to lord of Lou. He bestowed his own sword on the general and granted him the seal placing him in charge of the eighty-one areas of the six districts of the Southland as well as the districts of Jingzhou and giving him command of all armed forces. The king of Wu's final injunction to Lu Xun was, "I will take care of the home front; in the field you are in charge." Lu Xun accepted his command and descended from the altar. He ordered Xu Sheng and Ding Feng to serve as his guard; and that day he led forth the ground and naval forces.

Near Xiaoting, the news of the new Southland appointment alarmed Han Dang and Zhou Tai. "How could our lord put a pedant in charge of our forces?" they wondered aloud. By the time Lu Xun actually arrived at the front, no one was prepared to accept his authority. When Lu Xun held his first meeting in the command tent, the commanders participated grudgingly. Lu Xun began by saying, "The king has given me chief command to lead our forces in the destruction of the enemy. In the army there are unvarying regulations, which it would behoove you gentlemen to adhere to. For violators, the royal law shows no partiality. Do not do

遵守。违者王法无亲，勿致后悔。"众皆默然。周泰曰："目今安东将军孙桓，乃主上之侄，现困于彝陵城中，内无粮草，外无救兵；请都督早施良策，救出孙桓，以安主上之心。"逊曰："吾素知孙安东深得军心，必能坚守，不必救之。待吾破蜀后，彼自出矣。"众皆暗笑而退。韩当谓周泰曰："命此孺子为将，东吴休矣！——公见彼所行乎？"泰曰："吾聊以言试之，早无一计。——安能破蜀也！"

　　次日，陆逊传下号令，教诸将各处关防，牢守隘口，不许轻敌。众皆笑其懦，不肯坚守。次日，陆逊升帐唤诸将曰："吾钦承王命，总督诸军，昨已三令五申，令汝等各处坚守；俱不遵吾令，何也？"韩当曰："吾自从孙将军平定江南，经数百战；其余诸将，或从讨逆将军，或从当今大王，皆披坚执锐，出生入死之士。今主上命公为大都督，令退蜀兵，宜早定计，调拨军马，分头征进，以图大事；乃只令坚守勿战，岂欲待天自杀贼耶？吾非贪生怕死之人，奈何使吾等堕其锐气？"于是帐下诸将，皆应声而言曰："韩将军之言是也。吾等情愿决一死战！"陆逊听毕，掣剑在手，厉声曰："仆虽一介书生，今蒙主上托以重任者，以吾

anything you will regret." The assembled commanders kept silent until Zhou Tai said, "At this time the king's nephew, Sun Huan, General Who Secures the East, is under siege at Yiling. They have neither food nor provender, and no hope of rescue from outside. Would the chief commander kindly work out a plan as soon as possible to save him and relieve the king's anxiety?"

To this challenge Lu Xun responded, "I have no doubt that General Sun Huan has the complete confidence of his men. He will be able to defend his position without our assistance and will get out on his own after we have defeated the west." The commanders retired with mockery in their hearts. Han Dang said to Zhou Tai, "With this child for its leader, the Southland is doomed. You saw the way he conducted himself?" And Zhou Tai replied, "I was merely testing him. He had no plan at all! How could he defeat the west?"

The next day Lu Xun ordered the commanders to defend the several passes and avoid engaging the enemy. Mocking Lu Xun's caution, the commanders disdained to keep a strict guard. The following day Lu Xun called a meeting in his tent and said to them, "As royally appointed chief commander, I have repeatedly enjoined you to maintain the strictest defense at the various strongpoints. Why have you disregarded my orders?" Han Dang replied, "Since joining General Sun in the conquest of the Southland, I have been in hundreds of battles. Some commanders have served his elder brother Sun Ce; others have served His Majesty. Every one has seen long years of combat. Now the king commands your service as our chief in order to drive back the western army. A plan needs to be made at once for coordinating our forces in several lines of march so that our purposes can be accomplished. But all you have done is call for a strict defense and no fighting. Do you mean for us to wait until Heaven itself puts the enemy to death? We are not men who covet life and fear death. What is gained by depressing our spirits like this?"

The commanders in the tent responded in unison, "General Han Dang is right! A battle to the death is what we want!" Facing their demand, Lu Xun took Sun Quan's sword and cried harshly, "I may be no more than a pedant. But his lordship has appointed me because I have something to offer him; and I will suffer any humiliation, bear any burden required of

有尺寸可取，能忍辱负重故也。汝等只各守隘口，牢把险要，不许妄动，如违令者皆斩！"众皆愤愤而退。

却说先主自猇亭布列军马，直至川口，接连七百里，前后四十营寨，昼则旌旗蔽日，夜则火光耀天。忽细作报说："东吴用陆逊为大都督，总制军马。逊令诸将各守险要不出。"先主问曰："陆逊何如人也？"马良奏曰："逊虽东吴一书生，然年幼多才，深有谋略；前袭荆州，皆系此人之诡计。"先主大怒曰："竖子诡计，损朕二弟，今当擒之！"便传令进兵。马良谏曰："陆逊之才，不亚周郎，未可轻敌。"先主曰："朕用兵老矣，岂反不如一黄口孺子耶！"遂亲领前军，攻打诸处关津隘口。

韩当见先主兵来，差人报知陆逊。逊恐韩当妄动，急飞马自来观看，正见韩当立马于山上；远望蜀兵，漫山遍野而来，军中隐隐有黄罗盖伞。韩当接着陆逊，并马而观。当指曰："军中必有刘备，吾欲击之。"逊曰："刘备举兵东下，连胜十余阵，锐气正盛；今只乘高守险，不可轻出，出则不利。但宜奖励将士，广布守御之策，以观其变。今彼驰骋于平原广野之间，正自得志；我坚守不出，彼求战不得，必移屯于山林树木间。吾当以奇计胜之。"

me. You have only to defend the access points and take no rash action. Whoever disobeys, dies." The crowd withdrew indignantly.

*   *   *

Meanwhile, the Emperor (Liu Bei) had moved out from Xiaoting and reached the eastern border of the Riverlands. His forces stretched over a distance of seven hundred *li,* occupying forty base camps. By day their banners darkened the sun. By night their fires lit up the sky. Suddenly a spy sent in a report: "The Southland has given Lu Xun general command of their forces, and he has ordered his commanders to hold their strongpoints and not come out." The Emperor replied, "What kind of man is Lu Xun?" Ma Liang said, "Though he is a scholar, he has great talent for his youth and lays deep plans. It was he who planned their successful attack on Jingzhou." "By a boy's tricks I lost my second brother! I want him captured!" the Emperor said angrily and ordered a general advance. But Ma Liang remonstrated, "He is no less capable than Zhou Yu was! Do not risk a rash engagement." "I am seasoned in the ways of war," the Emperor replied. "Do you think a milksop of a child too much for me?" So saying, he took personal command of the forward contingent and attacked the various fords and passes.

Han Dang informed Lu Xun of the advance of the western forces; Lu Xun sped to the front to survey the situation and forestall any rash move on Han Dang's part. Lu Xun arrived when Han Dang, sitting astride his horse on a hilltop, was viewing the enemy swarming over the hills and covering the flatlands; dimly visible in the distance was a yellow silk umbrella. Han Dang received Lu Xun, and they reined in their horses side by side to observe. Pointing toward the umbrella, Han Dang said, "Liu Bei must be there. I want to attack." Lu Xun replied, "After more than ten victories on this eastern expedition, Liu Bei's fighting spirits are at their peak. All we can do now is occupy the highground and defend our strongpoints. If we go forth against them, we will suffer defeat. We need to whet the mettle of our officers and men, to broaden our defensive strategy until the situation changes. At the moment they enjoy control of the flat-lands before us. But by maintaining a strict defense, we deny them the engagement they seek, causing them to move into the wooded hills — that is when we shall take them by surprise."

韩当口虽应诺,心中只是不服。先主使前队搦战,辱骂百端。逊令塞耳休听,不许出迎,亲自遍历诸关隘口,抚慰将士,皆令坚守。先主见吴军不出,心中焦躁。马良曰:"陆逊深有谋略。今陛下远来攻战,自春历夏;彼之不出,欲待我军之变也。愿陛下察之。"先主曰:"彼有何谋?但怯敌耳。向者数败,今安敢再出!"先锋冯习奏曰:"即今天气炎热,军屯于赤火之中,取水深为不便。"先主遂命各营,皆移于山林茂盛之地,近溪傍涧;待过夏到秋,并力进兵。冯习遂奉旨,将诸寨皆移于林木阴密之处。马良奏曰:"我军若动,倘吴兵骤至,如之奈何?"先主曰:"朕令吴班引万余弱兵,近吴寨平地屯住;朕亲选八千精兵,伏于山谷之中。若陆逊知朕移营,必乘势来击,却令吴班诈败;逊若追来,朕引兵突出,断其归路,小子可擒矣。"文武皆贺曰:"陛下神机妙算,诸臣不及也!"

马良曰:"近闻诸葛丞相在东川点看各处隘口,恐魏兵入寇。陛下何不将各营移居之地,画成图本,问于丞相?"先主曰:"朕亦颇知兵法,何必又问丞相?"良曰:"古云:'兼听则明,偏

Han Dang, though he gave verbal assent to this plan , remained unconvinced. The Emperor sent his vanguard to provoke the southerners, reviling them in a hundred ways, Lu Xun ordered everyone to stuff up his ears, however, and would not permit any engagement of forces. He personally went to each control point to cheer the men and reaffirm his orders for maintaining the defense. No southern soldiers appeared, and the Emperor seethed with impatience. Ma Liang said to him, "Lu Xun is a deep planner; and Your Majesty has come a long distance to wage war. Spring has turned to summer. They are keeping behind their defenses, hoping that something will happen to our troops. Let Your Majesty look into this." The Emperor answered, "What can their plan be? They fear us, that's all. After their string of defeats, they don't dare show themselves." Vanguard Commander Feng Xi addressed the Emperor. "The weather is scorching hot," he said. "Camped in this burning plain, the army is having trouble getting water." Consequently, the Emperor commanded him to move into the lush hills, near the mountain streams, and deferred the attack until autumn. Feng Xi, as ordered, had the commanders shift all camps into the shade of the woods.

Ma Liang addressed the Emperor, saying, "If we make this move and the southerners come suddenly, what will you do?" "I have had Wu Ban take ten thousand inferior troops and position them on the plain near the southern defenses. I myself will take eight thousand elite troops and place them in ambush in the ravines. When Lu Xun learns of our move, he will not fail to strike. When he does, I have told Wu Ban to feign defeat. If Lu Xun pursues those inferior troops, I will charge in and seal off his retreat. The little devil will be ours!" All civil and military officials praised his plan, saying, "Your Majesty's ingenious designs and exquisite calculations are beyond us all!"

2037

Ma Liang said, "I heard recently that Prime Minister Zhuge is in the east Riverlands inspecting our defenses in anticipation of incursion by northern troops of Wei. Your Majesty, why not make a map of the positions you intend moving into for the prime minister to look over?" The Emperor replied, "I am versed in warfare well enough to do without his opinion." "There is an old saying, 'Broad consultation makes one wise; one-sided consideration makes one blind.' I hope Your Majesty will not

听则蔽。'望陛下察之。"先主曰："卿可自去各营,画成四至八道图本,亲到东川去向丞相。如有不便,可急来报知。"马良领命而去。于是先主移兵于林木阴密处避暑。早有细作报知韩当、周泰。二人听得此事,大喜,来见陆逊曰："目今蜀兵四十余营,皆移于山林密处,依溪傍涧,就水歇凉。都督可乘虚击之。"

正是:

蜀主有谋能设伏,吴兵好勇定遭擒。

未知陆逊可听其言否,且看下文分解。

ignore this," was Ma Liang's answer. The Emperor said, "Then chart the area yourself and go to the east Riverlands to show the prime minister your maps. Report to me at once anything unfavorable in them." Ma Liang departed with his orders.

And so the Emperor moved his army into the woods where the shade afforded some relief from summer's heat. Spies quickly informed Han Dang and Zhou Tai of these changes in the western position. And the two commanders were delighted to report to Lu Xun: "They have moved their camps, more than forty in all, into the wooded hills, where their proximity to mountain streams affords them drinking water and cooling relief. Chief Commander, now is the time to strike." Indeed:

> Planning to spring an ambush was the ruler of Shu,
> Sure of catching the bold and hardy troops of Wu.

Would Lu Xun accept the proposal?

Read on.

陸遜營燒七百里

西湖散人 圖

2041

第八十四回

陆逊营烧七百里　孔明巧布八阵图

　　却说韩当、周泰探知先主移营就凉，急来报知陆逊。逊大喜，遂引兵自来观看动静：只见平地一屯，不满万余人，大半皆是老弱之众，大书"先锋吴班"旗号。周泰曰："吾视此等兵如儿戏耳。愿同韩将军分两路击之。如其不胜，甘当军令。"陆逊看了良久，以鞭指曰："前面山谷中，隐隐有杀气起；其下必有伏兵，故于平地设此弱兵，以诱我耳。诸公切不可出。"众将听了，皆以为懦。

　　次日，吴班引兵到关前搦战，耀武扬威，辱骂不绝；多有解衣卸甲，赤身裸体，或睡或坐。徐盛、丁奉入帐禀陆逊曰："蜀兵欺我太甚！某等愿出击之！"逊笑曰："公等但恃血气之勇，未知孙、吴妙法。此彼诱敌之计也：三日后必见其诈矣。"徐盛曰："三日后，彼移营已定，安能击之乎？"逊曰："吾正欲令彼移营也。"诸将哂笑而退。过三日后，会诸将于关上观望，见吴班兵已退去。逊指曰："杀气起矣。——刘备必从山谷中出也。"言

Chapter 84

Lu Xun Burns a Seven-Hundred-*Li* Line of Camps
Kongming Deploys the Eightfold Ramparts Maze

Southern commanders Han Dang and Zhou Tai hurried to inform Lu Xun that the Emperor had shifted to cooler ground. Delighted, the chief commander came to the front to scan the field. There on the flats before him he found a single campsite with a mere ten thousand men, most of them unfit for service; their banner read, "Vanguard Wu Ban." Zhou Tai said to Lu Xun, "This looks like child's play. Allow General Han Dang and myself to attack with two companies. If we fail, we will welcome whatever punishment martial law imposes." After examining the enemy's position for some time, Lu Xun pointed with his whip and said, "In the distance ahead I detect lethal signs marking ambush points. They have purposely placed these troops on flat ground to lure us out. I absolutely forbid you to show yourselves." All took his caution for cowardice.

The next day Wu Ban led some troops to the pass and challenged the southerners, swaggering and casting scorn on them. Most of Wu Ban's men had slipped out of their battle gear and were lolling about half-naked. Xu Sheng and Ding Feng entered the command tent and petitioned Lu Xun. "The westerners' insults are unbearable," they cried. "Let us go out and attack them." Lu Xun smiled as he replied, "You are trusting to sheer physical courage and ignoring the fine points of warfare as taught by the masters. This is a trick to entice the enemy. In three days the deception will be apparent." Xu Sheng answered, "In three days their position will be too consolidated to attack." "I am waiting for them to complete the transfer," Lu Xun said. The commanders smirked as they withdrew.

After the three days had passed, Lu Xun gathered the commanders on the pass to survey the ground below. Wu Ban had already pulled back. Pointing ahead, Lu Xun said, "Those lethal signs are in the air. Liu Bei

2043

未毕，只见蜀兵皆全装惯束，拥先主而过。吴兵见了，尽皆胆裂。逊曰："吾之不听诸公击班者，正为此也。今伏兵已出，旬日之内，必破蜀矣。"诸将皆曰："破蜀当在初时；今连营五六百里，相守经七八月，其诸要害，皆已固守，安能破乎？"逊曰："诸公不知兵法。备乃世之枭雄，更多智谋，其兵始集，法度精专；今守之久矣，不得我便，兵疲意阻，取之正在今日。"诸将方才叹服。后人有诗赞曰：

　　　　虎帐谈兵按《六韬》，安排香饵钓鲸鳌。

　　　　三分自是多英俊，又显江南陆逊高。

　　却说陆逊已定了破蜀之策，遂修笺遣使奏闻孙权，言指日可以破蜀之意。权览毕，大喜曰："江东复有此异人，孤何忧哉！诸将皆上书言其懦，孤独不信。今观其言，果非懦也。"于是大起吴兵来接应。

　　却说先主于猇亭尽驱水军，顺流而下，沿江屯扎水寨，深入吴境。黄权谏曰："水军沿江而下，进则易，退则难。臣愿为前驱。陛下宜在后阵，庶万无一失。"先主曰："吴贼胆落，朕长驱大进，有何碍乎？"众官苦谏，先主不从。遂分兵两路：命黄权督江北之兵，以防魏寇；先主自督江南诸军，夹江分立营寨，以图

will be coming out from the gorges." As Lu Xun was speaking, lo and behold, the western army fully uniformed crossed before them, the Emperor in their midst. The sight struck panic in the southern troops. "This is why I could not listen to your advice," Lu Xun said to his commanders. "But now that the ambush is in the open, we will destroy the western army in ten days." "We should have done that to begin with," the commanders said. "Now their network of mutually defended camps stretches over five hundred *li,* and after these seven or eight months all strategic points are well fortified. How can we defeat them?" Lu Xun replied, "Gentlemen, you are unfamiliar with the art of war. Liu Bei is the craftiest owl of our day, the most cunning and ruthless of men. When he first deployed his forces, their order was precise, their discipline tight. Now after their long but fruitless wait, his men are worn down and frustrated in their aims. This is the moment for us to take them." Finally, Lu Xun convinced the commanders. A poet of later times left these lines of admiration for Lu Xun's qualities:

> He'd mastered war's six arts when he spoke before the chiefs;
> Angling for one mighty fish, he set a tasty bait.
> For this divided Kingdom now has paragons enough!
> And shining high above them all — Lu Xun of the south.

Having made his plans, Lu Xun dispatched a letter informing Sun Quan of the expected victory. Sun Quan read it with excitement. "The Southland has another genius like Zhou Yu!" he exclaimed. "My worries are over. The commanders' complaints of his cowardice never persuaded me. And now my confidence is confirmed." So saying, he mustered the southern army to support Lu Xun.

From Xiaoting the Emperor directed his entire naval force to proceed downstream. Pitching camp along the river, the mariners cut deeply into southern territory. Huang Quan raised an objection: "The marine forces are moving downriver easily enough, but retreat will prove difficult. Allow me to advance while you stay back — just in case." "The bastards of Wu have lost their nerve. Nothing can stop our massive onslaught," the Emperor replied, firmly rejecting all further appeals. He divided his forces into two field armies: one north of the river under Huang Quan, defending against Wei; one to the south, which he himself took charge of. Thus,

进取。细作探知，连夜报知魏主，言："蜀兵伐吴，树栅连营，纵横七百余里，分四十余屯，皆傍山林下寨；今黄权督兵在江北岸，每日出哨百余里，不知何意。"

魏主闻之，仰面笑曰："刘备将败矣！"群臣请问其故。魏主曰："刘玄德不晓兵法：岂有连营七百里，而可以拒敌者乎？包原隰险阻屯兵者，此兵法之大忌也。玄德必败于东吴陆逊之手。——旬日之内，消息必至矣。"群臣犹未信，皆请拨兵备之。魏主曰："陆逊若胜，必尽举吴兵去取西川；吴兵远去，国中空虚，朕虚托以兵助战，令三路一齐进兵，东吴唾手可取也。"众皆拜服。魏主下令，使曹仁督一军出濡须，曹休督一军出洞口，曹真督一军出南郡："三路军马会合日期，暗袭东吴。朕随后自来接应。"调遣已定。

不说魏兵袭吴。且说马良至川，入见孔明，呈上图本而言曰："今移营夹江，横占七百里，下四十余屯，皆依溪傍涧，林木茂盛之处。皇上令良将图本来与丞相观之。"孔明看讫，拍案叫苦曰："是何人教主上如此下寨？可斩此人！"马良曰："皆主上自为，非他人之谋。"孔明叹曰："汉朝气数休矣！"良问其故。孔明曰："包原隰险阻而结营，此兵家之大忌。倘彼用火攻，何

2047

they established separate camps on either shore to deliver the attack.

* * *

Spies soon told Cao Pi, ruler of Wei, "The army of Shu has gone to war against Wu. Their fortifications stretch in a line over seven hundred *li* long; they have built more than forty bases beside hills and woods. At present Huang Quan commands the forces on the northern shore, and their daily patrols range over one hundred *li*. We do not know what he is up to."

Cao Pi threw back his head and laughed at this report. "Liu Bei is done for!" he said. When his vassals pressed for an explanation, the Wei ruler continued, "Liu Xuande knows nothing of warfare. Camps strung out like that won't deter his enemy. And to pitch on such irregular, densely wooded ground is a classic blunder. Within ten days look for news of his defeat at Lu Xun's hands." The vassals, unconvinced, requested troops for preventive action. The Wei Emperor said, "If Lu Xun prevails, he will move ahead in force to take the Riverlands itself. With troops so far afield, the Southland will be left undefended. And we shall send down three armies, ostensibly as aid, which will make short work of them." The assembly voiced its admiration. The Wei Emperor ordered Cao Ren, Cao Xiu, and Cao Zhen to take command and move out from Ruxu, Dongkou, and Nanjun. The order read: "On the appointed day, coordinate a covert strike on the Southland. I will reinforce from the rear." Thus, Wei completed preparations for another southern campaign.

* * *

Ma Liang reached the Riverlands and presented Kongming with maps of the Emperor's positions. "At present we have more than forty bases on both sides of the river, covering a stretch of seven hundred *li*. Each is pitched close to a stream or creek near thick woods. His Majesty has sent me to show these sketches to Your Excellency." Kongming finished examining the documents and slammed his hand on the table. "Whoever," he cried in anguish, "whoever advised our lord to pitch camp in this way should be executed." Ma Liang responded, "It was entirely our lord's own doing. No one advised him." Kongming said with a sigh, "Then the vital cycle of the Han draws to a close."

Ma Liang asked the meaning of these words, and Kongming replied,

以解救？又，岂有连营七百里而可拒敌乎？祸不远矣！陆逊拒守不出，正为此也。汝当速去见天子，改屯诸营，不可如此。"良曰："倘今吴兵已胜，如之奈何？"孔明曰："陆逊不敢来追，成都可保无虞。"良曰："逊何故不追？"孔明曰："恐魏兵袭其后也。主上若有失，当投白帝城避之。吾入川时，已伏下十万兵在鱼腹浦矣。"良大惊曰："某于鱼腹浦往来数次，未尝见一卒，丞相何作此诈语？"孔明曰："后来必见，不劳多问。"马良求了表章，火速投御营来。孔明自回成都，调拨军马救应。

　　却说陆逊见蜀兵懈怠，不复提防，升帐聚大小将士听令曰："吾自受命以来，未尝出战。今观蜀兵，足知动静，故欲先取江南岸一营。谁敢去取？"言未毕，韩当、周泰、凌统等应声而出曰："某等愿往。"逊教皆退不用，独唤阶下末将淳于丹曰："吾与汝五千军，去取江南第四营：蜀将傅彤所守。今晚就要成功。吾自提兵接应。"淳于丹引兵去了，又唤徐盛、丁奉曰："汝等各领兵三千，屯于寨外五里。如淳于丹败回，有兵赶来，当出救之，却不可追去。"二将自引军去了。

"To pitch the camps like that violates every rule. If they attack by fire, he cannot be saved; nor can such a string of forts hold off the enemy. The end is not far off. Now I see why Lu Xun holds back so strictly and does not show himself. You must rush to the Son of Heaven and have him change the positions. They cannot be left like this." "And if the southerners have already overwhelmed them?" Ma Liang asked. "Lu Xun will not dare pursue. The capital is safe." "Why so?" Ma Liang asked. "Because they have the northern army behind them to worry about," Kongming explained. "If our lord finds himself in trouble, he should find safety in the city of Baidi.[1] When I came into the Riverlands, I left ten legions there at Fishbelly Meadow." Ma Liang was amazed. "I have been through Fishbelly Meadow any number of times and have never seen a single soldier. Why is Your Excellency trying to deceive me?" "You will find out later," Kongming replied. "Don't trouble yourself any further." Ma Liang took Kongming's written petition and sped back to the imperial camp. Kongming returned to Chengdu and prepared to rescue the Emperor.

* * *

Lu Xun observed that the troops of the Riverlands were beginning to flag and were growing negligent about their defenses. He gathered his commanders before his tent and told them, "Since assuming command, I have refrained from giving battle; but we now know enough about the enemy's movements. I want to capture a single camp on the southern side of the river. Who dares to do the job?" The sound of the chief commander's voice still hung in the air as Han Dang, Zhou Tai, and Ling Tong stepped forward to volunteer. But Lu Xun rejected their offer and instead summoned a subordinate commander from the lower ranks, Chunyu Dan. "I am giving you five thousand men," Lu Xun said to him. "Take the fourth camp on the southern side, the one Fu Tong is guarding. I want a victory this very evening. I will reinforce you." Chunyu Dan left to carry out his mission. Next, Lu Xun called Xu Sheng and Ding Feng and said to them, "Take three thousand men each and station them five *li* from our camp. If Chunyu Dan returns in defeat, go to his rescue. But whatever you do, do not pursue the enemy." The two commanders departed on their mission.

　　却说淳于丹于黄昏时分，领兵前进，到蜀寨时，已三更之后。丹令众军鼓噪而入。蜀营内傅彤引军杀出，挺枪直取淳于丹；丹敌不住，拨马便回。忽然喊声大震，一彪军拦住去路：为首大将赵融。丹夺路而走，折兵大半。正走之间，山后一彪蛮兵拦住：为首番将沙摩柯。丹死战得脱，背后三路军赶来。比及离营五里，吴军徐盛、丁奉二人两下杀来，蜀兵退去，救了淳于丹回营。丹带箭入见陆逊请罪。逊曰："非汝之过也。——吾欲试敌人之虚实耳。破蜀之计，吾已定矣。"徐盛、丁奉曰："蜀兵势大，难以破之，空自损兵折将耳。"逊笑曰："吾这条计，但瞒不过诸葛亮耳。天幸此人不在，使我成大功也。"

　　遂集大小将士听令：使朱然于水路进兵，来日午后东南风大作，用船装载茅草，依计而行；韩当引一军攻江北岸，周泰引一军攻江南岸，每人手执茅草一把，内藏硫黄焰硝，各带火种，各执枪刀，一齐而上，但到蜀营，顺风举火；蜀兵四十屯，只烧二十屯，每间一屯烧一屯。各军预带干粮，不许暂退，昼夜追袭，只擒了刘备方止。众将听了军令，各受计而去。

　　却说先主正在御营寻思破吴之计，忽见帐前中军旗幡，无风自倒。乃问程畿曰："此为何兆？"畿曰："今夜莫非吴兵来劫

As dusk fell, Chunyu Dan advanced, reaching the western camp after the third watch. As he penetrated the ambit, his men raised a wild din at his order. Fu Tong came forth, and the battle was joined. Fu Tong went straight for Chunyu Dan, who wheeled his mount round to retire, unable to withstand the charge. Suddenly the air rang with loud cries: a band of soldiers was blocking his retreat, General Zhao Rong at their head. Chunyu Dan now broke away and fled. Half his men were lost. A company of Man warriors blocked his way: their leader, Shamoke, the Qiang chieftain. Fighting for his life, Chunyu Dan struggled free again, the three enemy companies hot on his heels.

Five *li* from the camp, the Southland ambush was sprung. Xu Sheng and Ding Feng forced back the western army and then escorted Chunyu Dan back to the Southland side. Chunyu Dan, with an arrow lodged in him, went before Lu Xun to accept his punishment. "It was not your fault," Lu Xun reassured him. "I had to test the enemy's strength in order to form my plan for destroying Shu." "They are too strong for us to defeat," Xu Sheng and Ding Feng said, "We will lose men and leaders in vain." Lu Xun smiled as he replied, "My plan would never fool Kongming. But by Heavens's favor the man is not here, and this will help me to victory."

Again Lu Xun gathered his officers and men and issued his orders: "Zhu Ran is to advance on the river. Tomorrow after noon the southeast wind will blow strong. Load your boats with straw and proceed according to plan. Han Dang is to attack the north shore, Zhou Tai the south. In addition to spear and sword, each soldier is to carry a bundle of grass with sulphur and saltpeter inside and something to ignite it. Everyone is to advance together; as soon as you reach the enemy camps, use your torches according to the winds. They have forty encampments; fire every other one. Carry dry provisions and pursue them relentlessly day and night until you have taken Liu Bei." The commanders went severally to their ordered tasks.

* * *

In the main camp the Emperor was pondering his strategy, when the banner in front of his tent overturned even though there was no wind. He turned to Cheng Ji and asked, "What does this signify?" "The southerners

营？"先主曰："昨夜杀尽，安敢再来？"畿曰："倘是陆逊试敌，奈何？"正言间，人报山上远远望见吴兵尽沿山望东去了。先主曰："此是疑兵。"令众休动，命关兴、张苞各引五百骑出巡。黄昏时分，关兴回奏曰："江北营中火起。"先主急令关兴往江北，张苞往江南，探看虚实："倘吴兵到时，可急回报。"

二将领命去了。初更时分，东南风骤起。只见御营左屯火发。方欲救时，御营右屯又火起。风紧火急，树木皆着，喊声大震。两屯军马齐出，奔离御营中，御营军自相践踏，死者不知其数。后面吴兵杀到，又不知多少军马。先主急上马，奔冯习营时，习营中火光连天而起。江南、江北，照耀如同白日。冯习慌上马引数十骑而走，正逢吴将徐盛军到，敌住厮杀。先主见了，拨马投西便走。徐盛舍了冯习，引兵追来。先主正慌，前面又一军拦住，乃是吴将丁奉，两下夹攻。先主大惊，四面无路。忽然喊声大震，一彪军杀入重围，乃是张苞，救了先主，引御林军奔走。正行之间，前面一军又到，乃蜀将傅彤也，合兵一处而行。背后吴兵追至。先主前到一山，名马鞍山。张苞、傅彤请先主上的山时，山下喊声又起：陆逊大队人马，将马鞍山围住。张苞、傅彤死据山口。先主遥望遍野火光不绝，死尸重叠，塞江而下。

will raid tonight," Cheng Ji answered. "We put them to rout last night," the Emperor said. "They would not dare return." "And if it was a probe?" Cheng Ji replied. As they spoke, someone reported that hilltop sentinels had spotted southern troops in the distance moving eastward along the range of hills. "Decoys," the Emperor said and ordered his troops to take no action. Instead, he sent Guan Xing and Zhang Bao with five hundred riders each to reconnoitre. At dusk Guan Xing returned to report that fires had sprung up in the north shore encampments. The Emperor sent Guan Xing to the north shore and Zhang Bao to the south to investigate. "Tell me as soon as the southern troops arrive," the Emperor concluded.

The two commanders set off. At the first watch a southeast wind sprang up sharply. The camp to the left of the Emperor's burst into flame. Before anyone could go to its aid, the camp to the right of the Emperor's also began burning. The wind quickened and the fire sped in its wake. Trees and bushes caught fire; screams rent the air. Soldiers and horses dashed from the burning camps and away from the Emperor's campground, causing countless soldiers to trample one another to death. From behind, a mass of southern soldiers bore down for the kill.

The Emperor sprang into his saddle and raced to Feng Xi, but his camp was already an inferno. North and south of the river the glare was bright as day. Feng Xi dashed to his horse and led away a few score of cavalry, only to meet the murderous advance of Xu Sheng. The Emperor turned west and fled. Xu Sheng passed Feng Xi by and led his troops after the Emperor, around whom everything was in confusion. Ahead of him another troop — led by Ding Feng — blocked his advance. Trapped on either side, the Emperor panicked. Suddenly, amid thunderous shouts a band of soldiers led by Zhang Bao broke through and pulled him to safety; together with the Royal Guard they bolted away. Moments later General Fu Tong joined forces with the Emperor, and they proceeded together.

Pursued by southern troops, the Emperor came to Saddle Hill. Zhang Bao and Fu Tong urged him to the top. A tumult welled up from below as Lu Xun's massive contingents surrounded the base. Zhang Bao and Fu Tong fought to control the pathway up as the Emperor looked out upon the fires raging across the plain and the bodies of the dead choking the

次日，吴兵又四下放火烧山，军士乱窜，先主惊慌。忽然火光中一将引数骑杀上山来，视之，乃关兴也。兴伏地请曰："四下火光逼近，不可久停。陛下速奔白帝城，再收军马可也。"先主曰："谁敢断后？"傅彤奏曰："臣愿以死当之！"当日黄昏，关兴在前，张苞在中，留傅彤断后，保着先主，杀下山来。吴兵见先主奔走，皆要争功，各引大军，遮天盖地，往西追赶。先主令军士尽脱袍铠，塞道而焚，以断后军。正奔走间，喊声大震，吴将朱然引一军从江岸边杀来，截住去路。先主叫曰："朕死于此矣！"关兴、张苞纵马冲突，被乱箭射回，各带重伤，不能杀出。背后喊声又起，陆逊引大军从山谷中杀来。

先主正慌急之间，此时天色已微明，只见前面喊声震天，朱然军纷纷落涧，滚滚投岩：一彪军杀入，前来救驾。先主大喜，视之，乃常山赵子龙也。时赵云在川中江州，闻吴、蜀交兵，遂引军出；忽见东南一带火光冲天，云心惊，远远探视，不想先主被困，云奋勇冲杀而来。陆逊闻是赵云，急令军退。云正杀之间，忽遇朱然，便与交锋；不一合，一枪刺朱然于马下，杀散吴兵，救出先主，望白帝城而走。先主曰："朕虽得脱，诸将士将奈

river.

The following day the Southlanders set fires around the hill. The Emperor's troops scurried away in disorder, leaving him in extremity. But through the glare of the blaze, a few riders cut their way up the hill; their leader was Guan Xing. Kneeling before the Emperor, he said, "The flames press closer. We must move on. Make haste to Baidi, Your Majesty, where we can regroup." The Emperor said, "Who will hold the rear?" Fu Tong volunteered, and as darkness fell they battled their way down the slopes, Guan Xing in front, Zhang Bao in the middle, Fu Tong in the rear guarding the Emperor. The southern commanders, spotting the fleeing Emperor, vied eagerly for the glory of capturing him, and the hosts they led west across the battle ground darkened the sky and covered the earth.

The Emperor had his men discard their surcoats and armor, and burn them to clog the road and prevent pursuit. They were continuing west, when a hue and cry went up: the southern general Zhu Ran had led a company from theriverbank to block their way. The Emperor cried out, "Here I die!" Guan Xing and Zhang Bao, thrusting and surging, fell back before the flurries of arrows. Seriously wounded, they could not fight their way out. More shouts from behind told them that Lu Xun was bringing up the main army.

2055

Dawn broke on a desperate Emperor. Suddenly, he heard a great roar and watched as Zhu Ran's ranks started to disintegrate. Every which way they began dropping into the rushing creeks or tumbling wavelike down from the heights. A band of men cut through to rescue the Emperor, who, to his delight, recognized their leader, Zhao Zilong of Changshan. Zhao Zilong had been in Jiangzhou but came to the scene when he heard fighting had broken out. Seeing a field of flames licking the sky to the southeast, he anxiously investigated and to his astonishment found that the Emperor was trapped. Determined to save his lord, Zilong raced to the battleground. Lu Xun, hearing of Zhao Zilong's arrival, swiftly ordered a retreat. But in the thick of the struggle Zhao Zilong met up with Zhu Ran and killed him in a brief clash. He scattered the southern soldiers, took charge of the Emperor, and headed for Baidi. "I may be safely out of it," the Emperor said, "but what about my com-

何?"云曰:"敌军在后,不可久迟。陛下且入白帝城歇息,臣再引兵去救应诸将。"此时先主仅存百余人入白帝城。后人有诗赞陆逊曰:

持矛举火破连营,玄德穷奔白帝城。

一旦威名惊蜀魏,吴王宁不敬书生。

却说傅彤断后,被吴军八面围住。丁奉大叫曰:"川兵死者无数,降者极多,汝主刘备已被擒获。今汝力穷势孤,何不早降!"傅彤叱曰:"吾乃汉将,安肯降吴狗乎!"挺枪纵马,率蜀军奋力死战,不下百余合,往来冲突,不能得脱。彤长叹曰:"吾今休矣!"言讫,口中吐血,死于吴军之中。后人赞傅彤诗曰:

彝陵吴蜀大交兵,陆逊施谋用火焚。

至死犹然骂"吴狗",傅彤不愧汉将军。

蜀祭酒程畿,匹马奔至江边,招呼水军赴敌,吴兵随后追来,水军四散奔逃。畿部将叫曰:"吴兵至矣!程祭酒快走罢!"畿怒曰:"吾自从主上出军,未尝赴敌而逃!"言未毕,吴兵骤至,四下无路,畿拔剑自刎。后人有诗赞曰:

慷慨蜀中程祭酒,身留一剑答君王。

临危不改平生志,博得声名万古香。

manders and men?" "The enemy is too close," Zilong said. "We cannot delay. If Your Majesty will enter Baidi and rest, I will go back to relieve the commanders." At this time the Emperor entered Baidi with a retinue of little more than one hundred. A poet of later times has left these lines expressing admiration for Lu Xun:[2]

> Spears in hand they torched the western camps:
> A desperate Liu Bei dashed into Baidi.
> By this one stroke Xun frightened Wei and Shu.
> Could the king of Wu not honor scholar Lu?

Fu Tong, guarding the rear, was surrounded by the southern forces. Ding Feng shouted to him, "Countless Riverlands troops have fallen. Thousands have surrendered. Your lord, Liu Bei, has been captured. Your force is spent; your situation, extreme. A quick submission is advisable." But Fu Tong shouted back an angry rebuke: "No Han general would ever submit to the dogs of Wu!" Raising his spear, he rode forward, leading his men in a strenuous last effort. He fought more than a hundred bouts, driving and thrusting back and forth, but he could not break free. With a deep sigh, Fu Tong said, "Then it is over." Blood welled up in his mouth; he died in the heat of battle. A later poet left these lines in his praise:

> By Yiling, Shu met Wu in heavy strife;
> Then Lu Xun burned the western legions out.
> "Dogs of the south" was Fu Tong's final curse:
> This general of Han did his title proud.

2057

Riverlands Libationer Cheng Ji mounted, dashed to the edge of the river, and called for marine forces to assist. But the southern troops kept coming on, and the mariners scattered and fled. Cheng Ji's lieutenant called out to him, "Their men are here! Save yourself!" "Since campaigning with my lord, I have never fled the field," Cheng Ji retorted. As he spoke, the enemy bore swiftly down. Escape was impossible. He drew his sword and cut his own throat. Later these lines were written to praise him:

> The spirit-stirring elder lord of Shu
> By his sword to his liege stayed true!
> Till death his lifelong zeal did not abate;
> The name he passes on will never fade.

时吴班、张南久围彝陵城，忽冯习到，言蜀兵败，遂引军来救先主，孙桓方才得脱。张、冯二将正行之间，前面吴兵杀来，背后孙桓从彝陵城杀出，两下夹攻。张南、冯习奋力冲突，不能得脱，死于乱军之中。后人有诗赞曰：

冯习忠无二，张南义少双。

沙场甘战死，史册共流芳。

吴班杀出重围，又遇吴兵追赶；幸得赵云接着，救回白帝城去了。时有蛮王沙摩柯，匹马奔走，正逢周泰，战二十余合，被泰所杀。蜀将杜路、刘宁尽皆降吴。蜀营一应粮草器仗，尺寸不存。蜀将川兵，降者无数。时孙夫人在吴，闻猇亭兵败，讹传先主死于军中，遂驱车至江边，望西遥哭，投江而死。后人立庙江滨，号曰枭姬祠。尚论者作诗叹之曰：

先主兵归白帝城，夫人闻难独捐生。

至今江畔遗碑在，犹著千秋烈女名。

却说陆逊大获全功，引得胜之兵，往西追袭。前离夔关不远，逊在马上看见前面临山傍江，一阵杀气，冲天而起；遂勒马回顾众将曰："前面必有埋伏，三军不可轻进。"即倒退十余里，

Riverlands generals Wu Ban and Zhang Nan had had Yiling under siege for many days when Feng Xi arrived with news of the recent defeats. Wu Ban and Zhang Nan left Yiling at once to aid the Emperor; thus Sun Huan was finally relieved.[3] On the march Zhang Nan and Feng Xi were confronted by a southern force as Sun Huan came up behind them. Trapped between two attackers, Zhang Nan and Feng Xi fought mightily, only to fall in the melee. Later this verse was made in their honor:

> Than Feng Xi, who more loyal?
> Than Zhang Nan, few more true!
> On fighting fields full willingly they died.
> The histories will cast their virtue wide.

As he fought through the southern lines, Wu Ban was overtaken by another southern force when, luckily, Zhao Zilong arrived on the scene and escorted him safely to Baidi.

At this time the Man king Shamoke, fleeing alone, was accosted by Zhou Tai. He killed Shamoke in a battle of twenty bouts, and the western commanders Du Lu and Liu Ning gave themselves up. All the grain, provender, and equipment in the western camps thus fell into southern hands, and untold numbers of Shu commanders and soldiers surrendered.

In the Southland Lady Sun heard of the western defeat at Xiaoting. On receiving an erroneous report that the Emperor had perished in the fighting, she had herself transported to the riverbank, where she stood gazing into the west in sorrow for the husband she believed dead. Then she threw herself into the waters and was no more. Her memory was later honored by the Shrine to an Ill-starred Consort built along the river.[4] A commentator wrote a poem lamenting Lady Sun's death:

2059

> "To Baidi the army of Han's repaired" —
> She lay down her life when the tidings came.
> Today by the river there stands a stone
> To honor forever the martyr's name.[5]

Lu Xun, triumphant, rode west in swift pursuit. Approaching Kui Pass, he saw a lethal miasma arising from among the looming mountains and the river alongside. Turning, he said to his followers, "There must be an ambush ahead. The army must not advance." Lu Xun retreated ten *li* and

于地势空阔处，排成阵势，以御敌军；即差哨马前去探视。回报并无军屯在此，逊不信，下马登高望之，杀气复起。逊再令人仔细探视，哨马回报，前面并无一人一骑。逊见日将西沉，杀气越加，心中犹豫，令心腹人再往探看。回报江边止有乱石八九十堆，并无人马。逊大疑，令寻土人问之。须臾，有数人到。逊问曰："何人将乱石作堆？如何乱石堆中有杀气冲起？"土人曰："此处地名鱼腹浦。诸葛亮入川之时，驱兵到此，取石排成阵势于沙滩之上。自此常常有气如云，从内而起。"

陆逊听罢，上马引数十骑来看石阵，立马于山坡之上，但见四面八方，皆有门有户。逊笑曰："此乃惑人之术耳，有何益焉！"遂引数骑下山坡来，直入石阵观看。部将曰："日暮矣，请都督早回。"逊方欲出阵，忽然狂风大作，一霎时，飞沙走石，遮天盖地。但见怪石嵯峨，槎桠似剑；横沙立土，重叠如山；江声浪涌，有如剑鼓之声。逊大惊曰："吾中诸葛之计也！"急欲回时，无路可出。正惊疑间，忽见一老人立于马前，笑曰："将军欲出此阵乎？"逊曰："愿长者引出。"老人策杖徐徐而行，径出石阵，并无所碍，送至山坡之上。逊问曰："长者何人？"老人答曰："老夫乃诸葛孔明之岳父黄承彦也。昔小婿入川之时，于此布下石阵，名'八阵图'。反复八门，按遁甲休、生、伤、杜、景、死、

set up defensive formations on open ground. The scouts he sent to investigate came back with nothing to report. Lu Xun did not believe them. He
climbed a hill on foot and scanned the terrain: the same sensation of
danger made itself felt. He ordered a minute investigation, which turned
up neither man nor horse. As the sun began to set, the mysterious signs
seemed stronger. Still undecided, he sent one of his trusted followers to
examine the area. He reported finding only eighty or ninety chaotic rock
piles alongside the river, but no military forces.

But Lu Xun's doubts remained. He had some local people brought to
him for questioning. "Who made these piles," he asked them, "and why
does an aura of death seem to come from them?" One man replied, "This
is Fishbelly Meadow. When Zhuge Liang came to the Riverlands he sent
troops here to arrange these rock formations on the sandflats. Since then, a
kind of cloudlike effluvium seems to emanate from their interiors."

Lu Xun led a few score of cavalry to examine the rocks. From a
hillslope he could see openings on all sides. "A device to perplex whoever comes," Lu Xun said with a smile. "What use is it?" He guided his
men down from the slope directly into the formation to inspect it. A lieutenant said, "The sun is setting; we should return, Chief Commander."
But when Lu Xun tried to get out, violent winds came up from nowhere.
Instantly, streams of sand and stone covered the sky and the ground until
all Xun could see were monstrous rocks sawing the air, jagged like sword
blades, and the relentless sand heaping up and rising into mountains. The
voice of the river rumbled and rolled like the beating of war drums.[6]

In terror Lu Xun cried, "Trapped by Zhuge Liang!" He was searching
frantically for a way out, when an old man appeared in front of Lu Xun's
horse and said with a smile, "You desire to leave, General?" "Would you
lead us out, your reverence?" Lu Xun answered. The old man, supporting himself with a staff, slowly traversed the formations, escorting them
back without the slightest difficulty to the hillslope they had come from.
"Who are you, your reverence?" Lu Xun asked. "Huang Chengyan," he
replied, "father-in-law of Zhuge Kongming. My son-in-law passed here
on his way west and deployed these rocky ramparts, which he called the
Eightfold Maze. There are eight endlessly shifting openings arranged according to the 'Taboo Days' formula: Desist, Survived, Injure, Con-

惊、开。每日每时，变化无端，可比十万精兵。临去之时，曾分付老夫道：'后有东吴大将迷于阵中，莫要引他出来。'老夫适于山岩之上，见将军从'死门'而入，料想不识此阵，必为所迷。老夫平生好善，不忍将军陷没于此，故特自'生门'引出也。"逊曰："公曾学此阵法否？"黄承彦曰："变化无穷，不能学也。"逊慌忙下马拜谢而回。后杜工部有诗曰：

功盖三分国，名成八阵图。

江流石不转，遗恨失吞吴。

陆逊回寨，叹曰："孔明真'卧龙'也！吾不能及！"于是下令班师。左右曰："刘备兵败势穷，困守一城，正好乘势击之；今见石阵而退，何也？"逊曰："吾非惧石阵而退；吾料魏主曹丕，其奸诈与父无异，今知吾追赶蜀兵，必乘虚来袭。吾若深入西川，急难退矣。"遂令一将断后，逊率大军而回。退兵未及二日，三处人来飞报："魏兵曹仁出濡须，曹休出洞口，曹真出南郡：三路兵马数十万，星夜至境，未知何意。"逊笑曰："不出吾之所料。吾已令兵拒之矣。"

found, Exhibit, Perish, Surprise, and Liberate. During every time period of every day the openings move unpredictably, like ten crack legions in constant motion. As Kongming was leaving, he cautioned me, 'The time will come when a commanding general of the Southland will lose his way in this maze. Do not show him how to get out.' Just now from the cliffs I saw you go in by the gate called Perish and judged that you would be entrapped out of ignorance of the system. But I've always been disposed to do a good turn, and rather than see you get swallowed up in here, I came over to show you out by the gate Survive."

"Good sir," Lu Xun asked, "have you mastered this system of formations?" Huang Chengyan answered, "The transformations never end. They cannot be mastered." Lu Xun hurriedly dismounted, paid his respects to the old man, and returned to his camp.[7] The poet Du Fu has described Kongming's stone ramparts:

> Deeds to vault a thrice-torn realm,
> Fame at peak with the Eightfold Maze,
> Now steadfast stones in the river's run —
> Monument to his rue
> That his king had choked no Wu!

"Kongming's a 'Sleeping Dragon,' indeed — more than a match for me," Lu Xun conceded, and he gave the order to retreat. His advisers protested: "Liu Bei's army is ruined; his power is exhausted. We have him backed into a single walled town. This is our opportunity to attack. Why retire because of some rock formations?" Lu Xun responded, "I am not retreating for fear of the rocks. My guess is that Cao Pi, lord of Wei, is no less cunning than his father was. He knows we are pursuing the army of the Riverlands and will attack our undefended homeland. If we push too far west, it will be very difficult for us to pull back in time to defend it." And so Lu Xun assigned one general to block the rear while he led the main army back to the Southland. Less than two days after the retreat began, scouts urgently reported to Lu Xun the movements of the three northern armies: "Cao Ren has come down from Ruxu, Cao Xiu from Dongkiu, and Cao Zhen from Nanjun. There three armies numbering in the hundreds of thousands have reached our borders by swift night marches, but their intentions are as yet uncertain." Lu Xun smiled and

2063

正是：

　　　　雄心方欲吞西蜀，胜算还须御北朝。

未知如何退兵，且看下文分解。

said, "Exactly what I anticipated! I have already sent troops to check them." Indeed:

> Ambition to devour the west yieded to a wiser course:
> Contain the north.

How did Lu Xun retreat?
    Read on.

汉英经典文库

2066

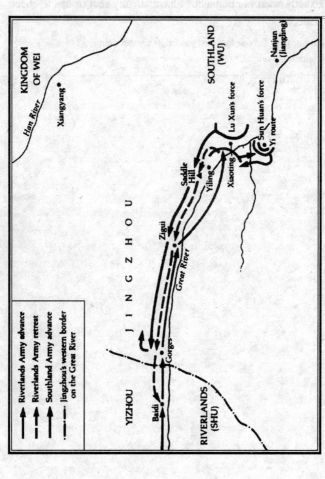

MAP 8. Liu Bei's defeat in the battle of Xiaoting. Source: Liu Chunfan, *Sanguo shihua* (Beijing: Beijing chubanshe, 1981), p. 154.

第八十五回

刘先主遗诏托孤儿　诸葛亮安居平五路

　　却说章武二年夏六月，东吴陆逊大破蜀兵于猇亭彝陵之地；先主奔回白帝城，赵云引兵据守。忽马良至，见大军已败，懊悔不及，将孔明之言，奏知先主。先主叹曰："朕早听丞相之言，不致今日之败！今有何面目复回成都见群臣乎！"遂传旨就白帝城住扎，将馆驿改为永安宫。人报冯习、张南、傅彤、程畿、沙摩柯等皆殁于王事，先主伤感不已。又近臣奏称："黄权引江北之兵，降魏去了。陛下可将彼家属送有司问罪。"先主曰："黄权被吴兵隔断在江北岸，欲归无路，不得已而降魏：是朕负权，非权负朕也。何必罪其家属？"仍给禄米以养之。

　　却说黄权降魏，诸将引见曹丕。丕曰："卿今降朕，欲追慕于陈、韩耶？"权泣而奏曰："臣受蜀帝之恩，殊遇甚厚，令臣督诸军于江北，被陆逊绝断。臣归蜀无路，降吴不可，故来投陛下。败军之将，免死为幸，安敢追慕于古人耶！"丕大喜，遂拜黄

Chapter 85

First Ruler Liu Finds a Guardian for His Heir
Zhuge Liang Calmly Holds Off Five Armies

It was the sixth month of the second year of Zhang Wu.[1] Lu Xun of the Southland had decisively beaten the Riverlands troops at Xiaoting and Yiling, and the Emperor was in sanctuary in Baidi, guarded by Zhao Zilong. Ma Liang arrived and, finding the army defeated, was overcome by a sense of futility and regret. He delivered Kongming's communication to the Emperor, who sighed and responded, "Had I heeded my prime minister in good time, today's defeat could have been avoided. How am I to return to Chengdu and face the assembly of the court?" He transmitted his wish to remain in Baidi and renamed his quarters the Palace of Enduring Peace. He grieved inconsolably when informed of the commanders who had perished in his service: Feng Xi, Zhang Nan, Fu Tong, Cheng Ji, and Shamoke.

A trusted vassal then reported: "Huang Quan has taken his troops from the north shore and defected to Wei. Your Majesty should deliver his entire clan to the authorities to answer for his conduct." But the Emperor replied, "Huang Quan was cut off by the southern army. He had no way to get back and surrendered to Wei against his will. It is I who have betrayed Huang Quan, not Huang Quan me. Why punish his family?" And he continued to provide for Huang Quan's family.

Meanwhile, Huang Quan has been taken before Cao Pi, who said, "In surrender, will you emulate Chen Ping and Han Xin and make war on Liu Bei while in my service?"[2] Huang Quan wept openly as he replied, "The Riverlands Emperor was generous to me beyond all measure. He gave me command of the forces north of the river, and there Lu Xun cut me off. I could not return to Shu; I would not submit to Wu — so I chose to take refuge with Your Majesty. For a defeated general to be spared is blessing enough. I have no desire to emulate the ancients." This answer

权为镇南将军。权坚辞不受。忽近臣奏曰："有细作人自蜀中来，说蜀主将黄权家属尽皆诛戮。"权曰："臣与蜀主，推诚相信，知臣本心，必不肯杀臣之家小也。"丕然之。后人有诗责黄权曰：

降吴不可却降曹，忠义安能事两朝？

堪叹黄权惜一死，紫阳书法不轻饶。

曹丕问贾诩曰："朕欲一统天下，先取蜀乎？先取吴乎？"诩曰："刘备雄才，更兼诸葛亮善能治国；东吴孙权，能识虚实，陆逊现屯兵于险要，隔江泛湖，皆难卒谋。以臣观之，诸将之中，皆无孙权、刘备敌手。虽以陛下天威临之，亦未见万全之势也。只可持守，以待二国之变。"丕曰："朕已遣三路大兵伐吴，安有不胜之理？"尚书刘晔曰："近东吴陆逊，新破蜀兵七十万，上下齐心，更有江湖之阻，不可卒制；陆逊多谋，必有准备。"丕曰："卿前劝朕伐吴，今又谏阻，何也？"晔曰："时有不同也。昔东吴累败于蜀，其势顿挫，故可击耳；今既获全胜，锐气百倍，未可攻也。"丕曰："朕意已决，卿勿复言。"遂引御林军亲往接应三路兵马。早有哨马报说东吴已有准备：令吕范引兵拒住曹

pleased Cao Pi. He would have appointed Huang Quan General Who Quells the South, but Quan firmly declined the honor. At that moment an attendant announced, "A spy from the west says that the lord of the Riverlands has put Huang Quan's clan to the sword." Huang Quan said, "The lord of the Riverlands and this vassal are perfectly honest with each other. He knows me too well to do such a thing." Cao Pi agreed. A poet of later times, however, criticized Huang Quan:

> Surrender not to Wu, then why to Cao?
> Loyalty is to serve a single throne!
> For Huang Quan thus to cherish his own life
> Is something Zhu Xi's *Gangmu* can't condone.

Cao Pi asked Jia Xu, "To fulfill my desire to unify the empire, should I take the Riverlands first or the Southland?" Jia Xu replied, "Liu Bei has prodigious ability and the added advantage of Zhuge Liang's great administrative skill. Sun Quan of the Southland has a keen eye for appraising his enemies. Lu Xun now controls the strategic points; the river and lakes give him protection and mobility. With no promising objectives and, in my view, no commanders to match those of the south or the west, not even Your awe-inspiring Majesty can ensure success. Better to maintain a defensive position and wait for new developments in the two kingdoms." Cao Pi said, "The three powerful armies we have sent south should prevail." However, Imperial Secretary Liu Ye said, "Recently Lu Xun has defeated seven hundred thousand Riverlanders. The southern army is unified in spirit and enjoys the protective advantage of various bodies of water. It will be quite difficult to overpower them. And Lu Xun is full of schemes and will be well prepared for us."

Cao Pi said, "Initially you urged me to attack. Now you raise objections. Why?" "A difference in the timing," Liu Ye continued. "Earlier, the southerners had suffered a string of defeats and were vulnerable because their force was blunted. Now after complete victory, with their morale heightened a hundredfold, they are proof against attack." "I have decided to attack. You need say no more," Cap Pi responded and went forth at the head of the Royal Guard to reinforce the three armies. Before long, the Wei ruler received intelligence that the southern commanders had drawn up their defense: Lü Fan to check Cao Xiu, Zhuge Jin to

休，诸葛瑾引兵在南郡拒住曹真，朱桓引兵当住濡须以拒曹仁。刘晔曰："既有准备，去恐无益。"丕不从，引兵而去。

却说吴将朱桓，年方二十七岁，极有胆略，孙权甚爱之；时督军于濡须，闻曹仁引大军去取羡溪，桓遂尽拨军守把羡溪去了，止留五千骑守城。忽报曹仁令大将常雕同诸葛虔、王双，引五万精兵飞奔濡须城来。众军皆有惧色。桓按剑而言曰："胜负在将，不在兵之多寡。兵法云：'客兵倍而主兵半者，主兵尚能胜于客兵。'今曹仁千里跋涉，人马疲困。吾与汝等，共据高城，南临大江，北背山险，以逸待劳，以主制客：此乃百战百胜之势。虽曹丕自来，尚不足忧，况仁等耶！"于是传令，教众军偃旗息鼓，只作无人守把之状。

且说魏将先锋常雕，领精兵来取濡须城，遥望城上并无军马。雕催军急进，离城不远，一声炮响，旌旗齐竖。朱桓横刀飞马而出，直取常雕。战不三合，被桓一刀斩常雕于马下。吴兵乘势冲杀一阵，魏兵大败，死者无数。朱桓大胜，得了无数旌旗军器战马。曹仁领兵随后到来，却被吴兵从羡溪杀出。曹仁大败而退，回见魏主，细奏大败之事。丕大惊。正议之间，忽探马报："曹真、夏侯尚围了南郡，被陆逊伏兵于内，诸葛瑾伏兵于外，

block Cao Zhen at Nanjun, and Zhu Huan to oppose Cao Ren at Ruxu. Liu Ye said to Cao Pi, "Since they are prepared, what's the good of our going?" But Cao Pi remained determined to proceed.

The southern general Zhu Huan, a mere twenty-seven years of age, was bold and resourceful; Sun Quan treasured him. While on duty at Ruxu, Zhu Huan heard that Cao Ren had moved to take Xianxi, so Zhu Huan sent the bulk of his force to defend Xianxi, keeping back only five thousand cavalry at Ruxu. Zhu Huan next learned that Cao Ren was sending a high commander, Chang Diao, to Xianxi, together with Zhuge Qian, Wang Shuang, and fifty thousand crack troops. The defenders began to give way to fear. But Zhu Huan rested his hand on his sword and said, "Leadership, not numbers, determines victory. The rules of war teach that a defender can prevail with only half an attacker's numbers. Cao Ren has come a hard thousand *li*. His men and horses are worn out. We command our high walls; we have the Great River directly south of us and formidable mountains to our north. When our well-rested troops give their fatigued forces the 'welcome' they deserve, victory will be certain. Cao Pi himself would pose no problem, let alone Cao Ren!" So saying, Zhu Huan ordered all banners downed and all drums stilled, thereby creating the impression that the town was undefended.

From the distance, the general of the approaching Wei vanguard, Chang Diao, and his crack force saw neither horse nor soldier on the walls of Ruxu. Diao hurried his troops along. As they drew near, a bombard sounded and banners sprang up. Broadsword leveled, Zhu Huan charged Chang Diao and swiftly cut him down from his horse. The southern soldiers made the most of their leader's victory, routing the northern mass and inflicting heavy losses. A triumphant Zhu Huan captured quantities of banners, military equipment, and war-horese. Cao Ren's army arrived late. The southern forces from Xianxi cut them to pieces and drove them from the field.

Cao Ren presented himself before the Wei ruler, Cao Pi, and recounted the details of the debacle. Cao Pi was astonished. During their discussion, a fresh report arrived: "Cao Zhen and Xiahou Shang have gone down to defeat. They had Nanjun surrounded when ambushers inside, led by Lu Xun, and outside, led by Zhuge Jin, closed in and decimated

内外夹攻，因此大败。"言未毕，忽探马又报："曹休亦被吕范杀败。"丕听知三路兵败，乃喟然叹曰："朕不听贾诩、刘晔之言，果有此败！"时值夏天，大疫流行，马步军十死六七，遂引军回洛阳。吴、魏自此不和。

却说先主在永安宫，染病不起，渐渐沉重。至章武三年夏四月，先主自知病入四肢，又哭关、张二弟，其病愈深；两目昏花，厌见侍从之人，乃叱退左右，独卧于龙榻之上。忽然阴风骤起，将灯吹摇，灭而复明。只见灯影之下，二人侍立。先主怒曰："朕心绪不宁，教汝等且退，何故又来！"叱之不退。先主起而视之，上首乃云长，下首乃翼德也。先主大惊曰："二弟原来尚在？"云长曰："臣等非人，乃鬼也。上帝以臣二人平生不失信义，皆敕命为神。哥哥与兄弟聚会不远矣。"先主扯定大哭。忽然惊觉，二弟不见。即唤从人问之，时正三更。先主叹曰："朕不久于人世矣！"遂遣使往成都，请丞相诸葛亮、尚书令李严等，星夜来永安宫，听受遗命。孔明等与先主次子鲁王刘永、梁王刘理，来永安宫见帝，留太子刘禅守成都。

且说孔明到永安宫，见先主病危，慌忙拜伏于龙榻之下。先主传旨，请孔明坐于龙榻之侧，抚其背曰："朕自得丞相，幸

them." While the envoy was speaking, another scout announced, "Cao Xiu has lost the field to Lü Fan." His three armies defeated, Cao Pi sighed deeply and said, "Had I only listened to Jia Xu and Liu Ye!"

It was midsummer. An epidemic was raging. Some seven-tenths of the soldiers, foot and mounted, had perished. At long last Cap Pi brought the armies back to Luoyang. Thereafter there was bad blood between Wei and Wu.

* * *

In the Palace of Enduring Peace the Emperor was confined to his bed by a worsening illness. In the fourth month of the third year of Zhang Wu (A.D. 223) the Emperor knew the disease had spread into his limbs. Weeping for his brothers had aggravated his symptoms. His vision grew dim. Disgusted with his attendants, he discharged them and lay back on his couch in solitude. A chill, gloomy wind sprang up. His lantern darkened, then flared. Two men stood in the circle of the shadow it cast. The Emperor spoke irritably: "I thought I had dismissed you to give my mind a moment's calm. What brings you again?" They ignored his dismissal. The Emperor arose to examine them: one was Lord Guan, the other Zhang Fei. "Then you are still alive!" the Emperor exclaimed. "We are ghosts, not men," responded Guan. "The supernal sovereign recognized that in our lifetimes we two never forsook our good faith or our allegiance, and so he has made gods of us. Elder brother, the time of our reunion is not far off."

2075

The Emperor reached for them, emitting a cry, then awoke with a spasm. The two were gone. He summoned his attendants to ask the hour. It was the third watch. The Emperor sighed, saying, "My time will be short in the world of men." He sent to Chengdu for Prime Minister Zhuge Liang, Imperial Secretary Li Yan, and other high officials, and they rushed to the Palace of Enduring Peace to receive his final instructions. Kongming and the Emperor's younger sons Liu Yong, king of Lu, and Liu Li, king of Liang, came before the Emperor. The heir apparent, Liu Shan, remained in Chengdu.

Kongming, seeing that the Emperor's condition was critical, prostrated himself at the royal couch with reverent haste. But the Emperor expressed his wish that the prime minister sit at the edge of the couch.

成帝业;何期智识浅陋,不纳丞相之言,自取其败。悔恨成疾,死在旦夕。嗣子孱弱,不得不以大事相托。"言讫,泪流满面。孔明亦涕泣曰:"愿陛下善保龙体,以副下天之望!"先主以目遍视,只见马良之弟马谡在傍,先主令且退。谡退出,先主谓孔明曰:"丞相观马谡之才何如?"孔明曰:"此人亦当世之英才也。"先主曰:"不然。朕观此人,言过其实,不可大用。丞相宜深察之。"分付毕,传旨召诸臣入殿,取纸笔写了遗诏,递与孔明而叹曰:"朕不读书,粗知大略。圣人云:'鸟之将死,其鸣也哀;人之将死,其言也善。'朕本待与卿等同灭曹贼,共扶汉室;不幸中道而别。烦丞相将诏付与太子禅,令勿以为常言。凡事更望丞相教之!"孔明等泣拜于地曰:"愿陛下将息龙体!臣等尽施犬马之劳,以报陛下知遇之恩也。"先主命内侍扶起孔明,一手掩泪,一手执其手,曰:"朕今死矣,有心腹之言相告!"孔明曰:"有何圣谕?"先主泣曰:"君才十倍曹丕,必能安邦定国,终定大事。若嗣子可辅,则辅之;如其不才,君可自为成都之主。"孔明听毕,汗流遍体,手足失措,泣拜于地曰:"臣安敢不竭股肱之力,尽忠贞之节,继之以死乎!"言讫,叩头流血。先主

Placing his hand gently on Kongming's back, he said, "Through you alone the imperial quest was achieved. How could I have foolishly rejected your advice and thus brought on this defeat? Wracked by remorse, I stand at death's door. My heir is an inconsequential weakling, and so I must entrust you with my cause." Tears covered his face.[3]

Kongming, also in tears, replied, "Your Majesty must preserve his dragon form to fulfill the hopes of the empire." The Emperor glanced around the room and, spotting Ma Liang's younger brother, Ma Su, told him to retire. The Emperor asked Kongming, "What is my prime minister's estimate of Ma Su's talents?" "Among the most splendid of the age," was the reply. "You are wrong," the Emperor said, "In my view he's braggart. Give him no important assignment. Take careful note of this, Prime Minister." Having issued this warning, the Emperor summoned his officials into his chamber and transcribed his testament before them. Handing it to Kongming, he said with a sigh, "I am no scholar; and my knowledge is crude and superficial. The Sage said, 'Doleful, the notes of a dying bird; precious, the words of a dying man.' Together we have tried to annihilate the traitor Cao and uphold the house of Han. Alas, midway in our undertaking we must part. I would trouble the prime minister to impart my edict to the heir and teach him its importance. I rely on you to guide him in all matters, Prime Minister."

Weeping, Kongming and the others bowed to the ground and said, "We beg Your Majesty to enjoy a measure of repose. Each of us will spare no pains in gratitude for your generous treatment." The Emperor ordered his attendants to raise Kongming up. Brushing his tearful eyes with one hand and taking Kongming's hand in the other, he said, "I am going to die, and I have something more to say." "What sacred instruction?" Kongming asked. The Emperor wept as he responded, "Your ability exceeds Cao Pi's by ten to one, and I know you will be able to secure and preserve the empire and in the end attain our goal. If my heir proves worthy of support, support him. If he proves unfit, take the kingship of the Riverlands yourself." Kongming broke into a sweat; in extreme agitation, he prostrated himself again. "Could I do otherwise," he said tearfully, "than serve him as aide and vassal, persevering in loyalty unto death?" He knocked his forehead to the ground until blood showed.

又请孔明坐于榻上,唤鲁王刘永、梁王刘理近前,分付曰:"尔等皆记朕言:朕亡之后,尔兄弟三人,皆以父事丞相,不可怠慢。"言罢,遂命二王同拜孔明。二王拜毕,孔明曰:"臣虽肝脑涂地,安能报知遇之恩也!"

先主谓众官曰:"朕已托孤于丞相,令嗣子以父事之。卿等俱不可怠慢,以负朕望。"又嘱赵云曰:"朕与卿于患难之中,相从到今,不想于此地分别。卿可想朕故交,早晚看觑吾子,勿负朕言。"云泣拜曰:"臣敢不效犬马之劳!"先主又谓众官曰:"卿等众官,朕不能一一分嘱,愿皆自爱。"言毕,驾崩,寿六十三岁。时章武三年夏四月二十四日也。后杜工部有诗叹曰:

蜀主窥吴向三峡,崩年亦在永安宫。

翠华想像空山外,玉殿虚无野寺中。

古庙杉松巢水鹤,岁时伏腊走村翁。

武侯祠屋长邻近,一体君臣祭祀同。

先主驾崩,文武官僚,无不哀痛。孔明率众官奉梓宫还成都。太子刘禅出城迎接灵柩,安于正殿之内。举哀行礼毕,开读遗诏。诏曰:

朕初得疾,但下痢耳;后转生杂病,殆不自济。朕闻"人年五十,不称夭寿"。今朕年六十有余,死复何恨?——

Again the Emperor called Kongming to sit on his couch. He summoned Liu Yong and Liu Li to approach and charged them: "Mark well my words. After I am gone, I want you and Liu Shan to serve the prime minister with all diligence and respect, as if he were your father." So saying, he ordered the two princes to prostrate themselves before Kongming. "Were I to lay my innards on the ground, I could never require the kindness Your Grace has shown me," Kongming concluded.

To the larger assembly the Emperor said, "I am entrusting my heir to the prime minister. I have instructed my heir to serve him as his father. Let none of you neglect this charge and betray my hopes." The Emperor turned to Zhao Zilong and said, "We have been through many a trial and ordeal together. Who could have anticipated such a parting? For the sake of our old friendship, will you keep a constant watch over my sons and honor my wishes?" Tearfully, Zhao Zilong prostrated himself and said, "I am bound to exert every fibre of my being in this service." Next, the Emperor said to the assembly, "I cannot give an individual charge to each one of you. But I hope you will all care well for yourselves and keep your self-respect." The Emperor finished speaking; then he was no more. He had reached the age of sixty-three. It was the twenty-fourth day of the fourth month of Zhang Wu 3.[4] Du Fu has left this poem lamenting the fate of Liu Bei:

> His view trained south, Shu's ruler graced Three Gorges
> And two years thence was dead, in Yong'an Palace still.
> Picture regal plumes upon those vacant hills;
> How blank and bare his hall of state in a country shrine!
> Fir and pine by the old fane keep cormorants[5]
> Till solstice feast days stir the old folks out:
> With Kongming's sanctum always right next door,
> In sacred union liege and man share the rites of worship.[6]

Grieving officials, led by Kongming, bore the royal coffin back to Chengdu, where Heir Apparent Liu Shan received them outside the city walls. He had his father's body placed in state in the main hall of the palace. After the rites and mourning the testament was read:

> It began with no more than severe stomach cramps, but complications developed, and recovery became less and less likely. They say, "After

但以卿兄弟之念耳。勉之！勉之！勿以恶小而为之，勿以善小而不为。惟贤惟德，可以服人；卿父德薄，不足效也。卿与丞相从事，事之如父，勿怠！勿忘！卿兄弟更求闻达。至嘱！至嘱！

群臣读诏已毕。孔明曰："国不可一日无君；请立嗣君，以承汉统。"乃立太子禅即皇帝位，改元建兴。加诸葛亮为武乡侯，领益州牧。葬先主于惠陵，谥曰昭烈皇帝。尊皇后吴氏为皇太后；谥甘夫人为昭烈皇后，糜夫人亦追谥为皇后。升赏群臣，大赦天下。

早有魏军探知此事，报入中原。近臣奏知魏主。曹丕大喜曰："刘备已亡，朕无忧矣。何不乘其国中无主，起兵伐之？"贾诩谏曰："刘备虽亡，必托孤于诸葛亮。亮感备知遇之恩，必倾心竭力，扶持嗣主。陛下不可仓卒伐之。"正言间，忽一人从班部中奋然而出曰："不乘此时进兵，更待何时？"众视之，乃司马懿也。丕大喜，遂问计于懿。懿曰："若只起中国之兵，急难取胜。须用五路大兵，四面夹攻，令诸葛亮首尾不能救应，然后可图。"

丕问何五路，懿曰："可修书一封，差使往辽东鲜卑国，见国王轲比能，赂以金帛，令起辽西羌兵十万，先从旱路取西平

fifty, one no longer dies young," so to die after sixty is hardly cause for regret, though you and your brothers still occupy my thoughts. Be vigilant! Be vigilant! If an evil is minor, resist it nonetheless. If a good deed is trifling, perform it all the same. Only wisdom and virtue can truly win men's devotion. My meagre virtue was unworthy of your emulation. Serve the prime minister as if he were your father; be neither negligent nor remiss. Seek to make a name for yourself. Such is my final charge.

After the reading of the will, Kongming said, "A dynasty cannot go a single day without a sovereign. Let us enthrone the heir in order to continue the line of Han unbroken." The assembly thus inaugurated Liu Shan emperor and changed the reign title to Jian Xing, "Commence the Revival." Zhuge Liang was made lord of Wuxiang and protector of Yizhou. The late Emperor was interred at Huiling and posthumously titled August Emperor Zhao Lie, or Reflected Glory.[7] The Empress, Lady Wu, was honored as queen mother. Lady Gan, the mother of Liu Shan, was posthumously honored as August Empress Zhao Lie. Lady Mi was posthumously remembered as Empress. The body of officials was promoted and rewarded; amnesty was proclaimed throughout the empire.[8]

* * *

News of Liu Bei's death soon made its way north, and imperial attendants informed the king. Cao Pi said delightedly, "With Liu Bei gone, my worries are over. Let us attack while they have no king." But Jia Xu remonstrated with him: "Liu Bei must have charged Zhuge Liang with the care of his son. Mindful of Liu Bei's kindness, Zhuge Liang will render to the heir the fullest measure of devotion. Your Majesty cannot invade precipitately." As Jia Xu spoke, someone stepped out from the rows of officials and cried with fervor, "Such an opportunity to attack will never come again!" The assembly turned to Sima Yi. The delighted Cao Pi asked his plan, and Sima Yi replied, "Troops from north China alone cannot succeed. To attain our objectives will require a vast force composed of five field armies concerted in an all-round attack to prevent Zhuge Liang from coordinating his van and his rear."

Questioned further by Cao Pi, Sima Yi explained, "Prepare a letter to the Xianbi nation in Liaodong. An envoy will take it to their king, Kebineng, together with gifts of gold and silk to get him to raise a force of

关：此一路也。再修书遣使赍官诰赏赐，直入南蛮，见蛮王孟获，令起兵十万，攻打益州、永昌、牂牁、越巂四郡，以击西川之南：此二路也。再遣使入吴修好，许以割地，令孙权起兵十万，攻两川峡口，径取涪城：此三路也。又可差使至降将孟达处，起上庸兵十万，西攻汉中：此四路也。然后命大将军曹真为大都督，提兵十万，由京兆径出阳平关取西川；此五路也。——共大兵五十万，五路并进，诸葛亮便有吕望之才，安能当此乎？"丕大喜，随即密遣能言官四员为使前去；又命曹真为大都督，领兵十万，径取阳平关。此时张辽等一班旧将，皆封列侯，俱在冀、徐、青及合淝等处，据守关津隘口，故不复调用。

　　却说蜀汉后主刘禅，自即位以来，旧臣多有病亡者，不能细说。凡一应朝廷选法、钱粮、词讼等事，皆听诸葛丞相裁处。时后主未立皇后，孔明与群臣上言曰："故车骑将军张飞之女甚贤，年十七岁，可纳为正宫皇后。"后主即纳之。

　　建兴元年秋八月，忽有边报说："魏调五路大兵，来取西川；第一路，曹真为大都督，起兵十万，取阳平关；第二路，乃反

one hundred thousand Qiang soldiers from Liaoxi as our first field army; let them take Xiping Pass by land. Write a second letter for an envoy to take to the land of the Southern Man along with new titles and rewards. Have their king, Meng Huo, muster another hundred thousand — the second field army — for an attack on the four southern districts of the Riverlands: Yizhou, Yongchang, Zangge, and Yuesui.[9] Next, send someone to the Southland to mend relations, promising them some territory to get Sun Quan to raise another hundred thousand soldiers — the third field army — for an attack on Three Gorges and the city of Fu. Then send an envoy to the general who has surrendered to us, Meng Da, so that one hundred thousand can be raised, in Shangyong for an attack to the west on Hanzhong. That will be the fourth field army. Finally, give Cao Zhen chief command of one hundred thousand — the fifth army — to proceed from Jingzhao to Yangping Pass for the capture of the Riverlands itself. Even if he had the talents of Lü Wang, Zhuge Liang could not contend with a concerted invasion by five hundred thousand."

Delighted, Cao Pi dispatched four persuasive envoys on their secret missions, and he made Cao Zhen chief commander of an army of one hundred thousand to take Yangping Pass. Zhang Liao and other members of Cao Cao's old guard who had been made honorary lords and posted to various strategic points in Jizhou, Xuzhou, Qingzhou, and Hefei were not assigned to join in this campaign.

* * *

Since the accession of the Second Ruler of Shu-Han, Liu Shan, many vassals of the old days had fallen ill and died; their particular fates may by passed over. All matters of state, appointment of officials, revenue and taxation, and judicial administration were left entirely in the hands of Prime Minister Zhuge Liang. The matter of an empress was still pending. Kongming and the courtiers petitioned the Emperor, "The daughter of Zhang Fei, late general of Chariots and Cavalry, is a worthy and virtuous woman. She is seventeen years and an acceptable consort for the new Emperor."[10] Liu Shan accepted the prime minister's choice.

In the eighth month of the first year of the new reign period, Jian Xing, a report form the border came in: "The kingdom of Wei has fielded five armies in order to conquer the Riverlands. The first, one hundred

将孟达，起上庸兵十万，犯汉中；第三路，乃东吴孙权，起精兵十万，取峡口入川；第四路，乃蛮王孟获，起蛮兵十万，犯益州四郡；第五路，乃番王轲比能，起羌兵十万，犯西平关。——此五路军马，甚是利害。已先报知丞相，丞相不知为何，数日不出视事。"后主听罢大惊，即差近侍赍旨，宣召孔明入朝。使命去了半日，回报："丞相府下人言，丞相染病不出。"后主转慌；次日，又命黄门侍郎董允、谏议大夫杜琼，去丞相卧榻前，告此大事。董、杜二人到丞相府前，皆不得入。杜琼曰："先帝托孤于丞相，今主上初登宝位，被曹丕五路兵犯境，军情至急，丞相何故推病不出？"良久，门吏传丞相令，言："病体稍可，明早出都堂议事。"董、杜二人叹息而回。次日，多官又来丞相府前伺候。从早至晚，又不见出。多官惶惶，只得散去。杜琼入奏后主曰："请陛下圣驾，亲往丞相府问计。"后主即引多官入宫，启奏皇太后。太后大惊，曰："丞相何故如此？有负先帝委托之意也！我当自往。"董允奏曰："娘娘未可轻往。臣料丞相必有高明之见。且待主上先往。如果怠慢，请娘娘于太庙中，召丞相问之未迟。"太后依奏。

thousand men under Chief Commander Cao Zhen, is marching to Yangping Pass. The second, under the rebel Meng Da, is attacking Hanzhong with one hundred thousand Shangyong soldiers. The third consists of Sun Quan's crack troops, numbering one hundred thousand; they are coming into the Riverlands through Three Gorges. The fourth army is led by the Southern Man king Meng Huo; its goal is Yizhou and the other three southern districts. The fifth is the army of the Qiang king Kebineng; it will go against Xiping Pass. These five armies pose a mortal threat. We have reported their movements to the prime minister, but for reasons unknown he has not conducted business for several days."

Alarmed by this report, the Second Emperor summoned Kongming to court. After a long while the messenger reported back, "According to his household staff, he is too ill to go out." The Second Emperor became more anxious. The next day he sent Inner Bureau Officer Dong Yun and Senior Court Counselor Du Qiong to announce the emergency to the prime minister in his sickroom. But the two men were not admitted to Kongming's residence. Du Qiong said to the gateman, "The late Emperor made the prime minister responsible for the heir. His Majesty has hardly assumed the throne, and Cao Pi's five armies have breached our borders. This is a military emergency. Why does the prime minister allege illness and not appear?" After a while the gateman conveyed the prime minister's answer: "As his indisposition had eased somewhat, he will be at the ministry tomorrow morning in his official capacity." The two dispirited envoys returned to the Emperor.

The next day the officials came before the prime minister's residence and waited. The day passed, and he did not appear. The officials departed apprehensively. Du Qiong addressed the Second Emperor: "I beg Your Majesty to go personally to the prime minister's residence and ask his plan." The Second Emperor immediately led his officials into the palace to explain the situation to the queen mother. The queen mother, startled by what she was told, said, "Why, the prime minister could never betray the late Emperor's trust. I will go to him myself." But Dong Yun said to her, "Royal Mother, do not be hasty. Surely, the prime minister has a higher end in view. Let His Majesty go to him first. If the prime minister is unresponsive, there will be time enough for you to summon

次日，后主车驾亲至相府。门吏见驾到，慌忙拜伏于地而迎。后主问曰："丞相在何处？"门吏曰："不知在何处。只有丞相钧旨，教挡住百官，勿得辄入。"后主乃下车步行，独进第三重门，见孔明独倚竹杖，在小池边观鱼。后主在后立久，乃徐徐而言曰："丞相安乐否？"孔明回顾，见是后主，慌忙弃杖，拜伏于地曰："臣该万死！"后主扶起，问曰："今曹丕分兵五路，犯境甚急，相父缘何不肯出府视事？"孔明大笑，扶后主入内室坐定，奏曰："五路兵至，臣安得不知？臣非观鱼，有所思也。"后主曰："如之奈何？"孔明曰："羌王轲比能，蛮王孟获，反将孟达，魏将曹真：此四路兵，臣已皆退去了也。止有孙权这一路兵，臣已有退之之计，但须一能言之人为使。因未得其人，故熟思之。陛下何必忧乎？"

后主听罢，又惊又喜，曰："相父果有鬼神不测之机也！愿闻退兵之策。"孔明曰："先帝以陛下付托与臣，臣安敢旦夕怠慢。成都众官，皆不晓兵法之妙——贵在使人不测，岂可泄漏于人？老臣先知西番国王轲比能，引兵犯西平关；臣料马超积祖西川人氏，素得羌人之心，羌人以超为神威天将军，臣已先遣一人，星夜驰檄，令马超紧守西平关，伏四路奇兵，每日交

him into the ancestral shrine." The queen mother abided by this counsel.

The next day the Second Emperor visited the ministerial residence. As His Majesty came into view, the gateman hurriedly prostated himself. "Where is the prime minister?" the Emperor asked. "I do not know." the gateman replied. "But we were instructed to admit no officials." The Second Emperor came down from his carriage and walked though the third archway. He found Kongming leaning on a bamboo staff and peering into a small fishpond. The Second Emperor stood behind him a good while before saying deliberately, "Are things well with Your Excellency?" Kongming looked back. Seeing the Emperor, he threw down his staff and prostrated himself. "I deserve to die ten thousand times!" he exclaimed.[11] The Emperor helped him to his feet and asked, "Cao Pi's armies have crossed our borders. The situation is serious. Prime Minister — Father — why will you not come out of seclusion and take care of this?"[12]

Kongming smiled broadly as he helped the Emperor to a seat in the rear chamber. The prime minister then addressed the sovereign: "I knew all about the arrival of the five armies. I was not really viewing the fish, but thinking my own thoughts." "What can we do?" the Emperor said. "I have already driven back four of the armies: that of the Qiang king, Kebineng; that of the Man king, Meng Huo; that of the rebel general, Meng Da; and that of the Wei general, Cao Zhen. But as for the last army, that of Sun Quan — though I have worked out a plan, I will need a capable spokesmen to send to him. I was pondering whom to send when you saw me at the fishpond. It is unnecessary for Your Majesty to worry."

2087

Amazed and delighted, the Emperor said, "Prime Minister and Second Father, your designs are indeed marvelous and unfathomable. I would know your plan." Kongming replied, "How could I treat Your Majesty, whom the late Emperor entrusted to my care, with the slightest negligence? None of the Chengdu officials knows much of the art of war. What mattered most was keeping anyone from guessing my plan. The details had to be secret. Early on I knew that the Qiang king Kebineng meant to attack Xiping Pass, so I took the following steps: Ma Chao and his forebears, Riverlands people for generations, have always enjoyed the friendship of the Qiang. The Qiang regard Ma Chao himself as a heavenly general with supernatural powers. So I sent a swift envoy with

换，以兵拒之：此一路不必忧矣。又南蛮孟获，兵犯四郡，臣亦飞檄遣魏延领一军左出右入，右出左入，为疑兵之计；蛮兵惟凭勇力，其心多疑，若见疑兵，必不敢进：此一路又不足忧矣。又知孟达引兵出汉中；达与李严曾结生死之交；臣回成都时，留李严守永安宫；臣已作一书，只做李严亲笔，令人送与孟达；达必然推病不出，以慢军心：此一路又不足忧矣。又知曹真引兵犯阳平关；此地险峻，可以保守，臣已调赵云引一军守把关隘，并不出战；曹真若见我军不出，不久自退矣。——此四路兵俱不足忧。臣尚恐不能全保，又密调关兴、张苞二将，各引兵三万，屯于紧要之处，为各路救应。此数处调遣之事，皆不曾经由成都，故无人知觉。只有东吴这一路兵，未必便动：如见四路兵胜，川中危急，必来相攻；若四路不济，安肯动乎？臣料孙权想曹丕三路侵吴之怨，必不肯从其言。虽然如此，须用一舌辩之士，径往东吴，以利害说之，则先退东吴；其四路之兵，何足忧乎？但未得说吴之人，臣故踌躇。何劳陛下圣驾来临？"后主曰："太后亦欲来见相父。今朕闻相父之言，如梦初觉，复何忧哉！"

orders for Ma Chao to guard Xiping Pass as tightly as possible and to place four units in ambush — to be rotated daily. That should take care of Kebineng, the first army.

"Now for the Man king, Meng Huo, whose troops threaten our four southern districts: I have dispatched orders to Wei Yan to keep moving his army left and right of Meng Huo as decoys; the Man troops, who rely only on courage, are so mistrustful that decoys will surely deter their advance. So that army should cause no anxiety.

"I also knew about Meng Da's advance on Hanzhong. Meng Da and Li Yan are friends to the death. When I got back to Chengdu, I left Li Yan guarding the Palace of Enduring Peace. I have written to Meng Da, copying Li Yan's hand. Meng Da will claim he is ill and will not join the action, thus weakening his troops' morale. That army, too, need occasion no further anxiety.

"Finally, Cao Zhen's coming assault on Yangping Pass. This is formidable terrain, easy to defend well. I have already dispatched Zhao Zilong to maintain defensive positions there. When Cao Zhen realizes our soldiers will not show themselves, he will retreat before long. Thus, none of the four enemy armies is worth worrying about. But for an extra measure of security I have secretly sent Guan Xing and Zhang Bao with thirty thousand troops each to reinforce our other units at crucial points. All these arrangements were made without going through Chengdu, so no one here has heard a thing.

2089

"That leaves the Southland army — but it should not make any major move. It would be likely to attack if the other four armies were winning and if the Riverlands encountered a crisis. But what will they do if the four armies are making no progress? My guess is that Sun Quan has not forgotten Cao Pi's invasion and will be reluctant to do his bidding. Nonetheless, I still need an able talker to go there and persuade them where their true interests lie: when the Southland backs out, the other four armies will pose no threat. But I have yet to find the man who can convince the south, and so I have been in a quandary. Forgive me for having troubled Your Majesty to make this visit." The Emperor replied, "The queen mother also meant to come and see you, prime minister and second father. Now your explanation has wakened me from a dream and relieved my anxieties."

孔明与后主共饮数杯，送后主出府。众官皆环立于门外，见后主面有喜色。后主别了孔明，上御车回朝。众皆疑惑不定。孔明见众官中，一人仰天而笑，面亦有喜色。孔明视之，乃义阳新野人，姓邓，名芝，字伯苗，现为户部尚书；汉司马邓禹之后。孔明暗令人留住邓芝。多官皆散，孔明请芝到书院中，问芝曰："今蜀、魏、吴鼎分三国，欲讨二国，一统中兴，当先伐何国？"芝曰："以愚意论之：魏虽汉贼，其势甚大，急难摇动，当徐徐缓图；今主上初登宝位，民心未安，当与东吴连合，结为唇齿，一洗先帝旧怨，此乃长久之计也。未审丞相钧意若何？"孔明大笑曰："吾思之久矣，奈未得其人。——今日方得也！"芝曰："丞相欲其人何为？"孔明曰："吾欲使人往结东吴。公既能明此意，必能不辱君命。使乎之任，非公不可。"芝曰："愚才疏智浅，恐不堪当此任。"孔明曰："吾来日奏知天子，便请伯苗一行，切勿推辞。"芝应允而退。至次日，孔明奏准后主，差邓芝往说东吴。芝拜辞，望东吴而来。

正是：

吴人方见干戈息，蜀使还将玉帛通。

未知邓芝此去若何，且看下文分解。

Kongming shared several cups with the Second Emperor and then escorted him from his residence. The waiting officials surrounding the gate watched doubtfully as the Emperor, looking pleased, bade Kongming good-bye and returned to court in his carriage. Kongming noticed one of the courtiers, Deng Zhi, looking upward and laughing. Deng Zhi (Bomiao), from Xinye in Yiyang, was secretary of the Agricultural Tax Department, a descendant of Marshal Deng Yu of the Han. Kongming had him quietly detained and invited him to his library after the other officials had departed.

Kongming asked Deng Zhi, "Now three kingdoms — Shu, Wei, and Wu — have formed. I want to wage war against the other two to unify the realm and restore the Han. Which kingdom should I attack first?" Deng Zhi responded, "In my humble opinion, Wei, though a traitor, is a formidable power, virtually unshakable. We should bide our time. The people's confidence in the new sovereign remains unsteady, so it seems sensible to unite again with the Southland for mutual defense, wiping clear the late Emperor's longstanding grievance against them. This is a plan for the long run. But what is Your Excellency's esteemed view?"

Kongming laughed as he said. "These have been my thoughts, too, for some time. I've been looking for the right man. Today I have found him!" "What do you wish him to do?" Deng Zhi inquired. Kongming responded, "I want to send him to the Southland to repair the alliance. Good sir, since you understand our thinking, you are sure to do justice to the royal command. You are the perfect man for the mission. There is no one else." "The task may be too much for my meagre talent and shallow knowledge," Deng Zhi protested. "Tomorrow," Kongming answered, "I will advise the Son of Heaven to request that you make the trip. I urge you to accept." Deng Zhi assented and withdrew.

The next day, as Kongming had advised, the Emperor delegated Deng Zhi as his representative to the Southland. Deng Zhi took leave and headed south. Indeed:

> No sooner had the Southland seen the end of war
> Than the Riverlands sent the gifts of peace.

What would be the outcome of Deng Zhi's mission?[13]

Read on.

2091

第八十六回

难张温秦宓逞天辩　破曹丕徐盛用火攻

　　却说东吴陆逊，自退魏兵之后，吴王拜逊为辅国将军、江陵侯，领荆州牧，自此军权皆归于逊。张昭、顾雍启奏吴王，请自改元。权从之，遂改为黄武元年。忽报魏主遣使至，权召入。使命陈说："蜀前使人求救于魏，魏一时不明，故发兵应之；今已大悔，欲起四路兵取川，东吴可来接应。若得蜀土，各分一半。"

　　权闻言，不能决，乃问于张昭、顾雍等。昭曰："陆伯言极有高见，可问之。"权即召陆逊至。逊奏曰："曹丕坐镇中原，急不可图；今若不从，必为仇矣。臣料魏与吴皆无诸葛亮之敌手。今且勉强应允，整军预备，只探听四路如何。若四路兵胜，川中危急，诸葛亮首尾不能救，主上则发兵以应之，先取成都，深为上策；如四路兵败，别作商议。"权从之，乃谓魏使曰："军需未办，择日便当起程。"使者拜辞而去。权令人探得西番兵出西平关，

Chapter 86

To Thwart Zhang Wen, Qin Mi Shows
Genius in Debate
To Defeat Cao Pi, Xu Sheng Employs
Fire in Attack

To mark Lu Xun's success in driving back the armies of Wei, the king of Wu honored him as General Who Upholds the Kingdom, lord of Jiangling, and protector of Jingzhou. Thereafter military authority was concentrated in Lu Xun's hands.

On the recommendation of Zhang Zhao and Gu Yong, the king of Wu established his own reign title, Huang Wu.[1] In the first year of the reign an envoy from the Wei ruler arrived unexpectedly and stated his purpose to Sun Quan: "Dearly we regret the mistake we made in giving military assistance to the Riverlands, but now we are mobilizing four armies to capture that territory, and half of it will be your prize if you back us up."[2] Sun Quan, uncertain how to respond to this proposal, put the question to his advisers Zhang Zhao and Gu Yong. Zhang Zhao said, "Lu Xun has greater insight. We can ask him."

Sun Quan summoned his chief commander, who said, "Cao Pi's hold on the heartland is firm enough to rule out a quick strike north. And should we refuse his proposal, we would become his enemy. I don't think Wei or Wu has a strategist to match Zhuge Liang, so I would say yes — reluctant as you may be — all the while enhancing our preparedness and gathering intelligence on the progress of their four armies. If their effort looks promising and the Riverlands is thrown into a crisis, and if Zhuge Liang's forces are disorganized, Your Majesty should send troops to aid Wei and try to take Chengdu. Such a plan is in our best interest. But if Wei's four armies are defeated, we shall have to reconsider."

Sun Quan accepted this advice and said to the envoy, "The army is still being provisioned. We will fix a day now to begin our expedition." The envoy left with his answer. Before long Sun Quan learned that the Qiang force attacking Xiping Pass had retreated before Ma Chao with-

...

见了马超，不战自退；南蛮孟获起兵攻四郡，皆被魏延用疑兵计杀退回洞去了；上庸孟达兵至半路，忽然染病不能行；曹真兵出阳平关，赵子龙拒住各处险道，果然"一将守关，万夫莫开"。曹真屯兵于斜谷道，不能取胜而回。

孙权知了此信，乃谓文武曰："陆伯言真神算也。孤若妄动，又结怨于西蜀矣。"忽报西蜀遣邓芝到。张昭曰："此又是诸葛亮退兵之计，遣邓芝为说客也。"权曰："当何以答之？"昭曰："先于殿前立一大鼎，贮油数百斤，下用炭烧。待其油沸，可选身长面大武士一千人，各执刀在手，从宫门前直摆至殿上，却唤芝入见。休等此人开言下说词，责以郦食其说齐故事，效此例烹之，看其人如何对答。"

权从其言，遂立油鼎，命武士立于左右，各执军器，召邓芝入。芝整衣冠而入。行至宫门前，只见两行武士，威风凛凛，各持钢刀、大斧、长戟、短剑，直列至殿上。芝晓其意，并无惧色，昂然而行。至殿前，又见鼎镬内热油正沸。左右武士以目视之，芝但微微而笑。近臣引至帘前，邓芝长揖不拜。权令卷起珠帘，大喝曰："何不拜！"芝昂然而答曰："上国天使，不拜小邦之主。"权大怒曰："汝不自料，欲掉三寸之舌，效郦生说齐乎！可速入油鼎！"芝大笑曰："人皆言东吴多贤，谁想惧一儒生！"权

out fighting; that Wei Yan, using decoy soldiers, had driven Southern Man leader Meng Huo and his troops back to their hollows, thus defeating his attack on the Riverlands' southern districts; that Meng Da had fallen ill en route and was unable to proceed; and that Cao Zhen had been checked by Zhao Zilong at Yangping Pass (giving fresh proof to the adage "A single commander at the pass can stop ten thousand men") and had turned back in frustration after posting his forces at Ye Gorge Road. Sun Quan then said to his counselors, "Lu Xun calculated perfectly. An ill-conceived action on my part would again have given the Riverlands good reason to hate us."

At this moment the Riverlands envoy, Deng Zhi, arrived.[3] Zhang Zhao said, "Another of Zhuge Liang's maneuvers to deflect enemy forces — sending Deng Zhi to win our cooperation." "How shall I answer him?" Sun Quan asked. Zhang Zhao replied, "Place a cauldron filled with several hundred *jin* of oil in front of the main hall and heat it with a charcoal fire. When the oil is bubbling, have a thousand tall, hard-faced soldiers, arms in hand, form a line from the main hall out to the palace gate. Summon Deng Zhi and before he can open his mouth, tell him you are going to boil him alive as the king of Qi boiled Li Yiji. See how he responds."[4]

Sun Quan set up the cauldron and detailed the soldiers as Zhang Zhao had advised. He then called for the envoy. Properly costumed, Deng Zhi came to the gate and saw the two lines of guards — with steel swords, battle-axes, halberds, and daggers — stretching up to the main hall. It was a chilling display. But Deng Zhi understood its purpose and, betraying no fear, strode up to the hall, where he found the giant cauldron of boiling oil. As the warriors to right and left eyed him, Deng Zhi smiled casually. The king's attendants led him to the curtain behind which the king sat. Deng Zhi bowed low from the waist but did not prostrate himself. Sun Quan had the curtain rolled up and shouted, "Why no obeisance?" With a confident air Deng Zhi responded, "The envoy of a great kingdom does not prostrate himself before the lord of a lesser one." Angrily Sun Quan responded, "You're asking for it! Try wagging that wordy little tongue of yours as well as Li Yiji and then throw yourself into the cauldron!"

Deng Zhi laughed loudly and said, "The Southland is supposed to be

转怒曰:"孤何惧尔一匹夫耶?"芝曰:"既不惧邓伯苗,何愁来说汝等也?"权曰:"尔欲为诸葛亮作说客,来说孤绝魏向蜀,是否?"芝曰:"吾乃蜀中一儒生,特为吴国利害而来。乃设兵陈鼎,以拒一使,何其局量之不能容物耶!"

权闻言惶愧,即叱退武士,命芝上殿,赐坐而问曰:"吴、魏之利害若何?愿先生教我。"芝曰:"大王欲与蜀和,还是欲与魏和?"权曰:"孤正欲与蜀主讲和;但恐蜀主年轻识浅,不能全始全终耳。"芝曰:"大王乃命世之英豪,诸葛亮亦一时之俊杰;蜀有山川之险,吴有三江之固;若二国连和,共为唇齿,进则可以兼吞天下,退则可以鼎足而立。今大王若委赞称臣于魏,魏必望大王朝觐,求太子以为内侍;如其不从,则兴兵来攻,蜀亦顺流而进取:如此则江南之地,不复为大王有矣。若大王以愚言为不然,愚将就死于大王之前,以绝说客之名也。"言讫,撩衣下殿,望油鼎中便跳。权急命止之,请入后殿,以上宾之礼相待。权曰:"先生之言,正合孤意。孤今欲与蜀主连和,先生肯为我介绍乎?"芝曰:"适欲烹小臣者,乃大王也;今欲使小臣者,

rich in worthy men. Who would have expected you to fear a mere scholar!"[5] "I, fear a reckless fool like you?" Sun Quan exclaimed. "If you don't fear the messenger, why worry about his message?" Was the reply. "Tell me the truth," Sun Quan said. "Has Zhuge Liang sent you to persuade me to break off with Wei and turn toward Shu?" "I am but a scholar from the Riverlands," Deng Zhi went on, "who has come to speak of what is in the interest of the Southland.[6] And you have set up a cauldron and soldiers to hold off a single envoy. It goes to show how petty you really are!"

Sun Quan, now regretting his ploy, dismissed the guards and ordered Deng Zhi to ascend to the hall, offered him a seat, and said, "Then I would learn from you, master, where our interest and Wei's interest lie." Deng Zhi replied, "Is it your wish to make peace with Wei or with Shu?"[7] Sun Quan said, "Our purpose is to negotiate a peace with Shu, but with a new ruler so young and inexperienced, I wonder if agreements can be carried through to the end."

To this Deng Zhi answered, "Your Highness is a splendid champion recognized by all, and Zhuge Liang an outstanding figure in his own right. Mountains and waterways afford the Riverlands ample protection; rivers keep the Southland secure. If our two kingdoms make peace for mutual defense, we can either devour the empire together or else enjoy the advantages of a three-way balance of power. If Your Highness sends presents of homage and declares subservience to Wei, they will demand your attendance at court and require the heir apparent to serve in their emperor's ranks. If you refuse, they will field an army and attack — in which case, the Riverlands army will come downstream and seize you territory.[8] The Southland will no longer be yours! If you think my humble views wrong, I will gladly die before you lest I become known as a glib troublemaker." So saying, he raised the lower part of his garment and descended from the hall toward the cauldron as if to jump in.

Sun Quan ordered Deng Zhi stopped and invited him to the rear chamber, where he received him as an honored guest. "Master," Sun Quan said, "your views and mine agree. I desire to conclude a peace with the ruler of Shu. Will you serve as my intermediary?"[9] "A moment ago," Deng Zhi responded, "you wanted to cook me. Now you want to recruit

2097

亦大王也：大王犹自狐疑未定，安能取信于人？"权曰："孤意已决，先生勿疑。"

于是吴王留住邓芝，集多官问曰："孤掌江南八十一州，更有荆楚之地，反不如西蜀偏僻之处也：蜀有邓芝，不辱其主；吴并无一人入蜀，以达孤意。"忽一人出班奏曰："臣愿为使。"众视之，乃吴郡吴人，姓张，名温，字惠恕，现为中郎将。权曰："恐卿到蜀见诸葛亮，不能达孤之情。"温曰："孔明亦人耳，臣何畏彼哉？"权大喜，重赏张温，使同邓芝入川通好。

却说孔明自邓芝去后，奏后主曰："邓芝此去，其事必成。吴地多贤，定有人来答礼。陛下当礼貌之，令彼回吴，以通盟好。吴若通和，魏必不敢加兵于蜀矣。吴、魏宁靖，臣当征南，平定蛮方，然后图魏。魏削则东吴亦不能久存，可以复一统之基业也。"后主然之。

忽报东吴遣张温与邓芝入川答礼。后主聚文武于丹墀，令邓芝、张温入。温自以为得志，昂然上殿，见后主施礼。后主赐锦墩，坐于殿左，设御宴待之。后主但敬礼而已。宴罢，百官送张温到馆舍。次日，孔明设宴相待。孔明谓张温曰："先帝在日，

me. If Your Highness is so indecisive, how can he win the confidence of others?"[10] "I am resolved," Sun Quan said. "Have no doubts, master."

The king of the Southland detained Deng Zhi and summoned his court into session. "My eighty-one Southland counties," he said, "coupled with Jingzhou, amount to less than the remote Riverlands, if only for the fact that they have a Deng Zhi, a man worthy of his king, while we lack a man of equal merit to represent our cause to Shu." At that moment a man stepped forth from the ranks and addressed the king: "I volunteer to be your envoy." The speaker was a southerner from Wujun district, Zhang Wen (Huishu), an Imperial Corps commander. Sun Quan said, "I am afraid that when Zhuge Liang receives you, you will not effectively convey my true sentiments." "Kongming is a man, after all," Zhang Wen replied. "Why should I fear him so?" And so Sun Quan gave Zhang Wen generous gifts with great pleasure and sent him with Deng Zhi to the Riverlands to negotiate the friendship between their two kingdoms.

* * *

After Deng Zhi had left for the Southland, Kongming addressed the Second Emperor: "Deng Zhi will succeed, and one of the many capable men in the south should soon be visiting us in reciprocal courtesy. Your Majesty, treat him with all due respect so that he will conclude the alliance when he goes back. If this peace is made, Wei will not dare military action against us. With quiet on the eastern and northern fronts, I will be able to march south and pacify the region of the Man peoples. After that, we can again make Wei our objective. And after Wei is whittled down, the Southland cannot long survive. In that way the unity of the empire can be reestablished."[11] The Emperor approved.

When the return mission of Deng Zhi and Zhang Wen was announced, the Emperor gathered his military and civil officials around him. He then permitted Deng Zhi and Zhang Wen to enter the throne chamber. With an air of pride and self-importance Zhang Wen strode into the hall and extended ritual greetings to the Emperor, who invited him to sit on a gorgeous damask hassock on the left side of the hall. A royal banquet was presented at which the Emperor played a merely formal role.[12] After the ceremonies officials escorted Zhang Wen to the guesthouse.

The next day Kongming invited Zhang Wen to dine and said to him,

与吴不睦，今已晏驾。当今主上，深慕吴王，欲捐旧忿，永结盟好，并力破魏。望大夫善言回奏。"张温领诺。酒至半酣，张温喜笑自若，颇有傲慢之意。

汉英经典文库

　　次日，后主将金帛赐与张温，设宴于城南邮亭之上，命众官相送。孔明殷勤劝酒。正饮酒间，忽一人乘醉而入，昂然长揖，入席就坐。温怪之，乃问孔明曰："此何人也？"孔明答曰："姓秦，名宓，字子勅，现为益州学士。"温笑曰："名称学士，未知胸中曾'学事'否？"宓正色而言曰："蜀中三尺小童，尚皆就学，何况于我？"温曰："且说公何所学？"宓对曰："上至天文，下至地理，三教九流，诸子百家，无所不通；古今兴废，圣贤经传，无所不览。"温笑曰："公既出大言，请即以天为问：天有头乎？"宓曰："有头。"温曰："头在何方？"宓曰："在西方。《诗》云：'乃眷西顾。'以此推之，头在西方也。"温又问："天有耳乎？"宓答曰："天处高而听卑。《诗》云：'鹤鸣九皋，声闻于天。'无耳何能听？"温又问："天有足乎？"宓曰："有足。《诗》云：'天步艰难。'无足何能步？"温又问："天有姓乎？"宓曰："岂得无姓！"温曰：

"When the late Emperor was alive, relations with the south were poor. But he is no more. Out of his deep admiration for the king of Wu, the present sovereign seeks to bury old grudges and form a long-term alliance in order to defeat Wei. I hope that you, my lord, will deliver our response with fair words."[13] Zhang Wen agreed to. As the wine eased their spirits, the envoy smiled and grew more expansive; he even became somewhat arrogant.

The next day the Emperor gave Zhang Wen gifts of gold and silk and told all courtiers to attend a banquet in his honor at the post station south of the capital. Kongming solicitously served wine to Zhang Wen. Suddenly, during the festivities a drunken man burst in and after a haughty gesture of salutation took a seat among the guests. Amazed, Zhang Wen asked Kongming who the man was. Kongming replied, "Qin Mi (styled Zilai), now an official scholar in Yizhou." "He may be called 'official scholar,'" Zhang Wen responded, "but I wonder if there is any 'scholarship' in him." Assuming a severe air, Qin Mi said, "Even the young lads of the Riverlands attend to their studies, not to speak of myself."

Zhang Wen continued, "Tell us what you have learned." "Astronomy and geography," Qin Mi replied, "the three teachings and the nine sects, the philosophers of every school — I have mastered them all. And I have read through the histories chronicling the rise and fall of many dynasties as well as the classics transmitted by sagely worthies." Zhang Wen laughed. "Since you take pride in your learning, good sir, allow me this question: does the sky have a head?" "It does," Qin Mi answered. "Where?" asked Zhang Wen. "In the west," Qin Mi answered again. "Inferring from the line in the *Book of Odes*, 'The High Ancestor looked to the west for a new king,' the head should be there."[14] "And does the sky have ears?" Zhang Wen asked next. "Heaven is located high above, but it hears those far below. As the *Book of Odes* says, 'The crane cries in the remote swamps, but its voice reaches Heaven above.' How could Heaven hear without ears?"[15] "And does Heaven have feet as well?" Zhang Wen pressed him. "Of course," Qin Mi answered. "The *Odes* says, 'Heaven advances step by step.'[16] That would be impossible without feet." Next, Zhang Wen asked, "And does Heaven have a surname?" "But of course," Qin Mi responded. "What name?" Zhang Wen

"何姓？"宓答曰："姓刘。"温曰："何以知之？"宓曰："天子姓刘，以故知之。"温又问曰："日生于东乎？"宓对曰："虽生于东，而没于西。"

此时秦宓语言清朗，答问如流。满座皆惊。张温无语。宓乃问曰："先生东吴名士，既以天事下问，必能深明天之理。昔混沌既分，阴阳剖判；轻清者上浮而为天，重浊者下凝而为地；至共工氏战败，头触不周山，天柱折，地维缺：天倾西北，地陷东南。天既轻清而上浮，何以倾其西北乎？又未知轻清之外，还是何物？愿先生教我。"张温无言可对，乃避席而谢曰："不意蜀中多出俊杰！恰闻讲论，使仆顿开茅塞。"孔明恐温羞愧，故以善言解之曰："席间问难，皆戏谈耳。足下深知安邦定国之道，何在唇齿之戏哉！"温拜谢。孔明又令邓芝入吴答礼，就与张温同行。张、邓二人拜辞孔明，望东吴而来。

却说吴王见张温入蜀未还，乃聚文武商议。忽近臣奏曰："蜀遣邓芝同张温入国答礼。"权召入。张温拜于殿前，备称后主、孔明之德，愿求永结盟好，特遣邓尚书又来答礼。权大喜，乃设宴待之。权问邓芝曰："若吴、蜀二国同心灭魏，得天下太

asked. "Liu," said Qin Mi. "How do you know?" Zhang Wen asked. "Because the Son of Heaven is surnamed Liu," was Qin Mi's reply. "And is the sun born in the east?" Zhang Wen queried. "Yes," Qin Mi answered. "But it 'dies' in the west."

In this exchange Qin Mi's articulate and fluent responses astonished the entire assembly and left Zhang Wen speechless. Qin Mi then asked him, "Master, you are a noted scholar of the Southland. Since you have condescended to ask me about Heaven, surely you have a profound grasp of its principles. In ancient times after the division of the primal substance, *yin* and *yang* were formed. The lighter, finer essence rose skyward to become Heaven. The grosser, darker essence congealed as earth. After Gong Gong lost the war, he butted Buzhou Mountain with his head, breaking the pillar of Heaven and one of the mainstays of the earth. This caused Heaven to tilt down in the northwest and earth to list to the southeast. Now, if Heaven was formed from a lighter, rising essence, how could it tilt down in the northwest? And secondly, what lies beyond the lighter essence? I am eager to learn from you."[17]

Unable to make any reply, Zhang Wen moved off his mat and said deferentially, "I am amazed that the Riverlands has such a paragon of erudition. Your arguments have been positively illuminating." Kongming intervened to save Zhang Wen from further embarrassment by saying, "The riddles posed during the banquet were in jest. Your knowledge of the means to keep a kingdom safe and sound has nothing to do with verbal jesting." Zhang Wen acknowledged the compliment, and Kongming ordered Deng Zhi to reciprocate the Southland's courtesy and accompany Zhang Wen home again. The two men took leave of the prime minister and headed back to the Southland.

2103

Sun Quan was in council when a personal attendant announced, "The Riverlands has sent Deng Zhi back with Zhang Wen as a gesture of reciprocity." Summoned before his lord, Zhang Wen praised in detail the virtue of the Second Emperor and Kongming; he conveyed their appeal for a lasting alliance, and told the king of the dispatch of Secretary Deng Zhi on a return visit. Delighted by these developments, Sun Quan held a banquet for Deng Zhi, during which he asked him, "Would it not be wonderful if our two kingdoms resolved to destroy Wei? It would bring

平,二主分治,岂不乐乎?"芝答曰:"'天无二日,民无二王。'如灭魏之后,未识天命所归何人。但为君者,各修其德;为臣者,各尽其忠:则战争方息耳。"权大笑曰:"君之诚款,乃如是耶!"遂厚赠邓芝还蜀。自此吴、蜀通好。

却说魏国细作人探知此事,火速报入中原。魏主曹丕听知,大怒曰:"吴、蜀连和,必有图中原之意也。不若朕先伐之。"于是大集文武,商议起兵伐吴。此时大司马曹仁、太尉贾诩已亡。侍中辛毗出班奏曰:"中原之地,土阔民稀,而欲用兵,未见其利。今日之计,莫若养兵屯田十年,足食足兵,然后用之,则吴、蜀方可破也。"丕怒曰:"此迂儒之论也!今吴、蜀连和,早晚必来侵境,何暇等待十年!"即传旨起兵伐吴。司马懿奏曰:"吴有长江之险,非船莫渡。陛下必御驾亲征,可选大小战船,从蔡、颍而入淮,取寿春,至广陵,渡江口,径取南徐:此为上策。"丕从之。于是日夜并工,造龙舟十只,长二十余丈,可容二千余人;收拾战船三千余只。魏黄初五年秋八月,会聚大小将士,令曹真为前部,张辽、张郃、文聘、徐晃等为大将先行,许褚、吕虔

peace to the empire, and the two sovereigns could share its governance."
Deng Zhi responded, "'The people have one king, as Heaven has one
sum.' After the destruction of Wei, to whom the mandate will revert is a
matter of conjecture. Whoever rules must cultivate his virtue. Whoever
serves must exhaust his loyalty. That will end the wars." "Your sincerity
is beyond question," Sun Quan said and sent Deng Zhi back to the
Riverlands laden with gifts. Thereafter Wu and Shu were on friendly
terms.

Spies swiftly brought word of these developments to the attention of
the Wei Emperor, Cao Pi. "An alliance between Wu and Shu will have
the north as its next objective. We should attack them first," he declared
angrily, and he called a general meeting of his officials and advisers to
discuss invading the Southland.

By this time Chief Commanding Officer Cao Ren and Grand Commandant Jia Xu had both passed away. Privy Counselor Xin Pi came
forward and addressed the sovereign: "War would ravage our northern
heartland, a broad territory on which the population is rather thinly settled.
A better plan would be to develop the armed forces and establish mili-
tary-agricultural colonies to ensure supplies of food and men. In ten years'
time Wu and Shu can be defeated." Angered by these words, Cao Pi
said, "That's how a pedant thinks! Wu and Shu are now allied, and their
armies will invade our land long before ten years have passed. I don't
have the luxury of waiting!" With that, the Wei Emperor ordered the
invasion to begin.

2105

Sima Yi addressed Cao Pi: "We'll need boats to cross the Great River,
the Southland's strategic defense. The best plan is for Your Majesty to
lead the expedition. Select a fleet of large and small craft, then enter the
Huai region from Cai and Ying and capture Shouchun. When you reach
Guangling, cross the river and capture Nanxu." Cao Pi adopted the plan.
He ordered nonstop preparation. Ten dragon boats were built, each over
two hundred spans long and able to hold over two thousand men. In addition, he commissioned some three thousand war-boats.[18]

In the autumn of the eighth month of the fifth year of Huang Chu,[19] the
entire northern command gathered. Cao Pi ordered Cao Zhen to lead the
vanguard; Zhang Liao, Zhang He, Wen Ping, and Xu Huang to serve as

为中军护卫，曹休为合后，刘晔、蒋济为参谋官。前后水陆军马三十余万，克日起兵。封司马懿为尚书仆射，留在许昌，凡国政大事，并皆听懿决断。

不说魏兵起程。却说东吴细作探知此事，报入吴国。近臣慌奏吴王曰："今魏王曹丕，亲自乘驾龙舟，提水陆大军三十余万，从蔡、颍出淮，必取广陵渡江，来下江南。甚为利害。"孙权大惊，即聚文武商议。顾雍曰："今主上既与西蜀连和，可修书与诸葛孔明，令起兵出汉中，以分其势；一面遣一大将，屯兵南徐以拒之。"权曰："非陆伯言不可当此大任。"雍曰："陆伯言镇守荆州，不可轻动。"权曰："孤非不知，奈眼前无替力之人。"言未尽，一人从班部内应声而出曰："臣虽不才，愿统一军以当魏兵。若曹丕亲渡大江，臣必生擒，以献殿下；若不渡江，亦杀魏兵大半，令魏兵不敢正视东吴。"权视之，乃徐盛也。权大喜曰："如得卿守江南一带，孤何忧哉！"遂封徐盛为安东将军，总镇都督建业、南徐军马。盛谢恩，领命而退；即传令教众官军多置器械，多设旌旗，以为守护江岸之计。

忽一人挺身出曰："今日大王以重任委托将军，欲破魏兵

lead generals; Xu Chu and Lü Qian to be Imperial Army superintendants;[20] Cao Xiu to coordinate the rear; and Liu Ye and Jiang Ji to serve as consulting officials. The land and naval forces, all told, came to more than three hundred thousand. A day was set to launch the invasion. Sima Yi, appointed supervisor of the Secretariat,[21] remained in Xuchang and assumed overall administrative responsibility.

* * *

Southland spies soon returned from the north to tell of the impending invasion, and a personal attendant communicated the news to the king of Wu: "The ruler of Wei, Cao Pi, is personally leading the imperial fleet and a combined land and naval force of more than three hundred thousand. They are coming into the Huai region from Cai and Yang, bent on seizing Guangling, crossing the river there, and descending upon the Southland — a serious threat." Sun Quan, deeply concerned, gathered his counselors. Gu Yong said, "Your Lordship has re-allied with the Riverlands. You might write to Kongming urging him to march into Hanzhong. That would force the northerners to fight on two fronts. At the same time post a top general to block the invaders at Nanxu." "No one but Lu Xun could undertake the task," Sun Quan said. Gu Yong replied, "He is defending Jingzhou and should stay there." "Well I know it," Sun Quan responded. "But whom do I have to take his place?"

At that moment someone stepped out to answer the call. "I may have little talent," he said, "but I volunteer to lead one detachment in the fight against Wei. If Cao Pi comes across the Great River, I will deliver him alive to the base of your throne hall. If he does not cross, I will destroy half the troops of Wei; the north will never defy us again." The volunteer was Xu Sheng. "With you to defend the regions south of the river, my worries are over," Sun Quan said with delight and appointed him General Who Makes the East Secure and chief commander of all forces in Jianye and Nanxu. Xu Sheng thanked Sun Quan, accepted his commission, and withdrew. He then issued orders for all armies to provide him with the weapons, flags, and banners necessary for defending the shores of the river.

Suddenly a man stood up and said, "General, today His Majesty has laid a heavy charge upon you, to defeat the northern army and capture

以擒曹丕,将军何不早发军马渡江,于淮南之地迎敌?直待曹丕兵至,恐无及矣。"盛视之,乃吴王侄孙韶也。韶字公礼,官授扬威将军,曾在广陵守御;年幼负气,极有胆勇。盛曰:"曹丕势大,更有名将为先锋,不可渡江迎敌。待彼船皆集于北岸,吾自有计破之。"韶曰:"吾手下自有三千军马,更兼深知广陵路势,吾愿自去江北,与曹丕决一死战。如不胜,甘当军令。"盛不从。韶坚执要去。盛只是不肯,韶再三要行。盛怒曰:"汝如此不听号令,吾安能制诸将乎?"叱武士推出斩之。刀斧手拥孙韶出辕门之外,立起皂旗。韶部将飞报孙权。权听知,急上马来救。武士恰待行刑,孙权早到,喝散刀斧手,救了孙韶。韶哭奏曰:"臣往年在广陵,深知地利;不就那里与曹丕厮杀,直待他下了长江,东吴指日休矣!"权径入营来。徐盛迎接入帐,奏曰:"大王命臣为都督,提兵拒魏;今扬威将军孙韶,不遵军法,违令当斩,大王何故赦之?"权曰:"韶倚血气之壮,误犯军法,万希宽恕。"盛曰:"法非臣所立,亦非大王所立,乃国家之典刑也。若以亲而免之,何以令众乎?"权曰:"韶犯法,本应任将军处治;奈此子虽本姓俞氏,然孤兄甚爱之,赐姓孙;于孤颇有劳

Cao Pi — why not send your men across the river first and meet the enemy in the Huai region? It may be too late to press your advantage if you wait for them to arrive." Xu Sheng turned to Sun Shao (Gongli), nephew of the king, recipient of the post of General Who Exhibits Power. He had once served in the defense at Guangling, and he was a headstrong youth, filled with sheer courage. Xu Sheng said to him, "Cao Pi has a vast fighting force and famous commanders in the vanguard. We cannot meet the enemy on the other side of the river. But after their fleet gathers on the north shore, I have a way to destroy them."

Sun Shao replied, "I have three thousand in my command, and I know the terrain around Guangling. I want to take the fight to the north side and finish Cao Pi there. If I fail, let military law be satisfied!" Xu Sheng would not agree; but Sun Shao would not relent. Xu Sheng refused permission; Sun Shao insisted. Finally, Xu Sheng angrily ordered Sun Shao removed and executed, saying, "If you ignore my command, how am I to control the other commanders?"

Armed guards forced Sun Shao outside the main gate of the camp and raised a black flag. One of Shao's lieutenants rushed the news to Sun Quan, who mounted at once and came to save him. As the executioners readied the knife, Sun Quan arrived, dispersed them with a shout, and rescued his nephew. Tearfully Sun Shao addressed the king: "Some years ago I became familiar with the terrain in Guangling. If instead of taking the battle to Cao Pi, we wait for him to cross the river, the Southland's days are numbered." Sun Quan went to the camp and was met by Xu Sheng, who showed him into his tent. "Your Highness," he said, "has appointed me chief commander with orders to stop Cao Pi's advance. Now Sun Shao, General Who Exhibits Power, shows no respect for military law. For disobeying orders he deserves to die. Why did Your Majesty pardon him?" "Sun Shao violated the law inadvertently; it was his rashness. I ask you to excuse his fault," Sun Quan replied. "I did not make the law," Xu Sheng went on, "nor did Your Majesty. It is law established by precedent in our kingdom. If he is exonerated as a member of the Sun family, what authority will we have to command others?" Sun Quan answered, "By all rights his offense should be punished, Gerneral. But there is a special circumstance here. Sun Shao was originally sur-

绩。今若杀之,负兄义矣。"盛曰:"且看大王之面,寄下死罪。"权令孙韶拜谢。韶不肯拜,厉声而言曰:"据吾之见,只是引军去破曹丕!便死也不服你的见识!"徐盛变色。权叱退孙韶,谓徐盛曰:"便无此子,何损于兵?今后勿再用之。"言讫自回。是夜,人报徐盛说:"孙韶引本部三千精兵,潜地过江去了。"盛恐有失,于吴王面上不好看,乃唤丁奉授以密计,引三千兵渡江接应。

却说魏主驾龙舟至广陵,前部曹真已领兵列于大江之岸。曹丕问曰:"江岸有多少兵?"真曰:"隔岸远望,并不见一人,亦无旌旗营寨。"丕曰:"此必诡计也。朕自往观其虚实。"于是大开江道,放龙舟直至大江,泊于江岸。船上建龙凤日月五色旌旗,仪銮簇拥,光耀射目。曹丕端坐舟中,遥望江南,不见一人,回顾刘晔、蒋济曰:"可渡江否?"晔曰:"兵法'实实虚虚'。彼见大军至,如何不作整备?陛下未可造次。且待三五日,看其动静,然后发先锋渡江以探之。"丕曰:"卿言正合朕意。"

是日天晚,宿于江中。当夜月黑,军士皆执灯火,明耀天地,恰如白昼。遥望江南,并不见半点儿火光。丕问左右曰:"此

named Yu; my brother granted him our surname because he was fond of the lad. He has done me important service. If you kill him, our fraternal bond will be violated."[22]

To this appeal Xu Sheng replied, "In deference to Your Highness, then, I will hold off on the penalty." Next, Sun Quan bade Sun Shao prostrate himself and admit has fault. Sun Shao would not perform the ritual bow, and instead cried out stridently, "The way I see it, there is no choice but to take the army to destroy Cao Pi. Death itself could not get me to accept your view." Xu Sheng turned pale. Sun Quan dismissed Sun Shao harshly and said to Xu Sheng, "Can't the army do without him? Don't use him from now on." With those words Sun Quan went back.

That night someone reported to Xu Sheng that Sun Shao had secretly taken his three thousand crack troops over the river. To guard against mishap and to avoid his king's displeasure, Xu Sheng went to Ding Feng, gave him a secret plan, and sent him across with three thousand men to back up Sun Shao.

* * *

During the night the dragon boat carrying the ruler of Wei reached Guangling, where the vanguard under Cao Zhen was already arrayed on the shore. "How many men on the opposite bank?" Cao Pi asked him. "I see none on the far shore," Cao Zhen replied, "no flags or campsites, either." "It's a trick," Cao Pi said. "I will go myself to explore the site." Cao Pi had the way cleared for his royal barge to come to the river. Moored on the northern shore, it flew multicolored banners bearing the dragon and the phoenix, the sun and the moon; its imperial regalia and its honor guard gleamed brilliantly. Seated amid this display, Cao Pi gazed at the southern shore. Seeing no one, he turned to Liu Ye and Jiang Ji and asked, "Can't we cross?" "Military science warns," Liu Ye replied, "that 'appearances often belie reality.' When they see us coming, they will prepare. Do not be hasty, Your Majesty. Take a few days to watch their movements before sending the vanguard across to probe their positions." "My thinking exactly," Cao Pi responded.

Cao Pi spent the night on the river. There was no moon, but the soldiers' lanterns turned night to day; over on the southern shore all was

2111

何故也？"近臣奏曰："想闻陛下天兵来到，故望风逃窜耳。"丕暗笑。及至天晓，大雾迷漫，对面不见。须臾风起，雾散云收，望见江南一带皆是连城：城楼上枪刀耀日，遍城尽插旌旗号带。顷刻数次人来报："南徐沿江一带，直至石头城，一连数百里，城郭舟车，连绵不绝，一夜成就。"曹丕大惊。原来徐盛束缚芦苇为人，尽穿青衣，执旌旗，立于假城疑楼之上。魏兵见城上许多人马，如何不胆寒？丕叹曰："魏虽有武士千群，无所用之。江南人物如此，未可图也！"

正惊讶间，忽然狂风大作，白浪滔天，江水溅湿龙袍，大船将覆。曹真慌令文聘撑小舟急来救驾。龙舟上人立站不住。文聘跳上龙舟，负丕下得小舟，奔入河港。忽流星马报道："赵云引兵出阳平关，径取长安。"丕听得，大惊失色，便教回军。众军各自奔走。背后吴兵追至。丕传旨教尽弃御用之物而走。龙舟将次入淮，忽然鼓角齐鸣，喊声大震，刺斜里一彪军杀到：为首大将，乃孙韶也。魏兵不能抵当，折其大半，淹死者无数。诸将奋力救出魏主。魏主渡淮河，行不三十里，淮河中一带芦苇，预

dark. Cao Pi asked why, and a personal attendant answered, "It would seem that, hearing of the arrival of your Heaven-ordained armies, they simply took flight." Cao Pi smiled to himself. By dawn a great fog had overspread the water, blotting out even the closest objects. Soon morning winds cleared the air and they saw a line of walled forts before them. On the towers spears and swords caught the sunlight; the walls bristled with signal flags and banners. Several scouts informed Cao Pi that from Nanxu to the City of Stones — a distance of hundreds of *li* along the river — an unbroken line of barrier walls, boats, and chariots had been put in place overnight. Cao Pi was astounded.

The defensive display had all been Xu Sheng's doing. He had fabricated straw men dressed in black and holding flags, and had stood them on false walls and decoy towers. But the deceived northerners panicked at the sight of so many soldiers on the wall, and Cao Pi said, "Although we have legions of soldiers, what use can we make of them? If the Southland has such forces, it is pointless for us to attack." As Cao Pi watched in amazement, a sudden gale sprang up and whipped the white waves skyward. The surges of the mighty Great River drenched Cao Pi's royal dragon robes and rocked the royal barge. Cao Zhen urgently ordered Wen Ping to punt a small craft onto the river to rescue the sovereign. On the dragon boat the men could not keep their footing. Wen Ping drew close, vaulted over to the imperial boat, and carried Cao Pi down to his own craft. Then they raced for a safe harbor.

Suddenly, a rider arrived with a message: "Zhao Zilong has come out of Yangping Pass to capture Chang'an." Blanching at the news of this new danger, Cao Pi ordered the army to return. His soldiers fled en masse. Southland troops pursued. Cao Pi ordered his men to abandon all articles for imperial use. As the dragon boat was about to enter the River Huai, drums and horns blasted in unison: a band of men headed by Sun Shao angled in for the kill, overwhelming the Wei troops, who offered no defense. More than half perished, untold numbers by drowning. The commanders, by strenuous effort, managed to save the ruler of Wei.

Cao Pi made it to the north side of the Huai; but before he had moved thirty *li*, his boat came to a stretch where reeds soaked in fish oil had been set to burn. The fire raged downstream in the wake of the wind,

灌鱼油，尽皆火着；顺风而下，风势甚急，火焰漫空，绝住龙舟。丕大惊，急下小船傍岸时，龙舟上早已火着。丕慌忙上马。岸上一彪军杀来：为首一将，乃丁奉也。张辽急拍马来迎，被奉一箭射中其腰，却得徐晃救了，同保魏主而走，折军无数。背后孙韶、丁奉夺得马匹、车仗、船只、器械，不计其数。魏兵大败而回。吴将徐盛全获大功，吴王重加赏赐。张辽回到许昌，箭疮迸裂而亡，曹丕厚葬之，不在话下。

却说赵云引兵杀出阳平关之次，忽报丞相有文书到，说益州耆帅雍闿结连蛮王孟获，起十万蛮兵，侵掠四郡；因此宣云回军，令马超坚守阳平关，丞相欲自南征。赵云乃急收兵而回。此时孔明在成都整饬军马，亲自南征。

正是：

　　　　方见东吴敌北魏，又看西蜀战南蛮。

未知胜负如何，且看下文分解。

whose force lifted the flames into the sky. The boat was cut off. Terri-fied, Cao Pi went down into a smaller craft and rowed for shore. His dragon boat had already gone up in flames.

Cao Pi hurriedly mounted, but on land another company — this commanded by Ding Feng — intercepted him. Cao Pi's veteran general, Zhang Liao, raced to his lord's defense, but an arrow shot by Ding Feng struck him in the torso. Xu Huang rescued Zhang Liao, and the two saw the ruler of Wei to safety. The northern army suffered untold losses. Behind them Sun Shao and Ding Feng made off with horses, carriages, boats, and weapons — who could know how many? The Wei troops went back badly defeated. Xu Sheng, the triumphant southern commander, was richly rewarded by Sun Quan. Zhang Liao returned to Xuchang, where he passed away from the open arrow wound. Cao Pi buried him with honors. Of this no more need be said.[23]

* * *

Zhao Zilong had led his men out of Yangping Pass, when an unex-pected letter from the prime minister recalled him to the capital. The letter explained that Yong Kai, a veteran commander of Yizhou, was plundering in the four southern districts of the Riverlands in collusion with the king of the Man nation, Meng Huo, at the head of one hundred thou-sand soldiers. Kongming added that he was ordering Ma Chao to hold Yangping Pass while he personally conducted the war against the Man. Zhao Zilong at once regathered his soldiers and returned to Chengdu where Kongming was preparing the new campaign. Indeed:

> First, we found eastern Wu at war with northern Wei;
> Next, western Shu was fighting the Southern Man.

How would the campaign turn out?[24]

Read on.

2115

第八十七回

征南寇丞相大兴师　抗天兵蛮王初受执

　　却说诸葛丞相在于成都，事无大小，皆亲自从公决断。两川之民，忻乐太平，夜不闭户，路不拾遗。又幸连年大熟，老幼鼓腹讴歌，凡遇差徭，争先早办：因此军需器械应用之物，无不完备；米满仓廒，财盈府库。

　　建兴三年，益州飞报："蛮王孟获，大起蛮兵十万，犯境侵掠。建宁太守雍闿，乃汉朝什方侯雍齿之后，今结连孟获造反。牂牁郡太守朱褒、越巂郡太守高定，二人献了城。止有永昌太守王伉不肯反。现今雍闿、朱褒、高定三人部下人马，皆与孟获为向导官，攻打永昌郡。今王伉与功曹吕凯，会集百姓，死守此城，其势甚急。"孔明乃入朝奏后主曰："臣观南蛮不服，实国家之大患也。臣当自领大军，前去征讨。"后主曰："东有孙权，北有曹丕，今相父弃朕而去，倘吴、魏来攻，如之奈何？"孔明曰："东吴方与我国讲和，料无异心；若有异心，李严在白帝城，此人可当陆逊也。曹丕新败，锐气已丧，未能远图；且有马超守

Chapter 87

The Prime Minister Musters a Massive Force
and Conquers the Southern Rebels
The Man King Leads a Heaven-defying Army
and Is Captured for the First Time

From the Riverlands capital of Chengdu, Prime Minister Zhuge Liang administered the government, personally handling affairs of state, whether great or small, in a spirit of fairness. The inhabitants of the region welcomed the reign of peace; a climate of honesty and mutual trust prevailed, and fortune favored the land with generous harvests several years in a row. Both old and young tapped their contented bellies rhythmically as they rejoiced in song. Compulsory labor service was eagerly undertaken, with the result that the army was amply supplied and the granaries and treasury overflowed.

In the third year of Jian Xing[1] a bulletin came to Yizhou announcing, "Meng Huo has led one hundred thousand Man tribesmen across our borders to plunder the villages. Governor of Jianning, Yong Kai, a descendant of Yong Chi, lord of Shifang under the Han, has leagued himself with Meng Huo. The governor of Zangge district, Zhu Bao, and the governor of Yuesui, Gao Ding, have already delivered their cities to the rebels. The governor of Yongchang, Wang Kang, remains loyal, but Meng Huo is attacking Yongchang, guided by the three rebel governors; meanwhile, Wang Kang and his deputy, Lü Kai, have rallied the population in a stout defense of Yongchang. Their situation is critical."

2117

Kongming entered the court and addressed the Second Emperor: "I shall go in force to suppress the Southern Man whose recalcitrance threatens the security of the dynasty." The Emperor replied, "What shall I do, prime minister and second father, if, after you have gone, Sun Quan strikes from the east or Cao Pi from the north?" Kongming answered, "We have recently made peace with the Southland, so they're not likely to break faith. But if they do attack, Li Yan in Baidi will be able to hold off Lu Xun. As for Cao Pi, he has no ambition to move after his latest

把汉中诸处关口，不必忧也。臣又留关兴、张苞等分两军为救应，保陛下万无一失。今臣先去扫荡蛮方，然后北伐，以图中原，报先帝三顾之恩，托孤之重。"后主曰："朕年幼无知，惟相父斟酌行之。"言未毕，班部内一人出曰："不可！不可！"众视之，乃南阳人也，姓王，名连，字文仪，现为谏议大夫。连谏曰："南方不毛之地，瘴疫之乡；丞相秉钧衡之重任，而自远征，非所宜也。且雍闿等乃疥癣之疾，丞相只须遣一大将讨之，必然成功。"孔明曰："南蛮之地，离国甚远，人多不习王化，收伏甚难，吾当亲去征之。可刚可柔，别有斟酌，非可容易托人。"

　　王连再三苦劝，孔明不从。是日，孔明辞了后主，令蒋琬为参军，费祎为长史，董厥、樊建二人为掾史；赵云、魏延为大将，总督军马；王平、张翼为副将；并川将数十员：共起川兵五十万，前望益州进发。忽有关公第三子关索，入军来见孔明曰："自荆州失陷，逃难在鲍家庄养病。每要赴川见先帝报仇，疮痕未合，不能起行。近已安痊，打探得东吴仇人已皆诛戮，径来西川见帝，恰在途中遇见征南之兵，特来投见。"孔明闻之，嗟讶

setback. But again, just in case, Ma Chao controls the key points in Hanzhong. You need not worry. In addition, I will leave Guan Xing and Zhang Bao in command of two support contingents to assure Your Majesty that nothing will go wrong. After I have made the region of the Southern Man safe, I will lead an expedition north to recover the heartland — this, to repay the late Emperor for the love and trust he showed by making three visits to my cottage in Longzhong and by placing you in my care."

The Second Emperor said, "I am too young to be wise. Act on your own judgment, prime minister and second father." As he spoke, a man stepped forward to protest. The assembly turned to Court Counselor Wang Lian (Wenyi) of Nanyang. "The south," he said, "a far-off wilderness of rampant pestilence, is no place for the prime minister, given his paramount position, to campaign. Yong Kai is a superficial problem; the prime minister needs but a single general to suppress him." "The territory of the Southern Man," Kongming replied, "lies too far from our kingdom to be affected by the civilizing influence of the imperial court. To win their allegiance I must first subdue them, and the required combination of harsh and lenient tactics is not to be lightly entrusted to anyone else."[2]

That day, notwithstanding Wang Lian's repeated appeals, Kongming took leave of the Emperor. He ordered Jiang Wan to serve as his adjutant, Fei Yi as his senior officer, and Dong Jue and Fan Jian as staff officers. Zhao Zilong and Wei Yan were made his chief generals and had overall command; Wang Ping and Zhang Yi were their lieutenants; and there were several dozen Riverlands commanders as well. In all, five hundred thousand Riverlands soldiers were mobilized for the march to Yizhou.

Unexpectedly, Guan Suo, Lord Guan's third son, came to see Kongming in camp. "Since escaping the Jingzhou catastrophe," he said, "I've been recuperating at Bao Hamlet. Many a time, aiming to avenge my father's murder, I wanted to go to the Riverlands and present myself to the late Emperor, but my wounds did not heal and I was unable to make the journey. After my recent recovery, however, I learned that all our Southland enemies had been put to the sword. I therefore came di-

不已；一面遣人申报朝廷，就令关索为前部先锋，一同征南。大队人马，各依队伍而行。饥餐渴饮，夜住晓行；所经之处，秋毫无犯。

却说雍闿听知孔明自统大军而来，即与高定、朱褒商议，分兵三路：高定取中路，雍闿在左，朱褒在右；三路各引兵五六万迎敌。于是高定令鄂焕为前部先锋。焕身长九尺，面貌丑恶，使一枝方天戟，有万夫不当之勇；领本部兵，离了大寨，来迎蜀兵。

却说孔明统大军已到益州界分。前部先锋魏延，副将张翼、王平，才入界口，正遇鄂焕军马。两阵对圆，魏延出马大骂曰："反贼早早受降！"鄂焕拍马与魏延交锋。战不数合，延诈败走，焕随后赶来。走不数里，喊声大震。张翼、王平两路军杀来，绝其后路。延复回，三员将并力拒战，生擒鄂焕。解到大寨，入见孔明。孔明令去其缚，以酒食待之。问曰："汝是何人部将？"焕曰："某是高定部将。"孔明曰："吾知高定乃忠义之士，今为雍闿所惑，以致如此。吾今放汝回去，令高太守早早归降，免遭

rectly west to be received by the Emperor. By luck, I met up with the southern expedition and have taken the opportunity to present myself to Your Excellency." Deeply touched by Guan Suo's story, Kongming informed the court and then gave Guan Suo command of the vanguard. Thus, Guan Suo joined the southern expedition. The vast army proceeded in well-organized sections with ample food and drink at its disposal; it rested nights and moved on at daybreak, never disturbing the people along the way.

* * *

On the news that Kongming was advancing in force, Yong Kai conferred at once with Gao Ding and Zhu Bao. The rebels formed three armies: Gao Ding took the center, Yong Kai the left, and Zhu Bao the right. With fifty or sixty thousand each, they went forward to meet the prime minister's force. Gao Ding had E Huan take the vanguard. E Huan, a man some nine spans tall with a crude, ugly face, wielded a halberd with double side blades and had the courage to fight against any odds. Commanding his own men, he left the main camp and set out to engage the Riverlands soldiers.

Kongming's host reached the Yizhou boundary. On entering the border zone, Vanguard Commander Wei Yan and his lieutenants, Zhang Yi and Wang Ping, encountered E Huan. The two units maneuvered into opposing positions, and Wei Yan rode forth to condemn the rebels. "Surrender quickly," he shouted. E Huan lashed his mount and closed with Wei Yan. After a short encounter, Wei Yan fled, feigning defeat, and E Huan followed in swift pursuit. A brief chase ensued, cries of war rent the air, and two armies, Zhang Yi's and Wang Ping's, closed in, cutting off E Huan's retreat. Wei Yan reversed direction, and the three commanders put up a stout fight and captured E Huan, whom they delivered in bonds to the main camp.

Kongming ordered the captive untied, offered him food and drink, and asked, "Whose subordinate are you?" "Gao Ding's," E Huan replied. "I know him," Kongming said, "a loyal and honorable man — whom Yong Kai has led astray and into rebellion. I shall release you now so you may get Governor Gao Ding to resubmit to our authority and spare himself the gravest consequences." Prostrating himself in grati-

大祸。"鄂焕拜谢而去，回见高定，说孔明之德。定亦感激不已。次日，雍闿至寨。礼毕，闿曰："如何得鄂焕回也？"定曰："诸葛亮以义放之。"闿曰："此乃诸葛亮反间之计：欲令我两人不和，故施此谋也。"定半信不信，心中犹豫。忽报蜀将搦战，闿自引三万兵出迎。战不数合，闿拨马便走，延率兵大进，追杀二十余里。次日，雍闿又起兵来迎。孔明一连三日不出。至第四日，雍闿、高定分兵两路，来取蜀寨。

　　却说孔明令魏延两路伺候；果然雍闿、高定两路兵来，被伏兵杀伤大半，生擒者无数，都解到大寨来。雍闿的人，囚在一边；高定的人，囚在一边。却令军士谣说："但是高定的人免死，雍闿的人尽杀。"众军皆闻此言。少时，孔明令取雍闿的人到帐前，问曰："汝等皆是何人部从？"众伪曰："高定部下人也。"孔明教皆免其死，与酒食赏劳，令人送出界首，纵放回寨。孔明又唤高定的人问之。众皆告曰："吾等实是高定部下军士。"孔明亦皆免其死，赐以酒食；却扬言曰："雍闿今日使人投降，要献汝主并朱褒首级以为功劳，吾甚不忍。汝等既是高定部下军，吾放汝等回去，再不可背反。若再擒来，决不轻恕。"

　　众皆拜谢而去；回到本寨，入见高定，说知此事。定乃密遣人去雍闿寨中探听，却有一般放回的人，言说孔明之德；因此

tude, E Huan returned to Gao Ding and told him of Kongming's mercy. Gao Ding, too, felt enormous gratitude.

The next day Yong Kai came to Gao Ding's camp. After the formalities Yong Kai asked, "How did E Huan manage to get back?" "Zhuge Liang freed him on his honor." "A trick to turn us against each other," Yong Kai said. Gao Ding, uncertain what to believe, hesitated to act. Suddenly it was announced that a Riverlands commander was issuing a challenge. Yong Kai, leading thirty thousand, went forth, but he turned and fled after engaging briefly. Wei Yan pursued boldly for a distance of twenty *li*, killing many. The next day Yong Kai returned to the field seeking combat. Kongming stayed behind his lines for three days. On the fourth day Yong Kai and Gao Ding, leading two armies, converged on the Riverlands base camp.

Kongming ordered Wei Yan to form two armies and lie in wait for a two-pronged attack. When Yong Kai and Gao Ding finally appeared, Wei Yan's ambush took a heavy toll in casualties and prisoners. The latter were escorted to Kongming's camp. Kongming had Yong Kai's men held on one side, Gao Ding's on the other. Rumors were spread among them to the effect that Gao Ding's men would be spared, Yong Kai's killed.

A while later Kongming summoned Yong Kai's met to his command tent and asked them whose unit they belonged to. "We are Gao Ding's men," they all responded. Kongming ordered them spared. He supplied food and drink, had them escorted back to the border, and freed them to return to their camp. Next, Kongming summoned Gao Ding's men; all declared themselves unquestionably Gao Ding's men. Again Kongming spared them and granted them food and drink. Then he informed them, "Today I received a man from Yong Kai who wanted to establish his merit by presenting the heads of Gao Ding and Zhu Bao. I did not have the heart to accept. Since you men serve Gao Ding, I shall let you go back. Do not rebel again. If I catch you, you will not be forgiven so lightly." The soldiers prostrated themselves and departed gratefully.

When the returning captives told Gao Ding what Kongming had said, Gao Ding sent a spy to Yong Kai's camp to gather information. The

雍闿部军,多有归顺高定之心。虽然如此,高定心中不稳,又令一人来孔明寨中探听虚实。被伏路军捉来见孔明。孔明故意认做雍闿的人,唤入帐中问曰:"汝元帅既约下献高定、朱褒二人首级,因何误了日期? 汝这厮不精细,如何做得细作!"军士含糊答应。孔明以酒食赐之,修密书一封,付军士曰:"汝持此书付雍闿,教他早早下手,休得误事。"细作拜谢而去,回见高定,呈上孔明之书,说雍闿如此如此。定看书毕,大怒曰:"吾以真心待之,彼反欲害吾,情理难容!"使唤鄂焕商议。焕曰:"孔明乃仁人,背之不祥。我等谋反作恶,皆雍闿之故;不如杀闿以投孔明。"定曰:"如何下手?"焕曰:"可设一席,令人去请雍闿。彼若无异心,必坦然而来;若其不来,必有异心。我主可攻其前,某伏于寨后小路候之:闿可擒矣。"高定从其言,设席请雍闿。闿果疑前日放回军士之言,惧而不来。是夜高定引兵杀投雍闿寨中。原来有孔明放回免死的人,皆想高定之德,乘时助战。雍闿军不战自乱。闿上马望山路而走。行不二里,鼓声响处,一彪军出,乃鄂焕也:挺方天戟,骤马当先。雍闿措手不及,被焕一戟刺于马下,就枭其首级。闿部下军士皆降高定。定引两部军来降孔明,献雍闿首级于帐下。孔明高坐于帐上,喝令

spy found Kongming's kindness widely praised and most of Yong Kai's men inclined to adhere to Gao Ding. Nevertheless, Gao Ding, still not convinced he should submit to the prime minister, sent another man to Kongming's camp to gather information. This spy was apprehended and taken to Kongming, who purposely mistook him for one of Yong Kai's men. Calling the spy inside, Kongming said, "Your chief commander promised me the heads of Gao Ding and Zhu Bao. Why have you missed the date? A good spy can't afford to be so careless!" The man answered evasively. Kongming offered him food and wine and then drafted a secret communication. "Take this to Yong Kai," Kongming said, entrusting the letter to the spy. "Tell him to act before it's too late." The spy prostrated himself in gratitude and departed. He delivered Kongming's letter to Gao Ding and imparted to him all Kongming had said concerning Yong Kai.

Angered by the letter, Gao Ding said, "I dealt with him in all sincerity, and now he tries to murder me. It is too much!" He called E Huan, who said, "To ignore a man of humanity like Kongming would be bad luck. All our conspiracies were instigated by Yong Kai. We are better off killing him and joining with Kongming." "How to proceed?" Gao Ding asked. "Hold a banquet," E Huan replied, "and invite Yong Kai. If he is sincere, he will come without hesitation. If he won't come, he means to betray us. My lord, attack him from the front. I will be waiting in hiding behind the camp. Yong Kai can be taken!"

Gao Ding invited Yong Kai to a banquet. But Yong Kai did not come, his fears stirred by the returnees' tales of the favor Kongming had shown those claiming to be Gao Ding's men. That night, his suspicions confirmed, Gao Ding led the raid on Yong Kai's camp. Most of the men Kongming had spared and released, mindful of their debt to Gao Ding, joined the raiders. Yong Kai's forces went to pieces without a fight, and he fled into the hills.

Yong Kai had traveled less than two *li*, when a band of soldiers burst into the open amid loud volleys of drums. It was E Huan, his halberd held high. He charged forward, catching Yong Kai off guard, speared him, and cut off his head. Yong Kai's force surrendered to Gao Ding, and Gao Ding led Yong Kai's army and his own in surrender to Kongming,

左右推转高定,斩首报来。定曰:"某感丞相大恩,今将雍闿首级来降,何故斩也?"孔明大笑曰:"汝来诈降。敢瞒吾耶!"定曰:"丞相何以知吾诈降?"孔明于匣中取出一缄,与高定曰:"朱褒已使人密献降书,说你与雍闿结生死之交,岂肯一旦便杀此人?吾故知汝诈也。"定叫屈曰:"朱褒乃反间之计也。丞相切不可信!"孔明曰:"吾亦难凭一面之词。汝若捉得朱褒,方表真心。"定曰:"丞相休疑。某去擒朱褒来见丞相,若何?"孔明曰:"若如此,吾疑心方息也。"

高定即引部将鄂焕并本部兵,杀奔朱褒营来。比及离寨约有十里,山后一彪军到,乃朱褒也。褒见高定军来,慌忙与高定答话。定大骂曰:"汝如何写书与诸葛丞相处,使反间之计害吾耶?"褒目瞪口呆,不能回答。忽然鄂焕于马后转过,一戟刺朱褒于马下。定厉声而言曰:"如不顺者皆戮之!"于是众军一齐拜降。定引两部军来见孔明,献朱褒首级于帐下。孔明大笑曰:"吾故使汝杀此二贼,以表忠心。"遂命高定为益州太守,总摄三郡;令鄂焕为牙将。三路军马已平。

于是永昌太守王伉出城迎接孔明。孔明入城已毕,问曰:"谁与公守此城,以保无虞?"伉曰:"某今日得此郡无危者,皆赖永昌不韦人,姓吕,名凯,字季平。皆此人之力。"孔明遂请吕

to whom he delivered Yong Kai's head.

Seated royally in his command tent, Kongming ordered his guards to remove and behead Gao Ding. Gao Ding protested, "Out of gratitude for Your Excellency's mercy I have surrendered bearing Yong Kai's head. Why execute me?" Kongming laughed loudly and said, "A false submission! Do you dare to fool me?" "What makes Your Excellency think that?" Gao Ding replied. Kongming drew a letter from a container and showed it to Gao Ding, saying, "I have a secret letter from Zhu Bao offering submission and stating that you and Yong Kai are friends to the death. How could you up and kill him? That's how I know you're lying." Defending himself against this unjust accusation, Gao Ding said, "That's Zhu Bao's ruse. Do not believe it, Your Excellency." "I am reluctant to rely on a one-sided report — but catching Zhu Bao for me would prove your sincerity." Gao Ding responded, "Have no doubt, Your Excellency. I will bring him to you." "It would quiet my suspicions," Kongming said.

Gao Ding led E Huan and his troops toward Zhu Bao's base. When they had come to within ten *li* of the perimeter, a band of soldiers emerged from behind a hill. The leader, Zhu Bao, tried desperately to talk to Gao Ding, but the latter denounced him: "How could you write to Prime Minister Zhuge to turn him against me?" Zhu Bao stared dumbly back, unable to answer. Suddenly E Huan swung round behind Zhu Bao and cut him down with a thrust of his halberd as Gao Ding shouted, "Whoever resists dies!" Zhu Bao's men prostrated themselves in a body and surrendered. Gao Ding let the two armies before Kongming and delivered Zhu Bao's head to his tent. Kongming laughed aloud, "You have proved your loyalty by killing those two rebels, which is what I wanted," he said, and he made Gao Ding governor of Yizhou with overall authority in three districts, E Huan was made the governor's garrison commander. Thus, the three rebellions were quelled.

After these events Wang Kang, governor of Yongchang, welcomed Kongming into the city, receiving him outside the walls. On entering, Kongming asked, "Who helped you defend against the rebels?" "Yongchang's safety," Wang Kang replied, "was ensured entirely by a man from Buwei, Lü Kai (styled Jiping). He made it all possible."

凯至。凯入见,礼毕。孔明曰:"久闻公乃永昌高士,多亏公保守此城。今欲平蛮方,公有何高见?"吕凯遂取一图,呈与孔明曰:"某自历仕以来,知南人欲反久矣,故密遣人入其境,察看可屯兵交战之处,画成一图,名曰'平蛮指掌图'。今敢献与明公。明公试观之,可为征蛮之一助也。"孔明大喜,就用吕凯为行军教授,兼向导官。于是孔明提兵大进,深入南蛮之境。

正行军之次,忽报天子差使命至。孔明请入中军,但见一人素袍白衣而进,乃马谡也。——为兄马良新亡,因此挂孝。——谡曰:"奉主上敕命,赐众军酒帛。"孔明接诏已毕,依命一一给散,遂留马谡在帐叙话。孔明问曰:"吾奉天子诏,削平蛮方;久闻幼常高见,望乞赐教。"谡曰:"愚有片言,望丞相察之;南蛮恃其地远山险,不服久矣;虽今日破之,明日复叛。丞相大军到彼,必然平服;但班师之日,必用北伐曹丕;蛮兵若知内虚,其反必速。夫用兵之道:'攻心为上,攻城为下;心战为上,兵战为下。'愿丞相但服其心足矣。"孔明叹曰:"幼常足知吾肺腑也!"于是孔明遂令马谡为参军,即统大兵前进。

却说蛮王孟获,听知孔明智破雍闿等,遂聚三洞元帅商

Kongming summoned Lü Kai. After the formalities of introduction Kongming asked him, "You have long been known to me as a wise scholar of Yongchang. Your help was a boon to the city. My desire now is to pacify the region of the Man tribes. Have you any advice for me?" Lü Kai showed Kongming a map and said, "From my first day in office I have known the Southern Man intended to rebel, so I sent a secret agent into their territory to investigate key sites for posting troops and for combat operations. I have made a chart entitled 'A Handy Guide for Pacifying the Man.' Today I venture to tender it, my lord, for whatever it may contribute to Your Lordship's campaign." Delighted, Kongming appointed Lü Kai military instructor and official guide. And so Kongming next led his army in a broad advance deep into the country of the Man.

During the march a messenger from the Son of Heaven suddenly arrived, and Kongming had him shown into the main tent. The man, Ma Su, entered wearing a white robe. (He was in mourning for Ma Liang, his older brother.) Ma Su said, "I bear His Majesty's command to give wine and silk to the soldiers." Kongming provided for the men in strict compliance with the edict he had received. He then detained Ma Su for an informal chat.

"The Son of Heaven has charged me to subdue the lands of the Man. For many years I have heard men speak of your wisdom, and I crave your counsel now." Ma Su replied, "I will venture one opinion, which I hope Your Excellency will consider. The Southern Man depend on their remoteness and inaccessibility in defying us. Even if you conquer them today, they will rebel tomorrow. Your Excellency's host will no doubt prevail; but after you have marched home and gone to war against Cao Pi, the Man will rebel the moment they learn the Riverlands is vulnerable. Follow the law of warfare: 'The enemy's mind is more important than his city: psychological struggle is superior to armed struggle.' I should think it sufficient for Your Excellency to subdue the minds of the Man." Kongming sighed as he said, "Ma Su, I am an open book to you." He appointed Ma Su military adviser and resumed the march south.

* * *

Learning of Kongming's ingenious defeat of his ally Yong Kai, the king of the Man, Meng Huo, gathered his chieftains from the three hol-

2129

议：第一洞乃金环三结元帅，第二洞乃董荼那元帅，第三洞乃阿会喃元帅。三洞元帅入见孟获，获曰："今诸葛丞相领大军来侵我境界，不得不并力敌之。汝三人可分兵三路而进。如得胜者，便为洞主。"于是分金环三结取中路，董荼那取左路，阿会喃取右路；各引五万蛮兵，依令而行。

却说孔明正在寨中议事，忽哨马飞报，说三洞元帅分兵三路到来。孔明听毕，即唤赵云、魏延至，却都不分付；更唤王平、马忠至，嘱之曰："今蛮兵三路而来，吾欲令子龙、文长去；此二人不识地理，未敢用之。王平可往左路迎敌，马忠可往右路迎敌。吾却使子龙、文长随后接应。今日整顿军马，来日平明进发。"二人听令而去。又唤张嶷、张翼分付曰："汝二人同领一军，往中路迎敌。今日整点军马，来日与王平、马忠约会而进。——吾欲令子龙、文长去取，奈二人不识地理，故未敢用之。"张嶷、张翼听令去了。

赵云、魏延见孔明不用，各有愠色。孔明曰："吾非不用汝二人，但恐以中年涉险，为蛮人所算，失其锐气耳。"赵云曰："倘我等识地理，若何？"孔明曰："汝二人只宜小心，休得妄动。"二人怏怏而退。赵云请魏延到自己寨内商议曰："吾二人为先锋，却说不识地理而不肯用。今用此后辈，吾等岂不羞乎？"延曰："吾二人只今就上马，亲去探之；捉住土人，便教引进，以敌蛮兵，大事可成。"云从之，遂上马径取中路而来。方行不数里，远远望见尘头大起。二人上山坡看时，果见数十骑蛮

lows. The chieftain of the first, Jinhuansanjie, of the second, Dongtuna, and of the third, Ahuinan, all came before Meng Huo, who said to them, "Prime Minister Zhuge has come into our territory with a mighty host. We must join forces to resist him. Divide yourselves into three armies and advance. The victor will rule the hollows." Meng Huo assigned the center route to Jinhuansanjie, the left to Dongtuna, and the right to Ahuinan. Each had fifty thousand Man soldiers and proceeded as ordered.

Kongming was deliberating in camp when a scout excitedly informed him that three Man armies under their chieftains were approaching from three directions. Kongming summoned Zhao Zilong and Wei Yan but gave them no orders. Next, he called Wang Ping and Ma Zhong and charged them: "I would prefer sending Zhao Zilong and Wei Yan against the Man, but neither knows the terrain well enough. I want Wang Ping to stand against their left army, and Ma Zhong against their right. Zhao Zilong and Wei Yan will reinforce you. Prepare for battle now and set out at dawn." The two men left to perform their mission.

Next, Kongming gave orders to Zhang Ni and Zhang Yi: "I want both of you to command a single army in the center. Organize the force today and start out tomorrow after you have worked out the timing with Wang Ping and Ma Zhong. I have decided not to use Zhao Zilong and Wei Yan because the terrain is unfamiliar to them." Zhang Ni and Zhang Yi went to carry out their orders.

Kongming, noting Zhao Zilong and Wei Yan's annoyance at being passed over, said to them, "I did mean to use you; but I thought you might, facing new hazards and past your prime, fall afoul of the Man and lose your mettle." "And if we knew the geography?" Zhao Zilong asked. "I'd rather you didn't take the risk," Kongming replied. The two men retired sullenly; Zhao Zilong invited Wei Yan to his camp. "We are the vanguard," he said to Wei Yan, "but His Excellency says we don't know the terrain and humiliates us by using our juniors." Wei Yan answered, "We can ride out ourselves and investigate. If we find some locals to show us how to proceed against the Man, we can accomplish our goal." Zhao Zilong agreed, and the two vanguard leaders took the central route.

After several *li,* Zhao Zilong and Wei Yan spied dust rising in the

兵，纵马而来。二人两路冲出。蛮兵见了，大惊而走。赵云、魏延各生擒几人，回到本寨，以酒食待之，却细问其故。蛮兵告曰："前面是金环三结元帅大寨，正在山口。寨边东西两路，却通五溪洞并董荼那、阿会喃各寨之后。"

赵云、魏延听知此话，遂点精兵五千，教擒来蛮兵引路。比及起军时，已是二更天气；月明星朗，趁着月色而行。刚到金环三结大寨之时，约有四更，蛮兵方起造饭，准备天明厮杀。忽然赵云、魏延两路杀入，蛮兵大乱。赵云直杀入中军，正逢金环三结元帅；交马只一合，被云一枪刺落马下，就枭其首级。余军溃散。魏延便分兵一半，望东路抄董荼那寨来。赵云分兵一半，望西路抄阿会喃寨来。比及杀到蛮兵大寨之时，天已平明。

先说魏延杀奔董荼那寨来：董荼那听知寨后有军杀至，便引兵出寨拒敌。忽然寨前门一声喊起，蛮兵大乱。原来王平军马早已到了。两下夹攻，蛮兵大败。董荼那夺路走脱，魏延追赶不上。

却说赵云引兵杀到阿会喃寨后之时，马忠已杀至寨前。两下夹攻，蛮兵大败，阿会喃乘乱走脱。各自收军，回见孔明。孔明问曰："三洞蛮兵，走了两洞之主；金环三结元帅首级安在？"赵云将首级献功。众皆言曰："董荼那、阿会喃皆弃马越岭而去，因此赶他不上。"孔明大笑曰："二人吾已擒下了。"赵、魏二

distance. Climbing to a height to survey the field, they saw dozens of Man horsemen racing toward them. From two angles the vanguard leaders fell upon the Man, put them to fearful flight, and returned to camp with several enemy warriors each. The commanders gave their captives food and drink and questioned them closely. The Man soldiers announced, "Ahead you'll find Chieftain Jinhuansanjie's main camp — just by the entrance to the hills. Two roads east and west of the camp run behind the Wuqi Hollows and the camps of Dongtuna and Ahuinan."

Provided with this information, Zhao Zilong and Wei Yan detailed five thousand crack troops for their captives to lead. By the second watch the force had set out under a clear, bright moon. By the fourth watch they had reached the main camp of Jinhuansanjie. The Man troops had begun to make the morning meal, intent on striking at dawn. Suddenly, Zhao Zilong and Wei Yan burst upon their ranks, scattering the Man. Zhao Zilong fought his way to the central command and came face-to-face with Chieftain Jinhuansanjie. The riders had scarcely engaged when Zhao Zilong speared the Man chieftain and beheaded him. The remaining Man troops bolted. Wei Yan detached half the force and headed for the camps of Dongtuna by the east road. Zhao Zilong led the other half to raid the camp of Ahuinan. By the time the Riverlands warriors reached the main Man camp, day had dawned.

Wei Yan attacked the rear of Dongtuna's camp. The chief met him and defended stoutly. Suddenly, to the front of the camp a shout went up, throwing the Man troops into confusion. It so happened that Wang Ping had arrived to reinforce Wei Yan, and their two-sided attack routed the Man. Dongtuna fled for his life; Wei Yan could not overtake him.

Meanwhile, as Zhao Zilong was attacking the rear of Ahuinan's base, Ma Zhong had already struck from the front. Caught in a squeeze, the Man troops suffered a heavy defeat. Ahuinan fled in the struggle. Wei Yan and Zhao Zilong recalled their forces and returned to Kongming, who said, "Of the three Man armies, the chiefs of two have escaped. But where is the head of Jinhuansanjie?" At that, Zhao Zilong held forth the head he had taken as a token of his merit, while his soldiers cried, "Dongtuna and Ahuinan abandoned their mounts and fled across the mountain range. That is why we could not catch them."

人并诸将皆不信。少顷，张嶷解董荼那到，张翼解阿会喃到。众皆惊讶。孔明曰："吾观吕凯图本，已知他各人下的寨子，故以言激子龙、文长之锐气，故教深入重地，先破金环三结，随即分兵左右寨后抄出，以王平、马忠应之。非子龙、文长不可当此任也。吾料董荼那、阿会喃必从便径往山路而走。故遣张嶷、张翼以伏兵待之，令关索以兵接应，擒此二人。"诸将皆拜伏曰："丞相机算，神鬼莫测！"

孔明令押过董荼那、阿会喃至帐下，尽去其缚，以酒食衣服赐之，令各自归洞，勿得助恶。二人泣拜，各投小路而去。孔明谓诸将曰："来日孟获必然亲自引兵厮杀，便可就此擒之。"乃唤赵云、魏延至，付与计策，各引五千兵去了。又唤王平、关索同引一军，授计而去。孔明分拨已毕，坐于帐上待之。

却说蛮王孟获在帐中正坐，忽哨马报来，说三洞元帅，俱被孔明捉将去了；部下之兵，各自溃散。获大怒，遂起蛮兵迤逦进发，正遇王平军马。两阵对圆，王平出马横刀望之：只见门旗开处，数百南蛮骑将两势摆开。中间孟获出马：头顶嵌宝紫金冠，身披缨络红锦袍，腰系碾玉狮子带，脚穿鹰嘴抹绿靴，骑一匹卷毛赤兔马，悬两口松纹镶宝剑，昂然观望，回顾左右蛮将

Kongming laughed and said, "I had those two long ago!" None of the commanders, including Zhao Zilong and Wei Yan, would believe this until Zhang Ni marched Dongtuna in and Zhang Yi entered with Ahuinan in custody. To the astonished assembly Kongming explained, "After locating the Man campsites on Lü Kai's charts, I provoked Zhao Zilong and Wei Yan, whetted their courage for a deep strike into enemy territory — first to defeat Jinhuansanjie, then to follow up with raids to his left and right. Wang Ping and Ma Zhong backed them up. No one but Zhao Zilong and Wei Yan could have succeeded. I anticipated that Dongtuna and Ahuinan would flee toward the mountains, and so I sent Zhang Ni and Zhang Yi to lie in ambush, with Guan Suo for support — and they took them." Hearing the explanation of his strategy, the commanders bowed to the ground and said, "Not even the gods could fathom Your Excellency's calculations!"

Kongming ordered Dongtuna and Ahuinan brought to his tent. He removed their bonds, provided them with food, drink, and clothes, and ordered them to return to their hollows, with his admonition never to abet a conspiracy again. The two men prostrated themselves and wept in gratitude; then they left, taking back trails. Kongming said to his commanders, "Tomorrow Meng Huo will personally lead an attack — giving us an opportunity to capture him." He called for Zhao Zilong and Wei Yan and instructed them to take five thousand troops each. He also called for Wang Ping and Guan Suo to carry out a second plan. After his assignments had been made, Kongming sat in his tent awaiting the outcome.

2135

*   *   *

The Man King, Meng Huo, sat in his tent as his scouts reported the capture of the three chieftains and the disintegration of their forces. Enraged, Meng Huo mustered his men, and they set out, company after company, for the site of the debacle. He soon encountered Wang Ping, and the two armies moved into fighting position. Wang Ping rode out from his line, sword leveled, only to find several hundred Man cavalry spread out before him. From the center came Meng Huo, crowned with a dark gold cap inlaid with gems. He wore a tasseled red damask surcoat, a lion-figured carved jade belt, and falcon-beak greendaubed boots. He

曰："人每说诸葛亮善能用兵；今观此阵，旌旗杂乱，队伍交错；刀枪器械，无一可能胜吾者；始知前日之言谬也。早知如此，吾反多时矣。谁敢去擒蜀将，以振军威？"言未尽，一将应声而出，名唤忙牙长；使一口截头大刀，骑一匹黄骠马，来取王平。二将交锋，战不数合，王平便走。孟获驱兵大进，迤逦追赶。关索略战又走，约退二十余里。孟获正追杀之间，忽然喊声大起，左有张嶷，右有张翼，两路兵杀出，截断归路。王平、关索复兵杀回。前后夹攻，蛮兵大败。孟获引部将死战得脱，望锦带山而逃。背后三路兵追杀将来。获正奔走之间，前面喊声大起，一彪军拦住：为首大将乃常山赵子龙也。获见了大惊，慌忙奔锦带山小路而走。子龙冲杀一阵，蛮兵大败，生擒者无数。孟获止与数十骑奔入山谷之中，背后追兵至近，前面路狭，马不能行，乃弃了马匹，爬山越岭而逃。忽然山谷中一声鼓响，乃是魏延受了孔明之策，引五百步军，伏于此处。孟获抵敌不住，被魏延生擒活捉了。从骑皆降。

　　魏延解孟获到大寨来见孔明。孔明早已杀牛宰羊，设宴在寨；却教帐中排开七重围子手，刀枪剑戟，灿若霜雪；又执御赐黄金钺斧，曲柄伞盖，前后羽葆鼓吹，左右排开御林军，布列得

rode a curly-maned red-hare horse and carried two swords inlaid with pine-grained jade. Looking proudly ahead, he turned to the commanders beside him and said, "How many times have I heard about the skillful tactician Zhuge Liang! Look at his formation — the disorder of his flags, the confusion among his ranks and files, his weapons no better than our own! Now I see the falsity of all I have been told. Had I only known this before, I would have rebelled ages ago! Who will take the Riverlands commander and show the foe our martial might?"

As he spoke, a commander stepped forth to answer the call: Mangyachang. Wielding a broadsword with a squared tip and riding a yellow charger, he took on Wang Ping. The two commanders crossed blade points. After the first clashes Wang Ping fled. Meng Huo motioned his soldiers to advance en masse, following the escaping Riverlands commander. Guan Suo, too, fought briefly and then retreated some twenty *li*. Meng Huo pursued hotly. Suddenly, amid the uproar of shouts, Zhang Ni and Zhang Yi surprised Meng Huo from two sides and cut off the road behind; Wang Ping and Guan Suo reversed course and joined the fighting. The Man troops, caught front and rear, were badly beaten; and Meng Huo, fighting for his life, fled toward the Brocade Belt Hills, barely ahead of the three Riverlands armies, only to be blocked in front by a shouting band of troops under Zhao Zilong. Astonished at finding the great warrior before him, Meng Huo hurriedly shifted to a side path and continued on toward the hills. Zhao Zilong set upon the Man soldiers, inflicting a serious defeat and taking many prisoners. Meng Huo entered the hills, a few score of riders still with him; his pursuers drew closer. The way narrowed, forcing him to abandon his horse, and he clambered over the hilltop. At that moment a volley of drums filled the ravine, announcing Wei Yan, who, following Kongming's plan, had placed five hundred foot soldiers there in ambush. Unable to resist further, Meng Huo was taken alive, and his companions surrendered.

Wei Yan delivered the prisoner to Kongming's camp, where the prime minister had already prepared a feast of slaughtered oxen and horses. The tent was lined by seven rings of yeomen; their swords and spears, sabers and halberds shone white. Beside Kongming, attendants held the imperially conferred golden broadaxe and the curve-handled canopy;

十分严整。孔明端坐于帐上,只见蛮兵纷纷穰穰,解到无数。孔明唤到帐中,尽去其缚,抚谕曰:"汝等皆是好百姓,不幸被孟获所拘,今受惊唬。吾想汝等父母、兄弟、妻子必倚门而望;若听知阵败,定然割肚牵肠,眼中流血。吾今尽放汝等回去,以安各人父母、兄弟、妻子之心。"言讫,各赐酒食米粮而遣之。蛮兵深感其恩,泣拜而去。孔明教唤武士押过孟获来。不移时,前推后拥,缚至帐前。获跪与帐下。孔明曰:"先帝待汝不薄,汝何敢背反?"获曰:"两川之地,皆是他人所占土地,汝主倚强夺之,自称为帝。吾世居此处,汝等无礼,侵我土地:何为反耶?"孔明曰:"吾今擒汝,汝心服否?"获曰:"山僻路狭,误遭汝手,如何肯服!"孔明曰:"汝既不服,吾放汝去,若何?"获曰:"汝放我回去,再整军马,共决雌雄;若能再擒吾,吾方服也。"孔明即令去其缚,与衣服穿了,赐以酒食,给与鞍马,差人送出路,径望本寨而去。

正是:

寇入掌中还放去,人居化外未能降。

未知再来交战若何,且看下文分解。

extending left and right of him in strict order were feather screens, drums and flutes, and the Royal Guard.

Kongming sat poised, watching the Man soldiers being herded in. He called for the captives' bonds to be removed and then said gently, "I know you are not hardened soldiers but well — intentioned folk who, unfortunately coerced by Meng Huo, now find yourselves in this present distress. I can imagine your parents, your brothers, your wives and children anxiously awaiting your return, suffering wrenching anguish and weeping in heartbreak as they learn of your defeat. But it is my purpose to set you free, so that you may return to your loved ones and rejoice with them." So saying, Kongming provided them with food and drink and sent them home with provisions. The Man troops, overwhelmed with gratitude, prostrated themselves and wept.

Next, Kongming called for Meng Huo; within moments guards had marched him in. Bound, Meng Huo kneeled before Kongming. "The late Emperor was more than generous to you," Kongming said. "Why have you broken faith and rebelled?" Meng Huo answered, "The whole of the Riverlands once belonged to another. Your lord seized it by force and proclaimed himself emperor. My ancestors held these lands, which you have encroached upon so barbarically. What 'rebellion' are you talking about?"

2139

Kongming said, "You are now my prisoner. Will you submit sincerely and willingly?" "No," Meng Huo replied. "I fell afoul of your tricks on a narrow mountain trail. Why should I submit?" "All the same," Kongming said, "I shall release you. What do you think of that?" "If you set me free," Meng Huo responded, "I shall reorder my forces for another trial at arms; but if you capture me again, I shall submit." At this point Kongming had Meng Huo's bonds removed and provided him with clothes, food, and drink. Meng Huo was given a saddle horse and escorted from the camp. Indeed:

> Kongming released the predator in hand;
> The man beyond the pale was not ready to surrender.

How would their next encounter turn out?

Read on.

第八十八回

渡泸水再缚番王　识诈降三擒孟获

　　却说孔明放了孟获，众将上帐问曰："孟获乃南蛮渠魁，今幸被擒，南方便定；丞相何故放之？"孔明笑曰："吾擒此人，如囊中取物耳。直须降伏其心，自然平矣。"诸将闻言，皆未肯信。

　　当日孟获行至泸水，正遇手下败残的蛮兵，皆来寻探。众兵见了孟获，且惊且喜，拜问曰："大王如何能勾回来？"获曰："蜀人监我在帐中，被我杀死十余人，乘夜黑而走；正行间，逢着一哨马军，亦被我杀之，夺了此马：因此得脱。"众皆大喜，拥孟获渡了泸水，下住寨栅，会集各洞酋长，陆续招聚原放回的蛮兵，约有十余万骑。此时董荼那、阿会喃已在洞中。孟获使人去请，二人惧怕，只得也引洞兵来。获传令曰："吾已知诸葛亮之计矣，不可与战，战则中他诡计。彼川兵远来劳苦，况即日天炎，彼兵岂能久住？吾等有此泸水之险，将船筏尽拘在南岸，一带皆筑土城，深沟高垒，看诸葛亮如何施谋！"众酋长从其计，尽拘船筏于南岸，一带筑起土城；有依山傍崖之地，高竖敌楼；

Chapter 88

Riverlands Forces Cross the Lu and Capture
Once Again the Foreign King
Zhuge Liang Sees Through a False Submission
and Makes the Third Capture

After Kongming had released Meng Huo, his commanders came to his tent and inquired of him, "We had the good fortune to catch the leading chieftain of the Southern Man; this could have brought the south under control. Why did Your Excellency set him free?" Kongming smiled as he replied, "I can catch him again with ease whenever I choose to. But pacification of the south requires that we subdue the hearts of the Man people." This explanation did not satisfy Kongming's commanders.

Reaching the River Lu that same day, Meng Huo met up with survivors of his shattered force still searching for him. Catching sight of their leader, the soldiers, astonished yet rejoicing, prostrated themselves. "How did Your Highness manage to get back?" they asked. "The Riverlanders," he replied, "confined me in a tent. But I killed some ten or more and got away in the dead of night. When their sentinel accosted me, I killed him too and seized his horse. That's how I escaped." The delighted soldiers followed Meng Huo across the river. They pitched camp and began gathering the chiefs of the various tribal areas, who, one after another, summoned back the men Kongming had released — over one hundred thousand riders in all.

2141

At this time Dongtuna and Ahuinan had already joined their own tribes. Meng Huo sent for the two chiefs, who, fearful of Huo's might, came with their men. Meng Huo issued an order: "I have seen through Zhuge Liang's tricks! We must not do battle with him and fall for another. The Riverlands troops, exhausted by long marches and plagued by fierce heat, will not abide here long. Protected by the River Lu, we can keep all boats and rafts on the south shore, raise a wall of earth there and other strong outworks. Let Zhuge Liang do what he likes!" The chiefs agreed, tied up all craft on the southern shore, and put up a wall. Prepar-

楼上多设弓弩炮石，准备久处之计。粮草皆是各洞供运。孟获以为万全之策，坦然不忧。

却说孔明提兵大进，前军已至泸水，哨马飞报说："泸水之内，并无船筏；又兼水势甚急，隔岸一带筑起土城，皆有蛮兵守把。"时值五月，天气炎热，南方之地，分外炎酷，军马衣甲，皆穿不得。孔明自至泸水边观毕，回到本寨，聚诸将至帐中，传令曰："今孟获兵屯泸水之南，深沟高垒，以拒我兵；吾既提兵至此，如何空回？汝等各各引兵，依山傍树，拣林木茂盛之处，与我将息人马。"乃遣吕凯离泸水百里，拣阴凉之地，分作四个寨子；使王平、张嶷、张翼、关索各守一寨，内外皆搭草棚，遮盖马匹，将士乘凉，以避暑气。参军蒋琬看了，入问孔明曰："某看吕凯所造之寨甚不好：正犯昔日先帝败于东吴时之地势矣。倘蛮兵偷渡泸水，前来劫寨，若用火攻，如何解救？"孔明笑曰："公勿多疑，吾自有妙算。"蒋琬等皆不晓其意。

忽报蜀中差马岱解暑药并粮米到。孔明令入。岱参拜毕，一面将米药分派四寨。孔明问曰："汝将带多少军来？"马岱曰："有三千军。"孔明曰："吾军累战疲困，欲用汝军，未知肯向前否？"岱曰："皆是朝廷军马，何分彼我？丞相要用，虽死不辞。"孔明曰："今孟获拒住泸水，无路可渡。吾欲先断其粮道，令彼

ing for a long stand, they built watchtowers on hills and high points, and placed crossbowmen and bombards inside; grain and fodder were brought in from the various tribes. Confident in his plan, Meng Huo felt invincible.

Meanwhile, Kongming had advanced in force to the Lu. His scouts reported back: "There's not a boat to be seen. The river is swift and rough, and they have built a wall on the far shore; troops are guarding it." It was the fifth month, the weather fiery hot. The punishing southern heat made it impossible to wear armor. After observing the enemy position from the riverbank, Kongming returned to camp, gathered his commanders, and told them: "Meng Huo occupies the south shore and is well dug in against us. But since we've come this far, how can we go home empty-handed? I want each of you to move to the hillsides and woods. Pick lush spots to rest your troops."

Next, Kongming sent Lü Kai to pitch four camps in a shady stretch one hundred *li* from the river; he then dispatched Wang Ping, Zhang Ni, Zhang Yi, and Guan Suo to defend them. In and around the camps thatched sheds were made for the horses and also for the commanders and their men. Inside the sheds the men found relief from the heat.

The military adviser Jiang Wan, after observing the sites, said to Kongming, "I don't think much of Lü Kai's position. He has his camps laid out exactly like the late Emperor did — exactly what enabled the Southland to defeat him. If the Man steal across the river and burn them, no one can save him." Kongming smiled an said, "You need not worry. I have an excellent plan." But neither Jiang Wan nor the others knew what Kongming was up to.[1]

At this moment Ma Dai arrived from the Riverlands with food grain and medication for heatstroke. Ma Dai was received and then presented himself to Kongming; the supply of food and medicine was shared among the four camps. Kongming asked him, "How many troops have you brought?" "Three thousand," Ma Dai replied. "Our men are worn out from battle," Kongming said. "I would like you to send your troops to the front if you are willing." "The Emperor's troops," Ma Dai said, "are neither yours nor mine. If Your Excellency needs them, I shall shirk no hardship, nor even death." Kongming said, "Meng Huo holds the river;

2143

军自乱。"岱曰："如何断得？"孔明曰："离此一百五十里，泸水下流沙口，此处水慢，可以扎筏而渡。汝提本部三千军渡水，直入蛮洞，先断其粮，然后会合董荼那、阿会喃两个洞主，便为内应。不可有误。"

马岱欣然去了，领兵前到沙口，驱兵渡水；因见水浅，大半不下筏，只裸衣而过，半渡皆倒；急救傍岸，口鼻出血而死。马岱大惊，连夜回告孔明。孔明随唤向导土人问之。土人曰："目今炎天，毒聚泸水，日间甚热，毒气正发：有人渡水，必中其毒；或饮此水，其人必死。若要渡时，须待夜静水冷，毒气不起，饱食渡之，方可无事。"孔明遂令土人引路，又选精壮军五六百，随着马岱，来到泸水沙口，扎起木筏，半夜渡水，果然无事。岱领着二千壮军，令土人引路，径取蛮洞运粮总路口夹山峪而来。那夹山峪，两下是山，中间一条路，止容一人一马而过。马岱占了夹山峪，分拨军士，立起寨栅。洞蛮不知，正解粮到，被岱前后截住，夺粮百余车。蛮人报入孟获大寨中。

此时孟获在寨中，终日饮酒取乐，不理军事，谓众酋长曰："吾若与诸葛亮对敌，必中奸计。今靠此泸水之险，深沟高垒以待之；蜀人受不过酷热，必然退走。那时吾与汝等随后击之，便可擒诸葛亮也。"言讫，呵呵大笑。忽然班内一酋长曰："沙口水浅，倘蜀兵透漏过来，深为利害；当分军守把。"获笑曰："汝是

there is no way we can cross. I want to cut off the grain supply and rout him." "How?" Ma Dai asked. "One hundred and fifty *li* away, in the lower reaches of the river, by Sandymouth where the current ebbs, it is possible to tie rafts together and get across. Take your own three thousand, get directly into the Man redoubts, and interdict their supply line. Then meet with Dongtuna and Ahuinan and make them our collaborators. Don't let anything go wrong."

Ma Dai set off eagerly. Reaching Sandymouth, he directed his men to cross the Lu. The water was shallow, and few took rafts; most went over naked. But in midstream they suddenly began falling over. Those who managed to get back to shore died all the same, blood flowing from their mouths and noses. Ma Dai was terrified and sent a report back to Kongming.

Kongming questioned native guides, who explained, "Now on the hottest days poisons concentrate in the river water: during the day malignant vapors attack anyone trying to cross; to drink the water is fatal. But you can cross unharmed in the dead of night when the water is cooler and the vapors clear. The men must eat well first." Kongming had the guides lead the way for Ma Dai and five or six hundred picked troops. At Sandymouth they put together a number of rafts, and at midnight the whole force crossed safely over as predicted. Next, Ma Dai had the natives lead two thousand of his men to Jiashan Defile on the main grain route for the Man tribal areas, where man and horse had to pass through singly on a path squeezed between two hills. Ma Dai occupied the defile, deploying his men and setting up barricades. Unaware of Ma Dai's movements, the Man tried to deliver the grain; but Ma Dai cut them off front and rear and seized more than a hundred cartloads. A report of the loss was dispatched to Meng Huo.

2145

Meng Huo spent his day in camp drinking and enjoying himself, paying little attention to military matters. To his chiefs he said, "If I go against Zhuge Liang, I will fall into a trap. Secure now behind the river, I will wait for the heat to force them to withdraw. An attack from the rear then will be sure to capture Zhuge Liang!" With that he laughed huskily. Suddenly one of the chiefs said, "If the Riverlanders slip across at the Sandymouth shallows, we will be in serious trouble. We should send a

本处土人，如何不知？吾正要蜀兵来渡此水，渡则必死于水中矣。"酋长又曰："倘有土人说与夜渡之法，当复何如？"获曰："不必多疑。吾境内之人，安肯助敌人耶？"正言之间，忽报蜀兵不知多少，暗渡泸水，绝断了夹山粮道，打着"平北将军马岱"旗号。获笑曰："量此小辈，何足道哉！"即遣副将忙牙长，引三千兵投夹山峪来。

却说马岱望见蛮兵已到，遂将二千军摆在山前。两阵对圆，忙牙长出马，与马岱交锋；只一合，被岱一刀，斩于马下。蛮兵大败走回，来见孟获，细言其事。获唤诸将问曰："谁敢去敌马岱？"言未毕，董荼那出曰："某愿往。"孟获大喜，遂与三千兵而去。获又恐有人再渡泸水，即遣阿会喃，引三千兵，去守把沙口。

却说董荼那引蛮兵到了夹山峪下寨，马岱引兵来迎。部内军有认得是董荼那，说与马岱如此如此。岱纵马向前大骂曰："无义背恩之徒！吾丞相饶汝性命，今又背反，岂不自羞！"董荼那满面惭愧，无言可答，不战而退。马岱掩杀一阵而回。董荼那回见孟获曰："马岱英雄，抵敌不住。"获大怒曰："吾知汝原受诸葛亮之恩，今故不战而退——正是卖阵之计！"喝教推出斩了。众酋长再三哀告，方才免死，叱武士将董荼那打了一百大棍，放归本寨。诸多酋长皆来告董荼那曰："我等虽居蛮方，未尝敢犯中国；中国亦不曾侵我。今因孟获势力相逼，不得已而

guard over there." But Meng Huo smiled as he answered, "A native like you should know that I want them to cross so they will die in the water." "And if someone tells them to cross at night?" the chief asked. "It is unlikely that any local person would help the enemy. Do not worry," Meng Huo answered. But at that moment Meng Huo was told that an unknown number of Riverlanders had secretly crossed the Lu and closed Jiashan Defile under a banner reading "Ma Dai, General Who Pacifies the North." Meng Huo smiled again. "I hardly think this young fellow a problem," he said, and he sent a lieutenant, Mangyachang, to the defile with three thousand men.

Sighting the Man troops, Ma Dai deployed his two thousand in front of the mountain. The two forces moved into opposing positions. Mangyachang rode forth and closed with Ma Dai. In a single exchange Ma Dai cut him down. The Man troops ran from the field in defeat. They reported to Meng Huo, who summoned his commanders and asked, "Who will fight Ma Dai?" Dongtuna stepped forward to volunteer. Meng Huo, delighted, gave him command of three thousand. He also sent Ahuinan to Sandymouth to prevent further enemy crossings.

After Dongtuna had camped near Jiashan Defile, Ma Dai came to engage him. Someone in his command had recognized Dongtuna and told Ma Dai something about the foe. Ma Dai subsequently raced forward and denounced Dongtuna: "Faithless ingrate! Villain! His Excellency spared your life, yet now you turn on us again! Where is your honor?" Dongtuna's face flushed with shame and he made no answer, but withdrew without fighting. Ma Dai delivered a single swift attack and then returned.

Dongtuna went back to Meng Huo and said, "I can't resist a hero like Ma Dai!" In a fury Meng Huo said, "I know Zhuge Liang once spared you. Now you refuse to fight. It is a sellout!" He ordered Dongtuna removed and executed. But when the chiefs all pleaded for his life, Meng Huo relented. He reduced the punishment to one hundred strokes and sent Dongtuna back to his camp.

The chiefs went to Dongtuna and said, "We live in the Man region, but we have never wanted to go against the middle kingdoms.[2] Nor have the middle kingdoms ever infringed on our territory. We rebelled only

造反。想孔明神机莫测，曹操、孙权尚自惧之，何况我等蛮方乎？况我等皆受其活命之恩，无可为报。今欲舍一死命，杀孟获去投孔明，以免洞中百姓涂炭之苦。"董荼那曰："未知汝等心下若何？"内有原蒙孔明放回的人，一齐同声应曰："愿往！"于是董荼那手执钢刀，引百余人，直奔大寨而来，时孟获大醉于帐中。董荼那引众人持刀而入，帐下有两将侍立。董荼那以刀指曰："汝等亦受诸葛丞相活命之恩，宜当报效。"二将曰："不须将军下手，某当生擒孟获，去献丞相。"于是一齐入帐，将孟获执缚已定，押到泸水边，驾船直过北岸，先使人报知孔明。

　　却说孔明已有细作探知此事，于是密传号令，教各寨将士，整顿军器，方教为首酋长解孟获入来，其余皆回本寨听候。董荼那先入中军见孔明，细说其事。孔明重加赏劳，用好言抚慰，遣董荼那引众酋长去了，然后令刀斧手推孟获入。孔明笑曰："汝前者有言：'但再擒得，便肯降服。'今日如何？"获曰："此非汝之能也；乃吾手下之人自相残害，以致如此：如何肯服？"孔明曰："吾今再放汝去，若何？"孟获曰："吾虽蛮人，颇知兵法；若丞相端的肯放吾回洞中，吾当率兵再决胜负。若丞相这番再擒得我，那时倾心吐胆归降，并不敢改移也。"孔明曰："这番生擒，如又不服，必无轻恕。"令左右去其绳索，仍前赐以

because Meng Huo forced us to do so. We don't think we can fathom Kongming's inspired tactics — why, Cao Cao himself feared him, and Sun Quan fears him still! What can we Man expect to do? Not to mention that we owe Kongming our lives! Whatever the risk, we want to kill Meng Huo and join Kongming. That will spare the people of our region untold misery." To this appeal Dongtuna replied, "What are your real thoughts?" Among the men were some whom Kongming had originally released, and in unison they cried, "Let's go to kill Meng Huo!"

At that, Dongtuna raised his steel sword and, at the head of a hundred men, rushed toward the main camp. Meng Huo lay drunk in his tent. Dongtuna approached, sword drawn. He found two commanders standing guard. Dongtuna pointed to them and said, "You two should show Prime Minister Zhuge gratitude for having spared your lives." "You need not take action, General," they replied. "We shall deliver Meng Huo to His Excellency." Then they burst into the tent. They tied Meng Huo up, brought him to the river, and ferried him to the northern shore, sending someone ahead to inform Kongming.

Apprised of Meng Huo's capture, Kongming issued secret orders to each camp to prepare their weapons for display before Dongtuna arrived with Meng Huo; Kongming then sent everyone back to his station. Dongtuna presented himself to Kongming and recounted the details of Meng Huo's capture. Kongming rewarded him well for his efforts, gave him kind and encouraging words, and sent him away at the head of the chiefs.

2149

Next, he had armed guards march Meng Huo in. With a smile Kongming said, "Remember your promise: 'If you catch me again, I will agree to submit.' What do you say now?" "You did not catch me by your own ability. My underlings turned on me. Why should I submit?" "And if I let you go again?" Kongming replied. "Even a Man knows something about the art of war. If Your Excellency actually sends me home, I will be back with my army to decide the day. And if you catch me again, I shall offer my allegiance with heartfelt unwavering sincerity." "Next time you're captured alive and refuse to submit," Kongming warned, "it will go hard with you." He had Meng Huo's bonds removed, provided food and drink as before, and invited the captive to sit with him in his

酒食，列坐于帐上。孔明曰："吾自出茅庐，战无不胜，攻无不取。汝蛮邦之人，何为不服？"获默然不答。

孔明酒后，唤孟获同上马出寨，观看诸营寨栅所屯粮草，所积军器。孔明指谓孟获曰："汝不降吾，真愚人也。吾有如此之精兵猛将，粮草兵器，汝安能胜吾哉？汝若早降，吾当奏闻天子，令汝不失王位，子子孙孙，永镇蛮邦。意下若何？"获曰："某虽肯降，怎奈洞中之人未肯心服。若丞相肯放回去，就当招安本部人马，同心合胆，方可归顺。"孔明忻然，又与孟获回到大寨。饮酒至晚，获辞去；孔明亲自送至泸水边，以船送获归寨。

孟获来到本寨，先伏刀斧手于帐下，差心腹人到董荼那、阿会喃寨中，只推孔明有使命至，将二人赚到大寨帐下，尽皆杀之，弃尸于涧。孟获随即遣亲信之人，守把隘口，自引军出了夹山峪，要与马岱交战，却并不见一人；及问土人，皆言昨夜尽搬粮草复渡泸水，归大寨去了。获再回洞中，与亲弟孟优商议曰："如今诸葛亮之虚实，吾已尽知，汝可去如此如此。"

孟优领了兄计，引百余蛮兵，搬载金珠、宝贝、象牙、犀角之类，渡了泸水，径投孔明大寨而来；方才过了河时，前面鼓角齐鸣，一彪军摆开：为首大将乃马岱也。孟优大惊。岱问了来

tent. After they were seated, Kongming said, "Since leaving my little thatched hut, I have won every battle I have engaged in; every attack has yielded victory. You of the Man nation — why not submit?" Meng Huo remained silent.

Afterward Kongming invited Meng Huo to ride out with him. Together they surveyed the storehouses stockpiled with grain and weapons. Kongming sad, "How foolish of you to resist these picked troops and fierce commanders so well provided for. Submit now and I will bring it to the attention of the Son of Heaven, who will reserve kingship over the Man nation for yourself and the generations after you in perpetuity. What do you think?" "Even if I did submit," the chief replied, "what of the other tribes whose hearts you have yet to win? Set me free, Your Excellency, and I will urge my men to offer unanimous allegiance." Kongming responded with enthusiasm. He returned to his camp with Meng Huo, and they drank late into the night. Then the chief took his leave. Kongming escorted him to the shore of the River Lu, and a boat provided by Kongming took Meng Huo across.[3]

On reaching his camp, Meng Huo posted armed guards in ambush and sent a trusted subordinate to the camps of Dongtuna and Ahuinan. The envoy, by pretending that Kongming had sent a messenger along, deceived the two chiefs into coming to the main camp. There Meng Huo had them executed and their bodies thrown into a stream. Next, Meng Huo dispatched reliable warriors to defend his strongpoints while he led his own men out of Jiashan Defile to do battle with Ma Dai; but he found no one at the defile. Local people told him that Ma Dai had gone back to the main camp after moving all provisions across the river the previous night. Meng Huo returned to his quarters and told his younger brother, Meng You, "By now I have a clear idea of Zhuge Liang's strong and weak points, so here is what you do..."

Meng You put his brother's plan into action: leading one hundred Man troops bearing gold and pearls, precious cowry shells, elephant tusks and gaur horn, he crossed the Lu. Meng You meant to go directly to Kongming's main camp; but the moment he landed on the northern shore, he was met by the sound of drums and horns as a band of soldiers — under Ma Dai — fanned out before him.

情，令在外厢，差人来报孔明。孔明正在帐中与马谡、吕凯、蒋琬、费祎等共议平蛮之事，忽帐下一人，报称孟获差弟孟优来进宝贝。孔明回顾马谡曰："汝知其来意否？"谡曰："不敢明言。——容某暗写于纸上，呈与丞相，看合钧意否？"孔明从之。马谡写讫，呈与孔明。孔明看毕，抚掌大笑曰："擒孟获之计，吾已差派下也。——汝之所见，正与吾同。"遂唤赵云入，向耳畔分付如此如此；又唤魏延入，亦低言分付；又唤王平、马忠、关索入，亦密密地分付。

各人受了计策，皆依令而去，方召孟优入帐。优再拜于帐下曰："家兄孟获，感丞相活命之恩，无可奉献，辄具金珠宝贝若干，权为赏军之资。续后别有进贡天子礼物。"孔明曰："汝兄今在何处？"优曰："为感丞相天恩，径往银坑山中收拾宝物去了，少时便回来也。"孔明曰："汝带多少人来？"优曰："不敢多带。只是随行百余人，皆运货物者。"孔明尽教入帐看时，皆是青眼黑面，黄发紫须，耳带金环，鬅头跣足，身长力大之士。孔明就令随席而坐，教诸将劝酒，殷勤相待。

却说孟获在帐中专望回音，忽报有二人回了；唤入问之，具说："诸葛亮受了礼物大喜，将随行之人，皆唤入帐中，杀牛宰羊，设宴相待。二大王令某密报大王：今夜二更，里应外合，以成大事。"

Meng You panicked. Ma Dai, after questioning him, had him wait in an outer area while he sent word to Kongming, who was in his tent deliberating the pacification of the Man with Ma Su, Lü Kai, Jiang Wan, Fei Yi, and others. Suddenly Meng You was announced. Kongming asked Ma Su, "Do you know his purpose?" "Rather than speak openly," Ma Su answered, "let me write it down and see if it accords with your own esteemed judgment." Kongming agreed. Ma Su handed his note to Kongming, who rubbed his palms together and laughed out loud. "Your plan has already been put in motion! Our views are one!" he said and called for Zhao Zilong, to whom he whispered certain instructions. He also called for Wei Yan and to him confided another charge. Wang Ping, Ma Zhong, and Guan Suo also received secret orders.

When each commander had left to perform his duty, Kongming called Meng You into his tent. Meng You prostrated himself and said, "My elder brother, Meng Huo, grateful to you for sparing his life and having until now presented no tribute to you, has ventured to prepare a number of treasures that may provisionally serve to reward your army. In the future there will be further presentations of ritual tribute to the Son of Heaven." "Where is your elder brother now?" Kongming asked him. "Thankful for Your Excellency's boundless kindness," Meng You replied, "my brother has gone to collect more valuables in the Silver Pit Hills. He should be back shortly." "How many came with you?" Kongming asked. "Not many. A retinue of no more than a hundred or so to transport our gifts," Meng You answered. Kongming had them all enter his tent. They were tall, strong men, disheveled and barefoot, with blue-green eyes and swarthy complexions, yellowish hair and purplish beards. Gold rings hung in each man's ear. Kongming had the bearers seat themselves and told his commanders to serve them wine and treat them all with full courtesy.

Meng Huo was waiting in his tent for news of the mission when two of Meng You's men came back and informed the chief, "Zhuge Liang, most pleased with the gifts, has slaughtered oxen and horses and feasted the whole retinue in his tent. The lesser king asked us to inform you that the action is set for the second watch tonight. Our men are inside their camp now, ready to support an attack from outside to achieve our goal."

2153

　　孟获听知甚喜，即点起三万蛮兵，分为三队。获唤各洞酋长分付曰："各军尽带火具。今晚到了蜀寨时，放火为号。吾当自取中军，以擒诸葛亮。"诸多蛮将，受了计策，黄昏左侧，各渡泸水而来。孟获带领心腹蛮将百余人，径投孔明大寨，于路并无一军阻当。前至寨门，获率众将骤马而入，——乃是空寨，并不见一人。获撞入中军，只见帐中灯烛荧煌，孟优并番兵尽皆醉倒。原来孟优被孔明教马谡、吕凯二人管待，令乐人搬做杂剧，殷勤劝酒，酒内下药，尽皆昏倒，浑如醉死之人。孟获入帐问之，内有醒者，但指口而已。获知中计，急救了孟优等一干人；却待奔回中队，前面喊声大震，火光骤起，蛮兵各自逃窜。一彪军杀到，乃是蜀将王平。获大惊，急奔左队时，火光冲天，一彪军杀到，为首蜀将乃是魏延。获慌忙望右队而来，只见火光又起，又一彪军杀到，为首蜀将乃是赵云。三路军夹攻将来，四下无路。孟获弃了军士、匹马望泸水而逃。正见泸水上数十个蛮兵，驾一小舟，获慌令近岸。人马方才下船，一声号起，将孟获缚住。原来马岱受了计策，引本部兵扮作蛮兵，撑船在此，诱擒孟获。

　　于是孔明招安蛮兵，降者无数。孔明一一抚慰，并不加害。就教救灭了余火。须臾，马岱擒孟获至；赵云擒孟优至；魏

Delighted by the news, Meng Huo called up thirty thousand Man soldiers, whom he divided into three armies. He charged the tribal chiefs: "Each soldier is to carry inflammable materials. When we reach the Riverlands camp tonight, fire will be the signal. I myself will take on their central army and capture Zhuge Liang!" The Man commanders were then given their orders. Toward the day's end they crossed the River Lu. Meng Huo, proceeding unopposed with a hundred mounted followers, reached the entrance to Kongming's main camp. But on bursting in, he and his commanders found the site deserted. In the main tent, lamps and candles surrounded the sprawled, drunken forms of Meng You and his Man troops.

This is what led up to the scene that Meng Huo found. Kongming had told Ma Su and Lü Kai to entertain Meng You. Accordingly, Ma Su and Lü Kai had plied Meng You and his men with wine while performances were put on for them. The wine being drugged, Meng You and his men were soon unconscious. And so when Meng Huo entered the tent to demand an explanation, those still awake simply pointed to their mouths. Meng Huo knew he had been fooled and tried to get Meng You and his men back to his camp, but ahead of them harsh war cries sounded and torchlights appeared.

The Man soldiers were scuttling off as Wang Ping led a band of men in for the kill. Meng Huo dashed frantically to his left force, but Wei Yan, leading Riverlands troops, accosted him as torches lit the sky. Meng Huo then raced desperately toward his right force, but again he met torchlights and hostile forces, this time under Zhao Zilong. Faced by three armies, with no avenue of escape, Meng Huo abandoned his men and fled alone on horseback to the River Lu. There he found a few score of Man soldiers steering a small ship. Meng Huo motioned them closer to land. But the moment man and mount boarded, a horn sounded and Meng Huo was seized and bound. This was Ma Dai's part in the plan. He had disguised his troops as Man soldiers and poled his craft into position to lure Meng Huo into being captured.

Kongming offered amnesty, and countless Man soldiers surrendered. Kongming cheered and encouraged one and all and, imposing no punishment, simply had them extinguish whatever fires they had started.

2155

延、马忠、王平、关索擒诸洞酋长至。孔明指孟获而笑曰:"汝先令汝弟以礼诈降,如何瞒得过吾!今番又被我擒,汝可服否?"获曰:"此乃吾弟贪口腹之故,误中汝毒,因此失了大事。吾若自来,弟以兵应之,必然成功。此乃天败,非吾之不能也:如何肯服!"孔明曰:"今已三次,如何不服?"孟获低头无语。孔明笑曰:"吾再放汝回去。"孟获曰:"丞相若肯放吾兄弟回去,收拾家下亲丁,和丞相大战一场:那时擒得,方才死心塌地而降。"孔明曰:"再若擒住,必不轻恕。汝可小心在意,勤攻韬略之书,再整亲信之士,早用良策,勿生后悔。"遂令武士去其绳索,放起孟获,并孟优及各洞酋长,一齐都放。孟获等拜谢去了。此时蜀兵已渡泸水。孟获等过了泸水,只见岸口陈兵列将,旗帜纷纷。获到营前,马岱高坐,以剑指之曰:"这番拿住,必无轻放!"孟获到了自己寨时,赵云早已袭了此寨,布列兵马。云坐于大旗下,按剑而言曰:"丞相如此相待,休忘大恩!"获嗻嗻连声而去。将出界口山坡,魏延引一千精兵,摆在坡上,勒马厉声而言曰:"吾今已深入巢穴,夺汝险要;汝尚自愚迷,抗拒大军!这回拿住,碎尸万段,决不轻饶!"孟获等抱头鼠窜,望本洞

Soon Ma Dai brought in Meng Huo, and Zhao Zilong brought in Meng You. Wei Yan, Ma Zhong, Wang Ping, and Guan Suo followed with the tribal chiefs in custody. Kongming smiled as he said to Meng Huo, "Did you expect to fool me by sending your brother with gifts, pretending to surrender? Now that I have caught you once again, are you willing to submit?" "You won because my brother overindulged a bit and fell victim to your poisoned wine. That's what ruined us. Had I come myself and left my brother to back me up, we would have succeeded. Heaven, not my failure, has defeated me — so why should I submit?"

"Why not?" Kongming asked. "It's the third time!" Meng Huo lowered his head and kept quiet. "I'll have to let you go again, then," Kongming said with a smile. "Your Excellency," Meng Huo responded, "release me and my brother and let us regather our own clansmen for a grand battle with you. If you succeed in capturing me again, I will submit to you and banish forever all thought of resistance." "It will not go easy with you the next time," Kongming warned. "Exercise extreme caution, study diligently the texts on the art of war, put your most reliable troops in fighting condition, and use sound tactics without delay to avoid further failures." With that, Kongming freed Meng Huo, Meng You, and the other chiefs. They bade a grateful good-bye and left.

By this time, Riverlands troops had already reached the Lu's southern bank. After Meng Huo had crossed over, he found Kongming's troops and commanders arrayed along the shore, their banners flying thickly overhead. When Meng Huo reached his base area camp, he found Ma Dai sitting in state. Pointing at the chief with his sword, Ma Dai declared, "This time you will not get off!" Coming to his own camp, Meng Huo found Zhao Zilong's troops in position and Zilong himself in control, sitting under a large banner, resting his hand on his sword. "Do not forget the great mercy His Excellency has shown you!" Zhao Zilong declared. Meng Huo murmured in agreement and left. He was about to enter the hills when Wei Yan, at the head of a line of a thousand picked troops deployed on a slope, reined in and shouted, "I have already penetrated your nests and dens. Your strategic places are in our hands but, stubborn and stupid, you resist the imperial legions. When we catch you again, your corpse will be sundered a thousand ways! There will be no mercy!"

而去。后人有诗赞曰：

　　　　五月驱兵入不毛，月明泸水瘴烟高。

　　　　誓将雄略酬三顾，岂惮征蛮七纵劳。

　　却说孔明渡了泸水，下寨已毕，大赏三军，聚众将于帐下曰："孟获第二番擒来，吾令遍观各营虚实，正欲令其来劫营也。吾知孟获颇晓兵法，吾以兵马粮草炫耀，实令孟获看吾破绽，必用火攻。彼令其弟诈降，欲为内应耳。吾三番擒之而不杀，诚欲服其心，不欲灭其类也。吾今明告汝等。——勿得辞劳，可用心报国。"众将拜伏曰："丞相智、仁、勇三者足备，虽子牙、张良不能及也。"孔明曰："吾今安敢望古人耶？皆赖汝等之力，共成功业耳。"帐下诸将听得孔明之言，尽皆喜悦。

　　却说孟获受了三擒之气，忿忿归到银坑洞中，即差心腹人赍金珠宝贝，往八番九十三甸等处，并蛮方部落，借使牌刀獠丁军健数十万，克日齐备，各队人马，云堆雾拥，俱听孟获调用。伏路军探知其事，来报孔明。孔明笑曰："吾正欲令蛮兵皆至，见吾之能也。"遂上小车而行。

Meng Huo and his leaders scurried off and headed home. A poet of later times left these lines in tribute to Kongming:

> A fifth-month march into the southern heath,
> On a moon-bright night as river vapors rose —
> His bold design requites Liu Bei's three calls.
> Unto seven times he dares to free his foes![4]

Meanwhile, Kongming had crossed the River Lu, pitched camp, and rewarded the armies. Gathering the commanders in his tent, he said, "The second time we caught Meng Huo, I let him see our entire base area in the hopes that he would attack. Since Meng Huo has some military knowledge, I gave him a good view of our weapons and provisions. My real purpose was to get him to notice our weak points, against which he was sure to use fire. His brother surrendered only so he could collaborate from within. After three captures I finally spared Meng Huo because what I really wanted was to subdue him mentally and not to have to exterminate his tribes. Today I can explain all this to you. Do not shirk future hardships. Apply yourselves in serving your kingdom."

The commanders bowed low and said, "Your Excellency is a man of humanity no less than wisdom, of courage no less than humanity. You excel even the famed advisers of antiquity, Jiang Ziya and Zhang Liang." "I am unworthy of the ancients," Kongming replied. "It is your collective strength that sustains me in our effort to accomplish our mission." The commanders were gratified by Kongming's words.

Meng Huo, frustrated by the three captures he had suffered, returned to the Silver Pit Hollow in an ugly mood. He sent trusted men bearing gifts of gold, pearls, and treasure to the ninety-three districts of the eight outer nations of the southwest as well as to the smaller tribes in the Man region. In response they sent several hundred thousand hardy warriors armed with shields and swords. On the appointed day the various details massed together like clouds to receive their instructions from Meng Huo. Sentinels on the roads reported the enemy's preparations to Kongming, who said, smiling, "I was hoping to draw the Man forces here to show them what we can do!" Kongming then mounted a small carriage and set out. Indeed:

> But for the fierce and awesome southwest tribal chiefs,

正是：

　　若非洞主威风猛,怎显军师手段高!

未知胜负如何,且看下文分解。

Could the director general have shown the world his skills?

Which side would prevail?

Read on.

第八十九回

武乡侯四番用计　南蛮王五次遭擒

　　却说孔明自驾小车，引数百骑前来探路。前有一河，名曰西洱河：水势虽慢，并无一只船筏。孔明令伐木为筏而渡，其木到水皆沉。孔明遂问吕凯，凯曰："闻西洱河上流有一山，其山多竹，大者数围。可令人伐之，于河上搭起竹桥，以渡军马。"孔明即调三万人入山，伐竹数十万根，顺水放下，于河面狭处，搭起竹桥，阔十余丈。乃调大军于河北岸一字儿下寨，便以河为壕堑，以浮桥为门，垒土为城；过桥南岸，一字下三个大营，以待蛮兵。

　　却说孟获引数十万蛮兵，恨怒而来。将近西洱河，孟获引前部一万刀牌獠丁，直扣前寨搦战。孔明头戴纶巾，身披鹤氅，手执羽扇，乘驷马车，左右众将簇拥而出。孔明见孟获身穿犀皮甲，头顶朱红盔，左手挽牌，右手执刀，骑赤毛牛，口中辱骂；手下万余洞丁，各舞刀牌，往来冲突。孔明急令退回本寨，四面紧闭，不许出战。蛮兵皆裸衣赤身，直到寨门前叫骂。诸将大怒，皆来禀孔明曰："某等情愿出寨决一死战！"孔明不许。诸将

Chapter 89

The Lord of Wuxiang Puts His Fourth
Plan to Work
The King of the Man Meets His Fifth Arrest

Guarded by a few hundred riders, Kongming guided his carriage along the road. Before them a river called the West Er ran sluggishly. Not a boat was on it. They made a raft, but it sank on launching. Kongming turned to Lü Kai, who said, "I'm told there's a hill upstream thick with bamboo, some of great thickness. Fell enough to make a bridge so our forces can cross."

Kongming sent thirty thousand men into the hills, where they cut down hundreds of thousands of bamboos and floated them downriver to a narrow point where Kongming's men built a bridge one hundred spans long. Next, he had a row of camps pitched on the northern shore. Now with the river as their moat and the bridge their gateway and a wall formed of heaped earth, they crossed to the southern shore and set up three large bases, there to await the Man army.

2163

Leading hundreds of thousands of warriors, Meng Huo came on in a towering fury. Approaching the West Er, he led a vanguard force of ten thousand blade-and-shield barbarians up to the Riverlands camp to issue a challenge to battle. Kongming was sitting in his four-mount carriage; he had a band wound round his head, crane plumes for a cloak, and a feather fan in his hand. His commanders clustered about him.

Kongming kept his eye on Meng Huo, who was armored in rhino hide and wore a red headpiece. In his left hand a shield and in his right a sword, he rode a red ox. Curses spewed from his mouth. The ten thousand brave men in his command came charging, whirling their weapons.

Kongming ordered an immediate retreat. He sealed the camp tight and forbade combat. The Man troops, stark naked, came up to the camp and let loose their cries and curses. The Riverlands commanders appealed heatedly to Kongming: "We volunteer to go out and fight them to

再三欲战，孔明止曰："蛮方之人，不遵王化，今此一来，狂恶正盛，不可迎也；且宜坚守数日，待其猖獗少懈，吾自有妙计破之。"

于是蜀兵坚守数日。孔明在高阜处探之，窥见蛮兵已多懈怠，乃聚诸将曰："汝等敢出战否？"众将欣然要出。孔明先唤赵云、魏延入帐，向耳畔低言，分付如此如此。二人受了计策先进。却唤王平、马忠入帐，受计去了。又唤马岱分付曰："吾今弃此三寨，退过河北；吾军一退，汝可便拆浮桥，移于下流，却渡赵云、魏延军马过河来接应。"岱受计而去。又唤张翼曰："吾军退去，寨中多设灯火。孟获知之，必来追赶，汝却断其后。"张翼受计而退。孔明只教关索护车。众军退去，寨中多设灯火。蛮兵望见，不敢冲突。

次日平明，孟获引大队蛮兵径到蜀寨之时，只见三个大寨，皆无人马，于内弃下粮草车仗数百余辆。孟优曰："诸葛弃寨而走，莫非有计否？"孟获曰："吾料诸葛亮弃辎重而去，必因国中有紧急之事：若非吴侵，定是魏伐。故虚张灯火以为疑兵，弃车仗而去也。可速追之，不可错过。"于是孟获自驱前部，直到西洱河边。望见河北岸上，寨中旗帜整齐如故，灿若云锦；沿河一带，又设锦城。蛮兵哨见，皆不敢进。获谓优曰："此是诸葛亮惧吾追赶，故就河北岸少住，不二日必走矣。"遂将蛮兵屯于河岸；又使人去山上砍竹为筏，以备渡河；却将敢战之兵，皆移

the death." But Kongming would not allow it. On their insistent protests he explained, "The Man disdain the sovereign's grace; in this mad rage they should be left alone. Better to hold back a few days longer and let them cool off. I have an excellent way to defeat them then."

For several more days the Riverlands troops continued defending their positions while from the vantage of a hilltop Kongming studied the enemy. At the first sign of slackness among the Man, he gathered his commanders and asked, "Are you ready?" The commanders were eager. Kongming first summoned Zhao Zilong and Wei Yan and whispered instructions to them; the two went boldly forth. Next, Wang Ping and Ma Zhong took their orders and left. Then Kongming said to Ma Dai, "I am going to abandon these three camps and withdraw to the north shore. As soon as I do, you are to take down the floating bridge and move it downstream so Zhao Zilong and Wei Yan can get across and stand ready to assist us." Ma Dai left, and Kongming called Zhang Yi. "When I withdraw," he told him, "light lamps all over the camp. Meng Huo will pursue once he finds out we've gone — and you will cut off his retreat." Zhang Yi retired with his instructions. Kongming had Guan Suo protect his carriage. As the army withdrew, the lights were lit.

The Man soldiers surveyed the western troops but dared not strike. The following dawn Meng Huo found the Riverlands' three camps deserted. Inside, several hundred grain and fodder wagons lay abandoned. Meng You said to him, "Zhuge has fled. This must be a trap — no?" Meng Huo replied, "I suppose Zhuge Liang left his supply train behind because of a crisis in Shu. The Southland may have invaded, or perhaps Wei has attacked. He lit these decoy lights to fool us and ran. He must not escape!"

Meng Huo himself marched the forward army to the bank of the West Er. On the far shore they saw flags and banners still in strict array, glorious as a brocade, a gorgeous, moving, multicolor wall extending along the river. The Man scouts would not advance. Meng Huo said to Meng You, "Zhuge Liang may linger on the northern shore, fearing pursuit. But in a day or so he'll be gone." Meng Huo stationed his army on the riverbank and sent troops into the hills to cut bamboo for rafts. Next, he moved his most daring soldiers to the front of his camp. Meng Huo had

于寨前面。——却不知蜀兵早已入自己之境。

是日，狂风大起。四壁厢火明鼓响，蜀兵杀到。蛮兵獠丁，自相冲突。孟获大惊，急引宗族洞丁杀开条路，径奔旧寨。忽一彪军从寨中杀出，乃是赵云。获慌忙回西洱河，望山僻处而走。又一彪军杀出，乃是马岱。孟获只剩得数十个败残兵，望山谷中而逃。见南、北、西三处尘头火光，因此不敢前进，只得望东奔走。方才转过山口，见一大林之前，数十从人，引一辆小车；车上端坐孔明，呵呵大笑曰："蛮王孟获！天败至此，吾已等候多时也！"获大怒，回顾左右曰："吾遭此人诡计，受辱三次；今幸得这里相遇。汝等奋力前去，连人带车砍为粉碎！"数骑蛮兵，猛力向前。孟获当先呐喊，抢到大林之前，趷踏一声，踏了陷坑，一齐塌倒。大林之内，转出魏延，引数百军来，一个个拖出，用索缚定。孔明先到寨中，招安蛮兵，并诸甸酋长洞丁——此时大半皆归本乡去了——除死伤外，其余尽皆归降。孔明以酒肉相待，以好言抚慰，尽令放回。蛮兵皆感叹而去。少顷，张翼解孟优至。孔明诲之曰："汝兄愚迷，汝当谏之。今被吾擒了四番，有何面目再见人耶！"孟优羞惭满面，伏地告求免死。孔明曰："吾杀汝不在今日。吾且饶汝性命，劝谕汝兄。"令武士解

no inkling that Riverlands forces had already entered his own territory.

That day strong winds blew. On four sides fires blazed and drums rolled. The Riverlands troops closed in, routing the Man braves, who overran each other in the confusion. Meng Huo panicked. Leading the warriors of his own hollow, he fought his way back to his original base camp — only to be met by Zhao Zilong and a band of troops coming out of it! In despair Meng Huo returned to the West Er and headed for a secluded point in the hills. But another band of troops stood before him, Ma Dai at their head. To Meng Huo there now remained only a few dozen battered soldiers. Seeing dust and fire to the south, north, and west, he fled eastward toward the ravines.

No sooner had Meng Huo turned into a valley than he saw a sizable wood ahead and several score of soldiers guiding a small carriage bearing Kongming, seated. Laughing aloud, Kongming said, "King of the Man! Heaven has sent you to your defeat! But how long you have kept me waiting!" Meng Huo turned furiously to those around him and cried, "Such vicious tricks have humiliated me thrice. Now I have the good fortune to meet up with him here. Charge! And hack man and carriage into a thousand pieces!" Several Man horsemen bolted forward. Meng Huo took the lead, shouting mightily to hearten them. But as they reached the ground before the woods, they found themselves flying head over heels into a pit. Wei Yan then emerged at the head of several hundred men, fished them out one at a time, and tied them up. By the time he was done, Kongming was already back in camp.

Kongming offered amnesty to the Man soldiers as well as to the tribal chieftains and braves (though the majority had gone back to their home areas), and all who survived tendered their submission. Kongming provided meat and drink, cheered them with friendly words, and sent them home. The Man soldiers roared in appreciation and departed.

Shortly after, Zhang Yi brought in Meng You. Kongming admonished him: "You must show your misguided elder brother the right thing to do. After his fourth capture what self-respect can he have?" Meng You, flushing with shame, flung himself to the ground and pleaded for mercy. "This is not the day for me to kill you," Kongming continued. "I shall spare your life. But I insist that you reason with your brother." He had

其绳索,放起孟优。优泣拜而去。

不一时,魏延解孟获至。孔明大怒曰:"你今番又被吾擒了,有何理说!"获曰:"吾今误中诡计,死不瞑目!"孔明叱武士推出斩之。获全无惧色,回顾孔明曰:"若敢再放吾回去,必然报四番之恨!"孔明大笑,令左右去其缚,赐酒压惊,就坐于帐中。孔明问曰:"吾今四次以礼相待,汝尚然不服,何也?"获曰:"吾虽是化外之人,不似丞相专施诡计,吾如何肯服?"孔明曰:"吾再放汝回去,复能战乎?"获曰:"丞相若再拿住吾,吾那时倾心降服,尽献本洞之物犒军,誓不反乱。"

孔明即笑而遣之。获忻然拜谢而去。于是聚得诸洞壮丁数千人,望南迤逦而行。早望见尘头起处,一队兵到:乃是兄弟孟优,重整残兵,来与兄报仇。兄弟二人,抱头相哭,诉说前事。优曰:"我兵屡败,蜀兵屡胜,难以抵当。只可就山阴洞中,退避不出。蜀兵受不过暑气,自然退矣。"获问曰:"何处可避?"优曰:"此去西南有一洞,名曰秃龙洞。洞主朵思大王,与弟甚厚,可投之。"于是孟获先教孟优到秃龙洞,见了朵思大王。朵思慌引洞兵出迎。孟获入洞,礼毕,诉说前事。朵思曰:"大王宽心。若

Meng You untied and released. Tearfully prostrating himself, Meng You departed.

When Wei Yan presently led in Meng Huo. Kongming was furious. "Once again I have caught you," he cried. "Have you anything to say for yourself?" "Your tricky scheme took me in." Meng Huo replied. "I will haunt you from my grave." Kongming commanded his guards to remove Meng Huo and behead him. Meng Huo's expression held no hint of fear. Boldly he flung back the words: "Dare to free me again and I will avenge all four disgraces at once." Kongming laughed and had his attendants untie him. He offered wine to calm the prisoner and gave him a seat in the tent. Kongming said, "This is the fourth time I have shown you civility. What makes you hold out?" Meng Huo answered, "I may be a man beyond the pale, but I would never resort to the knavish tricks that you use. Why should I consent?" "Will you war with us again if I free you now?" Kongming asked. "Your Excellency," he responded, "the next time you take me, I shall surrender in full sincerity and render as military tribute all the treasures of my hollows to confirm my vow to foreswear all sedition."

Kongming smiled and sent Meng Huo, gladly bowing and giving thanks, on his way. The Man leader then gathered the warriors of the hollows, several thousand of them, and led the throng south in a long procession. Soon after a contingent of soldiers rode up out of the dust, at their head Meng You, who had reorganized his battle-worn men to avenge Meng Huo. The reunited brothers muffled their heads and cried as they described their experiences. Meng You said, "We have suffered one defeat after another, and they have had many victories. How can we resist? What else can we do but take to the hills and avoid combat until the heat proves too much for them and they withdraw on their own?" "Where can we hide?" Meng Huo asked. "Bald Dragon Hollow, southwest of here," Meng You replied. "The leader, King Duosi, is my close friend and should take us in."

Meng Huo sent his brother ahead to Duosi. The chief then came out with an entourage of soldiers to welcome Meng Huo. Meng Huo entered the hollow and after the formalities described what had happened. "Set your mind at ease," Duosi said. "If the Riverlanders come, not one will

蜀兵到来,令他一人一骑不得还乡,与诸葛亮皆死于此处!"获大喜,问计于朵思。朵思曰:"此洞中止有两条路:东北上一路,就是大王所来之路,地势平坦,土厚水甜,人马可行;若以木石垒断洞口,虽有百万之众,不能进也。西北上有一条路,山险岭恶,道路窄狭;其中虽有小路,多藏毒蛇恶蝎;黄昏时分,烟瘴大起,直至已、午时方收,惟未、申、酉三时,可以往来;水不可饮,人马难行。此处更有四个毒泉:一名哑泉,其水颇甜,人若饮之,则不能言,不过旬日必死;二曰灭泉,此水与汤无异,人若沐浴,则皮肉皆烂,见骨必死;三曰黑泉,其水微清,人若溅之在身,则手足皆黑而死;四曰柔泉,其水如冰,人若饮之,咽喉无暖气,身躯软弱如绵而死。此处虫鸟皆无,惟有汉伏波将军曾到;自此以后,更无一人到此。今垒断东北大路,令大王稳居敝洞,若蜀兵见东路截断,必从西路而入;于路无水,若见此四泉,定然饮水:虽百万之众,皆无归矣。——何用刀兵耶!"孟获大喜,以手加额曰:"今日方有容身之地!"又望北指曰:"任诸葛神机妙算,难以施设!四泉之水,足以报败兵之恨也!"自此,孟获、孟优终日与朵思大王筵宴。

　　却说孔明连日不见孟获兵出,遂传号令教大军离西洱河,

go back — not a man, not a horse! They will die here, together with Zhuge
Liang!" Delighted, Meng Huo listened to Duosi's plan.

"This hollow has only two roads," Duosi said. "To the northeast, the
one Your Highness came by; the land lies flat; the soil is solid, and the
water sweet. It is a road easily traveled by man or horse. But if we bar
the way with timber and rocks, not even a million troops will be able to
work their way through. To the northwest is another route, a narrow
passage through arduous hills and nasty ridges. Poisonous snakes and
scorpions abound on the paths; as evening draws on, a miasma rises and
doesn't clear until late morning or past noon. Indeed, the only times suitable for travel on that route are the six afternoon hours. The water is not
potable and the going is rough. Moreover, there are four poisoned springs
along the route. The first, the Spring of the Mute, causes loss of speech;
whoever drinks from it (though the water be sweet) will perish in ten
days' time. The second, the Spring of Death, is hot, and bathing in it leads
to putrefaction of the flesh; death follows after the bones show through.
The third, the Black Spring, has somewhat clear water, but a few drops
can turn your hands and feet black, and death will follow. The fourth is
the Spring of Languor, whose icy water takes away the drinker's warm
breath while his body turns limp as cloth and he perishes. Neither birds
not insects live there. During the Han, the General Who Tames the Deeps
passed through; after him, the General Who Tames the Deeps passed
through; after him, no one.[1] Now we are going to blockade the northeast-
ern route to ensure Your Majesty's safe sojourn in our humble hollow.
Finding the east blocked, the Riverlands troops will come around to the
western route. There's no water on the way, so they will be sure to drink
at the four springs. Not one in a million will survive. Why waste military
force?"

Meng Huo was delighted and, putting his hand to his brow, said, "At
last I have found refuge!" Pointing to the north, he continued, "Zhuge
Liang's ingenious tricks are not going to work here! The waters of the
four springs will avenge the losses I have suffered!" Day after day Meng
Huo, Meng You, and King Duosi feasted and celebrated together.

*　*　*

Kongming watched for several days, but Meng Huo's troops did not

望南进发。此时正当六月炎天,其热如火。有后人咏南方苦热诗曰:

> 山泽欲焦枯,火光覆太虚。
>
> 不知天地外,署气更何如!

又有诗曰:

> 赤帝施权柄,阴云不敢生。
>
> 云蒸孤鹤喘,海热巨鳌惊。
>
> 忍舍溪边坐? 慵抛竹里行。
>
> 如何沙塞客,擐甲复长征!

孔明统领大军,正行之际,忽哨马飞报:"孟获退往秃龙洞中不出,将洞口要路垒断,内有兵把守;山恶岭峻,不能前进。"孔明请吕凯问之,凯曰:"某曾闻此洞有条路,实不知详细。"蒋琬曰:"孟获四次遭擒,既已丧胆,安敢再出? 况今天气炎热,军马疲乏,征之无益;不如班师回国。"孔明曰:"若如此,正中孟获之计也。吾军一退,彼必乘势追之。今已至此,安有复回之理!"遂令王平领数百军为前部;却教新降蛮兵引路,寻西北小径而入。前到一泉,人马皆渴,争饮此水。王平探有此路,回报孔明。比及到大寨之时,皆不能言,但指口而已。

孔明大惊,知是中毒,遂自驾小车,引数十人前来看时,见

emerge. He therefore ordered the main army to advance south of the West Er River. It was midsummer, the sixth month, and the weather hot as fire. A later poet sang of the cruel clime:

> A scorching heat to turn the marshes dry,
> A flaming sun that rules the empty sky —
> Who could find in any other land
> A zone of summer heat than this more damned?[2]

Another poem says:

> The fire god unleashes his torrid power;
> Upon the sky no shade of cloud dares show.
> In scalding mists the lonely heron pants;
> In steamy seas the giant tortoise frets.
> Who would for this forsake companionship by cooling streams
> Or idle walks through bamboo woods?
> What has brought me to this far frontier,
> On the march again, encased in gear?

Kongming's host was on the move when a scout reported: "Meng Huo has retreated inside Bald Dragon Hollow. He has sealed the approaches; soldiers within guard it. The hills are too arduous, the ridges too steep for us to advance." Kongming questioned Lü Kai, who said, "I've heard of a way into the area, but I don't know the exact route." Jiang Wan added, "After being captured four times, Meng Huo will not have the courage to show himself. And what of the heat? Our men and horses are fainting. We can gain nothing by attacking — better to withdraw and go home." To this Kongming replied, "That's what Meng Huo expects of us: we retreat, they pursue. No. We have come too far to turn back!" He commanded Wang Ping to take a few hundred soldiers of the van, with surrendered Man soldiers as guides, and go in search of the northwestern route into Meng Huo's lair.

At the first spring the men and horses, plagued by thirst, fought to get at the water. Wang Ping discovered the route and informed Kongming. But by the time they reached the main camp, the men had fallen mute and could communicate only by pointing to their mouths.

The astonished Kongming, realizing his men had been poisoned, went by carriage to examine the site: several score of followers attended him.

一潭清水，深不见底，水气凛凛，军不敢试。孔明下车，登高望之，四壁峰岭，鸟雀不闻，心中大疑。忽望见远远山冈之上，有一古庙。孔明攀藤附葛而到，见一石屋之中，塑一将军端坐，旁有石碑，乃汉伏波将军马援之庙；因平蛮到此，土人立庙祀之。孔明再拜曰："亮受先帝托孤之重，今承圣旨，到此平蛮；欲待蛮方既平，然后伐魏吞吴，重安汉室。今军士不识地理，误饮毒水，不能出声。万望尊神，念本朝恩义，通灵显圣，护佑三军！"

祈祷已毕，出庙寻土人问之。隐隐望见对山一老叟扶杖而来，形容甚异。孔明请老叟入庙，礼毕，对坐于石上。孔明问曰："丈者高姓？"老叟曰："老夫久闻大国丞相隆名，幸得拜见。蛮方之人，多蒙丞相活命，皆感恩不浅。"孔明问泉水之故，老叟答曰："军所饮水，乃哑泉之水也：饮之难言，数日而死。此泉之外，又有三泉：东南有一泉，其水至冷，人若饮水，咽喉无暖气，身躯软弱而死，名曰柔泉；正南有一泉，人若溅之在身，手足皆黑而死，名曰黑泉；西南有一泉，沸如热汤，人若浴之，皮肉尽脱而死，名曰灭泉。敝处有此四泉，毒气所聚，无药可治。又烟瘴甚起，惟未、申、酉三个时辰可往来；余者时辰，皆瘴气密布，

He found a clear pool so deep, the bottom was not visible. The water was piercing cold, and no one dared taste it. Kongming left his carriage, climbed to a high point, and scanned the surrounding peaks. Not a bird chirped. He was perplexed. On a distant ridge he saw an ancient shrine. Using vines and creepers, Kongming clambered up and found a stone chamber containing a statue of a general and a stone tablet. The shrine was dedicated to Ma Yuan, General Who Tames the Deeps. Local people had erected it in his memory after he pacified the Man of the region. Kongming prostrated himself twice in front of the image and said, "I am the guardian of the late Emperor's heir, by whose mandate I have come to pacify these Man. After that I shall invade Wei and devour Wu in order to make the house of Han secure again. My soldiers, ignorant of this land, were struck dumb after drinking at a poisoned spring. I pray you, revered spirit, remember the benign justice our court has always shown and by your divine presence keep our armies safe." [3]

His prayer finished, Kongming went out to find a native of the place. He spied a strange-looking old man coming toward him from the opposite hill, walking with the aid of a cane. Kongming invited the visitor into the shrine and after the formalities, when they had seated themselves on a stone ledge, asked him, "Your esteemed surname, master?" The old man replied, "Fortunate am I today to pay my respects to the prime minister of the great kingdom of Shu, a man of lasting fame. The people of the southern regions feel deep gratitude for your mercy in sparing their lives." Kongming asked about the spring. The old man answered, "Your soldiers drank from the Spring of the Mute, which causes loss of speech and, a few days later, death. There are three more springs besides this. To the southeast, one with icy water that drives the warm breath from your throat and causes death after enfeebling the body; it's called the Spring of Languor. Due south is another, the Black Spring. One touch of the water and you die after your hands and feet turn black. The spring to the southwest is like boiling water. If you bathe in it, your skin and flesh peel off; death follows swiftly. It's the Spring of Death. There is no cure for the lethal essences of the four springs in our humble regions. You must, moreover, pass only in the afternoon hours to avoid the fetid atmosphere of the springs. At all other times the miasma is thick,

2175

触之即死。"

孔明曰:"如此则蛮方不可平矣。蛮方不平,安能并吞吴、魏,再兴汉室? 有负先帝托孤之重,生不如死也!"老叟曰:"丞相勿忧。老夫指引一处,可以解之。"孔明曰:"老丈有何高见,望乞指教。"老叟曰:"此去正西数里,有一山谷,入内行二十里,有一溪名曰万安溪。上有一高士,号为'万安隐者';此人不出溪有数十余年矣。其草庵后有一泉,名安乐泉。人若中毒,汲其水饮之即愈。有人或生疥癞,或感瘴气,于万安溪内浴之,自然无事。更兼庵前有一等草,名曰'薤叶芸香'。人若口含一叶,则瘴气不染。丞相可速往求之。"孔明拜谢,问曰:"承丈者如此活命之德,感刻不胜。愿闻高姓?"老叟入庙曰:"吾乃本处山神,奉伏波将军之命,特来指引。"言讫,喝开庙后石壁而入。孔明惊讶不已,再拜庙神,寻旧路上车,回到大寨。

次日,孔明备信香、礼物,引王平及众哑军,连夜望山神所言去处,迤逦而进。入山谷小径,约行二十余里,但见长松大柏,茂竹奇花,环绕一庄;篱落之中,有数间茅屋,闻得馨香喷鼻。孔明大喜,到庄前叩户,有一小童出。孔明方欲通姓名,早有一人,竹冠草履,白袍皂绦,碧眼黄发,忻然出曰:"来者莫非汉丞相否?"孔明笑曰:"高士何以知之?"隐者曰:"久闻丞相大纛南征,安得不知!"遂邀孔明入草堂。礼毕,分宾主坐定。孔

and contact with it is fatal."

Kongming said, "The Man can never be conquered, then. Nor will we ever incorporate Wu and Wei in a restored Han dynasty, and my responsibility to my late emperor will never be fulfilled. Let me die rather than fail my cause!" "Do not despair, Your Excellency," the old man replied. "I can show you a place that will solve the problem." "I beg to receive your wisdom," Kongming said. "Several *li* due west of here," the old man began, "there is a valley. Twenty *li* inside the valley you will find the Stream of Eternal Peace. On the hilltop a man lives in seclusion, the Hermit of Eternal Peace. He has stayed by the stream for decades. Behind his thatched dwelling is the Spring of Peace and Joy, which counteracts the poisons of the other springs. A bath in its waters cures skin eruptions and miasma sickness. In addition, in the front of his hermitage you will find an herb called called 'leek-leaved rue.' Holding it in the mouth protects against the miasma. Your Excellency should go to seek it." Bowing in appreciation, Kongming said, "I remain forever grateful for receiving this life-saving kindness. May I know your honored surname?" The old man entered the temple and said, "I am the mountain spirit here, commanded by the General Who Tames the Deeps to give you guidance." Then at the old man's shout, the wall at the rear of the temple opened and he disappeared. The astonished Kongming bowed again to the temple god, made his way back to his carriage, and returned to camp.

The next day Kongming prepared incense and other ritual items and brought Wang Ping and his afflicted soldiers to the place the mountain spirit had indicated. Entering the valley by a small road, they had advanced about twenty *li* when they saw giant pines and cypresses, luxuriant bamboo, and rare blossoms enclosing a farm. A fine fragrance filled the air in the vicinity of a thatched cottage. Delighted, Kongming knocked on the front door, and a lad appeared. Before Kongming could introduce himself, a man followed promptly after the boy. He had a bamboo comb and straw slippers, a white robe girt with black, dark green eyes and yellowing hair. "Could my guest be the prime minister of the Han?" he asked. "How did you know, honored master?" Kongming replied, smiling. "Some time ago we heard that Your Excellency's grand army, impe-

2177

明告曰："亮受昭烈皇帝托孤之重，今承嗣君圣旨，领大军至此，欲服蛮邦，使归王化。不期孟获潜入洞中，军士误饮哑泉之水。夜来蒙伏波将军显圣，言高士有药泉，可以治之。望乞矜念，赐神水以救众兵残生。"隐者曰："量老夫山野废人，何劳丞相枉驾。此泉就在庵后。"教取来饮。

于是童子引王平等一起哑军，来到溪边，汲水饮之；随即吐出恶涎，便能言语。童子又引众军到万安溪中沐浴。隐者于庵中进柏子茶、松花菜，以待孔明。隐者告曰："此间蛮洞多毒蛇恶蝎，柳花飘入溪泉之间，水不可饮；但掘地为泉，汲水饮之方可。"孔明求"薤叶芸香"，隐者令众军尽意采取："各人口含一叶，自然瘴气不侵。"孔明拜求隐者姓名。隐者笑曰："某乃孟获之兄孟节是也。"孔明愕然。隐者又曰："丞相休疑，容伸片言：某一父母所生三人：长即老夫孟节，次孟获，又次孟优。父母皆亡。二弟强恶，不归王化。某屡谏不从，故更名改姓，隐居于此。今辱弟造反，又劳丞相深入不毛之地，如此生受，孟节合

rial plumes flying, had marched south. It was widely known," the hermit said as he invited Kongming into his dwelling.

After the formalities they took seats as host and guest. Kongming declared: "The late August Emperor Zhao Lie placed his heir apparent in my hands. Now, on the Second Emperor's authority I have marched my host here to subdue the land of the Man and win their adherence to the imperial way. Alas, Meng Huo has vanished into the depths of the coves and hollows and my troops have been poisoned at the Spring of the Mute. But last night I was honored by a visit from the living spirit of the General Who Tames the Deeps, and he told me that you, honored sir, possessed a medicinal spring. I humbly appeal for permission to use the holy water to save the lives of my men." "I am a useless old man of the mountain wilds, embarrassed to have troubled Your Excellency to visit. The stream you mention is right behind my hut," the recluse responded, and he invited Kongming to bring his soldiers to drink.

The young lad attending the hermit conducted Wang Ping and the troops who had lost their power of speech to the side of the stream. After drinking, they vomited some foul phlegm and recovered their voices. Next, the lad took the troops to bathe in the Stream of Eternal Peace, while in his dwelling the hermit served Kongming cedar tea and cypress fruits. The hermit said to him, "The hollows of the Man around here abound with scorpions and venomous snakes. And when the willow flowers drift into the streams and springs, they become unfit to drink from. You have to dig a well to find potable water." Kongming then requested the leek-leaved rue. The hermit told the soldiers to pick all they wanted, saying, "Keep a leaf in your mouth and the miasma will not affect you."

Kongming respectfully asked again who the hermit was. Smiling, he said, "Meng Huo's elder brother, Meng Jie." Kongming gasped in amazement. The hermit continued, "Your Excellency, contain your astonishment while I explain. We are three brothers of the same parents. I am the eldest; Meng Huo is next; the youngest is Meng You. Our parents are dead. My two brothers are wedded to their evil ways and despite my earnest appeals will not render homage to the imperial civilization. That is why I have changed my name and retired into seclusion. My shameless brothers have rebelled and burdened Your Excellency with the ne-

2179

该万死，故先于丞相之前请罪。"孔明叹曰："方信盗跖、下惠之事，今亦有之。"遂与孟节曰："吾申奏天子，立公为王，可乎？"节曰："为嫌功名而逃于此，岂复有贪富贵之意！"孔明乃具金帛赠之。孟节坚辞不受。孔明嗟叹不已，拜别而回。后人有诗曰：

　　　　高士幽栖独闭关，武侯曾此破诸蛮。

　　　　至今古木无人境，犹有寒烟锁旧山。

　　孔明回到大寨之中，令军士掘地取水。掘下二十余丈，并无滴水；凡掘十余处，皆是如此。军心惊慌。孔明夜半焚香告天曰："臣亮不才，仰承大汉之福，受命平蛮。今途中乏水，军马枯渴。倘上天不绝大汉，即赐甘泉！若气运已终，臣亮等愿死于此处！"是夜祝罢，平明视之，皆得满井甘泉。后人有诗曰：

　　　　为国平蛮统大兵，心存正道合神明。

　　　　耿恭拜井甘泉出，诸葛虔诚水夜生。

孔明军马既得甘泉，遂安然由小径直入秃龙洞前下寨。

　　蛮兵探知，来报孟获曰："蜀兵不染瘴疫之气，又无枯渴之患，诸泉皆不应。"朵思大王闻知不信，自与孟获来高山望之。

cessity of campaigning in these wilds, for which I consider myself deserving of ten thousand deaths. I come before Your Excellency now to answer for the offense."

Kongming sighed and said, "After this I can believe the ancient legend by which the robber Zhi and the worth Liu Xiahui were brothers; I have seen it myself today! If I petitioned the Son of Heaven to make you a king, would you accept?" Meng Jie answered, "Disdain for fame drove me here; what are wealth or position to me?" Kongming offered him gold and silk, but Meng Jie steadfastly declined the gifts. Kongming, profoundly moved, bowed low, said good-bye, and went back to his camp. In the words of a poet of later times,

> In that remotest vale the recluse dwelt,
> When Kongming worked the downfall of the Man.[4]
> Still unclaimed, those stately trees of yore,
> Where ancient hills by thawless mists stand barred.

Kongming returned to his main camp and had his men dig wells. At more than twenty feet, they found nothing. Ten other digs had the same result. The troops grew restive. At midnight Kongming burned incense and addressed Heaven: "Your servant Liang, though wanting in talent, has received the blessing of the mighty Han and its mandate to pacify the Man. Now midway in our course, man and horse are parched with thirst. If Heaven above means to sustain the cause of Han, then grant us one sweet spring! But if the time of Han has indeed expired, your servant begs for death here and now." His night incantation was done. At dawn they found the wells brimming. A poet of later times left these lines about the incident:

> In the name of Han he marched against the Man;
> The mind that dwells on truth may touch the gods.
> Geng Gong bowed to a well, and forth it flowed;[5]
> For Zhuge's constant heart these waters rose.

The Riverlands troops refreshed themselves and proceeded safely along the trails leading directly into Bald Dragon Hollow; they camped before it.

Man scouts informed Meng Hou: "The Riverlands troops resist the miasma and suffer no thirst. The springs have lost their power!" King

只见蜀兵安然无事，大桶小担，搬运水浆，饮马造饭。朵思见之，毛发耸然，回顾孟获曰："此乃神兵也！"获曰："吾兄弟二人与蜀兵决一死战，就殒于军前，安肯束手受缚！"朵思曰："若大王兵败，吾妻子亦休矣。当杀牛宰马，大赏洞丁，不避水火，直冲蜀寨，方可得胜。"

于是大赏蛮兵。正欲起程，忽报洞后迤西银冶洞二十一洞主杨锋引三万兵来助战。孟获大喜曰："邻兵助我，我必胜矣！"即与朵思大王出洞迎接。杨锋引兵入曰："吾有精兵三万，皆披铁甲，能飞山越岭，足以敌蜀兵百万；我有五子，皆武艺足备：愿助大王。"锋令五子入拜，皆彪躯虎体，威风抖擞。孟获大喜，遂设席相待杨锋父子。酒至半酣，锋曰："军中少乐，吾随军有蛮姑，善舞刀牌，以助一笑。"获忻然从之。须臾，数十蛮姑，皆披发跣足，从帐外舞跳而入，群蛮拍手以歌和之。杨锋令二子把盏。二子举杯诣孟获、孟优前。二人接杯，方欲饮酒，锋大喝一声，二子早将孟获、孟优执下座来。朵思大王却待要走，已被杨锋擒了。蛮姑横截于帐上，谁敢近前。获曰："'兔死狐悲，物伤其类'。吾与汝皆是各洞之主，往日无冤，何故害我？"锋曰：

Duosi, incredulous, went with Meng Hou to observe the invaders from a
high point. Lo, unharmed, they were providing for their horses and their
cooking with fresh water from vats and pole baskets. Duosi's hair stood
on end as he watched. Turning to Meng Huo, he said, "Those troops are
supernatural!" Meng Huo responded, "My brother Meng You and I shall
fight to the end. Better to die nobly on the field than surrender to the
foe!" Duosi said, "If Your Highness is defeated, my family and I are
done for. We must slaughter oxen and horses and feast the braves of our
tribes for a victorious drive on their camp. No danger must deter us!"

And so the Man army feasted grandly and then prepared to march.
Fresh support came from Yang Feng, chief of twenty-one tribes from
Silver Smelting Hollow, who arrived from the west at the head of a line of
thirty thousand. Meng Huo was delighted and said, "With our neighbor's
help, victory is assured." Meng Huo and King Duosi left the hollow to
meet Yang Feng.

Yang Feng led in his troops and said, "I have thirty thousand excellent
soldiers, all iron-armored and capable of traversing hill and ridge or holding back a million Riverlands men! My five sons, each a master of the
martial arts, desire to help Your Highness." Yang Feng summoned them
to pay their respects to the two kings. Their brawny, tigerlike physiques
radiated confidence and power. Delighted, Meng Huo set forth a banquet
for Yang Feng and his sons.

2183

The wine had already gone round many times when Yang Feng said,
"Let us not lack for music! And let the Man women following the army
who are expert at the sword-and-shield dance offer us some entertain-
ment." Meng Huo eagerly agreed. Moments later dozens of women
skipped into the tent, their hair hanging loose and their feet bare. The
Man host clapped and sang in accompaniment. Yang Feng had two of his
sons present cups of wine to Meng Huo and Meng You. As the brothers
raised the cups to their lips, Yang Feng gave a terrifying shout and his
sons pulled Meng Huo and Meng You down from their seats. King Duosi
tried to flee, but Yang Feng seized him. The Man women formed a barrier inside the tent, preventing all approach.

Meng Huo said to Yang Feng, "'The fox mourns the hare,' they say.
Things commiserate with their kind. You and I are leaders of our tribes.

"吾兄弟子侄皆感诸葛丞相活命之恩，无可以报。今汝反叛，何不擒献！"

于是各洞蛮兵，皆走回本乡。杨锋将孟获、孟优、朵思等解赴孔明寨来。孔明令人，杨锋等拜于帐下曰："某等子侄皆感丞相恩德，故擒孟获、孟优等呈献。"孔明重赏之，令驱孟获入。孔明笑曰："汝今番心服乎？"获曰："非汝之能，乃吾洞中之人，自相残害，以致如此。要杀便杀，只是不服！"孔明曰："汝赚吾入无水之地，更以哑泉、灭泉、黑泉、柔泉如此之毒，吾军无恙，岂非天意乎？汝何如此执迷？"获又曰："吾祖居银坑山中，有三江之险，重关之固。汝若就彼擒之，吾当子子孙孙，倾心服事。"孔明曰："吾再放汝回去，重整兵马，与吾共决胜负；如那时擒住，汝再不服，当灭九族。"叱左右去其缚，放起孟获。获再拜而去。孔明又将孟优并朵思大王皆释其缚，赐酒食压惊。二人悚惧，不敢正视。孔明令鞍马送回。

正是：

深临险地非容易，更展奇谋岂偶然！

未知孟获整兵再来，胜负如何，且看下文分解。

Between us no wrong has been done. Why would you injure me?" "My brothers, sons, and nephews," Yang Feng replied, "are grateful to His Excellency Zhuge for having spared their lives; they had to find a way to repay him. You have rebelled — why shouldn't we capture and deliver you?"

After this the Man soldiers all returned to their native regions. Yang Feng brought Meng Huo, Meng You, and Duosi in custody to Kongming's camp. Kongming invited them into his tent, where Yang Feng and his sons prostrated themselves and said, "Thankful for your merciful favor, we have delivered Meng Huo and Meng You." Kongming rewarded them handsomely and then had Meng Huo led in.

Smiling, Kongming said, "Ready to surrender now?" "This was not because of your ability," Meng Huo protested. "My fellow tribesmen betrayed me. Kill me if you wish — but I won't submit!" Kongming responded, "You fooled me into entering a land without water, and yet the poisons of the four springs have not affected my troops; they remain healthy. What could this be if not the will of Heaven? How long can you fool yourself?" But Meng Huo continued, "My forefathers dwelled in the Silver Pit Hills, secure behind three great rivers and multiple passes. If your can catch me there, I'll surrender with all my heart and for all generations to come." Kongming replied, "If I release you this time to reorganize your forces for the decision between us, and if I catch you and you still resist, I will exterminate your entire clan to the ninth degree."

2185

Kongming ordered Meng Huo freed, and the Man chieftain left after repeated prostrations. Kongming also released Meng You and King Duosi, giving them wine and food to quiet their anxieties. The two men were too frightened to look at the prime minister squarely. Kongming sent them home on saddled horses. Indeed:

> Campaigns deep in treacherous lands are never easy;
> Brilliant exploits are rarer still!

Would Meng Huo ever be subdued?

Read on.

2186

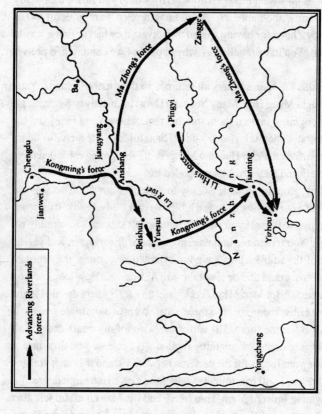

MAP 9. Kongming's southen campaign. The black arrows indicate the advancing Riverlands forces. Source: Liu Chunfan, *Sanguo Shihua* (Beijing: Beijing chubanshe, 1981), p. 173.

烧藤甲七擒孟获

2187

第九十回

驱巨兽六破蛮兵　烧藤甲七擒孟获

　　却说孔明放了孟获等一干人,杨锋父子皆封官爵,重赏洞兵。杨锋等拜谢而去。孟获等连夜奔回银坑洞。那洞外有三江:乃是泸水、甘南水、西城水。三路水会合,故为三江。其洞北近平坦三百余里,多产万物。洞西二百里,有盐井。西南二百里,直抵泸、甘。正南三百里,乃是梁都洞,洞中有山,环抱其洞;山上出银矿,故名为银坑山。山中置宫殿楼台,以为蛮王巢穴。其中建一祖庙,名曰"家鬼"。四时杀牛宰马享祭,名为"卜鬼"。每年常以蜀人并外乡之人祭之。若人患病,不肯服药,只祷师巫,名为"药鬼"。其处无刑法,但犯罪即斩。有女长成,却于溪中沐浴,男女自相混淆,任其自配,父母不禁,名为"学艺"。年岁雨水均调,则种稻谷;倘若不熟,杀蛇为羹,煮象为饭。每方隅之中,上户号曰"洞主",次曰"酋长"。每月初一、十五两日,皆在

Chapter 90

Giant Beasts Are Deployed in Kongming's
Sixth Victory
Rattan Shields Are Burned in Meng Huo's
Seventh Capture

After releasing the Man leaders, Kongming honored Yang Feng and
his sons with office and rank and richly rewarded the tribal warriors.
Yang Feng and his people prostrated themselves, expressed their gratitude, and departed.

Meng Huo and his companions hurried back to Silver Pit Hollow. On
its outskirts ran three rivers — the Lu, the Gannan, and the Xicheng —
which converged at a place called Three Rivers. North of the hollow
stretched a plain of some three hundred *li* that yielded a wide variety of
crops. Two hundred *li* due west were salt wells. Two hundred *li* to the
southwest ran the Li and the Gannan; three hundred *li* south, Liangdu
Hollow with its knolls was encircled by hills that contained silver ore; this
explains the name Silver Pit Hills.

On the hill stood a series of fine buildings, the sanctuary of the Man
king. One building housed an ancestral shrine called the family Spirits.
Each season the people there slaughtered an ox and a horse, which they
offered in sacrifice in a ceremony known as "divining the spirits." It was
also the custom to sacrifice Riverlanders or strangers from other places.
A native suffering from an affliction rarely took medicine, praying instead
to a shaman master known as the "medicine spirit." Criminal laws did
not exist; those who committed offenses were executed immediately.
When women grew to maturity, they bathed in a stream where male and
female mixed freely and coupled without parental prohibition, a practice
called "learning the art." When the rains were evenly distributed, they
planted rice. When the harvest did not ripen, they killed snakes for soup
and boiled elephant meat for their meals. In each and every corner of the
region the principal household was called "chief of the hollow" and the
second, "tribal elder." Market day was held on the first of each moon

2189

三江城中买卖,转易货物。其风俗如此。

却说孟获在洞中,聚集宗党千余人,谓之曰:"吾屡受辱于蜀兵,立誓欲报之。汝等有何高见?"言未毕,一人应曰:"吾举一人,可破诸葛亮。"众视之,乃孟获妻弟,现为八番部长,名曰"带来洞主"。获大喜,急问何人。带来洞主曰:"此去西南八纳洞,洞主木鹿大王,深通法术:出则骑象,能呼风唤雨,常有虎豹豺狼、毒蛇恶蝎跟随。手下更有三万神兵,甚是英勇。大王可修书具礼,某亲往求之。此人若允,何惧蜀兵哉!"获忻然,令国舅赍书而去。却令朵思大王守把三江城,以为前面屏障。

却说孔明提兵直至三江城,遥望见此城三面傍江,一面通旱;即遣魏延、赵云同领一军,于旱路打城。军到城下时,城上弓弩齐发:原来洞中之人,多习弓弩,一弩齐发十矢,箭头上皆用毒药;但有中箭者,皮肉皆烂,见五脏而死。赵云、魏延不能取胜,回见孔明,言药箭之事。孔明自乘小车,到军前看了虚实,回到寨中,令军退数里下寨。蛮兵望见蜀兵远退,皆大笑作贺,只疑蜀兵惧怯而退,因此夜间安心稳睡,不去哨探。

却说孔明约军退后,即闭寨不出。一连五日,并无号令。黄

and again on the fifteenth in the town at Three Rivers, where commodities circulated through barter. Such were the customs of the Man.

Back in his hollow, Meng Huo gathered more than a thousand of his clansmen and adherents and said to them, "For the many times the Riverlanders have put me to shame, I now swear vengeance! Are you with me?" One man responded, "Here is the man to defeat Zhuge Liang!" The assembly turned to the younger brother of Meng Huo's wife, the present leader of the Eight Outer Tribes and chief of Dailai Hollow. Meng Huo was delighted and asked whom he meant to recommend. The chief replied, "His Highness Mulu, chief of Bana Hollow southwest of here, a man thoroughly versed in the occult arts: he can use the elephant as his mount, summon wind and rain, and command the obedience of tiger, leopard, and wolf, scorpion and venomous snake. Thirty thousand superb troops of peerless courage follow him. Your Highness should compose a letter and prepare gifts; I will go myself to seek his help. If he consents, Riverlands soldiers need cause no fear." Meng Huo, delighted, had his brother-in-law carry the letter to King Mulu; he also had King Duosi fortify Three Rivers as a defensive barrier.

Approaching Three Rivers, Kongming saw that the citadel there fronted water on three sides. He immediately gave Wei Yan and Zhao Zilong joint command of an army for an attack from the land side. As they reached the city wall, waves of arrows greeted them. (The men of the hollow were skilled in the use of longbow and crossbow. A single crossbow launched ten arrows, each tipped with a poison that caused decomposition of the flesh and, ultimately, exposure of the inner organs and death.) Wei Yan and Zhao Zilong, unable to overcome the enemy, returned to Kongming and described the methods used against them.

Kongming rode to the front in a small carriage. After surveying the enemy's positions, he returned to camp and ordered the army to retire several *li* and recamp. The Man soldiers, seeing the Riverlanders pull so far back, began laughing and congratulating one another; thinking that the enemy had lost heart, they slept soundly that night and posted no sentinels.

Kongming had arranged for the soldiers to remain in their camps after the retreat and not show themselves. For five days he issued no com-

2191

昏左侧，忽起微风。孔明传令曰："每军要衣襟一幅，限一更时分应点。无者立斩。"诸将皆不知其意，众军依令预备。初更时分，又传令曰："每军衣襟一幅，包土一包。无者立斩。"众军亦不知其意，只得依令预备。孔明又传令曰："诸军包土，俱在三江城下交割。先到者有赏。"众军闻令，皆包净土，飞奔城下。孔明令积土为蹬道，先上城者为头功。于是蜀兵十余万，并降兵万余，将所包之土，一齐弃于城下。一霎时，积土成山，接连城上。一声暗号，蜀兵皆上城。蛮兵急放弩时，大半早被执下，余者弃城而走。朵思大王死于乱军之中。蜀将督军分路剿杀。孔明取了三江城，所得珍宝，皆赏三军。败残蛮兵逃回见孟获说："朵思大王身死，失了三江城。"获大惊。

正虑之间，人报蜀兵已渡江，现在本洞前下寨。孟获甚是慌张。忽然屏风后一人大笑而出曰："既为男子，何无智也？我虽是一妇人，愿与你出战。"获视之，乃妻祝融夫人也。夫人世居南蛮，乃祝融氏之后；善使飞刀，百发百中。孟获起身称谢。夫人忻然上马，引宗党猛将数百员、生力洞兵五万，出银坑宫阙，来与蜀兵对敌。方才转过洞口，一彪军拦住：为首蜀将，乃

mands. On the fifth, as dusk neared, a slight wind picked up. Kongming issued an order for every soldier, within the space of one watch, to report for roll call after tearing off a piece of his garment; those not complying would face execution. His commanders could not fathom his purpose but complied all the same. At the first watch he ordered every soldier to wrap a ball of earth with the torn cloth or face execution. The troops could not fathom his purpose, but followed the order. Kongming then issued another order for them to report with the wrapped earth to the wall around Three Rivers, offering a reward for the first to arrive. The soldiers wrapped up the soil and raced for the wall. Kongming had them pile it into a graded path and promised top honors to whoever climbed the wall first. The host of one hundred thousand Riverlands soldiers and more than ten thousand surrendered Man piled their clods of earth below the Three Rivers wall.

Soon the pile became a hill adjoining the wall. At a secret signal the Riverlands troops climbed up. The Man scrambled to loose their shafts, but the Riverlanders yanked them down in great numbers. The other defenders abandoned the wall and fled. King Duosi was killed in the confusion. In separate units the Riverlands commanders hunted down and killed their foe in all directions; Kongming occupied Three Rivers, rewarding the army with the spoils. The defeated Man troops returned to Meng Huo and said, "King Duosi is dead and Three Rivers is lost." Meng Huo could not believe it. The Man king was still bewildered when he learned that Riverlands troops had crossed the river and camped in front of his hollow.

2193

Meng Huo was too agitated to act. Suddenly from behind the screen someone stepped forward and, laughing loudly, said, "A man, and such a fool! I, a woman, will fight them for you!" Meng Huo set his eyes on Lady Zhurong, his wife, who was a descendant of Zhurong[1] and had always lived among the nations of the Man. She was skilled in knife throwing and never missed her mark. Meng Huo rose to express his thanks. Well pleased, Lady Zhurong mounted her horse and led several hundred commanders from her clan and its allies, combined with a fresh force of fifty thousand raised from the hollows, out of the gateway of Silver Pit Palace to do battle with the soldiers of the Riverlands.

是张嶷。蛮兵见之，却早两路摆开。祝融夫人背插五口飞刀，手挺丈八长标，坐下卷毛赤兔马。张嶷见之，暗暗称奇。二人骤马交锋。战不数合，夫人拨马便走。张嶷赶去，空中一把飞刀落下。嶷急用手隔，正中左臂，翻身落马。蛮兵发一声喊，将张嶷执缚去了。马忠听得张嶷被执，急出救时，早被蛮兵捆住。望见祝融夫人挺标勒马而立，忠忿怒向前去战，坐下马绊倒，亦被擒了。都解入洞中来见孟获。获设席庆贺。夫人叱刀斧手推出张嶷、马忠要斩。获止曰："诸葛亮放吾五次，今番若杀彼将，是不义也。且囚在洞中，待擒住诸葛亮，杀之未迟。"夫人从其言，笑饮作乐。

　　却说败残兵来见孔明，告知其事。孔明即唤马岱、赵云、魏延三人受计，各自领军前去。次日，蛮兵报入洞中，说赵云搦战。祝融夫人即上马出迎。二人战不数合，云拨马便走。夫人恐有埋伏，勒兵而回。魏延又引军来搦战，夫人纵马相迎。正交锋紧急，延诈败而逃，夫人只不赶。次日，赵云又引军来搦战，夫人领洞兵出迎。二人战不数合，云诈败而走，夫人按标不赶。欲收兵回洞时，魏延引军齐声辱骂，夫人急挺标来取魏延。延拨马便走。夫人忿怒赶来，延骤马奔入山僻小路。忽然

That moment a cohort rounded a hill and barred her path: the leader, Zhang Ni. Man troops fanned out in two divisions. Lady Zhurong had five throwing knives stuck into the gear on her back and an eighteen-span spear in her hand; she rode a curly-maned red-hare horse. Zhang Ni marveled quietly. The two dashed at one another and engaged. After several passes Lady Zhurong turned her mount and fled; Zhang Ni pursued hotly. A knife came flying through the air. Zhang Ni tried to deflect it, but it struck his left arm. He rolled off his horse, and screaming Man troops took him captive. Ma Zhong dashed out to rescue him, but Zhang Ni had already been taken and bound hand and foot. Lady Zhurong, lance held high, reined in and stood before him. Ma Zhong made one furious charge, but his horse was tripped, and he too was taken. The two captives were delivered to Meng Huo.

Meng Huo held a celebration feast at which Lady Zhurong ordered Zhang Ni and Ma Zhong executed. Meng Huo stopped the guards, however, saying, "Zhuge Liang spared me five times. It would not be honorable to kill his commanders. Hold them in our tribe for now; we can deal with them after Zhuge Liang is taken." His wife agreed, and they laughed and drank and made merry.

The Riverlanders reported their defeat to Kongming, who summoned Ma Dai, Zhao Zilong, and Wei Yan and gave them new assignments to fulfill. The next day Man soldiers reported to their leaders that Zhao Zilong had come to challenge them. Lady Zhurong mounted her horse and met him. After a brief clash Zhao Zilong turned and fled. Lady Zhurong, suspicious of ambush, halted and retired. Next, Wei Yan offered the challenge, and Lady Zhurong galloped forth to meet him. During an intense clash Wei Yan feigned defeat and ran off, but she refused to pursue.

The following day Zhao Zilong returned to the challenge, which she met again. After only a few exchanges Zhao Zilong halted combat and fled, but the lady, lance in hand, refused again to give chase. Lady Zhurong had already started to recall her troops when Wei Yan came forward. His troops vilified her raucously, and this time Lady Zhurong, spear raised high, raced for her opponent. Wei Yan fled as before. He raced onto a side path in the hills, the lady in hot pursuit. Suddenly he heard a high,

2195

背后一声响亮，延回头视之，夫人仰鞍落马：原来马岱埋伏在此，用绊马索绊倒。就里擒缚，解投大寨而来。蛮将洞兵皆来救时，赵云一阵杀散。孔明端坐于帐上，马岱解祝融夫人到，孔明急令武士去其缚，请在别帐赐酒压惊，遣使往告孟获，欲送夫人换张嶷、马忠二将。

　　孟获允诺，即放出张嶷、马忠，还了孔明。孔明遂送夫人入洞。孟获接入，又喜又恼。忽报八纳洞主到。孟获出洞迎接，见其人骑着白象，身穿金珠缨络，腰悬两口大刀，领着一班喂养虎豹豺狼之士，簇拥而入。获再拜哀告，诉说前事。木鹿大王许以报仇。获大喜，设宴相待。次日，木鹿大王引本洞兵带猛兽而出。赵云、魏延听知蛮兵出，遂将军马布成阵势。二将并辔立于阵前视之，只见蛮兵旗帜器械皆别：人多不穿衣甲，尽裸身赤体，面目丑陋；身带四把尖刀；军中不鸣鼓角，但筛金为号；木鹿大王腰挂两把宝刀，手执蒂钟，身骑白象，从大旗中而出。赵云见了，谓魏延曰："我等上阵一生，未尝见如此人物。"二人正沉吟之际，只见木鹿大王口中不知念甚咒语，手摇蒂钟。忽然狂风大作，飞砂走石，如同骤雨；一声画角响，虎豹豺狼，毒蛇

clear cry behind him and saw Lady Zhurong on the ground, prone across her saddle. Earlier, Ma Dai had set an ambush here, and the ropes he had strung had now tripped her horse. Ma Dai seized Lady Zhurong and took her as his prisoner back to the main camp. Man troops rode to her rescue, but Zhao Zilong dispersed them with fierce fighting.

Sitting solemnly in his tent where Ma Dai had brought Lady Zhurong before him, Kongming swiftly ordered the lady's bonds removed and sent her to another tent to drink some wine and compose herself. He also sent a man to Meng Huo, offering to exchange Lady Zhurong for the two commanders Zhang Ni and Ma Zhong. Meng Huo agreed to this proposal and sent the two commanders back to Kongming, who in turn sent Lady Zhurong back to her people. Meng Huo received her with both joy and anger in his heart.

Suddenly the leader of Bana Hollow was announced. Meng Huo received him outside his cove. The visitor rode a white elephant, and his garb was fringed with gold and pearls; large swords hung at his side. His retinue included a team of men who cared for his menagerie of tigers and panthers, jackals and wolves. The crowd entered Meng Huo's hollow.

Meng Huo prostrated himself and voiced his grief; then he recounted the previous events. King Mulu promised to assist him in exacting revenge, and Meng Huo showed his satisfaction by holding a banquet in Mulu's honor. The next day King Mulu led his own warriors and wild animals out to battle. Zhao Zilong and Wei Yan deployed their forces into fighting position. Riding side by side, they came before their line to view the enemy's strange banners and weapons. Few of the warriors wore armor; most were naked. Their faces were crude and ugly. Each carried four daggers. They sounded neither drum nor horn, signaling their troops by striking gongs. King Mulu had two swords hanging at his waist and a corolla-shaped bell in his hand. Surrounded by giant banners, he rode a white elephant.

"In all our days in the field," Zhao Zilong said to Wei Yan, "have we ever seen such a sight?" While the two watched in amazement, King Mulu uttered strange incantations and shook the bell. Suddenly fierce winds began to blow, driving sand and pebbles like hard rain, and a braying sound was heard: tigers and panthers, jackals and wolves, venomous

2197

猛兽,乘风而出,张牙舞爪,冲将过来。蜀兵如何抵当,往后便
退。蛮兵随后追杀,直赶到三江界路方回。赵云、魏延收聚败
兵,来孔明帐前请罪,细说此事。

　　孔明笑曰:"非汝二人之罪。吾未出茅庐之时,先知南蛮有
驱虎豹之法。吾在蜀中已办下破此阵之物也:随军有二十辆
车,俱封记在此。今日且用一半;留下一半,后有别用。"遂令左
右取了十辆红油柜车到帐下,留十辆黑油柜车在后。众皆不知
其意。孔明将柜打开,皆是木刻彩画巨兽,俱用五色绒线为毛
衣,钢铁为牙爪,一个可骑坐十人。孔明选了精壮军士一千余
人,领了一百,口内装烟火之物,藏在军中。次日,孔明驱兵大
进,布于洞口。蛮兵探知,入洞报与蛮王。木鹿大王自谓无敌,
即与孟获引洞兵而出。孔明纶巾羽扇,身衣道袍,端坐于车
上。孟获指曰:"车上坐的便是诸葛亮! 若擒住此人,大事定
矣!"木鹿大王口中念咒,手摇蒂钟。顷刻之间,狂风大作,猛兽
突出。孔明将羽扇一摇,其风便回吹彼阵中去了,蜀阵中假兽
拥出。蛮洞真兽见蜀阵巨兽口吐火焰,鼻出黑烟,身摇铜铃,张
牙舞爪而来,诸恶兽不敢前进,皆奔回蛮洞,反将蛮兵冲倒无

reptiles and ferocious beasts came riding on the winds, charging, with fangs bared and claws flexed. The Riverlands troops fell back; the Man pursued them all the way to the boundary of Three Rivers, killing many before withdrawing. Zhao Zilong and Wei Yan regathered their men and returned to Kongming's tent to confess their failure and recount the circumstances.

Kongming laughed and said, "It's not your fault. Even before I left my secluded thatched cottage, I knew about Man techniques for using wild animals in combat. Back in the Riverlands I devised some ways for foiling them. With the army I brought twenty wagons, which I had sealed and put away. Now is the time to put half of them to use; the other half we will save for another time." Kongming ordered his attendants to wheel out the ten wagons with red painted containers and leave the ten black ones behind. Everyone was puzzled. Kongming broke open the containers, which held enormous carved animals of colored wood with fur of multicolored yarn and teeth and claws of steel. Each animal was big enough to carry ten men. Kongming picked one thousand strong warriors and assigned them one hundred animals; these he had packed with incendiary materials and then concealed among the troops.

The next day Kongming advanced in force and deployed at the entrance to the hollow. Man scouts reported the enemy's movements to the kings. King Mulu, declaring himself invincible, went forth with Meng Huo to fight. Kongming, wearing his headband and Taoist robes, sat erect in his carriage, holding a feathered fan. Pointing at him, Meng Huo said to Mulu, "There's Zhuge Liang. If we catch him, our success is assured." King Mulu pronounced a curse and shook his bell. Shortly fierce winds sprang up and the wild beasts burst into view. But Kongming waved his fan, causing the wind to blow back toward the Man; from the Riverlands side the imitation monsters came forth.

The genuine animals of the Man region watched the opposing weird beasts belching fire and breathing black smoke, shaking their bronze clangers as they snarled and clawed. Daunted, the savage creatures of the Man turned and charged back to the hollow, trampling numerous men in their path. At this point Kongming signaled a general advance. Drum and horn sounded in unison as the Riverlanders pursued and killed count-

数。孔明驱兵大进,鼓角齐鸣,望前追杀。木鹿大王死于乱军之中。洞内孟获宗党,皆弃宫阙,扒山越岭而走。孔明大军占了银坑洞。

次日,孔明正要分兵缉擒孟获,忽报:"蛮王孟获妻弟带来洞主,因劝孟获归降,获不从,今将孟获并祝融夫人及宗党数百余人尽皆擒来,献与丞相。"孔明听知,即唤张嶷、马忠,分付如此如此。二将受了计,引二千精壮兵,伏于两廊。孔明即令守门将,俱放进来,带来洞主引刀斧手解孟获等数百人,拜于殿下。孔明大喝曰:"与吾擒下!"两廊壮兵齐出,二人捉一人,尽被执缚。孔明大笑曰:"量汝些小诡计,如何瞒得过我!汝见二次俱是本洞人擒汝来降,吾不加害;汝只道吾深信,故来诈降,欲就洞中杀吾!"喝令武士搜其身畔,果然各带利刀。孔明问孟获曰:"汝原说在汝家擒住,方始心服;今日如何?"获曰:"此是我等自来送死,非汝之能也。吾心未服。"孔明曰:"吾擒住六番,尚然不服,欲待何时耶?"获曰:"汝第七次擒住,吾方倾心归服,誓不反矣。"孔明曰:"巢穴已破,吾何虑哉!"令武士尽去其缚,叱之曰:"这番擒住,再若支吾,必不轻恕!"孟获等抱头鼠窜而去。

却说败残蛮兵有千余人,大半中伤而逃,正遇蛮王孟获。获收了败兵,心中稍喜,却与带来洞主商议曰:"吾今洞府已被蜀兵所占,今投何地安身?"带来洞主曰:"止有一国可以破

less Man. King Mulu fell in the confusion of battle. Inside their cove Meng Huo's clan and adherents abandoned their mansions and fled over the hills. Kongming's army occupied Silver Pit Hollow.

The next day as Kongming was preparing to divide his forces to find and capture Meng Huo, a messenger reported, "The younger brother of Meng Huo's wife, the chief of Dailai Hollow, urged Meng Huo to submit to you. Meng Huo refused, so the Dailai chief has seized Meng Huo, Lady Zhurong, and their families and will deliver them to Your Excellency." Kongming immediately summoned Zhang Ni and Ma Zhong and gave them instructions. After the two commanders had put two thousand able-bodied troops behind the passageways to Kongming's quarter, Kongming told the gate guards to admit Meng Huo's brother-in-law and his party. The chief of the Dailai, attended by guards with hidden weapons, delivered Meng Huo and several hundred others and prostrated himself before Kongming. "Seize them!" Kongming shouted.

From both sides husky soldiers rushed out — two on one — and tied up the prisoners. Laughing, Kongming said, "Did you expect to fool me with that little trick? Twice before, the people of your own hollow brought you in, but I did you no harm. You don't really think I would believe this false surrender, do you, and let you kill me right here in your own hollow?" Kongming ordered a search and found a sharp knife on each. Kongming asked Meng Huo, "You once promised that if I caught you in your own home, you would render sincere submission — what about now?" But Meng Huo replied, "This is a case of delivering ourselves to our own fate. Your skill played no part. My heart remains unsubdued." "Still, after six times?" Kongming said. "When will you submit?" "The seventh time," Meng Huo answered, "I will render wholehearted allegiance and swear never to rebel!" "With your sanctuary destroyed, there is no need to worry!" Kongming said and ordered the captives freed. "Next time," he added, "if you try to wriggle out of it, no further grace will be shown." Humiliated, Meng Huo and his followers scurried off.

King Meng Huo happened upon a mass of more than one thousand Man troops fleeing the Riverlanders; most of them were injured. When he had restored order among them, his spirits revived somewhat. He said to his brother-in-law, "The Riverlanders hold my cove. Where can we

2201

蜀。"获喜曰:"何处可去?"带来洞主曰:"此去东南七百里,有一国,名乌戈国。国主兀突骨,身长丈二,不食五谷,以生蛇恶兽为饭;身有鳞甲,刀箭不能侵。其手下军士,俱穿藤甲;其藤生于山涧之中,盘于石壁之上;国人采取,浸于油中,半年方取出晒之;晒干复浸,凡十余遍,却才造成铠甲;穿在身上,渡江不沉,经水不湿,刀箭皆不能入:因此号为'藤甲军'。今大王可往求之,若得彼相助,擒诸葛亮如利刀破竹也。"孟获大喜,遂投乌戈国,来见兀突骨。其洞无宇舍,皆居土穴之内。孟获入洞,再拜哀告前事。兀突骨曰:"吾起本洞之兵,与汝报仇。"获欣然拜谢。于是兀突骨唤两个领兵俘长:一名土安,一名奚泥,起三万兵,皆穿藤甲,离乌戈国望东北而来。行至一江,名桃花水,两岸有桃树,历年落叶于水中,若别国人饮之尽死,惟乌戈国人饮之,倍添精神。兀突骨兵至桃花渡口下寨,以待蜀兵。

　　却说孔明令蛮人哨探孟获消息,回报曰:"孟获请乌戈国主,引三万藤甲军,现屯于桃花渡口。孟获又在各番聚集蛮兵,并力拒战。"孔明听说,提兵大进,直至桃花渡口。隔岸望见蛮兵,不类人形,甚是丑恶;又问土人,言说即日桃叶正落,水不

find refuge?" The chief of the Dailai answered, "There is a kingdom that can defeat the Riverlands." "Where?" asked Meng Huo. "To the southeast, seven hundred *li* from here," the chief responded. "The Black Lance kingdom. Their chief, Wutugu, is some twelve spans tall, eats no grain, and survives on live snakes and vicious animals. His body is covered with scales no arrow or blade can pierce. The men in his command have rattan armor made from vines that grow in the ravines and wind around their rocky walls. Natives pick the vines, soak them in oil for half a year, then dry them in the sun. After being thoroughly dried, they are returned to the oil. The vines are dried and soaked this way ten times before being made into armor. The cured rattan keeps the body afloat and dry, as well as safe from arrow and blade; that's why they're called 'rattan-armored soldiers.' Your Highness should plead with their chief, for his help will make the capture of Zhuge Liang as sure as a 'sharp knife splits bamboo.'"

Delighted, Meng Huo headed for the Black Lance kingdom to meet Wutugu. He found the tribe had no roofed dwellings, as the members lived in caves in the earth. Meng Huo entered the hollow, prostrated himself, and related his bitter experiences. The chief said, "I will muster the men of my tribe and avenge you." Meng Huo eagerly prostrated himself again in gratitude. Thereupon Wutugu summoned Tu An and Xi Ni, two militia captains, and they mustered thirty thousand warriors in rattan armor for the campaign. Marching northeast, they reached the Peach Blossom, a river with peach trees lining its banks. Whenever the leaves dropped into the water, it became lethal to people of other kingdoms but a wondrous tonic to the people of the Black Lance. Wutugu's force camped at a crossing point of the Peach Blossom River to await the Riverlands army.

Certain Man natives whom Kongming had sent to gather information reported back: "In answer to Meng Huo's plea, the chief of the Black Lance kingdom has led thirty thousand rattan-armored troops into position at the crossing of the Peach Blossom. At the same time Meng Huo is recruiting troops from all the Man regions to join their war of resistance." At this news Kongming moved in force to the river. From the opposite shore he surveyed the Man warriors, who looked so repulsive that they

可饮。孔明退五里下寨,留魏延守寨。

次日,乌戈国主引一彪藤甲军过河来,金鼓大震。魏延引兵出迎。蛮兵卷地而至。蜀兵以弩箭射到藤甲之上,皆不能透,俱落于地;刀砍枪刺,亦不能入。蛮兵皆使利刀钢叉,蜀兵如何抵当,尽皆败走。蛮兵不赶而回。魏延复回,赶到桃花渡口,只见蛮兵带甲渡水而去;内有困乏者,将甲脱下,放在水面,以身坐其上而渡。魏延急回大寨,来禀孔明,细言其事。孔明请吕凯并土人问之。凯曰:"某素闻南蛮中有一乌戈国,无人伦者也。更有藤甲护身,急切难伤。又有桃叶恶水,本国人饮之,反添精神;别国人饮之即死:如此蛮方,纵使全胜,有何益焉? 不如班师早回。"孔明笑曰:"吾非容易到此,岂可便去! 吾明日自有平蛮之策。"于是令赵云助魏延守寨,且休轻出。

次日,孔明令土人引路,自乘小车到桃花渡口北岸山僻去处,遍观地理。山险岭峻之处,车不能行,孔明弃车步行。忽到一山,望见一谷,形如长蛇,皆光峭石壁,并无树木,中间一条大路。孔明问土人曰:"此谷何名?"土人答曰:"此处名为盘蛇谷。出谷则三江城大路,谷前名塔郎甸。"孔明大喜曰:"此乃天

hardly seemed human. A native informed him that peach leaves had fallen and made the water unsafe that day. Kongming retired five *li* and camped, leaving Wei Yan in command.

The next day the king of the Black Lances led a band of rattan-armored men across the river, gongs and drums resounding. Wei Yan went forth to meet them. The Man warriors swarmed, covering the terrain. The Riverlanders shot their crossbow bolts; but the rattan was impenetrable, and the arrows dropped harmlessly. Neither the strokes of their blades nor the thrusts of their spears could break through it. The Man wielded their sharp knives and steel forks against the Riverlanders, who, unable to defend themselves, eventually withdrew. The Man returned to camp without giving chase. Wei Yan turned back and rushed to the riverside, where he watched in amazement as the enemy crossed over in full armor: those taken by fatigue simply removed their armor and used it to float across.

Wei Yan raced back to the main camp and gave Kongming a detailed report. Kongming invited Lü Kai and some natives to his tent and asked them about the Black Lances and the Peach Blossom. "Long ago," Lü Kai explained, "I heard of a Black Lance kingdom among the southern Man, one bereft of human morality. Their rattan armor is almost impossible to pierce. Then there is the water poisoned by peach leaves; the natives are inured to it, but outsiders will die drinking it. That's what the southern region is like; the most complete victory would be of little use. It would be best to bring the army home." Kongming smiled and said, "After the trouble it took to get here, we can't simply leave. I have another plan to pacify the Man. Tomorrow." He ordered Zhao Zilong to guard the main camp with Wei Yan and to avoid going out.

The next day, with a native guide, Kongming took his carriage to a secluded spot on a hill north of the Peach Blossom River to survey the lay of the land. Where the road was too arduous for the carriage to pass, Kongming descended and proceeded on foot. He came to a hill where he saw a serpentine ravine with a wide road down its center and sheer, steep walls on which no tree or bush grew. "What is this valley called?" Kongming asked. "Winding Serpent Valley," the guide answered. "From the far side the road leads to Three Rivers. Before it is the region known

2205

赐吾成功于此也！"遂回旧路，上车归寨，唤马岱分付曰："与汝黑油柜车十辆，须用竹竿千条，柜内之物，如此如此。可将本部兵去把住盘蛇谷两头，依法而行。与汝半月限，一切完备。至期如此施设。倘有走漏，定按军法。"马岱受计而去。又唤赵云分付曰："汝去盘蛇谷后，三江大路口如此守把。所用之物，克日完备。"赵云受计而去。又唤魏延分付曰："汝可引本部兵去桃花渡口下寨。如蛮兵渡水来敌，汝便弃了寨，望白旗处而走。限半个月内，须要连输十五阵，弃七个寨栅。若输十四阵，也休来见我。"魏延领命，心中不乐，怏怏而去。孔明又唤张翼另引一军，依所指之处，筑立寨栅去了；却令张嶷、马忠引本洞所降千人，如此行之。各人都依计而行。

　　却说孟获与乌戈国主兀突骨曰："诸葛亮多有巧计，只是埋伏。今后交战，分付三军：但见山谷之中，林木多处，不可轻进。"兀突骨曰："大王说的有理。吾已知道中国人多行诡计。今后依此言行之。吾在前面厮杀，汝在背后教道。"两人商议已定。忽报蜀兵在桃花渡口北岸立起营寨。兀突骨即差二俘长引藤甲军渡了河，来与蜀兵交战。不数合，魏延败走。蛮兵恐有埋伏，不赶自回。次日，魏延又去立了营寨。蛮兵哨得，又引众军

as Talang Barrens." "Then Heaven grants us success here!" Kongming said with satisfaction and went back to the road he had taken.

Back at camp, Kongming summoned Ma Dai, whom he charged as follows: "I am going to give you the ten carriages with the black containers; you will need a thousand bamboo poles. Inside the containers you will find certain essential items. Have your own troops hold either end of Winding Serpent Valley and act according to our plan. You have half a month to prepare everything. At the prearranged time you are to proceed as instructed. Should anyone learn of this plan, the full weight of martial law will be imposed." Ma Dai received his instructions and left.

Next, Kongming summoned Zhao Zilong and charged him: "Go to the rear of Winding Serpent Valley; hold the main road into Three Rivers as instructed. Have everything you need ready by the appointed day." Zhao Zilong received his orders and left. Next, Wei Yan was called and charged: "Take your own troops and camp by the Peach Blossom River crossing. If Man troops come over to oppose you, abandon camp and race toward the white flag. Within half a month expect to lose fifteen battles and abandon as many as seven sites — but do not come to me until after the fifteenth defeat." With grave reservations, Wei Yan accepted his assignment and left in low spirits. Next, Kongming summoned Zhang Yi to take another contingent to a designated place and build a camp with barricades. He also ordered Zhang Ni and Ma Zhong to take charge of some one thousand surrendered Man for a special purpose. Everyone went to carry out his part of the plan.

Meng Huo said to the chief of the Black Lances, "Of Zhuge Liang's many tricks, ambush is his favorite. For future battles have all forces divide themselves into three units. And be most cautious about entering densely wooded valleys." Wutugu replied, "Your Highness speaks wisely. I know well the cunning of those from the middle kingdoms. From now on we will do what you say: I will move ahead and hunt them down; you will direct from behind ." Thus the two agreed.

When the Man kings learned that the Riverlanders had fortified the north bank, Wutugu sent two captains with rattan armored troops to cross the river and engage the enemy. After a brief battle Wei Yan fled. Fearing ambush, the Man soldiers returned south. The next day Wei Yan set

2207

渡过河来战。延出迎之。不数合，延败走。蛮兵追杀十余里，见四下并无动静，便在蜀寨中屯住。次日，二俘长请兀突骨到寨，说知此事。兀突骨即引兵大进，将魏延追一阵。蜀兵皆弃甲抛戈而走，只见前有白旗。延引败兵，急奔到白旗处，早有一寨，就寨中屯住。兀突骨驱兵追至，魏延引兵弃寨而走。蛮兵得了蜀寨。次日，又望前追杀。魏延回兵交战，不三合又败，只看白旗处而走，又有一寨，延就寨屯住。次日，蛮兵又至。延略战又走。蛮兵占了蜀寨。

话休絮烦，魏延且战且走，已败十五阵，连弃七个营寨。蛮兵大进追杀。兀突骨自在军前破敌，于路但见林木茂盛之处，便不敢进；却使人远望，果见树阴之中，旌旗招扬。兀突骨谓孟获曰："果不出大王所料。"孟获大笑曰："诸葛亮今番被吾识破！大王连日胜了他十五阵，夺了七个营寨，蜀兵望风而走。诸葛亮已是计穷；只此一进，大事定矣！"兀突骨大喜，遂不以蜀兵为念。至第十六日，魏延引败残兵，来与藤甲军对敌。兀突骨骑象当先，头戴日月狼须帽，身披金珠缨络，两肋下露出生鳞甲，眼目中微有光芒，手指魏延大骂。延拨马便走。后面蛮兵大进。魏延引兵转过了盘蛇谷，望白旗而走。兀突骨统引兵众，随

up another camp. The Man scouts discovered it, and more of them swarmed across to attack. Wei Yan met them in the field but again fled after a short engagement. The Man pursued more than ten *li*. Finding no enemy activity in the area, they occupied the Riverlands camp.

The next day the two Man captains led Wutugu to the captured camp and told him how the battle had gone. Wutugu pursued the Riverlanders with a large force until Wei Yan's retreating troops threw down their armor and spears and fled. Lo, a white flag flew ahead of them. Wei Yan led his men toward it; there they found a camp already pitched and settled into it. But as Wutugu's pursuing horde closed in, Wei Yan was forced to flee again, thus yielding the camp to the Man. The next day the Man resumed pursuit. The Riverlanders turned and fought, but defeated again in a brief clash, they fled in the direction of another white flag. On reaching it, they found a prepared site and camped down. The next day the Man arrived, and Wei Yan again fled after a halfhearted battle. The Man occupied the abandoned camp.

Wei Yan alternately fought and fled until he had quit fifteen engagements and abandoned seven bases. Ruthlessly the Man advanced to hunt him down, Wutugu out in front, striking at the enemy. Coming to a thick wood, he halted and sent scouts to reconnoitre. The scouts found insignia-bearing flags hanging slack in the depth of the shade. Wutugu said to Meng Huo, "Just as Your Highness predicted." Meng Huo smiled and replied, "So this is Zhuge Liang's game. Now that Your Highness has beat him in fifteen battles and seized seven of his camps, the Riverlanders flee on hearing of your approach. Zhuge Liang has no more tricks to play! With this next advance our cause carries!" Elated, Wutugu put all thought of danger out of his mind.

On the sixteenth day Wei Yan led his battle-worn men forth to oppose the rattan-armored Man. Riding an elephant, Wutugu took the lead. He wore a wolf-beard cap decorated with the sun and the moon. Gold and pearls laced his garment, through which his torso's hard-scaled skin showed. A subtle fire darted from his eyes. Pointing to Wei Yan, he pronounced his malediction. Wei Yan wheeled round and fled again. The Man gave chase in full force. Wei Yan maneuvered around into Winding Serpent Valley as he made for the white flag. Wutugu closed in for the

2209

后追杀。兀突骨望见山上并无草木，料无埋伏，放心追杀。赶到谷中，见数十辆黑油柜车在当路。蛮兵报曰："此是蜀兵运粮道路，因大王兵至，撇下粮车而走。"兀突骨大喜，催兵追赶。将出谷口，不见蜀兵，只见横木乱石滚下，垒断谷口。兀突骨令兵开路而进，忽见前面大小车辆，装载干柴，尽皆火起。兀突骨忙教退兵，只闻后军发喊，报说谷口已被干柴垒断，车中原来皆是火药，一齐烧着。兀突骨见无草木，心尚不慌，令寻路而走。只见山上两边乱丢火把，火把到处，地中药线皆着，就地飞起铁炮。满谷中火光乱舞，但逢藤甲，无有不着。将兀突骨并三万藤甲军，烧得互相拥抱，死于盘蛇谷中。孔明在山上往下看时，只见蛮兵被火烧的伸拳舒腿，大半被铁炮打的头脸粉碎，昏死于谷中，臭不可闻。孔明垂泪而叹曰："吾虽有功于社稷，必损寿矣！"左右将士，无不感叹。

却说孟获在寨中，正望蛮兵回报。忽然千余人笑拜于寨前，言说："乌戈国兵与蜀兵大战，将诸葛亮围在盘蛇谷中了。特请大王前去接应。我等皆是本洞之人，不得已而降蜀；今知大王前到，特来助战。"孟获大喜，即引宗党并所聚番人，连夜上马；就令蛮兵引路。方到盘蛇谷时，只见火光甚起，臭气难

kill; seeing the hills bare, he had assumed he was safe from ambush.

When he reached the middle of the valley, Wutugu saw several dozen wagons with black-painted containers blocking the road. A soldier reported, "This is the Riverlands grain transport route. Your Highness's arrival has caused them to flee and leave their carts." Wutugu triumphantly urged his warriors to press the chase to the other end of the valley. There they found no Riverlands troops; but great logs and volleys of rock crashed down, sealing the exit. Wutugu ordered his men to open the road. He had resumed his advance, when carts of all sizes loaded with burning wood loomed out of nowhere! Wutugu ordered immediate retreat. But from his rear ranks shouts went up: "The exit is blocked by dry tinder, and the carts, filled with powder, are in flames!" Wutugu remained calm because the site was too bare to conceal an ambush. He ordered his men to escape however they could. Then, lo, from both sides of the valley torches were hurled down, hitting fuses on the ground that ignited iron missiles. The whole valley began dancing wildly with fiery light, and the rattan armor caught fire when touched by the flames. Wutugu and his thirty thousand men perished in Winding Serpent Valley, huddled together in the inferno.

From a hilltop Kongming looked down upon the incinerated men strewn over the valley. Most of them had had their heads and faces pulverized by the falling missiles. An unbearable stench rose from their corpses. Kongming wept and sighed at the carnage. "Whatever service to the shrines of Han this represents, my life-span will be shortened for it," he said. His words deeply touched every officer and man.

In camp Meng Huo waited for his troops. Suddenly a thousand or more arrived and prostrated themselves before him. Smiling broadly, they said, "The army of the Black Lances has trapped the Riverlanders in Winding Serpent Valley. A major battle is under way. They need reinforcement, Your Highness. All of us are members of your hollow who surrendered against our will to the Riverlands, and we have come to help now that Your Highness is here." Meng Huo was delighted. With his clan, his adherents, and other outlanders he set out at once, using the returned Man as guides.

In Winding Serpent Valley a scene of fiery destruction and the stench

闻。获知中计,急退兵时,左边张嶷,右边马忠,两路军杀出。获方欲抵敌,一声喊起,蛮兵中大半皆是蜀兵,将蛮王宗党并聚集的番人,尽皆擒了。孟获匹马杀出重围,望山径而走。

正走之间,见山凹里一簇人马,拥出一辆小车;车中端坐一人,纶巾羽扇,身衣道袍,乃孔明也。孔明大喝曰:"反贼孟获!今番如何?"获急回马走。旁边闪过一将,拦住去路,乃是马岱。孟获措手不及,被马岱生擒活捉了。此时王平、张翼已引一军赶到蛮寨中,将祝融夫人并一应老小皆活捉而来。

孔明归到寨中,升帐而坐,谓众将曰:"吾今此计,不得已而用之,大损阴德。我料敌人必算吾于林木多处埋伏,吾却空设旌旗,实无兵马,疑其心也。吾令魏文长连输十五阵者,坚其心也。吾见盘蛇谷止一条路,两壁厢皆是光石,并无树木,下面都是沙土,因令马岱将黑油柜安排于谷中,车中油柜内,皆是预先造下的火炮,名曰'地雷',一炮中藏九炮,三十步埋之,中用竹竿通节,以引药线;才一发动,山损石裂。吾又令赵子龙预备草车,安排于谷口。又于山上准备大木乱石。却令魏延赚兀突骨并藤甲军入谷,放出魏延,即断其路,随后焚之。吾闻:'利于水者必不利于火。'藤甲虽刀箭不能入,乃油浸之物,见火必着。蛮兵如此顽皮,非火攻安能取胜?——使乌戈国之人不留

of slaughter greeted Meng Huo, and he knew he had been trapped. He tried to pull back, but Zhang Ni and Ma Zhong fell upon him to the left and right. As he began to defend himself, a war cry went up from his own ranks, and the bulk of his men now disclosed themselves to be Riverlands troops! They seized Meng Huo's clansmen and adherents as well as their regional allies and made them prisoners. Meng Huo himself managed to break out of the trap and raced toward the mountain paths.

While fleeing, he noticed a cluster of men with a small wagon emerging from a depression in the hills. Inside sat a man with bound hair, holding a feathered fan and garbed like a priest of the Tao. Kongming shouted, "Meng Huo, you rebel! How about it now?" Meng Huo turned swiftly to flee, but a commander darted out from the side and blocked his way. it was Ma Dai. Meng Huo, caught unprepared, was swiftly taken. By this time Wang Ping and Zhang Yi had already rushed the Man camp and captured Lady Zhurong and all the members of Meng Huo's family.

On reaching camp, Kongming took his place in the main tent. "This trick," Kongming told his commanders, "I used only because I had to; I shall lose much merit in the life to come for it. I guessed the enemy would be looking for an ambush in the woods, so I set up decoy banners there to confuse them. There were never any troops. Next, I had Wei Yan lose a series of battles to strengthen their confidence. I observed that Winding Serpent Valley had only one road between two sheer cliffs bare of vegetation, all sandy soil below. Accordingly, I ordered Ma Dai to deploy the black wagons in the valley — they had been loaded earlier with fire launchers called 'earth thunder,' each containing nine missiles. The mines were buried thirty paces apart and connected by fuses — bamboo tubes packed with powder. On firing, the hills crumbled and the rocks split.

"Next, I had Zhao Zilong prepare hay wagons and deploy them at the valley exit. On the slopes we had huge logs and rocks. After Wei Yan had lured Wutugu and his rattan armored troops into the valley and got free, we cut off the road and burned out the enemy. They say, 'What works with water doesn't work with fire': the rattan armor may be impervious to blade or arrow, but any article processed with oil is bound to be flammable. The Man warriors were so stubborn, how else could they have been defeated? But to have exterminated the Black Lances so com-

种类者，是吾之大罪也！"众将拜伏曰："丞相天机，鬼神莫测也！"孔明令押过孟获来。孟获跪于帐下。孔明令去其缚，教且在别帐与酒食压惊。孔明唤管酒食官至坐榻前，如此如此，分付而去。

　　却说孟获与祝融夫人并孟优、带来洞主、一切宗党在别帐饮酒。忽一人入帐谓孟获曰："丞相面羞，不欲与公相见。特令我来放公回去，再招人马来决胜负。公今可速去。"孟获垂泪言曰："七擒七纵，自古未尝有也。吾虽化外之人，颇知礼义，直如此无羞耻乎？"遂同兄弟妻子宗党人等，皆匍匐跪于帐下，肉袒谢罪曰："丞相天威，南人不复反矣！"孔明曰："公今服乎？"获泣谢曰："某子子孙孙皆感覆载生成之恩，安得不服！"孔明乃请孟获上帐，设宴庆贺，就令永为洞主。所夺之地，尽皆退还。孟获宗党及诸蛮兵，无不感戴，皆欣然跳跃而去。后人有诗赞孔明曰：

　　　　羽扇纶巾拥碧幢，七擒妙策制蛮王。
　　　　至今溪洞传威德，为选高原立庙堂。

pletely is a crime that weighs heavily on me." The commanders bowed low before him and said, "Your Excellency's marvelous ingenuity is more than even the gods and spirits could fathom!"

Kongming ordered Meng Huo brought before him. Meng Huo kneeled down, and Kongming had his bonds removed. To ease his fears, he had food and drink provided to the Man king in a separate tent. Finally, Kongming gave certain instructions to the commissary officer.

Meng Huo and Lady Zhurong, Meng You and the chief of Dailai Hollow, together with their clansmen and adherents, refreshed themselves. Suddenly an officer entered the tent and said to Meng Huo, "His Excellency was too embarrassed to see you, my lord, and has ordered me to release you. Go home and rally your forces for another trial of strength. Quickly, my lord." But Meng Huo, tears falling, replied, "Seven times captured, seven times freed! Such a thing has never happened![2] Though I stand beyond the range of the imperial grace, I am not utterly ignorant of ritual, of what propriety and honor require. No I am not so shameless!"

Having thus spoken, Meng Huo, his brother, his wife, and his other clansmen crawled to Kongming's tent. The king kenneled and exposed the upper half of his body, betokening his readiness to receive punishment. "Your Excellency's divine prestige ensures that the south will not rebel again," Meng Huo declared. "Then you submit?" Kongming responded. Weeping with gratitude, Meng Huo said, "For generations to come, our children and theirs after them will gratefully acknowledge your all-protecting, all-sustaining love, deep as Heaven, vast as earth. How can I not submit!" Kongming invited Meng Huo into his tent, where he held a feast confirming the king as chief of the hollows in perpetuity, and he relinquished to him all territories seized by the Riverlands troops. Meng Huo and his people, as well as the warriors of other Man nations, acclaimed his generosity, leaping and vaulting in unbounded excitement. A poet of later times left these lines in praise of Kongming:

> The feather fan, Taoist cap, and dark green canopy —
> Captured seven times, the Man king did his will —
> Those streams and hollows honor Kongming still,
> Raising to his virtue's force a hall upon a hill.

2215

长史费祎入谏曰："今丞相亲提士卒，深入不毛，收服蛮方；目今蛮王既已归服，何不置官吏，与孟获一同守之？"孔明曰："如此有三不易：留外人则当留兵，兵无所食，一不易也；蛮人伤破，父兄死亡，留外人而不留兵，必成祸患，二不易也；蛮人累有废杀之罪，自有嫌疑，留外人终不相信，三不易也。今吾不留人，不运粮，与相安于无事而已。"众人尽服。于是蛮方皆感孔明恩德，乃为孔明立生祠，四时享祭，皆呼之为'慈父'；各送珍珠金宝、丹漆药材、耕牛战马，以资军用，誓不再反。南方已定。

却说孔明犒军已毕，班师回蜀，令魏延引本部兵为前锋。延引兵方至泸水，忽然阴云四合，水面上一阵狂风骤起，飞沙走石，军不能进。延退兵回报孔明。孔明遂请孟获问之。

正是：

塞外蛮人方帖服，水边鬼卒又猖狂。

未知孟获所言若何，且看下文分解。

Senior Counselor Fei Yi entered and protested: "Your Excellency's campaign deep into the wilds has subjugated the Man region, and their king has tendered his allegiance. Is it not now appropriate to establish districts and officials so that we can rule together with Meng Huo?" "That poses three problems," Kongming replied. "First, if outsiders stay behind, troops must stay with them. But how are we to feed those troops? Second, the defeated Man have suffered grievously, losing fathers and brothers. To leave outsiders here without troops is bound to lead to trouble. And third, the Man nations have always been so politically unstable — the result of jealousies and suspicion — that they will never trust outsiders. If we leave no one, however, and ship no grain, we will find ourselves at peace with them for want of any cause of trouble." These arguments persuaded the commanders. In gratitude for Kongming's benevolence, the Man people set up a shrine at which offerings were made every season; the prime minister became known among them as "the kindly father." Each of the nations rendered tribute of pearls and precious metals, cinnabar, lacquer, medicinal herbs, water buffalo, and war-horses for military use. And the Man vowed not to rebel. Thus, the south was finally pacified.

After Kongming had feasted his army, the homeward march began. Wei Yan, in the vanguard, had reached the River Lu when sudden storm clouds bore down on him. Violent gusts sprang up on the water; and dust and stones swept through the army, preventing its advance. Wei Yan retreated and reported to Kongming, who turned to Meng Huo for advice. Indeed:

> The moment the Man were tamed,
> Angry spirits roiled the river.

What would Meng Huo say to Kongming?
Read on

伐原兵表
中密上
松涛

第九十一回

祭泸水汉相班师　伐中原武侯上表

　　却说孔明班师回国，孟获率引大小洞主酋长，及诸部落，罗拜相送。前军至泸水，时值九月秋天，忽然阴云布合，狂风骤起；兵不能渡，回报孔明。孔明遂问孟获，获曰："此水原有猖神作祸，往来者必须祭之。"孔明曰："用何物祭享？"获曰："旧时国中因猖神作祸，用七七四十九颗人头并黑牛白羊祭之，自然风恬浪静，更兼连年丰稔。"孔明曰："吾今事已平定，安可妄杀一人？"遂自到泸水岸边观看。果见阴风大起，波涛汹涌，人马皆惊。孔明甚疑，即寻土人问之。土人告说："自丞相经过之后，夜夜只闻得水边鬼哭神号。自黄昏直至天晓，哭声不绝。瘴烟之内，阴鬼无数。因此作祸，无人敢渡。"孔明曰："此乃我之罪愆也。前者马岱引蜀兵千余，皆死于水中；更兼杀死南人，尽弃此处：狂魂怨鬼，不能解释，以致如此。吾今晚当亲自往祭。"土人曰："须依旧例，杀四十九颗人头为祭，则怨鬼自散也。"孔明

Chapter 91

The Prime Minister Sacrifices to River Ghosts
Before Leading the Army Home
The Lord of Wu petitions for a Just War
Against the Northern Heartland

The Riverlands army started homeward; Meng Huo led the chiefs of the hollows and coves as well as other tribal leaders and tribesmen as they gathered around Kongming in obeisance to see him off. It was autumn, the ninth month of the year, when the vanguard reached the River Lu. Suddenly thick clouds darkened the sky and fierce winds blew. Told that the troops could not cross, Kongming turned to Meng Huo for advice. Meng Huo said, "An evil spirit has cursed this water; those who would pass must appease him by sacrifice." "What would please the spirit?" Kongming asked. "In olden times," Meng Huo explained, "when the god worked his wrath, they sacrificed forty-nine human heads — seven times seven — a black ox and a white sheep; then the winds would ease, the waters would subside, and years of plenty would follow."

"The campaign is over," Kongming said. "It would be wrong to kill." He went to the riverbank and found the army panicking as the storm raged and waves and breakers surged and swelled. Perplexed, Kongming sought out some natives to advise him. They said, "After Your Excellency first passed through, all we heard by the shore night after night was the moaning of ghosts and the howling of spirits. From day's end to dawn the cries went on. Shades beyond numbering, shrouded in the miasma, have hunted the waters after your passage, and now no man dares to cross."

"The cause is my grave crime." Kongming said. "Previously more than a thousand of Ma Dai's men perished in the River Lu, joined by the fallen southern warriors abandoned here. Those wronged souls, unable to find their final peace, now raise this disturbance. Tonight I must go and make offerings to them." The natives said, "Precedent must be followed. You must sacrifice forty-nine human heads before the wronged ghosts

曰:"本为人死而成怨鬼,岂可又杀生人耶?吾自有主意。"唤行厨宰杀牛马;和面为剂,塑成人头,内以牛羊等肉代之,名曰"馒头"。当夜于泸水岸上,设香案,铺祭物,列灯四十九盏,扬幡招魂;将馒头等物,陈设于地。三更时分,孔明金冠鹤氅,亲自临祭,令董厥读祭文。其文曰:

维大汉建兴三年秋九月一日,武乡侯、领益州牧、丞相诸葛亮,谨陈祭仪,享于故殁王事蜀中将校及南人亡者阴魂曰:

我大汉皇帝,威胜五霸,明继三王。昨自远方侵境,异俗起兵;纵虿尾以兴妖,恣狼心而逞乱。我奉王命,问罪遐荒;大举貔貅,悉除蝼蚁;雄军云集,狂寇冰消,才闻破竹之声,便是失猿之势。但士卒儿郎,尽是九州豪杰;官僚将校,皆为四海英雄:习武从戎,投明事主,莫不同申三令,共展七擒;齐坚奉国之诚,并效忠君之志。何期汝等偶失兵机,缘落奸计:或为流矢所中,魂掩泉台;或为刀剑所

will disperse." "Once they were living men," Kongming objected, "what good will more killing do? I have a better idea."

Kongming ordered his army cooks to slaughter oxen and horses and to compound a doughy preparation in the shape of a human head with a stuffing of beef and lamb; it was called "dough-head."[1] That night on the bank of the Lu, Kongming set up an incense stand, laid out the offerings, and lined up forty-nine lamps. He then raised streamers high to summon the lost souls and placed the dough-heads on the ground. At the third watch Kongming, wearing a gilded headdress and a cloak of crane feathers, personally officiated at·the sacrifice as Dong Jue read out the text. It said:

> On this first day of the ninth month of the third year of Jian Xing of the great Han,[2] lore of Wuxiang and protector of Yizhou, His Excellency Zhuge Liang, reverently conducts this sacrificial ceremony to sustain the shade-bound souls of the Riverlands commanders and lieutenants who have fallen in the imperial service, as well as the southern warriors who have perished.
>
> Hear Ye:
>
> When the domains of the August Emperor of the great Han, whose martial might excels the five hegemons' and whose wisdom makes him heir to the three sage kings of antiquity, recently suffered incursion from the barbarous hordes of remote regions — promoting subversion like scorpions flexing their tails, reveling in sedition like wolves — I, his vassal, bearing the royal mandate, visited these wilds to punish their crimes. We raised an army of heroes to sweep away the wretched vermin. Our brave warriors rallied, and these ungoverned predators, terrified by our swift victories, melted away like apes fleeing a wood on hearing a sword split bamboo.
>
> Our soldiers and yeomen, the bold spirits of the realm, our officials and commanders, heroes from around the empire, all were seasoned in the trials of war and committed to an enlightened lord. United, they carried out our commands and worked together in executing the seven captures. Firm in the sincerity with which they served the dynasty, they loyally strived in their sovereign's cause.
>
> Little did we expect, soldiers, that you would lose the military initiative and fall prey to the enemy's treacheries: some of you slain in volleys of arrows, your souls snatched off to the underworld; others killed by the

2223

伤,魄归长夜:生则有勇,死则成名。今凯歌欲还,献俘将及。汝等英灵尚在,祈祷必闻:随我旌旗,逐我部曲,同回上国,各认本乡,受骨肉之蒸尝,领家人之祭祀;莫作他乡之鬼,徒为异域之魂。我当奏之天子,使汝等各家尽露恩露,年给衣粮,月赐廪禄:用兹酬答,以慰汝心。至于本境土神,南方亡鬼,血食有常,凭依不远;生者既凛天威,死者亦归王化,想宜宁帖,毋致号啕。聊表丹诚,敬陈祭祀。呜呼,哀哉! 伏惟尚飨!

读毕祭文,孔明放声大哭,极其痛切,情动三军,无不下泪。孟获等众,尽皆哭泣。只见愁云怨雾之中,隐隐有数千鬼魂,皆随风而散。于是孔明令左右将祭物尽弃于泸水之中。

次日,孔明引大军俱到泸水南岸,但见云收雾散,风静浪平。蜀兵安然尽渡泸水,果然"鞭敲金镫响,人唱凯歌还"。行到永昌,孔明留王伉、吕凯守四郡;发付孟获领众自回,嘱其勤政驭下,善抚居民,勿失农务。孟获涕泣拜别而去。孔明自引大军

sword, your spirits sent home to everlasting night — brave in life, more splendid in death. Now we are about to return triumphant and deliver our prisoners to the Emperor.

As spiritual beings you still exist — therefore hear our prayer: follow our banners and flags, come after our army units, return with us to the great kingdom of Shu so that each may find his own native place and there receive the winter offerings from his flesh and blood and the ritual sacrifices of his family. Do not remain ghosts in a strange realm, lost souls in a foreign clime.

I shall address a petition to the Emperor, so that each of your families may share fully in the benevolent generosity of the sovereign, annual allowances of clothing and staples and monthly stipends of grain. By these means of redress we intend to pacify your discontent.

For the native spirits of this region, the homeless ghosts of the south, fresh animal sacrifices will be regularly maintained from the resources close at hand. If alive you felt the chilling awe of the divine majesty, in death you remain subject to the imperial aura. Be peaceful, then, and submissive, without indulging in these frightful shrieks, for I have come to demonstrate my sincerest reverence by conducting this sacrificial service. Heed this grieving voice of mine and partake of the feast we humbly lay before you.

LIBRARY OF CHINESE
AND ENGLISH CLASSICS

A sharp cry burst from Kongming after he had read the funerary address, and the whole army, joined by Meng Huo and his people, wept at his acute distress. And lo, amid the clouds of despair and the dark mists of discontent, thousands of ghostly souls, dimly visible, began to clear away in the wake of the winds as Kongming had his assistants cast sacrificial articles upon the waters of the Lu.

The next day Kongming led the army to the south shore. They found the clouds cleared, the mists scattered, the winds stilled, the waters calmed. The Riverlands soldiers crossed peacefully; as it is said, "To the crack of whip and the jingle of stirrup the men returned, celebrating their victories." When the march reached Yongchang, Kongming detailed Wang Kang and Lü Kai to defend the four districts; he directed Meng Huo to lead his people home, enjoining him to be conscientious in administration, to give guidance to his subordinates, and to deal gently with the local peoples so that they might never neglect their farms. Meng Huo tearfully

回成都。后主排銮驾出郭三十里迎接，下辇立于道傍，以候孔明。孔明慌下车伏道而言曰："臣不能速平南方，使主上怀忧，臣之罪也。"后主扶起孔明，并车而回，设太平筵会，重赏三军。自此远邦进贡来朝者二百余处。孔明奏准后主，将殁于王事者之家，一一优恤。人心欢悦，朝野清平。

却说魏主曹丕，在位七年，即蜀汉建兴四年也。丕先纳夫人甄氏，即袁绍次子袁熙之妇，前破邺城时所得。后生一子，名睿，字元仲，自幼聪明，丕甚爱之。后丕又纳安平广宗人郭永之女为贵妃，甚有颜色；其父尝曰："吾女乃女中之王也。"故号为"女王"。自丕纳为贵妃，因甄夫人失宠，郭贵妃欲谋为后，却与幸臣张韬商议。时丕有疾，韬乃诈称于甄夫人宫中掘得桐木偶人，上书天子年月日时，为魇镇之事。丕大怒，遂将甄夫人赐死，立郭贵妃为后。因无出，养曹睿为己子。虽甚爱之，不立为

prostrated himself; then he took leave and departed. Kongming led the army home to Chengdu.

The Second Emperor rode out thirty *li* in the royal carriage to welcome Kongming home. There he descended and stood by the side of the road to wait for the prime minister.[3] Kongming hurriedly stepped down from his own carriage, pressed his body to the ground, and said, "My failure to pacify the south swiftly has given Your Majesty concern, for which I take responsibility." The Emperor helped Kongming to his feet, and they returned to Chengdu, their carriages side by side. At a grand celebration for the end of the war the army was feasted and lavishly rewarded. Thereafter, more than two hundred minor kingdoms sent tribute and paid homage at court. Kongming petitioned the Emperor to show special consideration to each family that had lost a member in the recent service. The people rejoiced, and the court and the people basked in an aura of peace.

* * *

It was the fourth year of Jian Xing by the Shu-Han calendar.[4] The ruler of Wei, Cao Pi, had been on the throne for seven years. He had first married Lady Zhen (a fifth-rank concubine of Yuan Shao's second son, Xi) after Cao Cao conquered the city of Ye. Lady Zhen bore him a son named Rui (Yuanzhong), who showed great intellectual promise at an early age; Cao Pi doted on him. Later, Cao Pi took for ranking concubine a woman of great beauty, whose father was Guo Yong from Guangzong in Anping. Because her father had once said, "My daughter is a king among women," she was known as the "female king."

2227

Lady Zhen having lost Cao Pi's favor, Ranking Concubine Guo had begun plotting to become empress from the time of her elevation. The favored vassal Zhang Tao became her confidant in this matter. At one time Cao Pi fell ill, and Zhang Tao falsely declared that in Lady Zhen's palace he had dug up a human figure carved of paulownia wood and marked with the exact date and time of the Son of Heaven's birth to put him under a spell. In a fury Cao Pi had Lady Zhen condemned to death and Lady Guo installed as empress. Lady Guo, having no issue, raised Lady Zhen's son, Rui, as her own but did not make him heir despite her affection for the lad.

嗣。睿年至十五岁，弓马熟娴。当年春二月，丕带睿出猎。行于山坞之间，赶出子母二鹿，丕一箭射倒母鹿，回观小鹿驰于曹睿马前。丕大呼曰："吾儿何不射之？"睿在马上泣告曰："陛下已杀其母，臣安忍复杀其子也。"丕闻之，掷弓于地曰："吾儿真仁德之主也！"于是遂封睿为平原王。

　　夏五月，丕感寒疾，医治不痊，乃召中军大将军曹真、镇军大将军陈群、抚军大将军司马懿三人入寝宫。丕唤曹睿至，指谓曹真等曰："今朕病已沉重，不能复生。此子年幼，卿等三人可善辅之，勿负朕心。"三人皆告曰："陛下何出此言？臣等愿竭力以事陛下，至千秋万岁。"丕曰："今年许昌城门无故自崩，乃不祥之兆，朕故自知必死也。"正言间，内侍奏征东大将军曹休入宫问安。丕召入谓曰："卿等皆国家柱石之臣也，若能同心辅朕之子，朕死亦瞑目矣！"言讫，堕泪而薨。时年四十岁，在位七年。于是曹真、陈群、司马懿、曹休等，一面举哀，一面拥立曹睿为大魏皇帝。谥父丕为文皇帝，谥母甄氏为文昭皇后。封钟繇为太傅，曹真为大将军，曹休为大司马，华歆为太尉，王朗为司徒，陈群为司空，司马懿为骠骑大将军。其余文武官僚，各各封

By the age of fifteen Cao Rui was entirely at ease with the bow and the horse. In the second month of spring Cao Pi took Cao Rui with him to hunt. Riding through a dale, they flushed out two deer, fawn and doe. Cao Pi felled the mother with a single shot. Turning around, he saw the fawn racing before Cao Rui's horse. "Shoot, my son!" Cao Pi shouted. But Cao Rui, still on horseback, wept and said, "Your Majesty has slain the mother; can I bear to slay the child?" Cao Pi threw down his bow and said, "My son, you are indeed a magnanimous and virtuous prince." Cao Pi enfeoffed Cao Rui as prince of Pingyuan.

During summer, in the fifth month of the year, Cao Pi was afflicted with severe chills that the doctors could not control. He summoned three men to his resting chamber: Cao Zhen, supreme commander of the central army, Supreme Commander Chen Qun, controller of the army, and Supreme Commander Sima Yi, rallier of the army. Cao Pi then called for Cao Rui and, pointing at him, said to Cao Zhen and the two others, "Our illness is grave; recovery impossible. You three will have to guide this child and keep faith with my wishes." The three responded, "Do not speak this way, Your Majesty. Even without admonition we will always do our utmost in Your Majesty's service." Cao Pi said, "This year the main gate of Xuchang collapsed without cause, an omen which foretells my end." As he was speaking, an imperial attendant announced Supreme Commander Cao Xui, Conqueror of the East, who had come to inquire about the Emperor's health. Cao Pi summoned him in and said, "If you four, the pillars of our dynastic house, will support our son with undivided devotion, I shall die in peace." A last tear fell, and he passed from this world at the age of forty; he had reigned for seven years.

Cao Zhen, Chen Qun, Sima Yi, and Cao Xiu along with other high officials initiated the mourning ceremonies. At the same time they established Cao Rui as august emperor of the great Wei dynasty. Cao Pi was given the posthumous title August Emperor Wen and Lady Zhen the posthumous title August Empress Wen Zhao.[5] Zhong Yao was made imperial guardian, Cao Zhen regent-marshal,[6] Cao Xiu grand marshal, Hua Xin grand commandant, Wang Lang minister of the interior, Chen Qun minister of works, and Sima Yi chief general of the Flying Cavalry. Other civil and military officials and officers received fiefs and awards. An empire-

赠。大赦天下。时雍、凉二州缺人守把，司马懿上表乞守西凉等处。曹睿从之，遂封懿提督雍、凉等处兵马。领诏去讫。

早有细作飞报入川。孔明大惊曰："曹丕已死，孺子曹睿即位，余皆不足虑：司马懿深有谋略，今督雍、凉兵马，倘训练成时，必为蜀中之大患。不如先起兵伐之。"参军马谡曰："今丞相平南方回，军马疲敝，只宜存恤，岂可复远征？某有一计，使司马懿自死于曹睿之手，未知丞相钧意允否？"孔明问是何计，马谡曰："司马懿虽是魏国大臣，曹睿素怀疑忌。何不密遣人往洛阳、邺郡等处，布散流言，道此人欲反；更作司马懿告示天下榜文，遍贴诸处：使曹睿心疑，必然杀此人也。"孔明从之，即遣人密行此计去了。

却说邺城门上，忽一日见贴下告示一道。守门者揭了，来奏曹睿。睿观之，其文曰：

骠骑大将军总领雍、凉等处兵马事司马懿，谨以信义布告天下：昔太祖武皇帝，创立基业，本欲立陈思王子建为社稷主；不幸奸谗交集，岁久潜龙。皇孙曹睿，素无德

wide amnesty was proclaimed.

At this time the two provinces Yong and Liang needed someone to govern and defend them. Sime Yi petitoned to become defender of Xiliang and other points west. Cao Rui approved, and Sima Yi was appointed superintendent of Yong's and Liang's armed forces. Sima Yi accepted his edict of appointment and departed.

Riverlands spies swiftly reported these changes at the Wei court. Startled, Kongming said, "Cao Pi is dead, the boy Rui enthroned. There is little to concern us there. But Sima Yi, a man of deep strategy, has taken charge of the Liang and Yong armies; and once he has trained them, the Riverlands will have a serious problem. It would be best to act first and attack them!" The military adviser Ma Su said, "Your Excellency has hardly returned from conquering the south; the army is exhausted. Surely this is a time to consider our soldiers' welfare, not to make another expedition far afield. I have a plan that will cause Sima Yi to die at Cao Rui's hands, but I am not sure whether Your Excellency, in your profound judgment, will give me permission to try it."

Kongming asked the details, and Ma Su continued, "Although Sima Yi is a leading minister of the Wei court, Cao Rui has always regarded him with suspicion and fear. I recommend spreading rumors in Luoyang, Ye, and other key cities of Wei that Sima Yi is plotting to rebel. In addition, throughout the enemy's districts we can post forged proclamations by Sima Yi to the empire at large. That should unnerve Cao Rui enough to have him killed." Kongming approved the plan and sent secret agents to carry it out.

2231

* * *

Suddenly one day a proclamation was found attached to the main gate of Ye. The gatekeepers tore it down and brought it to Cao Rui. Cao Rui studied the text, which read:

> Cheif Commander Sima Yi of the Flying Cavalry, with overall command of the armed forces of Yong, Liang, and other regions, reverently and in good faith proclaims to the empire: originally our great ancestor, August Emperor Wu, founder of this house, wanted Cao Zhi to succeed as the lord of his shrine. Unfortunately, caught in the crosscurrents of treachery and calumny, Cao Zhi remained a submerged dragon for many years.[7] The

行，妄自居尊，有负太祖之遗意。今吾应天顺人，克日兴师，以慰万民之望。告示到日，各宜归命新君。如不顺者，当灭九族！先此告闻，想宜知悉。

曹睿览毕，大惊失色，急问群臣。太尉华歆奏曰："司马懿上表乞守雍、凉，正为此也。先时太祖武皇帝尝谓臣曰：'司马懿鹰视狼顾，不可付以兵权；久必为国家大祸。'今日反情已萌，可速诛之。"王朗奏曰："司马懿深明韬略，善晓兵机，素有大志；若不早除，久必为祸。"睿乃降旨，欲兴兵御驾亲征。忽班部中闪出大将军曹真奏曰："不可。文皇帝托孤于臣等数人，是知司马仲达无异志也。今事未知真假，遽尔加兵，乃逼之反耳。或者蜀、吴奸细行反间之计，使我君臣自乱，彼却乘虚而击，未可知也。陛下幸察之。"睿曰："司马懿若果谋反，将奈何？"真曰："如陛下心疑，可仿汉高伪游云梦之计。御驾幸安邑，司马懿必然来迎；观其动静，就车前擒之，可也。"睿从之，遂命曹真监国，亲自领御林军十万，径到安邑。

imperial grandson, Cao Rui, with no record of virtuous conduct, unconscionably placed himself upon the throne in violation of our founder Cao Cao's last wishes. But now, in response to Heaven's will and men's judgment, we have appointed the day for raising an army to satisfy the expectations of the millions. When this proclamation reaches you, let each man commit his allegiance to the new sovereign. Whosoever disobeys will be punished by clan-wide execution. Let this advance notice be made known far and wide.

After reading the text, Cao Rui, pale with distress, hastily consulted his ministers. Grand Commandant Hua Xin addressed his sovereign: "Now we see Sime Yi's true purpose in seeking military authority in the western provinces of Yong and Liang. I remember the great ancestor Cao Cao, August Emperor Wu, once telling me, 'Sima Yi has hungry eyes, like an eagle's or wolf's. Given military power, he will ruin the dynasty.' His revolt must be put down before it starts." Wang Lang addressed the Wei sovereign: "Sima Yi, with his deep comprehension of strategy and thorough understanding of military action, has long harbored grandiose ambitions. Remove him or suffer the consequences."

Cao Rui announced his intention to lead an armed force against Sima Yi. But suddenly Regent-Marshal Cao Zhen stepped forward and said, "I oppose it. The late sovereign, Cao Pi, entrusted the successor to my colleagues and me, and I am certain that Sima Yi has no subversive intent. The facts of the situation remain unclear, and precipitate military action will only force him into rebellion. It is possible that agents of the Riverlands or the Southland are attempting to sow discord between our sovereign and his subjects in order to create disorder before an attack. Your Majesty should inquire most carefully into this matter." Cao Rui said, "But what if Sima Yi is plotting to revolt?" "If Your Majesty is in doubt," Cao Zhen replied, "you might do what Han Gao Zu did when he traveled to Yunmeng.[8] If you proceed to Anyi, Sima Yi will have to receive you. Observe his movements carefully and you will be able to seize him when he comes before your carriage. It should work." Cao Rui approved the plan and commanded Cao Zhen to assume authority over the government. Taking personal command of the Royal Guard, one hundred thousand strong, Cao Rui went directly to Anyi.

司马懿不知其故，欲令天子知其威严，乃整兵马，率甲士数万来迎。近臣奏曰："司马懿果率兵十余万，前来抗拒，实有反心矣。"睿慌命曹休先领兵迎之。司马懿见兵马前来，只疑车驾亲至，伏道而迎。曹休出曰："仲达受先帝托孤之重，何故反耶？"懿大惊失色，汗流遍体，乃问其故。休备言前事。懿曰："此吴、蜀奸细反间之计，欲使我君臣自相残害，彼却乘虚而袭。某当自见天子辨之。"遂急退了军马，至睿车前俯伏泣奏曰："臣受先帝托孤之重，安敢有异心？必是吴、蜀之奸计。臣请提一旅之师，先破蜀，后伐吴，报先帝与陛下，以明臣心。"睿疑虑未决。华歆奏曰："不可付之兵权。可即罢归田里。"睿依言，将司马懿削职回乡，命曹休总督雍、凉军马。曹睿驾回洛阳。

却说细作探知此事，报入川中。孔明闻之大喜曰："吾欲伐魏久矣，奈有司马懿总雍、凉之兵。今既中计遭贬，吾有何忧！"次日，后主早朝，大会官僚，孔明出班，上《出师表》一

Sima Yi, unaware of the real reason for the Son of Heaven's visit and wishing to impress him with the extent of his power, put his armed forces in excellent order and led tens of thousands forth to welcome Cao Rui. A trusted attendant said to the Emperor, "Sima Yi is bringing more than one hundred thousand men to meet us. His real intent is to rebel." Cao Rui hurriedly ordered Cao Xiu to advance with troops and meet Yi in the field. When Sima Yi saw the army coming toward him, he assumed the Emperor was with it; he bowed low at the roadside to greet him. Cao Xiu came forward and said, "Sima Yi, you are one of those whom the late Emperor charged with the care of his heir apparent, now our sovereign. Why are you in rebellion?"

Sima Yi turned pale and sweat poured from him as he asked for an explanation. Cao Xiu recounted the preceding events, and Sima Yi said, "This is the work of Riverlands and Southland agents trying to turn an emperor and a loyal subject into mortal enemies so that they can exploit the chaos and attack us. I shall have to see the Son of Heaven and clarify this." Sima Yi ordered his army to withdraw. Then he went to Cao Rui's carriage and, bowing abjectly, tearfully addressed his sovereign: "Your late father entrusted you to me, and my thoughts could never be but wholly loyal. These slanders against me are the treachery of the Southland and the Riverlands. Grant me command of an expeditionary force, and I will defeat first Shu and then Wu to requite the late Emperor's and Your Majesty's grace and to manifest my loyalty."

Cao Rui, unsure what to do, made no decision. Hua Xin addressed the Emperor: "He should not have military authority. Relieve him of office and send him home at once." Accordingly, Cao Rui stripped Sima Yi of his office and ordered him back to his village. He gave Cao Xin command of the armed forces of Yong and Liang and returned to Luoyang.

* * *

Spies soon reported these events in the Riverlands, and Kongming received the news with delight. "I have long wanted to wage war against Wei," he said, "but could do nothing with Sima Yi leading the army in Yong and Liang. Now that he has fallen victim to this trap, my worries are over."

The next day the Second Emperor held court early in the day. Kongming

道。表曰:

　　臣亮言:先帝创业未半,而中道崩殂;今天下三分,益州罢敝,此诚危急存亡之秋也。然侍卫之臣,不懈于内;忠志之士,忘身于外者:盖追先帝之殊遇,欲报之于陛下也。诚宜开张圣听,以光先帝遗德,恢弘志士之气;不宜妄自菲薄,引喻失义,以塞忠谏之路也。宫中府中,俱为一体;陟罚臧否,不宜异同:若有作奸犯科,及为忠善者,宜付有司,论其刑赏,以昭陛下平明之治;不宜偏私,使内外异法也。侍中、侍郎郭攸之、费祎、董允等,此皆良实,志虑忠纯,是以先帝简拔以遗陛下:愚以为宫中之事,事无大小,悉以咨之,然后施行,必得裨补阙漏,有所广益。将军向宠,性行淑均,晓畅军事,试用之于昔日,先帝称之曰"能",是以众议举宠以为督:愚以为营中之事,事无大小,悉以咨之,必能使行阵和穆,优劣得所也。亲贤臣,远小人,此先汉所以兴隆也;亲小人,远贤臣,此后汉所以倾颓也。先帝在时,每与臣论此事,未尝不叹息痛恨于桓、灵

stepped forth and in front of the grand assembly submitted a memorial to the sovereign entitled "Petition on Taking the Field." It read:

Permit your servant, Liang, to observe: the late sovereign was taken from us while his life's work, the restoration of the Han, remained unfinished. Today, in a divided empire, our third, the province of Yizhou, war-worn and under duress, faces a season of crisis that threatens our very survival. Despite this, the officials at court persevere in their tasks, and loyal-minded officers throughout the realm dedicate themselves to you because one and all they cherish the memory of the exceptional treatment they enjoyed from the late sovereign and wish to repay it in service to Your Majesty.

Truly this is a time to widen your sagely audience in order to enhance the late Emperor's glorious virtue and foster the morale of your dedicated officers. It would be unworthy of Your Majesty to demean yourself by resorting to ill-chosen justifications that would block the avenues of loyal remonstrance.

The royal court and the ministerial administration constitute a single government.[9] Both must be judged by one standard. Those who do evil and violate the codes, as well as those who are loyal and good, must receive their due from the proper authorities. This will make manifest Your Majesty's fair and enlightened governance. Let no unseemly bias lead to different rules for the court and the administration.

Privy counselors and imperial attendants like Guo Youzhi, Fei Yi, and Dong Yun are all solid, reliable men, loyal of purpose, pure in motive. The late Emperor selected them for office so that they would serve Your Majesty after his demise. In my own humble opinion, consulting these men on palace affairs great or small before action is taken will prevent errors and shortcomings and maximize advantages. Xiang Chong, a general of fine character and fair-minded conduct, profoundly versed in military matters, proved himself in battle during the previous reign, and the late Emperor pronounced him capable. That is why the assembly has recommended him for overall command. In my humble opinion, General Xiang Chong should be consulted on all military matters large or small to ensure harmony in the ranks and the judicious use of personnel.[10]

The Former Han thrived because its emperors stayed close to worthy vassals and far from conniving courtiers. The opposite policy led the Later Han to ruin. Whenever the late Emperor discussed this problem with me, he decried the failings of Emperors Huan and Ling. Privy Coun-

也！侍中、尚书、长史、参军，此悉贞亮死节之臣也，愿陛下亲之、信之，则汉室之隆，可计日而待也。

臣本布衣，躬耕南阳，苟全性命于乱世，不求闻达于诸侯。先帝不以臣卑鄙，猥自枉屈，三顾臣于草庐之中，谘臣以当世之事，由是感激，遂许先帝以驱驰。后值倾覆，受任于败军之际，奉命于危难之间：尔来二十有一年矣。先帝知臣谨慎，故临崩寄臣以大事也。受命以来，夙夜忧虑，恐付托不效，以伤先帝之明；故五月渡泸，深入不毛。今南方已定，甲兵已足，当奖帅三军，北定中原，庶竭驽钝，攘除奸凶，兴复汉室，还于旧都：此臣所以报先帝而忠陛下之职分也。至于斟酌损益，进尽忠言，则攸之、祎、允之任也。愿陛下托臣以讨贼兴复之效，不效则治臣之罪，以告先帝之灵；若无兴复之言，则责攸之、祎、允等之咎，以彰其慢。陛下亦宜自谋，以谘诹善道，察纳雅言，深追先帝遗诏。臣不胜受恩感激！今当远离，临表涕泣，不知所云。

后主览表曰："相父南征，远涉艰难；方始回都，坐未安席；

selors Guo Youzhi and Fei Yi, Secretary Chen Zhen, Senior Adviser Zhang Yi, and Military Counselor Jiang Wan are all men of shining integrity and unshakable devotion. I beg Your Majesty to keep close to them and to trust them, for that will strengthen our hopes for the resurgence of the house of Han.

I began as a common man, toiling in my fields in Nanyang, doing what I could to keep body and soul together in an age of disorder and taking no interest in making a name for myself among the lords of the realm. Though it was beneath the dignity of the late Emperor to do so, he honored my thatched cottage to solicit my counsel on the events of the day. Grateful for his regard, I responded to his appeal and threw myself heart and soul into his service.

Hard times followed for the cause of the late Emperor. I assumed my duties at a critical moment for our defeated army, accepting assignment in a period of direst danger. Now twenty-one years have passed. The late Emperor always appreciated my meticulous caution and, as the end neared, placed his great cause in my hands. Since that moment, I have tormented myself night and day lest I prove unworthy of his trust and thus discredit his judgment.

That is why I crossed the River Lu in the summer heat and penetrated the barren lands of the Man. Now, the south subdued, our arms sufficing, it behooves me to marshal our soldiers to conquer the northern heartland and do my humble best to remove the hateful traitors, restore the house of Han, and return it to the former capital. This is the way I mean to honor my debt to the late Emperor and fulfill my duty to Your Majesty.

As for weighing the advantages of internal policy and making loyal recommendations to Your Majesty, that is the responsibility of Guo Youzhi, Fei Yi, and Dong Yun. My only desire is to obtain and execute your commission to chasten the traitors and restore the Han. Should I prove unfit, punish my offense and report it to the spirit of the late Emperor. If those three vassals fail to sustain Your Majesty's virtue, then their negligence should be publicized and censured.[11]

Your Majesty, take counsel with yourself and consult widely on the right course. Examine and adopt sound opinions, and never forget the last edict of the late Emperor. Overwhelmed with gratitude for the favor I have received from you, I now depart on a distant campaign. Blinded by my tears falling on this petition, I write I know not what.[12]

After reading the memorial, the Second Emperor said, "Prime minis-

今又欲北征，恐劳神思。"孔明曰："臣受先帝托孤之重，夙夜未尝有怠。今南方已平，可无内顾之忧；不就此时讨贼，恢复中原，更待何日？"忽班部中太史谯周出奏曰："臣夜观天象，北方旺气正盛，星曜倍明，未可图也。"乃顾孔明曰："丞相深明天文，何故强为？"孔明曰："天道变易不常，岂可拘执？吾今且驻军马于汉中，观其动静而后行。"谯周苦谏不从。于是孔明乃留郭攸之、董允、费祎等为侍中，总摄宫中之事。又留向宠为大将，总督御林军马；蒋琬为参军；张裔为长史，掌丞相府事；杜琼为谏议大夫；杜微、杨洪为尚书；孟光、来敏为祭酒；尹默、李譔为博士；郤正、费诗为秘书；谯周为太史：内外文武官僚一百余员，同理蜀中之事。

孔明受诏归府，唤诸将听令：前督部——镇北将军、领丞相司马、凉州刺史、都亭侯魏延；前军都督——领扶风太守张翼；牙门将——裨将军王平；后军领兵使——安汉将军、领建

ter and second father, your southern campaign was marked by ordeal and hardship, and you have still to settle down after your recent return. A northern campaign will strain you physically and mentally." Kongming replied, "My devotion to the late Emperor's charge to assist his heir remains undiminished. With the south pacified, we are free of internal troubles and must chasten the traitors and win back the north; this opportunity may never come again." Suddenly from the ranks Grand Historian Qiao Zhou stepped forth and addressed the Emperor, "Last night I was watching the heavenly correspondences: signs to the north suggest the height of vigor; the northern stars are doubly bright. This is no time to plan action there." Turning to Kongming, he went on, "Your Excellency has a deep knowledge of the constellations. Why do you persist?" Kongming answered, "The way of Heaven changes constantly. No one can cling to its patterns. I am going to post our forces in Hanzhong and observe the enemy's movements before advancing." Qiao Zhou's earnest objections were ignored.[13]

Kongming left Guo Youzhi, Dong Yun, and Fei Yi behind as privy counselors with authority over palace affairs. Xiang Chong remained as chief general with command of the Royal Guard. Jiang Wan was made military adviser. Zhang Yi, senior adviser, was put in charge of the affairs of the prime minister's office. Du Qiong became court counselor. Du Wei and Yang Hong were appointed to the Secretariat. Meng Guang and Lai Min were made libationers, Yin Mo and Li Zhuan scholars, Xi Zheng and Fei Shi secretaries, and Qiao Zhou became grand historian and archivist. Counting palace and administrative, civil and military personnel, there were over one hundred officials in charge of the affairs of the kingdom of Shu.[14]

2241

Kongming received the edict from the Emperor and returned to his quarters; he summoned his commanders and assigned them their commands.

> Forward command: General Wei Yan, controller of the North, commander of the Ministerial Forces, imperial inspector of Liangzhou, and lord of a Capital Precinct
>
> Chief inspector of the forward command: Zhang Ni, governor of Fufeng
>
> Garrison command: Subordinate General Wang Ping

宁太守李恢，副将——定远将军、领汉中太守吕义；兼管运粮左军领兵使——平北将军、陈仓侯马岱，副将——飞卫将军廖化；右军领兵使——奋威将军、博阳亭侯马忠、抚戎将军、关内侯张嶷；行中军师——车骑大将军、都乡侯刘琰；中监军——扬武将军邓芝；中参军——安远将军马谡；前将军——都亭侯袁绫；左将军——高阳侯吴懿；右将军——玄都侯高翔；后将军——安乐侯吴班；领长史——绥军将军杨仪；前将军——征南将军刘巴；前护军——偏将军、汉城亭侯许允；左护军——笃信中郎将丁咸；右护军——偏将军刘敏；后护军——典军中郎将官雝；行参军——昭武中郎将胡济；行参军——谏议将军阎晏；行参军——偏将军爨习；行参军——裨将军杜义，武略中郎将杜祺，绥戎都尉盛教；从事——武略中郎将樊岐；典军书记——樊建；丞相令史——董厥；帐前左护卫使——龙骧将

Rear command: General Li Hui, protector of the Han and governor of Jianning; and Li Hui's lieutenant, General Lü Yi, stabilizer of Remote Regions and governor of Hanzhong

Grain transport and command of the left army: General Who Calms the North Ma Dai, lord of Chencang; and Ma Dai's lieutenant, Flying Guard General Liao Hua

Command of the right army: General Who Exerts Might Ma Zhong, lord of Boyang precinct; and General Who Soothes the Barbarians Zhang Ni, honorary lord of the capital

Acting director of the central army: Chief General of Chariots and Cavalry Liu Yan, lord of Duxiang

Central military inspector: General Who Flourishes Armed Might Deng Zhi

Adviser of the central army: General Ma Su, protector of Distant Regions

Forward general: Yuan Lin, lord of a Capital Precinct

Left general: Wu Yi, lord of Gaoyang

Right general: Gao Xiang, lord of Xuandu

Rear general: Wu Ban, lord of Anle

Office of senior adviser: General Who Guides the Army Yang Yi

Forward general: General Liu Ba, conqueror of the South

Forward army personnel officer: Subordinate Commander Xu Yun, lord of Hancheng precinct

Left army personnel officer: Dedicated Imperial Corps Commander Ding Xian

Right army personnel officer: Subordinate General Liu Min

Rear army personnel officer: Imperial Corps Commander Directing the Army Guan Yong

Acting military counselor: Imperial Corps Commander Who Manifests Armed Might Hu Ji

Acting military counselor: General Who Remonstrates Yan Yan

Acting military counselor: Subordinate General Cuan Xi

Acting military counselors: Lieutenant General Du Yi, Imperial Corps Commander for Strategy Du Qi, and Provincial Commander Who Guides Foreign Peoples Sheng Bo

Army aides: Imperial Corps Commander for Strategy Fan Qi

Secretary for the army director: Fan Jian

Prime minister's cheif clerk: Dong Jue

Left guard of the command tent: Prancing Charger General Guan Xing

2243

军关兴；右护卫使——虎翼将军张苞。——以上一应官员，都随着平北大都督、丞相、武乡侯、领益州牧、知内外事诸葛亮。分拨已定，又檄李严等守川口以拒东吴。选定建兴五年春三月丙寅日，出师伐魏。忽帐下一老将，厉声而进曰："我虽年迈，尚有廉颇之勇，马援之雄。此二古人皆不服老，何故不用我耶？"众视之，乃赵云也。孔明曰："吾自平南回都，马孟起病故，吾甚惜之，以为折一臂也。今将军年纪已高，倘稍有参差，动摇一世英名，减却蜀中锐气。"云厉声曰："吾自随先帝以来，临阵不退，遇敌则先。大丈夫得死于疆场者，幸也，吾何恨焉？愿为前部先锋！"孔明再三苦劝不住。云曰："如不教我为先锋，就撞死于阶下！"孔明曰："将军既要为先锋，须得一人同去——"言未尽，一人应曰："某虽不才，愿助老将军先引一军前去破敌。"孔明视之，乃邓芝也。孔明大喜，即拨精兵五千，副将十员，随赵云、邓芝去讫。孔明出师，后主引百官送于北门外十里。孔明辞了后主，旌旗蔽野，戈戟如林，率军望汉中迤逦进发。

Right guard of the command tent: Winged Tiger General Zhang Bao

All of the above-mentioned officials were under the authority of Prime Minister Zhuge Liang, first field marshal for the pacification of the north, lord of Wuxiang, and protector of the Riverlands with responsibility for domestic and foreign affairs.

When Kongming had completed his dispositions, he sent instructions to Li Yan and other commanders defending the gateways to the Riverlands to bar any Southland forces. Then he selected the third cyclical day of the third month of Jian Xing 5 to commence the expedition against the north.[15] Suddenly, a veteran commander came forward in the command tent and said sternly, "Though advanced in years, I still have the valor of a Lian Po and the heroism of Ma Yuan, two men of antiquity who did not accept the limitations of age. Why have you passed me by?" The assembly turned to Zhao Zilong. Kongming said, "Since our return from the southern campaign, Ma Chao has died of illness. I miss him as I would miss a lost brother. Now you, General, are advanced in years. If anything should go amiss and affect your heroic name, morale throughout the Riverlands would suffer." Zhao Zilong responded impatiently, "Since becoming the late Emperor's follower I have never shied from battle. I have always been the first to meet the enemy. For a self-respecting warrior to die on the field is an honor, not a cause for regret. I volunteer for the vanguard of the forward army."

2245

Kongming was unable to dissuade him. "If you refuse me," Zhao Zilong went on, "I will dash out my brains before your eyes." "To serve in the vanguard," Kongming said, "you will need a backup." Before Kongming could finish, a man said, "Though of little ability, I volunteer to help the veteran general defeat the enemy." Delighted by the offer, Kongming turned to the speaker: it was Deng Zhi. Next, Kongming selected five thousand crack troops and ten lieutenant commanders to back up Zhao Zilong and Deng Zhi.

When Kongming went forth with the main army, the Second Emperor and his entire court escorted him ten *li* beyond the north gate. Kongming took leave of his sovereign and led the army toward Hanzhong. His flags and banners covered the plain; his spears and halberds stood thick as a forest.[16]

　　却说边庭探知此事,报入洛阳。是日曹睿设朝,近臣奏曰:"边官报称:诸葛亮率领大兵三十余万,出屯汉中,令赵云、邓芝为前部先锋,引兵入境。"睿大惊,问群臣曰:"谁可为将,以退蜀兵?"忽一人应声而出曰:"臣父死于汉中,切齿之恨,未尝得报。今蜀兵犯境,臣愿引本部猛将,更乞陛下赐关西之兵,前往破蜀:上为国家效力,下报父仇,臣万死不恨!"众视之,乃夏侯渊之子夏侯楙也。楙字子休;其性最急,又最吝;自幼嗣与夏侯惇为子。后夏侯渊为黄忠所斩,曹操怜之,以女清河公主招楙为驸马,因此朝中钦敬。虽掌兵权,未尝临阵。当时自请出征,曹睿即命为大都督,调关西诸路军马前去迎敌。司徒王朗谏曰:"不可。夏侯驸马素不曾经战,今付以大任,非其所宜。更兼诸葛亮足智多谋,深通韬略,不可轻敌。"夏侯楙叱曰:"司徒莫非结连诸葛亮,欲为内应耶? 吾自幼从父学习韬略,深通兵法。汝何欺我年幼? 吾若不生擒诸葛亮,誓不回见天子!"王朗等皆不敢言。夏侯楙辞了魏主,星夜到长安,调关西诸路军马

* * *

Wei border stations, informed of these developments, sent reports to Luoyang. They arrived as Cao Rui was holding court; his attendants addressed him: "Border officers report that Zhuge Liang has set out with his host — more than three hundred thousand strong now camped in Hanzhong — and that Zhao Zilong and Deng Zhi have already entered our territory." Cao Rui was astonished and asked his officials, "Who will take the lead in driving off the Riverlands forces?" One man rose in response and said, "Since my father's death in the fighting in Hanzhong, my own undying hatred has remained unsatisfied. If Riverlands troops have crossed our borders, I volunteer to lead the valiant commanders of my own unit — to which I pray Your Majesty will add troops from west of the pass — in destroying the enemy. To die serving the dynasty and striving to avenge my father will be to die with no regret."

The assembly turned to Xiahou Mao (Zixiu), son of Xiahou Yuan.[17] Xiahou Mao had a fiery temper. He was also extremely stingy. As a young boy he was adopted by Xiahou Dun. Later, when Xiahou Yuan was killed by Huang Zhong, Cao Cao was moved to invite him to become an imperial son-in-law through marriage to his daughter, Princess Qinghe. Thus, he enjoyed the court's respect and had a military command though he had never seen battle.

2247

In response to Xiahou Mao's offer to lead the expedition, Cao Rui appointed him first field marshal. Cao Rui also ordered several armies in the region west of the pass to proceed against the Riverlanders. Minister of the Interior Wang Lang objected, however. "This will not do," he said. "Imperial Son-in-Law Xiahou has no experience in the field and should not be given so important a command. Moreover, Your Majesty should be cautious about engaging Zhuge Liang; he's a shrewd strategist thoroughly versed in the ways of war." Xiahou Mao denounced his critic, saying, "I'd hate to think that the minister of the interior is in league with Zhuge Liang, or perhaps serving as a collaborator. As a child I studied warfare by my father's side. It is an art I know perfectly well. Will you make fun of my age? If I do not take Zhuge Liang alive, I vow never to return to the Son of Heaven!" Wang Lang and the others dared say no more.

Xiahou Mao took leave of the ruler of Wei and went immediately to

二十余万，来敌孔明。

正是：

　　　　欲秉白旄麾将士，却教黄吻掌兵权。

未知胜负如何，且看下文分解。

Chang'an to see to the transfer of two hundred thousand men for the war with Kongming. Indeed:

Given the white banner that directs the army,
Could this callow youth command his forces on the field?

Could he conquer the warriors of the west?

Read on.

汉英经典文库

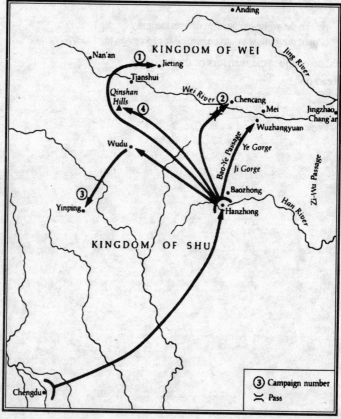

MAP 10. Kongming's northern campaigns. Source: Liu Chunfan, *Zhuge Liang zhuan* (Beijing: Zhongguo qingnian chubanshe, 1986), p. 129.

稍甲龍身
軒五須

西泠布衣

第九十二回

赵子龙力斩五将　诸葛亮智取三城

　　却说孔明率兵前至沔阳，经过马超坟墓，乃令其弟马岱挂孝，孔明亲自祭之。祭毕，回到寨中，商议进兵。忽哨马报道："魏主曹睿遣驸马夏侯楙，调关中诸路军马，前来拒敌。"魏延上帐献策曰："夏侯楙乃膏粱子弟，懦弱无谋。延愿得精兵五千，取路出褒中，循秦岭以东，当子午谷而投北，不过十日，可到安长。夏侯楙若闻某骤至，必然弃城望横门邸阁而走。某却从东方而来，丞相可大驱士马，自斜谷而进：如此行之，则咸阳以西，一举可定也。"孔明笑曰："此非万全之计也。汝欺中原无好人物，倘有人进言，于山僻中以兵截杀，非惟五千人受害，亦大伤锐气。决不可用。"魏延又曰："丞相兵从大路进发，彼必尽起关中之兵，于路迎敌：则旷日持久，何时而得中原？"孔明曰：

Chapter 92

Zhao Zilong Slaughters Five Generals
Zhuge Liang Snares Three Cities

Kongming advanced to Mianyang.[1] On the way he had come to the tomb of Ma Chao and offered sacrifice to his memory; attired in mourning, Ma Dai, Ma Chao's younger cousin, had assisted. After the ceremony Kongming had returned to camp to plan the next phase of the invasion.

Mounted scouts brought Kongming fresh news: "The ruler of Wei, Cao Rui, has sent Imperial Son-in-Law Xiahou Mao[2] against us; several field armies, mobilized in the land within the passes, support him." Wei Yan went directly to the command tent and proposed a plan: "Xiahou Mao, the pampered child of a wealthy family, is an incapable coward. I request five thousand crack troops to follow the route out of Baozhong and eastward along the Qinling Mountains. Once I turn north at Zi-Wu Pass, I'll be ten days from Chang'an. When Xiahou Mao learns of this swift approach, he will vacate the city, head for the military depots at Broad Gate to the northwest, and flee. I will move in from the east, and Your Excellency can advance in force from Ye Gorge. This way we can take everything west of Xianyang[3] in a single action."

Kongming smiled and said, "This method leaves too much to chance. You do the northerners an injustice to say they have no capable men. If someone there were to propose intercepting you in a remote part of the mountains, your five thousand troops could be lost and the morale of the whole army gravely impaired. We cannot adopt your plan." Wei Yan responded: "If Your Excellency's troops advance on the main road, the enemy will be able to mobilize all its forces within the passes to slow us down. With time working against us, we will never take the northern heartland." Kongming answered, "I am going to take the flat road from Longyou and move on from there, as accepted military tactics dictate, for

"吾从陇右取平坦大路,依法进兵,何忧不胜!"遂不用魏延之计。魏延怏怏不悦。孔明差人令赵云进兵。

　　却说夏侯楙在长安聚集诸路军马。时有西凉大将韩德,善使开山大斧,有万夫不当之勇,引西羌诸路兵八万到来;见了夏侯楙,楙重赏之,就遣为先锋。德有四子,皆精通武艺,弓马过人:长子韩瑛,次子韩瑶,三子韩琼,四子韩琪。韩德带四子并西羌兵八万,取路至凤鸣山,正遇蜀兵。两阵对圆。韩德出马,四子列于两边。德厉声大骂曰:"反国之贼,安敢犯吾境界!"赵云大怒,挺枪纵马,单搦韩德交战。长子韩瑛,跃马来迎;战不三合,被赵云一枪刺死于马下。次子韩瑶见之,纵马挥刀来战。赵云施逞旧日虎威,抖擞精神迎战。瑶抵敌不住。三子韩琼,急挺方天戟骤马前来夹攻。云全然不惧,枪法不乱。四子韩琪,见二兄战云不下,也纵马抡两口日月刀而来,围住赵云。云在中央独战三将。少时,韩琪中枪落马,韩阵中偏将急出救去。云拖枪便走。韩琼按戟,急取弓箭射之,连放三箭,皆被云用枪拨落。琼大怒,仍绰方天戟纵马赶来;却被云一箭射中面门,落马而死。韩瑶纵马举宝刀便砍赵云。云弃枪于地,闪过

2254

that will assure victory." And so — to Wei Yan's dismay — Kongming set aside his plan and issued Zhao Zilong the order to advance.[4]

* * *

In Chang'an, Xiahou Mao had gathered several armies; one of their leaders, a ranking general from Xiliang, was Han De, an expert at wielding a "mountain-splitting battle-axe" and a man of supreme courage. He had arrived with eighty thousand Qiang troops and presented himself to Xiahou Mao, who rewarded him richly and sent him to the vanguard. Han De had four sons, all masters of the martial arts and superior in horsemanship and archery. The eldest was Han Ying, the second Han Yao, the third Han Qiong, and the fourth Han Qi. Han De and his four sons together with their eighty thousand Qiang troops took the road to Phoenix Call Mountain, where they encountered the Riverlands army.

The two armies consolidated their formations. Han De rode forth flanked by his four sons. "Traitor to the dynasty!" Han De shouted, "how dare you violate our border?" A wrathful Zhao Zilong raised his spear and raced forth, challenging Han De to single combat. The eldest son, Han Ying, charged out to meet him. The clash was brief. Zhao Zilong thrust his man through, and he dropped from his horse. Next Han Yao, the second son, took the field, flourishing his sword.

Zhao Zilong displayed the ferocity and power for which he was famed, and Han Yao fell back, shaken by Zilong's spirit and energy. The third son, Han Qiong, charged out with double-bladed halberd to assist his brother. Zhao Zilong was utterly unfazed, and his spear handling never missed a stroke. The fourth son, Han Qi, seeing that his two brothers could not subdue Zhao Zilong, charged onto the field wheeling a pair of sun-and-moon swords. The three surrounded Zhao Zilong, who fought unaided from the center. When Han Qi dropped wounded from his horse and a lieutenant commander rode out from Han De's line to save the fallen general, Zhao Zilong withdrew, his spear raised behind him.

Han Qiong put his halberd by and shot three arrows in swift succession, but Zhao Zilong deflected them neatly with his spear. Furious, Han Qiong picked up his halberd again and gave chase. But a single arrow from Zhao Zilong caught him in the forehead, and he fell dead. Han Yao now came forth, his sword carried high to cut down Zhao Zilong. Zhao

宝刀,生擒韩瑶归阵,复纵马取枪杀过阵来。韩德见四子皆丧于赵云之手,肝胆皆裂,先走入阵去。西凉兵素知赵云之名,今见其英勇如昔,谁敢交锋?赵云马到处,阵阵倒退。赵云匹马单枪,往来冲突,如入无人之境。后人有诗赞曰:

忆昔常山赵子龙,年登七十建奇功。

独诛四将来冲阵,犹似当阳救主雄。

邓芝见赵云大胜,率蜀兵掩杀,西凉兵大败而走。韩德险被赵云擒住,弃甲步行而逃。云与邓芝收军回寨。芝贺曰:"将军寿已七旬,英勇如昨。今日阵前力斩四将,世所罕有!"云曰:"丞相以吾年迈,不肯见用,吾故聊以自表耳。"遂差人解韩瑶,申报捷书,以达孔明。

却说韩德引败军回见夏侯楙,哭告其事。楙自统兵来迎赵云。探马报入蜀寨,说夏侯楙引兵到。云上马绰枪,引千余军,就凤鸣山前摆成阵势。当日,夏侯楙戴金盔,坐白马,手提大砍刀,立在门旗之下。见赵云跃马挺枪,往来驰骋,楙欲自战。韩德曰:"杀吾四子之仇,如何不报!"纵马轮开山大斧,直取赵云。云奋怒挺枪来迎;战不三合,枪起处,刺死韩德于马下,急

Zilong threw down his spear and drew his own sword; he captured Han Yao alive and took him back to his line. Then he galloped out again and took a heavy toll of the enemy with his spear.

Han De, seeing his four sons lost at Zhao Zilong's hands, fled in panic back to his line. The Qiang troops had long known Zhao Zilong's name and had now seen that his splendid valor was undiminished. Who had the courage to face him? Wherever Zhao Zilong struck, the enemy gave way. A single mounted warrior, Zhao Zilong plunged here and thrust there as if moving through undefended land. Later a poet left these lines in his praise:

> Who could forget Changshan's Zhao Zilong,
> Winning his laurels even at three-score-ten?
> He breaks the enemy line — four generals down! —
> Unchanged since he saved his lord at Dangyang town.

Seeing Zhao Zilong's triumph, Deng Zhi led the Riverlands troops in a sudden attack on the Qiang, who fled in defeat. Barely escaping Zhao Zilong, Han De threw down his armor and ran off. Zhao Zilong and Deng Zhi rallied their men and returned to camp. Deng congratulated Zhao Zilong: "General, at three-score-ten, you still have the brilliance and the courage of the old days. Your exploits before the lines are something rare in this age." Zhao Zilong replied, "His Excellency wouldn't use me because of my years; I wanted to show him what I could do." He detailed a man to take custody of Han Yao, and he reported the victory to Kongming.[5]

* * *

2257

Han De led his troops back to Xiahou Mao and reported the painful defeat. Xiahou Mao took command himself and went to oppose Zhao Zilong; Riverlands scouts reported his arrival. Zhao Zilong, spear held high, brought a thousand men to Phoenix Call Mountain and deployed them in front. That day Xiahou Mao wore a gilded helmet and rode a white horse. Carrying a large saber, he stood beneath the banners at the entrance to his line. The sight of Zhao Zilong, spear raised, charging back and forth on his prancing horse, stirred the fight in him. But Han De said, "I shall avenge my four sons!" And he rode straight for Zhao Zilong, flourishing his mountain-splitting battle-axe. With furious energy Zhao

拨马直取夏侯楙。楙慌忙闪入本阵。邓芝驱兵掩杀，魏兵又折一阵，退十余里下寨。楙连夜与众将商议曰："吾久闻赵云之名，未尝见面；今日年老，英雄尚在，方信当阳长坂之事。似此无人可敌，如之奈何？"参军程武——乃程昱之子也——进言曰："某料赵云有勇无谋，不足为虑。来日都督再引兵出，先伏两军于左右；都督临阵先退，诱赵云到伏兵处；都督却登山指挥四面军马，重叠围住，云可擒矣。"楙从其言，遂遣董禧引三万军伏于左，薛则引三万军伏于右：二人埋伏已定。

次日，夏侯楙复整金鼓旗幡，率兵而进。赵云、邓芝出迎。芝在马上谓赵云曰："昨夜魏兵大败而走，今日复来，必有诈也。老将军防之。"子龙曰："量此乳臭小儿，何足道哉！吾今日必当擒之！"便跃马而出。魏将潘遂出迎，战不三合，拨马便走。赵云赶去，魏阵中八员将一齐来迎。放过夏侯楙先走，八将陆续奔走。赵云乘势追杀，邓芝引兵继进。赵云深入重地，只听得四面喊声大震。邓芝急收军退回，左有董禧，右有薛则，两路兵杀到。邓芝兵少，不能解救。赵云被困在垓心，东冲西突，魏

Zilong raised his spear and met his foe. The fight was brief. The spear went up and then sank into Han De. He fell dead from his horse. Zhao Zilong next made swiftly for Xiahou Mao, who ducked back into his line.

Under fresh attacks directed by Deng Zhi, the Wei troops suffered further losses. They fell back ten *li* and camped. Xiahou Mao hastily took counsel with his commanders. "Though Zhao Zilong's name had long been known to me," he said, "I had never seen him face-to-face. Now he is old; but seeing the hero in action, I can well believe the legend of his triumph at Steepslope in Dangyang. It seems that no one is his match. What shall we do?" The military adviser Cheng Wu (the son of Cheng Yu) put forth a proposal: "Zhao Zilong has courage, but no strategy; he poses no real threat. Tomorrow, Chief Commander, lead the troops out again after two flank contingents have been placed in ambush, then retreat to entice Zhao Zilong into the trap. You, Chief Commander, can climb a hill and direct the forces surrounding the enemy. As the multiple rings close around them, Zhao Zilong will be taken." Xiahou Mao adopted this plan and sent Dong Xi with thirty thousand to the left, and Xue Ze with another thirty thousand to the right; the two established their ambush positions.

The next day Xiahou Mao, gongs, drums, flags, and streamers all in order, led forth his army. Zhao Zilong and Deng Zhi met him in the field. Deng Zhi on horseback turned to Zhao Zilong and said, "Yesterday the northern troops fled after a major defeat. Their return today must be a trick. Take care, old veteran!" "The babe had the stink of mother's milk about him," Zhao Zilong replied. "It is nothing. I will take him today." With that he raced ahead.

The Wei general Pan Sui met him in combat but fled after a brief clash. Zhao Zilong gave chase. Eight commanders from the northern side rode forth to engage him. They let Xiahou Mao run by first, then one after another the eight followed in his tracks. Zhao Ziling, riding on the momentum, closed in for the kill, Deng Zhi following close behind.

When Zhao Zilong entered the ambush site, he heard thunderous shouts on every side. Deng Zhi urgently gathered his men and retreated as Dong Xi and Xue Ze fell upon Zhao Zilong's men from two sides. Deng Zhi had too few troops to rescue Zhao Zilong. Caught in the middle, he

兵越厚。时云手下止有千余人，杀到山坡之下，只见夏侯楙在
山上指挥三军。赵云投东则望东指，投西则望西指：因此赵云
不能突围——乃引兵杀上山来。半山中擂木炮石打将下来，不
能上山。赵云从辰时杀至酉时，不得脱走，只得下马少歇，且待
月明再战。却才卸甲而坐，月光方出，忽四下火光冲天，鼓声大
震，矢石如雨，魏兵杀到，皆叫曰："赵云早降！"云急上马迎
敌。四面军马渐渐逼近，八方弩箭交射甚急，人马皆不能向
前。云仰天叹曰："吾不服老，死于此地矣！"忽东北角上喊声大
起，魏兵纷纷乱窜：一彪军杀到，为首大将持丈八点钢矛，马项
下挂一颗人头。云视之，乃张苞也。苞见了赵云，言曰："丞相恐
老将军有失，特遣某引五千兵接应。闻老将军被困，故杀透重
围。正遇魏将薛则拦路，被某杀之。"云大喜，即与张苞杀出西
北角来。只见魏兵弃戈奔走：一彪军从外呐喊杀入，为首大将
提偃月青龙刀，手挽人头。云视之，乃关兴也。兴曰："奉丞相之
命，恐老将军有失，特引五千兵前来接应。却才阵上逢着魏将
董禧，被吾一刀斩之，枭首在此。丞相随后便到也。"云曰："二

fought fiercely on all sides; but the Wei lines only grew more dense. At the same time Zhao Zilong had only a thousand men in his command. He fought his way to the slope of a hill, on top of which he saw Xiahou Mao directing the northern army, pointing east when he headed east, west when he headed west. Zhao Zilong could not break through the enemy lines, and so he headed uphill.

Zhao Zilong was midway up the slope when timber and other missiles come hurtling down, checking his advance. Held down from early morning until dusk, he dismounted, intending to rest and wait for the moon to rise before resuming the struggle. Zhao Zilong was sitting without his armor as the moon came up. Suddenly from four sides flames shot skyward; drums roared in the air, and arrows and stones came raining down on him again. The Wei soldiers closed in, shouting, "Surrender now, Zhao!" Zhao Zilong swiftly mounted and took on the foe. But on all sides the northmen pressed closer, and crossbow bolts flew toward him with increasing frequency from every corner. His forces pinned, Zhao Zilong looked up and sighed, "I chose not to retire, and now it is over for me!"

Suddenly from the northeast voices rang out in the air; the northern soldiers began to break and scatter as a band of warriors attacked. Leading them was a commander with an eighteen-span spear in his grasp and a human head hanging from his horse's neck. It was Zhang Bao! Seeing Zhao Zilong, he said, "His Excellency sensed something might go wrong, General, and sent me with five thousand men to support you. When I heard you were in trouble, I cut through the encirclement and slew the Wei general, Xue Ze, who was blocking the road." Zhao Zilong was overjoyed. He and Zhang Bao cut their way out of the northwest corner.

The two watched amazed as the Wei troops flung down their spears and fled before another band of soldiers that was outside the enemy line and cutting their way in, shouting fiercely. The general at their head wielded a crescent-moon blade, Green Dragon; a human head swung from his free hand; it was Guan Xing. "The prime minister charged me to bring five thousand here in case the veteran general ran into trouble and needed support," Guan Xing said. "Just now," he went on, "I met up with the Wei general Dong Xi and cut him down. This is his head. His Excellency is close behind and should be arriving momentarily." "The extraordinary

2261

将军已建奇功，何不趁今日擒住夏侯楙，以定大事？"张苞闻言，遂引兵去了。兴曰："我也干功去。"遂亦引兵去了。云回顾左右曰："他两个是吾子侄辈，尚且争先干功；吾乃国家上将，朝廷旧臣，反不如此小儿耶？吾当舍老命以报先帝之恩！"于是引兵来捉夏侯楙。当夜三路兵夹攻，大破魏军一阵。邓芝引兵接应，杀得尸横遍野，血流成河。夏侯楙乃无谋之人，更兼年幼，不曾经战，见军大乱，遂引帐下骁将百余人，望南安郡而走。众军因见无主，尽皆逃窜。兴、苞二将闻夏侯楙望南安郡去了，连夜赶来。楙走入城中，令紧闭城门，驱兵守御。兴、苞二人赶到，将城围住；赵云随后也到：三面攻打。少时，邓芝亦引兵到。一连围了十日，攻打不下。忽报丞相留后军住沔阳，左军屯阳平，右军屯石城，自引中军来到。赵云、邓芝、关兴、张苞皆来拜问孔明，说连日攻城不下。

孔明遂乘小车亲到城边周围看了一遍，回寨升帐而坐。众将环立听令。孔明曰："此郡壕深城峻，不易攻也。吾正事不在此城，汝等如只久攻，倘魏兵分道而出，以取汉中，吾军危矣。"邓芝曰："夏侯楙乃魏之驸马，若擒此人，胜斩百将。今困于此，岂可弃之而去？"孔明曰："吾自有计。——此处西连天水郡，北

service you two generals have rendered," Zhao Zilong said, "now gives us the opportunity to capture Xiahou Mao and achieve our goal. What do you say?" At these words Zhang Bao started off with his band, and Guan Xing followed, saying, "I intend to distingusih myself as well."

Turning to his attendants, Zhao Zilong said, "If those two nephews of mine thirst for fame, how can a senior general of the royal house like me, a venerable vassal of the court, show any less zeal? What do I care for the days left to me, if I can requite the love of the former Emperor!" So saying, Zhao Zilong joined the effort to catch Xiahou Mao.

That night the three armies attacked and defeated the northern troops in battle. Deng Zhi joined the fighting, which went on until the field was strewn with corpses and drenched with blood. Xiahou Mao was not a resourceful man. Young and inexperienced in war, he responded to the rout of his forces by fleeing to Nan'an district with a hundred or more of the valiant cavaliers under him, whereupon the mass of Wei soldiers, left leaderless, scurried from the field themselves.

Zhang Bao and Guan Xing followed Xiahou Mao to Nan'an. Entering the city, Xiahou Mao sealed the gates and posted guards. When Guan Xing and Zhang Bao arrived, they surrounded the city. Zhao Zilong arrived shortly after, and the three generals besieged Nan'an on three sides. In a short while Deng Zhi too reached Nan'an. The siege went on for ten days, but the defenders continued to hold out. Suddenly it was reported that the prime minister had come with the central army after leaving the rear army in Mianyang, the left army in Yangping, and the right army in Shicheng. Zhao Zilong, Deng Zhi, Guan Xing, and Zhang Bao came to receive Kongming and discuss their failure to take the city.

Kongming went in a small carriage to the city wall and examined the situation closely. Then he returned to his tent and seated himself. The commanders stood in a circle around him, awaiting orders. Kongming said, "Its deep moat and steep walls make this city difficult to attack. In any event, Nan'an is not my main concern. If you remain here too long, I am afraid the Wei will take Hanzhong by other routes and endanger our forces." Deng Zhi protested, "But Xiahou Mao is an imperial son-in-law. His capture would be worth more to us than beheading a hundred of their commanders. How can we let him go when we have him?" "I have an

抵安定郡：二处太守，不知何人？"探卒答曰："天水太守马遵，安定太守崔谅。"孔明大喜，乃唤魏延受计，如此如此；又唤关兴、张苞受计，如此如此；又唤心腹军士二人受计，如此行之。各将领命，引兵而去。孔明却在南安城外，令军运柴草堆于城下，口称烧城。魏兵闻知，皆大笑不惧。

　　却说安定太守崔谅，在城中闻蜀兵围了南安，困住夏侯楙，十分慌惧，即点军马约共四千，守住城池。忽见一人自正南而来，口称有机密事。崔谅唤入问之，答曰："某是夏侯都督帐下心腹将裴绪。今奉都督将令，特来求救于天水、安定二郡。南安甚急，每日城上纵火为号，专望二郡救兵，并不见到；因复差某杀出重围，来此告急。可星夜起兵为外应。都督若见二郡兵到，却开城门接应也。"谅曰："有都督文书否？"绪贴肉取出，汗已湿透；略教一视，急令手下换了乏马，便出城望天水而去。不二日，又有报马到，告天水太守已起兵救援南安去了，教安定早早接应。崔谅与府官商议。多官曰："若不去救，失了南安，送了夏侯驸马，皆我两郡之罪也：只得救之。"谅即点起人马，离城而去，只留文官守城。崔谅提兵向南安大路进发，遥望见火

idea," Kongming answered. "West of here is Tianshui. To the north, Anding. Who are the governors of these two districts?" A spy replied, "Ma Zun is governor of Tianshui, Cui Liang of Anding." Delighted, Kongming summoned Wei Yan and gave him certain instructions. Next, he called Guan Xing and Zhang Bao to give them their instructions. Last, he called two trusted officers and instructed them. Every commander led his men off to carry out his assignment. Meanwhile, Kongming remained outside the walls of Nan'an, ordering the soldiers to heap up twigs and dry grass at the base of the wall and to proclaim that they were going to burn the city. Inside, the Wei troops laughed bravely at the threat.

Cui Liang, governor of Anding, however, was apprehensive about the Riverlands siege of Nan'an and Xiahou Mao's plight. Accordingly, he detailed four thousand men to defend his own city. Suddenly a man arrived from a southerly direction, claiming to have secret information. Questioned by the governor, the man said, "I am Pei Xu, a confidential agent for Chief Commander Xiahou Mao. My orders are to seek the assistance of Tianshui and your city of Anding for the emergency in Nan'an. Every day from the wall we have signaled with fire and have anticipated relief from the two district towns, but nothing has come. I have been sent through the lines to report our condition to you. Raise an army at once to assist us. If the chief commander sees troops from the two towns, he will open the gates and join the battle too." "Do you have a document from the chief commander?" Cui Liang asked. Pei Xu produced a letter, now soaked in sweat after being held against his skin. He let the governor read it quickly and then headed for Tianshui on a fresh horse.

The second day another rider came to announce that the governor of Tianshui had sent troops to relieve Nan'an, and he called for swift assistance from Anding. Cui Liang conferred with his ministers, who argued, "If we send no relief, we will lose Nan'an, and the imperial son-in-law will be doomed. Our two towns will have to answer for it. We have no choice." Cui Liang consequently mustered a force and, leaving Anding guarded by civilian officials, set out on the main road for Nan'an. He saw flames rising into the sky in the distance and urged his force to make haste.

光冲天，催兵星夜前进。离南安尚有五十余里，忽闻前后喊声大震，哨马报道："前面关兴截住去路，背后张苞杀来！"安定之兵，四下逃窜。谅大惊，乃领手下百余人，往小路死战得脱，奔回安定。方到城壕边，城上乱箭射下来。蜀将魏延在城上叫曰："吾已取了城也！何不早降？"原来魏延扮作安定军，黄夜赚开城门，蜀兵尽入，因此得了安定。

　　崔谅慌投天水郡来。行不到一程，前面一彪军摆开。大旗之下，一人纶巾羽扇，道袍鹤氅，端坐于车上。谅视之，乃孔明也，急拨回马走。关兴、张苞两路兵追到，只叫："早降！"崔谅见四面皆是蜀兵，不得已遂降，同归大寨。孔明以上宾相待。孔明曰："南安太守与足下交厚否？"谅曰："此人乃杨阜之族弟杨陵也；与某邻郡，交契甚厚。"孔明曰："今欲烦足下入城，说杨陵擒夏侯楙，可乎？"谅曰："丞相若令某去，可暂退军马，容某入城说之。"孔明从其言，即时传令，教四面军马各退二十里下寨。崔谅匹马到城边叫开城门，入到府中，与杨陵礼毕，细言其事。陵曰："我等受魏主大恩，安忍背之？可将计就计而行。"遂引崔谅到夏侯楙处，备细说知。楙曰："当用何计？"杨陵曰："只

When Cui Liang came within fifty *li* of Nan'an, he suddenly heard a great tumult both before and behind him. Mounted scouts reported, "Guan Xing has cut off the road ahead. Zhang Bao is coming from behind." The Anding troops fled in fear. Cui Liang panicked; he led a hundred of his own men in retreat, and by desperate fighting they managed to flee to Anding by back roads. But when they reached the city wall, they were greeted by barrages of arrows. Wei Yan, the Riverlands general, shouted down, "Your city is in my hands! Surrender at once." Wei Yan had disguised his troops as Anding men and in the dead of the night had fooled the guards into opening the gate to them. The Riverlanders had then entered and taken the town.

In desperation Cui Liang fled toward Tianshui. But before he had made one stage of the march, he found the road ahead barred by a band of soldiers holding a broad banner aloft. Beneath it was a carriage carrying a man, sitting poised, with bound hair and a feather fan, a Taoist robe and a crane-feather cloak. Recognizing Kongming, Cui Liang turned and fled. Guan Xing and Zhang Bao pursued with their men, calling out, "Surrender now!" Cui Liang, encircled now by Riverlands troops, could only comply, and he returned with Guan Xing and Zhang Bao to the main camp.

Kongming treated Cui Liang as an honored guest and said to him, "The governor of Nan'an and you are close friends, I believe?" "Governor Yang Ling is a cousin of Yang Fu. The governor is from the neighboring district. Our relations are extremely close," Cui Liang responded. Kongming continued, "I would trouble Your Honor to go into Nan'an and convince Yang Ling to seize Xiahou Mao. Is it possible?" "If Your Excellency orders me to go," Cui Liang answered, "pull back your troops for the time being, and I will go into the city to persuade him." Kongming approved and immediately ordered all contingents to withdraw twenty *li* and camp.

Cui Liang rode to the wall of Nan'an and was admitted into the city. He presented himself before the governor and explained the situation fully. Yang Ling said, "We cannot turn against the ruler of Wei whose favor we have enjoyed. Let's fight fire with fire." Yang Ling had Cui Liang inform Xiahou Mao of the circumstances. Xiahou Mao responded,

推某献城门，赚蜀兵入，却就城中杀之。"

崔谅依计而行，出城见孔明，说："杨陵献城门，放大军入城，以擒夏侯楙。杨陵本欲自捉，因手下勇士不多，未敢轻动。"孔明曰："此事至易：今有足下原降兵百余人，于内暗藏蜀将扮作安定军马，带入城去，先伏于夏侯楙府下；却暗约杨陵，待半夜之时，献开城门，里应外合。"崔谅暗思："若不带蜀将去，恐孔明生疑。且带入去，就内先斩之，举火为号，赚孔明入来；杀之可也。"因此应允。孔明嘱曰："吾遣亲信将关兴、张苞随足下先去，只推救军杀入城中，以安夏侯楙之心；但举火，吾当亲入城去擒之。"时值黄昏，关兴、张苞受了孔明密计，披挂上马，各执兵器，杂在安定军中，随崔谅来到南安城下。杨陵在城下撑起悬空板，倚定护心栏，问曰："何处军马？"崔谅曰："安定救军来到。"谅先射一号箭上城，箭上带着密书曰："今诸葛亮先遣二将，伏于城中，要里应外合；且不可惊动，恐泄漏计策。待入府中图之。"杨陵将书见了夏侯楙，细言其事。楙曰："既然诸葛亮中计，可教刀斧手百余人，伏于府中。如二将随崔太守到府下马，闭门斩之；却于城上举火，赚诸葛亮入城。伏兵齐出，亮

"What plan should we use?" Yang Ling said, "Tell them I will surrender the city. We will trick them into entering and will slaughter them once they are inside."

Accordingly, Cui Liang left the city, met with Kongming, and said, "Yang Ling will surrender and allow your army to enter Nan'an and capture Xiahou Mao — a step Yang Ling has not taken only because his force is too small." "That should be easy enough to remedy," Kongming answered. "You already have the more than one hundred who have surrendered. Conceal among them Riverlands commanders disguised as Anding soldiers; and after entering the town, hide them in Xiahou Mao's quarters. Then secretly arrange with Yang Ling to deliver the city in the middle of the night so that our soldiers outside can coordinate with yours inside."

Cui Liang reflected, "If I don't take their commanders, Kongming will get suspicious. Anyway, we can kill them once inside, raise the fire signal, and trick Kongming into coming in." And so Cui Liang accepted Kongming's suggestion. Next, Kongming told Cui Liang, "I will first send my most trusted commanders Guan Xing and Zhang Bao to follow you in. To allay Xiahou Mao's suspicions, simply pose as a rescue force entering the city. The moment you signal with fire, I will come in myself and capture Xiahou Mao."

2269

It was nearly dark. Guan Xing and Zhang Bao had Kongming's secret instructions. Armed and mounted, they mingled with the Anding soldiers and followed Cui Liang to Nan'an. Inside, Yang Ling had suspended a platform over the city wall. Now he leaned against its protective railing. "Where is your army from?" he asked. Cui Liang responded, "We are a rescue force from Anding." Cui Liang shot an arrow onto the wall bearing a secret message: "Zhuge Liang has sent two commanders to wait in ambush in our city and collaborate with the outside force. Remain calm so our plan is not divulged. When they are inside, we can deal with them."

Yang Ling showed the letter to Xiahou Mao and explained the situation. Xiahou Mao said, "Since he has fallen for the trap, have a hundred men armed with swords and axes hide in the government buildings. If the two commanders following Governor Cui Liang dismount there, shut the

可擒矣。”安排已毕，杨陵回到城上言曰：“既是安定军马，可放入城。”关兴跟崔谅先行，张苞在后。杨陵下城，在门边迎接。兴手起刀落，斩杨陵于马下。崔谅大惊，急拨马奔到吊桥边，张苞大喝曰：“贼子休走！汝等诡计，如何瞒得丞相耶！”手起一枪，刺崔谅于马下。关兴早到城上，放起火来。四面蜀兵齐入。夏侯楙措手不及，开南门并力杀出。一彪军拦住，为首大将，乃是王平；交马只一合，生擒夏侯楙于马上，余皆杀死。

　　孔明入南安，招谕军民，秋毫无犯。众将各各献功。孔明将夏侯楙囚于车中。邓芝问曰：“丞相何故知崔谅诈也？”孔明曰：“吾已知此人无降心，故意使入城。彼必尽情告与夏侯楙，欲将计就计而行。吾见来情，足知其诈，复使二将同去，以稳其心。此人若有真心，必然阻当；彼忻然同去者，恐吾疑也。他意中度二将同去，赚入城内杀之未迟；又令吾军有托，放心而进。吾已暗嘱二将，就城门下图之。城内必无准备，吾军随后便到：此出其不意也。”众将拜服。孔明曰：“赚崔谅者，吾使心

gates and kill them; light a fire on the wall, lure Kongming in, and spring the ambush. Zhuge Liang can be taken!" These arrangements completed, Yang Ling returned to the wall and said, "If these are Anding troops, then let them in." Guan Xing followed Cui Liang into the town; Zhang Bao followed. When Yang Ling descended to welcome them inside the gate, Guan Xing's arm rose, his blade struck, and Yang Ling fell dead. Stunned, Cui Liang turned his horse and raced to the drawbridge. Zhang Bao shouted to him, "Halt, traitor! How could you ever fool His Execllency?" With a single thrust of his spear, he killed Cui Liang. Guan Xing had already given the fire signal from the wall, and the Riverlands troops were swarming in. Xiahou Mao, caught unprepared, opened the southern gate and tried to fight his way out; but a band of troops led by Wang Ping cut him off. After a brief struggle, Wang Ping captured Xiahou Mao. All his followers had been killed.

Kongming entered Nan'an and informed the people of the change of rule; his highly disciplined troops committed no offense against the city residents. The Riverlands commanders had rendered exceptional service; and Xiahou Mao had been imprisoned in a cage-cart. Deng Zhi asked Kongming, "How did Your Excellency come to know Cui Liang's plan?" "I knew he never meant to surrender," Kongming replied, "so I purposely sent him back into the town, certain that he would tell Xiahou Mao everything he had agreed to with me and devise counter-measures. When he came to me again, his deceit was evident; I sent the two commanders back with him to reassure him.

2271

"If Yang Ling had been sincere, he would have refused the commanders. He took them eagerly only to avoid arousing my suspicions, thinking he would have ample time to get rid of them once inside the city and that we would enter unsuspecting if we had those two on the inside to rely on. But I had already given Guan Xing and Zhang Bao secret orders to take care of them once inside the gate, where there would be no preparations. Then my army followed directly after, something they had not counted on at all." The Riverlands commanders expressed great admiration for Kongming's planning. "To fool Cui Liang," Kongming continued, "I had my trusted agent impersonate the Wei commander Pei Xu. Another agent was sent to deceive the governor at Tianshui, but he has not

腹人诈作魏将裴绪也。吾又去赚天水郡，至今未到，不知何故。今可乘势取之。"乃留吴懿守南安，刘琰守安定，替出魏延军马去取天水郡。

　　却说天水郡太守马遵，听知夏侯楙困在南安城中，乃聚文武官商议。功曹梁绪、主簿尹赏、主记梁虔等曰："夏侯驸马乃金枝玉叶，倘有疏虞，难逃坐视之罪。太守何不尽起本部兵以救之？"马遵正疑虑间，忽报夏侯驸马差心腹将裴绪到。绪入府，取公文付马遵，说："都督求安定、天水两郡之兵，星夜救应。"言讫，匆匆而去。次日又有报马到，称说："安定兵已先去了，教太守火急前来会合。"马遵正欲起兵，忽一人自外而入曰："太守中诸葛亮之计矣！"众视之，乃天水冀人也，姓姜名维，字伯约。父名冏，昔日曾为天水郡功曹，因羌人乱，没于王事。维自幼博览群书，兵法武艺，无所不通；奉母至孝，郡人敬之；后为中郎将，就参本郡军事。当日姜维谓马遵曰："近闻诸葛亮杀败夏侯楙，困于南安，水泄不通，安得有人自重围之中而出？又且裴绪乃无名下将，从不曾见；况安定报马，又无公文：以此察之，此人乃蜀将诈称魏将。赚得太守出城，料城中无

returned, for reasons still unknown. Now we are in a position to take Tianshui." Leaving Wu Yi to defend Nan'an and Liu Yan to defend Anding, Kongming dispatched Wei Yan with a force to capture the district of Tianshui.

The governor of Tianshui was Ma Zun. Hearing that Xiahou Mao was trapped in Nan'an, he had convened his council. Liang Xu of the Merit Bureau, Yin Shang, his first secretary, and Liang Qian, the official clerk, as well as others argued, "Imperial Son-in- Law Xiahou Mao is a part of the royal family; the slightest negligence will be punished as willful indifference to his fate. Governor, shouldn't you muster all the troops you have to save him?"

Ma Zun was in a quandary when Pei Xu, Xiahou Mao's trusted agent, was announced. The man entered the governor's residence, handed Ma Zun a document, and said, "Chief Commander Xiahou demands immediate relief from both Tianshui and Anding districts." So saying, he hurried away. The next day another rider arrived and announced, "The Anding force has already left. Have the governor hasten on to meet them." Ma Zun was about to call up his troops, when someone rushed in and cried, "Don't fall into Zhuge Liang's trap!" The assembly turned to Jiang Wei (Boyue), a native of Jicheng in Tianshui district.

Jiang Wei's father, Jiong, had once headed the Bureau of Merit in Tianshui but died serving the dynasty during the uprisings of the Qiang people. Since childhood Jiang Wei had read and studied widely and was a master of both military affairs and martial arts. He served his mother with unstinting filial love and had earned wide respect for it throughout the district. Later he was appointed Imperial Corps commander and in that capacity advised the governor's military force.

Jiang Wei said to Ma Zun, "I have just heard that Zhuge Liang has defeated Xiahou Mao and that Nan'an is sealed off. How could anyone have gotten out to come here? Pei Xu is a minor captain, completely unknown. We have never met him. Then there is a rider from Anding, who has no documents. As I analyze it, this man is not a Wei commander, but a Riverlands commander in disguise whose intention is to trick Your Lordship into leaving Tianshui. I am sure that if we leave our city undefended, they will place an ambush force close by to await the right mo-

备,必然暗伏一军于左近,乘虚而取天水也。"马遵大悟曰:"非伯约之言,则误中奸计矣!"维笑曰:"太守放心。某有一计,可擒诸葛亮,解南安之危。"

　　正是:

　　　　运筹又遇强中手,斗智还逢意外人。

　　未知其计如何,且看下文分解。

ment to capture it." Ma Zun suddenly realized the actual situation. "If not for Jiang Wei," he said, "I would have fallen into the trap!" With a smile Jiang Wei responded, "The governor need not worry. I have a plan to capture Zhuge Liang and relieve Nan'an." Indeed:

> In spinning cunning plans, one will meet one's master;
> In the battle of the minds, one finds an unexpected man.[6]

Would Jiang Wei's ploy succeed?

Read on.

2277

第九十三回

姜伯约归降孔明　武乡侯骂死王朗

　　却说姜维献计于马遵曰："诸葛亮必伏兵于郡后，赚我兵出城，乘虚袭我。某愿请精兵三千，伏于要路。太守随后发兵出城，不可远去，止行三十里便回；但看火起为号，前后夹攻，可获大胜。如诸葛亮自来，必为某所擒矣。"遵用其计，付精兵与姜维去讫，然后自与梁虔引兵出城等候；只留梁绪、尹赏守城。原来孔明果遣赵云引一军埋伏于山僻之中，只待天水人马离城，便乘虚袭之。当日细作回报赵云，说天水太守马遵，起兵出城，只留文官守城。赵云大喜，又令人报与张翼、高翔，教于要路截杀马遵。——此二处兵亦是孔明预先埋伏。

　　却说赵云引五千兵，径投天水郡城下，高叫曰："吾乃常山赵子龙也！汝知中计，早献城池，免遭诛戮！"城上梁绪大笑曰："汝中吾姜伯约之计，尚然不知耶？"云恰待攻城，忽然喊声大震，四面火光冲天。当先一员少年将军，挺枪跃马而言曰："汝见天水姜伯约乎！"云挺枪直取姜维。战不数合，维精神倍长。

Chapter 93

Jiang Wei Submits to Kongming
Kongming's Invective Kills Wang Lang

Jiang Wei offered Ma Zun this plan: "Zhuge Liang's force is waiting nearby to surprise Tianshui — if he can trick us into leaving. Let me have three thousand crack troops to place in ambush on the main road. Then, Your Lordship, come out of the city with the main army, not too far — turn back after thirty *li*. The moment you see fire, we will catch the enemy between us and defeat them. Let Zhuge Liang come himself: we will capture him." Ma Zun adopted the plan, and Jiang Wei left with a crack force. After that, Ma Zun and Liang Qian led their troops out of the city to await the enemy; and Liang Xu and Yin Shang remained to guard Tianshui.

Prior to these events Kongming had sent Zhao Zilong with a company of troops to hide in the hills and wait for the governor to leave Tianshui open to attack. On the day the defending troops marched out, spies reported the move to Zhao Zilong; they also told him that civil officials but no military officers had remained behind to hold the city. Delighted, Zhao Zilong communicated the news to Zhang Yi and Gao Xiang and had them intercept Ma Zun. (Their two contingents had earlier been placed in ambush by Kongming.)

2279

Zhao Zilong led five thousand men straight for Tianshui and, reaching the wall, shouted out, "Zhao Zilong of Changshan is here! You have fallen into a trap! Surrender the city at once and spare a bloodletting." But from the wall Liang Xu laughed aloud and said, "You have fallen into Jiang Wei's trap in case you don't know it!" As Zhao Zilong began the attack, shouts rang out and all around fire shot skyward. A young commander took the lead. His spear poised, his horse straining, he declared, "Jiang Wei of Tianshui! Here before you!"

Zhao Zilong raised his spear and took on his man. They battled sev-

云大惊，暗忖曰："谁想此处有这般人物！"正战时，两路军夹攻来，乃是马遵、梁虔引军杀回。赵云首尾不能相顾，冲开条路，引败兵奔走，姜维赶来。亏得张翼、高翔两路军杀出，接应回去。赵云归见孔明，说中了敌人之计。孔明惊问曰："此是何人，识吾玄机？"有南安人告曰："此人姓姜，名维，字伯约，天水冀人也；事母至孝，文武双全，智勇足备，真当世之英杰也。"赵云又夸奖姜维枪法，与他人大不同。孔明曰："吾今欲取天水，不想有此人。"遂起大军前来。

　　却说姜维回见马遵曰："赵云败去，孔明必然自来。彼料我军必在城中。今可将本部军马，分为四枝：某引一军伏于城东，如彼兵到则截之。太守与梁虔、尹赏各引一军城外埋伏。梁绪率百姓在城上守御。"分拨已定。

　　却说孔明因虑姜维，自为前部，望天水郡进发。将到城边，孔明传令曰："凡攻城池，以初到之日，激励三军，鼓噪直上。若迟延日久，锐气尽隳，急难破矣。"于是大军径到城下。因见城上旗帜整齐，未敢轻攻。候至半夜，忽然四下火光冲天，喊声震地，正不知何处兵来。只见城上亦鼓噪呐喊相应，蜀兵乱窜。孔明急上马，有关兴、张苞二将保护，杀出重围。回头看时，正东

eral bouts. Jiang Wei's martial spirits rose; Zhao Zilong reflected in surprise, "Imagine finding such a fighter here!" As they fought on, the two Tianshui contingents led by Ma Zun and Liang Qian turned back and closed in. Zhao Zilong and his men, caught in between, forced an opening and fled. Jiang Wei pursued, but Zhang Yi and Gao Xiang came on the scene with two contingents and saw Zilong safely back.

Zhao Zilong came before Kongming and explained how the enemy had trapped him. Anxiously Kongming asked, "Who was it that saw through my scheme?" Someone from Nan'an answered, "Jiang Wei (styled Boyue) from Jicheng in Tianshui. He is a man filial to his mother, full of wisdom and courage, and as expert in civil as in military science. Truly a bold hero of the age." Zhao Zilong also gave high praise to Jiang Wei's excellent technique in spear fighting. Kongming said, "When I decided to take Tianshui, I never expected to find such a man!" He summoned the army and went forward against the city.

*　*　*

Meanwhile, Jiang Wei had returned and told Ma Zun: "Zhao Zilong's defeat will surely bring Kongming, and he will expect our army to be inside the city. So let us divide it into four units. I will take one and place it in ambush to the east. If the enemy comes that way, I will cut them off from behind. You, Governor, as well as Liang Qian and Yin Shang, should hide your forces outside the city; and from the wall Liang Xu can direct the defenders within." Thus, Jiang Wei completed the disposition of forces.

Wary of Jiang Wei, Kongming led the forward army himself. Nearing Tianshui, he issued an order: "We must beat the war drums the day we arrive to spur the army to advance and attack the wall. The slightest delay will hurt morale, and the attack will fail." Accordingly, the army moved directly to the base of the wall. But the Riverlanders, impressed by the strict array of flags above them, hesitated until the middle of the night. Suddenly flames shot up all around, and the cries of a vast host shook the ground. The Riverlands soldiers could not tell from which direction the enemy would strike. The clamor of the drums on the walls and the cheers of the population below heartened the northern soldiers; the westerners slunk away in disorder.

Kongming took to his horse and, protected by Guan Xing and Zhang

上军马,一带火光,势若长蛇。孔明令关兴探视,回报曰:"此姜维兵也。"孔明叹曰:"兵不在多,在人之调遣耳。此人真将才也!"收兵归寨,思之良久,乃唤安定人问曰:"姜维之母,现在何处?"答曰:"维母今居冀县。"孔明唤魏延分付曰:"汝可引一军,虚张声势,诈取冀县。若姜维到,可放入城。"又问:"此地何处紧要?"安定人曰:"天水钱粮,皆在上邽;若打破上邽,则粮道自绝矣。"孔明大喜,教赵云引一军去攻上邽。孔明离城三十里下寨。早有人报入天水郡,说蜀兵分为三路:一军守此郡,一军取上邽,一军取冀城。姜维闻之,哀告马遵曰:"维母现在冀城,恐母有失。维乞一军往救此城,兼保老母。"马遵从之,遂令姜维引三千军去保冀城;梁虔引三千军去保上邽。

却说姜维引兵至冀城,前面一彪军摆开,为首蜀将,乃是魏延。二将交锋数合,延诈败奔走。维入城闭门,率兵守护,拜见老母,并不出战。赵云亦放过梁虔入上邽城去了,孔明乃令人去南安郡,取夏侯楙至帐下。孔明曰:"汝惧死乎?"楙慌拜伏乞命。孔明曰:"目今天水姜维现守冀城,使人持书来说:'但得驸马在,我愿归降。'吾今饶汝性命,汝肯招安姜维否?"楙曰:

Bao, fought his way out of the encircling force. Turning back, he saw due east a serpentine band of fiery light hovering over the enemy troops. Kongming had Guan Xing investigate. "Jiang Wei's troops," he reported. Kongming sighed deeply. "Warfare depends not on the number of one's men alone, but on how one directs them. This man's talent as a general is great."

Kongming rallied his men and returned to camp, where he pondered the situation. Then he questioned a man from Anding: "Where is Jiang Wei's mother?" The reply was, "She lives in Jicheng." Kongming summoned Wei Yan and instructed him: "Take one company and bruit it about that you are going to capture Jicheng. If Jiang Wei arrives, let him enter the city." Then Kongming asked the Anding man, "What's the key point to Tianshui?" The man replied, "Their coin and grain are in Shanggui. Conquer Shanggui and their supply line will be cut." Kongming was delighted and had Zhao Zilong attack the town. Kongming himself camped about thirty *li* away.

Word soon reached Tianshui that the Riverlands army had split into three units: one to guard the district capital, Tianshui; one to take Shanggui; and one to attack Jicheng. When Jiang Wei learned of these moves, he appealed in anguish to Ma Zun: "My mother is in Jicheng. Before anything happens to her, give me a company to rescue the town." Ma Zun granted Jiang Wei three thousand soldiers and ordered him to rescue Jicheng. Tianshui Commander Liang Qian went to Shanggui with another three thousand.

Advancing toward Jicheng, Jiang Wei encountered a band of soldiers arrayed before him; their commander was Wei Yan. The two leaders exchanged spear thrusts until Wei Yan, feigning defeat, fled the field. Jiang Wei entered the town, sealed the gates, and deployed his men defensively while he went to pay his respects to his mother. Zhao Zilong permitted Liang Qian to pass and enter Shanggui.[1]

At this point Kongming had Xiahou Mao brought from Nan'an and put before him. "Do you fear death?" Kongming asked him. Xiahou Mao fell to the ground and prostrated himself, pleading for his life. "Jiang Wei of Tianshui," Kongming said, "presently guarding Jicheng, has sent a letter saying that if we spare you, the imperial son-in-law, he will agree to

"情愿招安。"孔明乃与衣服鞍马,不令人跟随,放之自去。楸得脱出寨,欲寻路而走,奈不知路径。正行之间,逢数人奔走。楸问之,答曰:"我等是冀县百姓;今被姜维献了城池,归降诸葛亮,蜀将魏延纵火劫财,我等因此弃家奔走,投上邽去也。"楸又问曰:"今守天水城是谁?"土人曰:"天水城中乃马太守也。"楸闻之,纵马望天水而行。又见百姓携男抱女远来,所说皆同。楸至天水城下叫门,城上人认得是夏侯楸,慌忙开门迎接。马遵惊拜问之。楸细言姜维之事;又将百姓所言说了。遵叹曰:"不想姜维反投蜀矣!"梁绪曰:"彼意欲救都督,故以此言虚降。"楸曰:"今维已降,何为虚也?"正踌躇间,时已初更,蜀兵又来攻城。火光中见姜维在城下挺枪勒马,大叫曰:"请夏侯都督答话!"夏侯楸与马遵等皆到城上,见姜维耀武扬威大叫曰:"我为都督而降,都督何背前言?"楸曰:"汝受魏恩,何故降蜀?有何前言耶?"维应曰:"汝写书教我降蜀,何出此言?汝要脱身,却将我陷了!我今降蜀,加为上将,安有还魏之理?"言

surrender and submit. I am prepared to pardon you. Are you willing to go and ask Jiang Wei to accept our terms?" "More than willing," was the reply.

Kongming accordingly provided Xiahou Mao with clothes and a saddled horse and set him free. But Xiahou Mao was unattended and uncertain of the way. Riding alone, he met up with some men running pell-mell. Questioned by Xiahou Mao, they said, "We are commoners from Jicheng. Jiang Wei has surrendered the city and gone over to Zhuge Liang. After Riverlands Commander Wei Yan torched the city and stole our goods, we fled our homes, hoping to reach Shanggui." Xiahou Mao asked further, "Who defends Tianshui?" "Governor Ma Zun," a local man responded. Xiahou Mao turned and rode for Tianshui. He came upon another group of commoners with their children who had evidently been traveling a fair distance. They confirmed what the other refugees had told him. On reaching the wall of Tianshui, Xiahou Mao shouted up, and the men on the wall, recognizing Xiahou Mao, hastened to admit him. Surprised, Ma Zun bowed to Xiahou Mao and asked him what was going on. Mao related the story of Jiang Wei's surrender, as well as all that the refugees had told him. With a sigh Ma Zun responded, "Who would have expected Jiang Wei to betray us and join the Riverlands?" Liang Xu said to Xiahou Mao, "He must have pretended to submit in an attempt to save you, Chief Commander." But Xiahou Mao said, "Jiang Wei has submitted. What is there to 'pretend'?"

As the leaders in Tianshui pondered Jiang Wei's motives, the Riverlands troops for the second time attacked Tianshui during the first watch. Amid flames the defenders saw Jiang Wei near the wall, his spear raised, his horse reined to a halt. He shouted out, "Let Chief Commander Xiahou appear!" Xiahou Mao and Ma Zun climbed to the top of the wall to find Jiang Wei below flaunting his prowess and shouting, "I submitted for the sake of the chief commander. Why has he broken his promise?" "You have received the love of the house of Wei," Xiahou Mao retorted, "how could you surrender to the Riverlands? What promise do you speak of?" Jiang Wei answered, "What are you talking about? You're the one who wrote a letter telling me to surrender. You only want to escape and trap me! After I surrendered, they made me a high commander. It is

讫，驱兵打城，至晓方退。——原来夜间妆姜维者，乃孔明之计，令部卒形貌相似者，假扮姜维攻城，因火光之中，不辨真伪。

孔明却引兵来攻冀城。城中粮少，军食不敷。姜维在城上，见蜀军大车小辆，搬运粮草，入魏延寨中去了。维引三千兵出城，径来劫粮。蜀兵尽弃了粮车，寻路而走。姜维夺得粮车，欲要入城，忽然一彪军拦住，为首蜀将张翼也。二将交锋，战不数合，王平引一军又到，两下夹攻。维力穷抵敌不住，夺路归城；城上早插蜀兵旗号：原来已被魏延袭了。维杀条路奔天水城，手下尚有十余骑；又遇张苞杀了一阵，维止剩得匹马单枪，来到天水城下叫门。城上军见是姜维，慌报马遵，遵曰："此是姜维来赚我城门也。"令城上乱箭射下。姜维回顾蜀兵至近，遂飞奔上邽城来。城上梁虔见了姜维，大骂曰："反国之贼，安敢来赚我城池！吾已知汝降蜀矣！"遂乱箭射下。姜维不能分说，仰天长叹，两眼泪流，拨马望长安而走。行不数里，前至一派大树茂林之处，一声喊起，数千兵拥出：为首蜀将关兴，截住去路。维人困马乏，不能抵当，勒回马便走。忽然一辆小车从山坡中

pointless to return to Wei!" So saying, he sent his men against the town; the battle lasted until dawn.

The truth of the situation was that during the night someone had impersonated Jiang Wei. Following a plan of Kongming's, a soldier resembling Jiang Wei was ordered by Kongming to attack the city posing as the Imperial Corps commander. In the shadowlight of the fires no one detected the deception. Next Kongming led his troops in an attack on Jicheng. Inside, grain was too scarce to keep the defending soldiers fed. From the wall surrounding Jicheng the real Jiang Wei watched the Riverlands army moving wagons and carts of grain into Wei Yan's camp and subsequently led three thousand men out of the city to try and seize the supplies. The Riverlands soldiers abandoned their burdens and fled for their lives, letting Jiang Wei take the wagons. He was about to reenter the city when a band of soldiers led by Zhang Yi cut him off. The two commanders crossed spears. After a brief clash Wang Ping, leading a company, came to Zhang Yi's aid, and Jiang Wei, too spent to resist, made his way back to Jicheng — only to find the flags of Shu flying on the walls: Wei Yan had surprised the city.

Jiang Wei forced a way through and fled to Tianshui. With hardly a dozen riders left in his command, he met and fought with Zhang Bao. After the battle, Jiang Wei had not a single follower left; he arrived alone at the gates of Tianshui and demanded entry. The defenders recognized him and quickly informed Ma Zun, who said, "He has come to trick me into opening the city," and ordered the defenders to shower Jiang Wei with arrows. With the Riverlanders closing in from behind, Jiang Wei dashed to Shanggui.

At the wall of Shanggui, Liang Qian denounced Jiang Wei: "Traitor to your house! Do you think you can take the city by trickery? I know you have surrendered to Shu!" Fresh volleys of arrows descended. What more could Jiang Wei say? Looking at the heavens, he sighed deeply, tears standing in his eyes. Then he wheeled about and rode for Chang'an. After several *li* he came to a large, flourishing grove, out of which poured thousands of wildly yelling soldiers. At their lead, barring his way, stood Guan Xing. Jiang Wei was too fatigued, his horse too spent, to offer resistance. Again he wheeled and fled. But suddenly a small carriage came

转出。其人头戴纶巾，身披鹤氅，手摇羽扇，乃孔明也。孔明唤姜维曰："伯约此时何尚不降？"维寻思良久，前有孔明，后有关兴，又无去路，只得下马投降。孔明慌忙下车而迎，执维手曰："吾自出茅庐以来，遍求贤者，欲传授平生之学，恨未得其人。今遇伯约，吾愿足矣。"维大喜拜谢。

孔明遂同姜维回寨，升帐商议取天水、上邽之计。维曰："天水城中尹赏、梁绪，与某至厚；当写密书二封，射入城中，使其内乱，城可得矣。"孔明从之。姜维写了二封密书，拴在箭上，纵马直至城下，射入城中。小校拾得，呈与马遵。遵大疑，与夏侯楙商议曰："梁绪、尹赏与姜维结连，欲为内应，都督宜早决之。"楙曰："可杀二人。"尹赏知此消息，乃谓梁绪曰："不如纳城降蜀，以图进用。"是夜，夏侯楙数次使人请梁、尹二人说话。二人料知事急，遂披挂上马，各执兵器，引本部军大开城门，放蜀兵入。夏侯楙、马遵惊慌，引数百人出西门，弃城投羌胡城而去。梁绪、尹赏迎接孔明入城。安民已毕，孔明问取上邽之计。梁绪曰："此城乃某亲弟梁虔守之，愿招来降。"孔明大喜。绪当日到上邽唤梁虔出城来降孔明。孔明重加赏劳，就令梁绪为天水太守，尹赏为冀城令，梁虔为上邽令。孔明分拨已

into sight from around a hillside. Binding the passenger's head was a plaited band; cloaked in crane plumes, he held a feather fan. Kongming hailed Jiang Wei: "Must you keep us waiting so long for your surrender, Jiang Wei?" Jiang Wei took stock: ahead, Kongming; behind, Guan Xing. He dismounted and surrendered. Kongming hurried down to welcome him and, taking his hand, said, "Since leaving my poor home, I have looked far and wide for an able and worthy man to whom I could hand down my teachings. Alas, I never found him; but now my wish is granted." Overjoyed, Jiang Wei prostrated himself in gratitude.

Kongming and Jiang Wei returned to camp together and went into the main tent to plan the capture of Tianshui and Shanggui. "Let me write to Yin Shang and Liang Xu," Jiang Wei said, "my good friends in Tianshui. Shot over the wall, the letters should create enough confusion in the city for us to take it." Kongming approved, and Jiang Wei wrote two letters. He attached them to arrows, rode to the base of the wall, and shot them over. A petty officer picked them up and showed them to Ma Zun.

Perplexed, Ma Zun conferred with Xiahou Mao. "Liang Xu and Yin Shang," he said, "are agents collaborating with Jiang Wei. Chief Commander, we must do something at once." "Have them killed," Xiahou Mao answered. Yin Shang learned of Xiahou Mao's decision and said to Liang Xu, "Better for us to deliver the city to the Riverlands and surrender — that at least will earn us promotion." During the night Xiahou Mao called the two to a meeting several times; they knew things had come to a head. Fully armored, weapons in hand, they rode with their men to the city gate and threw it open. The Riverlands soldiers entered.

2289

Panicked, Xiahou Mao and Ma Zun led several hundred men out the west gate and headed toward Qianghu as Liang Xu and Yin Shang welcomed Kongming into the city. Kongming first reassured the population, then asked the commanders how to capture Shanggui. Liang Xu replied, "The defender of Shanggui is my brother Liang Qian. I will invite him to surrender." Kongming was delighted.

That day Liang Xu went to Shanggui and induced Liang Qian to surrender. Kongming rewarded Qian well; he then made Liang Xu governor of Tianshui, Yin Shang prefect of Jicheng, and Liang Qian prefect of Shanggui. After completing the reorganization of the district administra-

毕,整兵进发。诸将问曰:"丞相何不去擒夏侯楙?"孔明曰:"吾放夏侯楙,如放一鸭耳。今得伯约,得一凤也!"

　　孔明自得三城之后,威声大震,远近州郡,望风归降。孔明整顿军马,尽提汉中之兵,前出祁山,兵临渭水之西。细作报入洛阳。

　　时魏主曹睿太和元年,升殿设朝。近臣奏曰:"夏侯驸马已失三郡,逃窜羌中去了。今蜀兵已到祁山,前军临渭水之西,乞早发兵破敌。"睿大惊,乃问群臣曰:"谁可为朕退蜀兵耶?"司徒王朗出班奏曰:"臣观先帝每用大将军曹真,所到必克;今陛下何不拜为大都督,以退蜀兵?"睿准奏,乃宣曹真曰:"先帝托孤与卿,今蜀兵入寇中原,卿安忍坐视乎?"真奏曰:"臣才疏智浅,不称其职。"王朗曰:"将军乃社稷之臣,不可固辞。老臣虽驽钝,愿随将军一往。"真又奏曰:"臣受大恩,安敢推辞?但乞一人为副将。"睿曰:"卿自举之。"真乃保太原阳曲人,姓郭,名淮,字伯济,官封射亭侯,领雍州刺史。睿从之,遂拜曹真为大都督,赐节钺;命郭淮为副都督,王朗为军师。——朗时年已七

tions, Kongming put the troops in order for his next advance. The commanders asked, "Why not capture Xiahou Mao, Your Excellency?" "Letting him go we lose a duck. In Jiang Wei we have gained a phoenix," Kongming replied.

The taking of these three cities heightened Kongming's reputation in the region, and many joined his side. His forces in order, Kongming levied all soldiers in Hanzhong and advanced to the hills of Qishan, putting his troops within striking distance of the west bank of the River Wei. Spies carried word of these movements to Luoyang.

* * *

In the first year of the Tai He reign period (A.D. 227), Cao Rui, ruler of Wei, held court in his audience hall. A high vassal submitted a proposal: "Imperial Son-in-Law Xiahou Mao has slipped away to Qiangzhong after losing three districts, and the Riverlands army vanguard now overlooks the west bank of the Wei from Qishan. I beg you, send the army out at once and defeat the foe." Cao Rui turned in alarm to the assembly of vassals and asked, "Who can drive back the enemy for us?"[2] Minister of the Interior Wang Lang stepped forward and addressed the Emperor: "I remember how successful Cao Zhen was whenever the late Emperor sent him into battle. Why not make him first field marshal now, Your Majesty, to repel the Riverlands army?"

Cao Rui approved this proposal; he called in Cao Zhen and said, "My father, the late Emperor, placed me in your care. Have you the heart to sit back and watch while a Riverlands army pillages our home territory?" Cao Zhen said in response, "Deficient in talent and meagre in knowledge, I am unequal to the task." Wang Lang said, "General, as a vassal of the sacred shrines you may not refuse. Though worn out and unfit for use, I volunteer to join you." Cao Zhen continued: "In view of the great favor I have received, I shall accept. All I request is a deputy commander." "Name him yourself," Cao Rui answered. The man Cao Zhen recommended was Guo Huai (Boji) from Yangqu county in Taiyuan; he had been enfeoffed lord of Sheting and served as imperial inspector of Yongzhou. Cao Rui approved the choice.

Cao Rui appointed Cao Zhen first field marshal and presented him with the battle-axe representing imperial authority. He also appointed Guo

十六岁矣。——选拨东西二京军马二十万与曹真。真命宗弟曹遵为先锋，又命荡寇将军朱赞为副先锋。当年十一月出师，魏主曹睿亲自送出西门之外方回。

　　曹真领大军来到长安，过渭河之西下寨。真与王朗、郭淮共议退兵之策。朗曰："来日可严整队伍，大展旌旗。老夫自出，只用一席话，管教诸葛亮拱手而降，蜀兵不战自退。"真大喜，是夜传令：来日四更造饭，平明务要队伍整齐，人马威仪，旌旗鼓角，各按次序。当时使人先下战书。次日，两军相迎，列成阵势于祁山之前。蜀军见魏兵甚是雄壮，与夏侯楙大不相同。

　　三军鼓角已罢，司徒王朗乘马而出。上首乃都督曹真，下首乃副都督郭淮；两个先锋压住阵角。探子马出军前，大叫曰："请对阵主将答话！"只见蜀兵门旗开处，关兴、张苞分左右而出，立马于两边；次后一队队骁将分列；门旗影下，中央一辆四轮车，孔明端坐车中，纶巾羽扇，素衣皂绦，飘然而出。孔明举目见魏阵前三个麾盖，旗上大书姓名：中央白髯老者，乃军师、

Huai deputy commander and Wang Lang — at the age of seventy-five —
director general. From the two capitals a force of two hundred thousand
assembled under Cao Zhen's command. Cao Zhen named his cousin
Cao Zun leader of the vanguard, and Bandit-Clearing General Zhu Zan,
deputy vanguard leader. In the eleventh month of that year (early A.D.
228) Cao Rui, ruler of Wei, escorted this army beyond the west gate and
out of the capital.

Cao Zhen advanced to Chang'an, crossed the River Wei, and pitched
camp on the western side. The three leaders then conferred on dislodging
the Riverlands forces from the hills of Qishan. Wang Lang said, "Tomorrow set the ranks in grand array exhibiting all flags. Let this old man go
forth first, for a single dialogue with Zhuge Liang should suffice to convince him to submit quietly and the Riverlands army to retreat without a
battle." Cao Zhen was delighted and issued orders that night: "Tomorrow, mess at the fourth watch; at daybreak, all ranks to be in place with
their units and all insignia, including flags, banners, drums, and horns, in
perfect order."

At this time Cao Zhen sent a man with the call to battle. The next day
the two armies met and deployed in formation before the Qishan hills.
The Riverlands soldiers saw that these troops were quite formidable, utterly unlike those of Xiahou Mao.

2293

Drums and horns resounded as Minister of the Interior Wang Lang
rode forth. Behind him, in the place of honor, rode Cao Zhen, the field
commander, and beside him Guo Huai, his deputy. The opposing vanguards secured their positions. Advance riders raced ahead of their lines
and shouted, "Let the opposing leader come forth and parley!" The bright-
bannered entrance to the Riverlands army widened, and Guan Xing and
Zhang Bao rode forth, one to each side, and halted; following them, teams
of commanders formed a handsome line. In the center, in the shadows of
the entrance banners, a four-wheeled carriage held Kongming; he sat
poised, a plaited band wound around his head and a feather fan in his
hand. He wore plain beige garb belted with black silk cording. Gracefully,
he advanced.

Kongming raised his gaze to the three command umbrellas in front of
the northern army. Each banner bore a name writ large. In the center, old

司徒王朗。孔明暗忖曰："王朗必下说词，吾当随机应之。"遂教推车出阵外，令护军小校传曰："汉丞相与司徒会话。"王朗纵马而出。孔明于车上拱手，朗在马上欠身答礼。朗曰："久闻公之大名，今幸一会。公既知天命、识时务，何故兴无名之兵？"孔明曰："吾奉诏讨贼，何谓无名？"朗曰："天数有变，神器更易，而归有德之人，此自然之理也。曩自桓、灵以来，黄巾倡乱，天下争横。降至初平、建安之岁，董卓造逆，催、汜继虐；袁术僭号于寿春，袁绍称雄于邺土；刘表占据荆州，吕布虎吞徐郡：盗贼蜂起，奸雄鹰扬，社稷有累卵之危，生灵有倒悬之急。我太祖武皇帝，扫清六合，席卷八荒；万姓倾心，四方仰德：非以权势取之，实天命所归也。世祖文帝，神文圣武，以膺大统，应天合人，法尧禅舜，处中国以临万邦，岂非天心人意乎？今公蕴大才、抱

and white-bearded, was the director general, Minister of the Interior Wang Lang. Kongming sized up the situation. "Wang Lang will try and talk his way around me. I must answer in kind," he mused, and he had his carriage pushed forward. The officer guarding him relayed his message: "The prime minister of the Han will speak with the minister of the interior." Wang Lang galloped out. Without leaving his carriage, Kongming folded his hands in salute, while from horseback Wang Lang bowed, reciprocating the courtesy.

Wang Lang said, "After lifelong admiration of Your Lordship's magnificent reputation, fortune rewards me with this meeting. Your Lordship knows the meaning of Heaven's Mandate and the nature of the times. Why have you put an army in the field with no justification?"

Kongming replied, "I hold an edict to chastise rebels. Is that not justification?" "By the turn of Heaven's ordained periods," Wang Lang said, "the sacred instruments of power have changed hands, reverting to a man of virtue, as must happen in the normal course of things. Since the reigns of Emperors Huan and Ling the sedition incited by the Yellow Scarves has kept the empire in turmoil. During the reign periods Chu Ping and Jian An, Dong Zhuo rebelled, and Li Jue and Guo Si continued his savage practices. Yuan Shu usurped the imperial title in Shouchun, and Yuan Shao declared himself an independent power in Ye. Liu Biao occupied Jingzhou; Lü Bu swallowed Xuzhou. As bandits and rebels arose like hornets and villainous predators hovered above, the sacred shrines stood in imminent peril, and the common people faced grave perils.

"Our great ancestor, Cao Cao, August Emperor Wu, cleared all corners of the realm and took control of its farthest reaches. Millions eagerly gave him their allegiance, and in all quarters men admired his virtue. Nor was this by dint of his power and position; it was rather because the Mandate of Heaven had found in him its proper place. The next sovereign, Cao Pi, the Emperor Wen, divine in the civil and sage in the military arts, undertook the great succession in response to Heaven, in accord with men, and in faithfulness to the model of Yao's yielding to Shun. He positioned himself in the northern heartland and presided over the whole of the realm. Did this not show Heaven's intent and man's wish? Your

2295

大器,自欲比于管、乐,何乃强欲逆天理、背人情而行事耶?岂不闻古人曰:'顺天者昌,逆天者亡。'今我大魏带甲百万,良将千员。谅腐草之萤光,怎及天心之皓月?公可倒戈卸甲,以礼来降,不失封侯之位。国安民乐,岂不美哉!"

孔明在车上大笑曰:"吾以为汉朝大老元臣,必有高论,岂期出此鄙言!吾有一言,诸军静听:昔日桓、灵之世,汉统陵替,宦官酿祸;国乱岁凶,四方扰攘。黄巾之后,董卓、傕、汜等接踵而起,迁劫汉帝,残暴生灵。因庙堂之上,朽木为官,殿陛之间,禽兽食禄,狼心狗行之辈,滚滚当道,奴颜婢膝之徒,纷纷秉政。以致社稷丘墟,苍生涂炭。吾素知汝所行:世居东海之滨,初举孝廉入仕;理合匡君辅国,安汉兴刘;何期反助逆贼,同谋篡位!罪恶深重,天地不容!天下之人,愿食汝肉!今幸天意不

Lordship has nourished a great talent and possesses great abilities. You have compared yourself to Guan Zhong and to Yue Yi. It is difficult to believe that you would defy divine principle and turn against true human sentiment. You cannot have forgotten the words 'Conform to Heaven and prosper; oppose it and fall.' Today our great Wei dynasty numbers a million shields; our excellent commanders are as many as a thousand. I hardly think the flicker of a firefly in moldering hay can rival the clear moon at the zenith. Your Lordship, lay down your arms and submit as ceremonial courtesy dictates, and your enfeoffment as a lord will follow. What could be more excellent than a dynasty at peace, its people rejoicing?"

From his carriage Kongming laughed. "I would have expected loftier argument from a venerable minister of the Han court, not these debased words. I have one thing to say to all officers and men. Hear me in silence. A long time ago in the age of Emperors Huan and Ling, the succession of the royal house fell into disorder and the evils wrought by the eunuchs resulted in widespread disaster. Misgovernment of the royal house and successive years of famine engulfed the four corners of the realm in turmoil. The Yellow Scarves were followed by Dong Zhuo and his generals, Li Jue and Guo Si. They kidnaped the Emperor and plundered the people. Corrupt officials served in the royal household, wild beasts in the imperial court. Men of wolfish heart and violent conduct controlled the public highways, while craven, servile sorts held every kind of administrative office.

"The sacred shrines stand now in ruin, the common people in extremity. I have long known the record of your conduct: after dwelling by the shore of the eastern sea, you first entered office by election for filial devotion and personal integrity. It is unthinkable that you — you whose proper function was to shield your sovereign and uphold his house, to secure the Han and help the Liu to thrive — should have turned and aided renegades and rebels, plotting with them the usurpation of the dynasty! Heaven will not countenance such sins. Nothing but the taste of your flesh will satisfy the people's claim against you.

"Fortunately, Heaven decided to continue the fire-signed Han dynasty in the person of the August Emperor Zhao Lie of the Riverlands. Today I

2297

绝炎汉，昭烈皇帝继统西川。吾今奉嗣君之旨，兴师讨贼。汝既为诌谀之臣，只可潜身缩首，苟图衣食；安敢在行伍之前，妄称天数耶！皓首匹夫！苍髯老贼！汝即日将归于九泉之下，何面目见二十四帝乎！老贼速退！可教反臣与吾共决胜负！"

王朗听罢，气满胸膛，大叫一声，撞死于马下。后人有诗赞孔明曰：

> 兵马出西秦，雄才敌万人。
>
> 轻摇三寸舌，骂死老奸臣。

孔明以扇指曹真曰："吾不逼汝。汝可整顿军马，来日决战。"言讫回车。于是两军皆退。曹真将王朗尸首，用棺木盛贮，送回长安去了。副都督郭淮曰："诸葛亮料吾军中治丧，今夜必来劫寨。可分兵四路：两路兵从山僻小路，乘虚去劫蜀寨；两路兵伏于本寨外，左右击之。"曹真大喜曰："此计与吾相合。"遂传令唤曹遵、朱赞两个先锋分付曰："汝二人各引一万军，抄出祁山之后。但见蜀兵望吾寨而来，汝可进兵去劫蜀寨。如蜀兵不动，便撤兵回，不可轻进。"二人受计，引兵而去。真谓淮曰："我两个各引一枝军，伏于寨外，寨中虚堆柴草，只留数人。如蜀兵到，放火为号。"诸将皆分左右，各自准备去了。

却说孔明归帐，先唤赵云、魏延听令。孔明曰："汝二人各

bear the imperial order of his legitimate heir to field an army and chastise the rebels. There is nothing for groveling vassals like you but to get back out of sight and to see if you can somehow salvage your own miserable means of sustenance. How dare you step before the army lines to rant about 'changes in Heaven's ordained periods'? White-haired old fool! Grey-bearded villain! When you go home to the netherworld — any day now — how will you face the twenty-four sovereigns of the Han? Back, old villain, and have the turncoats settle the score with me."

At Kongming's denunciation Wang Lang's chest heaved with rage. A loud cry broke from him, and he fell dead from his horse. A poet of later times wrote of Kongming thus:

> Forth from a land once known as Qin,
> With mettle to match a thousand times ten.
> He came with his light and limber tongue
> And lashed to death the false Wang Lang.

Kongming next pointed his fan at Cao Zhen and said, "I shall not press you. Put your troops in order, and tomorrow we will settle it." With that, he returned to his line, and the two armies retired.[3]

Cao Zhen had Wang Lang's body encoffined and taken back to Chang'an. Deputy Field Marshal Guo Huai said, "Zhuge Liang will surely strike tonight, expecting the army to hold mourning ceremonies. Let us make four units: two to take the mountain byroads and raid the Riverlands camp, and two to wait outside our camp to attack the enemy from the other side." Delighted, Cao Zhen said, "My thinking, exactly." He summoned Cao Zun and Zhu Zan, the two vanguard leaders, and charged them: "Take ten thousand men each and scour the area behind the Qishan hills. The moment you see Riverlands troops moving toward our camp, advance and raid theirs. If the enemy keeps its positions, withdraw. Do not risk engagement." The two left to carry out their orders.

Cao Zhen then said to Guo Huai, "Let's each take a contingent outside the camp, leaving only piles of kindling and straw and a few men inside to signal with fire should the enemy come." The commanders went their several ways and saw to their preparations.

Back in his command tent, Kongming summoned Zhao Zilong and Wei Yan for further instructions: "Take your own troops and raid the Wei

引本部军去劫魏寨。"魏延进曰："曹真深明兵法，必料我乘丧劫寨。他岂不提防？"孔明笑曰："吾正欲曹真知吾去劫寨也。彼必伏兵在祁山之后，待我兵过去，却来袭我寨；吾故令汝二人，引兵前去，过山脚后路，远下营寨，任魏兵来劫吾寨。汝看火起为号，分兵两路：文长拒住山口；子龙引兵杀回，必遇魏兵，却放彼走回，汝乘势攻之，彼必自相掩杀。可获全胜。"二将引兵受计而去。又唤关兴、张苞分付曰："汝二人各引一军，伏于祁山要路；放过魏兵，却从魏兵来路，杀奔魏寨而去。"二人引兵受计去了。又令马岱、王平、张翼、张嶷四将，伏于寨外，四面迎击魏兵。孔明乃虚立寨栅，居中堆起柴草，以备火号；自引诸将退于寨后，以观动静。

　　却说魏先锋曹遵、朱赞黄昏离寨，迤逦前进。二更左侧，遥望山前隐隐有军行动。曹遵自思曰："郭都督真神机妙算！"遂催兵急进。到蜀寨时，将及三更。曹遵先杀入寨，却是空寨，并无一人。料知中计，急撤军回。寨中火起。朱赞兵到，自相掩杀，人马大乱。曹遵与朱赞交马，方知自相践踏。急合兵时，忽四面喊声大震，王平、马岱、张嶷、张翼杀到。曹、朱二人引心腹军百余骑，望大路奔走。忽然鼓角齐鸣，一彪军截住去路，为首大将乃常山赵子龙也，大叫曰："贼将那里去？早早受死！"曹、朱二

camp." "Cao Zhen is too well schooled in the art of warfare," Wei Yan commented, "not to prepare for our attack during the funeral services." Kongming smiled and replied, "That is exactly what I want him to think — that we will raid his camp. He will put troops in ambush behind the hills of Qishan, waiting for us to pass so that he can attack our camp. That's why I want you two to advance, cross the back road at the foot of the mountains, and pitch camp farther along — so the enemy will feel free to attack. When we signal with fire, divide your men into two companies. You, Wei Yan, hold the approach to the hills. Zilong, you come back ready for battle. You will meet up with the Wei army; let them run, but attack when you have the advantage. They will mostly kill one another in the confusion, giving us the victory." The two commanders departed to carry out Kongming's plan.

Next, Kongming ordered Ma Dai, Wang Ping, Zhang Yi, and Zhang Ni to take up positions in ambush on all sides of the camp and prepare to counterattack the Wei army. Kongming himself remained at the empty base where he had kindling and straw piled high to give the signal by fire. He then withdrew behind the site with a few commanders to observe.

* * *

The Wei vanguard, Cao Zun and Zhu Zan, left camp at dusk and snaked forward. During the second watch, they spied soldiers on their left, hardly visible, moving in the distance. Cao Zun reflected, "Field Marshal Guo is really a marvel!" and urged his men forward. It was almost the third watch when he reached the Riverlands camp. Cao Zun charged in but found it empty. Assuming a trap, he retreated quickly. Flames shot up inside the camp just as his partner Zhu Zan arrived, and the two companies fell upon each other in a wild melee. Not until Cao Zun and Zhu Zan had found each other did they realize what was happening. As they hurried to regroup, shouts rang out on all sides of them, and Wang Ping, Ma Dai, Zhang Yi, and Zhang Ni closed in for the kill.

Cao Zun and Zhu Zan were leading about one hundred trusted riders toward the main road when suddenly drums and horns sounded in unison: a band of soldiers barred their way. At their head, Zhao Zilong of Changshan. "Where to, rebels?" he shouted. "Submit quickly or die!" Cao Zun and Zhu Zan fled by the nearest route, but they were accosted

2301

人夺路而走。忽喊声又起，魏延又引一彪军杀到。曹、朱二人大败，夺路奔回本寨。守寨军士，只道蜀兵来劫寨，慌忙放起号火。左边曹真杀至，右边郭淮杀至，自相掩杀。背后三路蜀兵杀到：中央魏延，左边关兴，右边张苞，大杀一阵。魏兵败走十余里，魏将死者极多。孔明全获大胜，方始收兵。曹真、郭淮收拾败军回寨，商议曰："今魏兵势孤，蜀兵势大，将何策以退之？"淮曰："胜负乃兵家常事，不足为忧。某有一计，使蜀兵首尾不能相顾，定然自走矣。"

正是：

可怜魏将难成事，欲向西方索救兵。

未知其计如何，且看下文分解。

at once by Wei Yan's company amid shouts and cries. Utterly defeated, Cao Zun and Zhu Zan returned to their base camp. There the defenders mistook them for Riverlands soldiers and signaled with fire, causing Cao Zhen and Guo Huai to attack from either side. As the Wei forces were slaughtering one another, the real Riverlands attack began from the rear: in the center, Wei Yan; on the left, Guan Xing; on the right, Zhang Bao. They struck in force, and the Wei army retreated ten *li,* having lost many commanders.

His triumph complete, Kongming recalled his army. Cao Zhen and Guo Huai gathered up their beaten troops and returned to the camp. The two commanders shared their appraisal: "Now the Wei army is isolated, and the Shu army is stronger than ever. How can we drive them back?" Then Guo Huai said, "Defeat is a commonplace for the military man. Do not be discouraged. I have a plan to disorganize the Riverlands army and force them to flee." Indeed:

> Pity the Wei leaders who, having failed in their task,
> Must seek their relief from the west!

What was Guo Huai's plan?
Read on.

第九十四回

诸葛亮乘雪破羌兵　司马懿克日擒孟达

　　却说郭淮谓曹真曰："西羌之人，自太祖时连年入贡，文皇帝亦有恩惠加之；我等今可据住险阻，遣人从小路直入羌中求救，许以和亲，羌人必起兵袭蜀兵之后。吾却以大兵击之，首尾夹攻，岂不大胜？"真从之，即遣人星夜驰书赴羌。

　　却说西羌国王彻里吉，自曹操时年年入贡；手下有一文一武：文乃雅丹丞相，武乃越吉元帅。时魏使赍金珠并书到国，先来见雅丹丞相，送了礼物，具言求救之意。雅丹引见国王，呈上书礼。彻里吉览了书，与众商议。雅丹曰："我与魏国素相往来，今曹都督求救，且许和亲，理合依允。"彻里吉从其言，即命雅丹与越吉元帅起羌兵一十五万，皆惯使弓弩、枪刀、蒺藜、飞锤等器；又有战车，用铁叶裹钉，装载粮食军器什物：或用骆驼驾车，或用骡马驾车，号为'铁车兵'。二人辞了国王，领兵直扣西平关。守关蜀将韩祯，急差人赍文报知孔明。

　　孔明闻报，问众将曰："谁敢去退羌兵？"张苞、关兴应曰：

Chapter 94

Zhuge Liang Defeats the Qiang in a Snowstorm
Sima Yi Captures Meng Da in Good Time

Guo Huai disclosed his plan to Cao Zhen: "From the time of the Great Ancestor, Emperor Wu (Cao Cao), the Western Qiang have submitted annual tribute; Emperor Wen (Cao Pi) was shown them especial kindness and generosity. Let us maintain our defense at this strategic point and send to the Qiang for help. An alliance by marriage should persuade them to strike the Riverlands army from behind as we attack in force. Engaged on two fronts, the enemy will yield!" Cao Zhen approved and sent a messenger to the Qiang.

King Cheliji of the Western Qiang had presented yearly tribute to the Han court since the era of Cao Cao. He was served on the civil side by Prime Minister Yadan, and by Marshal Yueji on the military. On arriving with Cao Zhen's letter together with gifts of gold and pearls, the Wei emissary went first to Prime Minister Yadan to deliver the ritual gifts and explain Cao Zhen's purposes. Yadan conducted the man into the presence of King Cheliji, who accepted the letter and gifts and then conferred with his chiefs. "We have long maintained an unbroken friendship with the kingdom of Wei," Yadan said to them. "Now Field Marshal Cao seeks our help and promises a marriage to strengthen the alliance. There is no reason to refuse his request." Cheliji approved and ordered Yadan and Yueji to muster one hundred and fifty thousand Qiang, warriors skilled in bow and crossbow, spear and sword, studded mace and flying hammer. They also had "iron wagons" — war chariots protected with iron armor — to transport their food and equipment. Some were drawn by camel, some by mule. Yadan and Yueji bade their king good-bye and led their troops to Xiping Pass. The Shu commander guarding the pass, Han Zhen, dispatched a report to Kongming.

Informed of the threat, Kongming asked his commanders, "Who will

2305

"某等愿往。"孔明曰："汝二人要去,奈路途不熟。"遂唤马岱曰："汝素知羌人之性,久居彼处,可作向导。"便起精兵五万,与兴、苞二人同往。兴、苞等引兵而去。行有数日,早遇羌兵。关兴先引百余骑登山坡看时,只见羌兵把铁车首尾相连,随处结寨;车上遍排兵器,就似城池一般。兴睹之良久,无破敌之策,回寨与张苞、马岱商议。岱曰："且待来日见阵,观看虚实,另作计议。"次早,分兵三路:关兴在中,张苞在左,马岱在右,三路兵齐进。羌兵阵里,越吉元帅手挽铁锤,腰悬宝雕弓,跃马奋勇而出。关兴招三路兵径进。忽见羌兵分在两边,中央放出铁车,如潮涌一般,弓弩一齐骤发。蜀兵大败,马岱、张苞两军先退;关兴一军,被羌兵一裹,直围入西北角上去了。

兴在垓心,左冲右突,不能得脱;铁车密围,就如城池。蜀兵你我不能相顾。兴望山谷中寻路而走。看看天晚,但见一簇皂旗,蜂拥而来,一员羌将,手提铁锤大叫曰："小将休走!吾乃越吉元帅也!"关兴急走到前面,尽力纵马加鞭,正遇断涧,只得回马来战越吉,兴终是胆寒,抵敌不住,望涧中而逃;被越吉赶到,一铁锤打来,兴急闪过,正中马胯。那马望涧中便倒,兴

drive the invaders back?" Zhang Bao and Guan Xing volunteered. "How will you manage, not knowing the roads?" Kongming asked, and he summoned Ma Dai. "You know the ways of the Qiang," he said, "and have lived among them long enough to serve as a guide." Kongming called up fifty thousand well-trained men and placed them under Zhang Bao and Guan Xing; the two set out and within several days had met up with the Qiang troops. Guan Xing led a hundred horsemen up a slope and observed the enemy linking their iron-paneled wagons together and pitching campsites here and there. The wagons, on which weapons were arrayed, functioned like a barrier defending a city. Guan Xing watched for a long time; but having no plan of attack, he returned to his camp to confer with Zhang Bao and Ma Dai. Ma Dai said, "Tomorrow look for weaknesses in their formation. Then we can plan further." The next morning, their forces divided into three — Guan Xing in the center, Zhang Bao on the left, and Ma Dai on the right — they advanced together.

From the Qiang line Marshal Yueji sprang forward brave and smart, a steel hammer in his hand, a figured bow at his waist. Guan Xing motioned the three companies ahead. Suddenly, the Qiang line parted and the iron wagons came surging through like a tide as their crossbowmen filled the air with bolts. The Riverlands troops suffered a stunning defeat, and Ma Dai and Zhang Bao, the two wings, retreated. Guan Xing's company, however, had been enveloped by the Qiang and forced toward the northwest.

Surrounded, Guan Xing thrust left and right but could not get past the wall of iron wagons. The Riverlands troops were unable to look out for one another, and Guan Xing fled, hoping to find a way out of the valley. Evening was fast approaching. He spied a cluster of black flags swarming toward him. A Qiang commander, armed with a steel hammer, shouted, "I am Marshal Yueji. Go no farther, little general!" Guan Xing dashed ahead, laying on the whip, but a swift stream blocked his way, forcing him to turn and do battle with Yueji.

Guan Xing's courage deserted him. Unable to hold his ground, he plunged into the stream. Yueji overtook him and swung his heavy hammer, striking the horse squarely on the hipbone; the horse toppled, throwing Guan Xing into the water. Suddenly he heard a voice ring out as Yueji

落于水中。忽听得一声响处，背后越吉连人带马，平白地倒下水来。兴就水中挣起看时，只见岸上一员大将，杀退羌兵。兴提刀待砍越吉，吉跃水而走。关兴得了越吉马，牵到岸上，整顿鞍辔，绰刀上马。只见那员将，尚在前面追杀羌兵。兴自思此人救我性命，当与相见，遂拍马赶来。看看至近，只见云雾之中，隐隐有一大将，面如重枣，眉若卧蚕，绿袍金铠，提青龙刀，骑赤兔马，手绰美髯——分明认得是父亲关公。兴大惊。忽见关公以手望东南指曰："吾儿可速望此路去。吾当护汝归寨。"言讫不见。关兴望东南急走。至半夜，忽一彪军到，乃张苞也，问兴曰："你曾见二伯父否？"兴曰："你何由知之？"苞曰："我被铁车军追急，忽见伯父自空而下，惊退羌兵，指曰：'汝从这条路去救吾儿。'因此引军径来寻你。'关兴亦说前事，共相嗟异。二人同归寨内。马岱接着，对二人说："此军无计可退。我守住寨栅，你二人去禀丞相，用计破之。"于是兴、苞二人，星夜来见孔明，备说此事。

孔明随命赵云、魏延各引一军埋伏去讫；然后点三万军，带了姜维、张翼、关兴、张苞，亲自来到马岱寨中歇定。次日上高阜处观看，见铁车连络不绝，人马纵横，往来驰骤。孔明曰："此不难破也。"唤马岱、张翼分付如此如此。二人去了，乃唤姜维曰："伯约知破车之法否？"维曰："羌人惟恃一勇力，岂知妙

and his horse for no apparent reason went flying into the water, too. Guan Xing struggled against the waves to get a look. There on the bank he saw a powerful general driving off the Qiang soldiers. Guan Xing raised his sword to cut down Yueji, but he leaped from the water and fled.

Guan Xing took Yueji's horse, drew it up to the bank, and rearranged the gear on it. Then hefting his sword, he mounted, all the while watching that same unknown general up ahead still pursuing the Qiang. Thinking to meet the man who had saved his life, Guan Xing rode hard after him, but as he drew close — lo! in swirls of mist he discerned the dim figure of a mighty general, his face dark as dates, his eyebrows like sleeping silkworms; in green battle gown and metal armor, he held his sword high, a Green Dragon; the horse he rode was a Red Hare; he fingered his beard gently. All doubt vanished. It was his late father! The astounded Guan Xing watched Lord Guan point southeast and say, "Flee that way, my son. I will protect you until you reach camp." With that, he was gone.

Guan Xing fled in the direction the apparition had indicated. Toward midnight a band of troops approached him, led by Zhang Bao, who asked, "Did you see Second Uncle?" "How did you know?" Guan Xing asked in reply. "A force of iron wagons was chasing me, when I saw him descend from the sky and drive off the Qiang troops. He said, 'Take this road and save my son.' So I led my troops straight here to find you." Guan Xing then recounted his experience to their mutual amazement. As the two returned to camp, Ma Dai welcomed them, saying, "There is no way to repel the enemy. I will defend the campsite while you two petition the prime minister for a plan to defeat them." Accordingly, Guan Xing and Zhang Bao went to Kongming and gave him a full report.

Kongming ordered Zhao Zilong and Wei Yan each to hide one company in ambush outside camp. He then mustered thirty thousand soldiers and marched to Ma Dai's camp, together with Jiang Wei, Zhang Yi, Guan Xing, and Zhang Bao; there he rested his forces. The next day from a hilltop he watched the enemy's iron wagons and infantry and cavalry moving in every direction with dispatch. "This will not be difficult to break up," Kongming said, and he gave Ma Dai and Zhang Yi certain instructions. After they had left, he asked Jiang Wei, "Do you see a way to defeat them?" Jiang Wei replied, "The Qiang rely on raw courage and

计乎？"孔明笑曰："汝知吾心也。今彤云密布，朔风紧急，天将降雪，吾计可施矣。"便令关兴、张苞二人引兵埋伏去讫；令姜维领兵出战：但有铁车兵来，退后便走；寨口虚立旌旗，不设军马。准备已定。

　　是时十二月终，果然天降大雪。姜维引军出，越吉引铁车兵来。姜维即退走。羌兵赶到寨前，姜维从寨后而去。羌兵直到寨外观看，听得寨内鼓琴之声，四壁皆空竖旌旗，急回报越吉。越吉心疑，未敢轻进。雅丹丞相曰："此诸葛亮诡计，虚设疑兵耳。可以攻之。"越吉引兵至寨前，但见孔明携琴上车，引数骑入寨，望后而走。羌兵抢入寨栅，直赶过山口，见小车隐隐转入林中去了。雅丹谓越吉曰："这等兵虽有埋伏，不足为惧。"遂引大兵追赶。又见姜维兵俱在雪地之中奔走。越吉大怒，催兵急追。山路被雪漫盖，一望平坦。正赶之间，忽报蜀兵自山后而出。雅丹曰："纵有些小伏兵，何足惧哉！"只顾催趱兵马，往前进发。忽然一声响，如山崩地陷，羌兵俱落于坑堑之中；背后铁车正行得紧溜，急难收止，并拥而来，自相践踏。后兵急要回时，左边关兴，右边张苞，两军冲出，万弩齐发；背后姜维、马

strength alone. What do they care for clever tactics?" "How well you know my thinking," Kongming said with a smile. "The thick clouds and rising north wind presage snow; and once we have snow, my plan will work." Kongming ordered Guan Xing and Zhang Bao to ambush the enemy, and Jiang Wei to give battle openly but to withdraw if the iron wagon force was deployed. Lastly, by the entrance to the camp Kongming had decoy banners planted but deployed no troops. He thus completed the preparations.

It was winter, the end of the twelfth month.[1] The snow Kongming had expected began to fall. Jiang Wei advanced, then retreated as Yueji brought on his iron wagons. The Qiang troops pursued him to Kongming's camp, but Jiang Wei escaped through its rear. The Qiang had advanced to the edge of the camp, when they heard the sound of a zither being strummed from inside. On all four walls of the stockade they saw the decoy banners flying, and hurried back to Yueji to report. Puzzled, Yueji chose not to advance.

Prime Minister Yadan said to Marshal Yueji, "Zhuge Liang's decoys. Let the attack continue." Yueji led his force to the front of the Riverlands camp, where he found Kongming climbing onto his chariot, a zither under his arm; sparsely attended, he left by the rear gate. The Qiang soldiers forced their way into the site and pursued Kongming, passing the gateway to the mountain. Ahead in the distance a small chariot seemed to be turning into a wood. "Even if there's an ambush, it will be nothing to be afraid of," Yadan said to Yueji, and continued to pursue Kongming in force. They saw Jiang Wei's troops dashing forward in the snow. Yueji angrily pressed forward. The snow had blanketed the pathways, smoothing out the landscape. Yueji was informed that Riverlands troops were coming from behind a hill. Yadan said, "A few troops in hiding. Nothing to worry about," and raced ahead.

Suddenly a rumbling sound like an avalanche filled the air as the Qiang troops tumbled into a moat. The iron wagons went out of control and slid down after them, one crashing into the next. Troops farther behind tried to turn back but were attacked by Guan Xing and Zhang Bao from both sides as ten thousand crossbowmen let fly their bolts. From the rear the corps under Jiang Wei, Ma Dai, and Zhang Yi moved in for the kill. The

岱、张冀三路兵又杀到。铁车兵大乱。越吉元帅望后面山谷中而逃，正逢关兴；交马只一合，被兴举刀大喝一声，砍死于马下。雅丹丞相早被马岱活捉，解投大寨来。羌兵四散逃窜。孔明升帐，马岱押过雅丹来。孔明叱武士去其缚，赐酒压惊，用好言抚慰。雅丹深感其德。孔明曰："吾主乃大汉皇帝，今命吾讨贼，尔如何反助逆？吾今放汝回去，说与汝主：吾国与尔乃邻邦，永结盟好，勿听反贼之言。"遂将所获羌兵及车马器械，尽给还雅丹，俱放回国。众皆拜谢而去。孔明引三军连夜投祁山大寨而来，命关兴、张苞引军先行；一面差人赍表奏报捷音。

却说曹真连日望羌人消息，忽有伏路军来报说："蜀兵拔寨收拾起程。"郭淮大喜曰："此因羌兵攻击，故尔退去。"遂分两路追赶。前面蜀兵乱走，魏兵随后追袭。先锋曹遵正赶之间，忽然鼓声大震，一彪军闪出，为首大将乃魏延也，大叫曰："反贼休走！"曹遵大惊，拍马交锋；不三合，被魏延一刀斩于马下。副先锋朱赞引兵追赶，忽然一彪军闪出，为首大将乃赵云也。朱赞措手不及，被云一枪刺死。曹真、郭淮见西路先锋有失，欲收兵回；背后喊声大震，鼓角齐鸣：关兴、张苞两路兵杀出，围了曹真、郭淮，痛杀一阵。曹、郭二人，引败兵冲路走脱。

iron wagon force had fallen apart. Marshal Yueji ducked into a recess behind but fell to Gaun Xing's sword in a brief clash. Prime Minister Yadan was captured alive by Ma Dai and brought to the main camp. The Qiang soldiers scurried off in the four directions.

Kongming took his seat in the command tent, and Ma Dai led the prisoner in. Kongming had Yadan freed, allowed him wine to relieve his fears, and spoke kind and comforting words to him. Yadan's gratitude was boundless. Kongming said, "The lord I serve, August Emperor of the great Han, commands me to chastise rebels and traitors. How dare you abet their sedition contrary to your proper duty? I shall let you return to tell this to your lord: 'My kingdom and yours are neighbors, pledged to eternal amity. Give no heed to the counsel of traitors.'" So saying, Kongming permitted all the captured Qiang as well as their wagons, horses, and equipment to return home with Yadan. The entire Qiang army prostrated itself in gratitude and departed. Directly afterward, Kongming led his three armies to the main camp in the hills of Qishan. He commanded Guan Xing and Zhang Bao to lead the way; and he sent a formal report of the victory to the court in Chengdu.

* * *

Meanwhile, the days had gone by while Cao Zhen waited for news from the Qiang. Suddenly, a soldier from the ambush corps reported: "The Riverlands army has broken camp and begun marching." Most pleased, Guo Huai said, "They are retreating because of the Qiang attack," and he sent two companies in pursuit. Ahead the Riverlands army fled chaotically, and the Wei army gave chase. Cao Zun was in the vanguard, when drumbeats began to shake the ground and a band of troops flashed into sight; their leader, Wei Yan. "Halt, traitors!" he cried. An astonished Cao Zun laid on the whip and engaged Wei Yan, who swiftly cut him down from his horse. The deputy vanguard leader Zhu Zan then entered the imbroglio, but a group under Zhao Zilong sprang into action, spearing Zhu Zan before he could defend himself.

Cao Zhen and Guo Huai saw the two companies weakening and tried to recall them; but from behind shouts erupted, and drums and horns announced Guan Xing and Zhang Bao: their two corps surrounded Cao Zhen and Guo Huai. The two northern commanders withstood the fierce

蜀兵全胜,直追到渭水,夺了魏寨。曹真折了两个先锋,哀伤不已;只得写本申朝,乞拨援兵。

却说魏主曹睿设朝,近臣奏曰:"大都督曹真,数败于蜀,折了两个先锋,羌兵又折了无数,其势甚急。今上表求救,请陛下裁处。"睿大惊,急问退军之策。华歆奏曰:"须是陛下御驾亲征,大会诸侯,人皆用命,方可退也。不然,长安有失,关中危矣!"太傅钟繇奏曰:"凡为将者,智过于人,则能制人,孙子云:'知彼知己,百战百胜。'臣量曹真虽久用兵,非诸葛亮对手。臣以全家良贱,保举一人,可退蜀兵。未知圣意准否?"睿曰:"卿乃大老元臣;有何贤士,可退蜀兵,早召来与朕分忧。"钟繇奏曰:"向者,诸葛亮欲兴师犯境,但惧此人,故散流言,使陛下疑而去之,方敢长驱大进。今若复用之,则亮自退矣。"睿问何人。繇曰:"骠骑大将军司马懿也。"睿叹曰:"此事朕亦悔之。今仲达现在何地?"繇曰:"近闻仲达在宛城闲住。"睿即降诏,遣使持节,复司马懿官职,加为平西都督,就起南阳诸路军马,

assault, however, and managed to lead their defeated force away. The triumphant Riverlands army pursued them to the River Wei and plundered the northern army's main camp. Cao Zhen, in despair over the loss of both vanguards, could only appeal in writing to the Wei court for reinforcement.

The ruler of Wei, Cao Rui, was at court session when a personal attendant brought the news: "First Field Marshal Cao Zhen has suffered successive defeats in the Riverlands. His vanguards are lost, and the Qiang have taken heavy losses too. In dire straits, he petitions for aid and requests Your Majesty's decision." In alarm, Cao Rui demanded a plan for driving back the Riverlands force. Hua Xin addressed him: "The only way is for Your Majesty himself to lead the campaign; gather the lords in a general assembly to ensure that your command will be universally obeyed. Otherwise, Chang'an may fall, endangering the land within the passes."

Imperial Guardian Zhong Yao also addressed the sovereign: "To command men means to control them through superior knowledge. Sunzi has said, 'Know the enemy, know yourself; never know defeat!' In my opinion, Cao Zhen, despite his long experience in war, is no match for Zhuge Liang. I will guarantee with the lives of my family members and household servants the one man who can force back the Riverlands army. I wonder if Your Majesty in his sagely wisdom might approve my recommendation." Cao Rui answered, "You are a trusted elder, my lord. If you know a man capable of repelling the foe, summon him at once so that he may share our burden." Zhong Yao said to Cao Rui: "This is the man Zhuge Liang feared most when he planned to march across our borders, the man whose loyalty Zhuge Liang induced Your Majesty to suspect by spreading rumors about his motives. Your Majesty removed him, and Zhuge Liang advanced in force. Summon this man back, and Zhuge Liang will retreat on his own."

Cao Rui asked the man's name. Zhong Yao replied, "Regent-Marshal and General of the Flying Cavalry Sima Yi." Cao Rui sighed. "The incident was regrettable," he said. "Where is Sima Yi now?" "Idle in Wancheng, according to the latest report," was the reply. Cao Rui issued an edict conferring general military authority on Sima Yi, restoring his former office, and adding the title of Field Marshal Who Conquers the

前赴长安。睿御驾亲征,令司马懿克日到彼聚会。使命星夜望宛城去了。

　　却说孔明自出师以来,累获全胜,心中甚喜;正在祁山寨中,会聚议事,忽报镇守永安宫李严令子李丰来见。孔明只道东吴犯境,心甚惊疑,唤入帐中问之。丰曰:"特来报喜。"孔明曰:"有何喜?"丰曰:"昔日孟达降魏,乃不得已也。彼时曹丕爱其才,时以骏马金珠赐之,曾同辇出入,封为散骑常侍,领新城太守,镇守上庸、金城等处,委以西南之任。自丕死后,曹睿即位,朝中多人嫉妒,孟达日夜不安,常谓诸将曰:'我本蜀将,势逼于此。'今累差心腹人,持书来见家父,教早晚代禀丞相:前者五路下川之时,曾有此意;今在新城,听知丞相伐魏,欲起金城、新城、上庸三处军马,就彼举事,径取洛阳;丞相取长安,两京大定矣。今某引来人并累次书信呈上。"孔明大喜,厚赏李丰等。忽细作人报说:"魏主曹睿,一面驾幸长安;一面诏司马懿

West, in which capacity he was immediately to march all troops in Nanyang to Chang'an. Cao Rui took personal command of the expedition; Sima Yi was to meet him in Chang'an at a fixed date. A messenger set out directly for Wancheng.

*　*　*

Since leading his hosts forth, Kongming had gone from victory to victory, and he rejoiced inwardly. During a meeting in the Qishan camp he was informed of a visit by Li Feng, paid at the behest of his father, Li Yan, chief guardian of the Palace of Enduring Peace.[2] Kongming was alarmed, thinking that the Southland was invading Shu territory, when he summoned Li Feng into his tent.

Li Feng said, "I bring good news." "What news?" Kongming asked. "Meng Da's defection to Wei was not of his own volition. At that time Cao Pi so admired his abilities that he presented him with many gifts of fine horses, gold, and pearls. He also shared the royal carriage with Meng Da and, after appointing him detached imperial cavalier and regular attendant,[3] made him governor of Xincheng with authority over Shangyong and Jincheng and responsibility for dealing with the Riverlands. However, when Cao Pi died and Cao Rui came to power, the widening jealousies at court caused Meng Da endless anxiety, and he was always saying to his generals, 'I am a Riverlands general. Circumstances compelled me to this.'

2317

"Lately he has more than once sent trusted men bearing letters to my father asking him to intercede with the prime minister at the earliest chance. When the five northern armies descended upon us, Meng Da already had this in mind. Now at Xincheng, hearing of Your Excellency's campaign against Wei, he proposes to mobilize Jincheng, Xincheng, and Shangyong and take action then and there against Luoyang. If Your Excellency seizes Chang'an at the same time; the two capitals will be conquered. I've brought Meng Da's envoy; and I have the letters my father has received to submit to Your Excellency." Delighted, Kongming rewarded Li Feng and the others. At that moment a spy delivered an unexpected report: "The ruler of Wei, Cao Rui, is coming to Chang'an himself after having restored Sime Yi to his former position, making him Field Marshal Who Conquers the West. Cao Rui has raised his own army and will rendez-

复职，加为平西都督，起本处之兵，于长安聚会。"孔明大惊。参军马谡曰："量曹睿何足道！若来长安，可就而擒之。丞相何故惊讶？"孔明曰："吾岂惧曹睿耶？所患者惟司马懿一人而已。今孟达欲举大事，若遇司马懿，事必败矣。达非司马懿对手，必被所擒。孟达若死，中原不易得也。"马谡曰："何不急修书，令孟达提防？"孔明从之，即修书令来人星夜回报孟达。

却说孟达在新城，专望心腹人回报。一日，心腹人到来，将孔明回书呈上。孟达拆封视之。书略曰：

> 近得书，足知公忠义之心，不忘故旧，吾甚喜慰。若成大事，则公汉朝中兴第一功臣也。然极宜谨密，不可轻易托人。慎之！戒之！近闻曹睿复诏司马懿起宛、洛之兵，若闻公举事，必先至矣。须万全提备，勿视为等闲也。

孟达览毕，笑曰："人言孔明心多，今观此事可知矣。"乃具回书，令心腹人来答孔明。孔明唤入帐中。其人呈上回书。孔明拆封视之。书曰：

> 适承钧教，安敢少怠。窃谓司马懿之事，不必惧也：宛城离洛阳约八百里，至新城一千二百里。若司马懿闻达举事，须表奏魏主：往复一月间事，达城池已固，诸将与三军皆在深险之地。司马懿即来，达何惧哉？丞相宽怀，惟听捷报！

孔明看毕，掷书于地而顿足曰："孟达必死于司马懿之手矣！"马谡问曰："丞相何谓也？"孔明曰："兵法云：'攻其不备，出其不意。'岂容料在一月之期？曹睿既委任司马懿，逢寇即

vous with Sime Yi in Chang'an."

The news of the northern ruler's advance alarmed Kongming. His military adviser, Ma Su, said, "Cao Rui is not much of a threat. If he comes to Chang'an, we will capture him directly. You have nothing to fear, Your Excellency." "You think I fear Cao Rui?" Kongming replied. "I worry about Sima Yi! Meng Da wants to make a break, but he's no match for Sima Yi; he will only be captured. After that the central heartland will be all the harder to regain." Ma Su said, "What about forewarning Meng Da?" Kongming adopted this suggestion and that night sent Meng Da's envoy off with a letter to Meng Da, who was in Xincheng eagerly awaiting his envoy's return. Before long Meng Da had Kongming's letter. In essence it read:

> Your recent letters amply manifest Your Lordship's loyal and honorable heart. That you still remember former friends gives me joy and comfort. If we succeed, you will be the foremost vassal of the Han restoration. But extreme caution is essential: no one is to be lightly trusted. Be on guard. Be forewarned. I have learned that Cao Rui has called on Sima Yi to mobilize Wancheng and Luoyang. If he hears you have taken action, he will move against you first. The most comprehensive defense preparation is required. Do not look on this as a routine situation.

Reading the text, Meng Da smiled and said, "Kongming is known for being excessively cautious. Having read this letter, I now understand why." He prepared a reply, which his messenger took back to Kongming. In essence it read:

> Having received this weighty charge, I dare not relax. In my humble view, Sima Yi is not to be feared. Wancheng is about eight hundred *li* from Luoyang and twelve hundred *li* from Xincheng. If Sima Yi finds out I mean to act, he will have to submit a memorial to the Wei ruler. That would take a month. My fortifications are sound; my leaders and their forces are established in strategic recesses. Let Sima Yi come. What have I to fear? Rest easy, Your Excellency, and prepare for reports of victory!

2319

Kongming threw the letter to the ground and, stamping his foot, cried, "He will die at Sima Yi's hands!" "What does Your Excellency mean?" Ma Su asked. "The art of war tells us to 'attack the enemy where he's unprepared; appear where he does not expect you.' How can he count on a month's delay? Cao Rui has already empowered Sima Yi to clear

除,何待奏闻?若知孟达反,不须十日,兵必到矣,安能措手耶?"众将皆服。孔明急令来人回报曰:"若未举事,切莫教同事者知之;知则必败。"其人拜辞,归新城去了。

却说司马懿在宛城闲住,闻知魏兵累败于蜀,乃仰天长叹。懿长子司马师,字子元;次子司马昭,字子尚:二人素有大志,通晓兵书。当日侍立于侧,见懿长叹,乃问曰:"父亲何为长叹?"懿曰:"汝辈岂知大事耶?"司马师曰:"莫非叹魏主不用乎?"司马昭笑曰:"早晚必来宣召父亲也。"言未已,忽报天使持节至。懿听诏毕,遂调宛城诸路军马。忽又报金城太守申仪家人,有机密事求见。懿唤入密室问之,其人细说孟达欲反之事。更有孟达心腹人李辅并达外甥邓贤,随状出首。司马懿听毕,以手加额曰:"此乃皇上齐天之洪福也!诸葛亮兵在祁山,杀得内外人皆胆落;今天子不得已而幸长安,若旦夕不用吾时,孟达一举,两京休矣!此贼必通谋诸葛亮:吾先擒之,诸葛亮定然心寒,自退兵也。"长子司马师曰:"父亲可急写表申奏天子。"懿曰:"若等圣旨,往复一月之间,事无及矣。"即传令教人马起程,一日要行二日之路,如迟立斩;一面令参军梁畿赍

out rebels wherever he finds them: he won't be waiting for any memorials. Ten days after learning of Meng Da's defection, he will attack, long before Meng Da is ready." The commanders saw the truth of Kongming's comment. Kongming swiftly penned an order to Meng Da: "Until you act, let no one know your mind — or defeat is certain." Meng Da's courier took formal leave and returned to Xincheng with this order.

*   *   *

Biding his time in Wancheng, Sima Yi heard of the Wei army's defeats and sent a long, despairing sigh Heavenward. Sima Yi's eldest son, Sima Shi (Ziyuan), as well as his second son, Sima Zhao (Zishang), harbored grand ambitions and had acquainted themselves with the works of military science. That day standing beside Sima Yi, they asked, "What makes you sigh so deeply, Father?" "What do you know of our great cause?" he answered them. Sima Shi said, "Could it be because the ruler of Wei has left you to languish?" Sima Zhao smiled and said, "The Emperor will soon send for you." Even as he spoke, the imperial envoy arrived.

In accordance with the new edict, Sima Yi assigned several field armies to Wancheng in the west. Suddenly he had report that a kinsman of Shen Yi, governor of Jincheng, was seeking audience on a secret matter. Sima Yi received the envoy in his chambers and learned from him the details of Meng Da's intended defection back to Shu. As evidence, the envoy had with him the written confessions of Li Fu, Meng Da's trusted companion, and Deng Xian, Meng Da's nephew. Sima Yi clapped his hand to his brow and said, "What marvelous good fortune for my sovereign! Zhuge Liang's army is now in Qishan. Their recent victories have struck terror in the hearts of all and compelled the Son of Heaven to grace Chang'an himself. He must send me into action before Meng Da defects and the two capitals fall in a single stroke. The traitor connives with Zhuge Liang. But timely capture will dampen Zhuge Liang's enthusiasm and induce him to retreat."

Sima Shi, the eldest son, said "Father, write for the Emperor's approval at once." "And wait a month for the edict?" Sima Yi exclaimed. He ordered the army to march double time and to execute laggards. At the same time, to forestall Meng Da's suspicions, Sima Yi dispatched

檄星夜去新城,教孟达等准备征进,使其不疑。梁畿先行,懿随后发兵。行了二日,山坡下转出一军,乃是右将军徐晃。晃下马见懿,说:"天子驾到长安,亲拒蜀兵,今都督何往?"懿低言曰:"今孟达造反,吾去擒之耳。"晃曰:"某愿为先锋。"懿大喜,合兵一处。徐晃为前部,懿在中军,二子押后。又行了二日,前军哨马捉住孟达心腹人,搜出孔明回书,来见司马懿。懿曰:"吾不杀汝,汝从头细说。"其人只得将孔明、孟达往复之事,一一告说。懿看了孔明回书,大惊曰:"世间能者所见皆同。吾机先被孔明识破。幸得天子有福,获此消息:孟达今无能为矣。"遂星夜催军前行。

却说孟达在新城,约下金城太守申仪、上庸太守申耽,克日举事。耽、仪二人佯许之,每日调练军马,只待魏兵到,便为内应;却报孟达言:军器粮草,俱未完备,不敢约期起事。达信之不疑。忽报参军梁畿来到,孟达迎入城中。畿传司马懿将令曰:"司马都督今奉天子诏,起诸路军以退蜀兵。太守可集本部军马听候调遣。"达问曰:"都督何日起程?"畿曰:"此时约离宛

Military Adviser Liang Ji to Xincheng with orders for Meng Da to prepare to join the expedition. Liang Ji set out first; Sima Yi followed with the army.

When they had been on the march for two days, a company of men appeared from behind a hill: it was General of the Right Xu Huang and his men. Xu Huang dismounted and came before Sima Yi. "The Son of Heaven is now in Chang'an confronting the Riverlands army," he said. "Where is the field marshal headed?" Sima Yi replied in a low voice, "Meng Da is in revolt. I am going to get him." "Then put me in the vanguard," Xu Huang said. Pleased by this offer, Sima Yi combined the two forces. Xu Huang led the forward army, Sima Yi the center, and his two sons the rear.

After another two days, scouts from the forward army captured Meng Da's trusted envoy. They discovered Kongming's reply on his person and brought him before Sima Yi, who said, "Tell all and I'll spare you." The envoy disclosed the entire exchange between Kongming and Meng Da. On reading Kongming's reply, Sima Yi said in astonishment, "Able men think alike. Kongming saw through my devices. Luckily for the Son of Heaven, we have come by this information. Meng Da will be helpless now." He resumed the advance at a rapid pace.

From Xincheng, Meng Da had fixed the time to strike with the governor of Jincheng, Shen Yi, and the governor of Shangyong, Shen Dan, both of whom feigned agreement. Each day they trained their forces while waiting for the arrival of the Wei army, with whom they meant to collaborate; but to Meng Da they protested that they lacked the equipment and provisions to enable them to move at the appointed time. Meng Da accepted their story.

Liang Ji arrived, and Meng Da welcomed the unexpected visitor into the city. Liang Ji delivered Sima Yi's order, saying, "Field Commander Sima holds the edict of the Son of Heaven directing him to muster several field armies and repel the Riverlands army. Gather your forces, Governor, and await instructions." "When will he set out?" Meng Da asked. "He should have left Wancheng for Chang'an by now," was the reply. Meng Da thought to himself, "My cause will succeed!" He feted Liang Ji and escorted him out of the city. Next, he notified Shen Dan and Shen

2323

城,望长安去了。"达暗喜曰:"吾大事成矣!"遂设宴待了梁畿,送出城外,即报申耽、申仪知道,明日举事,换上大汉旗号,发诸路军马,径取洛阳。忽报:"城外尘土冲天,不知何处兵来。"孟达登城视之,只见一彪军,打着"右将军徐晃"旗号,飞奔城下。达大惊,急扯起吊桥。徐晃坐下马收拾不住,直来到壕边,高叫曰:"反贼孟达,早早受降!"达大怒,急开弓射之,正中徐晃头额,魏将救去。城上乱箭射下,魏兵方退。孟达恰待开门追赶,四面旌旗蔽日,司马懿兵到。达仰天长叹曰:"果不出孔明所料也!"于是闭门坚守。

　　却说徐晃被孟达射中头额,众军救到寨中,取了箭头,令医调治;当晚身死,时年五十九岁。司马懿令人扶柩还洛阳安葬。次日,孟达登城遍视,只见魏兵四面围得铁桶相似。达行坐不安,惊疑未定,忽见两路兵自外杀来,旗上大书"申耽"、"申仪"。孟达只道是救军到,忙引本部兵大开城门杀出。耽、仪大叫曰:"反贼休走!早早受死!"达见事变,拨马望城中便走,城上乱箭射下。李辅、邓贤二人在城上大骂曰:"吾等已献了城也!"达夺路而走,申耽赶来。达人困马乏,措手不及,被申耽一枪刺于马下,枭其首级。余军皆降。李辅、邓贤大开城门,迎接司马懿入城。抚民劳军已毕,遂遣人奏知魏主曹睿。睿大喜,教将孟达首级去洛阳城市示众;加申耽、申仪官职,就随司马懿征进;命李辅,邓贤守新城、上庸。

Yi to be ready the following day to raise the banner of Han and march east on Luoyang.

It was with surprise, therefore, that Meng Da learned that an unidentified army was approaching. He climbed the wall, but all he could make out was a band of soldiers racing toward him under a banner reading "General of the Right Xu Huang." Alarmed, Meng Da had the drawbridge raised as Xu Huang, making no attempt to rein in, rode directly to the moat and shouted: "Traitor Meng Da! Surrender now!" Meng Da shot Xu Huang through the forehead, and the Wei commanders carried him away; volleys of bolts from the wall drove the Wei troops back. Meng Da ordered the gates opened so he could pursue, but all at once banners darkened the sky on every side: the army of Sima Yi had come. Meng Da lifted his face to the sky, sighed in despair, and said, "Just as Kongming anticipated." He then sealed the gates.

Xu Huang was carried to camp and treated by a surgeon, but he died that night at the age of fifty-nine. Sima Yi had the coffin returned to Luoyang for proper burial. The next day Meng Da ascended the wall and saw the Wei troops ringing the city as tightly as iron hoops around a bucket. Fear and doubt tormented him. Suddenly he saw two companies approaching in the distance; their banners read "Shen Dan" and "Shen Yi." Thinking rescue at hand, Meng Da hastily opened the gates and came out fighting. But the two governors shouted, "Traitor! Halt! Prepare to die!" Meng Da realized that a coup had occurred and rode back toward the city; but arrows now rained upon him, and Li Fu and Deng Xian shouted down, "We have delivered the city." Meng Da fled by the nearest road, Shen Dan in pursuit. Exhausted, his mount spent, Meng Da could not defend himself. Shen Dan speared him and severed his head,[4] and his companions surrendered. Li Fu and Deng Xian flung wide the city gates and welcomed Sima Yi, who reassured the people and rewarded the soldiers; then he notified the Wei ruler of the victory. Overjoyed, Cao Rui had Meng Da's head brought to Luoyang and shown to the populace. The two governors, Shen Dan and Shen Yi, were promoted and told to accompany Sima Yi on the campaign against the Riverlands; Li Fu and Deng Xian were ordered to defend Xincheng and Shangyong.[5]

Sima Yi marched to Chang'an, pitched camp before its walls, and

2325

却说司马懿引兵到长安城外下寨。懿入城来见魏主。睿大喜曰:"朕一时不明,误中反间之计,悔之无及。今达造反,非卿等制之,两京休矣!"懿奏曰:"臣闻申仪密告反情,意欲表奏陛下,恐往复迟滞,故不待圣旨,星夜而去。若待奏闻,则中诸葛亮之计也。"言罢,将孔明回孟达密书奉上。睿看毕,大喜曰:"卿之学识,过于孙、吴矣!"赐金钺斧一对,后遇机密重事,不必奏闻,便宜行事。就令司马懿出关破蜀。懿奏曰:"臣举一大将,可为先锋。"睿曰:"卿举何人?"懿曰:"右将军张郃,可当此任。"睿笑曰:"朕正欲用之。"遂命张郃为前部先锋,随司马懿离长安来破蜀兵。

正是:

　　既有谋臣能用智,又求猛将助施威。

未知胜负如何,且看下文分解。

entered the city. On receiving him, the ruler of Wei said, "For a time I was fooled by the enemy's plot to turn me against you. But regrets are pointless now. Meng Da's revolt could have cost us both capitals had you not brought him under control." Sima Yi said to the ruler, "It was Shen Yi who secretly revealed Meng Da's plot. I had intended to petition Your Majesty before acting, but rather than lose time waiting for your sagely instruction, I decided to set out at once to deal with the traitor. Otherwise, I would have fallen into Zhuge Liang's trap." So saying, he handed up to Cao Rui Kongming's secret letter of reply to Meng Da. Cao Rui read it and said, "You surpass the great strategists of ancient times, Sunzi and Wu Qi." He bestowed on Sima Yi a pair of gold-knobbed maces authorizing him to act on his own judgment in future crises without recourse to imperial petition. He then ordered Sima Yi to march west through the passes to defeat the army of Shu.

Sima Yi said to his master, "May I recommend a commander for the vanguard?" "Whom?" Cao Rui asked. "General of the Right Zhang He is fit for the task," Sima Yi replied. "Exactly the man I was going to employ," Cao Rui said smiling, and he made the assignment. Sima Yi left Chang'an with Zhang He to do battle with the Riverlands army. Indeed:

> First the cunning counselor worked his plan;
> Next he found a fierce commander to expand his power.

Would the north or the west prevail?

Read on.

2327

武侯彈琴退仲達

侶鶴散人題書

2329

第九十五回

马谡拒谏失街亭　武侯弹琴退仲达

　　却说魏主曹睿令张郃为先锋，与司马懿一同征进；一面令辛毗、孙礼二人领兵五万，往助曹真。二人奉诏而去。且说司马懿引二十万军，出关下寨，请先锋张郃至帐下曰："诸葛亮平生谨慎，未敢造次行事。若是吾用兵，先从子午谷径取长安，早得多时矣。他非无谋，但怕有失，不肯弄险，今必出军斜谷，来取郿城。若取郿城，必分兵两路，一军取箕谷矣。吾已发檄文，令子丹拒守郿城，若兵来不可出战；令孙礼、辛毗截住箕谷道口，若兵来则出奇兵击之。"郃曰："今将军当于何处进兵？"懿曰："吾素知秦岭之西，有一条路，地名街亭；傍有一城，名列柳城：此二处皆是汉中咽喉。诸葛亮欺子丹无备，定从此进。吾与汝径取街亭，望阳平关不远矣。亮若知吾断其街亭要路，绝其粮道，则陇西一境，不能安守，必然连夜奔回汉中去也。彼若回动，吾提兵于小路击之，可得全胜；若不归时，吾却将诸处小路，尽皆垒断，俱以兵守之。一月无粮，蜀兵皆饿死，亮必被吾擒矣。"张郃大悟，拜伏于地曰："都督神算也！"懿曰："虽然如

Chapter 95

Rejecting Advice, Ma Su Loses Jieting
Strumming His Lute, Kongming Drives Off Sima

Cao Rui, ruler of Wei, had ordered Zhang He to the vanguard of Sima Yi's expedition. Next, he ordered Xin Pi and Sun Li to take fifty thousand troops and support Cao Zhen; the two commanders received their edicts of authorization and left.

Sima Yi led two hundred thousand through the pass. He pitched camp and summoned Zhang He to his tent. "Zhuge Liang moves with extreme caution," he said, "and never takes chances. In his place, I would head straight for Chang'an from Zi-Wu Gorge — the quickest route. But he won't risk it, despite his remarkable ingenuity; he'll go by Ye Gorge first and seize the city of Mei. Next, if he succeeds, he will detail one contingent to take Winnow Basket Gorge. I have instructed Cao Zhen to guard Mei but to refuse battle; and I have ordered Sun Li and Xin Pi to close Winnow Basket Gorge and launch a surprise attack on the enemy if they come."

Zhang He said, "How far should we advance?" "I recall a road running through a place called Jieting, west of Qinling," Sima Yi answered. "Nearby there's a town called Willow Rows. These are the two choke points of Hanzhong. Zhuge Liang will assume that Cao Zhen is unprepared and will advance that way. You and I should capture Jieting directly to put Yangping Pass in range. Once Kongming finds out we have cut the main road at Jieting stopping their grain supply and threatening the whole of Longxi, he will hurry back to Hanzhong. The moment he turns, we will harass him on the paths and complete the rout. If he does not turn, I will seal those same roads and hold them under guard. Inside of a month the Riverlands army will starve, and Zhuge Liang will fall into my hands."

Zhang He understood Sima Yi's logic and, prostrating himself, said,

此,诸葛亮不比孟达。将军为先锋,不可轻进。当传与诸将:循山西路,远远哨探。如无伏兵,方可前进。若是急忽,必中诸葛亮之计。"张郃受计引军而行。

　　却说孔明在祁山寨中,忽报新城探细人来到。孔明急唤入问之,细作告曰:"司马懿倍道而行,八日已到新城,孟达措手不及;又被申耽、申仪、李辅、邓贤为内应:孟达被乱军所杀。今司马懿撤兵到长安,见了魏主,同张郃引兵出关,来拒我师也。"孔明大惊曰:"孟达做事不密,死固当然。今司马懿出关,必取街亭,断吾咽喉之路。"便问:"谁敢引兵去守街亭?"言未毕,参军马谡曰:"某愿往。"孔明曰:"街亭虽小,干系甚重:倘街亭有失,吾大军皆休矣。汝虽深通谋略,此地奈无城郭,又无险阻,守之极难。"谡曰:"某自幼熟读兵书,颇知兵法。岂一街亭不能守耶?"孔明曰:"司马懿非等闲之辈;更有先锋张郃,乃魏之名将:恐汝不能敌之。"谡曰:"休道司马懿、张郃,便是曹睿亲来,有何惧哉!若有差失,乞斩全家。"孔明曰:"军中无戏言。"谡曰:"愿立军令状。"孔明从之。谡遂写了军令状呈上。孔明曰:"吾与汝二万五千精兵,再拨一员上将,相助你去。"即唤王平分付曰:"吾素知汝平生谨慎,故特以此重任相托。汝可

"A marvelous calculation, Field Marshal." "Nevertheless," Sima Yi went on, "Zhuge Liang is no Meng Da. As vanguard commander, you must exercise caution. Order your commanders to follow the western paths and send advance patrols far ahead. If there is no ambush, move forward. The slightest negligence will deliver you to Zhuge Liang." Zhang He left with his troops to carry out the plan.

* * *

A spy freshly back from Xincheng reported to Kongming in his Qishan camp: "Sima Yi reached Xincheng in eight days marching double-time. Meng Da had no time to defend himself. Shen Dan, Shen Yi, Li Fu, and Deng Xian all collaborated with the enemy, and Meng Da was killed by soldiers in revolt. Sima Yi pulled back to Chang'an, had an audience with the ruler of Wei, and then, joined by Zhang He, came through the passes to oppose our army." Kongming reacted strongly, saying, "Meng Da failed to keep his activities secret and sealed his own fate. Sima Yi will try to take Jieting and cut off our main route. Who will lead a force to Jieting to defend it?" He had hardly finished speaking, when Military Adviser Ma Su stepped forward to volunteer. "However insignificant Jieting may seem," Kongming continued, "it is vital to the survival of our main army. I know you are thoroughly versed in strategy; but with no wall of natural defenses, the place will be most difficult to hold."

2333

Ma Su replied, "Lifelong study of military science has given me a good understanding of warfare. I hardly think it beyond my abilities to hold a Jieting." "Sima Yi is no ordinary general," Kongming warned. "Furthermore, he has one of Wei's top commanders, Zhang He, in the vanguard. I don't think you are a match for them."

Ma Su replied, "Never mind Sima Yi and Zhang He. Let Cao Rui himself come: it won't daunt me. If anything goes wrong, you can put my whole family to the sword." "The army is no place for extravagant boasts!" Kongming warned. "You'll have my oath!" Ma Su said. Kongming agreed, and a written pledge was submitted. "I shall allow you twenty-five thousand of our finest men and select a leading commander to assist you," Kongming said. He summoned Wang Ping. "You have been chosen for this task," Kongming instructed him, "because you are known to be a man of extreme caution. Guard that place with the great-

小心谨守此地：下寨必当要道之处，使贼兵急切不能偷过。安营既毕，便画四至八道地理形状图本来我看。凡事商议停当而行，不可轻易。如所守无危，则是取长安第一功也。戒之！戒之！"二人拜辞引兵而去。

孔明寻思，恐二人有失，又唤高翔曰："街亭东北上有一城，名列柳城，乃山僻小路，此可以屯兵扎寨。与汝一万兵，去此城屯扎。但街亭危，可引兵救之。"高翔引兵而去。孔明又思：高翔非张郃对手，必得一员大将，屯兵于街亭之右，方可防之，遂唤魏延引本部兵去街亭之后屯扎。延曰："某为前部，理合当先破敌，何故置某于安闲之地？"孔明曰："前锋破敌，乃偏裨之事耳。今令汝接应街亭，当阳平关冲要道路，总守汉中咽喉：此乃大任也，何为安闲乎？汝勿以等闲视之，失吾大事。切宜小心在意！"魏延大喜，引兵而去。孔明恰才心安，乃唤赵云、邓芝分付曰："今司马懿出兵，与旧日不同。汝二人各引一军出箕谷，以为疑兵。如逢魏兵，或战、或不战，以惊其心。吾自统大军，由斜谷径取郿城；若得郿城，长安可破矣。"二人受命而去。孔明令姜维作先锋，兵出斜谷。

却说马谡、王平二人兵到街亭，看了地势。马谡笑曰："丞相何故多心也？量此山僻之处，魏兵如何敢来！"王平曰："虽然魏兵不敢来，可就此五路总口下寨；却令军士伐木为栅，以图

est care. Pitch camp along the main road to prevent the enemy from slipping past. After the position is secured, send me a map of the surrounding terrain. While there, make no move until it has been discussed and agreed upon. Leave nothing to chance. Defending Jieting is a contribution of the first order to the capture of Chang'an. Take care ! Take care!" The two men withdrew respectfully and set off with their forces.

To supplement these measures, Kongming summoned Gao Xiang and said to him, "Northeast of Jieting is the town of Willow Rows on a small road screened by the hills. Place troops there — I'll give you ten thousand — and pitch camp. If there's trouble in Jieting, go to the rescue." Gao Xiang left with his troops. But Kongming, still not satisfied that Gao Xiang could deal with Zhang He, decided to augment Jieting's defense with a force on the east. Accordingly, he instructed another commander, Wei Yan, to position himself behind Jieting. Wei Yan replied, "The vanguard leads the attack. Why give me such a safe assignment?" Kongming said, "The van attack is a lesser service. I want you to reinforce Jieting, to cover the main route to Yangping Pass, and to defend the choke points of Hanzhong. This is a major responsibility, not a 'safe' assignment. Don't take this for some routine affair, or you will undo everything. And keep caution foremost in your thoughts!" Assuaged, Wei Yan left with his force.

Content with his preparations at last, Kongming summoned Zhao Zilong and Deng Zhi. "Sima Yi has taken the field," he told them, "and that changes everything. I want each of you to lead a company of men through Winnow Basket Gorge as decoys. If you encounter any northern troops, give battle only intermittently to unnerve them. I will lead the main army through Ye Gorge and seize Mei. Chang'an will fall." The two men left to carry out their orders. Kongming had Jiang Wei command the van as he moved through the gorge.

* * *

Ma Su and Wang Ping reached Jieting and studied the lay of the land. With a smile Ma Su said, "What could have made His Excellency so uneasy? The Wei army is unlikely to come to this forsaken spot." Wang Ping said, "All the same, we had better camp at the intersection of these five roads and then have the men fell trees for palings for a strategic

2335

久计。"谡曰:"当道岂是下寨之地?此处侧边一山,四面皆不相连,且树木极广,此乃天赐之险也:可就山上屯军。"平曰:"参军差矣。若屯兵当道,筑起城垣,贼兵总有十万,不能偷过;今若弃此要路,屯兵于山上,倘魏兵骤至,四面围定,将何策保之?"谡大笑曰:"汝真女子之见!兵法云:'凭高视下,势如劈竹。'若魏兵到来,吾教他片甲不回!"平曰:"吾累随丞相经阵,每到之处,丞相尽意指教。今观此山,乃绝地也:若魏兵断我汲水之道,军士不战自乱矣。"谡曰:"汝莫乱道!孙子云:'置之死地而后生。'若魏兵绝我汲水之道,蜀兵岂不死战?以一可当百也。吾素读兵书,丞相诸事尚问于我,汝奈何相阻耶!"平曰:"若参军欲在山上下寨,可分兵与我,自于山西下一小寨,为掎角之势。倘魏兵至,可以相应。"马谡不从。忽然山中居民,成群结队,飞奔而来,报说魏兵已到。王平欲辞去。马谡曰:"汝既不听吾令,与汝五千兵自去下寨。待吾破了魏兵,到丞相面前须分不得功!"王平引兵离山十里下寨,画成图本,星夜差人去禀孔明,具说马谡自于山上下寨。

　　却说司马懿在城中,令次子司马昭去探前路:若街亭有兵守御,即当按兵不行,司马昭奉令探了一遍,回见父曰:"街亭

defense." But Ma Su replied, "The road is no place for a camp, with an isolated hill so near and all four fronts impossible to link. Also, the broad woods offer a natural strategic advantage. The army should move to the hilltop." "Surely you are mistaken, Military Adviser," Wang Ping replied. "If we station the army along the road and build a wall, not even one hundred thousand rebels will be able to get by us. But if we abandon this key point for the hilltop and the northerners charge in and surround us, nothing will save us." Ma Su laughed out loud and retorted, "That's really a woman's way of seeing things! The laws of warfare state, 'Depend on heights, surveying all below, and the enemy will be like bamboo to a cleaver.' Let them come! I won't let a shield go back!"

Wang Ping persisted, "How many times have I been with His Excellency when he managed formations? At every new site he would give exhaustive directions. If we isolate our men on this hill and the northerners come and sever the water lines, the army will collapse without a battle." "Enough of your stupidity!" Ma Su cried. "Sunzi has said, 'Soldiers always survive when threatened by death.' If they cut the conduits, won't the Riverlanders fight for their very lives, one of ours a match for a hundred of theirs? I know my military texts. Even His Excellency has come to me with questions. Don't make things difficult!"

Wang Ping said, "Would you be willing, Adviser, to form two camps, one on top and one below, giving me a portion of the troops to place at the west foot of the hill so we can create a pincer formation? Then we can deal with the northerners should they come." Ma Su refused.

Suddenly, dwellers from the hills came thronging to report the arrival of the northerners. Wang Ping wanted to take his leave. Ma Su said, "Since you will not obey my orders, take five thousand and pitch camp where you will. But after my victory, you will not get a scrap of credit when we stand before the prime minister." Wang Ping led his men ten *li* from the hill and camped. Then he prepared maps and had them carried to Kongming along with a description of Ma Su's hilltop position.

* * *

From the city, Sima Yi sent his second son, Sima Zhao, to explore the road ahead, instructing him not to proceed if he found soldiers defending Jieting. After making his survey, Sima Zhao said to his father, "There are

有兵守把。"懿叹曰："诸葛亮真乃神人，吾不如也！"昭笑曰："父亲何故自堕志气耶？——男料街亭易取。"懿问曰："汝安敢出此大言？"昭曰："男亲自哨见，当道并无寨栅，军皆屯于山上，故知可破也。"懿大喜曰："若兵果在山上，乃天使吾成功矣！"遂更换衣服，引百余骑亲自来看。是夜天晴月朗，直至山下，周围巡哨了一遍，方回。马谡在山上见之，大笑曰："彼若有命，不来围山！"传令与诸将："倘兵来，只见山顶上红旗招动，即四面皆下。"

　　却说司马懿回到寨中，使人打听是何将引兵守街亭。回报曰："乃马良之弟马谡也。"懿笑曰："徒有虚名，乃庸才耳！孔明用如此人物，如何不误事！"又问："街亭左右别有军否？"探马报曰："离山十里有王平安营。"懿乃命张郃引一军，当住王平来路。又令申耽、申仪引两路兵围山，先断了汲水道路；待蜀兵自乱，然后乘势击之。当夜调度已定。次日天明，张郃引兵先往背后去了。司马懿大驱军马，一拥而进，把山四面围定。马谡在山上看时，只见魏兵漫山遍野，旌旗队伍，甚是严整。蜀兵见之，尽皆丧胆，不敢下山。马谡将红旗招动，军将你我相推，无一人敢动。谡大怒，自杀二将。众军惊惧，只得努力下山来冲魏

soldiers protecting Jieting." In a tone of resignation Sima Yi said, "Zhuge Liang is marvelous! Far beyond me!" "Don't despair, Father," Sima Zhao said with a smile. "Jieting looks easy enough to capture." "Is this an empty boast?" asked Sima Yi. "When I scouted the road, I saw no fortifications — all their men had been put on the hill — so I am sure we can defeat them." Delighted, Sima Yi said, "If that's true, then Heaven itself ensures our success." He dressed in war gear and, attended by a hundred cavalry, went to inspect the site himself.

It was a clear night; the moon shone bright. Sima Yi and his son rode straight to the foot of the hill, explored all around it, and went back. From the hill Ma Su watched it all, smiling. "They are doomed if they surround this hill," he said, and he issued orders to his commanders: if the enemy comes, swoop down on all sides when you see a red flag waving on the summit.

Sima Yi got back to camp and sent a man to find out who the Reverlands commander at Jieting was. "Ma Su," was the answer, "younger brother of Ma Liang." Sima Yi smiled and said, "A man with an undeserved reputation. If Kongming is using men of such commonplace abilities, he will defeat only himself." Then he asked another question: "Have they any other forces near Jieting?" The scout reported: "Wang Ping is camped ten *li* away." Sima Yi accordingly ordered Zhang He to block Wang Ping's position with a corps of men. He also ordered Shen Dan and Shen Yi to take two contingents to surround the mountain and cut off the water conduits. Sima Yi intended to strike after the Riverlands forces had become disorderly; that night he completed his deployment.

The following dawn Zhang He led his men behind the mountain as Sima Yi advanced in force, cordoning the base with his troops. Ma Su looked down on the swarm of northerners spreading over hill and dale, their flags and ranks in perfect order. His Riverlands troops lost heart and refused to go down. Ma Su raised the red flag to signal the attack, but none of the commanders or soldiers would take the initiative. Enraged by this show of resistance, Ma Su personally killed two commanders. The soldiers, afraid for their lives, halfheartedly descended and attacked. But the Wei troops held firm, and soon the Riverlanders retreated uphill. Ma

兵。魏兵端然不动。蜀兵又退上山去。马谡见事不谐,教军紧守寨门,只等外应。

　　却说王平见魏兵到,引军杀来,正遇张郃;战有数十余合,平力穷势孤,只得退去。魏兵自辰时困至戌时,山上无水,军不得食,寨中大乱。嚷到半夜时分,山南蜀兵大开寨门,下山降魏。马谡禁止不住。司马懿又令人于沿山放火,山上蜀兵愈乱。马谡料守不住。只得驱残兵杀下山西逃奔。司马懿放条大路,让过马谡。背后张郃引兵追来。赶到三十余里,前面鼓角齐鸣,一彪军出,放过马谡,拦住张郃;视之,乃魏延也。延挥刀纵马,直取张郃。郃回军便走。延驱兵赶来,复夺街亭。赶到五十余里,一声喊起,两边伏兵齐出:左边司马懿,右边司马昭,却抄在魏延背后,把延困在垓心。张郃复来,三路兵合在一处。魏延左冲右突,不得脱身,折兵大半。正危急间,忽一彪军杀入,乃王平也。延大喜曰:"吾得生矣!"二将合兵一处,大杀一阵,魏兵方退。二将慌忙奔回寨时,营中皆是魏兵旌旗。申耽、申仪从营中杀出。王平、魏延径奔列柳城,来投高翔。此时高翔闻知街亭有失,尽起列柳城之兵,前来救应,正遇延、平二人,诉说前事。高翔曰:"不如今晚去劫魏寨,再复街亭。"当时三人在山坡下商议已定。待天色将晚,兵分三路。魏延引兵先进,径到街

Su, seeing his situation worsening, ordered a tight defense of the camp until outside help had arrived.

Meanwhile, Wang Ping saw the Wei troops approaching and led his men forth. Zhang He opposed him, and they battled until, exhausted and isolated, Wang Ping withdrew. The Wei troops held the ring tight from dawn to dusk. The Riverlanders had no water to cook with, and panic broke out in the camps. The commotion lasted well into the night. On the south slope Riverlands troops opened the gate to their fortifications and went down to surrender; Ma Su could do nothing to stop them. Sima Yi ringed the foot of the hill with fires, increasing the confusion of the hill-bound troops. Realizing his position was untenable, Ma Su drove his men down in a final desperate assault and fled westward where Sima Yi had made way for him to pass. Zhang He pursued hotly for thirty *li* until he encountered a band of soldiers, drums and horns resounding, who stopped him after letting Ma Su through. Their commander was Wei Yan.

Flourishing his sword, Wei Yan raced for Zhang He; Zhang He turned back to his line and fled. Wei Yan continued his drive and retook Jieting. But when Wei Yan had gone more than fifty *li* beyond the town, voices roared as ambushers emerged on either side: to the left Sima Yi, to the right Sima Zhao. They had managed to slip behind Wei Yan and were now encircling him as Zhang He reversed his flight to join the attack. Wei Yan threw himself against the northerners but could not break free; more then half his men perished.

At this critical moment a band of troops led by Wang Ping joined the battle. Thankfully, Wei Yan cried, "I am saved!" The two western commanders forced the Wei army to retreat after heavy fighting and rushed back to their camps. But they found the colors of Wei already flying there. When Shen Dan and Shen Yi came forth to do battle, Wang Ping and Wei Yan dashed for the town of Willow Rows to take refuge with Gao Xiang.

By this time Gao Xiang had learned of the fall of Jieting and had summoned the townsmen to arms. On his way to rescue Wang Ping and Wei Yan, he came upon them. They told him what had passed, and Gao Xiang said, "Raid their camp tonight, and we will recover Jieting!" The three sat down on the slope of a hill and made their plans. As the sky

2341

亭，不见一人，心中大疑，未敢轻进，且伏在路口等候。忽见高翔兵到，二人共说魏兵不知在何处。正没理会，又不见王平兵到。忽然一声炮响，火光冲天，鼓起震地：魏兵齐出，把魏延、高翔围在垓心。二人往来冲突，不得脱身。忽听得山坡后喊声若雷，一彪军杀入，乃是王平，救了高、魏二人，径奔列柳城来。比及奔到城下时，城边早有一军杀到，旗上大书"魏都督郭淮"字样。原来郭淮与曹真商议，恐司马懿得了全功，乃分淮来取街亭；闻知司马懿、张郃成了此功，遂引兵径袭列柳城。正遇三将，大杀一阵。蜀兵伤者极多。魏延恐阳平关有失，慌与王平、高翔望阳平关来。

　　却说郭淮收了军马，乃谓左右曰："吾虽不得街亭，却取了列柳城，亦是大功。"引兵径到城下叫门，只见城上一声炮响，旗帜皆竖，当头一面大旗，上书"平西都督司马懿"。懿撑起悬空板，倚定护心木栏干，大笑曰："郭伯济来何迟也？"淮大惊曰："仲达神机，吾不及也！"遂入城。相见已毕，懿曰："今街亭已失，诸葛亮必走。公可速与子丹星夜追之。"郭淮从其言，出城而去。懿唤张郃曰："子丹、伯济，恐吾全获大功，故来取此城

began to darken, they formed three units. Wei Yan advanced to Jieting but, finding it deserted, cautiously had his men outside rather than enter. Gao Xiang arrived, but neither he nor Wei Yan could figure out where the troops of Wei had gone. And Wang Ping's troops were nowhere to be seen.

Suddenly a bombard sounded; flames mounted to the heavens and the beating of drums shook the ground as the northerners came forth and surrounded Wei Yan and Gao Xiang. The two leaders charged back and forth but could not break through. Next, thunderous shouts from behind a slope announced the arrival of Wang Ping's force; these troops opened a fresh battle and succeeded in getting Gao Xiang and Wei Yan safely out. The western forces hurried to Willow Rows only to find an army in position there, waiting for them under a banner that read "Guo Huai, Field Marshal of Wei." This move resulted from a decision by Cao Zhen and Guo Huai to have Guo Huai capture Jieting and thus prevent Sima Yi from taking all the credit for the victories of the day. Hearing of the victories of Sima Yi and Zhang He, however, Guo Huai had surprised and seized Willow Rows instead. Now he confronted the three Riverlands commanders, and in the ensuing battle dealt the Riverlands armies a grave defeat. Wei Yan, fearing the loss of Yangping Pass, hurried there with Wang Ping and Gao Xiang.

2343

As Guo Huai's men regrouped around him, he said, "Though we failed to take Jieting, the capture of Willow Rows will be a great distinction for us!" Marching to the gate, he demanded entrance but was met instead by the roar of bombards from the wall. And standing among the proud pennons on the wall was a flag reading "Sima Yi, Field Marshal Who Conquers the West." Sima Yi himself leaned against a wooden railing on a suspended platform and said with a loud laugh to Guo Huai, "What took you so long to get here?" "Sima Yi, you are a man of amazing genius!" the astonished Guo Huai replied. He then entered the town and presented himself to Sima Yi, who said, "Now that he has lost Jieting, Kongming is sure to flee. You, sir, and Cao Zhen should pursue him at once." Guo Huai left the town of Willow Rows to carry out his assignment.

Next, Sima Yi called Zhang He and said to him, "Guo Huai and Cao

池。吾非独欲成功，乃侥幸而已。吾料魏延、王平、马谡、高翔等辈，必先去据阳平关。吾若去取此关，诸葛亮必随后掩杀，中其计矣。兵法云：'归师勿掩，穷寇莫追。'汝可从小路抄箕谷退兵。吾自引兵当斜谷之兵。若彼败走，不可相拒，只宜中途截住：蜀兵辎重，可尽得也。"张郃受计，引兵一半去了。懿下令："竟取斜谷，由西城而进。——西城虽山僻小县，乃蜀兵屯粮之所，又南安、天水、安定三郡总路。——若得此城，三郡可复矣。"于是司马懿留申耽、申仪守列柳城，自领大军望斜谷进发。

　　却说孔明自令马谡等守街亭去后，犹豫不定。忽报王平使人送图本至。孔明唤入，左右呈上图本。孔明就文几上拆开视之，拍案大惊曰："马谡无知，坑陷吾军矣！"左右问曰："丞相何故失惊？"孔明曰："吾观此图本，失却要路，占山为寨。倘魏兵大至，四面围合，断汲水道路，不须二日，军自乱矣。若街亭有失，吾等安归？"长史杨仪进曰："某虽不才，愿替马幼常回。"孔明将安营之法，一一分付与杨仪。——正待要行，忽报马到来，说："街亭、列柳城，尽皆失了！"孔明跌足长叹曰："大事去矣！——此吾之过也！"急唤关兴，张苞分付曰："汝二人各引三千

Zhen came to take Willow Rows because they thought I wanted the credit for this campaign all for myself. That is not true. I took this place through an accident of war. My thought is that our enemies, Wei Yan, Wang Ping, Ma Su, and Gao Xiang, will try now to hold Yangping Pass. If I take the pass myself, Zhuge Liang will surprise me from the rear and trap me. The rules of warfare say, 'Don't surprise a retreating army; don't chase an exhausted foe.' So you are to take the bypaths and harass the troops of Zhao Zilong and Deng Zhi as they retire from Winnow Basket Gorge. I will cover Ye Gorge myself. If they flee, don't oppose them; simply raid them along the way to seize their supplies."

Zhang He received Sima Yi's orders and departed with half of the troops. Then Sima Yi commanded: "After we have Ye Gorge, advance through Xicheng. Though a small and remote mountain town, it is a grain depot for the westerners, and it connects to the three district capitals of Nan'an, Tianshui, and Anding. The capture of Xicheng will mean the recovery of the three districts." With that, Sima Yi left Shen Dan and Shen Yi guarding Willow Rows and set out in force for Ye Gorge.

*　*　*

Meanwhile, after ordering Ma Su to hold Jieting, Kongming could not decide on a course of action. Suddenly he was told that Wang Ping's sketch of the Jieting defenses had come. Kongming received the sketch from his attendants and unrolled it on his table. Examining it, he struck the table in consternation. He cried, "The fool, Ma Su, has led my army to its doom!" "Why is Your Excellency so excited?" his attendants asked. "I can see from the map that Ma Su has abandoned the main roads and fortified the hilltop," Kongming replied. "If the northerners of Wei come in strength to surround him and cut off his water, our men will go to pieces in two days. And where can we retreat to if Jieting falls?" Senior Adviser Yang Yi advanced a proposal: "Despite my lack of talent, permit me to go and replace Ma Su." Kongming subsequently gave the adviser explicit instructions on preparing the ground for the camp at Jieting.

Yang Yi was about to leave, when Kongming was told of the fall of both Jieting and Willow Rows. He stamped his foot in despair and sighed. "Our cause is lost and it is my doing!" he cried, and he summoned Guan Xing and Zhang Bao. "Take three thousand crack troops each," he or-

2346

精兵，投武功山小路而行。如遇魏兵，不可大击，只鼓噪呐喊，为疑兵惊之。彼当自走，亦不可追。待军退尽，便投阳平关去。"又令张翼先引军去修理剑阁，以备归路。又密传号令，教大军暗暗收拾行装，以备起程。又令马岱、姜维断后，先伏于山谷中，待诸军退尽，方始收兵。又差心腹人，分路报与天水、南安、安定三郡官吏军民，皆入汉中。又遣心腹人到冀县搬取姜维老母，送入汉中。

孔明分拨已定，先引五千兵退去西城县搬运粮草。忽然十余次飞马报到，说："司马懿引大军十五万，望西城蜂拥而来！"时孔明身边别无大将，只有一班文官，所引五千兵，已分一半先运粮草去了，只剩二千五百军在城中。众官听得这个消息，尽皆失色。孔明登城望之，果然尘土冲天，魏兵分两路望西城县杀来。孔明传令，教"将旌旗尽皆隐匿；诸军各守城铺，如有妄行出入，及高言大语者，斩之！大开四门，每一门用二十军士，扮作百姓，洒扫街道。如魏兵到时，不可擅动，吾自有计。"孔明乃披鹤氅，戴纶巾，引二小童携琴一张，于城上敌楼前，凭栏而坐，焚香操琴。

却说司马懿前军哨到城下，见了如此模样，皆不敢进，急

dered them, "and head for the bypaths of the Wugong Hills. If you run into Wei troops, don't launch any major action; just beat the drums and howl to the skies so they'll think you are a decoy force. If they go, do not pursue. When they withdraw, head for Yangping Pass." At the same time Kongming had Zhang Yi ready Saber Gateway for the return of the army to Shu; he issued secret instructions for the main army to prepare quietly for the march home; he had Ma Dai and Jiang Wei secure the rear of his retreat route by placing ambushes in the valleys with orders not to pull back until the main forces had withdrawn. He also sent trusted agents to Tianshui, Nan'an, and Anding to inform the officers and men as well as officials and townsmen that they should move into Hanzhong; and finally, he sent a trusted agent to Jicheng to move Jiang Wei's mother into Hanzhong.

After making these arrangements, Kongming took five thousand men back to Xicheng to move grain and provender. Suddenly a dozen mounted couriers arrived and reported: "Sima Yi is leading a multitude of one hundred and fifty thousand toward Xicheng." At this point Kongming had no commanders of importance beside him — only a group of civil officials — and half the five thousand in his command had been detailed to move food supplies, leaving a mere twenty-five hundred troops in the town. The officials turned pale at the news of Sima Yi's approach. When Kongming mounted the city wall to observe, he saw dust clouds in the distance rising skyward as the two northern field armies advanced for battle.

2347

Kongming ordered all flags and banners put out of sight and instructed the wall sentries to execute anyone who tried to pass in or out without authority or who raised his voice. Next, Kongming ordered the town's four gates opened wide; at each a squad of twenty, disguised as commoners, swept the roadway. The soldiers had been told to make no untoward move when the Wei army arrived, as Kongming was following a plan of his own. After this Kongming put on his crane-feather cloak, wrapped a band around his head, and, followed by two lads bearing his zither, sat down on the wall. He propped himself against the railing in front of a turret and began to strum as incense burned.

Meanwhile, Sima Yi's scouts had reached the wall of Xicheng. Find-

报与司马懿。懿笑而不信，遂止住三军，自飞马远远望之。果见孔明坐于城楼之上，笑容可掬，焚香操琴。左有一童子，手捧宝剑；右有一童子，手执麈尾。城门内外，有二十余百姓，低头洒扫，傍若无人。懿看毕大疑，便到中军，教后军作前军，前军作后军，望北山路而退。次子司马昭曰："莫非诸葛亮无军，故作此态？父亲何故便退兵？"懿曰："亮平生谨慎，不曾弄险。今大开城门，必有埋伏。我兵若进，中其计也。汝辈岂知？宜速退。"于是两路兵尽皆退去。孔明见魏军远去，抚掌而笑。众官无不骇然，乃问孔明曰："司马懿乃魏之名将，今统十五万精兵到此，见了丞相，便速退去，何也？"孔明曰："此人料吾生平谨慎，必不弄险；见如此模样，疑有伏兵，所以退去。吾非行险，盖因不得已而用之。此人必引军投山北小路去也。吾已令兴、苞二人在彼等候。"众皆惊服曰："丞相之机，神鬼莫测。若某等之见，必弃城而走矣。"孔明曰："吾兵止有二千五百，若弃城而走，必不能远遁。得不为司马懿所擒乎？"后人有诗赞曰：

　　瑶琴三尺胜雄师，诸葛西城退敌时。

　　十五万人回马处，土人指点到今疑。

言讫，拍手大笑，曰："吾若为司马懿，必不便退也。"遂下令，教西城百姓，随军入汉中：司马懿必将复来。于是孔明离西城望

ing the scene as described, they advanced no further but reported at once to their commander. Sima Yi laughed and dismissed the report. He then halted his army and rode forward himself to view the town from a distance. There indeed was Kongming sitting by the turret, smiling as ever and burning incense as he played. To his left, a lad held a fine sword; to his right, another held a yak-tail whisk. By the gate two dozen sweepers plied their brooms with lowered heads, as if no one else were about.

Puzzled, Sima Yi turned his army around and retreated toward the hills to the north. His second son, Sima Zhao, asked, "What makes you sure Kongming isn't putting this on because he has no troops? Why simply retreat, Father?" Sima Yi answered, "Kongming has always been a man of extreme caution, never one to tempt the fates. He opened the gates because he had set an ambush. On entering, we would have been trapped. You are too young to know! Hurry the retreat!" Thus the two Wei armies withdrew.[1]

After the retreating army was well into the distance, Kongming rubbed his palms together and laughed; but his officials were left amazed. One of them asked, "Why did a famous Wei general like Sima Yi with one hundred fifty thousand in his command withdraw after one look at Your Excellency?" "The man," Kongming replied, "assumed I was too cautious to tempt fate. He saw my preparations, suspected ambush, and withdrew. It was not recklessness. What choice had I? Sima Yi is sure to head for the northern hills. I have already told Guan Xing and Zhang Bao to be waiting for him there." The astonished officials acknowledged his genius, saying, "The very gods could not outwit Your Excellency. We would have abandoned the town!" "Could I have gotten far enough with twenty-five hundred men," Kongming asked, "to escape Sima Yi?" A poet of later times has left these lines of admiration:

> A zither three spans long subdued a puissant host
> When Liang dismissed his foe at Xicheng town.
> A hundred fifty thousand turned themselves around —
> And townsmen at the spot still wonder how!

His explanation made, Kongming clapped his hands and laughed aloud. "But were I Sima Yi, I would not have gone back!" he said. Next, he ordered the people of Xicheng to follow the troops into Hanzhong in view

2349

汉中而走。天水、安定、南安三郡官吏军民,陆续而来。

却说司马懿望武功山小路而走。忽然山坡后喊杀连天,鼓声震地。懿回顾二子曰:"吾若不走,必中诸葛亮之计矣。"只见大路上一军杀来,旗上大书"右护卫使虎冀将军张苞"。魏兵皆弃甲抛戈而走。行不到一程,山谷中喊声震地,鼓角喧天,前面一杆大旗,上书"左护卫使龙骧将军关兴"。山谷应声,不知蜀兵多少;更兼魏军心疑,不敢久停,只得尽弃辎重而去。兴、苞二人皆遵将令,不敢追袭,多得军器粮草而归。司马懿见山谷中皆有蜀兵,不敢出大路,遂回街亭。此时曹真听知孔明退兵,急引兵追赶。山背后一声炮响,蜀兵漫山遍野而来:为首大将,乃是姜维、马岱。真大惊,急退军时,先锋陈造已被马岱所斩。真引兵鼠窜而还。蜀兵连夜皆奔回汉中。

却说赵云、邓芝伏兵于箕谷道中。闻孔明传令回军,云谓芝曰:"魏军知吾兵退,必然来追。吾先引一军伏于其后,公却引兵打吾旗号,徐徐而退。吾一步步自有护送也。"

却说郭淮提兵再回箕谷道中,唤先锋苏颙分付曰:"蜀将赵云,英勇无敌。汝可小心提防。彼军若退,必有计也。"苏颙欣然曰:"都督若肯接应,某当生擒赵云。"遂引前部三千兵,奔

of the expected return of Sima Yi. And so Kongming set out for Hanzhong from Xicheng, followed by the officials, officers soldiers, and people of the three districts Tianshui, Anding, and Nan'an.

Meanwhile, Sima Yi was heading for the Wugong Hills. Suddenly from behind a slope murderous shouts rent the air and drumbeats shook the ground. "Had I stayed, I would have fallen into Zhuge Liang's trap," Sima Yi was saying, when he saw a company of men advancing upon him; their banner read "Winged Tiger General Zhang Bao of the Right Guard." The Wei soldiers flung down their shields and weapons and fled. But they had hardly gone one stage when fresh cries came thundering out of another valley. Drum and horn rent the air and before them a banner held high on a pole bore the words "Prancing Dragon General Guan Xing of the Left Guard." Their clamor echoed in the valley; no one could tell how many Riverlands troops there were. Too confused to take up positions, the Wei army abandoned their wagons and fled. As instructed, the two warriors did not pursue; they took quantities of grain and weapons and withdrew.

Seeing that the valleys were filled with Riverlands soldiers, Sima Yi did not dare come out on the main road but retreated to Jieting. By this time Cao Zhen had learned of Kongming's retreat and gave eager chase. But behind a nearby hill bombards sounded, and Riverlands troops spread over the terrain: their leaders, Jiang Wei and Ma Dai. Cao Zhen, surprised, quickly withdrew; his vanguard commander, Chen Zao, had already been slain by Ma Dai. Cao Zhen led his army in a race for safety; and the Riverlands troops hurried back that night without halt to Hanzhong.

* * *

When Zhao Zilong and Deng Zhi, waiting in ambush along the roads of Winnow Basket Gorge, received Kongming's orders to retreat, Zilong said to Deng Zhi, "If the Wei army knows of this, they will give chase. I am going to move a company into ambush to the rear; you retreat slowly and show my flag. I will protect you step by step."

Meanwhile, Guo Huai had taken Wei troops back into Winnow Basket Gorge and commanded his vanguard Su Yong: "There is no general braver than Zhao Zilong. Keep up your guard. If he retreats, it means a trap." Su Yong answered with enthusiasm, "Field Marshal, if you will

入箕谷。看看赶上蜀兵，只见山坡后闪出红旗白字，上书"赵云"。苏颙急收兵退走。行不到数里，喊声大震，一彪军撞出；为首大将，挺枪跃马，大喝曰："汝识赵子龙否！"苏颙大惊曰："如何这里又有赵云？"措手不及，被云一枪刺死于马下。余军溃散。云迤逦前进，背后又一军到，乃郭淮部将万政也。云见魏兵追急，乃勒马挺枪，立于路口，待来将交锋。——蜀兵已去三十余里。——万政认得是赵云，不敢前进。云等得天色黄昏，方才拨回马缓缓而进。郭淮兵到，万政言赵云英勇如旧，因此不敢近前。淮传令教军急赶，政令数百骑壮士赶来。行至一大林，忽听得背后大喝一声曰："赵子龙在此！"惊得魏兵落马者百余人，余者皆越岭而去。万政勉强来敌，被云一箭射中盔缨，惊跌于涧中。云以枪指之曰："吾饶汝性命回去！快教郭淮赶来！"万政脱命而回。云护送车仗人马，望汉中而去，沿途并无遗失。曹真、郭淮复夺三郡，以为己功。

　　却说司马懿分兵而进。此时蜀兵尽回汉中去了，懿引一军复到西城，因问遗下居民及山僻隐者，皆言孔明止有二千五百

back me up, I can take him alive." He rushed ahead with a force of three thousand into Winnow Basket Gorge and was soon bidding to overtake the Riverlands troops. But when he saw red banners inscribed in white with the words "Zhao Zilong" appear from behind a slope, Su Yong quickly recalled his men. He had withdrawn only a few *li* before a band of men charged at him, all noise and war cries. The leader, a great figure of a general, hoisted his spear and urged his horse forward, shouting, "Do you know me or not? I am Zhao Zilong!" The astonished Su Yong said, "How could you be here as well?" Before he could defend himself, Zhao Zilong had dropped him from the saddle with a thrust of his spear. Su Yong's men scattered, and Zilong pressed forward.

Behind Zilong another Wei commander appeared, Wan Zheng, a lieutenant of Guo Huai. Seeing the Wei forces draw near, Zilong halted and raised his spear, ready to engage Wan Zheng. (By now, the Riverlands troops were already thirty *li* away.) But Wan Zheng recognized Zhao Zilong and would not go forward. Zilong waited until the sky had darkened; then he turned his horse round again and withdrew with studied slowness.

Guo Huai arrived, and Wan Zheng protested that he could not advance against a Zhao Zilong as formidable now as ever. But on Guo Huai's direct order Wan Zheng pursued with several hundred cavaliers. Reaching a broad wood, the cavaliers heard a hearty shout behind them: "Zhao Zilong stands here!" More than a hundred of them fell in panic from their saddles; the rest fled over a hill. Wan Zheng rashly confronted Zilong, whose arrow grazed the straps of Wan Zheng's helmet, causing him to stumble into a nearby stream. Aiming his spear, Zilong said, "I shall spare you. Go and tell Guo Huai to come after us!" Wan Zheng escaped with his life. Zhao Zilong continued to protect the retreating Riverlands forces, and they headed back toward Hanzhong without incident. Cao Zhen and Guo Huai claimed full credit for recapturing the three districts Nan'an, Tianshui, and Anding.

Meanwhile, Sima Yi was advancing with a fresh detachment; but the Riverlands army had already completed its return to Hanzhong. So Sima Yi led the detachment back to Xicheng, where he learned from the few remaining residents and some mountain recluses that Kongming had had

2353

军在城中，又无武将，只有几个文官，别无埋伏。武功山小民告曰："关兴、张苞，只各有三千军，转山呐喊，鼓噪惊追，又无别军，并不敢厮杀。"懿悔之不及，仰天叹曰："吾不如孔明也！"遂安抚了诸处官民，引兵径还长安，朝见魏主。睿曰："今日复得陇西诸郡，皆卿之功也。"懿奏曰："今蜀兵皆在汉中，未尽剿灭。臣乞大兵并力收川，以报陛下。"睿大喜，令懿即便兴兵。忽班内一人出奏曰："臣有一计，足可定蜀降吴。"

　　正是：

　　　　蜀中将相方归国，魏地君臣又逞谋。

　　未知献计者是谁，且看下文分解。

汉英经典文库

only twenty-five hundred men in the city, no commanders, a few civil officials, and of course no ambush in readiness. And at the Wugong Hills the commoners told him, "Guan Xing and Zhang Bao had only three thousand men each. They came round the hill yelling and drumming to frighten off pursuers, but they had no other forces and no intention of engaging in battle." Sima Yi looked ruefully into the heavens and said with a sigh, "Kongming's the better man!" After attending to the interests of the officials and inhabitants in the various areas where his army had been, he withdrew directly to Chang'an.

Cao Rui received him and said, "Thanks to you alone we have recovered the districts of Longxi." Sima Yi addressed the Wei ruler, saying, "The Riverlands army, now in Hanzhong, must be rooted out. Your vassal appeals for a large force to capture the Riverlands in gratitude for Your Majesty's generosity." Cao Rui was delighted and gave the order for Sima Yi to mobilize. But suddenly someone stepped forward from the ranks and said to the Wei ruler, "This vassal has a different plan for conquering the Riverlands and winning the submission of the Southland." Indeed:

> The Riverlands commanders and advisers had barely gone home,
> When the ruler and vassals of Wei were proffering fresh schemes.[2]

Who proposed the plan?
Read on.

2355

第九十六回

孔明挥泪斩马谡　周鲂断发赚曹休

汉英经典文库

2356

　　却说献计者，乃尚书孙资也。曹睿问曰："卿有何妙计？"资奏曰："昔太祖武皇帝收张鲁时，危而后济；常对群臣曰：'南郑之地，真为天狱，'中斜谷道为五百里石穴，非用武之地。今若尽起天下之兵伐蜀，则东吴又将入寇。不如以现在之兵，分命大将据守险要，养精蓄锐。不过数年，中国日盛，吴、蜀二国必自相残害：那时图之，岂非胜算？乞陛下裁之。"睿乃问司马懿曰："此论若何？"懿奏曰："孙尚书所言极当。"睿从之，命懿分拨诸将守把险要，留郭淮、张郃守长安。大赏三军，驾回洛阳。

　　却说孔明回到汉中，计点军士，只少赵云、邓芝，心中甚忧；乃令关兴、张苞，各引一军接应。二人正欲起身，忽报赵云、邓芝到来，并不曾折一人一骑；辎重等器，亦无遗失。孔明大喜，亲引诸将出迎。赵云慌忙下马伏地曰："败军之将，何劳丞相远接？"孔明急扶起，执手而言曰："是吾不识贤愚，以致如

Chapter 96

Shedding Tears, Kongming Executes Ma Su
Cutting Hair, Zhou Fang Deceives Cao Xiu

The chief of the Secretariat, Sun Zi, offered a plan. "What good counsel have you got for us?" Cao Rui asked. Sun Zi replied, "Many years ago, your great ancestor Cao Cao, the August Emperor Wu, regained Hanzhong from Zhang Lu — but he paid a heavy price. Describing the experience later, he would say, 'Nanzheng is harder to enter than a prison designed by Heaven itself.' Along the Ye Gorge trail you'll find rock caves for five hundred *li*; it's no place to wage war. If we commit all the imperial armies to the attack on the Riverlands, the Southland will raid our territory. A better course would be to direct your main commanders to hold the crucial passes to the west with troops already in the field while we rebuild our fighting strength at home. In a few years, after the north is flourishing once more, Shu and Wu should be mortal enemies again; that will be the time to aim for Shu. It is for Your Majesty to decide."

Turning to Sima Yi, Cao Rui asked, "And what is your view?" Sima Yi voiced agreement, and the ruler of Wei approved Sun Zi's suggestion. He deployed several commanders to the passes and assigned Guo Huai and Zheng He to defend Chang'an. Then, after providing generously for the army, Cao Rui returned to Luoyang.

* * *

Kongming reached Hanzhong and tallied up his forces. He was distressed to find Zhao Zilong and Deng Zhi still missing and sent Guan Xing and Zhang Bao off to render aid if needed. But as the two were about to leave, Zhao Zilong and Deng Zhi arrived, their forces and supplies intact. A delighted Kongming led the commanders out to greet them. Zhao Zilong hurriedly dismounted and prostrated himself. "What right has a defeated general," he said, "to be received by Your Excellency like this?" Kongming raised him up and took his hand. "My own poor judgment," he admitted,

此！——各处兵将败损，惟子龙不折一人一骑，何也？"邓芝告曰："某引兵先行，子龙独自断后，斩将立功，敌人惊怕，因此军资什物，不曾遗弃。"孔明曰："真将军也！"遂取金五十斤以赠赵云，又取绢一万匹赏云部卒。云辞曰："三军无尺寸之功，某等俱各有罪；若反受赏，乃丞相赏罚不明也。且请寄库，候今冬赐与诸军未迟。"孔明叹曰："先帝在日，常称子龙之德，今果如此！"乃倍加钦敬。

忽报马谡、王平、魏延、高翔至。孔明先唤王平入帐，责之曰："吾令汝同马谡守街亭，汝何不谏之，致使失事？"平曰："某再三相劝，要在当道筑土城，安营守把。参军大怒不从，某因此自引五千军离山十里下寨。魏兵骤至，把山四面围合，某引兵冲杀十余次，皆不能入。次日土崩瓦解，降者无数。某孤军难立，故投魏文长求救。半途又被魏兵困在山谷之中，某奋死杀出。比及归寨，早被魏兵占了。及投列柳城时，路逢高翔，遂分兵三路去劫魏寨，指望克复街亭。因见街亭并无伏路军，以此心疑。登高望之，只见魏延、高翔被魏兵围住，某即杀入重围，救出二将，就同参军并在一处。某恐失却阳平关，因此急来回

"caused all this. We have had losses all around. Only you have returned whole. What is the reason?" Deng Zhi explained, "I led my men ahead while Zilong guarded the rear. He took such a toll of the enemy commanders that they shrank from combat, and none of our materiel had to be abandoned." "A true commander!" marveled Kongming, and he presented Zhao Zilong with fifty catties of gold; he also allotted ten thousand rolls of silk to his soldiers. But Zhao Zilong declined the gifts. "My army has accomplished nothing deserving the name of merit. With blame enough to go around, for us to accept such bounty would confuse Your Excellency's standards of reward and punishment. I suggest that the gifts be placed in the treasury for distribution this winter. That will be soon enough." With a sigh Kongming said, "The late Emperor always praised Zilong's virtue — with good reason!" The prime minister felt added respect for Zhao Zilong.

Suddenly the arrival of Ma Su, Wang Ping, Wei Yan, and Gao Xiang was announced. Kongming summoned Wang Ping first and said to him, "I ordered you to help Ma Su defend Jieting. Couldn't you have prevented this loss?" Wang Ping replied, "I pleaded with him over and over to construct an earth wall on the road and to fortify it. But Military Adviser Ma Su refused to listen and only grew angrier, so I led five thousand men off and camped ten *li* from the mountain. The Wei army came suddenly and surrounded the hill. I made more than ten attempts to break through their line, but without success. The next day our main position fell apart and great numbers surrendered. Unable to maintain my isolated position, I went to Wei Yan for help, but on the way some northern troops trapped me in a valley. I fought for my life and broke free; but the Wei had already taken my camp by the time I got back to it, so I headed for Willow Rows and met Gao Xiang on the way. We subsequently formed three separate units — Wei Yan, Gao Xiang, and I — and raided the camp; our goal, to retake Jieting. I was surprised to see no enemy troops lying in wait on the road. This puzzled me, so I climbed a hill and looked around. Lo! Wei Yan and Gao Xiang were already trapped by Wei troops. I plunged through their line and plucked the two commanders to safety; then we reunited with Military Adviser Ma Su. I was afraid that Yangping Pass would be lost next and hurried back to defend it. I did all I could to per-

守。——非某之不谏也。丞相不信，可问各部将校。"孔明喝退，又唤马谡入帐。谡自缚跪于帐前。孔明变色曰："汝自幼饱读兵书，熟谙战法。吾累次丁宁告戒：街亭是吾根本。汝以全家之命，领此重任。汝若早听王平之言，岂有此祸？今败军折将，失地陷城，皆汝之过也！若不明正军律，何以服众？汝今犯法，休得怨吾。汝死之后，汝之家小，吾按月给与禄粮，汝不必挂心。"叱左右推出斩之。谡泣曰："丞相视某如子，某以丞相为父。某之死罪，实已难逃；愿丞相思舜帝殛鲧用禹之义，某虽死亦无恨于九泉！"言讫大哭。孔明挥泪曰："吾与汝义同兄弟，汝之子即吾之子也，不必多嘱。"左右推出马谡于辕门之外，将斩。参军蒋琬自成都至，见武士欲斩马谡，大惊，高叫："留人！"入见孔明曰："昔楚杀得臣而文公喜。今天下未定，而戮智谋之臣，岂不可惜乎？"孔明流涕而答曰："昔孙武所以能制胜于天下者，用法明也。今四方分争，兵戈方始，若复废法，何以讨贼耶？合当斩之。"须臾，武士献马谡首级于阶下。孔明大哭不

汉英经典文库

suade Ma Su. The commanders and lieutenants will bear me out."

Kongming dismissed Wang Ping and summoned Ma Su, who placed ropes around himself and knelt before the prime minister. Kongming, wearing an angry expression, said, "From your youth you have read your fill of military texts and have been thoroughly versed in battle tactics. Time and again I warned you that Jieting was a vital base when you took the responsibility of defending it, pledging the lives of your family. Had you listened to Wang Ping, you could have avoided this disaster. You must bear the blame for our defeated army, our fallen commanders, our abandoned territory, and our lost towns. If military regulations are not clear and correct, how can I discipline the soldiers? Your violation of the rules was no fault of mine. Your family, however, will be provided with a monthly allowance of cash and grain; therefore set your mind at rest." So saying, Kongming ordered Ma Su removed and executed.

Ma Su wept and said, "You have been a father to me, and I a son to you. My punishment is unavoidable. I ask only that Your Excellency remember the legend of Shun, who employed Yu after executing Gun, and I shall bear you no grudge in the netherworld below."[1] With that, Ma Su wept loudly. Kongming brushed away his tears, saying, "Brothers could not be closer than we two. Your son will be my son. Say no more."

The guards took Ma Su outside the main gate of the camp and were about to perform their duty, when Military Adviser Jiang Wan arrived from Chengdu. Seeing the execution being prepared, he cried out in alarm, "Spare him!" He went before Kongming and said, "In ancient times the leader of Chu killed General Cheng Dechen after a great defeat and gave Duke Wen of Jin, Chu's enemy, great satisfaction thereby. With the empire so unstable, it is surely a shame to put a wise counselor to death." Weeping freely, Kongming replied, "In ancient times Sunzi was able to impose his control over the empire because his applictation of the laws was clear and unmistakable. Now strife afflicts every part of the empire, and warfare is constantly breaking out. If the law is set aside, how can we continue the campaign against the rebels? It is necessary to execute Ma Su."

Soon after, the guards presented Ma Su's head to the prime minister's attendants. Kongming wept long and loud. Jiang Wan said to him, "The

2361

已。蒋琬问曰:"今幼常得罪,既正军法,丞相何故哭耶?"孔明曰:"吾非为马谡而哭。吾想先帝在白帝城临危之时,曾嘱吾曰:'马谡言过其实,不可大用。'今果应此言。乃深恨己之不明,追思先帝之言,因此痛哭耳!"大小将士,无不流涕。马谡亡年三十九岁,时建兴六年夏五月也。后人有诗曰:

> 失守街亭罪不轻,堪嗟马谡枉谈兵。
>
> 辕门斩首严军法,拭泪犹思先帝明。

却说孔明斩了马谡,将首级遍示各营已毕,用线缝在尸上,具棺葬之,自修祭文享祀;将谡家小加意抚恤,按月给与禄米。于是孔明自作表文,令蒋琬申奏后主,请自贬丞相之职。琬回成都,入见后主,进上孔明表章。后主拆视之。表曰:

> 臣本庸才,叨窃非据,亲秉旄钺,以励三军。不能训章明法,临事而惧,至有街亭违命之阙,箕谷不戒之失。咎皆在臣,授任无方。臣明不知人,恤事多阇。《春秋》责帅,臣职是当。请自贬三等,以督厥咎。臣不胜惭愧,俯伏待命!

后主览毕曰:"胜负兵家常事,丞相何出此言?"侍中费祎奏曰:"臣闻治国者,必以奉法为重。法若不行,何以服人?丞相

law has punished Ma Su for his crime. Why do you lament, Your Excellency?" "It's not for Ma Su that I weep," he answered. "I am thinking of the late Emperor — at Baidi when the end was near — warning me not to use this man because his deeds would not match his boasts. The late king's words have proved too true, leaving me now to rue my blindness. I weep to recall it." Senior and junior commanders and officers wept with him. Ma Su died at the age of thirty-nine during the summer, in the fifth month of Jian Xing 6 (A. D. 228). A later poet left these lines:

> Ma Su, for losing Jieting — no small crime —
> Earned only scorn for his claims of skill
> And paid before the camp the law's full due
> As tearful Kongming thought, how much the late king knew!

After the execution Kongming had Ma Su's head displayed in all the camps and then sewn back on his corpse that it might be interred whole. Kongming personally prepared the memorial text and the sacrificial offering; he showed Ma Su's family especial concern and provided them with cash and grain each month.

Kongming then wrote a petition for Jiang Wan to present to the Second Emperor requesting his own demotion from the position of prime minister. Jiang Wan returned to Chengdu and presented the document to his lord. It read:

2363

> Though a man of commonplace ability, I came to hold a position far beyond my scope. I tried my best to inspire the army as bearer of the imperial battle-axe and flag of command; but I failed to enforce the statutes, to clarify the laws, and to act with prudence. The result was the loss of Jieting, when my command was violated, and of Winnow Basket Gorge, when my warnings were ignored. The fault rests with me for delegating authority so wrongly. Clearly, I did not choose well and made grave mistakes in affairs entrusted to me. In the *Spring and Autumn Annals* it is the commander who bears responsibility when things go wrong; it is thus fitting that I be demoted three grades to punish my fault. Overcome with shame, this vassal prostrates himself awaiting your decision.

Having read the petition, the Second Emperor said, "Victory and defeat are commonplace to the master of warfare. Why does His Excellency make this statement to us?" Privy Counselor Fei Yi said to the Emperor, "It is this vassal's understanding that in government nothing

败绩,自行贬降,正其宜也。"后主从之,乃诏贬孔明为右将军,行丞相事,照旧总督军马,就命费祎赍诏到汉中。孔明受诏贬降讫,祎恐孔明羞赧,乃贺曰:"蜀中之民,知丞相初拔四县,深以为喜。"孔明变色曰:"是何言也!得而复失,与不得同。公以此贺我,实足使我愧赧耳。"祎又曰:"近闻丞相得姜维,天子甚喜。"孔明怒曰:"兵败师还,不曾夺得寸土,此吾之大罪也。量得一姜维,于魏何损?"祎又曰:"丞相现统雄师数十万,可再伐魏乎?"孔明曰:"昔大军屯于祁山、箕谷之时,我兵多于贼兵,而不能破贼,反为贼所破:此病不在兵之多寡,在主将耳。今欲减兵省将,明罚思过,较变通之道于将来;如其不然,虽兵多何用?自今以后,诸人有远虑于国者,但勤攻吾之阙,责吾之短,则事可定,贼可灭,功可翘足而待矣。"费祎诸将皆服其论。费祎自回成都。孔明在汉中,惜军爱民,励兵讲武,置造攻城渡水之器,聚积粮草,预备战筏,以为后图。细作探知,报入洛阳。

outweighs reverence for the law. When the law is not applied, authority is not accepted. For the prime minister to demote himself after a grave defeat is entirely appropriate." The Second Emperor accepted Fai Yi's judgment and issued an edict demoting Kongming to general of the Right and acting prime minister but preserving his overall military authority. The Emperor then sent Fei Yi to Hanzhong to deliver the edict.

After Kongming had received the edict, Fei Yi tried to spare the prime minister's feelings by saying in a complimentary tone, "The people of the Riverlands rejoice in Your Excellency's capture of the four northwest counties." Kongming, visibly angry, replied, "What are you saying! To lose what one wins is not to win. This compliment of yours humiliates!" But Fei Yi persisted, saying, "And the Son of Heaven rejoiced to hear that Jiang Wei has joined us." Frankly angered now, Kongming said, "The army comes home defeated, not a scrap of land won. The blame is mine. How much of a loss to the enemy is one Jiang Wei?"

Fei Yi went on, "The army Your Excellency commands numbers several hundred thousand; will it be possible to attack the north again?" Kongming answered, "When our forces occupied Qishan and Winnow Basket Gorge, an enemy inferior in numbers defeated us. The problem was not the size of our army but the leadership. My present purpose is to reduce the army's size and relieve some of the commanders, to punish openly those who deserve it while reflecting on our own mistakes, and to revise our tactics for the future. Unless we do this, simply increasing our forces won't help. Henceforth, those of you genuinely concerned for our kingdom's ultimate fate must vigorously attack my errors and hold me responsible for my failures. Then our direction can be set, the rebels destroyed, and an early victory anticipated." Fei Yi and the other commanders accepted this view. Fei Yi returned to Chengdu.

2365

Kongming remained in Hanzhong, where he treated the army and the populace with solicitude and had the troops put through rigorous training. He also arranged for the construction of equipment for laying siege and for crossing rivers; he stockpiled grain and provender; and he readied rafts for battle. Northern spies reported these war preparations to Luoyang.

魏主曹睿闻知，即召司马懿商议收川之策。懿曰："蜀未可攻也。方今天道亢炎，蜀兵必不出；若我军深入其地，彼守其险要，急切难下。"睿曰："倘蜀兵再来入寇，如之奈何？"懿曰："臣已算定今番诸葛亮必效韩信暗度陈仓之计。臣举一人往陈仓道口，筑城守御，万无一失：此人身长九尺，猿臂善射，深有谋略。若诸葛亮入寇，此人足可当之。"睿大喜，问曰："此何人也？"懿奏曰："乃太原人，姓郝，名昭，字伯道，现为杂号将军，镇守河西。"

睿从之，加郝昭为镇西将军，命守把陈仓道口，遣使持诏去讫。忽报扬州司马大都督曹休上表，说东吴鄱阳太守周鲂，愿以郡来降，密遣人陈言七事，说东吴可破，乞早发兵取之。睿就御床上展开，与司马懿同观。懿奏曰："此言极有理，吴当灭矣！臣愿引一军往助曹休。"忽班中一人进曰："吴人之言，反覆不一，未可深信。周鲂智谋之士，必不肯降。此特诱兵之诡计也。"众视之，乃建威将军贾逵也。懿曰："此言亦不可不听，机会亦不可错失。"魏主曰："仲达可与贾逵同助曹休。"二人领命去讫。于是曹休引大军径取皖城；贾逵引前将军满宠、东莞太

* * *

Apprised of these developments, Cao Rui summoned Sima Yi to plan the conquest of the Riverlands. "It is not the time for an attack," Sima Yi counseled. "Now, at the very height of summer, the Riverlands troops will hold back. And if we go too deeply into their territory while they sit tight in their strongpoints, we will be a long time defeating them." Cao Rui asked, "And what if the Riverlands troops raid our territory?" "I, your vassal," Sima Yi answered, "have already concluded that Zhuge Liang is bound to follow Han Xin's example and secretly aim for Chencang.[2] I am recommending someone who can fortify our position there so that there will not be the slightest chance of losing it. He stands nine spans tall and has the powerful arms of a champion marksman as well as a profound understanding of strategy. He will be able to stop Zhuge Liang's invasion."

Delighted, Cao Rui asked the man's name, and Sima Yi responded, "Hao Zhao (styled Bodao) of Taiyuan, presently controlling Hexi as a commander with various titles." In accordance with Sima Yi's recommendation, Cao Rui sent an edict appointing Hao Zhao General Who Controls the West and assigning him to defend the road to Chencang. At that moment the Wei ruler received an unexpected report from First Field Marshal Cao Xiu, military authority in Yangzhou.[3] It said that Zhou Fang, the Southland's governor in Poyang, was offering to surrender his district and that he had sent a secret emissary enumerating seven conditions for breaking the power of the Southland along with his appeal for Wei troops to take over Poyang.

Cao Rui unrolled the document on his platform, and he and Sima Yi examined it. Sima Yi said, "This appeal should be answered. The Southland will be destroyed. Give me a company to assist Cao Xiu." Suddenly someone stepped forward from the assembly's ranks and said, "The men of the Southland always go back on what they say; I wouldn't place much faith in this offer. Zhou Fang is too cunning to be surrendering. It must be a trick to lure our soldiers in." All eyes turned to Jia Kui, General Who Establishes Dynastic Authority. Sima Yi said to him, "This appeal must be heeded lest an opportunity be missed." The ruler of Wei said, "Let both of you, Sima Yi and Jia Kui, assist Cao Xiu." The two generals left to execute the order. Following this, Cao Xiu marched in force directly to

守胡质,径取阳城,直向东关;司马懿引本部军径取江陵。

却说吴主孙权,在武昌东关,会多官商议曰:"今有鄱阳太守周鲂密表,奏称魏扬州都督曹休,有入寇之意。今鲂诈施诡计,暗陈七事,引诱魏兵深入重地,可设伏兵擒之。今魏兵分三路而来。诸卿有何高见?"顾雍进曰:"此大任非陆伯言不敢当也。"权大喜,乃召陆逊,封为辅国大将军、平北都元帅,统御林大兵,摄行王事:授以白旄黄钺,文武百官,皆听约束。权亲自与逊执鞭。逊领命谢恩毕,乃保二人为左右都督,分兵以迎三道。权问何人,逊曰:"奋威将军朱桓,绥南将军全琮,二人可为辅佐。"权从之,即命朱桓为左都督,全琮为右都督。于是陆逊总率江南八十一州并荆湖之众七十余万,令朱桓在左,全琮在右,逊自居中,三路进兵。朱桓献策曰:"曹休以亲见任,非智勇之将也。今听周鲂诱言,深入重地,元帅以兵击之,曹休必败。

the city of Huan; Jia Kui led Forward Commander Man Chong and the governor of Dongwan, Hu Zhi, directly to East Pass to capture Yangcheng; and Sima Yi led his troops to seize Jiangling.[4]

* * *

At this time the ruler of the Southland, Sun Quan, was meeting with his officials at East Pass in Wuchang. He told them, "I have a secret petition from Zhou Fang, governor of Poyang. It states that Wei's governor of Yangzhou, Cao Xiu, plans to invade our district. Zhou Fang has put into action a cunning plan to lure the enemy into a fortified area where we can ambush and capture Cao Xiu. Wei troops — three field armies — are on their way. What are you views?"

Gu Yong offered his opinion: "The only man who can stop them is Lu Xun!" Delighted with this suggestion, Sun Quan summoned the general[5] and honored him with the titles First Field Marshal Who Sustains the Kingdom and Generalissimo Who Pacifies the North. As commander of the Royal Guard, Lu Xun was empowered to act in the King's behalf. He received the yak-tail standard and the golden mace before the assembled officials, who listened gravely. Sun Quan personally handed Lu Xun the whip for his mount.

Lu Xun received Sun Quan's mandate and thanked his sovereign for his favor. Before dispatching forces to meet the invaders, Lu Xun recommended two men to serve as his lieutenants so that the army could be split into three divisions and advanced along three routes. Sun Quan asked for their names, and Lu Xun replied, "Zhu Huan, General Who Invigorates Our Prestige, and Quan Zong, General Who Calms the South. These two will support my command." Sun Quan approved and appointed Zhu Huan field marshal of the Left and Quan Zong field marshal of the Right. Following this, Lu Xun took command of a vast host of more than seven hundred thousand troops recruited from the eighty-one departments of the Southland and from the Jingzhou region as well. With Zhu Huan leading the left route army and Quan Zong leading the right route army, Lu Xun advanced, leading the central army himself.

Zhu Huan proposed a plan: "Cao Xiu was sent on his mission only because he is an imperial relation. He has neither the brains nor the courage to command. Zhou Fang's scheme has lured him into a key area.

败后必走两条路：左乃夹石，右乃挂车。此二条路，皆山僻小径，最为险峻。某愿与全子璜各引一军，伏于山险，先以柴木大石塞断其路，曹休可擒矣。若擒了曹休，便长驱直进，唾手而得寿春，以窥许、洛，此万世一时也。"逊曰："此非善策，吾自有妙用。"于是朱桓怀不平而退。逊令诸葛瑾等拒守江陵，以敌司马懿。诸路俱各调拨停当。

却说曹休兵临皖城，周鲂来迎，径到曹休帐下。休问曰："近得足下之书，所陈七事，深为有理，奏闻天子，故起大军三路进发。若得江东之地，足下之功不小。有人言足下多谋，诚恐所言不实。——吾料足下必不欺我。"周鲂大哭，急掣从人所佩剑欲自刎。休急止之。鲂仗剑而言曰："吾所陈七事，恨不能吐出心肝。今反生疑，必有吴人使反间之计也。若听其言，吾必死矣。吾之忠心，惟天可表！"言讫，又欲自刎。曹休大惊，慌忙抱住曰："吾戏言耳，足下何故如此！"鲂乃用剑割发掷于地曰："吾以忠心待公，公以吾为戏，吾割父母所遗之发，以表此心！"曹休乃深信之，设宴相待。席罢，周鲂辞去。忽报建威将军贾逵

Marshal, if you attack, he is bound to fall back and then flee by one of two routes — Gorge of Rock on the left or Hanging Wagon on the right — both treacherous mountain paths. Let Quan Zong and myself each set a detachment in ambush at these points after we have blocked the road with rocks and branches. Cao Xiu will be taken. That done, we will advance directly and seize Shouchun, bringing Xuchang and Luoyang within striking distance, a once-in-a-lifetime opportunity!" "I'm afraid it's not a good plan," Lu Xun replied. "I have some clever ploys of my own." Thereupon Zhu Huan withdrew, resentful of the way his views had been received. Lu Xun ordered Zhuge Jin and others to hold Jiangling and oppose Sima Yi. All the field armies were positioned exactly as Lu Xun directed.

*　*　*

Meanwhile, as Cao Xiu approached the city of Huan, Zhou Fang went forth to greet him, proceeding directly to Cao Xiu's tent. Cao Xiu said, "Your recent communication stating seven conditions seemed entirely reasonable, and your appeal was submitted to the Son of Heaven. He has mustered the whole army for an expedition south; and if we take the Southland, your contribution will have played no small part. Some contend you are full of schemes and some doubt the truth of what you say, but I feel confident you are not deceiving us."

Zhou Fang let out a sharp cry, seized a follower's sword, and attempted to cut his own throat. Cao Xiu swiftly checked him. Bracing himself on the sword, Zhou Fang said, "I made seven points and will now prove my sincerity with my blood. Some southerner is provoking suspicion to turn you against me. Give him credence, and I shall die. Let Heaven vouch for my loyalty." So saying, Zhou Fang again tried to kill himself. In alarm Cao Xiu restrained him, saying, "I spoke in jest. There is no need for such demonstrations." Zhou Fang then cut off his hair with the sword and flung the tangle to the ground. He said, "I come to you with a loyal heart, and you treat me in jest. To show my true heart, I have severed the hair that comes from the parents who gave me life." Thus, Zhou Fang convinced Cao Xiu of his sincerity. Cao Xiu held a grand banquet in his honor; the festivities ended, and Zhou Fang excused himself.

Suddenly Jia Kui, General Who Establishes Dynastic Authority, was

来见,休令入,问曰:"汝此来何为?"逵曰:"某料东吴之兵,必尽屯于皖城。都督不可轻进,待某两下夹攻,贼兵可破矣。"休怒曰:"汝欲夺吾功耶?"逵曰:"又闻周鲂截发为誓,此乃诈也,——昔要离断臂,刺杀庆忌——未可深信。"休大怒曰:"吾正欲进兵,汝何出此言以慢军心!"叱左右推出斩之。众将告曰:"未及进兵,先斩大将,于军不利。且乞暂免。"休从之,将贾逵兵留在寨中调用,自引一军来取东关。时周鲂听知贾逵削去兵权,暗喜曰:"曹休若用贾逵之言,则东吴败矣!今天使我成功也!"即遣人密到皖城,报知陆逊。逊唤诸将听令曰:"前面石亭,虽是山路,足可埋伏。早先去占石亭阔处,布成阵势,以待魏军。"遂令徐盛为先锋,引兵前进。

　　却说曹休命周鲂引兵而进,正行间,休问曰:"前至何处?"鲂曰:"前面石亭也,堪以屯兵。"休从之,遂率大军并车仗等器,尽赴石亭驻扎。次日,哨马报道:"前面吴兵不知多少,据住山口。"休大惊曰:"周鲂言无兵,为何有准备?"急寻鲂问之。人报周鲂引数十人,不知何处去了。休大悔曰:"吾中贼之计矣!——虽然如此,亦不足惧!"遂令大将张普为先锋,引数千兵来与吴兵交战。两阵对圆,张普出马骂曰:"贼将早降!"徐盛

announced. Cao Xiu ordered him to appear and asked him, "What have you come for?" Jia Kui replied, "I believe the Southland has massed troops at Huan. Field Marshal, do not risk an advance before I try to defeat the enemy with flank attacks." Cao Xiu replied angrily, "Are you trying to rob me of this achievement?" But Jia Kui went on, "Zhou Fang cut his hair to deceive you — as Yao Li did in ancient times when he cut off his arm to win Qing Ji's trust before murdering him. Give him no credence!"

In rising anger Cao Xiu asked, "Would you sap our morale at the very moment I am preparing to march?" He ordered his guards to remove and execute Jia Kui. The other commanders appealed in his behalf: "To kill a leading commander on the eve of the expedition will do our army no good. Spare him for now." Cao Xiu relented; he held Jia Kui's men in camp pending deployment and took a company ahead to capture East Pass. When Zhou Fang heard that Jia Kui had been stripped of his command, he said to himself with satisfaction, "Had Cao Xiu heeded Jai Kui, the Southland would have been done for. But Heaven brings us victory this day!"

Zhou Fang sent a secret emissary to the city of Huan to report these developments to Lu Xun. Lu Xun summoned his commanders and delivered his orders to them: "Stonetown lies ahead. The roads are hilly, suitable enough for an ambush. Go and occupy the open ground first, then deploy and await the Wei army." Finally, Lu Xun ordered Xu Sheng to move up as vanguard.

Meanwhile, Cao Xiu had ordered Zhou Fang to advance. On the march Cao Xiu asked him, "What place lies ahead?" "Stonetown," Zhou Fang replied. "A good place to occupy." Following this advice, Cao Xiu led his main force, complete with impedimenta and regalia, and stationed it at Stonetown. The next day lookouts reported to him, "Southland troops in undetermined numbers bar our way into the hills." "But Zhou Fang assured me," Cao Xiu said in alarm. "How could there be troops waiting?" Cao Xiu raced to find Zhou Fang but was told he had ridden off with a few dozen men, no one knew where. "I have fallen into a trap, but there's no need to panic," Cao Xiu exclaimed, and he ordered General Zhang Pu to lead the vanguard into battle against the southern army.

出马相迎。战无数合，普抵敌不住，勒马收兵，回见曹休，言徐盛勇不可当。休曰："吾当以奇兵胜之。"——就令张普引二万军伏于石亭之南，又令薛乔引二万军伏于石亭之北——"明日吾自引一千兵搦战，却佯输诈败，诱到北山之前，放炮为号，三面夹攻，必获大胜。"二将受计，各引二万军到晚埋伏去了。

却说陆逊唤朱桓、全琮分付曰："汝二人各引三万军，从石亭山路抄到曹休寨后，放火为号；吾亲率大军从中路而进：可擒曹休也。"当日黄昏，二将受计引兵而进。二更时分，朱桓引一军正抄到魏寨后，迎着张普伏兵。普不知是吴兵，径来问时，被朱桓一刀斩于马下。魏兵便走。桓令后军放火。全琮引一军抄到魏寨后，正撞在薛乔阵里，就那里大杀一阵。薛乔败走，魏兵大损，奔回本寨。后面朱桓、全琮两路杀来。曹休寨中大乱，自相冲击。休慌上马，望夹石道奔走。徐盛引大队军马，从正路杀来。魏兵死者不可胜数，逃命者尽弃衣甲。曹休大惊，在夹石道中，奋力奔走。忽见一彪军从小路冲出，为首大将，乃贾逵也。休惊慌少息，自愧曰："吾不用公言，果遭此败！"逵曰："都

The two sides deployed in formation. Zhang Pu rode forth and de-nounced the enemy commander: "Surrender now, traitor!" Xu Sheng rode forth to engage him. After a brief clash Zhang Pu, unable to with-stand the assault, reined in and recalled his men. He returned to Cao Xiu and told him that Xu Sheng was too bold to confront. "I will defeat him with a surprise attack," Cao Xiu boasted, and he ordered Zhang Pu to put twenty thousand men in ambush south of Stonetown. At the same time Cao Xiu ordered Xue Qiao to lay another twenty thousand in ambush north of the town. "Tomorrow," Cao Xiu told them, "I will go forth with one thousand men and provoke battle. Then I will feign defeat to draw the enemy near the northern hills. At the signal of a bombard we will attack from three sides — and a great victory will be ours." The two commanders went to carry out their orders.

Meanwhile, Lu Xun had summoned his lieutenants Zhu Huan and Quan Zong and instructed them: "Take thirty thousand troops each and harass Cao Xiu's camp from the rear; then signal with fire. I will advance in force on the main road. Cao Xiu can be taken!" At dusk the two com-manders moved forward according to plan. During the second watch Zhu Huan led a company behind Cao Xiu's camp, where he fell upon Zhang Pu's ambush. But Zhang Pu did not realize the troops were hostile and rode forward to make inquiry; Zhu Huan cut him down with a stroke of the sword. The Wei force fled, and Zhu Huan ordered the rear com-pany to light a fire. At this signal Quan Zong, leading his company to worry the rear of Cao Xiu's camp, came to grips with the soldiers of Xue Qiao. In the ensuing slaughter Xue Qiao fled in defeat; and the Wei troops ran headlong back to camp, having suffered grave losses.

From the rear Zhu Huan and Quan Zong, leading separate units, moved in for the kill. Cao Xiu's camp became so disorganized that his troops began attacking one another. Cao Xiu leaped to his horse and raced to-ward the Stonetown road. With a sizable force Xu Sheng moved along the main road killing countless Wei troops; those who escaped abandoned their battle garments and shields. Cao Xiu was in a panic, racing for his life down the Stonetown road, when a band of men burst into his view from a bypath, their commander Jia Kui. Cao Xiu recovered slightly and in a tone of self-reproach said, "I suffered this defeat because I ignored

督可速出此道：若被吴兵以木石塞断，吾等皆危矣！"于是曹休骤马而行，贾逵断后。逵于林木盛茂处，及险峻小径，多设旌旗以为疑兵。及至徐盛赶到，见山坡下闪出旗角，疑有埋伏，不敢追赶，收兵而回。——因此救了曹休。司马懿听知休败，亦引兵退去。

　　却说陆逊正望捷音，须臾，徐盛、朱桓、全琮皆到，所得车仗、牛马、驴骡、军资、器械，不计其数，降兵数万余人。逊大喜，即同太守周鲂并诸将班师还吴。吴主孙权，领文武官僚出武昌城迎接，以御盖覆逊而入。诸将尽皆升赏。权见周鲂无发，慰劳曰："卿断发成此大事，功名当书于竹帛也。"即封周鲂为关内侯；大设筵会，劳军庆贺。陆逊奏曰："今曹休大败，魏已丧胆；可修国书，遣使入川，教诸葛亮进兵攻之。"权从其言，遂遣使赍书入川去。

　　正是：

　　　　只因东国能施计，致令西川又动兵。

　　未知孔明再来伐魏，胜负如何，且看下文分解。

your advice." "Leave this road at once, Field Marshal," Jia Kui urged. "If the southerners block it with rocks and branches, we will be in grave danger." Cao Xiu galloped off. Jia Kui protected the rear and planted decoy banners both in the thick of the woods and along precarious hill paths. Racing up in pursuit, Xu Sheng glimpsed the banners on the slopes and chose to recall his troops and return rather than press the chase and risk ambush. Thus, Cao Xiu was rescued; and Sima Yi, hearing of Cao Xiu's defeat, withdrew.

Lu Xun was awaiting news of victory when Xu Sheng, Zhu Huan, and Quan Zong returned, having captured huge quantities of chariots, carts, draft animals, materiel, and weapons in addition to tens of thousands of enemy soldiers. Delighted with the outcome of the day's action, Field Marshal Lu Xun brought the army back to the Southland, followed by Governor Zhou Fang and the Principal lieutenant commanders. The lord of the Southland, Sun Quan, led his officials and officers out of Wuchang to greet Lu Xun, whom he placed beside him under the imperial umbrella for the ride back into the city. All the lieutenant commanders were promoted and rewarded.

Noticing that Zhou Fang was missing some hair, Sun Quan cheered him, saying, "You will go down in history for what you accomplished today." He then made Zhou Fang an honorary lord and held a grand banquet to feast the army and celebrate the victory. Lu Xun addressed his sovereign, saying, "Cao Xiu's defeat has daunted the Wei. Now is the time to send a letter to the Riverlands urging Zhuge Liang to march against them." Sun Quan approved the proposal and sent an emissary off to Shu. Indeed:

> A sound plan from the eastern kingdom
> Would cause the western kingdom to mobilize again.

How would Kongming's next campaign against Wei turn out?
Read on.

2377

第九十七回

讨魏国武侯再上表　破曹兵姜维诈献书

　　却说蜀汉建兴六年秋九月，魏都督曹休被东吴陆逊大破于石亭，车仗马匹，军资器械，并皆罄尽。休惶恐之甚，气忧成病，到洛阳，疽发背而死。魏主曹睿敕令厚葬。司马懿引兵还，众将接入问曰："曹都督兵败，即元帅之干系，何故急回耶？"懿曰："吾料诸葛亮知吾兵败，必乘虚来取长安。倘陇西紧急，何人救之？吾故回耳。"众皆以为惧怯，哂笑而退。

　　却说东吴遣使致书蜀中，请兵伐魏，并言大破曹休之事：一者显自己威风，二者通和会之好。后主大喜，令人持书至汉中，报知孔明。时孔明兵强马壮，粮草丰足，所用之物，一切完备，正要出师。听知此信，即设宴大会诸将，计议出师。忽一阵大风，自东北角上而起，把庭前松树吹折。众皆大惊。孔明就占一课，曰："此风主损一大将！"诸将未信。正饮酒间，忽报镇南

Chapter 97

Kongming Appeals Again for an Expedition Against Wei
Jiang Wei Defeats the Cao Army by Offering
a False Letter

It was autumn, the ninth month of Jian Xing 6 (A.D. 228) by the Shu-Han calendar, when the Southland general Lu Xun defeated the Wei field Marshal Cao Xiu at Stonetown and seized his chariots, livestock, and fighting equipment. Despair over these losses caused Cao Xiu to develop an ulcer on his back; he died on reaching Luoyang. The ruler of Wei, Cao Rui, had him buried with full honors.

When Sima Yi returned with his troops, the assembled commanders asked him, "Field Marshal Cao's defeat was as much your responsibility, Commander, as his — why have you rushed back?" "Zhuge Liang might exploit our defeat to take Chang'an," he replied. "Who else can meet an emergency to our west? That is why I came home." But the commanders thought Sima Yi afraid, and snickered as they withdrew.

* * *

2379

Meanwhile, the Southland emissary had delivered Sun Quan's letter to the Shu capital. Its appeal for the Riverlands to attack Wei and its account of the defeat of Cao Xiu bespoke Sun Quan's intention to demonstrate the Southland's strength and to promote good relations with the Riverlands. The Second Emperor was delighted with the letter and had it carried to Kongming in Hanzhong.

Preparing for another offensive, Kongming had brought his armed forces to full strength, laid in supplies, and readied all equipment and materiel. When the Second Emperor's courier arrived with Sun Quan's letter, Kongming convened a grand banquet for planning the campaign with his commanders. Suddenly, a violent gust of wind from the northeast blew down a prine tree in front of Kongming's quarters. Before a startled assembly Kongming divined by tossing coins and said, "This portends the fall of a great general." The commanders were skeptical of this predic-

将军赵云长子赵统、次子赵广，来见丞相。孔明大惊，掷杯于地曰："子龙休矣！"二子入见，拜哭曰："某父昨夜三更病重而死。"孔明跌足而哭曰："子龙身故，国家损一栋梁，吾去一臂也！"众将无不挥涕。孔明令二子入成都面君报丧。后主闻云死，放声大哭曰："朕昔年幼，非子龙则死于乱军之中矣！"即下诏追赠大将军，谥封顺平侯，敕葬于成都锦屏山之东；建立庙堂，四时享祭。后人有诗曰：

> 常山有虎将，智勇匹关张。
> 汉水功勋在，当阳姓字彰。
> 两番扶幼主，一念答先皇。
> 青史书忠烈，应流百世芳。

却说后主思念赵云昔日之功，祭葬甚厚；封赵统为虎贲中郎，赵广为牙门将，就令守坟。二人辞谢而去。忽近臣奏曰："诸葛丞相将军马分拨已定，即日将出师伐魏。"后主问在朝诸臣，诸臣多言未可轻动。后主疑虑未决。忽奏丞相令杨仪赍出师表

tion, and the banquet continued. Suddenly Zhao Tong, eldest son of Zhao Zilong, General Who Controls the South, and Zhao Guang, the Second son, came to present themselves before the prime minister. Astonished, Kongming threw his cup to the ground and cried, "We have lost Zhao Zilong!" The two sons entered Kongming's presence, flung themselves to the ground, and wept. "Father died last night at the third watch," they cried, "after his illness had taken a turn for the worse." Kongming stamped his foot on the ground. Tearfully, he said, "In Zilong the dynasty had a pillar; and I, my right arm!" All the assembled commanders wept.

Kongming sent the sons of Zhao Zilong to Chengdu to report their father's demise. On receiving the news, the Second Emperor emitted a sharp cry and shed tears. "Long ago, when I was still an infant," he said, "Zhao Zilong plucked me from certain death during a chaotic retreat of our forces." The Second Emperor issued an edict posthumously honoring Zhao Zilong as regent-marshal and lord of Shunping and ordered him interred east of the Damask Screen Hills outside Chengdu. An ancestral temple was built on the site for the offering of sacrifice each season. A poet of later times left these lines in Zhao Zilong's memory:

Tiger General from Changshan
With the wit and courage of Zhang and Guan!
Your triumph at Hanshui stands today;[1]
Your name at Dangyang all acclaimed.
Twice you saved the baby prince
In service to his sacred sire.
History honors those whom duty claims,
Conferring a glory that never wanes.

2381

Mindful of Zhao Zilong's past achievements, the Second Emperor buried him with rich and splendid ceremony. He assigned Zhao Tong to the Imperial Tiger Escort and appointed Zhao Guang garrison commander, ordering them to stand watch at the graveside in honor of their late father's memory.

The two sons took their leave and departed. Suddenly an imperial attendant informed the Emperor, "Prime Minister Zhuge Liang is ready to resume the campaign against Wei." The Second Emperor turned to the officials at court; they advocated a more cautious policy. The Em-

至。后主宣入,仪呈上表章。后主就御案上拆视,其表曰:

先帝虑汉、贼不两立,王业不偏安,故托臣以讨贼也。以先帝之明,量臣之才,故知臣伐贼,才弱敌强也。然不伐贼,王业亦亡。惟坐而待亡,孰与伐之?是故托臣而弗疑也。臣受命之日,寝不安席,食不甘味;思惟北征,宜先入南:故五月渡泸,深入不毛,并日而食。——臣非不自惜也:顾王业不可偏安于蜀都,故冒危难以奉先帝之遗意。而议者谓为非计。今贼适疲于西,又务于东,兵法“乘劳”:此进趋之时也。谨陈其事如左:

高帝明并日月,谋臣渊深,然涉险被创,危然后安;今陛下未及高帝,谋臣不如良、平,而欲以长策取胜,坐定天下:此臣之未解一也。刘繇、王朗,各据州郡,论安言计,动引圣人,群疑满腹,众难塞胸;今岁不战,明年不征,使孙权坐大,遂并江东:此臣之未解二也。曹操智计,殊绝于

peror was struggling to reach a decision, when he was told that the prime minister had sent Yang Yi with a petition. The Second Emperor summoned Yang Yi, who presented the document for his examination. The text read:

Painfully recognizing that either the kingdom of Han or the kingdom of Wei must fall and that our royal rule would never know security if confined to a part of the realm, the late Emperor empowered me to wage righteous war against the northern traitors. Accurately appraising his vassal's abilities, he knew full well what feeble talent I had to pit against so strong an enemy; but not to go forward spelled our doom. To arms, rather than to bow to fate! Thus, the late Emperor charged me, and he never wavered in that commitment.

The day I received his mandate, I neither slept nor ate; the northern expedition occupied my thoughts. But first we had to move into the region south of us. In the fifth month I crossed the River Lu and penetrated deep into aboriginal territory, going without food for days at a time — not because I threw caution to the winds but because, knowing that Your Majesty's rule could never have survived confined to the Shu capital, we would have faced any danger, any difficulty, to carry out the late Emperor's last wishes. Critics have complained of this plan. Now, when the traitors are spent in the west and occupied in the east, military logic tells us to exploit their distress. It is time to move forward. Allow me to present further details of this case.

The founder of the Han, Emperor Gao Zu, had wisdom of a heavenly scale and advisers of great depth and subtlety. Yet he tested treacherous terrain and suffered painful defeats, gaining security only after many trials and ordeals. Your Majesty will never surpass Emperor Gao Zu; your advisers will never surpass Zhang Liang and Chen Ping. How Your Majesty could seek a long-range plan for conquering the empire from a passive position is the first thing I fail to understand.

Imperial Inspector Liu Yao and Governor Wang Lang each held imperial territory.[2] They were concerned for their security and worked out plans, freely citing the ancient sages. But a crowd of doubts filled their breasts, innumerable obstacles impeded their thinking, and they put off military action from year to year. That they thus allowed Sun Ce to wax in power unhampered and eventually engross the whole of the Southland in the second thing I fail to understand.

Cao Cao — no shrewder planner than he — waged war in a manner

2384

人，其用兵也，仿佛孙、吴，然困于南阳，险于乌巢，危于祁连，逼于黎阳，几败北山，殆死潼关，然后伪定一时耳；况臣才弱，而欲以不危而定之：此臣之未解三也。曹操五攻昌霸不下，四越巢湖不成，任用李服而李服图之，委任夏侯而夏侯败亡，先帝每称操为能，犹有此失；况臣驽下，何能必胜：此臣之未解四也。自臣到汉中，中间期年耳，然丧赵云、阳群、马玉、阎芝、丁立、白寿、刘郃、邓铜等，及曲长屯将七十余人，突将无前，賨、叟、青羌，散骑武骑一千余人，此皆数十年之内，所纠合四方之精锐，非一州之所有；若复数年，则损三分之二也。——当何以图敌：此臣之未解五也。今民穷兵疲，而事不可息；事不可息，则住与行，劳费正等；而不及今图之，欲以一州之地，与贼持久：此臣之未解六也。

　　夫难平者，事也。昔先帝败军于楚，当此之时，曹操拊手，谓天下已定。——然后先帝东连吴、越，西取巴、蜀，举兵北征，夏侯授首：此操之失计，而汉事将成也。——然后吴更违盟，关羽毁败，秭归蹉跌，曹丕称帝：凡事如是，难可逆见。臣鞠躬尽瘁，死而后已；至于成败利钝，非臣之明所能逆睹也。

worthy of Sunzi and Wu Qi. Nonetheless, his enemies trapped him at Nanyang, put him in straits in Wuchao, imperiled his life at Qilian, pressed him hard at Liyang, nearly ruined him at Beishan, and almost killed him at Tong Pass. After all that, he enjoyed a brief period of false security. How then this vassal, Liang, with so much less talent than Cao Cao, could ever conquer the north without running risks is the third thing I fail to understand.

Cao Cao attacked Changba five times but could not subdue it. He tried to cross Lake Chao four times and failed. He took Li Fu into his service, but Li Fu conspired against him. He gave authority to Xiahou Yuan, but Xiahou Yuan died. The late Emperor always acknowledged Cao Cao's capabilities, yet he had his failures too. How then one so inferior as this vassal could guarantee a victory is the fourth thing I fail to appreciate.

Alas, since arriving in Hanzhong, in one year we have lost Zhao Zilong,[3] Yang Qun, Ma Yu, Yan Zhi, Ding Li, Bo Shou, Liu He, Deng Tong, and others, in addition to unit leaders and positional commanders totaling more than seventy. We also lost more than a thousand of our special forces — shock troops, units of the Cong, Sou, and Black Qiang nations, rangers and armed cavalry. To assemble these elite forces from around the realm took many decades; no single province can make up the loss. And in a few more years, we will lose another two-thirds of them. How to deal with the enemy then is the fifth thing I fail to understand.

At present, though the population is strained to the utmost and the armed forces near exhaustion, events will not stand still; and in their swift course, action is no dearer than restraint. Not to act when the hour beckons, trying instead to sustain a protracted struggle with the resources of but a single province is the sixth thing I fail to understand.

Events are the hardest things to control. Once the late Emperor lost a battle in Jingzhou, and Cao Cao gleefully rubbed his hands together, confident that he had conquered the empire. But then the late Emperor allied himself with Wu and Yue in the east, took Ba and Shu in the west, and marched against the north. Xiahou Yuan fell. This was something Cao Cao failed to reckon on and a promise of success for the cause of Han. But the Southland turned on its Riverlands ally; Lord Guan perished, Zigui fell, and Cao Pi proclaimed a new dynasty. That's how things happen; it is difficult to anticipate things to come. Humbly I shall toil to the last ounce of my strength, until my end; but whether the outcome will favor us or not is beyond my powers of prediction.[4]

后主览表甚喜,即敕令孔明出师。孔明受命,起三十万精兵,令魏延总督前部先锋,径奔陈仓道口而来。

早有细作报入洛阳。司马懿奏知魏主,大会文武商议。大将军曹真出班奏曰:"臣昨守陇西,功微罪大,不胜惶恐。今乞引大军往擒诸葛亮。臣近得一员大将,使六十斤大刀,骑千里征宛马,开两石铁胎弓,暗藏三个流星锤,百发百中,有万夫不当之勇,乃陇西狄道人,姓王,名双,字子全。臣保此人为先锋。"睿大喜,便召王双上殿。视之,身长九尺,面黑睛黄,熊腰虎背。睿笑曰:"朕得此大将,有何虑哉!"遂赐锦袍金甲,封为虎威将军、前部大先锋。曹真为大都督。真谢恩出朝,遂引十五万精兵,会合郭淮、张郃,分道守把隘口。

却说蜀兵前队哨至陈仓,回报孔明,说:"陈仓口已筑起一城,内有大将郝昭守把,深沟高垒,遍排鹿角,十分谨严;不如弃了此城,从太白岭鸟道出祁山甚便。"孔明曰:"陈仓正北是街亭;必得此城,方可进兵。"命魏延引兵到城下,四面攻之。连

The Second Emperor was delighted with Kongming's petition and issued orders for the expedition to begin. Kongming accepted the imperial command. He put three hundred thousand of his finest troops into the field and made Wei Yan commander of the vanguard of the first unit. Then he headed striaght for the road to Chencang.

* * *

Spies soon reported these movements to Sima Yi in Luoyang, and he informed the ruler of Wei, who called a court conference to discuss the matter. Regent-MarshalCao Zhen stepped forward and addressed the Emperor: "This vassal's recent defense of Longxi was a humiliating failure. To redeem myself, I request a large force to go and capture Zhuge Liang. I have lately acquired the services of an important commander who wields a sword of sixty *jin* and rides a champion war-horse. He can pull an iron bow more than two hundred pounds strong, and with three concealed 'meteor hammers' he can hit his target every time. Ten thousand fighters could not equal him in courage. This man comes from Didao in Longxi. His name is Wang Shuang (styled Ziquan). I recommend him for the vanguard." Cao Rui was delighted and summoned Wang Shuang to the elevated hall. Cao Rui studied his nine-span frame, his swarthy face and yellowish eyes, his bearlike waist and tigerlike back. With a smile Cao Rui said, "So great a commander eases my cares." He bestowed on him a silk surcoat, golden armor, and the titles Tiger-Fearsome General and vanguard of the first unit. Cao Zhen was the chief commander of the expedition. After thanking the ruler, Cao Zhen left the court and, at the head of one hundred and fifty thousand picked troops, met with Guo Huai and Zhang He; then they went to defend different strongpoints.

* * *

The advance reconnaissance unit of the Riverlands army reached Chencang and then reported back to Kongming: "They have walled Chencang. Inside, General Hao Zhao commands a well-fortified complex surrounded by an impenetrable network of branches and staves. It would be easier for us to reach Qishan through the narrow mountain path in the Taibo Range and leave Chencang alone." "Due north of Chencang stands Jieting, the town we must take before we advance," was

日不能破。魏延复来告孔明，说城难打。孔明大怒，欲斩魏延。忽帐下一人告曰："某虽无才，随丞相多年，未尝报效。愿去陈仓城中，说郝昭来降，不用张弓只箭。"众视之，乃部曲靳祥也。孔明曰："汝用何言以说之？"祥曰："郝昭与某，同是陇西人氏，自幼交契。某今到彼，以利害说之，必来降矣。"孔明即令前去。靳祥骤马径到城下，叫曰："郝伯道故人靳祥来见。"城上人报知郝昭。昭令开门放入，登城相见。昭问曰："故人因何到此？"祥曰："吾在西蜀孔明帐下，参赞军机，待以上宾之礼。特令某来见公，有言相告。"昭勃然变色曰："诸葛亮乃我国仇敌也！吾事魏，汝事蜀：各事其主，昔时为昆仲，今时为仇敌！汝再不必多言，便请出城！"靳祥又欲开言，郝昭已出敌楼上了。魏军急催上马，赶出城外。祥回头视之，见昭倚定护心木栏杆。祥勒马以鞭指之曰："伯道贤弟，何太情薄耶？"昭曰："魏国法度，兄所知也。吾受国恩，但有死而已，兄不必下说词。早回见诸葛亮，教快来攻城：吾不惧也！"祥回告孔明曰："郝昭未等某开言，便先阻却。"孔明曰："汝可再去见他，以利害说之。"祥又到城下，请郝昭相见。昭出到敌楼上。祥勒马高叫曰："伯道贤弟，听吾忠言：汝据守一孤城，怎拒数十万之众？今不早降，后悔无

Kongming's reply, and he ordered Wei Yan to march to the wall and lay siege to Chencang.

After pressing the attack for several days, Wei Yan returned and told Kongming that he could not take Chencang. Kongming would have exceuted Wei Yan, but someone stepped forward and declared, "I have followed Your Excellency for many years without performing worthy service. Inept as I am, I beg to enter Chencang for the purpose of persuading Hao Zhao to submit. Not an arrow need be wasted." The assembly turned to unit commander Jin Xiang. "And how will you convince him?" Kongming asked. "Both of us come from Longxi," Jin Xiang replied, "and have been close since childhood. If I show him where his advantage lies, he will submit." Kongming ordered Jix Xiang to proceed.

Jin Xiang galloped to Chencang and shouted up to the wall: "An old friend of Hao Zhao's!" Guards reported to Hao Zhao, who ordered the visitor admitted. Jin Xiang mounted the wall and the two met. "What brings my old friend?" Hao Zhao asked. "At present I am under Kongming of the Riverlands," Jin Xiang replied, "engaged in military planning, for which I am treated most cordially. It is he who sends me with a message for you." Hao Zhao's expression turned severe as he said, "Zhuge Liang is my kingdom's foe. I serve Wei; you serve Shu. Each serves his lord. Brothers once, we are mortal enemies now. Say no more, but leave Chencang at once!"[5] Jin Xiang tried to speak further, but Hao Zhao had already left the watchtower. The Wei army urged the envoy to his mount and chased him off.

Looking back, Jin Xiang watched Hao Zhao leaning against the high protective railing of the wall. Jin Xiang reined in and pointed at Hao Zhao with his whip as he cried out, "Worthy brother, why do you treat me so shabbily?" "You know the law of Wei," Hao Zhao answered. "I will honor my duty as long as I live. Waste no more breath on your persuasions. Hurry back and tell Zhuge Liang I await his attack!"

Jin Xiang returned to Kongming and said, "Hao Zhao turned me away before I could open my mouth." "Try again," Kongming said. Jin Xiang went back to Chencang and requested to see Hao Zhao. When Hao Zhao appeared at the tower, Jin Xiang reined in and shouted, "Worthy brother, heed these loyal words. How will you hold off an army of hun-

及！且不顺大汉而事奸魏，抑何不知天命、不辨清浊乎？愿伯道思之。"郝昭大怒，拈弓搭箭，指靳祥而喝曰："吾前言已定，汝不必再言！可速退！——吾不射汝！"

　　靳祥回见孔明，具言郝昭如此光景。孔明大怒曰："匹夫无礼太甚！岂欺吾无攻城之具耶？"随叫土人问曰："陈仓城中，有多少人马？"土人告曰："虽不知的数，约有三千人。"孔明笑曰："量此小城，安能御我！休等他救兵到，火速攻之！"于是军中起百乘云梯，一乘上可立十数人，周围用木板遮护。军士各把短梯软索，听军中擂鼓，一齐上城。郝昭在敌楼上，望见蜀兵装起云梯，四面而来，即令三千军各执火箭，分布四面；待云梯近城，一齐射之。孔明只道城中无备，故大造云梯，令三军鼓噪呐喊而进；不期城上火箭齐发，云梯尽着，梯上军士多被烧死。城上矢石如雨，蜀兵皆退。孔明大怒曰："汝烧吾云梯，吾却用'冲车'之法！"于是连夜安排下冲车。次日，又四面鼓噪呐喊而进。郝昭急命运石凿眼，用葛绳穿定飞打，冲车皆被打折。孔明又令人运土填城壕，教廖化引三千锹镢军，从夜间掘地道，暗入城去。郝昭又于城中掘重壕横截之。如此昼夜相攻，二十余日，无计可破。孔明正在营中忧闷，忽报："东边救兵到了，旗上

dreds of thousands from an isolated town? Surrender now, for future regrets will be futile. Disobedient to Han, you serve the seditious Wei. Do you not know the Mandate of Heaven, nor the difference between black and white? Consider well, good brother." In great anger Hao Zhao fit an arrow to his bow and shouted back, "What I have said still stands. Say no more but withdraw at once, and I shall not shoot."

Jin Xiang returned to Kongming and described Hao Zhao's behavior. In great anger Kongming responded, "That fool's insult goes too far, imagining we don't have the means to take his town!" He asked a resident of the area the size of the force in Chencang, and was told, "It's hard to say precisely: about three thousand." Kongming said with a smile, "I doubt this little town can hold us off! But let's attack before help is able to reach them." Kongming ordered up one hundred assault towers — each holding a dozen men — and had them screened with boards. His soldiers took short ladders and ropes and prepared to storm the wall at the sound of the drum.

From his observation tower Hao Zhao watched the Riverlands soldiers erect their assault towers and approach from four sides, and he ordered his three thousand archers to the four walls to direct burning arrows at the approaching engines.[6] Assuming the town to be unprepared, Kongming forced the pace of the assault towers and ordered the army to beat the drums and shout as they bore down. To Kongming's surprise, masses of burning arrows set his towers aflame, killing most of the troops inside them. Arrows and stones poured down from the wall, forcing the Riverlands troops to retreat.[7] Kongming angrily cried, "Burn my assault towers? Then I'll use battering rams!"

Kongming prepared the batteries and sent his troops drumming and screaming against the town the next day. Hao Zhao swiftly ordered his men to smash the rams by using long hemp ropes to sling giant stones. In response Kongming ordered his men to fill the moat with earth and then had Liao Hua direct three thousand sappers in the digging of a hidden tunnel into the city. But Hao Zhao cut them off by making a transverse trench inside the wall. Thus, the battle continued for twenty days, with Kongming unable to find a way to reduce Chencang.

Kongming was brooding in his camp when he was informed, "The

2391

书:'魏先锋大将王双'。"孔明问曰:"谁可迎之?"魏延出曰:
"某愿往。"孔明曰:"汝乃先锋大将,未可轻出。"又问:"谁敢迎
之?"裨将谢雄应声而出。孔明与三千军去了。孔明又问曰:"谁
敢再去?"裨将龚起应声要去。孔明亦与三千兵去了。孔明恐
城内郝昭引兵冲出,乃把人马退二十里下寨。

　　却说谢雄引军前行,正遇王双;战不三合,被双一刀劈
死。蜀兵败走,双随后赶来。龚起接着,交马只三合,亦被双所
斩。败兵回报孔明。孔明大惊,忙令廖化、王平、张嶷三人出
迎。两阵对圆,张嶷出马,王平、廖化压住阵角。王双纵马来与
张嶷交马,数合不分胜负。双诈败便走,嶷随后赶去。王平见张
嶷中计,忙叫曰:"休赶!"嶷急回马时,王双流星锤早到,正中
其背。嶷伏鞍而走,双回马赶来。王平、廖化截住,救得张嶷回
阵。王双驱兵大杀一阵,蜀兵折伤甚多。嶷吐血数口,回见孔
明,说:"王双英雄无敌;如今将二万兵就陈仓城外下寨,四围
立起排栅,筑起重城,深挖壕堑,守御甚严。"孔明见折二将,张
嶷又被打伤,即唤姜维曰:"陈仓道口这条路不可行。别求何
策?"维曰:"陈仓城池坚固,郝昭守御甚密,又得王双相助,实
不可取。不若令一大将,依山傍水,下寨固守;再令良将守把要

enemy's rescue force has arrived on the east with banners reading 'General Wang Shuang, Vanguard of the Wei.'" Kongming asked, "Who will take them on?" and Wei Yan volunteered. "You are the vanguard commander," Kongming said. "We cannot risk sending you out now." He called for another volunteer. Lieutenant Commander Xie Xiong responded promptly, and Kongming gave him three thousand men. Kongming asked again for a volunteer to follow Xie Xiong, and Lieutenant Commander Gong Qi also came forward and received a command of three thousand men. Kongming subsequently pulled back twenty *li* and camped in case of a surprise attack by Hao Zhao.

Xie Xiong advanced, but General Wang Shuang sliced him through in a brief clash. The Riverlands forces fled in defeat, pursued by the Wei general. Gong Qi joined the battle but fell to Wang Shuang's sword after two or three passes. When returning troops informed Kongming, he was astonished and ordered Liao Hua, Wang Ping, and Zhang Ni forward to the front. The opposing lines — the Riverlands' and Wei's — formed, and Zhang Ni rode forth while Wang Ping and Liao Hua guarded the two wings. Wang Shuang raced out and engaged Zhang Ni, but they fought to a draw. Wang Shuang feigned defeat and fled; Zhang Ni gave chase. Wang Ping saw Zhang Ni being led into a trap, and he cried out, "Stop the chase!" As Zhang Ni turned sharply, Wang Shuang threw a hammer with lightning speed, hitting him square in the back. Zhang Ni slumped forward but galloped on. Wang Ping and Liao Hua interposed and escorted him safely back to camp. Wang Shuang's men swept down on the Riverlands troops, taking a heavy toll.

Zhang Ni spit mouthfuls of blood. He told Kongming: "Wang Shuang is a mighty warrior; none can match him. Wei's defense is formidable: they have twenty thousand camped outside Chencang, palisades on four sides, strong walls, and a deep moat." Kongming had lost two commanders, and Zhang Ni was badly wounded, so he summoned Jiang Wei and told him, "We cannot move down the road to Chencang. Is there any other way to get at them?" "With its fortifications, Hao Zhao's tight defense, and Wang Shuang's help," Jiang Wei said, "Chencang indeed cannot be taken. Another way might be to send a commander to set up a solid base in the hills hard by a stream and to have a second commander

道，以防街亭之攻；却统大军去袭祁山，某却如此如此用计，可捉曹真也。"孔明从其言，即令王平、李恢，引二枝兵守街亭小路；魏延引一军守陈仓口。马岱为先锋，关兴、张苞为前后救应使，从小径出斜谷望祁山进发。

却说曹真因思前番被司马懿夺了功劳，因此到洛阳分调郭淮、孙礼东西守把；又听的陈仓告急，已令王双去救。闻知王双斩将立功，大喜，乃令中护军大将费耀，权摄前部总督，诸将各自守把隘口。忽报山谷中捉得细作来见。曹真令押入，跪于帐前。其人告曰："小人不是奸细，有机密来见都督，误被伏路军捉来。乞退左右。"真乃教去其缚，左右暂退。其人曰："小人乃姜伯约心腹人也。蒙本官遣送密书。"真曰："书安在？"其人于贴肉衣内取出呈上。真拆视曰：

罪将姜维百拜，书呈大都督曹麾下：维念世食魏禄，忝守边城；叨窃厚恩，无门补报。昨日误遭诸葛亮之计，陷身于巅崖之中。思念旧国，何日忘之！今幸蜀兵西出，诸葛亮甚不相疑。赖都督亲提大兵而来：如遇敌人，可以诈败；维当在后，以举火为号，先烧蜀人粮草，却以大兵翻身掩

hold the main road to guard against another attack from Jieting. You, then, would take the main army quietly to Qishan while I took certain steps — Cao Zhen could be captured."

Kongming approved Jiang Wei's plan, sending Wang Ping and Li Hui to defend the road near Jieting with two contingents, and Wei Yan to post forces on the road to Chencang. Ma Dai had the vanguard; Guan Xing and Zhang Bao coordinated front and rear reinforcement. Kongming's army set out on bypaths through Ye Gorge and headed for the hills of Qishan.

* * *

Cao Zhen had never forgotten how Sima Yi had robbed him of his laurels in the previous campaign. Accordingly, after reaching Luoyang he assigned Guo Huai and Sun Li to establish defensive positions east and west of the capital. Afterward, he sent Wang Shuang to relieve the emergency at Chencang. Delighted now with the reports of Wang Shuang's exploits, he sent General Fei Yao, the central defender of the Army, to serve provisionally as commander of the Forward Army. Cao Zhen had other commanders secure the various strongpoints.

Suddenly the capture of a spy was announced, and Cao Zhen had the man brought in. Kneeling, the man said, "This humble one is no spy. I come on a secret mission to the field marshal. Troops posted on the road took me by mistake. Please dismiss your attendants." Cao Zhen had the man's arms freed and sent his attendants away. The man went on, "I am in the service of Jiang Wei and carry a secret message from him." At Cao Zhen's request the courier drew the message from an inside garment and presented it. Cao Zhen opened it. The text read:

> From Jiang Wei, the deserting commander, one hundred prostrations and this letter, submitted to the field marshal of the Cao banners. Because I have long been supported as a servant of the Wei, I was dispatched to defend a border town. Favored by your generosity, I found no way to repay it. Recently I fell into Zhuge Liang's trap and had to find a way to survive a desperate situation. How could I ever forget my former kingdom? Now by good fortune the Riverlands troops have moved west, and Zhuge Liang trusts me implicitly. I am counting on you, Field Marshal, to come with a large force. If you meet up with the enemy, feign defeat, I will

之,则诸葛亮可擒也。非敢立功报国,实欲自赎前罪。倘蒙照察,速赐来命。

曹真看毕,大喜曰:"天使吾成功也!"遂重赏来人,便令回报,依期会合。真唤费耀商议曰:"今姜维暗献密书,令吾如此如此。"耀曰:"诸葛亮多谋,姜维智广,或者是诸葛亮所使,恐其中有诈。"真曰:"他原是魏人,不得已而降蜀,又何疑乎?"耀曰:"都督不可轻去,只守定本寨。某愿引一军接应姜维。如成功,尽归都督;倘有奸计,某自支当。"真大喜,遂令费耀引五万兵,望斜谷而进。行了两三程,屯下军马,令人哨探。当日申时分,回报:"斜谷道中,有蜀兵来也。"耀忙催兵进。蜀兵未及交战先退。耀引兵追之,蜀兵又来。方欲对阵,蜀兵又退:如此者三次,俄延至次日申时分。魏军一日一夜,不曾敢歇,只恐蜀兵攻击。方欲屯军造饭,忽然四面喊声大震,鼓角齐鸣,蜀兵漫山遍野而来。门旗开处,闪出一辆四轮车,孔明端坐其中,令人请魏军主将答话。耀纵马而出,遥见孔明,心中暗喜,回顾左右曰:"如蜀兵掩至,便退后走。若见山后火起,却回身杀去,自有兵来相应。"分付毕,跃马出呼曰:"前者败将,今何敢又来!"孔

be to their rear and will signal with fire; first we'll burn out their supplies, then you will fall upon them, Field Marshal, in a surprise attack. Zhuge Liang can be captured. I seek no distinction in serving my kingdom, only the redemption of my former crime. If I receive favorable consideration, send your command with all speed.[8]

Delighted by this opportunity, Cao Zhen cried, "Heaven sends me success!" After rewarding the courier, he sent him back to report that he would cooperate at the time indicated. Cao Zhen summoned General Fei Yao to discuss the matter. "Jiang Wei has sent a secret communication," he said, "and would have us take certain steps..." "Zhuge Liang is all tricks!" Fei Yao warned, "and Jiang Wei is shrewder than most. Zhuge Liang could be behind this. It may be a trap!" Cao Zhen replied, "Jiang Wei was a man of Wei to start with and defected only because he had no other choice. Your suspicions are groundless." "Do not risk it, Field Marshal," Fei Yao persisted. "Sit tight here in camp. I will take a detachment and receive Jiang Wei. If I succeed, the credit will go to you. If there is treachery here, I will deal with it myself." Pleased with this plan, Cao Zhen ordered Fei Yao to move toward Ye Gorge with fifty thousand soldiers.

After marching several stages, Fei Yao camped and sent out scouts. That afternoon a report came back: "Riverlands troops are moving through Ye Gorge." Fei Yao advanced at full speed. The Riverlands troops retreated without engaging; Fei Yao pursued. More Riverlands troops came but withdrew again without assuming battle formation. The Riverlanders approached and withdrew — three times all told — until late afternoon of the following day. During this time the northern troops could not rest for fear of being attacked. As the Wei troops finally settled in to prepare their meal, thunderous shouts surrounded them and drums and horns sounded out as the Riverlands troops swarmed over hill and plain.

The bannered front of the Riverlands line parted, revealing a four-wheeled carriage bearing Kongming sitting erect. He sent a man to call on the Wei commander to meet with him. Fei Yao galloped forth and, spotting Kongming, rejoiced in his heart. Turning to his followers, he said, "If they move against us, withdraw and flee. When you see fire behind the hill, turn back again and slaughter them. Troops are coming to back

明曰:"唤汝曹真来答话!"耀骂曰:"曹都督乃金枝玉叶,安肯与反贼相见耶!"孔明大怒,把羽扇一招,左有马岱,右有张嶷,两路兵冲出。魏兵便退。行不到三十里,望见蜀兵背后火起,喊声不绝。费耀只道号火,便回身杀来。蜀兵齐退。耀提刀在前,只望喊处追赶。将次近火,山路中鼓角喧天,喊声震地,两军杀出:左有关兴,右有张苞。山上矢石如雨,往下射来。魏兵大败。费耀知是中计,急退军望山谷中而走,人马困乏。背后关兴引生力军赶来,魏兵自相践踏及落涧身死者,不知其数。耀逃命而走,正遇山坡口一彪军,乃是姜维。耀大骂曰:"反贼无信!吾不幸误中汝奸计也!"维笑曰:"吾欲擒曹真,误赚汝矣!速下马受降!"耀骤马夺路,望山谷中而走。忽见谷口火光冲天,背后追兵又至。耀自刎身死,余众尽降。孔明连夜驱兵,直出祁山前下寨,收住军马,重赏姜维。维曰:"某恨不得杀曹真也!"孔明亦曰:"可惜大计小用矣。"

　　却说曹真听知折了费耀,悔之不及,遂与郭淮商议退兵之策。于是孙礼、辛毗星夜具表申奏魏主,言蜀兵又出祁山,曹真

you up." Having issued these instructions, Fei Yao charged boldly out on his high-stepping mount and shouted: "A defeated general dares to show himself again?" "Have Cao Zhen come and talk to me!" Kongming responded. Fei Yao taunted him: "Field Marshal Cao belongs to the royal family. He would never lower himself to meet traitor!" In great anger Kongming motioned with his feathered fan, and two forces, led by Ma Dai on the right and Zhang Yi on the left, charged onto the field.

The Wei troops withdrew; but before they had gone thirty *li,* they saw flames behind the Riverlands army. Shouting voices were everywhere. Thinking it was the fire signal, Fei Yao reversed course and began to slaughter the Riverlanders. When the Riverlands troops retreated, Fei Yao raised his sword and led the chase on toward the source of. the shouting. But as they approached the site of the flames, the hillside paths echoed with the beat of drums and the blast of horns. The earth shook as two Riverlands companies sprang forth: on the left Guan Xing, on the right Zhang Bao. From above, shafts and stones pelted the northerners, and their ranks disintegrated. Fei Yao, realizing he was caught, ordered a swift retreat into the valleys; but his forces were spent. From behind, Guan Xing swept down with fresh troops. The Wei soldiers trampled one another, and many others drowned.

Fei Yao fled for his life. But on a hillslope he encountered a band of troops led by Jiang Wei. "Faithless, treacherous villain!" Fei Yao shouted. "By bad luck I fell into your fiendish trap!" Jiang Wei smiled and said, "I was trying to capture Cao Zhen and did not mean to entrap you. Dismount and submit." Without responding, Fei Yao bolted toward a valley but found himself facing a towering wall of flame; behind, the enemy was closing in. Fei Yao cut his own throat, and his followers surrendered.

Kongming urged the Riverlands troops on until they had pushed through the hills of Qishan. After pitching camp on the farther eastern side, he gathered in his forces and rewarded Jiang Wei. "If only we had killed Cao Zhen," Jiang Wei remarked ruefully. "It is too bad that our grand plan came to so little," Kongming replied.

The news of Fei Yao's death caused Cao Zhen deep regret. With Guo Huai he began planning anew how to force the Riverlanders back. Sun Yi and Xin Pi dispatched a memorial to Luoyang to inform the ruler

2399

损兵折将，势甚危急。睿大惊，即召司马懿入内曰："曹真损兵折将，蜀兵又出祁山。卿有何策，可以退之？"懿曰："臣已有退诸葛亮之计。不用魏军扬武耀威，蜀兵自然走矣。"

正是：

已见子丹无胜术，全凭仲达有良谋。

未知其计如何，且看下文分解。

of Wei that the Shu army had come through the Qishan hills and that Cao Zhen had suffered heavy losses of men and commanders, with the result that the northerners' overall position was in danger. In alarm Cao Rui called for Sima Yi and said to him, "Cao Zhen defeated, and the Riverlanders on this side of the mountains! How can we push them back?" "Your servant," Sima Yi responded, "has a plan to force Zhuge Liang back. Without any show of force by the Wei army, the enemy will flee of its own accord." Indeed:

> Since Cao Zhen had no means to win,
> He had to count on Sima Yi's plan.

What was the plan?
Read on.

第九十八回

追汉军王双受诛　袭陈仓武侯取胜

　　却说司马懿奏曰："臣尝奏陛下，言孔明必出陈仓，故以郝昭守之，今果然矣。彼若从陈仓入寇，运粮甚便。今幸有郝昭、王双守把，不敢从此路运粮。其余小道，搬运艰难。臣算蜀兵行粮止有一月，利在急战。我军只宜久守。陛下可降诏，令曹真坚守诸路关隘，不要出战。不须一月，蜀兵自走。那时乘虚而击之，诸葛亮可擒也。"睿欣然曰："卿既有先见之明，何不自引一军以袭之？"懿曰："臣非惜身重命，实欲存下此兵，以防东吴陆逊耳。孙权不久必将僭号称尊；如称尊号，恐陛下伐之，定先入寇也：臣故欲以兵待之。"正言间，忽近臣奏曰："曹都督奏报军情。"懿曰："陛下可即令人告戒曹真：凡追赶蜀兵，必须观其虚实，不可深入重地，以中诸葛亮之计。"睿即时下诏，遣太常卿韩暨持节告戒曹真："切不可战，务在谨守；只待蜀兵退去，方才击之。"司马懿送韩暨于城外，嘱之曰："吾以此功让与子丹；

Chapter 98

Wang Shuang Is Executed While Pursuing
the Han Army
Kongming Is Victorious After Raiding Chencang

Sima Yi addressed his ruler: "In a previous petition I predicted that Kongming would come through Chencang; I therefore sent Hao Zhao to defend it. Now my prediction has been confirmed. The enemy needs Chencang to supply its invasion. Fortunately, Hao Zhao and Wang Shuang hold it, blocking the enemy's grain line, and all other routes are too narrow for easy transport. The Riverlands army should have no more than a month's grain and will be eager for an early encounter. Delay will thus work to our advantage. Your Majesty, issue an edict ordering Cao Zhen to defend the key routes and strongpoints but to avoid battle; within a month the Riverlanders will be gone, and we can strike and capture Zhuge Liang!"

Cao Rui said enthusiastically, "Since you can see so far ahead, why not take your own army to surprise the enemy?" Sima Yi responded, "My own life means little to me, but I want to keep my force intact to check any move from the south by Lu Xun. Before long Sun Quan is bound to declare himself emperor; and when he does, he will strike north to preempt an attack by Your Majesty. I would prefer to be ready for him." Even as Sima Yi was speaking, a privileged attendant announced to the throne, "Field Marshal Cao's report on the military situation." "Your Majesty," Sima Yi said, "warn Cao Zhen at once that all who pursue the Riverlands troops must beware of the enemy's strengths and not enter fortified areas, or they will fall into one of Zhuge Liang's traps."

Cao Rui readily authorized his master of ceremony, Han Ji, to bear this warning to Cao Zhen: "Avoid Riverlands troops under all circumstances; concentrate on vigilant defense; attack only after the enemy retreats." Sima Yi escorted Han Ji outside the capital and left him with this instruction: "I want credit for the victory to go to Cao Zhen. So when

2403

公见子丹，休言是吾所陈之意，只道天子降诏，教保守为上。追赶之人，大要仔细，勿遣性急气躁者追之。"暨辞去。

却说曹真正升帐议事，忽报天子遣太常卿韩暨持节至。真出寨接入，受诏已毕，退与郭淮、孙礼计议，淮笑曰："此乃司马仲达之见也。"真曰："此见若何？"淮曰："此言深识诸葛亮用兵之法。久后能御蜀兵者，必仲达也。"真曰："倘蜀兵不退，又将如何？"淮曰："可密令人去教王双，引兵于小路巡哨，彼自不敢运粮。待其粮尽兵退，乘势追击，可获全胜。"孙礼曰："某去祁山虚妆做运粮兵，车上尽装干柴茅草，以硫黄焰硝灌之，却教人虚报陇西运粮到。若蜀人无粮，必然来抢。待入其中，放火烧车，外以伏兵应之，可胜矣。"真喜曰："此计大妙！"即令孙礼引兵依计而行。又遣人教王双引兵于小路上巡哨，郭淮引兵提调箕谷、街亭，令诸路军马守把险要。真又令张辽子张虎为先锋，乐进子乐綝为副先锋，同守头营，不许出战。

却说孔明在祁山寨中，每日令人挑战，魏兵坚守不出。孔明唤姜维等商议曰："魏兵坚守不出，是料吾军中无粮也。今陈

you see him, there's no need to mention that I suggested these tactics. Simply say that the Son of Heaven has authorized by edict a policy of strict defense. And remember: whoever he sends to pursue the Riverlanders must exercise great care. Tell him not to use anyone rash or excitable." Han Ji took leave and departed.

Cao Zhen had hardly entered his command tent to meet with his commanders, when the imperially authorized emissary, Master of Ceremony Han Ji, was announced. Cao Zhen welcomed him in front of his camp. After receiving the edict, he withdrew and took counsel with Guo Huai and Sun Li. With a smile Guo Huai said, "Sounds like Sima Yi's idea." "What do you think of it?" Cao Zhen asked. "It shows deep understanding of Zhuge Liang's methods of warfare. In the future Sima Yi will be the man to stop the Shu troops." "But what do we do if the Riverlands troops do not retreat?" Cao Zhen asked. "Then," Guo Huai answered, "we'll have secret orders sent to Wang Shuang to patrol the hill paths and stop the enemy from moving in grain. After their grain is gone, they will retreat, the tactical advantage will pass to us, and we will win a complete victory."

Sun Li said, "I'll go into the Qishan hills with troops pretending to be moving grain — the carts will actually be carrying twigs and straw soaked with sulphur and saltpeter and we'll spread word that the grain has arrived from Longxi. If the Riverlanders are out of food, they will come to seize the grain. Once they get among the carts, we'll set them afire and move in with troops already in hiding. Victory will be ours!" "A great plan!" Cao Zhen exclaimed and had Sun Li set the scheme in motion. At the same time Cao Zhen sent Wang Shuang to patrol the roads, posted Guo Huai to Winnow Basket Gorge and Jieting, and ordered the various commanders to reinforce all strongpoints. Finally, Cao Zhen had Zhang Liao's son Zhang Hu serve as the vanguard, with Yue Jin's son Yue Chen as his lieutenant, their task to guard the front position and prevent direct engagement with the western forces.

* * *

Kongming remained in his Qishan camp. He sent men out every day to challenge the Wei troops, but he provoked no response. Kongming summoned Jiang Wei and others and said to them, "The enemy refuses

仓转运不通，其余小路盘涉艰难，吾算随军粮草，不敷一月用度，如之奈何？"正踌躇间，忽报："陇西魏军运粮数千车于祁山之西，运粮官乃孙礼也。"孔明曰："其人如何？"有魏人告曰："此人曾随魏主出猎于大石山，忽惊起一猛虎，直奔御前，孙礼下马拔剑斩之。从此封为上将军。——乃曹真心腹人也。"孔明笑曰："此是魏将料吾乏粮，故用此计：车上装载者，必是茅草引火之物。吾平生专用火攻，彼乃欲以此计诱我耶？彼若知吾军去劫粮车，必来劫吾寨矣。可将计就计而行。"遂唤马岱分付曰："汝引三千军径到魏兵屯粮之所，不可入营，但于上风头放火。若烧着车仗，魏兵必来围吾寨。"又差马忠、张嶷各引五千兵在外围住，内外夹攻。三人受计去了。又唤关兴、张苞分付曰："魏兵头营接连四通之路。今晚若西山火起，魏兵必来劫吾营。汝二人却伏于魏寨左右，只等他兵出寨，汝二人便可劫之。"又唤吴班、吴懿分付曰："汝二人各引一军伏于营外。如魏兵到，可截其归路。"孔明分拨已毕，自在祁山上凭高而坐。魏兵探知蜀兵要来劫粮，慌忙报与孙礼。礼令人飞报曹真。真遣人去头营分付张虎、乐綝："看今夜山西火起，蜀兵必来救应。

to engage because they think we're out of grain. Nothing can be shipped through Chencang now, and the other roads are practically impassable. I doubt the grain we have with us will last another month. What are we to do?" At this moment of uncertainty there came an unexpected report: "The Wei army in Longxi is moving thousands of grain carts west of Qishan. The officer in charge is Sun Li." "What kind of man is he?" Kongming asked. A man of Wei told him, "He once accompanied the ruler of Wei on a hunt on Great Stone Mountain. Suddenly a tiger confronted them and charged the ruler. Sun Li dismounted and slew it with his sword. The ruler honored him as a senior commander. He is a man Cao Zhen trusts implicitly."

With a smile Kongming said, "That report of grain carts is a trick. The Wei commander thinks we're running out of grain — they must have packed inflammable materials on the carts. Do they expect to fool someone like me, who has specilized in attacks by fire all his life? But if they think our troops have gone to raid the grain carts, then they will come to raid our camp. So we can beat them at their own game!"

Kongming summoned Ma Dai and instructed him: "Take three thousand men to the Wei army grain depot. Do not enter the site; only set fires upwind. If the carts burn, the enemy will come to surround our camp." Next, he had Ma Zhong and Zhang Ni post five thousand men in a ring removed from the camp so that the enemy could be caught between them and the defenders within. The three — Ma Dai, Ma Zhong, and Zhang Ni — left to execute their orders. Kongming then instructed Guan Xing and Zhang Bao: "The enemy's forward position intersects the main roads. Tonight when fire breaks out on the west hill, they will raid our position. I want you two to lie in ambush on either side of the Wei camp. When their troops come out, attack." Next, Kongming instructed Wu Ban and Wu Yi: "Take one company each, hide outside our camp, and cut off their route back if they come." His deployment completed, Kongming rested, secure in the heights of the Qishan hills.

Wei soldiers hurried back to Sun Li with the news that Riverlands troops intended to come for the grain; and Sun Li swiftly informed Cao Zhen. Cao Zhen ordered Zhang Hu and Yue Chen: "When you see fire west of the hills, it will mean Shu is coming to reinforce. Go into the field,

可以出军，如此如此。"二将受计，令人登楼专看号火。

却说孙礼把军伏于山西，只待蜀兵到。是夜二更，马岱引三千兵来，人皆衔枚，马尽勒口，径到山西。见许多车仗，重重叠叠，攒绕成营，车仗虚插旌旗。正值西南风起，岱令军士径去营南放火，车仗尽着，火光冲天。孙礼只道蜀兵到魏寨内放号火，急引兵一齐掩至。背后鼓角喧天，两路兵杀来：乃是马忠、张嶷，把魏军围在垓心。孙礼大惊。又听的魏军中喊声起，一彪军从火光边杀来，乃是马岱。内外夹攻，魏兵大败。火紧风急，人马乱窜，死者无数。孙礼引中伤军，突烟冒火而走。

却说张虎在营中，望见火光，大开寨门，与乐綝尽引人马，杀奔蜀寨来，——寨中却不见一人。急收军回时，吴班、吴懿两路兵杀出，断其归路。张、乐二将急冲出重围，奔回本寨，只见土城之上，箭如飞蝗，——原来却被关兴、张苞袭了营寨。魏兵大败，皆投曹真寨来。方欲入寨，只见一彪败军飞奔而来，乃是孙礼；遂同入寨见真，各言中计之事。真听知，谨守大寨，更不出战。蜀兵得胜，回见孔明。

孔明令人密授计与魏延，一面教拔寨齐起，杨仪曰："今已大胜，挫尽魏兵锐气，何故反欲收军？"孔明曰："吾兵无粮，利在急战。今彼坚守不出，吾受其病矣。彼今虽暂时兵败，中原必

and..." On these orders, the two front commanders sent men into the watchtowers to look for the fire signal. Sun Li hid his troops west of the hills and waited for the Riverlanders.

During the second watch Ma Dai approached with three thousand men. Both horses and men wore gags as they moved straight toward their destination. They noticed a large number of bannered carts clustered around the site in multiple rings. As a southwest wind began to blow, Ma Dai had his men set fires on the south side of the camp. The carts were consumed in flames that stretched into the sky.

Sun Li thought that the fire he saw rose from within the Riverlands camp, and he moved in swiftly. Riverlands forces closed in on him from behind. As drumbeat and horn blast charged the air, Ma Zhong and Zhang Ni encircled the Wei troops. Sun Li panicked. He heard fresh shouts from inside the Wei army: a band of men emerged from the flames, led by Ma Dai coming out for the kill. Caught on two sides, the Wei army was badly defeated; men and horses fled the field in confusion, leaving countless casualties as the wind sped the flames. Sun Li, braving fire and smoke, led his mauled soldiers out and they ran from the battle.

Meanwhile, Zhang Hu was ready in his camp. Seeing the flames, he opened wide the camp entrance and with Yue Chen led his forces against the Riverlands base — but it was deserted. As they began pulling back, Wu Ban and Wu Yi moved in and blocked all retreat. The northern commanders succeeded in charging through the enemy line and dashed back to their base, only to encounter swarms of arrows whizzing down at them from the wall: Guan Xing and Zhang Bao had already surprised the camp. The Wei army, totally routed, headed for Cao Zhen's camp. As they started to enter, Sun Li's defeated corps rode up and the two defeated commanders went in together. They came before Cao Zhen, and each told how he had been trapped. Cao Zhen heard them out, then mounted strict guard over his camp, refusing all battle. The victorious Riverlands troops returned to Kongming.

Kongming conveyed secret plans to Wei Yan and subsequently had all positions decamp. Yang Yi objected. "We had a great victory," he said. "The Wei army is shattered. Why are we pulling back?" "We don't have the grain," Kongming explained. "A quick battle was what we

有添益;若以轻骑袭吾粮道,那时要归不能。今乘魏兵新败,不敢正视蜀兵,便可出其不意,乘机退去。所忧者但魏延一军,在陈仓道口拒住王双,急不能脱身;吾已令人授以密计,教斩王双,使魏人不敢来追。只令后队先行。"当夜,孔明只留金鼓守在寨中打更。一夜兵已尽退,只落空营。

却说曹真正在寨中忧闷,忽报左将军张郃领军到。郃下马入帐,谓真曰:"某奉圣旨,特来听调。"真曰:"曾别仲达否?"郃曰:"仲达分付云:'吾军胜,蜀兵必不便去;若吾军败,蜀兵必即去矣。'今吾军失利之后,都督曾往哨探蜀兵消息否?"真曰:"未也。"于是即令人往探之,果是虚营,只插着数十面旌旗,兵已去了二日也。曹真懊悔无及。

且说魏延受了密计,当夜二更拔寨,急回汉中。早有细作报知王双。双大驱军马,并力追赶。追到二十余里,看看赶上,见魏延旗号在前,双大叫曰:"魏延休走!"蜀兵更不回头。双拍马赶来。背后魏兵叫曰:"城外寨中火起,恐中敌人奸计。"双急勒马回时,只见一片火光冲天,慌令退军。行到山坡左侧,忽一骑马从林中骤出,大喝曰:"魏延在此!"王双大惊,措手不及,被延一刀砍于马下。魏兵疑有埋伏,四散逃走。延手下止有三

wanted, but the enemy will not show themselves again. And that works against us. Their homeland will make good their losses. If their light horsemen raid our grain routes, we won't be able to get back at all. Their latest defeat gives us some room to maneuver, to do what they least expect: withdraw. My one concern is Wei Yan and his men, who are at Chencang holding off Wang Shuang. They may not make it away safely. I have sent Wei Yan secret plans for killing Wang Shuang and preventing pursuit by the Wei. I want our rear squadrons to turn back first." That night Kongming left only the watchmen in camp to mark the watch with gong and drum. All the troops were evacuated.

Cao Zhen was brooding in his camp when the arrival of Zhang He, general of the Left, was announced. The commander dismounted, entered the leader's tent, and said, "I have been instructed by our lord to place myself at your disposal." Cao Zhen asked, "Did you take leave of Sima Yi?" "He said to me," Guo Huai replied, "'If we win the field, the Riverlanders will remain; if we lose, they will leave.' Now that our army has suffered defeat, Field Marshal, have you surveyed the enemy's positions?" "Not yet," Cao Zhen answered. He sent scouts to the Shu camp and learned from them that the troops had left two days ago; only a few dozen banners remained to mark the site. Cao Zhen regretted his inaction acutely.

Meanwhile, Wei Yan, pursuant to his secret orders, quit camp at the second watch and hastened back toward Hanzhong, a move spies soon reported to Wang Shuang. Wang Shuang pursued the retreating Riverlanders in force for about twenty *li,* and soon Wei Yan's banners were before him. "Halt, Wei Yan!" he cried. But the Riverlanders never stopped to look back. Wang Shuang galloped hard after them; behind him Wei troops shouted, "Flames outside the wall and inside the camp! Look out for the enemy's trap!" Wang Shuang quickly turned and rode back, only to meet a wall of living flame stretching higher and higher. He ordered a swift retreat. As he reached a hillslope, a group of riders erupted from a wood. "Here is Wei Yan!" their leader cried. Wang Shuang panicked and fell to Wei Yan's blade before he could defend himself. Fearing an ambush, the northern troops dispersed and fled; but Wei Yan had had only thirty horsemen. Slowly he resumed his march to Hanzhong. A

十骑人马,望汉中缓缓而行。后人有诗赞曰:

　　　孔明妙算胜孙庞,耿若长星照一方。

　　　进退行兵神莫测,陈仓道口斩王双。

原来魏延受了孔明密计:先教存下三十骑,伏于王双营边;只待王双起兵赶时,却去他营中放火;待他回寨,出其不意,突出斩之。魏延斩了王双,引兵回到汉中见孔明,交割了人马。孔明设宴大会,不在话下。

　　且说张郃追蜀兵不上,回到寨中。忽有陈仓城郝昭差人申报,言王双被斩。曹真闻知,伤感不已,因此忧成疾病,遂回洛阳;命郭淮、孙礼、张郃守长安诸道。

　　却说吴王孙权设朝,有细作人报说:"蜀诸葛丞相出兵两次,魏都督曹真兵损将亡。"于是群臣皆劝吴王兴师伐魏,以图中原。权犹疑未决。张昭奏曰:"近闻武昌东山,凤凰来仪;大江之中,黄龙屡现。主公德配唐、虞,明并文、武:可即皇帝位,然后兴兵。"多官皆应曰:"子布之言是也。"遂选定夏四月丙寅日,筑坛于武昌南郊。是日,群臣请权登坛即皇帝位,改黄武八年为黄龙元年。谥父孙坚为武烈皇帝,母吴氏为武烈皇后,兄

poet of later times celebrated Kongming's ingenuity in these lines:

> He excelled Sun and Pang with subtle schemes;
> In his zone of sky, a fixed star gleams.
> His moves, which baffled all surmise,
> On Chencang road Shuang's doom devised.

Kongming's original plan that Wei Yan carried out was this: Wei Yan was to place thirty cavalry in hiding alongside Wang Shuang's camp; the moment he came out to pursue Wei Yan's men, Yan was to enter the camp and light fires; on Wang Shuang's return, Wei Yan was to surprise him and kill him. After killing Wang Shuang, Wei Yan led his men back to Kongming and officially tendered his forces. Kongming held a grand banquet to celebrate his victorious return.

Having failed to overtake the Riverlands army, Zhang He returned to his camp. Suddenly a man from Hao Zhao in Chencang reported Wang Shuang's death, news that so pained Cao Zhen that he took sick and went back to Luoyang, leaving Guo Huai, Sun Li, and Zhang He to defend the Chang'an roads.

* * *

Sun Quan, king of the Southland, was holding court when a spy reported: "Prime Minister Zhuge of Shu has taken the field twice, inflicting heavy losses of fighters and captains on Cao Zhen's Wei army." After this report the assembly of vassals urged the king to wage war against Wei for the purpose of taking the northern heartland. Sun Quan wavered, unable to come to a decision. Zhang Zhao addressed him: "I have heard recently that in the hills east of Wuchang a phoenix has displayed itself, and that in the Great River a tawny dragon has been sighted several times. Your Lordship's virtue matches that of Yao and Shun, your wisdom matches that of kings Wen and Wu. Ascend the imperial seat first; then send forth the army." Many officials echoed Zhang Zhao's view. Thus they selected the third cyclical[1] day of the fourth month for the enthronement and erected an altar in the southern suburb of Wuchang.

2413

On the appointed day, pursuant to the petition of the assembled officials, Sun Quan ascended the imperial seat. The reign year was changed from Huang Wu 8 to Huang Long 1.[2] Sun Quan's father, Sun Jian, was

孙策为长沙桓王。立子孙登为皇太子。命诸葛瑾长子诸葛恪为太子左辅，张昭次子张休为太子右弼。

恪字元逊，身长七尺，极聪明，善应对。权甚爱之。年六岁时，值东吴筵会，恪随父在座。权见诸葛瑾面长，乃令人牵一驴来，用粉笔书其面曰："诸葛子瑜"。众皆大笑。恪趋至前，取粉笔添二字于其下曰："诸葛子瑜之驴"。满座之人，无不惊讶。权大喜，遂将驴赐之。又一日，大宴官僚，权命恪把盏。巡至张昭面前，昭不饮，曰："此非养老之礼也。"权谓恪曰："汝能强子布饮乎？"恪领命，乃谓昭曰："昔姜尚父年九十，秉旄仗钺，未尝言老。今临阵之日，先生在后；饮酒之日，先生在前：何谓不养老也？"昭无言可答，只得强饮。权因此爱之，故命辅太子。张昭佐吴王，位列三公之上，故以其子张休为太子右弼。又以顾雍为丞相，陆逊为上将军，辅太子守武昌。权复还建业。群臣共议伐魏之策。张昭奏曰："陛下初登宝位，未可动兵。只宜修文

posthumously honored as Emperor Wu Lie, or Martial Glory; his mother, Lady Wu, as Empress Wu Lie; his brother, Sun Ce, as King Huan of Changsha. Sun Deng, Quan's son, was designated crown prince, and Zhuge Ke, eldest son of Zhuge Jin, became his principal guide; Zhang Xiu, younger son of Zhang Zhao, became the heir apparent's first assistant.

Zhuge Ke (Yuansun)[3] was seven spans tall; he had unusual intelligence and great skill in repartee, and he enjoyed the favor of Sun Quan. At the age of six Zhuge Ke accompanied his father to a royal banquet at which Sun Quan observed that Zhuge Jin had an elongated face. He had a donkey led in and chalked the words "Zhuge Jin" on its nose, whereupon the assembly burst into laughter. Zhuge Ke dashed up to the animal, took the chalk, and added "'s donkey." The guests were astonished, and Sun Quan was so amused that he gave Ke the donkey as a gift.

Another day at a feast for the officials, Sun Quan asked Zhuge Ke to pass around the wine. When he came to Zhang Zhao, Zhang Zhao refused to drink, saying, "This is not the proper form for the ceremony of nourishing an elder." Sun Quan said to Zhuge Ke, "Get Zhang Zhao to drink for me." On receiving this command, Zhuge Ke said to Zhang Zhao, "Long, long ago the great counselor Jiang Ziya — at the age of ninety — grasped the signal banner, steadied the battle-axe, and never once called himself 'old.' On days of trial by arms, you are always in the rear; on days of banqueting, you are always in the front. What do you mean, I have failed to 'nourish an elder'?"[4] At a loss for an answer, Zhang Zhao was constrained to drink. After this incident Sun Quan prized Zhuge Ke more than ever and consequently made him the guide to his heir apparent.

Zhang Zhao had served Sun Quan as senior counselor and held a position second only to the king himself. Thus, his son Zhang Xiu was made first assistant to the heir. Further appointments on the occasion were Gu Yong, prime minister; and Lu Xun, senior general, guardian to the heir, and governor of Wuchang. Afterwards, Sun Quan returned to Jianye where the court deliberated on the war policy. Zhang Zhao addressed Sun Quan: "It is wrong to mobilize so soon after Your Majesty has taken the throne. You should develop your civil rule and lay down the

2415

偃武,增设学校,以安民心;遣使入川,与蜀同盟,共分天下,缓缓图之。"

权从其言,即令使命星夜入川,来见后主。礼毕,细奏其事。后主闻知,遂与群臣商议。众议皆谓孙权僭逆,宜绝其盟好。蒋琬曰:"可令人问于丞相。"后主即遣使到汉中问孔明。孔明曰:"可令人赍礼物入吴作贺,乞遣陆逊兴师伐魏。魏必命司马懿拒之。懿若南拒东吴,我再出祁山,长安可图也。"后主依言,遂令太尉陈震,将名马、玉带、金珠、宝贝,入吴作贺。震至东吴,见了孙权,呈上国书。权大喜,设宴相待,打发回蜀。权召陆逊入,告以西蜀约会兴兵伐魏之事。逊曰:"此乃孔明惧司马懿之谋也。既与同盟,不得不从。今却虚作起兵之势,遥与西蜀为应。待孔明攻魏急,吾可乘虚取中原也。"即时下令,教荆襄各处都要训练人马,择日兴师。

却说陈震回到汉中,报知孔明。孔明尚忧陈仓不可轻进,先令人去哨探。回报说:"陈仓城中郝昭病重。"孔明曰:"大事成矣。"遂唤魏延、姜维分付曰:"汝二人领五千兵,星夜直奔陈仓城下;如见火起,并力攻城。"二人俱未深信,又来告曰:"何

汉英经典文库

weapons of war. Establish schools to settle the people's minds. Renew the alliance with the Riverlands, agreeing to share the empire between you. Take your time planning the conquest of the north."

Sun Quan accepted Zhang Zhao's advice and sent a swift messenger to the Riverlands. After the Second Emperor had formally received the envoy and taken note of his detailed petition, he took counsel with his court. Their consensus was that relations should be severed with Sun Quan because he was a usurper and a rebel. Jiang Wan, however, suggested asking the prime minister's opinion. Accordingly, the Second Emperor sent an envoy to Hanzhong to get Kongming's view. Kongming said: "Send gifts to the Southland to congratulate Sun Quan and urge them to send Lu Xun into the field against Wei: Wei will order Sima Yi to block them; and with Sima Yi occupied to the south, I will be able to strike Chang'an from Qishan." The Second Emperor approved this suggestion and sent Grand Commandant Chen Zhen to the Southland with prize horses, a jade belt, gold, pearls, and other gems as congratulatory gifts.

On reaching the Southland, Chen Zhen was received by Sun Quan, to whom he presented the letter from the Shu court. Delighted, Sun Quan feasted the representative and sent him back to the Riverlands. He then summoned Lu Xun and informed him that he had agreed to march against Wei. "This is a scheme of Kongming's, devised out of fear of Sima Yi," said the veteran general. "But since you have allied with Shu, we must abide by what you have agreed. We will simply appear to invade, however, and try to involve the Riverlands. If Kongming launches an all-out attack on Wei, we will have the opportunity to take the northern heartland for ourselves." Sun Quan issued the order for northern Jingzhou to begin training local forces in preparation for mobilization.

* * *

Chen Zhen went back to Hanzhong and reported to Kongming on his mission south. But Kongming, still hesitant to move against Chencang, simply had scouts survey the town. They reported back, "Hao Zhao is in the town, seriously ill." "Our plan will work!" Kongming responded. He summoned Wei Yan and Jiang Wei and instructed them: "Take five thousand men to the walls of Chencang as fast as you can. When you see fire, attack in concert." Somewhat surprised, the two commanders asked

日可行?"孔明曰:"三日都要完备;不须辞我,即便起行。"二人受计去了。又唤关兴、张苞至,附耳低言,如此如此。二人各受密计而去。

且说郭淮闻郝昭病重,乃与张郃商议曰:"郝昭病重,你可速去替他。我自写表申奏朝廷,别行定夺。"张郃引着三千兵,急来替郝昭。时郝昭病危,当夜正呻吟之间,忽报蜀军到城下了。昭急令人上城守把。时各门上火起,城中大乱。昭听知惊死。蜀兵一拥入城。

却说魏延、姜维领兵到陈仓城下看时,并不见一面旗号,又无打更之人。二人惊疑,不敢攻城。忽听得城上一声炮响,四面旗帜齐竖。只见一人纶巾羽扇,鹤氅道袍,大叫曰:"汝二人来的迟了!"二人视之,乃孔明也。二人慌忙下马,拜伏于地曰:"丞相真神计也!"孔明令放入城,谓二人曰:"吾打探得郝昭病重,吾令汝三日内领兵取城,此乃稳众人之心也。吾却令关兴、张苞,只推点军,暗出汉中。吾即藏于军中,星夜倍道径到城下,使彼不能调兵。吾早有细作在城内放火、发喊相助,令魏兵惊疑不定。兵无主将,必自乱矣。吾因而取之,易如反掌。兵法云:'出其不意,攻其无备。'正谓此也。"魏延、姜维拜伏。孔明

Kongming, "What day shall we set out?" "You have three days to get ready," Kongming replied. "No need to take formal leave. Just start out." The two left to perform their assignment. Next, Kongming called in Guan Xing and Zhang Bao and whispered certain instructions to them. They too departed to carry out their orders.

Meanwhile, Guo Huai had learned of Hao Zhao's illness. "You had better go and replace Hao Zhao at once," he told Zhang He. "I will petition the court for a final decision." Zhang He took three thousand men to Chencang. Hao Zhao was dying. One night as he lay groaning, he was told of the arrival of the Riverlands force and swiftly ordered men to hold the wall. But the gates had already been torched and the town was in confusion. Hao Zhao expired on hearing the news. The Riverlanders stormed Chencang.

When Wei Yan and Jiang Wei reached the walls of Chencang, they found not a single banner nor anyone to sound the watch. Puzzled, they hesitated to attack. Suddenly they heard the sound of bombards from the town and saw flags and banners standing straight all around the wall. Lo! in silk headgear, holding a feathered fan, wearing a crane-plumed robe, a Taoist appeared. "You are late!" Kongming shouted down to them. The two swiftly dismounted and prostrated themselves before him, saying, "Your Excellency's plan was truly more than human!" Kongming bade them enter Chencang.

2419

"When I found out how sick Hao Zhao really was," Kongming told Wei Yan and Jiang Wei, "I gave you three days to take the town. But that was simply to firm up morale. At the same time I had Guan Xing and Zhang Bao call up some troops — among whom I concealed myself — and slip out of Hanzhong. We marched to Chencang double-time, before the enemy could reinforce. Spies planted earlier in the town aided us by lighting fires and shouting war cries to unsettle the Wei army. Without leadership, their troops lost all discipline. This enabled me to take Chencang handily. The rules of warfare tell us to appear where they least expect you, strike where they are least prepared. And that's just what I did!" Wei Yan and Jiang Wei prostrated themselves before him. Kongming, in consideration of the death of Hao Zhao, allowed Zhao's wife and children to bear his coffin home to Wei, thereby signifying the dead man's

怜郝昭之死,令彼妻小扶灵柩回魏,以表其忠。

孔明谓魏延、姜维曰:"汝二人且莫卸甲,可引兵去袭散关。把关之人,若知兵到,必然惊走。若稍迟便有魏兵至关,即难攻矣。"魏延、姜维受命,引兵径到散关。把关之人,果然尽走。二人上关才要卸甲,遥见关外尘头大起,魏兵到来。二人相谓曰:"丞相神算,不可测度!"急登楼视之,乃魏将张郃也。二人乃分兵守住险道。张郃见蜀兵把住要路,遂令退军。魏延随后追杀一阵,魏兵死者无数,张郃大败而去。延回到关上,令人报知孔明。孔明先自领兵,出陈仓斜谷,取了建威。后面蜀兵陆续进发。后主又命大将陈式来助。孔明驱大兵复出祁出。安下营寨,孔明聚众言曰:"吾二次出祁山,不得其利;今又到此,吾料魏人必依旧战之地,与吾相敌。彼意疑我取雍、郿二处,必以兵拒守;吾观阴平、武都二郡,与汉连接,若得此城,亦可分魏兵之势。何人敢取之?"姜维曰:"某愿往。"王平应曰:"某亦愿往。"孔明大喜,遂令姜维引兵一万取武都,王平引兵一万取阴平。二人领兵去了。

再说张郃回到长安,见郭淮、孙礼,说:"陈仓已失,郝昭已亡,散关亦被蜀兵夺了。今孔明复出祁山,分道进兵。"淮大惊曰:"若如此,必取雍、郿矣!"乃留张郃守长安,令孙礼保雍

loyalty to his sovereign.

Kongming told Wei Yan and Jiang Wei, "Keep your armor on. I want you to surprise San Pass. Those holding it will flee the moment our troops arrive; but the slightest delay will give the Wei troops time to get there, making capture difficult." Wei Yan and Jiang Wei carried out Kongming's orders, and the pass guards fled. The two commanders climbed up and were about to shed their armor, when they spotted the dust clouds of approaching troops in the distance. It was the Wei army. The two acknowledged to one another: "The prime minister's marvelous calculations surpass all reckoning!" Swiftly climbing the watchtower, they looked down on General Zhang He and deployed their forces to the key approaches in order to hold off his army.

Zhang He retreated once he realized that Shu troops now held the pass. Wei Yan pursued and took a heavy toll of the northerners. The Wei general quit the field; and Wei Yan, after returning to the pass, informed Kongming of the latest developments. The prime minister, for his part, had already led his own troops out of Chencang and Ye Gorge and had seized Jianwei; behind him in swift succession followed the forces of Shu as well as General Chen Shi, whom the Second Emperor had sent to aid him. Kongming emerged from the Qishan hills in full force, pitched camp, and then spoke to the assembled army: "My first two sorties from these mountains ended badly. Now we find ourselves on this ground again. I feel certain that the northerners will oppose us here as they have before. They mean to deceive us into trying to take Yong and Mei, which they will have well fortified. But Yinping and Wudu offer access to Hanzhong; by taking those towns, we can split the Wei force. Who dares to try?" Jiang Wei volunteered, followed by Wang Ping. Well pleased, Kongming assigned ten thousand troops to Jiang Wei to capture Wudu, and ten thousand to Wang Ping to capture Yinping. The two departed with their forces.

* * *

Zhang He returned to Chang'an and presented himself to Guo Huai and Sun Li. "Chencang is lost," he informed them, "and Hao Zhao is dead. The westerners have sized San Pass. Kongming has sallied forth again from Qishan along several routes." Guo Huai was astonished. "In that case, he will try to take Yong and Mei," he said. Guo Huai left Zhang

城。淮自引兵星夜来郿城守御，一面上表入洛阳告急。

却说魏主曹睿设朝，近臣奏曰："陈仓城已失，郝昭已亡，诸葛亮又出祁山，散关亦被蜀兵夺了。"睿大惊。忽又奏满宠等有表，说："东吴孙权僭称帝号，与蜀同盟。今遣陆逊在武昌训练人马，听候调用。只在旦夕，必入寇矣。"睿闻知两处危急，举止失措，甚是惊慌。此时曹真病未痊，即召司马懿商议。懿奏曰："以臣愚意所料，东吴必不举兵。"睿曰："卿何以知之。"懿曰："孔明尝思报猇亭之仇，非不欲吞吴也，只恐中原乘虚击彼，故暂与东吴结盟。陆逊亦知其意，故假作兴兵之势以应之，实是坐观成败耳。陛下不必防吴，只须防蜀。"睿曰："卿真高见！"遂封懿为大都督，总摄陇西诸路军马，令近臣取曹真总兵将印来。懿曰："臣自去取之。"遂辞帝出朝，径到曹真府下，先令人入府报知，懿方进见。问病毕，懿曰："东吴、西蜀会合，兴兵入寇，今孔明又出祁山下寨，明公知之乎？"真惊讶曰："吾家人知我病重，不令我知。似此国家危急，何不拜仲达为都督，以

He in charge of Chang'an's defenses, ordered Sun Li to the town of Yong, and hurried to the town of Mei with his own forces. At the same time he sent a petition to the capital announcing the emergency to Cao Rui.

Cao Rui was holding court when a personal vassal told him, "Chencang is lost, Hao Zhao dead. Zhuge Liang has again taken the field, and his army has seized San Pass." The Wei ruler expressed alarm. A fresh petition then arrived from Man Chong: "Sun Quan has usurped the title of emperor and formed an alliance with Shu. He has sent Lu Xun to Wuchang to train the army and await orders. We expect them to invade at any moment." Thus beset on either side, Cao Rui felt himself sliding into despair, unable to decide what course to take. Since at the time Cao Zhen had not yet recovered his health, Cao Rui consulted Sima Yi.

Sima Yi addressed the sovereign: "In my own humble estimation, the Southland will make no move." "How do you know?" Cao Rui responded.[5] "Kongming," he replied, "has never abandoned his desire to avenge the defeat at Jieting and has every intention of devouring the Southland. But he also has us to worry about. That's why he has made an alliance of opportunity with the Riverlands. But of course Lu Xun knows the score and is simply making 'invasion' gestures to satisfy Kongming. In fact, the south means to wait and watch the outcome. So, Your Majesty, no defense is needed against Wu — only against Shu!" "A suggestion of great insight!" Cao Rui exclaimed and made Sima Yi first field marshal of the forces, including the Longxi armies. He ordered a personal vassal to obtain the seal of command from Cao Zhen for Sima Yi. But Sima Yi said, "I'll go for it myself."[6]

Sima Yi took leave of the Emperor and went directly from the court to Cao Zhen's headquarters. After having himself announced, Sima Yi entered, inquired about Cao Zhen's illness, and then said, "The Southland and the Riverlands are joining forces for an invasion of our territory. Kongming has already camped on the eastern side of the Qishan hills. Is Your Lordship aware of this?" Cao Zhen gulped in amazement. "Those around me," he answered, "have kept this from me, knowing I was ill. It seems that the dynasty is in dire peril. Zhongda, you should be made field marshal for the purpose of driving back the western army." Sima Yi

退蜀兵耶?"懿曰:"某才薄智浅,不称其职。"真曰:"取印与仲达。"懿曰:"都督少虑。某愿助一臂之力,——只不敢受此印也。"真跃起曰:"如仲达不领此任,中国必危矣!吾当抱病见帝以保之!"懿曰:"天子已有恩命,但懿不敢受耳。"真大喜曰:"仲达今领此任,可退蜀兵。"懿见真再三让印,遂受之,入内辞了魏主,引兵往长安来与孔明决战。

正是:

旧帅印为新帅取,两路兵惟一路来。

未知胜负如何,且看下文分解。

2424

replied, "My meagre talent and shallow knowledge are hardly adequate
to such an office." Cao Zhen went on, "Have the seal handed to
Zhongda." "Spare yourself the anxiety, Field Marshal," Sima Yi answered.
"I shall lend what strength I have — only I can't bring myself to accept
the seal." Cao Zhen leaped from his bed and cried, "Unless you undertake the task, Zhongda, the northland is doomed. Sick as I am, I shall
betake myself to the Emperor to recommend you for this post." Sima Yi
then told him: "The Son of Heaven's gracious command has already
been given, but I could not bear to accept it." Well pleased, Cao Zhen
said, "Under your command, we can push back the western army." Cao
Zhen offered the seal twice, then a third time; finally Sima Yi accepted it.
After taking leave of the ruler of Wei, Sima Yi marched to Chang'an for
the showdown with Kongming. Indeed:

> As a new commander received the old seal,
> Two great armies became unified.[7]

Would the north prevail, or the west?
Read on.

NOTES

Chapter 74

[1] Mao: "Yu Jin's jealousy is retribution for Pang De's betrayal of Ma Chao."

[2] The word for fish, *yu,* is a homophone for the *yu* of Yu Jin.

[3] Mao: "I suspect that Pang De refused to surrender in order to protect his wife and children in the capital. Pang De had killed his sister-in-law and severed relations with his brother. But his wife and children, it seems, he could not abandon." According to his biography, Pang De's last words to Lord Guan were: "You miserable wretch! Why should I surrender? The whole empire respects the awful might of the king of Wei and his million-fold hosts. That Liu Bei of yours, with his mediocre ability, is no match for the king. I would be a ghost of this dynasty before I'd be a general of rebels and traitors" (*SGZ*, p.546).

[4] Mao: "If not for Man Chong's good counsel, Lord Guan would surely have taken Fan and controlled all the land below the Yellow River. And from such a superior position, Lord Guan would have been able to cope with the southern attack. But Man Chong advised, and Cao Ren heeded; is that not Heaven's will at work?"

[5] Mao (introductory note): "That Fan does not fall means that Heaven will not restore the Han. When Shan Fu captured Fan [chap.36] for Liu Bei, he lacked the military strength to hold the city and ended up abandoning it. But when Lord Guan laid siege to Fan, he had more than enough resources to take it , and the season, too, favored him. Reading how an arrow stopped him in mid-course makes one sigh and sigh again."

Chapter 75

[1] Mao's introductory note suggests that Hua Tuo and Ji Ping (the physician killed in chapter 21 for an attempt on Cao Cao's life) are "one person" in their devotion to righteousness.

[2] Mao (introductory note): "Cao Ren wanted to abandon Fan: Man Chong stopped him. Cao Cao wanted to leave the capital at Xuchang: Sima Yi stopped him. Had Cao Ren abandoned Fan, the region south of the Yellow River would have been thrown into turmoil. Had Cao Cao moved the capital, the region north of the Yellow River would have been thrown into turmoil....Word of Lord Guan's victory over Xiangyang was sufficient to snatch the initiative from Cao Cao....Guan failed to complete the conquest only because the right moment to act eluded him."

[3] Mao (introductory note): "When Sun Quan took Lü Meng's advice, he became as much a traitor to the Han as Cao Cao, king of Wei. If Sun Quan had taken advantage of Lord Guan's siege of Fan to conquer Xuzhou, thus dividing the north, the house of Han could have been restored and Cao Cao's treason crushed. But he forgot his oath, went back on his original covenant, and made a secret deal with Cao Cao to attack Lord Guan. And the cause? Nothing more than his struggle to gain Jingzhou!"

[4] Mao (introductory note): "While Zhou Yu lived, Liu and Sun were antagonists. When Zhou Yu died, Liu and Sun had cooperative relations. While Lu Su was in office, Liu and Sun·

cooperated. When Lu Su died [and Lü Meng succeeded him], their relations became antago-
nistic again."

⁵ The *TS* (p.726) renders the scene with dialogue: grateful to have been spared, the
station guards cooperate and suggest a means of deception for entering the city. Presumably,
Mao Zonggang wants to make the willingness of Lord Guan's men to betray him less
obvious; by shifting from dialogue to prose narrative, he also reduces the vividness of the
scene. The attack took place in the autumn of A.D. 219.

⁶ Apparently Jiangling, not Gong'an, was the functional provincial capital of this time;
Xiangyang had been in Cao Cao's hands until Lord Guan recaptured it to prepare his attack
on Fan.

⁷ See chapter 73.

⁸ Mao (introductory note): "This chapter begins with a description of Lord Guan suffering from his wound but acting as if uninjured. Then we go directly to a description of Lü
Meng feigning an illness. First, we have Hua Tuo treating a real injury; then we have Lu Xun
curing Lü Meng's feigned illness. Hua Tuo recognized the poison on the arrow and got rid of
it — a case of using medicine against medicine. Lu Xun knew that Lü Meng was feigning
illness and consequently told him to resign alleging illness — a case of using illness to cure
illness. And there are even more remarkable things to come! Lord Guan had an ailing arm,
and an ailing attitude as well — namely, his overestimation of himself and his arrogance
toward all others. If Lu Xun had a method for eliminating Lü Meng's illness, he also had a
method for aggravating Lord Guan's ailment — namely, rich gifts and honeyed words. Lü
Meng resigned his office, and Lord Guan assumed he was free of a problem, a greater relief
than the cure of his arm. And so he pulled out his southern defenses [for the siege at Fan].
But by so doing, Lord Guan was more severely poisoned than by the arrow!"

"Kongming cured Zhou Yu with a borrowed wind, and Pang Tong 'cured' the northern
soldiers ［seasickness］ by getting Cao Cao to link up his boats. Lu Xun worked both types
[the cure and the 'cure']."

Chapter 76

¹ In the *TS* (p.728), Lord Guan threatens severe beatings for a delay of one or two days,
death for a delay of three.

² In the *TS* (p.731), Cao Ren wants to pursue Lord Guan, but is dissuaded by an adviser,
who argues, "Qriginally Sun Quan allied himself to Lord Guan.... Now Lord Guan is defeated
and his much — reduced army on the run. Let him survive for a while; it'll be a threat to Sun
Quan! If you chase him and fail to capture him, Sun Quan may shift his hopes to him and
start to look on us as his enemy again."

³ A Western Han general sent by Emperor Jing (r.156-140 B.C.) to suppress the southern
rebellion organized by Liu Bi, king of Wu.

⁴ Ma Liang and Yi Ji have been sent to Chengdu for help. The *PH* (pp. 123-24) says that
Liu Feng blocked the messengers as his revenge on Lord Guan for backing Shan instead of
himself as heir to Xuande.

⁵ Mao (introductory note): "Zhang Liang used the songs of Chu to cause the troops ［of

Xiang Yu] to flee.... Lü Meng uses the men of Jingzhou to call away the men of Jingzhou." In this famous tragic scene Han Gao Zu incited desertion in the ranks of his main opponent, Xiang Yu, king of Chu, by having men of Chu in his own army sing songs in the Chu dialect. After this victory the way was clear to the establishment of the Han dynasty. The verse in the *TS* makes the same historical allusion.

⁶ In the *TS* (p.735) this speech is fuller. Lord Guan is reported as saying, "Succession through the legitimate son is a time-honored principle. Why ask me such a question? Liu Feng is adopted. Send him off to a remote town and spare yourself great trouble in the family."

⁷ There is trouble underneath the question of Liu Bei's succession. In the *PH*, Kongming refuses to tell Liu Bei whether he prefers Liu Shan or Liu Feng and suggests that Liu Bei take the question to Lord Guan. Lord Guan favors Liu Shan, and so Liu Feng (who expected to succeed Liu Bei as ruler of Shu) believes Lord Guan has wronged him and vows to settle the score. He does so by blocking aid to Jingzhou when Lord Guan is defeated. In the *SGZ*, Liu Feng's adoption precedes the birth of Liu Shan, *Three Kingdoms* reverses this sequence, thus giving Liu Shan seniority of position (though not of age), in order to spare Liu Bei criticism for choosing the cadet brother as his heir. See Afterword, pp.1523-24.

Earlier, when Jingzhou was being threatened by Wei and Wu jointly, Guan Ping had urged his father to get help from Liu Bei. But Lord Guan said no, embarrassed at having won no honors in the western campaigns. Ignoring his father's wishes, Guan Ping wrote to Liu Bei, but his letters of appeal were all intercepted by Liu Feng. This is the *PH* version of the events leading to Lord Guan's fall. At an earlier point, when Lord Guan was fighting Cao Cao (at Qingni), Liu Bei at Jiameng received Sun Quan's appeal for help against Cao Cao. Unfortunately for Lord Guan, Liu Bei refused Sun Quan's appeal, choosing first to conquer Chengdu and hence the Riverlands.

⁸ The name of a hexagram in the *Book of Changes*. The top three lines, *kun,* stand for earth; the boottom three, *kan,* for water.

Chapter 77

¹ The text here reads hai, the last earthly branch, which corresponds to the hours 9:00 to 11:00 p.m., and to the direction northwest.

² Mai, downriver from Linju on the River Ju, was roughly between Dangyang and Jiangling.

³ This was the place where Pujing had once saved Lord Guan. See chapter 27.

⁴ The *TS* (p.741) has Pujing saying, "In terms of your own particular conduct, long ago at Baima defile you stabbed to death an altogether unprepared and unsuspecting Yan Liang. How can he not bear rancor toward you down in the netherworld? What right have you to quibble about the treachery by which Lü Meng did you in? Why should this puzzle you?" The *TS* is referring to its own version of how Lord Guan killed Cao Cao's general Yan Liang: Yan Liang comes forth to parley and is suddenly cut down. See chapter 25 n. 14.

⁵ This plays on various connotations of the word *chi* (red, ruddy). Red was the symbolic color of Han.

⁶ The play hear is on various meanings of *qing*, the color of nature: the clear lamp, the color of bamboo (served as paper, hence written history), the light of day, the east, and the *Yang* strength of Lord Guan's sword, Green Dragon.

⁷ Hu Sanxing, principal editor of the *ZZTJ*, representing an early Yuan, pro-Cao view, argues (p.2166) that Lord Guan would have been defeated by Cao Cao without the participation of the southern forces and that therefore Cao Cao was simply setting the two bandits (Lord Guan and Lü Meng) against each other.

⁸ Mao: "The very words that Cao spoke to Lord Guan at the Huarong Pass〔when Lord Guan spared him; see chapter 50〕."

⁹ Huai Ying, daughter of Duke Mu of Qin, married Zi Yu, duke of Jin. After Zi Yu's death she was given to his uncle Chong Er, who became Duke Wen of Jin, the famed hegemon of the late seventh century B.C.

¹⁰ Mao (introductory note): "That phrase, 'Lord Guan, what has become of you?' is the equivalent of the profound teaching of the whole *Diamond Sutra*. For that matter, what has become of the Southland, the Riverlands, the kingdom of Wei, the division of the realm, and the greats who lived in those times? All who have existed cease to exist. And only those who do not 'exist' have permanent existence. To know what has become of Lord Guan means that his existence is eternal."

Chapter 78

¹ The *TS* chapter title differs somewhat: "Cao Cao Kills the Superb Physician Hua Tuo; The Wei Crown Prince Cao Pi Seizes Power."

² Mao: "Kongming shows resentment because Lord Guan ignored his advice to maintain amity with the Southland."

³ Mao: "Forgetting Wei, he mentions the south along."

⁴ Mao: "Kongming speaks of Wei and Wu〔north and south〕together."

⁵ The heaven-touching sacred tree is a symbol of a dynasty's contact with and acceptance by Heaven.

⁶ See chapters 20 and 21.

⁷ Han rules by the symbolic element of fire; "on the fire" implies usurping the Han.

⁸ The *TS* (p.751) adds the phrase "since the reign of Emperor An [A.D. 107-26]."

⁹ The original petition is in the Wei lüe; see *SGZ*, pp.52-53.

¹⁰ Mao: "The implication is that the usurpation will be left to his son Pi." Zhou Wenwang refrained from overthrowing the reigning Shang dynasty even though he held two-thirds of the realm. His son, Wuwang, carried out the conquest and established the reign of Zhou.

¹¹ Cao Cao had killed Ma Teng, and Teng's son Chao had vowed revenge. See chapter 57. Mao: "The dream must have occurred before Ma Teng's death.... Even before Cao Pi's usurpation, there is an omen of the Sima clan."

¹² *Lu* means good luck, salary, food (an ancient form of pay for officials). In fact, the omen refers to the Sima clan, which overthrew the Wei dynasty of the Cao clan and founded the Jin dynasty; i.e., the Ma (*ma*, "horse"),who are employed by the Cao, will feed upon the

Cao (*cao,* "trough"). The three horses also refer to the three leaders of the *Sima* clan.

[13] The Sima clan will establish the Jin dynasty after usurping the Wei dynasty in A.D. 263, then go on to absorb the Riverlands in A.D. 265 and the Southland in A.D. 280.

[14] Mao: "To speak only of his house and not the imperial line shows the old traitor's cunning."

[15] This luxurious touch is not found in the "Wudi ji" of the *SGZ* (p.53), which emphasizes Cao's austerity in life and death: "They dressed his body in the clothes appropriate to the season; no valuables were buried with him." See also the *Wei shu* passage in the commentary on p.54.

Mao (introductory note): "Some claim that in dividing the perfume among the women and then ordering them to sell shoes, Cao Cao was departing from his lifelong love of deception. They fail to realize this too was one of his deceptions... At the brink of death what question could be more important than the imperial succession. [i.e., of the Han Emperor Xian]. But Cao Cao, who provided to the smallest detail for each of his women, had not one word to say about the Han throne. This can only be because he wanted the world and later generations to believe that he had no thought of usurping the dynasty; rather, he let his progeny bear the blame that he avoided. That is what he meant by comparing himself to King Wen of the Zhou."

The presentation of perfume and the order to weave shoes are not in the *TS*. This is one of a small category of striking events that Mao Zonggang has added.

[16] Mao (introductory note): "Cao Cao died in a *gengzi* year of the cycle 〔the five *zi* years in any sixty-year cycle have the sign of the rat〕. And the month is *xuyin* [*yin* carries the sign of the tiger]. So the year of Cao's death was forecast by Zuo Ci when he spoke of an 'earth rat and a metal tiger' ten chapters back." He died March 15, a *gengzi* day.

[17] This ode does not appear in the *TS*.

[18] Mao: "There is no longer any interest in an imperial mandate."

[19] Mao: "From the man who broke down a wall and dragged out the imperial consort, another instance of 'loyalty'" The text of the decree appears in the *TS* (p.756) dated Jian An 25, second month (A.D.220). Hua Xin acted to prevent any interference in Cao Pi's accession through Emperor Xian.

2431

Chapter 79

[1] The *TS* chapter title differs: "In Anger the King of Hanzhong 〔Liu Xuande〕 Has Liu Feng Killed."

[2] *Jianyidaifu* was the lowest grade of *daifu,* or imperial officer attending the emperor. All four grades of *daifu* were under the *guangluxun* (director of the palace), who managed the palace bureaucracy.

[3] Mao (introductory note): "To see how the Cao clan was spared internecine struggle is to understand that Heaven no longer wished to preserve the sacrifices of the Han royal house. The weakling Cao Xiong is not worth mentioning; but Cao Zhang had some pretentions to valor and strategy, appearing at the city of Ye with a puissant force. And Cao Zhi, through his talent and reputation, had assembled many literary men in Linzi. They came

perilously close to a civil war over Cao Pi's succession. If fraternal strife had broken out — such as that between Yuan Shao's sons, Tan and Shang, or Liu Biao's sons, Zong and Qi — the king of Hanzhong could have exploited the divisions and attacked."

The Cao clan applied the rule *li jian wei hou,* "Establish empresses from families without wealth and status," in an attempt to control strife within the clan.

⁴It is as Emperor Wu (Wudi) that Cao Cao passes into history: the *SGZ* opens with the annals of Emperor Wu ("Wudi ji"). Mao (introductory note) discusses Cao Cao's posthumous title: "A name cannot be falsely appropriated; and a fact cannot be lied out of existence. Cao Cao had bequeathed to his son the task of the Zhou dynasty's King Wu [the Martial; i.e., the task of actually overthrowing the reigning dynasty], while comparing himself to King Wen [the Civil: i.e., the king who refrains from military action and remains loyal to the dynasty in power despite his own overwhelming popularity]. Nonetheless, Cao Pi saw things in the opposite way. He did not regard his father Cao Cao as a King Wen but gave him the posthumous title of King Wu. Certainly, Cao Cao tried to avoid the reputation of overthrower for himself and leave it for his successor. But the successor Pi, to avoid the name of overthrower, returned it to his ancestor. In that way the Wei dynasty's usurpation of the Han became Cao Cao's doing, not Cao Pi's. Cao Cao tried to fool others, but he couldn't fool his son. He tried to cover up his deed, but his son wouldn't cooperate."

⁵Fa Zheng died in A.D. 220 at the age of forty-five after Cao Cao's armies were driven from Hanzhong; it was he who had arranged Liu Bei's takeover of the Riverlands. See *SGZ,* p.961. Fa Zheng's historical importance is somewhat overshadowed in the novel by the large role Zhuge Liang plays. See He You, "Zhuge Liang yu Fa Zheng," in Chengdushi Zhuge Liang yanjiuhui, ed., *Zhuge Liang yanjiu* (Chengdu:. Ba Shu shushe, 1985), pp.289-95.

⁶At this point in the novel two titles are used for Xuande, king of Hanzhong and First Ruler (*xianzhu*). The latter name (which appears in the title of his biography in the *SGZ*) is a posthumous recognition of his place as the first ruler of the Shu-Han dynasty. For simplicity's sake the word "king" is used in most cases. The *ZZTJ* uses the universal Hanzhu (ruler of Han) over the regional Xianzhu (first ruler), reflecting Liu Bei's conception of himself.

⁷Fan Li served the king of Yue, but after the king achieved his goal, Li left his service and went into obscurity, saying, "The king is not one to enjoy victory with." Zifan, uncle to Patriarch Wen of Jin, accompanied his nephew through nineteen years of exile. When the patriarch was about to cross the river to return to his state, Uncle Fan took his leave, fearing that his faults alone would be remembered.

⁸Wu Zixu, originally of the state of Chu, helped the king of Wu defeat the king of Yue during the Spring and Autumn period; later, calumny drove him to suicide. Meng Tian, despite fine service on the northern frontier, was driven to suicide by the slanders of Zhao Gao. Yue Yi served the state of Yan during a time of dramatic victories over Qi during the Spring and Autumn period.

⁹A Wei title, created by combining two Qin offices, *sanqi* (detached cavalry) and *changshi* (regular attendant).

¹⁰I.e., northern Jingzhou. The Wei formed a new imperial district called Xiangyangjun.

¹¹In this document (cited in the *TS,* p. 763) Meng Da makes these points to Liu Feng: (1)

he, Feng, has had many conflicts with his foster father, Xuande; (2) he and Xuande are unrelated; (3) selection of Ah Dou (Xuande's natural son, Liu Shan) as heir apparent "has embittered men of true understanding"; (4) submitting to Cao Pi is wise and honorable, while resisting is foolishly dangerous; and (5) he can expect an excellent reception from the king of Wei.

¹² Mao (introductory note): "Liu Feng's rebuff of Meng Da and Mi Fang's acquiescence to Fu Shiren [who turned Fang against Lord Guan and helped Cao Cao gain Jingzhou] are altogether different. But if Liu Feng rebuffed Meng Da in the end, why didn't he to begin with? If Liu Feng was capable of executing Meng Da's messenger and not surrendering to the north, why did he originally listen to Meng Da's slander and refuse to help Lord Guan?... From Shangyong he could easily have helped Lord Guan in Mai. Not listening to Meng Da would not have cost him his life. It is too bad he didn't size up the situation earlier."

¹³ Mao (introductory note): "Despite Liu Feng's offense, the first Ruler [of Shu — Han, Xuande] was unjustified in killing him. Liu Feng's refusal to aid Lord Guan justified punishment, but his refusal to surrender to the Cao clan would have justified forgiveness. And his final rebuff of Meng Da was praiseworthy. Thus, his regrettable earlier acquiescence in Meng Da's treachery is pardonable. After losing an adopted brother, Xuande went on and killed an adopted son — a dubious idea. Further, Xuande did not [merely] summon Liu Feng and put him to death; instead, he caused the loss of fifty thousand soldiers and the territory of Shangyong, thereby compounding his error...something he would regret to the end of his days."

¹⁴ Mao (introductory note): "Comparing the circumstances in the Liu and Cao houses, what a gap there is in terms of depth of feeling. Xuande, a 'brother' of another surname, grieved for his younger brother's death. By contrast, Cao Pi, a brother of the same womb, was eager for his brothers' deaths. Xuande felt pain for the loss of an adopted brother and was heedless of compassion for his adopted son. Cao Pi sought his true brothers' deaths and was heedless of his natural mother's feelings of love."

¹⁵ This was Cao Cao's native district.

2433

Chapter 80

¹ The two elements of the graph *wei*, read individually, mean "[Han] consigned to the dead."

² The name "Xuchang" for the city of Xu begins with Cao Pi's reign.

³ The *TS* has more lines spoken by Hua Xin, including the motif phrase, "The empire belongs to no one man but to all in the empire" (pp.767-68). The abdication process went on from September to December of A.D. 220.

⁴ Cao Cao had married his daughter Jie to Emperor Xian.

⁵ Mao has transformed the *TS* here. On p. 768 the Empress says, "You call my brother a usurping traitor! What was your Supreme Ancestor [Liu Bang] if not a drunken lout, without standing, a nobody! Yet he stole the empire from the Qin! My father [Cao Cao] cleared the realm of rebels. My brother has many achievements to his credit. Why shouldn't he become emperor? You could never have held the throne in safety for more than thirty

years without my father and brother." Here Luo Guanzhong is true to the *PH* tradition of hostility toward Liu Bang. Compare the opening of the *Qian Hanshu pinghua* as well as the *Sanguozhi pinghua*. Mao's depiction of Empress Cao is based on her annals in the *HHS*, p.455; however, this portrait of virtue and loyalty is rejected as spurious by the commentator of the *ZZTJ*, Hu Sanxing (p.2182).

[6] This poem is added by Mao. The "Canon of Yao" describing Yao's legendary transfer of power to Shun, bypassing his own son, opens the canonical *Shu jing*. This abdication (*shan*) myth was often cited by usurpationists in the Cao court to justify the removal of Emperor Xian. In the *TS* (p.767), Hua Xin draws the analogy between Cao and Shun.

[7] Mao: "He did not say that the throne could not be yielded. He said, 'Seek elsewhere.' Thus, he intended that the Emperor vacate the throne."

[8] The *TS* (pp. 769-70) records Wang Lang's memorial. It reads in part: "Reverently I have received your edict... abdicating to this vassal without merit. Respectfully I call your attention to the example of Xu You, who went into hiding rather than accept Yao's offer of the throne. For this Xu You was acclaimed ever after. This vassal, of little talent and slight virtue, could never receive the mandate of rule. In this plenteous age I beseech you to seek some man of great gifts to receive the abdication and thus spare me the censure of history."

Following this, Hua Xin suggests another part of the Yao-Shun myth for Emperor Xian to follow: "In ancient times Yao of Tang had two daughters....When he offered to abdicate to Shun, Shun declined, and so Yao married both daughters to him. For this later ages hailed Yao for the virtue of great sagehood. Now Your Majesty, too, has two daughters. Why not emulate Yao and give them in marriage to the king of Wei [Cao Pi]?'...The two princesses were conveyed by carriage into the palace of the king of Wei." See the closing lines of the "Canon of Yao" (*Shu jing*, "Yao dian"), which describe Yao's sending his daughters to marry into Shun's clan. Emperor Xian's second edict to Cao Pi is dated November 25, A.D.220.

[9] The *PH* (p.126) places responsibility for the abdication directly on Cao Cao. Advising Emperor Xian concerning the succession problem, Cao Cao says, "Has not Your Majesty heard of Yao, Shun, Yu, and Tang, who came to power because they had virtue?... All in the empire declare that your subject Cao Pi is worthy to be Son of Heaven." The *SGZ*, however, describes the abdication as devised by Cao Pi and carried out by Hua Xin and Zhang Yin.

[10] Achilles Fang makes this December 10 in Ssu-ma Kuang [Sima Guang], *The chronicle of the Three Kingdoms*, trans. and annot. Achilles Fang, Harvard-Yenching Institute Studies, no. 6 (Cambridge: Harvard University Press, 1952-65), 1:37. Sima Guang follows other sources and dates the abdication of Emperor Xian to Cao Pi to the *yimao* day, the fifty-second of the cycle, or November 25.

[11] From the standpoint of Wei chronology, Yan Kang is the name of the reign period that spans the death of Cao Cao (March 15, A.D. 220) and the usurpation of Cao Pi (December 10). As far as Wei is concerned, Yan Kang is the last Han reign period, and the last Jian An year is 24 (A.D. 219). The first Wei reign period, Huang Chu, is declared in the tenth month but retroactively covers the whole year, thus displacing Yan Kang in general chronologies. The words Huang Chu signify earth (associated with the color yellow) sup-

planting fire; that is, the inauguration of a new era according to Five Agents theory. The use of Jian An 25 for much of A.D.220 by the Riverlands court signifies the continuation of Han chronology in defiance of Wei chronology.

[12] Qiao Zhou was the teacher of Chen Shou, author of the *SGZ*. The *Jin shu* contains a biography of Chen Shou.

[13] "The vapour of the Emperor appears red inside and yellow outside, and shows uniformity all round. It indicates the rise of an Emperor whenever it makes its appearance." Ho Peng Yoke, *The Astronomical Chapters of the Chin Shu*, Le monde d'outre-mer passé et présent, sér 2: Documents, n° 9 (Paris: Mouton & Co.,1966), p.144.

[14] I.e., the middle of the western quarter of the sky.

[15] *Zhong* and *yi*. The *TS* (p.774) has xiao (filial piety) for yi.

[16] The *ZZTJ* (p. 2185) gives prominence to the protest made by Fei Shi: "Your Majesty has traveled far and wide gathering a loyal army to smite the traitors who have usurped the Han. Now to make yourself emperor before your great enemy is conquered is likely to confuse people. In the years before Han was founded, the Supreme Ancestor and Xiang Yu swore that the first to defeat Qin would be king of that region. But after the Supreme Ancestor had taken Xiangyang and captured Ziying [the last Qin emperor], Xiang Yu still refused the honor due him. How much less should Your Majesty covet the emperorship when he has not been beyond the palace [of late]. Your course is unwise." This criticism was not welcomed by Liu Bei, and he demoted Fei Shi. See his biography in *SGZ*, p.1016. The *PH, TS,* and *Three Kingdoms* do not contain this passage.

[17] Northwest of Chengdu, according to the *TS* note.

[18] May 15, A.D. 221.

[19] Still preserving Emperor Xian's reign period, Jian An.

[20] Not Lady Sun of Wu (the Southland), but the wife of the late Liu Mao, brother of Liu Zhang, from whom Xuande took the Riverlands. See *ZZTJ*, p.2129.

[21] From here on, Xianzhu, or First Ruler, is Three Kingdoms' designation for Liu Xuande, following the usage of the *SGZ. ZZTJ* uses the term Hanzhu, or Ruler of Han. Xianzhu will be sometimes translated Emperor.

Chapter 81

[1] In the *PH* (p.126), Kongming directly expresses opposition to an invasion of Wu.

[2] Mao: "He protests Liu Bei's leading the expedition, not the expedition itself."

[3] *TS* (p.778): "The Emperor said, 'I will hold the army while a different plan is considered.'"

[4] Here the *TS* adds: "Moreover, Lord Guan slighted the worthy and treated scholars with arrogance. He was rigid and self-important. That is what cost him his life; no Heaven ordained it."

[5] *TS* "The first year of Zhang Wu, the fifth month [A.D.221]."

[6] 221. Achilles Fang gives August 6 to September 4 for the seventh month; see Ssu-ma Kuang [Sima Guang], *The Chronicle of the Three Kingdoms,* trans. and annot. Achilles Fang, Harvard-Yenching Institute Studies, no. 6 (Cambridge: Harvard University Press, 1952-

65),1:50. The thirteenth day of the cycle, *hingzi* (not bingyin), would match August 14.

[7] See chapter 2. Liu Xuande's first appointment was to Anxi.

[8] Mao: "Liu Bei ignored Kongming's advice on taking over the Riverlands, but he took Fa Zheng's; so Fa Zheng should have been able to get Liu Bei to stop the march."

[9] "Azure" (*qing,* the color of ever-renewing nature) implies eternal youth in Taoist mythology.

[10] Mao (introductory note): "The First Ruler [Liu Bei] was determined to attack Wu. Kongming, having failed to dissuade him, hoped to use the old sage of Azure City Mountain to prevent him."

[11] Mao (introductory note): "After the revered Lord Guan's ghost manifested itself, the story could have moved to the death of Liu Feng at the First Ruler's hands. Instead, between these two incidents the author unexpectedly inserted Cao Cao's illness, the killing of Hua Tuo, Cao Pi's establishment as heir to Cao Cao, king of Wei, and Cao Zhi's poem of protest."

"After the execution of Liu Feng, the story could have moved to the murder of Zhang Fei followed by Liu Bei's invasion of the Southland. However, the author inserted the abdication of Emperor Xian, the usurpation of Cao Pi, the reaction in Chengdu, and Kongming's arguments for attacking Wei. Among these crossing branches and overlapping leaves of the narrative the seams are never apparent; not a line is out of place in these interwoven stories. Such technique recalls the great historian Sima Qian."

Chapter 82

[1] The northern part of Jingzhou, called Xiangyang, had been held by Cao Cao all along.

[2] I.e., Liu Bei.

[3] Mao (introductory note): "The present Sun Quan is utterly unlike the former. How bold the first Sun Quan, when he drew his sword and sheared off a piece of a table [to demonstrate his determination to resist Cao Cao]! How feeble the present Sun Quan, bowing his head and submitting to Wei! Why the change? His blunder in Jingzhou and his split with Liu Bei."

Sun Quan's reference to the founder of the Han suggests that he had large ambitions. Xiang Yu gave the Han founder, Gao Zu, the kingship of Han (i.e., the land west of the River Han) as a consolation after denying him the prize rightfully his: the land within the passes. Gao Zu had to accept the inferior kingdom of Han, but he soon moved east again, conquered the land within the passes, overcame Xiang Yu's armies, and within four years established the new dynasty of Han. See the "Xiang Yu benji" and "Gao Zu benji" in the *SJ*.

[4] The year after Liu Bei became king of Hanzhong, he named Huang Zhong one of the "Five Tiger Generals," thus putting him on a par with Lord Guan, Zhang Fei, Ma Chao, and Zhao Zilong. The following year the historical Huang Zhong died (*SGZ*, p.948). The author of *Three Kingdoms* has fictionally extended Huang Zhong's life. Similarly, the exploits of Guan Xing and Zhang Bao, the sons of Lord Guan and Zhang Fei, are fictional additions. At the end of this chapter it is A.D.222.

Chapter 83

[1] See chapter 68 for the pre-raid feast and for Gan Ning's reconciliation with Ling Tong, whose father he had killed.

[2] Mao (introductory note): "The Emperor's campaign against Sun Quan makes it certain that he will not spare Mi Fang [younger brother of the wife who threw herself into the well so that Zhao Zilong could save Ah Dou]. For if he Showed no leniency toward Sun Quan, whose sister [Lady Sun, a later wife of Liu Bei] still lived, he would hardly show leniency to Mi Fang, whose sister was already dead. Looking at the situation another way, the Emperor's execution of Mi Fang meant that he would never relax his determination to destroy the Southland. If the Emperor would not spare Mi Fang, whose sister had sacrificed her life for An Dou, he would hardly forgive the brother of Lady Sun [Sun Quan], who had left his house without telling him."

[3] The TS (p.800) "...destroy Wu first, then take over Wei, emulating the restoration of Guang Wu [the first Later Han emperor] — this is my desire."

Chapter 84

[1] The name means "White Emperor", as noted in chapter 82; later the town was renamed Yong'an, "Enduring Peace." See chap, 34, n.11.

[2] Mao (introductory note): "Compare Zhou Yu's use of fire to attack Cao Cao and Lu Xun's use of fire to attack Liu Bei: Lu Xun had more problems than Zhou Yu. In the first place, Zhou Yu received his command when the southern army was fittest, while Lu Xun received his command when the southern army had already suffered several reverses. In the second place, Zhou Yu had the support of Liu Bei against the northern enemy, while Lu Xun had a watchful predator to his north, Cao Pi. And in the third place, Zhou Yu had the help of Kongming, Pang Tong, Huang Gai, Kan Ze, and Gan Ning; Lu Xun had to contend with the doubts of Zhang Zhao, Gu Yong, Bu Zhi, Han Dang, and Zhou Tai..."

2437

"Lord Guan failed only because he disregarded Kongming's advice to maintain amity with Sun Quan. The Emperor was defeated for the same reason.... Zhuge Jin tried twice to persuade Lord Guan [to cooperate with the south] and tried once to persuade the Emperor. Although less talented than his brother Zhuge Liang, his understanding of the situation was largely the same."

The battle of Yiling has very little source material behind it in the SGZ; the majority of it is found in Lu Xun's biography. An introduction to the battle may be found in Cao Xuewei's article "Yiling zhi zhan de qingjie he renwu chuangzao," in XK 2 (1986):254-63.

[3] Mao: "Lu Xun had reckoned that no outside aid would be needed to end the siege of Yiling."

[4] The words also mean "consort of a treacherous owl"; "treacherous owl" was an epithet applied to Liu Bei.

[5] This poem and the notice of Lady Sun's suiclde are not in the TS, which says earlier that Lady Sun returned to the Southland. By this revision Mao Zonggang seeks to turn her into a devoted Confucian wife who follows her lord in death. For this he claims a historical basis in the Xiao ji zhuan (Tales of ill-fated consorts).

In Mao Zonggang's list of emendations, he mentions this revision (paragraph 2), together with his revision of the *TS* account of the conduct of Emperor Xian's consort (see chap. 80). Mao's text note says. "How firm of purpose was Lady Sun when she denounced the ［pursuing］ Southland soldiers! Her will may have weakened when she tried to take Ah Dou south with her, but her suicide here in grief for her husband ［Liu Bei］ shows her chaste honor undiminished."

⁶ There is a powerful description of the noise caused by the rolling of boulders on the floor of the Yangzi in John Hersey's *A Single Pebble* (New York: Knopf, 1956), p.43.

⁷ Mao: "Lord Guan obligated Cao Cao when he released him on the Huarong Trail. Here Huang Chengyan similarly obligates Lu Xun at Fishbelly Meadow."

Chapter 85

¹ A.D. 222. The reign title Zhang Wu, which the kingdom of Shu proclaimed, began in 221. Prior to that, Shu loyally followed the reign titles of Han Xiandi; thus, 220 was Jian An 25, and 221 was Jian An 26 (see *TS*, p.775); Jian An 26 retroactively became Zhang Wu 1, which was proclaimed in May of that year. The *ZZTJ* follows the reign titles of Wei under Cao Pi: Huang Chu 1 is A.D.220. *Three Kingdoms*, following Zhu Xi's *Gangmu*, indicates its support for the cause of Liu Bei when it uses Shu-Han reign titles. But at times in the narrative the reign titles of the other kingdoms will be found.

² Both generals served Xiang Yu before joining Liu Bang's cause and helping him defeat Xiang Yu.

³ In the *TS* (p.817) Liu Bei says to Kongming: "I must request that Your Excellency take responsibility for our cause." The *PH* says (p.128): "The heir apparent was summoned before his father, who bade him prostrate himself before the lord of Wu [Kongming]. The lord of Wu attempted to raise the lad up, but the Emperor held his son down. The lord of Wu said, 'It is a capital offense for your vassal [to receive the heir apparent's obeisance].' The First Ruler said, 'The director general knows the story of Dan, duke of Zhou, who ［as regent］ protected King Cheng.' The First Ruler continued, 'Ah Dou is too young to bear rule. If it is fitting, place him in power; if not, rule yourself.' The lord of Wu said, 'What virtue have I for that? If Your Majesty entrusted the heir to me, my death would not suffice to requite the honor.' The heir apparent [rose], advanced on his knees, and then prostrated himself. The Emperor said, 'Whenever the heir apparent has official business, let him consult with the director general.' With these words, the Emperor passed away." The *SGZ* says that Liu Bei named Li Yan, chief of the Secretariat, as Ah Dou's second guardian (p. 891).

⁴ June 10, A.D. 220.

⁵ Cranes and herons are thought to return to the same nest in successive years.

⁶ This seven-character regulated verse is the fourth of a five-ode sequence, *Yonghuai guji*, "Songs to Remember Historic Sites," by the renowned mid-Tang poet Du Fu. A translation and discussion of the five poems may be found in Hans Frankel, *The Flowering Plum and the Palace Lady* (New Haven and London: Yale University Press, 1976), pp. 116-24. The first three poems of the sequence lament, in turn, two poets and a palace beauty who suffer owing either to their sovereign's neglect or his misfortune. Mao Zonggang

has substituted this one poem for a group of prose compositions and verses extolling Liu Bei (*TS*, pp. 818-20). The effect is to echo Liu Bei's tragic recognition that he should never have ignored Kongming's warnings about invading the Southland. The last line reads *Yiti junchen jisi tong;* one literal translation would be "As one body, liege and liege man, sacrificial services shared." The words *yiti,* "as one body," come from the *Yili,* "Sangfu zhuan," which explains that father and son, husband and wife, and brothers are "as one body" when their spirits are worshiped, hence the translation "in sacred union." Liege and vassal (*junchen*) are not included in the list, however; thus the line may be Du Fu's way of saying that the worshipers at the two neighboring shrines were treating Kongming as Liu Bei's true son or brother and therefore co-recipient of services to the late emperor. The phrase *yiti* occurs early in chapter 81 when Liu Bei says of the excuted Lord Guan, "Yunchang is I — in sacred union," implying that he will be ritually remembered jointly with Lord Guan.

[7] The *ZZTJ* always refers to Liu Bei as Hanzhu (ruler of Han), not Xianzhu (First Ruler) as in *SGZ*, or Shuzhu (ruler of Shu). Sima Guang was simply following the usage of the Shu leadership, not acknowledging Liu Bei as the legitimate Han emperor. Note that on occasion *Three Kingdoms* refers to the western kingdom as Shu-Han; note also that the second word in Liu Bei's posthumous temple title, Zhao Lie, contains the fire element. Liu Shan is called Houzhu, Later Ruler, usually translated here as Second Ruler or Second Emperor; he reigned until A.D. 263.

[8] Mao (introductory note): "from the First Ruler's words committing Liu Shan to Kongming's guidance, we can tell that the campaign against Wei was more important to him than the campaign against Wu. The ruler said to Kongming. 'You are ten times more able than Cao Pi.' Why did he not say 'than Sun Quan'? I would answer, because the Cao clan's Wei dynasty was Han's mortal enemy. When the First Ruler said, 'If Liu Shan deserves support, support him; if not, assume the throne yourself,' it was as if he were saying 'If he is able to suppress the rebels, support him; if not, then take over.' The emphasis is on suppressing the rebels, [in the north].... Did the First Ruler really mean for Kongming to assume his throne? In one sense, yes; in another, no. To have Kongming usurp as Cao Pi did is something the First Ruler could never have permitted himself to suggest. He had to have said what he did to Kongming in order to strengthen his commitment to support Liu Shan, but also to let Liu Shan know that he had to respect and obey Kongming absolutely." According to Li Yan's biography (*SGZ*, p.999), the dying Liu Xuande decreed by edict that Li Yan and Zhuge Liang should jointly support and guide the new ruler, Liu Shan.

The *SGZ* and the *ZZTJ* as well as *Three Kingdoms* (especially the *TS*) suggest some opposition in the Riverlands to an offensive strategy against the north. However, there is no record of the kind of full-scale debate in the Riverlands over the war policy that took place in the Southland between Zhang Zhao and Zhou Yu before the battle at Red Cliffs.

[9] In the next several chapters Kongming will settle the potential conflict between the Southern Man people and the new Riverlands government. In their civil wars the Chinese used Man nations as early as the Spring and Autumn period (see *HHS*, p.2831). In A.D. 223 uprisings in the Riverlands had already begun under Huang Yong after he learned of Liu Bei's illness; later, the news of Liu Bei's death led to outbreaks in the Nanzhong districts in the

south of the province. See Ssu-ma Kuang [Sima Guang], Achilles Fang, trans, *The Chronicle of the Three Kingdoms* 1:153,160.

[10] Liu Shan was also seventeen.

[11] It was lese majesty for Kongming to have caused the Emperor to come to him.

[12] Mao (introductory note): "Yi Yin [served the king of Shang] after three invitations; Kongming [agreed to serve] after three visits [from a humbled Liu Bei], making him another Yi Yin. Lü Wang [i.e., Jiang Ziya] was angling in the river [when called to serve the king]; Kongming is contemplating fish, making him another Lü Wang."

[13] Mao (introductory note): "Gao Zu slew the white serpent and founded his career. Guang Wu arose in White Water Village and revived the Han. The First Ruler entered White Emperor city [Baidi] to die and gave his son into the care of Kongming....From the peach garden to this point is one great line of development. The First Ruler's life ends here; Kongming's will commence a new phase. His previous conquest of the Riverlands and Hanzhong fulfilled [the forecast he made] when Liu Bei visited him in his thatched hut. His subsequent achievements — capturing Meng Huo and leading the army out of Qishan — stem from his acceptance of responsibility for the orphan heir. Thus, this chapter marks the transition between two large portions of the story."

Chapter 86

[1] A.D.222. The reign title Huang Wu combines the first character of Wei's reign title (Huang Chu) and the second of Shu's (Zhang Wu), as if to acknowledge neutrally both calendars in Wu's own. Sun Quan did not formally declare himself emperor until A.D.229. At the end of 221, Emperor Cao Pi of Wei ordered Sun Quan made king (*wang*), rejecting the alternative course of advancing Sun Quan in military rank and honoring him as a lord (*hou*) with a fief of ten thousand households (*ZZTJ*,p.2193).

[2] The narrative goes back to the Southland court when Cao Pi was organizing an invasion of the west (see chap.85).

[3] Deng Zhi's arrival is dated by the *ZZTJ* (p.2217) to the tenth month of A.D. 223, five months after Liu Shan succeeded Liu Bei.

[4] Li Yiji went to Qi to persuade the king of Qi, Tian Guang, to submit to Liu Bang. The king agreed and suspended military preparations. Han Xin, Liu Bang's general, chose this moment to attack, and the king boiled Li Yiji alive, thinking he had betrayed him.

At this time Sun Quan owed fealty to Cao Pi.

[5] Mao: "He not only shows no fear, he speaks of the Southland's fear! How artful!"

[6] Mao: "He speaks of the Southland's interest, not the Riverlands'. How artful!"

[7] Mao: "Deng Zhi asks first to know Sun Quan's mind. In this lies his art."

[8] Mao: "Deng Zhi's art lies in reverting to hard words."

[9] Mao: "Deng Zhi contrives to have Sun Quan make the request to him. Artful beyond description!"

[10] Mao: "Deng Zhi is the one posing difficulties! Exquisitely artful!"

[11] Mao: "This shows Kongming's continuing concern for the late Emperor's wish to attack the Southland."

[12] Mao: "And said not a word."

[13] Mao: "Speaking before the king of the Southland, Deng Zhi never once alluded to the Riverlands' attack on the Southland. But here, to the Southland envoy, Kongming repairs the 'omission.'"

[14] From *Shi jing*, ode 241, "Huang yi."

[15] From *Shi jing*, ode 184, "He ming."

[16] From *Shi jing*, ode 229, "Bai hua."

[17] This version of the mythological war between Gong Gong and Zhuan Xu comes from the "Tian wen" section of the *Huainan zi*.

[18] Mao: "At the Battle of Red Cliffs Cao Cao already had Jingzhou, so his forces could cross from there. In this case Jingzhou was in Sun Quan's hands, so northern forces on the Huai had to come across from Guangling."

[19] A.D. 224; the year is named by the Wei calendar.

[20] *Zhongjun huwei:* a Wei, not a Han, title.

[21] *Shangshu puye:* traditionally, the Secretariat's principal authority was the *ling;* the *puye* was second to him.

Throughout the Han and into the Wei the secretariat was increasing in staff and complexity of functions. See Yang Hongnian, *Han Wei zhidu congkao* (Wuhan: Wuhan daxue chubanshe, 1985), pp. 91-93.

[22] Mao: "Unlike Cao Pi, Sun Quan is deeply devoted to his brothers."

[23] In the tenth month of 224 the Emperor returned to Xuchang (*ZZTJ*, p.2221).

[24] In the late summer of 223 in Yizhou district (present-day Jinning of Yunnan province), Yong Kai initiated an armed rebellion. At the critical moment when Liu Shan succeeded Liu Bei, Yong Kai murdered the Shu-Han-appointed governor of Yizhou, Zheng Mao, then arrested Zheng Mao's successor, Zhang Yi, and sent him to the Southland in exchange for Sun Quan's support. Sun Quan reciprocated by appointing Yong Kai governor of Yongchang. The *SGZ* (p.894) places Deng Zhi's visit to the Southland to reestablish friendship with the Riverlands *after* Yong Kai's rebellion.

According to the *ZZTJ* (p. 2216), the chief official at Yongchang, Lü Kai, barred Yong Kai's entrance. As a result, Yong Kai had a native of the district, Meng Huo, incite the southern tribes against Lü Kai.

2441

Chapter 87

[1] The year is A.D.225. Jian Xing ("Commence the [Dynastic] Revival" or simply "New Beginning") is the reign title of Liu Bei's son Liu Shan, Second Emperor of Shu-Han. Kongming will return to Chengdu from these wars in the fall of the same year (chap.91).

[2] Mao (introductory note): "After the peace with Wu, Kongming should have followed up with an attack on Wei. Instead, he began the southern march. Why? I would reply, Cao Pi wanted to borrow Sun Quan's army to attack the Riverlands. Cao Pi also wanted to borrow Meng Huo's Man troops to attack the Riverlands. The Riverlands had succeeded in turning the Southland troops north against Wei but could not do the same with Meng Huo's troops. Rather, Kongming had to invest all his efforts in eliminating the threat Meng Huo

posed, because a precipitate attack on the north would have exposed the Riverlands to Meng Huo from the south. Thus, both in concluding peace with Wu and in attacking the Man, Kongming's ultimate objective remained Wei."

The Man had also approached the Southland for troops. After the Riverlands' first successful downriver attacks on the Southland, Man agents from Wuqi in Wuling sought military assistance from Sun Quan (ZZTJ,p.2191).

Chapter 88

[1] Mao: "One may conclude that Kongming 〔unlike Liu Bei〕 would never have been burned out at Xiaoting." Mao's preceding note says, "At Xiaoting, Liu Bei also pitched camp in a shady wood; Kongming's camps, however, are not connected."

[2] The Han sphere.

[3] Mao (introductory note): "Kongming's purpose in showing Meng Huo around the base area is actually to lure him into making an attack."

[4] By the Tang poet Hu Zeng (TS, p. 853). The "three calls" on Kongming refer to Liu Bei's visits to his Longzhong farm to solicit his service (chap. 37).

Chapter 89

[1] Ma Yuan, who reconquered the area (the former Southern Viet kingdom) for the Chinese in A.D. 44 after the uprising of the Trung sisters. The first General Who Tames the Deeps in this area was Lu Bode; he overcame the Southern Viets for Han Wudi in 111 B.C.

[2] According to the TS, this poem is by Sima Wen.

[3] The TS (p.859) has the last line read: "Remember the gravity of the cause of Han." Mao Zonggang tends to "correct" the TS's secular language of political power with the moralistic language of imperial authority.

[4] The poem uses "Wu hou" (lord of Wu), not "Kongming."

[5] Geng Gong was the hero of a desperate battle against the northern Xiongnu during the reign of Han Mingdi (A.D. 58-75).

Chapter 90

[1] The legendary fire god.

[2] Typically, Han conquerors controlled minority regions by establishing districts and appointing Han bureaucrats to govern them. Kongming's strategy of psychological subjugation (fuxin) aimed at "going to the local chieftains and giving them office." See the extract from the Han Jin chunqiu in SGZ, p.921. The description of Kongming's strategy in Three Kingdoms is historical. But according to the slightly different picture presented in the SGZ, the original rebellion of Yong Kai did not attract many adherents and some Man peoples aided Kongming in suppressing the rebels. Three Kingdoms has enhanced the scale of the rebellion, as well as Kongming's methods of suppressing it. See Liu Chunfan, Zhuge Liang zhuan (Beijing: Zhongguo qingnian chubanshe, 1986), pp. 102-15.

The PH account differs significantly from the Three Kingdoms account: "Half a year after Liu Shan succeeded Liu Bei as emperor, the Man king Meng Huo sent a Man general for the ten legions that Liu Bei had ﹇earlier﹈ borrowed. The Man general said, 'What are you trying to get from up?' Director General Kongming kept him for fifteen days in a guesthouse before sending him away with valuable gifts. The young ruler ﹇Liu Shan﹈ asked Kongming to devise measures against the Man general should he come again."

The *PH* says further that Meng Huo instigated three district governors (*taishou*) — Yong Kai, Lü Kai, and Du Qi — to revolt against the Riverlands on account of the ten unreturned legions. During one battle Du Qi said to Kongming, "Zhuge, you are unprincipled. You killed our sovereign Liu Zhang. Why shouldn't I revolt?" (pp.129-30).

According to the Han *Jin chunqiu*, however, Kongming had no military or economic support from the Man until after his successful southern campaign; *Three Kingdoms* follows this source.

Qiu Zhensheng points out elements of superstition and Han chauvinism in *Three King-doms'* treatment of the campaign and notes that certain minorities reverse the legend by celebrating Meng Huo for organizing various local peoples in the struggle against Zhuge Liang and for capturing and releasing Zhuge Liang seven times. See *ZHT*, pp. 238-39; and cf. the "obligating release" of Cao Cao by Lord Guan.

Chapter 91

[1] The familiar mantou or steamed buns.

[2] A.D. 225: Jian Xing (Commence the Revival) is the Second Emperor's first reign period.

[3] *TS* (p.876): "... as if waiting to serve his father." Mao: "The situation resembles Emperor Xian's reception of Cao Cao."

[4] A.D.226. The *TS* (p.877) first gives the year according to the Wei calendar: Huang Chu 7.

[5] *Wen,* a basic term for Chinese culture, may be translated as "civil order" ; it forms a contrastive pair with the term *wu,* "martial might." Cao Cao, Pi's father, was posthumously titled Wu Huangdi, August Emperor Wu. The Chinese word *huang* conventionally trans-lated "august" literally means "high and shining like the sun." It is the-nō in the Japanese tennō, "emperor." Cao Cao's temple name was Tai Zu, or Great Ancestor, just as Liu Bang was called Gao Zu, or Supreme Ancestor. Cao Pi's death is dated to June 29. Wen *Zhao* means Reflector of Emperor Wen; *zhao* contains the graph for sun.

[6] The title *dajiangjun* is translated "supreme commander" in military contexts; in earlier chapters it was translated "regent" or "regent-marshal." Since Cao Zhen had respon-sibility for the heir, the translation "regent-marshal" is used in his case.

[7] "Submerged dragon" suggests a potential sovereign.

[8] Liu Bang suspected Han Xin of disloyalty and on the pretext of a pleasure tour went to Yunmeng to see him. There Liu Bang tricked Han Xin into receiving him, and then arrested him on the spot. Later Liu Bang released him and made him lord of Huaiyin. See Ssu-ma Ch'ien [Sima Qian], *Records of the Grand Historian of China* (New York: Columbia Univer-sity Press, 1961), 1:109,229.

⁹ Mao: "Kongming's instruction to the Second Emperor concerns two institutions, the palace and the ministries. If the Emperor lets the palace [or court] officials become too intimate, and the ministerial [or bureau] officials become estranged, then opportunists will have access to him but worthy men will not. This is how emperors Huan and Ling came to grief."

¹⁰ Xiang Chong was the only commander to bring his forces home intact after the disastrous campaign against the Southland.

¹¹ Slightly amended, following the text in Zhuge Liang's biography in the SGZ, p.920.

¹² Mao's introductory note says: "The *Gangmu* headline reads, 'The Han prime minister, Zhuge Liang, lord of Wuxiang, orders the army to wage just war on Wei.' Thus, this memorial first expresses the great principle [*dayi*] of smiting the traitor [Cao clan]." According to the Wei calendar, it was the third month of Tai He (Grand Harmony) or A.D.227. The Wei reign title changed with the accession of the new emperor, Cao Rui.

¹³ Qiao Zhou was the mentor of Chen Shou, author of the SGZ.

¹⁴ These offices mainly replicate the Han bureaucracy; most bureaucratic innovations were made in the Wei kingdom.

¹⁵ The fourth or fifth day of May in A.D. 227.

¹⁶ According to Pei Songzhi's interlinear note to the biography of Li Yan, citing Chen Shou's *Zhuge Liang ji* (SGZ, p.999), Li Yan urged Zhuge Liang to assume the Nine Dignities (i.e., become king, or *wang*). Zhuge Liang rejected the idea and reiterated his dedication to the Second Emperor. On the awarding of the Nine Dignities to Cao Cao, see chapter 61 n. 5; on the awarding of the Nine Dignities to Sun Quan, see chapter 82.

¹⁷ Xiahou Yuan died in battle in A.D. 218 when Liu Bei drove Cao Cao's forces from Hanzhong.

Chapter 92

¹ Summer, the fourth month of the fifth year of the Shu-Han reign period Jian Xing (A.D.227) (TS, p.885).

² Cao Cao's son-in-law.

³ I.e., Chang'an.

⁴ Wei Yan is a character of particular importance for understanding the last years of Kongming's career as well as the events after his death. Liu Bei had made him responsible for Hanzhong, or "East Riverlands," the crucial region between Shu and Guanzhong, and he knew the terrain well. See Shen Bojun, "Lun Wei Yan," in *LWJ*, p.176.

⁵ Mao (introductory note): "In this chapter we find the military exploits of Zhao Zilong, which are the 'consummation of his purposes.' What does this phrase mean? When the First Ruler assumed the throne, Zhao Zilong urged him to attack Wei at once. When the First Ruler attacked Wu [instead], he put Zhao Zilong in the rear because his heart was not in waging war on Wu. But in the campaign against Wei, Kongming put Zhao Zilong in the van because the warrior's heart was in it."

⁶ Mao (introductory note): "In Jiang Wei the Riverlands and someone who ultimately took up arms against the Wei as an heir to Kongming's policy. Even before Kongming's

Qishan campaigns against the Wei, the author inserts the man who will campaign against the Wei [after the six Qishan campaigns]. Intending later to use a character positively, the author introduces him in a negative light — as an enemy of the Riverlands in the service of the Wei....Thus, we come to a realization of the author's method of narrative organization."

Chapter 93

[1] Mao (introductory note): "Kongming used Jiang Wei's mother to control him in much the same way that Cao Cao used Shan Fu's mother to control him. But Cao cao forged the mother's letter to lure the son; Kongming did not have to forge a letter.... Shan Fu yielded only to his mother, but not to Cao Cao. Jiang Wei yields not only to his mother, but also to Kongming."

[2] Imperial and nonimperial locutions are mixed here. *Three Kingdoms* refers here to Cao Rui as *zhu* (ruler) instead of *di or tianzi* (emperor), and uses his *ming* (name) in order to deny his universal (*tianxia*) legitimacy.

[3] Wang Lang's death is dated by the *ZZTJ* to the second year of Tai He, eleventh month, i.e., late 228 or early 229. The cause and circumstances are not mentioned, but it is unlikely that he accompanied Cao Zhen on this campaign. Indeed, judging from the *ZZTJ* as well as Cao Zhen's biography (*SGZ*, p.281), the revolt of the three towns is followed directly by the crucial defeat of Kongming's picked commander Ma Su. Why has Luo Guanzhong interposed a dramatic rhetorical duel between Kongming and Wang Lang?

It was Wang Lang who, together with Hua Xin, persuaded Cao Pi to create the Wei regime; Lang's long years of loyal service to Han and Wei and his intrepid opposition to the "Shu traitors" (*SGZ*, p.411) are detailed in his biography. Advancing his death one year and giving Kongming a memorable moral victory over the venerable Wei vassal perhaps cushions the humiliating defeat at Jieting — which came at a time of growing doubt in the Riverlands about Kongming's pursuit of Liu Bei's original quest.

Chapter 94

[1] I.e., in February of A.D. 228.

[2] The Palace of Enduring Peace was where Liu Bei had passed away.

[3] *Sanji changshi* is a Wei title. "The Qin dynasty appointed *sanji*, detached cavalry, and *changshi*, regular attendants. The former rode behind the imperial carriage; the latter had personal access to the sovereign. Both offices were held in addition to another appointment [jia guan]. Early in the Eastern Han the position of *sanji* was abolished, and all *changshi* positions were filled by eunuchs. Now the *sanji* has been reestablished and combined with the *changshi* to form one office whose function is to offer moral remonstrance, not to take charge of administrative business." From note to *ZZTJ*, p.2178, under Huang Chu 1, the first reign year for Cao Pi (A.D. 220).

[4] Mao: "Meng Da's murder of Liu Feng is avenged." Sima Yi captured Xincheng and killed Meng Da between February 23 and March 23, A.D.228.

[5] Mao (introductory note): "Had the Wei ruler not employed Sima Yi again, Meng Da

would have survived and the two capitals [Chang'an and Luoyang] could have been attacked. If the two capitals had been attacked, the Cao dynasty, Wei, could have been destroyed. That the dynasty was not destroyed then and there was Sima Yi's achievement. Nonetheless, the saving of Wei led directly to the usurping of Wei. So by using the Sima Yi to counter Han [Shu, or the Riverlands], the Wei barred the tiger at the front only to admit the wolf at the rear. At the outset of Sima Yi's renewed service to the Wei, the author introduces Yi's brave and forthright sons not, it would seem, because they aided the Wei, but rather because they foreshadow its doom."

Meng Da's last stand is treated differently in the *PH* (p.133): Meng Da agrees to rejoin the Riverlands camp; Sima Yi marches against him. Meng Da writes Zhuge Liang for help; Zhuge Liang does not come. Meng Da writes Liang a second time; still he does not come. Meng Da realizes Zhuge Liang's purpose and speaks of falling into his trap; Meng Da hangs himself.

In the longer view, the civil wars between Wei and Shu created the conditions for Qiang and Di (another non-Han people) dominance in northern China in the fourth century.

Chapter 95

[1] Mao (introductory note): "With this chapter the opposition between Sima Yi and Kongming begins. Engagement is in Kongming's interest; avoidance of battle works to Sima Yi's advantage."

[2] Mao (introductory note): "The previous chapter told how Meng Da lost Shangyong by ignoring Kongming's advice. This chapter tells how Ma Su lost Jieting by ignoring Kongming's advice. The loss of Shangyong left Kongming without hope of advancing. The loss of Jieting nearly left him without a place of retreat. Why? Without Jieting, Yangping Pass was not secure. If Yangping Pass was not safe, advance became fruitless and retreat costly....Thus, Nan'an, Anding, and Tianshui had to be sacrificed; Winnow Basket Gorge had to be evacuated; and the stores at Xicheng had to be removed. The previous victories, from the capture of Xiahou Mao... to the defeat of Cao Zhen [all that Kongming had achieved since returning from the southern expedition against the Man] now came to naught, Alas."

The Zi-Wu Gorge was a passage cut in the Wang Mang era across the Southern or Qinling Mountains, which divide Guanzhong from Hanzhong to the south. See Pan Ku [Ban Gu], *History of the Former Han Dynasty*, trans. Homer H. Dubs (Baltimore: The Waverly press, 1938-55),3:212.

The historical Sima Yi was not at the western front for the "vacant city ruse" but at the more important southern front with the Southland. Sima Yi did not come to the western front until Kongming's fourth offensive (see chap. 100). The fictional tradition tends to attach more importance to the Wei-Shu conflict than to the Wei-Wu conflict, and *Three Kingdoms* accordingly builds up the Kongming-Sima Yi rivalry and the events of A.D.228.

Chapter 96

[1] Gun was executed for failing to control the floods, but his son Yu (or Great Yu), mastered the waters and subsequently succeeded Shun as emperor. The *SGZ* (p.984) says that Ma Su died in prison. Historically, the defeat at Jieting may have cost Kongming a speedy conquest of Chang'an. The defeat resulted directly from his assignment of Jieting's defense to Ma Su. In making this assignment, Kongming not only went against Liu Xuande's warning about Ma Su; he also ignored the majority of his advisers who had argued that Wei Yan, not Ma Su, be given authority to defend Jieting. Ma Su was the younger brother of Ma Liang, with whom Kongming had had an extremely close relationship; see the note by Pei Songzhi, *SGZ*, p.983.

[2] In 206 B.C., at the start of his campaign against Xiang Yu, Liu Bang needed to slip his forces past Chencang. To help Liu Bang accomplish this maneuver, Han Xin built a cliffside plank road that diverted Xiang Yu's attention, allowing Liu Bang to reach his destination. See SJ, "Gao Zu benji."

[3] Yangzhou was the official Han (and now Wei) provincial name for the Southland region.

[4] Huan was the main city of Lujiang, a district which was the center of a long strip of Southland territory above the Yangzi. The northern part of Lujiang was in Wei hands.

[5] Lu Xun was renowned for foiling Liu Bei's invasion of the Southland (chap. 84.)

Chapter 97

[1] The triumph at Hanshui refers to Zilong's rescue of Kongming. On the eve of the battle at Red Cliffs, Zilong picked up Kongming and ferried him out of the Southland. For the rescue of the Second Emperor (Ah Dou), see chapter 41.

[2] This refers to the early years of Emperor Xian's reign; Liu Yao was made inspector of Yangzhou in A.D.194. A few lines below, the translation follows the *TS* (p. 936), which reads Sun Ce, not Sun Quan.

[3] Mao (introductory note): "The first petition was to guide Liu Shan, the second petition to answer critics... The first petition concerned itself with domestic issues, the second with external affairs."

Many scholars doubt the authenticity of Kongming's second petition, in part because Zhao Zilong's death is dated in his *SGZ* biography to the following year. The document is preserved in the *Han Jin chunqiu* of Xi Zuochi, via Pei Songzhi's notes to the *SGZ* (p.923). Neither the *SGZ* itself nor the Wen xuan includes it; Sima Guang, however, places it in the *ZZTJ* under the year A.D.228. Ma Zhijie, "Hou chu shi biao de zuozhe wenti," attributes the piece to Zhuge Liang's nephew, Zhuge Ke; see *Wen shi*, no. 17 (1983): 264-69. Also see Zhuge Ke's biography in the *SGZ*, especially p. 1435.

The Cong and the Sou, mentioned a few lines below, are non-Han peoples who come from the Ba and Shu regions, respectively, of the Riverlands. The Black Qiang were named for the color of their clothing.

[4] Dated in the *TS* to the eleventh month of Jian Xing 6 (between December 14, A.D. 228, and January 12, A.D. 229). Mao (introductory note): "Since the defeat at Jieting and the execution of Ma Su, voices in the Riverlands had been raised in favor of maintaining

peace in the kingdom and opposing the war against Wei. Kongming, however, held that only by waging war against Wei could peace in the Riverlands be made secure."

[5] Mao: "Sima Yi is a fine judge of men if this is the kind he recommends."

[6] Mao: "Ma Su could not hold Jieting with thirty thousand; but Hao Zhao held Chencang with three thousand — because Jieting had no wall and Chencang did."

[7] Mao: "Sima Yi took Jieting, but Kongming could not take Chencang. The reason lies in the difference between the defenders as well as the site." Chencang commands the middle section of the Wei River; father west, Tianshui and then Nan'an command the river's western end.

[8] Mao (introductory note): "Zhou Fang 'surrendered' to Wei, and Cao Xiu believed him. Jiang Wei 'surrendered' to Wei, and Cao Zhen believed him. The incidents are analogous, except that Zhou Fang 'surrendered' by letter and in person, Jiang Wei only by letter...."

"Meng Da gave allegiance to Shu as a man of Shu, and Kongming believed him. Jiang Wei gave allegiance to Wei as a man of Wei, and Cao Zhen believed him. The incidents are analogous, except that Kongming judged rightly, Cao Zhen wrongly. Meng Da's surrender was genuine, but his plan failed; Jiang Wei's surrender was false, but his plan worked. In this respect the incidents are not analogous."

Chapter 98

[1] It was not the third day of the cycle (bingyin), but the thirty-third (bingshen), according to the SGZ (p.1134). Achilles Fang equates it to June 23, A.D.229; see Ssu-ma Kuang [Sima Guang], The Chronicle of the Three Kingdoms, trans. and annot. Achilles Fang, Harvard-Yenching Institute Studies, no. 6 (Cambridge: Harvard University Press, 1952-65), 1:291.

[2] From "Imperial [huang, yellow] Might" to "Imperial Dragon."

[3] Zhuge Ke, a nephew of Zhuge Liang, is often supposed to be the author of Kongming's "Second Petition on Taking the Field" (chap.97) because it resembles Ke's polemic against Wei, the "Zheng Wei lun." See SGZ, p.1134; see also chap. 97, n.3. Zhuge Ke's anti-Wei militance and Sun Quan's anti-Wei leadership come through more sharply in the historical than in the fictional traditions.

[4] Zhuge Ke alludes here to Zhang Zhao's long record of favoring accommodation with the north (note his conflict with Zhou Yu before the battle at Red Cliffs). The reference to Jiang Ziya, the military leader who guided the Zhou dynasty founder to power, emphasizes Zhang Zhao's timidity.

[5] In the TS (p.951), Sima Yi begins with these words: "Years before, Sun Quan defended Wu from below the Great River with help from no one. He was satisfied [to hold his region] and harbored no further ambition. After that, when Lu Xun took Jingzhou, Sun Quan said he had gone too far. Now however, Sun Quan has declared himself emperor, but his people remain uneasy. He will not dare to risk military action."

[6] Mao: "Not wanting the Emperor to reclaim the seal but wanting Cao Zhen instead to yield the seal on his own demonstrates Sima Yi's skill in handling Cao Zhen. Not waiting for the Emperor to confer the seal but saying instead, 'I'll go for it myself', demonstrates Sima

Yi's contempt for the Emperor."

⁷ Mao (introductory note): "The descriptions of Kongming's seven captures and seven releases of Meng Huo form a sequence, and herein lies their genius. The descriptions of Kongming's six offensives from the Qishan hills are not connected however, and therein lies their genius. Between the first and second offensives comes Lu Xun's defeat of Wei....Between the second and third, Sun Quan declares himself emperor....We often find that the *Zuo zhuan* narratives concerning a particular kingdom branch out to include narratives of other kingdoms, thus providing richer detail. And Sima Qian's *Shi ji* often branches out to lateral events in a particular narrative, thus making its accounts fuller. *Three Kingdoms* holds its own with those great histories."

"Among [the rulers of] the three kingdoms, Sun Quan was the last to declare himself emperor. Why? Because circumstances barred it. Sun Quan did not declare himself emperor while Cao Cao still lived simply because Cao Cao would have used the authority of Emperor Xian to attack him. When Cao Pi declared himself emperor, Sun Quan could have done so too, but with Shu attacking Wu, such a rash move would have added strength to the attackers and cut off aid from Wei. But once Shu befriended Wu, and Wei separated from Wu; once Shu felt pressure from Wei, and Wei suffered defeat by Shu, *then* Sun Quan seized the chance to become the Son of Heaven...."

"Wu had acknowledged itself a vassal to Wei and received the Nine Dignities from Wei because Wu was seeking Wei's aid in attacking Shu. But once Sun Quan declared himself emperor, Wu and Wei could never cooperate again.... This meant the isolation of Wu as well as Wei. Thus , Kongming's plan to befriend Wu may be rightly regarded as a plan to devour Wu."

Sometime in July of A.D. 229, "the leader of the Southland and the representative of Han [i.e., Shu] formally divided the territory of Wei between them. The treaty assigned Yuzhou, Qingzhou, Xuzhou, and Youzhou to the south; and Yanzhou, Jizhou, Bingzhou, and Liangzhou to Han. The administrative district [i.e., the sizhou, the territory that contained the two capitals] was divided at Hangu Pass" (ZZTJ, p.2254). The account of this agreement in the SGZ (p.1134) is even fuller and depicts Sun Quan personally dividing the territory of Wei. A trace of this agreement between Wu and Shu remains in the TS (p.949); no indication whatever remains in the Mao edition of this formal acceptance by Shu-Han of Wu's equal sovereignty. However, the primary southern source, the "Wuzhu zhuan" (Life of Sun Quan), contains the text of this "Han-Wu" covenant. (Clearly, the Riverlands — Shu — called itself Han.) The covenant is based on a common moral denunciation of the third Wei emperor, Cao Rui, for stealing power in the manner of Cao Pi, and it concludes with a provision for mutual military assistance (SGZ, pp. 1134-35). The personal preeminence of Sun Quan, uncontested after Liu Bei's death, is expressed in these pages of the SGZ.

2449